THE CRITICS RAVING

"Barth works his corner of our land, reconstructs it with ALL THE INTENSITY OF MORRIS RE-IMAGINING NEBRASKA, HEMINGWAY UPPER MICHIGAN, FAULKNER NORTHERN MISSISSIPPI, OR WHITMAN (IN HIS LESS COSMIC MOMENTS) BROOKLYN . . . What he discovers is scandal and terror and disreputable joy—which is to say the human condition . . . The book is a joke-book, an endless series of gags. But the biggest joke of all is that BARTH SEEMS FINALLY TO HAVE WRITTEN SOMETHING CLOSER TO THE 'GREAT AMERICAN NOVEL' THAN ANY OTHER BOOK OF THE LAST DECADES."

—Leslie Fiedler,
The New Leader

JOHN BARTH

THE SOT-WEED FACTOR

BANTAM BOOKS
TORONTO · NEW YORK · LONDON · SYDNEY

*This low-priced Bantam Book
has been completely reset in a type face
designed for easy reading, and was printed
from new plates. It contains the complete
text of the original hard-cover edition.*
NOT ONE WORD HAS BEEN OMITTED.

THE SOT-WEED FACTOR

*A Bantam Book / published by arrangement with
Doubleday & Company, Inc.*

PRINTING HISTORY

*Doubleday edition published 1960
Doubleday revised edition published 1967*

Bantam edition / May 1969

2nd printing	*April 1970*	6th printing	*August 1974*
3rd printing	*April 1971*	7th printing	*June 1975*
4th printing	*April 1972*	8th printing ..	*September 1976*
5th printing	*July 1973*	9th printing ..	*February 1978*
	10th printing	*April 1980*	

ISBN 0–553–14079–5

Published simultaneously in the United States and Canada

PRINTED IN THE UNITED STATES OF AMERICA

19 18 17 16 15 14 13 12 11

Foreword to the Second Edition

I'VE TAKEN THE OPPORTUNITY to reread *The Sot-Weed Factor* with an eye to emending and revising the text of the original edition before its reissue, quite as Ebenezer Cooke himself did in 1731 with the poem from which this novel takes its title. The cases differ in that Cooke's objective was to blunt the barbs of his original satire, he having dwelt by then many years among its targets, but mine is merely, where possible, to make this long narrative a quantum swifter and more graceful.

John Barth

Buffalo, New York
1966

Contents

PART I: THE MOMENTOUS WAGER

1

*The Poet Is Introduced, and Differentiated
from His Fellows*

IN THE LAST YEARS of the Seventeenth Century there was to
be found among the fops and fools of the London coffee-
houses one rangy, gangling flitch called Ebenezer Cooke,
more ambitious than talented, and yet more talented than
prudent, who, like his friends-in-folly, all of whom were supposed to be educating at Oxford or Cambridge, had found
the sound of Mother English more fun to game with than her
sense to labor over, and so rather than applying himself to
the pains of scholarship, had learned the knack of versifying,
and ground out quires of couplets after the fashion of the
day, afroth with *Joves* and *Jupiters*, aclang with jarring
rhymes, and string-taut with similes stretched to the snap-
ping-point.

As poet, this Ebenezer was not better nor worse than his
fellows, none of whom left behind him anything nobler than
his own posterity; but four things marked him off from them.
The first was his appearance: pale-haired and pale-eyed,
raw-boned and gaunt-cheeked, he stood—nay, *angled*—nineteen hands high. His clothes were good stuff well tailored, but
they hung on his frame like luffed sails on long spars. Heron

3

of a man, lean-limbed and long-billed, he walked and sat with loose-jointed poise; his every stance was angular surprise, his each gesture half flail. Moreover there was a discomposure about his face, as though his features got on ill together: heron's beak, wolf-hound's forehead, pointed chin, lantern jaw, wash-blue eyes, and bony blond brows had minds of their own, went their own ways, and took up odd postures, which often as not had no relation to what one took as his mood of the moment. And these configurations were short-lived, for like restless mallards the features of his face no sooner were settled than *ha!* they'd be flushed, and *hi!* how they'd flutter, and no man could say what lay behind them.

The second was his age: whereas most of his accomplices were scarce turned twenty, Ebenezer at the time of this chapter was more nearly thirty, yet not a whit more wise than they, and with six or seven years' less excuse.

The third was his origin: Ebenezer was born American, though he'd not seen his birthplace since earliest childhood. His father, Andrew Cooke 2nd, of the Parish of St. Giles in the Fields, County of Middlesex—a red-faced, whitechopped, stout-winded old lecher with flinty eye and withered arm—had spent his youth in Maryland as agent for an English manufacturer, as had his father before him, and having a sharp eye for goods and a sharper for men, had added to the Cooke estate by the time he was thirty some one thousand acres of good wood and arable land on the Choptank River. The point on which this land lay he called Cooke's Point, and the small manor-house he built there, Malden. He married late in life and conceived twin children, Ebenezer and his sister Anna, whose mother (as if such an inordinate casting had cracked the mold) died bearing them. When the twins were but four Andrew returned to England, leaving Malden in the hands of an overseer, and thenceforth employed himself as a merchant, sending his own factors to the plantations. His affairs prospered, and the children were well provided for.

The fourth thing that distinguished Ebenezer from his coffee-house associates was his manner: though not one of them was blessed with more talent than he needed, all of Ebenezer's friends put on great airs when together, declaiming their verses, denigrating all the well-known poets of their time (and any members of their own circle who happened to be not on hand), boasting of their amorous conquests and their prospects for imminent success, and otherwise behaving

4

in a manner such that, had not every other table in the coffee-house sported a like ring of coxcombs, they'd have made great nuisances of themselves. But Ebenezer himself, though his appearance rendered inconspicuousness out of the question, was bent to taciturnity. He was even chilly. Except for infrequent bursts of garrulity he rarely joined in the talk, but seemed content for the most part simply to watch the other birds preen their feathers. Some took this withdrawal as a sign of his contempt, and so were either intimidated or angered by it, according to the degree of their own self-confidence. Others took it for modesty; others for shyness; others for artistic or philosophical detachment. Had it been in fact symptom of any one of these, there would be no tale to tell; in truth, however, this manner of our poet's grew out of something much more complicated, which warrants recounting his childhood, his adventures, and his ultimate demise.

2

The Remarkable Manner in Which Ebenezer Was Educated, and the No Less Remarkable Results of That Education

EBENEZER AND ANNA had been raised together. There happening to be no other children on the estate in St. Giles, they grew up with no playmates except each other, and hence became unusually close. They played the same games together and were educated in the same subjects, since Andrew was wealthy enough to provide them with a tutor, but not with separate tutoring. Until the age of ten they even shared the same bedroom—not that space was lacking either in Andrew's London house, on Plumtree Street, or in the later establishment at St. Giles, but because Andrew's old housekeeper, Mrs. Twigg, who was for some years their governess, had in the beginning been so taken with the fact of their twinship that she'd made a point of keeping them together, and then later, when their increased size and presumed awareness began to embarrass her, they had come so to enjoy each other's company that she was for a time unable to resist their combined protests at any mention of separate chambers. When the separation was finally effected, at Andrew's orders, it was merely to adjoining rooms, between which the door was normally left open to allow for conversation.

In the light of all this it is not surprising that even after puberty there was little difference, aside from the physical manifestations of their sex, between the two children. Both were lively, intelligent, and well-behaved. Anna was the less timid of the two, and even when Ebenezer naturally grew to be the taller and physically stronger, Anna was still the quicker and better coordinated, and therefore usually the winner in the games they played: shuttlecock, fives, or *paille maille;* squails, Meg Merrilies, jackstraws, or shove ha'penny. Both were great readers, and loved the same books: among the classics, the *Odyssey* and the *Metamorphoses,* the *Book of Martyrs* and the *Lives of the Saints;* the romances of Valentine and Orson, Bevis of Hampton, and Guy of Warwick; the tales of Robin Good-Fellow, Patient Grisel, and the Foundlings in the Wood; and among the newer books, Janeway's *Token for Children,* Batchiler's *Virgins Pattern,* and Fisher's *Wise Virgin,* as well as *Cacoethes Leaden Legacy, The Young Mans Warning-Peece, The Booke of Mery Riddles,* and, shortly after their publication, *Pilgrim's Progress* and Keach's *War with the Devil.* Perhaps had Andrew been less preoccupied with his merchant-trading, or Mrs. Twigg with her religion, her gout, and her authority over the other servants, Anna would have been kept to her dolls and embroidery-hoops, and Ebenezer set to mastering the arts of hunting and fencing. But they were seldom subjected to direction at all, and hence drew small distinction between activities proper for little girls and those proper for little boys.

Their favorite recreation was play-acting. Indoors or out, hour after hour, they played at pirates, soldiers, clerics, Indians, royalty, giants, martyrs, lords and ladies, or any other creatures that took their fancy, inventing action and dialogue as they played. Sometimes they would maintain the same role for days, sometimes only for minutes. Ebenezer, especially, became ingenious at disguising his assumed identity in the presence of adults, while still revealing it clearly enough to Anna, to her great delight, by some apparently innocent gesture or remark. They might spend an autumn morning playing at Adam and Eve out in the orchard, for example, and when at dinner their father forbade them to return there, on account of the mud, Ebenezer would reply with a knowing nod, "Mud's not the worst of't: I saw a snake as well." And little Anna, when she had got her breath back, would declare, "It didn't frighten *me*, but Eben's forehead hath been sweating ever since," and pass her brother the bread. At night, both before and after their separation into two rooms, they would either continue to make-believe (necessarily confining themselves to dialogue, which they found it easy to carry on in the dark) or else play word-games; of these they had a great variety, ranging from the simple "How many words do you know beginning with *S?*" or "How many words rhyme with *faster?*" to the elaborate codes, reverse pronunciations, and homemade languages of their later childhood.

In 1676, when they were ten, Andrew employed for them a new tutor named Henry Burlingame III—a wiry, brown-eyed, swarthy youth in his early twenties, energetic, intense, and not unhandsome. This Burlingame had for reasons unexplained not completed his baccalaureate; yet for the range and depth of his abilities he was little short of an Aristotle. Andrew had found him in London unemployed and undernourished, and, always a good businessman, was thus for a miserly fee able to provide his children with a tutor who could sing the tenor in a Gesualdo madrigal as easily as he dissected a field-mouse or conjugated ἐιμί. The twins took an immediate liking to him, and he in turn, after only a few weeks, grew so attached to them that he was overjoyed when Andrew permitted him, at no increase in salary, to convert the little summer-pavilion on the grounds of the St. Giles estate into a combination laboratory and living-quarters, and devote his entire attention to his charges.

He found both to be rapid learners, especially apt in natural philosophy, literature, composition, and music; less so in languages, mathematics, and history. He even taught them how to dance, though Ebenezer by age twelve was already too ungainly to do it well. First he would teach Ebenezer to play the melody on the harpsichord; then he would drill Anna in the steps, to Ebenezer's accompaniment, until she mastered them; next he would take Ebenezer's place at the instrument so that Anna could teach her brother the steps; and finally, when the dance was learned, Ebenezer would help Anna master the tune on the harpsichord. Aside from its obvious efficiency, this system was in keeping with the second

7

of Master Burlingame's three principles of pedagogy; to wit, that one learns a thing best by teaching it. The first was that of the three usual motives for learning things—necessity, ambition, and curiosity—simple curiosity was the worthiest of development, it being the "purest" (in that the value of what it drives us to learn is terminal rather than instrumental), the most conducive to exhaustive and continuing rather than cursory or limited study, and the likeliest to render pleasant the labor of learning. The third principle, closely related to the others, was that this sport of teaching and learning should never become associated with certain hours or particular places, lest student and teacher alike (and in Burlingame's system they were much alike) fall into the vulgar habit of turning off their alertness, except at those times and in those places, and thus make by implication a pernicious distinction between learning and other sorts of natural behavior.

The twins' education, then, went on from morning till night. Burlingame joined readily in their play-acting, and had he dared ask leave would have slept with them as well, to guide their word-games. If his system lacked the discipline of Locke's, who would have all students soak their feet in cold water, it was a good deal more fun: Ebenezer and Anna loved their teacher, and the three were great companions. To teach them history he directed their play-acting to historical events; to sustain their interest in geography he produced volumes of exotic pictures and tales of adventure; to sharpen their logical equipment he ran them through Zeno's paradoxes as one would ask riddles, and rehearsed them in Descartes' skepticism as gaily as though the search for truth and value in the universe were a game of Who's Got the Button. He taught them to wonder at a leaf of thyme, a line of Palestrina, the configuration of Cassiopeia, the scales of a pilchard, the sound of *indefatigable,* the elegance of a sorites.

The result of this education was that the twins grew quite enamored of the world—especially Ebenezer, for Anna, from about her thirteenth birthday, began to grow more demure and less demonstrative. But Ebenezer could be moved to shivers by the swoop of a barn-swallow, to cries of laughter at the lace of a cobweb or the roar of an organ's pedal-notes, and to sudden tears by the wit of *Volpone,* the tension of a violin-box, or the truth of the Pythagorean Theorem. By age eighteen he had reached his full height and ungainliness; he was a nervous, clumsy youth who, though by this time he far excelled his sister in imaginativeness, was much her inferior

8

in physical beauty, for though as twins they shared nearly identical features, Nature saw fit, by subtle alterations, to turn Anna into a lovely young woman and Ebenezer into a goggling scarecrow, just as a clever author may, by delicate adjustments, parody a beautiful style.

It is a pity that Burlingame could not accompany Ebenezer when, at eighteen, the boy made ready to matriculate at Cambridge, for though a good teacher will teach well regardless of the theory he suffers from, and though Burlingame's might seem to have been an unusually attractive one, yet there is no perfect educational method, and it must be admitted that at least partly because of his tutoring Ebenezer took quite the same sort of pleasure in history as in Greek mythology and epic poetry, and made little or no distinction between, say, the geography of the atlases and that of fairy-stories. In short, because learning had been for him such a pleasant game, he could not regard the facts of zoology or the Norman Conquest, for example, with genuine seriousness, nor could he discipline himself to long labor at tedious tasks. Even his great imagination and enthusiasm for the world were not unalloyed virtues when combined with his gay irresolution, for though they led him to a great sense of the arbitrariness of the particular real world, they did not endow him with a corresponding realization of its finality. He very well knew, for instance, that "France is shaped like a teapot," but he could scarcely accept the fact that there was actually in existence *at that instant* such a place as France, where people were speaking French and eating snails whether he thought about them or not, and that despite the virtual infinitude of imaginable shapes, this France would have to go on resembling a teapot forever. And again, though the whole business of Greece and Rome was unquestionably delightful, he found the notion preposterous, almost unthinkable, that this was the *only* way it happened: that made him nervous and irritable, when he thought of it at all.

Perhaps with continued guidance from his tutor he could in time have overcome these failings, but one morning in July of 1684 Andrew simply announced at breakfast, "No need to go to the summer-house today, Ebenezer. Thy lessons are done."

Both children looked up in surprise.

"Do you mean, sir, that Henry will be leaving us?" Ebenezer asked.

9

"I do indeed," Andrew replied. "In fact, if I be not greatly in error he hath already departed."

"But how is that? With never a fare-thee-well? He spoke not a word of leaving us!"

"Gently, now," said Andrew. "Will ye weep for a mere schoolmaster? 'Twas this week or the next, was't not? Thou'rt done with him."

"Did you know aught of't?" Ebenezer demanded of Anna. She shook her head and fled from the room. "You ordered him off, Father?" he asked incredulously. "Why such suddenness?"

" 'Dslife!" cried Andrew. "At your age I'd sooner have drunk him good riddance than raised such a bother! The fellow's work was done and I sacked him, and there's an end on't! If he saw fit to leave at once 'tis his affair. I must say 'twas a more manly thing than all this hue and cry!"

Ebenezer went at once to the summer-pavilion. Almost everything was there exactly as it had been before: a half-dissected frog lay pinned out upon its beech-board on the work-table; books and papers were spread open on the writing-desk; even the teapot stood half-full on the grate. But Burlingame was indeed gone. While Ebenezer was looking about in disbelief Anna joined him, wiping her eyes.

"Dear Henry!" Ebenezer lamented, his own eyes brimming. " 'Tis like a bolt from Heaven! Whatever shall we do without him?"

Anna made no reply, but ran to her brother and embraced him.

For this reason or another, then, when not long afterwards Ebenezer bade good-bye to his father and Anna and established himself in Magdalene College, at Cambridge, he proved a poor student. He would go to fetch Newton's lectures *De Motu Corporum* from the library, and would spend four hours reading Esquemeling's *History of the Buccaneers* instead, or some Latin bestiary. He took part in few pranks or sports, made few friends, and went virtually unnoticed by his professors.

It was during his second year of study that, though he did not realize it at the time, he was sore bit by the muse's gadfly. Certainly he did not at the time think of himself as a poet, but it got so that after hearing his teachers argue subtly and at length against, say, philosophical materialism, he would leave the lecture-hall with no more in his notebook than:

> *Old* Plato *saw both Mind and Matter;*
> Thomas Hobbes, *naught but the latter.*
> *Now poor Tom's Soul doth fry in Hell:*
> *Shrugs* GOD, *"'Tis immaterial."*

or:

> *Source of Virtue, Truth, and All is*
> *Each Man's* Lumen Naturalis.

As might be expected, the more this affliction got hold of him, the more his studies suffered. The sum of history became in his head no more than the stuff of metaphors. Of the philosophers of his era—Bacon, Hobbes, Descartes, Spinoza, Leibnitz, Locke—he learned little; of its scientists—Kepler, Galileo, Newton—less; of its theologians—Lord Herbert, Cudworth, More, Smith, Glanvill—nothing. But *Paradise Lost* he knew inside out; *Hudibras* upside down. At the end of the third year, to his great distress, he failed a number of examinations and had to face the prospect of leaving the University. Yet what to do? He could not bear the thought of returning to St. Giles and telling his formidable father; he would have to absent himself quietly, disappear from sight, and seek his fortune in the world at large. But in what manner?

Here, in his difficulty with this question, the profoundest effects of Burlingame's amiable pedagogy become discernible: Ebenezer's imagination was excited by every person he met either in or out of books who could do with skill and understanding anything whatever; he was moved to ready admiration by expert falconers, scholars, masons, chimneysweeps, prostitutes, admirals, cutpurses, sailmakers, barmaids, apothecaries, and cannoneers alike.

Ah, God, he wrote in a letter to Anna about this time, *it were an easy Matter to choose a Calling, had one all Time to live in! I should be fifty Years a Barrister, fifty a Physician, fifty a Clergyman, fifty a Soldier! Aye, and fifty a Thief, and fifty a Judge! All Roads are fine Roads, beloved Sister, none more than another, so that with one Life to spend I am a Man bare-bumm'd at Taylors with Cash for but one pair of Breeches, or a Scholar at Bookstalls with Money for a single Book: to choose ten were no Trouble; to choose one, impossible! All Trades, all Crafts, all Professions are wondrous, but*

11

none is finer than the rest together. I cannot choose, sweet Anna: twixt Stools my Breech falleth to the Ground!

He was, that is to say, temperamentally disinclined to no career, and, what is worse (as were this not predicament enough), he seemed consistently no special sort of person: the variety of temperaments and characters that he observed at Cambridge and in literature was as enchanting to him as the variety of life-works, and as hard to choose from among. He admired equally the sanguine, the phlegmatic, the choleric, the melancholic, the splenetic, and the balanced man, the fool and the sage, the enthusiast and the stick-in-the-mud, the talkative and the taciturn, and, most dilemmal of all, the consistent and the inconsistent. Similarly, it seemed to him as fine a thing to be fat as to be lean, to be short as tall, homely as handsome. To complete his quandary—what is probably an effect of the foregoing—Ebenezer could be persuaded, at least notionally, by any philosophy of the world, even by any strongly held opinion, which was either poetically conceived or attractively stated, since he appeared to be emotionally predisposed in favor of none. It was as pretty a notion to him that the world was made of water, as Thales declared, as that it was air, *à la* Anaximines, or fire, *à la* Heraclitus, or all three and dirt to boot, as swore Empedocles; that all was matter, as Hobbes maintained, or that all was mind, as some of Locke's followers were avowing, seemed equally likely to our poet, and as for ethics, could he have been all three and not just one he'd have enjoyed dying once a saint, once a frightful sinner, and once lukewarm between the two.

The man (in short), thanks both to Burlingame and to his natural proclivities, was dizzy with the beauty of the possible; dazzled, he threw up his hands at choice, and like ungainly flotsam rode half-content the tide of chance. Though the term was done he stayed on at Cambridge. For a week he simply languished in his rooms, reading distractedly and smoking pipe after pipe of tobacco, to which he'd become addicted. At length reading became impossible; smoking too great a bother: he prowled restlessly about the room. His head always felt about to ache, but never began to.

Finally one day he did not deign even to dress himself or eat, but sat immobile in the window seat in his nightshirt and stared at the activity in the street below, unable to choose a motion at all even when, some hours later, his untutored bladder suggested one.

3

Ebenezer Is Rescued, and Hears a Diverting Tale Involving Isaac Newton and Other Notables

LUCKILY FOR HIM (else he might have mossed over where he sat), Ebenezer was roused from his remarkable trance shortly after dinner-time by a sudden great commotion at his door.

"Eben! Eben! Prithee admit me quickly!"

"Who is it?" called Ebenezer, and jumped up in alarm: he had no friends at the College who might be calling on him.

"Open and see," the visitor laughed. "Only hurry, I beg of thee!"

"Do but wait a minute. I must dress."

"What? Not dressed? 'Swounds, what an idle fellow! No matter, boy; let me in at once!"

Ebenezer recognized the voice, which he'd not heard for three years. "Henry!" he cried, and threw open the door.

" 'Tis no other," laughed Burlingame, giving him a squeeze. "Marry, what a lout thou'rt grown to! A good six feet! And abed at this hour!" He felt the young man's forehead. "Yet you've no fever. What ails thee, lad? Ah well, no matter. One moment——" He ran to the window and peered cautiously below. "Ah, there's the rascal! Hither, Eben!"

Ebenezer hurried to the window. "Whatever is't?"

"Yonder, yonder!" Burlingame pointed up the street. "Coming by the little dram-shop! Know you that gentleman with the hickory-stick?"

Ebenezer saw a long-faced man of middle age, gowned as a don, making his way down the street.

"Nay, 'tis no Magdalene Fellow. The face is strange."

"Shame on thee, then, and mark it well. 'Tis Isaac himself, from Trinity."

"Newton!" Ebenezer looked with sharper interest. "I've not

13

seen him before, but word hath it the Royal Society is bringing out a book of his within the month that will explain the workings of the entire universe! I'faith, I thank you for your haste! But did I hear you call him *rascal?*"

Burlingame laughed again. "You mistake the reason for my haste, Eben. I pray God my face hath altered these fifteen years, for I'm certain Brother Isaac caught sight of me ere I reached your entryway."

"Is't possible you *know* him?" asked Ebenezer, much impressed.

"Know him? I was once near raped by him. Stay!" He drew back from the window. "Keep an eye on him, and tell me how I might escape should he turn in at your door."

"No difficulty: the door of this chamber lets onto an open stairway in the rear. What in Heav'n's afoot, Henry?"

"Don't be alarmed," Burlingame said. " 'Tis a pretty story, and I'll tell it all presently. Is he coming?"

"One moment—he's just across from us. There. Nay, wait now—he is saluting another don. Old Bagley, the Latinist. There, now, he's moving on."

Burlingame came to the window, and the two of them watched the great man continue up the street.

"Not another moment, Henry," Ebenezer declared. "Tell me at once what mystery is behind this hide-and-seek, and behind thy cruel haste to leave us three years past, or watch me perish of curiosity!"

"Aye and I shall," Burlingame replied, "directly you dress yourself, lead us to food and drink, and give full account of yourself. 'Tis not I alone who have excuses to find."

"How! Then you know of my failure?"

"Aye, and came to see what's what, and perchance to birch some sense into you."

"But how can that be? I told none but Anna."

"Stay, you'll hear all, I swear't. But not a word till I've a spread of sack and mutton. Let not excitement twist thy values, lad—come on with you!"

"Ah, bless you, thou'rt an Iliad Greek, Henry," Ebenezer said, and commenced dressing.

They went to an inn nearby, where over small beer after dinner Ebenezer explained, as best he could, his failure at the College and subsequent indecisions. "The heart of't seems to be," he concluded, "that in no matter of import can I make up my mind. Marry, Henry, how I've needed thy counsel! What agonies you might have saved me!"

14

"Nay," Burlingame protested. "You well know I love you, Eben, and feel your afflictions as my own. But advice, I swear't, is the wrong medicine for your malady, for two reasons: first, the logic of the problem is such that at some remove or other you'd have still to choose, inasmuch as should I counsel you to come with me to London, you yet must choose whether to follow my counsel; and should I farther counsel you to follow my first counsel, you must yet choose to follow my second—the regress is infinite and goes nowhere. Second, e'en could you choose to follow my counsel, 'tis no cure at all, but a mere crutch to lean upon. The object is to put you on your feet, not to take you off them. 'Tis a serious affair, Eben; it troubles me. What are your own sentiments about your failure?"

"I must own I have none," Ebenezer said, "though I can fancy many."

"And this indecision: how do you feel about yourself?"

"Marry, I know not! I suppose I'm merely curious."

Burlingame frowned and called for a pipe of tobacco from a winedrawer working near at hand. "You were indeed the picture of apathy when I found you. Doth it not gall or grieve you to lose the baccalaureate, when you'd approached so near it?"

"In a manner, I suppose," Ebenezer smiled. "And yet the man I most respect hath got on without it, hath he not?"

Burlingame laughed. "My dear fellow, I see 'tis time I told you many things. Will it comfort you to learn that I, too, suffer from your disease, and have since childhood?"

"Nay, that cannot be," Ebenezer said. "Ne'er have I seen thee falter, Henry: thou'rt the very antithesis of indecision! 'Tis to you I look in envy, and despair of e'er attaining such assurance."

"Let me be your hope, not your despair, for just as a mild siege of smallpox, though it scar a man's face, leaves him safe forever from dying of that ailment, so inconstancy, fickleness, a periodic shifting of enthusiasms, though a vice, may preserve a man from crippling indecision."

"*Fickleness*, Henry?" Ebenezer asked in wonderment. "Is't fickleness explains your leaving us?"

"Not in the sense you take it," Burlingame said. He fetched out a shilling and called for two more tankards of beer. "I say, did you know I was an orphan child?"

"Why, yes," Ebenezer said, surprised. "Now you mention it, I believe I did, though I can't recall your ever telling us.

15

Haply we just assumed it. I'faith, Henry, all the years we've known you, and yet in sooth we know naught of you, do we? I've no idea when you were born, or where reared, or by whom."

"Or why I left you so discourteously, or how I learned of your failure, or why I fled the great Mister Newton," Burlingame added. "Very well then, take a draught with me, and I shall uncloak the mystery. There's a good fellow!"

They drank deeply, and Burlingame began his story.

"I've not the faintest notion where I was born, or even when—though it must have been about 1654. Much less do I know what woman bore me, or what man got me on her. I was raised by a Bristol sea-captain and his wife, who were childless, and 'tis my suspicion I was born in either America or the West Indies, for my earliest memories are of an ocean passage when I was no more than three years old. Their name was Salmon—Avery and Melissa Salmon."

"I am astonished!" Ebenezer declared. "I ne'er dreamed aught so extraordinary of your beginnings! How came you to be called Burlingame, then?"

Burlingame sighed. "Ah, Eben, just as till now you've been incurious about my origin, so till too late was I. Burlingame I've been since earliest memory, and, as is the way of children, it ne'er occurred to me to wonder at it, albeit to this day I've met no other of that surname."

"It must be that whomever Captain Salmon received you from was your parent!" Ebenezer said. "Or haply 'twas some kin of yours, that knew your name."

"Dear Eben, think you I've not racked myself upon that chance? Think you I'd not forfeit a hand for five minutes' converse with my poor Captain, or gentle Melissa? But I must put by my curiosity till Judgment Day, for they both are in their graves."

"Unlucky fellow!"

"All through my childhood," Burlingame went on, " 'twas my single aim to go to sea, like Captain Salmon. Boats were my only toys; sailors my only playmates. On my thirteenth birthday I shipped as messboy on the Captain's vessel, a West Indiaman, and so taken was I by the mariner's life that I threw my heart and soul into my apprenticeship. Ere we raised Barbados I was scrambling aloft with the best of 'em, to take in a stuns'l or tar the standing rigging, and was as handy with a fid as any Jack aboard. Eben, Eben, what a life for a lad—e'en now it shivers me to think on't! Brown as a coffee-

16

bean I was, and agile as a monkey, and ere my voice had left off changing, ere my parts were fully haired—at an age when most boys have still the smell of the womb on 'em, and dream of traveling to the neighboring shire—I had dived for sheepswool sponges on the Great Bahaman Banks and fought with pirates in the Gulf of Paria. What's more, after guarding my innocence in the fo'c'sle with a fishknife from a lecherous old Manxman who'd offered two pounds for't, I swam a mile through shark-water from our mooring off Curaçao to squander it one August night with a mulatto girl upon the beach. She was scarce thirteen, Eben—half Dutch, half Indian, lissome and trembly as an eight-month colt—but on receipt of a little brass spyglass of mine, which she'd taken a great fancy to in the village that morning, she fetched up her skirts with a laugh, and I deflowered her under the sour-orange trees. I was not yet fifteen."

"Gramercy!"

"No man e'er loved his trade more than I," Burlingame continued, "nor slaved at it more diligently; I was the apple of the Captain's eye, and would, I think, have risen fast through the ranks."

"Then out on't, Henry, how is't you claim my failing? For I see naught in thy tale here but a staggering industry and singlemindedness, the half of which I'd lose an ear to equal."

Burlingame smiled and drank off the last of his beer. *"Inconstancy*, dear fellow, inconstancy. That same singlemindedness that raised me o'er the other lads on the ship was the ruin of my nautical career."

"How can that be?"

"I made five voyages in all," Burlingame said. "On the fifth —the same voyage on which I lost my virginity—we lay becalmed one day in the horse latitudes off the Canary Islands, and quite by chance, looking about for something wherewith to occupy myself, I happened on a copy of Motteux's *Don Quixote* among a shipmate's effects; I spent the remainder of the day with it, for though Mother Salmon had taught me to read and write, 'twas the first real storybook I'd read. I grew so entranced by the great Manchegan and his faithful squire as to lose all track of time and was rebuked by Captain Salmon for reporting late to the cook.

"From that day on I was no longer a seaman, but a student. I read every book I could find aboard ship and in port —bartered my clothes, mortgaged my pay for books, on any subject whatever, and reread them over and over when no new ones could be found. All else went by the board; what work I could be made to do I did distractedly, and in careless haste. I took to hiding, in the rope-locker or the lazarette, where I could read for an hour undisturbed ere I was found. Finally Captain Salmon could tolerate it no more: he ordered the mate to confiscate every volume aboard, save only the charts, the ship's log, and the navigational tables, and pitched 'em to the sharks off Port-au-Prince; then he gave me such a hiding for my sins that my poor bum tingled a fortnight after, and forbade me e'er to read a printed page aboard his vessel. This so thwarted and aggrieved me, that at the next port (which happened to be Liverpool) I jumped ship and left career and benefactor forever, with not a thank-ye nor a fare-thee-well for the people who'd fed and clothed me since babyhood.

"I had no money at all, and for food only a great piece of hard cheese I'd stolen from the ship's cook: therefore I very soon commenced to starve. I took to standing on street-corners and singing for my supper: I was a pretty lad and knew many a song, and when I would sing *What Thing Is Love?* to the ladies, or *A Pretty Duck There Was* to the gentlemen, 'twas not often they'd pass me by without a smile and tuppence. At length a band of wandering gypsies, traveling down from Scotland to London, heard me sing and invited me to join them, and so for the next year I worked and lived with those curious people. They were tinkers, horse-traders, fortune-tellers, basket-makers, dancers, troubadours, and thieves. I dressed in their fashion, ate, drank, and slept with them, and they taught me all their songs and tricks. Dear Eben! Had you seen me then, you'd ne'er have doubted for an instant I was one of them!"

"I am speechless," Ebenezer declared. " 'Tis the grandest adventure I have heard!"

"We worked our way slowly, with many digressions, from Liverpool through Manchester, Sheffield, Nottingham, Leicester, and Bedford, sleeping in the wagons when it rained or out under the stars on fine nights. In the troupe of thirty souls I was the only one who read and wrote, and so was of great assistance to them in many ways. Once to their great delight I read them tales out of Boccaccio—they all love to tell and hear stories—and they were so surprised to learn that books contain such marvelous pleasantries, a thing which erst they'd not suspected, that they began to steal every book they could find for me: I seldom lacked reading that year! It happened one day they turned up a primer, and I taught the lot of 'em their letters, for which services they were unimaginably grateful. Despite my being a 'gorgio' (by which name they call non-gypsies) they initiated me into their most privy matters and expressed the greatest desire for me to marry into their group and travel with them forever.

"But late in 1670 we arrived here in Cambridge, having wandered down from Bedford. The students and several of the dons took a great fancy to us, and though they made too free with sundry of our women, they treated us most cordially, even bringing us to their rooms to sing and play for them. Thus were my eyes first opened to the world of learning and scholarship, and I knew on the instant that my interlude with the gypsies was done. I resolved to go no farther: I bid adieu to my companions and remained in Cambridge, determined to starve upon the street-corners rather than leave this magnificent place."

"Marry, Henry!" Ebenezer said. "Thy courage brings me nigh to weeping! What did you then?"

"Why, so soon as my belly commenced to rumble I stopped short where I was (which happened to be over by Christ's College) and broke into *Flow My Tears*, it being of all the songs I knew the most plaintive. And when I had done with the last verse of it—

> *Hark! yon Shadows that in Darkness dwell,*
> *Learn to contemn Light.*
> *Happy, happy they that in Hell*
> *Feel not the World's Despite.*

—when I had done, I say, there appeared at a nearby window a lean frowning don, who enquired of me, What manner of Cainite was I, that I counted them happy who must fry forever in the fires of Hell? And another, who came to the window beside him, a fat wight, asked me, Did I not know where I was? To which I answered, 'I know no more, good masters, than that I am in Cambridge Town and like to perish of my belly!' Then the first don, who all unbeknownst to me was having a merry time at my expense, told me I was in Christ's College, and that he and all his fellows were powerful divines, and that for lesser blasphemies than mine they had caused men to be broke upon the wheel. I was a mere sixteen then, and not a little alarmed, for though I'd read enough scarce to credit their story, yet I knew not but what

19

they could work me some injury or other, e'en were't something short of the wheel. Therefore I humbly craved their pardon, and pled 'twas but an idle song, the words of which I scarce attended; so that were there aught of blasphemy in't, 'twas not the singer should be racked for't but the author Dowland, who being long since dead, must needs already have had the sin rendered out of him in Satan's try-works, and there's an end on't! At this methinks the merry dons had like to laugh aloud, but they put on sterner faces yet and ordered me into their chamber. There they farther chastised me, maintaining that while my first offense had been grievous enough, in its diminution of the torments of Hell, this last remark of mine had on't the very smell of the stake. 'How is that?' I asked them. 'Why,' the lean one cried, 'to hold as you do that they who perpetuate another's sin, albeit witlessly, are themselves blameless, is to deny the doctrine of Original Sin itself, for who are Eve and Adam but the John Dowlands of us all, whose sinful song all humankind must sing willy-nilly and die for't?' 'What is more,' the fat don declared, 'in denying the mystery of Original Sin you scorn as well the mystery of Vicarious Atonement—for where's the sense of Salvation for them that are not lost?'

" 'Nay, nay!' said I, and commenced to sniffling. 'Marry, masters, 'twas but an idle observation! Prithee take no notice of't!'

" 'An idle observation!' the first replied, and laid hold of my arms. ' 'Swounds, boy! You scoff at the two cardinal mysteries of the Church, which like twin pillars bear the entire edifice of Christendom; you as much as call the Crucifixion a vulgar Mayfair show; and to top all you regard such unspeakable blasphemies as idle observations! 'Tis a more horrendous sin yet! Whence came thee here, anyhow?'

" 'From Bedford,' I replied, frightened near out of my wits, 'with a band of gypsies.' On hearing this the dons feigned consternation, and declared that every year at this time the gypsies passed through Cambridge for the sole purpose, since they are heathen to a man, of working some hurt on the divines. Only the year before, they said, one of my cohorts had sneaked privily into the Trinity brew-house and poisoned a vat of beer, with the result that three Senior Fellows, four Scholars, and a brace of idle Sizars were done to death ere sundown. Then they asked me, What was my design? And when I told them I had hoped to attach myself to one of their number as a serving-boy, the better to improve my mind, they made out I was come to poison the lot of 'em. So saying, they stripped me naked on the spot, despite my protestations of innocence, and on pretext of seeking hidden phials of vitriol they poked and probed every inch of my person, and pinched and tweaked me in alarming places. Nay, I must own they laid lecherous hands upon me, and had soon done me a violence but that their sport was interrupted by another don—an aging, saintlike gentleman, clearly their superior—who bade them stand off and rebuked them for molesting me. I flung myself at his feet, and, raising me up and looking at me from top to toe, he enquired, What was the occasion of my being disrobed? I replied, I had but sung a song to please these gentlemen, the which they had called a blasphemy, and had then so diligently searched me for phials of vitriol, that I looked to be costive the week through.

"The old don then commanded me to sing the song at once, that he might judge of its blasphemy, and so I fetched up my guitar, which the gypsies had taught me the use of, and as best I could (for I was weeping and shivering with fright) I once again sang *Flow My Tears*. Throughout the piece my savior smiled on me sweetly as an angel, and when I was done he spoke not a word about blasphemy, but kissed me upon the forehead, bade me dress, and after reproving again my tormentors, who were mightily ashamed at being thus surprised in their evil prank, he commanded me to go with him to his quarters. What's more, after interrogating me at length concerning my origin and my plight, and expressing surprise and pleasure at the extent of my reading, he then and there made me a member of his household staff, to serve him personally, and allowed me free use of his admirable library."

"I must know who this saintly fellow was," Ebenezer interrupted. "My curiosity leaps its banks!"

Burlingame smiled and raised a finger. "I shall tell thee, Eben; but not a word of't must you repeat, for reasons you'll see presently. Whate'er his failings, 'twas a noble turn he did me, and I'd not see his name besmirched by any man."

"Never fear," Ebenezer assured him. " 'Twill be like whispering it to thyself."

"Very well, then. I shall tell thee only that he was Platonist to the ears, and hated Tom Hobbes as he hated the Devil, and was withal so fixed on things of the spirit—on *essential spissitude* and *indiscerptibility* and *metaphysical extension* and the like, which were as real to him as rocks and cow-pat-

21

ties—that he scarce lived in this world at all. And should these be still not sufficient clues, know finally that he was at that time much engrossed in a grand treatise against the materialist philosophy, which treatise he printed the following year under the title *Enchiridion Metaphysicum*."

" 'Sheart!" Ebenezer whispered. "My dear friend, was't Henry More himself you sang for? I should think 'twould be thy boast, not an embarrassment!"

"Stay, till I end my tale. 'Twas in sooth great More himself I lived with! None knows more than I his noble character, and none is more a debtor to his generosity. I was then perhaps seventeen: I tried in every way I knew to be a model of intelligence, good manners, and industry, and ere long the old fellow would allow no other servant near him. He took great pleasure in conversing with me, at first about my adventures at sea and with the gypsies, but later on matters of philosophy and theology, with which subjects I made special effort to acquaint myself. 'Twas plain he'd conceived a great liking for me."

"Thou'rt a lucky wight, i'faith!" Ebenezer sighed.

"Nay; only hear me out. As time went on he no longer addressed me as 'Dear Henry,' or 'My boy,' but rather 'My son,' and 'My dear'; and after that 'Dearest thing,' and finally 'Thingums,' 'Precious laddikins,' and 'Gypsy mine' in turn. In short, as I soon guessed, his affection for me was Athenian as his philosophy—dare I tell you he more than once caressed me, and called me his little Alcibiades?"

"I am amazed!" said Ebenezer. "The scoundrel rescued you from the other blackguards, merely to have you for his own unnatural lusts!"

"Oh la, 'twas not at all the same thing, Eben. The others were men in their thirties, full to bursting (as my master himself put it) with *the filth and unclean tinctures of corporeity*. More, on the other hand, was near sixty, the gentlest of souls, and scarce realized himself, I daresay, the character of his passion: I had no fear of him at all. And here I must confess, Eben, I did a shameful thing: so intent was I on entering the University, that instead of leaving More's service as soon as tact would permit, I lost no opportunity to encourage his shameful doting. I would perch on the arm of his chair like an impudent lass and read over his shoulder, or cover his eyes for a tease, or spring about the room like a monkey, knowing he admired my energy and grace. Most of all I sang and played on my guitar for him: many's the night—I blush

22

to tell it!—when I would let him come upon me, as though by accident; I would laugh and blush, and then as if to make a lark of't, take my guitar and sing *Flow My Tears*.

"Need I say the poor philosopher was simply ravished? His passion so took governance o'er his other faculties, he grew so entirely enamored of me, that upon my granting him certain trifling favors, which I knew he'd long coveted but scarce hoped for, he spent nearly all his meager savings to outfit me like the son of an earl, and enrolled me in Trinity College."

Here Burlingame lit another pipe, and sighed in remembrance.

"I was, I believe, uncommonly well-read for a boy my age. In the two years with More I'd mastered Latin, Greek, and Hebrew, read all of Plato, Tully, Plotin, and divers other of the ancients, and at least perused most of the standard works of natural philosophy. My benefactor made no secret that he looked for me to become as notable a philosopher as Herbert of Cherbury, John Smith, or himself—and who knows but what I might have been, had things turned out happily? But alas, Eben, that same shamelessness by virtue of which I reached my goal proved my undoing. 'Twas quite poetic."

"What happened, pray?"

"I was not strong in mathematics," Burlingame said, "and for that reason I devoted much of my study to that subject, and spent as much time as I could with mathematicians—especially with the brilliant young man who but two years before, in 1669, had taken Barrow's place as Lucasian Professor of Mathematics, and holds the office yet. . . ."

"Newton!"

"Aye, the wondrous Isaac! He was twenty-nine or thirty then, as I am now, with a face like a pure-bred stallion's. He was thin and strong and marvelous energetic, much given to moods; he had the arrogance that oft goes with great gifts, but was in other ways quite shy, and seldom overbearing. He could be merciless with others' theories, yet was himself inordinately sensitive to criticism. He was so diffident about his talents 'twas with great reluctance he allowed aught of his discoveries to be printed; yet so vain, the slightest suggestion that someone had antedated him would drive him near mad with rage and jealousy. Impossible, splendid fellow!"

"Marry, he frightens me!" Ebenezer said.

"Now you must know that at that time More and Newton had no love whatever for each other, and the cause of their enmity was the French philosopher Renatus Descartes."

"Descartes? How can that be?"

"I know not how well you've heeded your tutors," Burlingame said; "you might know that all these Platonical gentlemen of Christ's and Emmanuel Colleges are wont to sing the praises of Descartes, inasmuch as he makes a great show of pottering about in mathematics and the motions of heavenly bodies, like any Galileo, and yet unlike Tom Hobbes he affirms the real existence of God and the soul, which pleases them no end. The more for that the lot of 'em are Protestants: this much-vaunted rejection of the learning of his time, that Renatus brags of in his *Discourse on Method:* this searching of his innards for his axioms—is't not the first principle of Protestantism? Thus it is that Descartes' system is taught all over Cambridge, and More, like the rest, praised and swore by him as by a latter-day saint. Tell me, Eben: how is't, d'you think, that the planets are moved in their courses?"

"Why," said Ebenezer, " 'tis that the cosmos is filled with little particles moving in vortices, each of which centers on a star; and 'tis the subtle push and pull of these particles in our solar vortex that slides the planets along their orbs—is't not?"

"So saith Descartes," Burlingame smiled. "And d'you haply recall what is the nature of light?"

"If I have't right," replied Ebenezer, " 'tis an aspect of the vortices—of the press of inward and outward forces in 'em. The celestial fire is sent through space from the vortices by this pressure, which imparts a transitional motion to little light globules——"

"Which Renatus kindly hatched for that occasion," Burlingame interrupted. "And what's more he allows his globules both a rectilinear and a rotatory motion. If only the first occurs when the globules smite our retinae, we see white light; if both, we see color. And as if this were not magical enough —*mirabile dictu!*—when the rotatory motion surpasseth the rectilinear, we see blue; when the reverse, we see red; and when the twain are equal, we see yellow. What fantastical drivel!"

"You mean 'tis not the truth? I must say, Henry, it sounds reasonable to me. In sooth, there is a seed of poetry in it; it hath an elegance."

"Aye, it hath every virtue and but one small defect, which is, that the universe doth not operate in that wise. Marry, 'tis no crime, methinks, to teach the man's skeptical philosophy or his analytical geometry—both have much of merit in 'em.

24

But his cosmology is purely fanciful, his optics right bizarre; and the first man to prove it is Isaac Newton."

"Hence their enmity?" asked Ebenezer.

Burlingame nodded. "By the time Newton became Lucasian Professor he had already spoilt Cartesian optics with his prism experiments—and well do I recall them from his lectures!—and he was refuting the theory of vortices by mathematics, though he hadn't as yet published his own cosmical hypotheses. But his loathing for Descartes goes deeper yet: it hath its origin in a difference betwixt their temperaments. Descartes, you know, is a clever writer, and hath a sort of genius for illustration that lends force to the wildest hypotheses. He is a great hand for twisting the cosmos to fit his theory. Newton, on the other hand, is a patient and brilliant experimenter, with a sacred regard for the facts of nature. Then again, since the lectures *De Motu Corporum* and his papers on the nature of light have been available, the man always held up to him by his critics is Descartes.

"So, then, no love was lost 'twixt Newton and More; they had in fact been quietly hostile for some years. And when I became the focus of't, their antagonism boiled over."

"*You?* But you were a simple student, were you not? Surely two such giants ne'er would stoop to fight their battles with their students."

"Must I draw a picture, Eben?" Burlingame said. "I was out to learn the nature of the universe from Newton, but knowing I was More's protégé, he was cold and incommunicative with me. I employed every strategy I knew to remove this barrier, and, alas, won more than I'd fought for—in plain English, Eben, Newton grew as enamored of me as had More, with this difference only, that there was naught Platonical in his passion."

"I know not what to think!" cried Ebenezer.

"Nor did I," said Burlingame, "albeit one thing I knew well, which was that save for the impersonal respect I bare the twain of 'em, I cared not a fart for either. 'Tis a wise thing, Eben, not to confuse one affection with another. Well, sir, as the months passed, each of my swains came to realize the passions of the other, and both grew as jealous as Cervantes' *Celoso Extremeño*. They carried on shamefully, and each threatened my ruination in the University should I not give o'er the other. As for me, I paid no more heed than necessary to either, but wallowed in the libraries of the colleges like a dolphin in the surf. 'Twas job enough for me to re-

25

member to eat and sleep, much less fulfill the million little obligations they thought I owed 'em. I'faith, a handsome pair!"

"Prithee, what was the end of it?"

Burlingame sighed. "I played the one against the other for above two years, till at last Newton could endure it no longer. The Royal Society had by this time published his experiments with prisms and reflecting telescopes, and he was under fire from Robert Hooke, who had light theories of his own; from the Dutchman Christian Huygens, who was committed to the lens telescope; from the French monk Pardies; and from the Belgian Linus. So disturbed was he by the conjunction of this criticism and his jealousy, that in one and the same day he swore ne'er to publish another of his discoveries, and confronted More in the latter's chambers with the intent of challenging him to settle their rivalry for good and all by means of a duel to the death!"

"Ah, what a loss to the world, whate'er the issue of't," observed Ebenezer.

"As't happened, no blood was let," Burlingame said: "the tale ends happily for them both, if not for the teller. After much discourse Newton discovered that his rival's position was uncertain as his own, and that I seemed equally indifferent to both—which conclusion, insofar as't touches the particular matters they had in mind, is as sound as any in the *Principia*. In addition More showed to Newton his *Enchiridion Metaphysicum*, wherein he plainly expressed a growing disaffection for Descartes; and Newton assured More that albeit 'twas universal gravitation, and not angels or vortices, that steered the planets in their orbits, there yet remained employment enough for the Deity as a first cause to set the cosmic wheels a-spin, e'en as old Renatus had declared. In fine, so far from dueling to the death, they so convinced each other that at the end of some hours of colloquy—all which I missed, being then engrossed in the library—they fell to tearful embraces, and decided to cut me off without a penny, arrange my dismissal from the College, and move into the same lodgings, where, so they declared, they would couple the splendors of the physical world to the glories of the ideal, and listen ravished to the music of the spheres! This last they never did in fact, but their connection endures to this day, and from all I hear, More hath washed his hands entirely of old Descartes, while Newton hath caught a foolish infatuation with theology, and seeks to explain the Apocalypse by

26

application of his laws of series and fluxions. As for the first two of their resolves, they fulfilled 'em to the letter—turned me out to starve, and so influenced all and sundry against me that not a shilling could I beg, nor eat one meal on credit. 'Twas off to London I went, with not a year 'twixt me and the baccalaureate. Thus was it, in 1676, your father found me; and playing fickle to the scholar's muse, I turned to you and your dear sister all the zeal I'd erst reserved for my researches. Your instruction became my First Good, my Primary Cause, which lent all else its form and order. And my fickleness is thorough and entire: not for an instant have I regretted the way of my life, or thought wistfully of Cambridge."

"Dear, dear Henry!" Ebenezer cried. "How thy tale moves me, and shames me, that I let slip through idleness what you strove so hard in vain to reach! Would God I had another chance!"

"Nay, Eben, thou'rt no scholar, I fear. You have perchance the schoolman's love of lore, but not the patience, not the address, not I fear that certain nose for relevance, that grasp of the world, which sets apart the thinker from the crank. There is a thing in you, a set of the grain as 'twere, that would keep you ingenuous even if all the books in all the libraries of Europe were distilled in your brain. Nay, let the baccalaureate go; I came here not to exhort you to try again, or to chide you for failing, but to take you with me to London for a time, until you see your way clearly. 'Twas Anna's idea, who loves you more than herself, and I think it wise."

"Precious Anna! How came she to know thy whereabouts?"

"There, now," laughed Burlingame, "that is another tale entirely, and 'twill do for another time. Come with me to London, and I'll tell it thee in the carriage."

Ebenezer hesitated. " 'Tis a great step."

" 'Tis a great world," replied Burlingame.

"I fear me what Father would say, did he hear of't."

"My dear fellow," Burlingame said, "we sit here on a blind rock careening through space; we are all of us rushing headlong to the grave. Think you the worms will care, when anon they make a meal of you, whether you spent your moment sighing wigless in your chamber, or sacked the golden towns of Montezuma? Lookee, the day's nigh spent; 'tis gone careering into time forever. Not a tale's length past we lined our bowels with dinner, and already they growl for more. We are dying men, Ebenezer: i'faith, there's time for naught but bold resolves!"

"You lend me courage, Henry," Ebenezer said, rising from the table. "Let us begone."

4

Ebenezer's First Sojourn in London, and the Issue of It

BURLINGAME SLEPT THAT NIGHT in Ebenezer's room, and the next day they left Cambridge for London by carriage.

"I think you've not yet told me," the young man said en route, "how it is you left St. Giles so suddenly, and how Anna came to know your whereabouts."

Burlingame sighed. "'Tis a simple mystery, if a sad one. The fact is, Eben, your father fancies I have designs upon your sister."

"Nay! Incredible!"

"Ah, now, as for that, 'tis not so incredible; Anna is a sweet and clever girl, and uncommon lovely."

"Yet think of your ages!" Ebenezer said. "'Tis absurd of Father!"

"Think you 'tis absurd?" Burlingame asked. "Thou'rt a candid fellow."

"Ah, forgive me," Ebenezer laughed; "'twas a rude remark. Nay, 'tis not absurd at all: thou'rt but thirty-odd, and Anna twenty-one. I daresay 'tis that you were our teacher made me think of you as older."

"'Twere no absurd suspicion, methinks, that *any* man might look with love on Anna," Burlingame declared, "and I did indeed love the both of you for years, and love you yet; nor did I ever try to hide the fact. 'Tis not that which distresses me; 'tis Andrew's notion that I had vicious designs on the girl. 'Sheart, if anything be improbable, 'tis that so mar-

28

velous a creature as Anna could look with favor on a penni-less pedagogue!"

"Nay, Henry, I have oft heard her protest, that by compar-ison to you, none of her acquaintances was worth the labor of being civil to."

"Anna said that?"

"Aye, in a letter not two months past."

"Ah well, whate'er the case, Andrew took my regard for her as lewd intent, and threatened me one afternoon that should I not begone ere morning he'd shoot me like a dog and horsewhip dear Anna into the bargain. I had no fear for myself, but not to risk bringing injury to her I left at once, albeit it tore my heart to go."

Ebenezer sat amazed at this revelation. "How she wept that morning! and yet neither she nor Father told me aught of't!"

"Nor must you speak of it to either," Burlingame warned, "for 'twould but embarrass Anna, would it not? And anger Andrew afresh, for there's no statute of limitations within a family. Think not you'll reason him out of his notion: he is convinced of it."

"I suppose so," Ebenezer said doubtfully. "Then Anna has been in correspondence with you since?"

"Not so regularly as I could wish. Egad, how I've yearned for news of you! I took lodgings on Thames Street, between Billingsgate and the Customs-House—far cry from the sum-mer-pavilion at St. Giles, you'll see!—and hired myself as tutor whenever I could. For two years and more I was unable to communicate with Anna, for fear your father would hear of't, but some months ago I chanced to be engaged as a tutor in French to a Miss Bromly from Plumtree Street, that re-membered you and Anna as playmates ere you removed to St. Giles. Through her I was able to tell Anna where I live, and though I dare not write to her, she hath contrived on two or three occasions to send me letters. 'Twas thus I learned the state of your affairs, and I was but too pleased to act on her suggestion that I fetch you out of Cambridge. She is a dear girl, Eben!"

"I long to see her again!" Ebenezer said.

"And I," said Burlingame, "for I esteem her as highly as thee, and 'tis three years since I've seen her."

"Think you she might visit us in London?"

"Nay, I fear 'tis out of the question. Andrew would have none of it."

29

"Yet surely I cannot resign myself to never seeing her again! Can you, Henry?"

" 'Tis not my wont to look that far ahead," Burlingame said. "Let us consider rather how you'll occupy yourself in London. You must not sit idle, lest you slip again into languishment and stupor."

"Alas," said Ebenezer, "I have no long-term goals toward which to labor."

"Then follow my example," advised Burlingame, "and set as your long-term goal the successful completion of all your short-term goals."

"Yet neither have I any short-term goal."

"Ah, but you will ere long, when your belly growls for dinner and your money's gone."

"Unhappy day!" laughed Ebenezer. "I've no skill in any craft or trade whatever. I cannot even play *Flow My Tears* on the guitar."

"Then 'tis plain you'll be a teacher, like myself."

" 'Sheart! 'Twould be the blind leading the blind!"

"Aye," smiled Burlingame. "Who better grasps the trials of sightlessness than he whose eyes are gone?"

"But what teach? I know something of many things, and enough of naught."

"I'faith, then the field is open, and you may graze where you list."

"Teach a thing I know naught of?" exclaimed Ebenezer.

"And raise thy fee for't," replied Burlingame, "inasmuch as 'tis no chore to teach what you know, but to teach what you know naught of requires a certain application. Choose a thing you'd greatly like to learn, and straightway proclaim yourself professor of't."

Ebenezer shook his head. " 'Tis still impossible; I am curious about the world in general, and ne'er could choose."

"Very well, then: I dub thee Professor of the Nature of the World, and as such shall we advertise you. Whate'er your students wish to learn, that will you teach them."

"Thou'rt jesting, Henry!"

"If't be a jest," replied Burlingame, " 'tis a happy one, I swear, for just so have I lined my belly these three years. B'm'faith, the things I've taught! The great thing is always to be teaching something to someone—a fig for *what* or *to whom*. 'Tis no trick at all."

No matter what Ebenezer thought of this proposal, he had not the wherewithal to reject it: immediately on arriving in

London he moved into Burlingame's chambers by the river and was established as a full partner. A few days after that, Burlingame brought him his first customer—a lout of a tailor from Crutched Friars who happily desired to be taught nothing more intricate than his A B Cs—and for the next few months Ebenezer earned his living as a pedagogue. He worked six or seven hours a day, both in his rooms and at the homes of his students, and spent most of his free time studying desperately for the following day's lessons. What leisure he had he spent in the taverns and coffeehouses with a small circle of Burlingame's acquaintances, mostly idle poets. Impressed by their apparent confidence in their talent, he too endeavored on several occasions to write poems, but abandoned the effort each time for want of anything to write about.

At his insistence a devious correspondence was established with his sister through Miss Bromly, Burlingame's pupil, and after two months Anna contrived to visit them in London, using as excuse the illness of a spinster aunt who lived near Leadenhall. The twins were, as may be imagined, overjoyed to see each other again, for although conversation did not come so readily since Ebenezer's departure from St. Giles three years before, each still bore, abstractly at least, the greatest affection and regard for the other. Burlingame, too, Anna expressed considerable but properly decorous pleasure in seeing again. She had changed somewhat since Ebenezer had seen her last: her brown hair had lost something of its shine, and her face, while still fair, was leaner and less girlish than he remembered it.

"My dear Anna!" he said for the fourth or fifth time. "How good it is to hear your voice! Tell me, how did you leave Father? Is he well?"

Anna shook her head. "Well on the way to Bedlam, I fear, or to driving me there. 'Tis your disappearance, Eben; it angers and frightens him at once. He knows not the cause of't, or whether to comb the realm for you or disown you. A dozen times daily he demands of me whether I know aught of your whereabouts, or else rails at me for keeping things from him. He is grown hugely suspicious of me, and yet sometimes asks of you so plaintively as to move my tears. He has aged much these past weeks, and though he blows and blusters no less than before, his theart is not in it, and it saps his strength."

"Ah, God, it pains me to hear that!"

"And me," said Burlingame, "for though old Andrew hath small love for me, I wish him no ill."

"I do think," Anna said to Ebenezer, "that you should strive to establish yourself in some calling, and communicate with him directly you find a place; for despite the abuse he'll surely heap on you, 'twill ease his soul to learn thou'rt well, and well established."

"And 'twould ease mine to ease his," Ebenezer said.

"Marry, and yet 'tis your own life!" Burlingame cried impatiently. "Filial love be damned, it galls me sore to see the pair of you o'erawed by the pompous rascal!"

"Henry!" Anna chided.

"You must pardon me," Burlingame said; "I mean no harm by't. But lookee, Anna, 'tis not alone Andrew's health that suffers. Thou'rt peaked thyself, and wan, and I mark a sobering of your spirits. You too should flee St. Giles for London, as your aunt's companion or the like."

"Am I wan and solemn?" Anna asked gently. "Haply 'tis mere age, Henry: one-and-twenty is no more a careless child. But prithee ask me not to leave St. Giles; 'tis to ask Father's death."

"Or belike she hath a suitor there," Ebenezer said to Burlingame. "Is't not so, Anna?" he teased. "Some rustic swain, perchance, that hath won your heart? One-and-twenty is no child, but 'twere a passing good wife, were't not? Say, Henry, see the girl blush! Methinks I've hit on't!"

"'Twere a lucky bumpkin, b'm'faith," Burlingame remarked.

"Nay," said Anna, "twit me no more on't, Brother."

She was so plainly overwrought that Ebenezer at once begged her forgiveness for his tease.

Anna kissed his cheek. "How shall I marry, when the man I love best hath the bad sense to be my brother? What say the books at Cambridge, Eben? Was e'er a maid less lucky?"

"Nay, i'faith!" laughed Ebenezer. "You'll live and die a maiden ere you find my like! Yet I commend my friend here to your attention, who though something gone in years yet sings a creditable tenor, and is the devil's own good fellow!"

As soon as he spoke it Ebenezer realized the tactlessness of his remark in the light of what Burlingame had told him weeks before of Andrew's suspicions; both men blushed at once, but Anna saved the situation by kissing Burlingame lightly on the cheek as she had kissed her brother, and saying

32

easily, " 'Twere no mean catch, if you speak truly. Doth he know his letters?"

"What matter?" Burlingame asked, joining the raillery. "Whate'er I lack, this fellow here can teach me, or so he vaunts."

" 'Swounds, that reminds me," Ebenezer said, jumping up, "I must run to Tower Hill this minute, to give young Farmsley his first recorder lesson!" He fetched an alto recorder from the mantelpiece. "Quickly, Henry, how doth one blow the thing?"

"Nay, not quickly: slowly," Burlingame said. " 'Twere a grievous error to learn an art too fast. On no account must thy Farmsley blow a note ere he's spent an hour fondling the instrument, holding it properly, taking it apart and fitting it together. And never, *never* should the master show off his own ability, lest the student grow discouraged at the distance he must travel. I'll teach you the left-hand notes tonight, and you can play *Les Bouffons* for him on the morrow."

"Must you go?" Anna asked.

"Aye, or 'tis stale bread come Sunday, for Henry hath no scholars of his own this week. I shall trust you to his care till I return."

Anna remained a week in London, slipping away from her aunt's bedside as often as possible to visit Ebenezer and Burlingame. At the end of that time, the aunt having recuperated sufficiently to manage for herself, she announced her intention to return to St. Giles, and to Burlingame's considerable surprise and distress, Ebenezer declared that he was going with her—nor could any amount of expostulation change his mind.

" 'Tis no good," he would say, shaking his head. "I am not a teacher."

"Damn me," Burlingame cried, "if thou'rt not fleeing responsibility!"

"Nay. If I flee, I flee *to* it. 'Twas a coward's act to hide from Father's wrath. I shall ask his pardon and do whate'er he requires of me."

"A pox on his anger! 'Tis not responsibility to him I speak of at all, but responsibility to thyself. 'Twere a noble act, on the fact of't, to beg his pardon and take your birching like a man, but 'tis no more than an excuse for dropping the reins of your own life. 'Sheart, 'tis a manlier matter to set your goal and swallow the consequences!"

Ebenezer shook his head. "Put what face you will upon it, Henry, I must go. Can a son stand by and watch his father fret to an early grave?"

"Think no ill of't, Henry," Anna pleaded.

"Surely *you* don't believe it a wise move also?" Burlingame asked incredulously.

"I cannot judge the wisdom of't," Anna replied, "but certain 'twere not a *wrong* thing to do."

"Marry, I have done with the twain of you!" Burlingame cried. "Praise Heav'n I know not my own father, if this be how they shackle one!"

"I pray Heav'n rather you may someday find him," Anna said calmly, "or word of him, at least. A man's father is his link with the past: the bond 'twixt him and the world he's born to."

"Then again I thank Heav'n I'm quit of mine," said Burlingame. "It leaves me free and unencumbered."

"It doth in sooth, Henry," Anna said with some emotion, "for better or worse."

When the time came to leave, Ebenezer asked, "When shall we see you again, Henry? I shall miss you painfully."

But Burlingame only shrugged and said, "Stay here now, if't pain you so."

"I shall visit as often as I can."

"Nay, risk not your father's displeasure. Besides, I may be gone."

"Gone?" asked Anna, with mild alarm. "Gone whither, Henry?"

He shrugged again. "There's naught to keep me here. I care not a fig for any of my pupils, save to pass the time till something else absorbs me."

After making their good-byes, which their friend's bitterness rendered awkward, Ebenezer and Anna hired a carriage to fetch then to St. Giles in the Fields. The little journey, though uneventful, they both enjoyed, for despite the fact that Anna was disturbed to the point of occasional tears over Burlingame's attitude, and Ebenezer grew more anxious by the mile at the prospect of confronting his father, the carriage-ride was the twins' first opportunity in some time to converse privately and at length. When finally they arrived at the Cooke estate they found to their alarm that Andrew had taken to his bed three days before, at the direction of his physician, and was being cared for by Mrs. Twigg, the housekeeper, like an invalid.

"Dear God!" cried Anna. "And I in London all the while!"

" 'Tis no fault of yours, my dear," said Mrs. Twigg. "He told us not to send for you. 'Twould do him good to see you, though, I'm certain."

"I shall go too," Ebenezer declared.

"Nay, not just yet," Anna said. "Let me see what state he's in, and how 'twill strike him. 'Twere best to prepare him for it, don't you think?"

Ebenezer agreed, somewhat reluctantly, for he feared his courage would fail him should he postpone the move too long. That same day, however, Andrew's physician paid a call to the estate, and after learning what the situation was and assuring Ebenezer that his father was too weak to make a scene, he took it upon himself to announce to Andrew, as tactfully as possible, that his son had returned.

"He desires to see you at once," the physician reported afterwards to Ebenezer.

"Is he terribly wroth?" Ebenezer asked.

"I think not. Your sister's return raised his spirits, and I recalled to him the story of the prodigal son."

Ebenezer went upstairs and into his father's bedchamber, a room he had entered not more than thrice in his life. He found his father anything but the figure he'd feared: lying wigless and thin in bed, he looked nearer seventy than fifty; his cheeks were hollow, his eyes pale; his hair was turning white, his voice querulous. At the sight of him Ebenezer quite forgot a small speech of apology he'd concocted; tears sprang to his eyes, and he knelt beside the bed.

"Get up, son, get up," Andrew said with a sigh, "and let me look at ye. 'Tis good to see ye again, I swear it."

"Is't possible thou'rt not enraged?" Ebenezer asked, speaking with difficulty. "My conduct warrants it."

"I'faith, I've no longer the heart for't. Thou'rt my son in any case, and my only son, and if I could wish a better, you too might wish a better father. 'Tis no light matter to be a good one."

"I owe you much explanation."

"Mark the debt canceled," Andrew said, "for I've not the strength for that either. 'Tis the bad child's grace to repent, and the bad father's to forgive, and there's an end on't. Stay, now, I've a deal to say to you and small wind to say it in. In yonder table lies a paper I drafted yesterday, when the world looked somewhat darker than it doth today. Fetch it hither, if't please ye."

Ebenezer did as he was instructed.

"Now," said his father, holding the paper away from Ebenezer's view, "ere I show ye this, say truly: are ye quite ready to have done with flitting hither and yon, and commence to carry a man's portion like a man? If not, ye may put this back where ye fetched it."

"I shall do whate'er you wish, sir," Ebenezer said soberly.

"Marry, 'tis almost too much to hope! Mrs. Twigg has oft maintained that English babies ne'er should take French tit, and lays as the root o' your prodigality the pull and tug of French milk with English blood. Yet I have e'er hoped, and hope still, that soon or late I'll see ye a man, in sooth an *Ebenezer* for our house."

"Beg pardon, sir! I must own I lose you in this talk of French milk and Ebenezers. Surely my mother wasn't French?"

"Nay, nay, thou'rt English sired and English foaled, ye may be certain. Damn that doctor, anyway! Fetch me a pipe and sit ye down, boy, and I shall lay your history open to ye once for all, and the matter I'm most concerned with."

"Is't not unwise to tire yourself?" Ebenezer inquired.

"La," Andrew scoffed, "by the same logic 'tis folly to live. Nay, I'll rest soon enough in the grave." He raised himself a bit on the bed, accepted a pipe from Ebenezer, and after sampling it with pleasure, commenced his story:

" 'Twas in the summer of 1665," he said, "when I came to London from Maryland to settle some business with the merchant Peter Paggen down by Baynard's Castle, that I met and married Anne Bowyer of Bassingshawe, your mother. 'Twas a brief wooing, and to escape the great Plague we sailed at once to Maryland on the brig *Redoubt*, cargoed with dry goods and hardware. We ran into storms from the day we left the Lizard, and headwinds from Flores to the Capes; fourteen weeks we spent a-crossing, and when at last we stepped ashore at St. Mary's City in December, poor Anne was already three months with child! 'Twas an unhappy circumstance, for you must know that every newcomer to the plantations endures a period of seasoning, some weeks of fitting to the clime, and hardier souls than Anne have succumbed to't. She was a little woman, and delicate, fitter for the sewing parlor than the 'tween decks: we'd been not a week at St. Mary's ere a cold she'd got on shipboard turned to a frightful ague. I fetched her o'er the Bay to Malden at once, and the room I'd built for her bridal-chamber became her sick-room—she languished there for the balance of her term, weak and feverish."

Ebenezer listened with considerable emotion, but could think of nothing to say. His father drew again on his pipe.

"My whole house," he continued, "and I as well, looked for Anne to miscarry, or else deliver the child still-born, by reason of her health. Nonetheless I took it upon myself to seek a wet nurse on the chance it might live, for I knew well poor Anne could ne'er give suck. As't happened, one day in February I chanced to be standing on the wharf where Cambridge is now, bargaining with some planters, when I heard a great splash in the Choptank behind me, and turned around in time to see a young lady's head go under the ice."

"Mercy!"

"I was a passing good swimmer in those days, despite my arm, and as no one else seemed inclined to take a cold bath I jumped in after her, periwig and all, and held her up till the others fetched us out. But think ye I got so much as a thank-ee for my pains? The wench was no sooner herself again than she commenced to bewail her rescue and berate me for not letting her drown. This surprised the lot of us no end, inasmuch as she was a pretty young thing, not above sixteen or seventeen years old.

" 'How is't ye wish to end what you've scarce begun?' I asked her. 'Many's the merry tale hath a bad beginning.'

" 'No matter the cause of't,' she replied. 'In sooth I've little to thank ye for; in saving me from a short death by drowning, you but condemn me to a long one by freezing, or a longer by starving.'

"I was about to press her farther for the cause, but I chanced to observe what I'd not remarked ere then—that though her face and arms were peaked and thin, her belly was a-bloom for fair.

" 'Ah, I see't now,' I said. 'Belike your master had sent ye to feel of the sot-weed, whether 'twas dry enough for casking, and some field-hand rogered ye in the curing-house?'

"This I said by way of a tease, inasmuch as I guessed by her ragged dress and grimy skin she was a servant girl. She made no answer, but shook her head and wept e'en harder.

" 'Welladay, then,' I said to her, 'if not a field-hand, why, the master himself, and if not the curing-house, then the linen closet or the cowshed. Such a belly as thine is not got in church, I swear! And now the planter's not stayed to lay by his harvest, I'll wager.'

"After some farther enquiry the girl owned she had indeed been *supping ere the priest said grace,* as young folks will; but only once, and this not by force at the hands of a servingman, but rather at the entreaty of a planter's son who'd sworn his love for her. Nor was't a mere silly milkmaid's maidenhead he took, i'faith, for she was Roxanne Edouard, the orphan of the great French gentleman Cecile Edouard of Edouardine, upriver from Cooke's Point. She'd been reared since her parents' death by a wealthy uncle in Church Creek, down-county, who was so concerned for her noble blood that he permitted her no suitors from among the young men of the place. 'Twas her bad luck to fall in love with the eldest son of her uncle's neighbor, another planter, and he in turn was so taken with her that he begged her to marry him. She was a dutiful enough child not to wed a young man against the wishes of her guardian, but not so dutiful that she didn't let him have first go at her anyhow, in the bilge of a piragua out on the river. Afterwards she refused to see him farther, and the young fool was so distressed as to give up his patrimony and go to sea a common sailor, ne'er to be heard from again. Anon she found herself with child, and straightway confessed the whole matter to her uncle, who turned her off the place at once."

"How!" Ebenezer cried. " 'Tis a nice concern he bore her, indeed! Heav'n protect a child from such solicitude! I cannot fathom it!"

"Nor I," said Andrew, "but thus it happened, or so I heard it. What's more, he threatened violence to any who took her in, and so poor Roxanne was soon brought to direst straits. She tried to indent herself as a domestic, though 'twas little she knew of work; but masters had small inclination for a servant who would herself need service ere many months passed. Everyone knew her and her plight, and many a man who'd been turned from her uncle's door for paying her the merest cordiality before, made her the filthiest proposals now she was down on her luck."

" 'Sheart! Had the wretches no pity for her state?"

"Nay, e'en here her belly undid her, for so far from discouraging, it seemed rather the more to enflame 'em, the plainer it showed. Have ye not yourself observed——" He glanced at his son. "Nay, no matter. In short, she saw naught ahead save harlotry and disgrace on the one hand, or rape and starvation on the other, and being ashamed of the former

38

and afraid of the latter, she chose a third in lieu of either, which was, to leap into the Choptank."

"And, prithee, what did she after you saved her?" Ebenezer asked.

"Why, what else but strive with might and main to leap in again?" Andrew replied. "At last it occurred to me to invite her to join my house, since she looked to lighten but a week ere poor Anne; I agreed to keep her well and provide for her confinement on condition she suckle our babe, if it should live, with her own. She agreed, we drafted the indenture-papers, and I fetched her back to Malden.

"Now your mother, God rest her, grew worse all the time. She was a wondrous Protestant, much giv'n to Bible-reading, and whene'er I showed her pity she was wont to reply, 'Fear not, husband: the Lord will help us.' "

"Bless her!" said Ebenezer.

" 'Twas her conceit," Andrew went on, "to regard her several infirmities as an enemy host, and late and soon she was after me to read her from the Old Testament of God's military intercessions in behalf of the Israelites. Hence when her ague passed off without killing her (albeit it left her pitifully weak), she was proud as any general who sees a flank of the enemy turned, and she declared like the prophet Samuel upon the rout of the Philistines, 'Thus far hath the Lord helped us!' At length her time arrived, and after frightful labor she brought forth Anna, eight pounds and a half. She named her after her own mother, and said again to me, 'Thus far hath the good Lord helped us!' Not a soul then but thought her trials were done, and even I, who was no Catholic saint nor Protestant either, thanked God for her delivery. But not an hour after bearing Anna her travail commenced again, and after much clamor and hollowing she brought you to light, nigh as big as your sister. Seventeen pounds of child she dropped in all, from a—well, from a frame so delicate, simple flatulence gave her pain. 'Twas no wonder she passed into a coma ere your shoulders cleared, and ne'er recovered from it! That same night she died, and the weather being unseasonably hot for May, I fetched her down next day and buried her 'neath a great loblolly pine tree on the Bay side of the point, where she lies yet."

"God help me!" Ebenezer wept. "I am not worthy of't!"

" 'Twould be dishonest not to own," Andrew said, "that such exactly were my sentiments at the time, God forgive

39

me. E'en as the burial service was read I could hear the twain of you a-squalling up in the house, and when I placed a boulder atop the sandy grave, against the time our mason could letter a headstone, it recalled to me those verses in the Book of Samuel where God smites the Philistines and Samuel dedicates the token of His aid—the stone the Hebrews called *Ebenezer*. 'Twas then, boy, in bitterness and sacrilege, I gave ye that name: I baptized ye myself, ere Roxanne could stay me, with the dregs of a flagon of perry, and declared to the company of Malden, 'Thus far hath the Lord helped us!' "

"Ah, dear Father, berate thyself no more for't," Ebenezer begged—though Andrew had displayed no particular emotion. "I understand and forgive!"

Andrew tapped out his pipe in a spittoon beside the bed and, after resting a moment, resumed his story.

"In any case," he said calmly, "you and your sister ne'er wanted mothering. The girl Roxanne had borne her own child, a daughter, eight days before, but the babe had strangled ere its first cry with the navel-cord round its neck; so that maugre the fact there were two of ye, instead of one, she had no more mouths to feed than breasts to feed 'em with, and there was milk aplenty for all. She was e'er a healthy wench once on her feed again—ruddy-faced, full-breasted, and spirited as a dairymaid for all her fine blood. For the four years of her indenture she raised ye as her own. Mrs. Twigg declared no good could come of mixing French pap and English blood, but ye grew fat and merry as any babes in Dorset.

"In 1670, the last year of Roxanne's service, I resolved to leave Malden for London. I was weary of factoring, for one thing; I saw no chance to improve my tobacco-holdings, for another; and though Cooke's Point is of all places on earth dearest to my heart, and my first and largest property, yet 'twas e'er a heartache to live a widower in the house I'd raised for my bride. Moreover, I must own my position with regard to Roxanne had got somewhat delicate since poor Anne's death. That she thought no ill o' me I took for granted, for she was bound to me by gratitude as well as legal instrument. I in turn was more than a little obliged to her, in that she'd not only suckled twice as many of my children as she was legally bound to, but done it with a mother's love, and had taken on most of Mrs. Twigg's duties as governess as well, out of pure affection for ye. I've said already she was an uncommon pretty piece, and I at that time was a strapping

40

wight of thirty-three, prosperous and it may be not unhandsome, who by reason of poor Anne's affliction and death had perforce slept alone and uncomforted since my arrival in the province. Hence, 'tis not surprising some small-minded busybodies should have it Roxanne was filling Anne's place in the bedchamber as well as the nursery—more especially since they themselves had lechered after her. 'Tis e'er the way of men, I've learned, to credit others with the sins themselves want either the courage or the means to commit."

"But marry, what vicious gossip!"

"Aye," Andrew said, "but *As well be a sinner as known for one.* What a man is in the eyes of God means little to the world of men. All things considered, I thought it well to release her; yet I could by no means send her back to death or harlotry, and so 'twas a pleasant surprise when, one day on that selfsame landing where I'd met her, I was approached by a man who introduced himself as Roxanne's uncle, and asked most solicitously after his niece."

"I pray the fellow had tempered his wrath by then."

"He had," Andrew said, "to the point where the very thought of his former unkindness started him to tears, and when I told him of Roxanne's subsequent straits and of the death of her infant, he near tore his hair in remorse. There was no end to his expressions of gratitude for my having saved and cared for her; he declared himself eager to make amends for his severity, and entreated me to prevail upon Roxanne to return to his house. I reminded him that it was his unreasonableness in the matter of suitors for his niece that had driven her to her former disgrace, and he replied that so far from persisting in that unreasonableness, he had in mind at that very moment an excellent match for her with a wealthy fellow of the neighborhood, who had e'er looked kindly upon her.

"You can imagine Roxanne's surprise when she learned of all this. She was pleased to hear of her uncle's change of heart, and yet 'twas like giving up two of her own to let you and Anna go. She wept and wailed, as women will at any great change in their circumstances, and pleaded with me to take her to London, but it seemed to me 'twould be a disservice to the twain of us to maintain any longer our connection, more especially since her uncle had a substantial match arranged for her. Thus was it that on the same day when I gave Roxanne my half of her indenture-bond, signifying the end of her service, her uncle drove out to Malden in a buckboard and fetched her away, and that was that. Not a fortnight later I too made my last farewells to Malden, and left Maryland forever. Think not 'twas an easy matter to go: 'tis a rarity indeed when Life presents ye with a clean choice, i'faith! 'Tis more her wont to arrange things in such fashion that de'il the course ye choose, 'twill give ye pain. *Eheu!* I've rambled and digressed till I'm near out of wind! Here now," he said, handing Ebenezer the document he'd been toying and gesturing with throughout his narration. "Read this whilst I catch my breath."

Ebenezer took the paper, curious and uneasy, and read, among other things:

> Andrew Cooke of the parish of St. Giles in the Fields in the County of Middlesex, Gentleman doe make this my last will and Testament as followeth . . . Imprimus I give to my Son Ebenezer Cooke and Anna Cooke my daughter all my Right and Title of and to . . . all my Land called Cookes Poynt lyng at the mouth of great Choptank River lyng in Dorchester County in Maryland . . . share and share alike. . . .

"Dost see't, boy?" Andrew demanded. "Dost grasp it, damn ye? 'Tis Cooke's Point; 'tis my dear sweet Malden, where the twain of ye saw daylight and your mother lies yet! There's this house too, and the place on Plumtree Street, but Cooke's Point's where my heart lies; Malden's my darling, that I raised out o' the wilderness. 'Tis your legacy, Eben, your inheritance; 'tis your personal piece o' the great wide world to husband and to fructify—and a noble legacy 'tis, b'm'faith! 'Share and share alike,' but the job of managing an estate is man's work, not woman's. 'Twas for this I got, reared, and schooled ye, and 'tis for this ye must work and gird yourself, damn ye, to make ye worthy of't, and play no more at shill I, shall I!"

Ebenezer blushed. "I am sensible I have been remiss, and I've naught to say in my defense, save that 'twas not stupidity undid me at Cambridge, but feckless indirection. Would God I'd had dear Henry Burlingame to steer and prod me!"

"Burlingame!" cried Andrew. "Fogh! He came no nearer the baccalaureate than yourself. Nay, 'twas your dear rascal Burlingame ruined ye, methinks, in not teaching ye how to work." He waved the draft of his will. "Think ye your Burlingame will ever have a Malden to bequeath? Fie on that scoundrel! Mention his name no more to me, an't please ye, lest I suffer a stroke!"

"I am sorry," said Ebenezer, who had mentioned Burlingame's name intentionally to observe his father's reaction: he now concluded it would be impolitic to describe in any detail his sojourn in London. "I know no way to show you how your magnanimity shames me for my failure. Send me back to Cambridge, if you will, and I swear on oath I'll not repeat my former errors."

Andrew reddened. "Cambridge my arse! 'Tis *Maryland* shall be your Cambridge, and a field of sot-weed your library! And for diploma, if ye apply yourself, haply you'll frame a bill of exchange for ten thousandweight of Oronoco!"

"You mean to send me to Maryland, then?" Ebenezer asked uncomfortably.

"Aye, to till the ground that spawned ye, but thou'rt by no means fit for't yet; I fear the University hath so addled and debilitated ye, you've not the head to manage an estate nor the back to till it. 'Twill take some doing to sweat Burlingame and the college out o' ye, but *A man must walk ere he runs.* What ye want's but an honest apprenticeship: I mean to send ye forthwith to London, to clerk for the merchant Peter Paggen. Study the ins and outs of the plantation trade, as did I and my father before me, and I swear 'twill stand ye in better stead than aught ye heard at Cambridge, when time comes for ye to take your place at Malden!"

Now this course of life was not one that Ebenezer would have chosen for himself—but then neither was any other. Moreover, when he reflected upon it, he was not blind to a certain attractiveness about the planter's life as he envisioned it: he could see himself inspecting the labor of the fields from the back of his favorite riding-horse; smoking the tobacco that made him wealthy; drinking quince or perry from his own distillery with a few refined companions; whiling away the idle evenings on the gallery of his manor-house, remarking the mallards out on the river, and perhaps composing occasional verses of ease and dignity. He was, alas, not blind to the attractiveness of any kind of life. And more immediately, the prospect of returning to London with a clear conscience pleased him.

Therefore he said, halfheartedly but not cheerlessly, "Just as you wish, Father. I shall try to do well."

"Why, thank Heav'n for that!" Andrew declared, and even

contrived a thin smile. "'Thus far hath the Lord helped us!' Leave me now for the nonce, ere I collapse from very weariness."

Andrew settled back in bed, turned his face to the wall, and said no more.

5

Ebenezer Commences His Second Sojourn in London, and Fares Unspectacularly

BECAUSE OF THE great unrest in the nation at this time, occasioned by the conflict between James II and William of Orange, Ebenezer, at his father's advice, did not return to London until the winter of 1688, by which time William and Mary were securely established on the throne of England. The idle year at St. Giles was, although he had no way of realizing it at the time, perhaps Ebenezer's nearest approach to happiness. He had nothing at all to do except read, walk about the countryside or London-without-the-walls, and talk at length with his sister. Although he could not look to his future with enthusiasm, at least he had not to bear the responsibility of having chosen it himself. In the spring and summer, when the weather turned fine, he grew too restless even to read. He felt full to bursting with ill-defined potentialities. Often he would sit a whole morning in the shade of a pear tree behind the house playing airs on the tenor recorder, whose secret he had learned from Burlingame. He cared for no sports; he wished not even to see anyone, except Anna. The air, drenched with sun and clover, made him volatile. On several occasions he was so full of feeling as to fear he'd swoon if he could not empty himself of it. But often as he tried to set down verses, he could not begin: his fancy would not settle on stances and conceits. He spent the warm months in a kind of nervous exaltation which, while more upsetting than pleasurable at the moment, left a sweet taste in

44

his mouth at day's end. In the evenings, often as not, he would watch meteors slide down the sky till he grew dizzy.

And though again he could not know it at the time, this idle season afforded him what was to be his last real communion with his sister for many a year. Even so, it was for the most part inarticulate; somewhere they'd lost the knack of talking closely to each other. Of the things doubtless most important to each they spoke not at all—Ebenezer's failure at Cambridge and his impending journey; Anna's uncertain past connection with Burlingame and her present isolation from and lack of interest in suitors of any sort. But they walked together a great deal, and one hot forenoon in August, as they sat under a sycamore near a rocky little steam-branch that ran through the property, Anna clutched his right arm, pressed her forehead to it, and wept for several minutes. Ebenezer comforted her as best he could without inquiring the reason for her tears: he assumed it was some feeling about their maturity that grieved her. At this time, in their twenty-second year of life, Anna looked somewhat older than her brother.

Andrew, once his son's affairs seemed secure, grew gradually stronger, and by autumn was apparently in excellent health again, though for the rest of his life he looked older than his years. In early November he declared the political situation stable enough to warrant the boy's departure; a week later Ebenezer bade the household good-bye and set out for London.

The first thing he did, after finding lodging for himself in a Pudding Lane boardinghouse, was visit Burlingame's address, to see how his old friend fared. But to his surprise he found the premises occupied by new tenants—a draper and his family—and none of the neighbors knew anything of Henry's whereabouts. That evening, therefore, when he'd seen to the arrangement of his belongings, he went to Locket's, hoping to find there, if not Burlingame himself, at least some of their mutual acquaintances who might have news of him.

He found three of the group to which Burlingame had introduced him. One was Ben Oliver, a great fat poet with beady eyes and black curly hair, a very rakehell, who some said was a Jew. Another was Tom Trent, a short sallow boy from Christ's College, also a poet: he'd been sent to prepare for the ministry, but had so loathed the idea that he caught French pox from a doxy he kept in his quarters by way of contempt for his calling, and was finally dismissed upon his spreading the contagion to his tutor and at least two professors who had befriended him. Since then he'd come to take a great interest in religion: he liked no poets save Dante and Milton, maintained a virtual celibacy, and in his cups was wont to shout verses of Scripture at the company in his great bass voice. The third, Dick Merriweather, was despite his surname a pessimist, ever contemplating suicide, who wrote only elegiac verse on the subject of his own demise. Whatever the disparity in their temperaments, however, the three men lived in the same house and were almost always found together.

"I'God, 'tis Eben Cooke the scholar!" cried Ben upon seeing him. "Have a bottle with us, fellow, and teach us the Truth!"

"We thought you dead," said Dick.

Tom Trent said nothing: he was unmoved by greetings and farewells.

Ebenezer returned their greetings, drank a drink with them, and, after explaining his return to London, inquired after Burlingame.

"We've seen none of him for a year," Ben said. "He left us shortly after you did, and I'd have said the twain of you were off together on some lark."

"I recall hearing he'd gone to sea again," Dick Merriweather said. "Belike he's at the bottom of't now, or swimming in the belly of a whale."

"Stay," said Ben. "Now I think on't, didn't I have it from Tom here 'twas Trinity College Henry went back to, to earn his baccalaureate?"

" 'Twas what I had from Joan Toast, that had it from Henry the last night ere he left," Tom said indifferently. "I'll own I pay scant heed to gossip of goings and comings, and 'tis not impossible I misheard her."

"Who is this Joan Toast then, pray, and where might I find her?" asked Ebenezer.

"No need to seek *her*," Ben laughed; "she's but a merry whore of the place, and you may ask what you will of her anon, when she comes in to find a bedfellow."

Ebenezer waited until the girl arrived, and learned only that Burlingame had spoken of his intention to ransack the libraries of Cambridge for a fortnight—for what purpose she did not know, nor did any amount of inquiry around the winehouse shed more light on his intentions or present whereabouts. During the next week Ebenezer lost no opportunity to ask after his friend, but when it became clear that no clues were to be found, he reluctantly abandoned his efforts, wrote Anna a distressed note informing her of the news, and in the following months and years came almost to forget Henry's existence—though to be sure, he felt the loss acutely whenever the name occurred to him.

Meanwhile, he presented himself at the establishment of the merchant Peter Paggen, and, on producing letters from his father, was set to totting up accounts with the junior apprentices at a little desk among many others in a large room. It was understood that if he applied himself diligently and showed some ability in his work, he would be promoted after a week or so to a post from which he could observe to better advantage the workings of the plantation trade (Mr. Paggen had extensive dealings in Maryland and Virginia). Unfortunately, this promotion was never granted him. For one thing, no matter how hard he tried, Ebenezer could not concentrate his attention on the accounts. He would begin to add a column of totally meaningless figures and realize five minutes later that he'd been staring at a wen on the neck of the boy in front of him, or rehearsing in his mind a real or imaginary conversation between himself and Burlingame, or drawing mazes on a bit of scratch-paper. For the same reason, though he had by no means the troublemaker's temperament, his untamable fancy more than once led him to be charged with irresponsibility: one day, for example, scarcely conscious of what he was about, he involved himself entirely in a game with a small black ant that had wandered across the page. The rule of the game, which he invested with the inexorability of natural law, was that every time the ant trod unwittingly upon a 3 or a 9, Ebenezer would close his eyes and tap the page thrice, smartly and randomly, with the point of his quill. Although his role of *Deus civi Natura* precluded mercy, his sentiments were unequivocally on the side of the ant: with an effort that brought sweat to his brow he tried by force of thought to steer the hapless creature from dangerous numbers; he opened his eyes after every series of taps, half afraid to look at the paper. The game was profoundly exciting. After some ten or fifteen minutes the ant had the bad luck to be struck by a drop of ink not a half inch from the 9 that had triggered the bombardment: flailing blindly, he inked a tiny trail straight back to the 9 again, and this time, after being bracketed by the first two taps, he was smitten squarely with the third. Ebenezer looked down to find him curled and dying in the loop of the digit. Tears of compassion, tempered with vast understanding and acceptance of the totality of life and the unalterable laws of the universe, welled in his eyes; his genital stiffened. At last the ant expired. Suddenly self-conscious, Ebenezer glanced around to see whether anyone had noticed him, and everyone in the room laughed aloud: they had witnessed the whole performance. From that day on they regarded him as more or less mad instead of simply odd; luckily for Ebenezer, however, they believed him to have some special connection with their employer Mr. Paggen, and so made little of the incident except among themselves.

But it would not be fair to suggest that Ebenezer was entirely responsible for his impasse. There were a few occasions during the first year when he managed to do his work satisfactorily, even intelligently, for several weeks running, and yet no mention was made of transferring him to the promised post. Only once did he muster courage enough to inquire about it: Mr. Paggen made him a vague reply which he accepted eagerly, in order to terminate the interview, and never spoke of it again. Actually, except for infrequent twinges of conscience, Ebenezer was quite content to languish among the junior apprentices: he had learned the job and was frightened at the prospect of learning another. Moreover, he found the city suited to his languor; his free hours he spent with his friends in the coffee-houses, taverns, or theaters. Now and again he devoted a Sunday, without much success, to his writing-desk. And in general he came quite to forget what it was he was supposed to be doing in London.

It was withal a curious time in his life. If not actually satisfying, the routine was at any rate in no way unpleasant, and Ebenezer floated along in it like a fitful sleeper in a warm wash of dreams. Often, chameleonlike, he was but a reflection of his situation: were his companions boasting the tenuousness of their positions he might declare, in a burst of camaraderie, "Should old Andy discover *my* situation, 'twould be off to Maryland with me, sirs, and no mistake!" As often he went out of his way to differ with them, and half-yearned for the bracing life of the plantations. Still other times he'd sit like a stuffed stork all the afternoon without a word. So, one day cocksure, one day timorous; one day fearless, one craven; now the natty courtier, now the rumpled poet—and devil the hue that momently colored him, he'd look a-fidget at the rest of the spectrum. What's red to a rainbow?

All of which is to say, if you wish, that insofar as to *be* is to be in essence the Johnny-come-Friday that was John o' Thursday, why, this Ebenezer Cooke was no man at all. As for Andrew, he must have been incurious about his boy's life in London, or else believed that *A good post is worth a long wait.* The idyl lasted not for one, but for five or six years, or until 1694—in the March of which, when a disastrous wager brought it to a sudden end, our story begins.

6

The Momentous Wager Between Ebenezer
and Ben Oliver, and Its Uncommon Result

PIMP IN EBENEZER'S CIRCLE was one wiry, red-haired, befreckled ex-Dubliner named John McEvoy, twenty-one years old and devoid of school education, as long in energy and resourcefulness as short in money and stature, who spent his days abed, his evenings pimping for his privileged companions, and the greater part of his nights composing airs for the lute and flute, and who from the world of things that men have valued prized none but three: his mistress Joan Toast (who, whore as well, was both his love and his living), his music, and his liberty. No one-crown frisker Joan, but a two-guinea hen well worth the gold to bed her, as knew every man among them but Ebenezer; she loved her John for all he was her pimp, and he her truly too for all she was his whore. —for no man was ever *just* a pimp, nor any woman *merely* whore. They seemed, in fact, a devoted couple, and jealous.

All spirit, imagination, and brave brown eyes, small-framed, large-breasted, and tight-skinned (though truly somewhat coarse-pored, and stringy in the hair, and with teeth none of the best), this Joan Toast was his for the night who'd two guineas to take her for, and indignify her as he would, she'd give him his gold's worth and more, for she took that pleasure in her work as were she the buyer and he the ven-

49

dor; but come morning she was cold as a fish and back to her Johnny McEvoy, and should her lover of the night past so much as wink eye at her in the light of day, there was no more Joan Toast for *him* at any price.

Ebenezer had of course observed her for some years as she and his companions came and went in their harlotry, and from the talk in the coffee-house had got to know about her in great detail at second hand a number of things that his personal disorganization precluded learning at first. When in manly moments he thought of her at all it was merely as a tart whom, should he one day find himself single-minded enough, it might be sweet to hire to initiate him at long last into the mysteries. For it happened that, though near thirty, Ebenezer was yet a virgin, and this for the reason explained in the previous chapters, that he was no person at all: he could picture any kind of man taking a woman—the bold as well as the bashful, the clean green boy and the dottering gray lecher—and work out in his mind the speeches appropriate to each under any of several sorts of circumstances. But because he felt himself no more one of these than another and admired all, when a situation presented itself he could never choose one role to play over all the rest he knew, and so always ended up either turning down the chance or, what was more usually the case, retreating gracelessly and in confusion, if not always embarrassment. Generally, therefore, women did not give him a second glance, not because he was uncomely—he had marked well that some of the greatest seducers have the faces of goats and the manner of lizards—but because, a woman having taken in his ungainly physique, there remained no other thing for her to notice.

Indeed he might have gone virgin to his grave—for there are urgencies that will be heeded if not one way then perforce another, and that same knuckly hand that penned him his couplets took no wooing to make his quick mistress—but on this March night in 1694 he was noticed by Joan Toast, in the following manner: the gallants were sitting in a ring at Locket's, as was their custom, drinking wine, gossiping, and boasting their conquests, both of the muse and of lesser wenches. There were Dick Merriweather, Tom Trent, and Ben Oliver already well wined, Johnny McEvoy and Joan Toast out for a customer, and Ebenezer incommunicado.

"Heigh-ho!" sighed Dick at a lull in their talk. " 'Twere a world one could live in did wealth follow wit, for gold's the best bait to snare sweet conies with, and then we poets were fearsome trappers all!"

"No need gold," replied Ben, "did God but give women half an eye for their interests. What makes your good lover, if not fire and fancy? And for whom if not us poets are fire and fancy the very stock in trade? From which 'tis clear, that of all men the poet is most to be desired as a lover: if his mistress have beauty, his is the eye will most be gladdened by't; if she have it not, his is the imagination that best can mask its lack. If she displease him, and he slough her off shortly, she hath at least had for a time the best that woman can get; if she please him, he will haply fix her beauty for good and all in verse, where neither age nor pox can spoil it. And as poets as a class are to be desired in this respect over other sorts of fellows, so should the best poet prove the best lover; were women wise to their interests they'd make seeking him out their life-work, and finding him would straight lay their favors a-quiver in his lap—nay, upon his very writing-desk—and beg him to look on 'em kindly!"

"Out on't, then!" said Dick to Joan Toast. "Ben speaks truly, and 'tis you shall pay *me* two guineas this night! Marry, and were't not that I am poor as any church mouse this week and have not long to live, you'd not buy immortality so cheap! My counsel is to snatch the bargain while it lasts, for a poet cannot long abide this world."

To which Joan rejoined without heat, "Fogh! Could any man of ye rhyme as light as talk, or swive grand as swagger, why, your verse'd be on every lip in London and your arse in every bed, I swear! But *Talk pays no toll:* I look to pacify nor ear nor bum with aught o' ye but my sweet John, who struts not a strut nor brags no brags, but saves words for his melodies and strength for the bed."

"Hi!" applauded Ben. "Well put!"

"If ill timed," John McEvoy added, frowning lightly upon her. "Let no such sentiments come 'twixt thee and two guineas this night, love, or thy sweet John'll have nor strength nor song, but a mere rumbly gut to bed ye with on the morrow."

" 'Sblood!" remarked Tom Trent without emotion. "If Lady Joan reason rightly, there's one among us who far more merits her favor than you, McEvoy, for as you speak one word to our two, so speak you ten to his one: I mean yon Ebenezer, who for lack of words should be chiefest poet and cocks-

51

man in this or any winehouse—John Milton and Don Juan Tenorio in a single skin!"

"Indeed he may be," vowed Joan, who, being by chance seated next to Ebenezer, gave him a pat on the hand.

"At any rate," smiled McEvoy, "having heard not a line of his making, I've no evidence he's not a poet."

"Nor I he's not that other," Joan added smartly, "and 'tis more praise on both counts than I can praise the rest o' ye." Then she colored somewhat and added: "I must own I've heard it said, *Marry fat but love lean*, for as how your fat fellow is most often a jolly and patient husband, but your bony lank is long all over and springy in the bed. Howbeit, I've no proof of the thing."

"Then 'sdeath, you shall have it!" cried Ben Oliver, "for there's more to extension than simple length. When the subject in hand's the tool of love, prithee give weight to the matter of diameter, for diameter's what gives weight to love's tool—whether 'tis in hand or in the subject, for that matter! Nay, lass, I'll stick by my fat, as't hath stuck by me. *A plump cock's the very devil of the hen house*, so they say: he treads 'em with authority!"

" 'Tis too weighty a question to leave unsettled," declared McEvoy. "What think you, Tom?"

"I take no interest in affairs of the flesh," said Tom, "but I have e'er observed that women, like men, have chiefest relish in things forbidden, and prize no conquest like that of a priest or saint. 'Tis my guess, moreover, that they find their trophy doubly sweet, inasmuch as 'tis hard come by to begin with, and when got 'tis fresh and potent as vintage brandy, for having been so long bottled and corked."

"Dick?"

"I see no sense in it," Merriweather said. " 'Tis not a man's weight, but his circumstances, that make him a lover. The sweetest lover of all, I should think, is the man about to end his life, who would by the act of love bid his adieu to this world, and at the moment of greatest heat pass on the next."

"Well, now," McEvoy said, "ye owe it to England to put an answer to't. What I propose is this, that ye put each your best foot forward, so to speak, this same night, and let Joan take eight guinea from him she names loser. Thus the winner gets glory for him and his kind and a swiving to boot; the losers get still a swiving—ay, a double swiving!—and my good woman and I get chops instead of chitterlings for a day. Done?"

"Not I," said Tom. " 'Tis a sorry sport, is lust, that makes man a slavering animal on embracing his mistress and a dolorous vegetable after."

"Nor I," said Dick, "for had I eight guineas I'd hire three trollops and a bottle of Madeira for one final debauch ere I end my life."

"Mary, 'tis done for all 'o' me," said Ben, "and heartily, too, for your Joan's had none of old Ben these two months past."

"Nor shall I more," swore Joan cheerfully, "for thou'rt a sweatbox and a stinkard, sir. My memory of our last will serve as *your* performance, when I came away bruised and abused as a spaniel bitch from a boar's pen, and had need of a course of liniments to drive out the aches and a course of hot baths to carry off the smell. For the rest of the wager, 'tis Mr. Cooke's to yea or nay."

"So be't," shrugged Ben, "though had I known at the time 'twas that studding I'd be judged by, you'd have found me more bull than boar and haply have a Minotaur to show for't. What say you, Ebenezer?"

Now Ebenezer had followed this raillery intently and would have joined in it, perhaps, but that from his overstocked wardrobe no particular style came readily to hand. Then, when Joan Toast touched him, the hand she touched tingled as if galvanized, and on the instant Ebenezer felt his soul rise up in answer. Had not Boyle shown, and Burlingame taught, that electrical attraction takes place in a vacuum? Well, here was Boyle figured in the empty poet: the pert girl worked some queer attraction in him, called forth a spark from the vacuum of his character, and set him all suddenly a-burn and a-buzz.

But did this prick-up afford the man identity? On the contrary: as he saw the direction the twitting took and heard McEvoy give birth to the wager, he but buzzed and burned the more; his mind ran madly to no end like a rat in a race and could not engage the situation. His sensibility all erected, he could feel the moment coming when the eyes of all would swing to bear on him with some question which he'd be expected to answer. It was the wait for it, together with the tingle of Joan Toast's touch and the rush to find a face to meet the wager with, that made him sick when his ears heard Ben's "What say you, Ebenezer?" and his two eyes saw ten look to him for reply.

What say? What say? His windpipe glotted with a surfeit of alternatives; but did he urge one up like a low-pressured

53

belch, the suck of the rest ungassed it. Eyes grew quizzical; smiles changed character. Ebenezer reddened, not from embarrassment but from internal pressure.

"What ails ye, friend?" McEvoy.

"Speak up, man!" Ben Oliver.

"Swounds! He'll pop!" Dick Merriweather.

One Cooke eyebrow fluttered. A mouth-corner ticked. He closed and unclosed his hands and his mouth, and the strain near retched him, but it was all a dry heave, a false labor: no person issued from it. He gaped and sweated.

"*Gah*," he said.

"'Sblood!" Tom Trent. "He's ill! 'Tis the vapors! The fellow wants a clyster!"

"*Gah*," said Ebenezer again, and then froze tight and said no more, nor moved a single muscle.

By this time his behavior had been noticed by the other patrons of the winehouse, and a number of the curious gathered round him where he sat, now rigid as a statue.

"Hi, there, throw't off!" demanded one fellow, snapping his fingers directly before Ebenezer's face.

" 'Tis the wine has dagged him, belike," a wag suggested, and tweaked the poet's nose, also without effect. "Aye," he affirmed, "the lad's bepickled himself with't. Mark ye, 'tis the fate awaits us all!"

"As you please," declared Ben Oliver with a grin; "I say 'tis a plain case of the staggering fearfuls, and I claim the victory by default, and there's an end on't."

"Aye, but what doth it profit you?" Dick Merriweather asked.

"What else but Joan Toast this night?" laughed Ben, slapping three guineas onto the table. "Upon your honor as judge, John McEvoy, will you refuse me? Test my coins, fellow: they'll ring true as the next man's, and there's three of 'em."

McEvoy shrugged his shoulders and looked inquiringly at his Joan.

"Not in a pig's arse," she sniffed. She flounced from her chair and with a wink at the company flung her arms around Ebenezer's neck and caressed his cheek.

"Ah, me ducky, me dove!" she cooed. "Will ye leave me to the mercies of yon tub o' suet, to lard like any poor partridge? Save me, sir!"

But Ebenezer sat unmoved and unmoving.

" 'Tis no lardoon thou'rt in for," Ben said. " 'Tis the very spit!"

"Ah! Ah!" cried Joan as though terrified and, clambering onto Ebenezer's lap, hid her face in his neck. "I shake and I shiver!"

The company shouted with delight. Joan grasped one of Ebenezer's large ears in each hand and drew his face nose to nose with her own.

"Carry me off!" she implored him.

"To the spit with her!" urged an onlooker. "Baste the hussy!"

"Aye!" said Ben, and crooked his finger at her. "Come along now, sweetmeat."

"As ye be a man and a poet, Eben Cooke," Joan scolded, jumping to her feet and shouting in his ear, "I lay it upon ye to match this rascal's gold with your own and have done with't. If ye will not speak up and act the man, I'm Ben's and be damned t'ye!"

Ebenezer gave a slight start and suddenly stood up, blinking as if just roused from bed. His features twitched, and he alternately blushed and paled as he opened his mouth to speak.

"I had five guineas but this morning by messenger from my father," he said weakly.

"Thou'rt a fool," said Dick Merriweather. "She asks but three, and had you spoke sooner 'twould've cost you but two!"

"Will ye raise him two bob, Ben?" asked John McEvoy, who had been watching the proceedings serenely.

"Indeed he shan't!" snapped Joan. "Is this a horse auction, then, and I a mare to be rid by the high bidder?" She took Ebenezer's arm fondly. "Only match Ben's three guineas, ducky, and speak no more of't. The night's near done, and I am ill o' this lewd raillery."

Ebenezer gawked, swallowed, and shifted his weight.

"I cannot match it here," he said, "for I've but a crown in my purse." He glanced around him wildly. "The money is in my rooms," he added, teetering as if to swoon. "Come with me there, and you shall have't all."

"Hello, the lad's no fool!" said Tom Trent. "He knows a thing or two!"

"'Sblood, a very Jew!" agreed Dick Merriweather.

"Better a fowl in hand than two flying," Ben Oliver

laughed, and jingled his three guineas. " 'Tis a hoax and fraud, to lure honest women to their ruin! What would your father say, Ebenezer, did he get wind of't? Shame, shame!"

"Pay the great ass no heed," said Joan.

Ebenezer swayed again, and several of the company tittered.

"I swear to you——" he began.

"Shame! Shame!" cried Ben once more, wagging a fat finger at him to the company's delight.

Ebenezer tried again, but could do no more than raise his hand and let it fall.

"Stand off!" someone warned uneasily. "He is starching up again!"

"*Shame!*" roared Ben.

Ebenezer goggled at Joan Toast for a second and then lurched full speed across the room and out of the winehouse.

7

*The Conversation Between Ebenezer and
the Whore Joan Toast, Including the Tale
of the Great Tom Leech*

As a rule Ebenezer would after such a bumble have been in for some hours of motionless reflection in his room. It was his habit (for such rigidities as this at Locket's were not new to him) upon recovering himself to sit at his writing-desk, looking-glass in hand, and stare fish-eyed at his face, which only during such spells was still. But this time, though he did indeed take up his vis-à-vis, the face he regarded was anything but vacant: on the contrary, where typically he'd have seen a countenance blank as an owl's, now he saw a roil as of swallows round a chimney pot; whereas another time he'd have heard in his head but a cosmic rustle, as though his skull were a stranded wentletrap, now he sweated, blushed, and dreamed two score ragged dreams. He studied the ears

56

Joan Toast had touched, as though by study to restore their tingle, and when he could by no means succeed, he recognized with alarm that it was his heart she now had hands on.

"Ah God," he cried aloud, "that I'd risen to the wager!"

The manly sound of his voice arrested him. Moreover, it was the first time he'd ever spoken to himself aloud, and he failed to be embarrassed by it.

"Had I but another chance," he declared to himself, " 'twould be no chore to snatch the moment! Lord, into what ferment have those eyes put me! Into what heat those bosoms!"

He took up the glass again, made himself a face, and inquired, "Who art thou *now*, queer fellow? Hi, there is a twitch in thy blood, I see—a fidget in thy soul! 'Twere a right manly man Joan Toast would taste, were the wench but here to taste him!"

It occurred to him to return to Locket's to seek her out, on the chance she'd not have succumbed to Ben Oliver's entreaties. But he was reluctant to confront his friends so soon after his flight, in the first place, and in the second——

"Curse me for my innocence!" he railed, pounding his fist upon some blank papers on the writing-desk. "What knowledge have I of such things? Suppose she should come with me? 'Sblood! What then?

"Yet 'tis now or never," he told himself grimly. "This Joan Toast sees in me what no woman hath before, nor I myself: a man like other men. And for aught I know she hath made me one, for when else have I talked to myself? When else felt so potent? To Locket's," he ordered himself, "or go virgin to the grave!"

Nevertheless he did not get up, but lapsed instead into lecherous, complicated reveries of rescue and gratitude; of shipwreck or plague and mutual survivorship; of abduction, flight, and violent assault; and, sweetest of all, of towering fame and casual indulgence. When at length he realized that he was not going to Locket's at all, he was overcome with self-loathing and returned, in despair, once more to the mirror.

He calmed at the sight of the face in it.

"Odd fellow, there! *Ooo-ooo!* Hey-nonny-nonny! *Fa-la!*"

He leered and mouthed into the glass until his eyes brimmed with tears, and then, exhausted, buried his face in his long arms. Presently he fell asleep.

There came, an uncertain time later, a knocking at the

entrance door below, and before Ebenezer was awake enough to wonder at it, his own door was opened by his servant, Bertrand, who had been sent to him just a few days earlier by his father. This Bertrand was a thin-faced, wide-eyed bachelor in his later forties whom Ebenezer knew scarcely at all, for Andrew had hired him while the young man was still at Cambridge. With him, when he had come from the St. Giles establishment, he had brought the following note from Andrew, in an envelope sealed with wax:

Ebenezer,
　　The Bearer of this note is Bertrand Burton, my Valet since 1686, and now yours, if you want him. He is a diligent enough fellow, if something presumptuous, and will make you a good man if you hold him to his place. Mrs Twigg and he got on ill together, to the point where I had either to sack him or lose her, without whom I could scarce manage my house. Yet deeming it a hard matter to sack the fellow outright, whose only fault is, that though he never forgets his work, he oft forgets his place, I have promoted him out of my service into yours. I shall pay him his first quarters wage; after that, if you want him, I presume your post with Paggen will afford him.

Though his current wage from Peter Paggen, which was precisely what it had been in 1688, was barely adequate to keep himself, Ebenezer nonetheless had welcomed Bertrand's service, at least for the three months during which it was to cost him nothing. Luckily, the room adjoining his own was unoccupied at the time, and he had arranged with his landlord for Bertrand to lodge there, where he was always within call.

Now the man stepped into the room in nightshirt and cap, all smiles and winks, said, "A lady to see you, sir," and, to Ebenezer's great surprise, ushered Joan Toast herself into the room.

"I shall retire at once," he announced, winking again, and left them before Ebenezer could recover sufficiently to protest. He was extremely embarrassed and not a little alarmed at being alone with her, but Joan, not a whit disturbed, came over to where he still sat at the writing table and bussed him lightly upon the cheek.

"Say not a word," she ordered, taking off her hat. "I know well I'm tardy, and I ask your pardon for't."

Ebenezer sat dumb, too astonished to speak. Joan strode blithely to the windows, closed the curtains, and commenced undressing.

" 'Tis your friend Ben Oliver's to blame, with his *three* guineas, and his *four* guineas, and his *five* guineas, and his great hands both a-clench to lay hold on me! But a shilling o'er your five he couldn't offer, or wouldn't, and since 'twas you first offered it, I'm quit o' the brute with conscience clear."

Ebenezer stared at her, head afire.

"Come along now, sweet," Joan said presently, and turned to him entirely unclothed. "Put thy guineas upon the table and let's to bed. Faith, but there's a nip in the air this night! *Brrr!* Jump to't, now!" She sprang to the bed and snuggled under the coverlets, drawing them up around her chin.

"Come along!" she said again, a bit more briskly.

"Ah God, I cannot!" Ebenezer said. His face was rapturous, his eyes were wild.

"Ye *what?*" Joan cried, throwing back the covers and sitting up in alarm.

"I cannot pay thee," Ebenezer declared.

"Not pay me! What prank is this, sir, ye make me butt of, when I have put off Ben Oliver and his five gold guineas? Out with thy money now, Master Cooke, and off with thy breeches, and prank me no pranks!"

" 'Tis no prank, Joan Toast," said Ebenezer. "I cannot pay thee five guineas, or four guineas, or three. I cannot pay thee a shilling. Nay, not so much as a farthing."

"What! Are ye paupered, then?" She gripped his shoulders as if to shake him. "Marry, sir, open wide those great cow's eyes, that I may claw them from out their sockets! Think ye to make a fool o' me?" She swung her legs over the side of the bed.

"Nay, nay, lady!" Ebenezer cried, falling to his knees before her. "Nay, I have the five guineas, and more. But how price the priceless? How buy Heaven with simple gold? Ah, Joan Toast, ask me not to cheapen thee so! Was't for gold that silver-footed Thetis shared the bed of Peleus, Achilles' sire? Think thee Venus and Anchises did their amorous work on consideration of five guineas? Nay, sweet Joan, a man seeks not in the market for the favors of a goddess!"

"Let foreign bawds run their business as't please 'em," Joan declared, somewhat calmer. " 'Tis five guineas the night for this one, and pay ere ye play. Do ye reckon it cheap, then pleasure in thy bargain: 'tis all one to me. What a temper ye put me in with thy *not a farthing!* I had near leaped ye! Come along, now, and save thy conceits for a love sonnet in the morning."

"Ah, dear God, Joan, wilt thou not see?" said Ebenezer, still down upon his knees. " 'Tis not for common sport I crave thee, as might another: such lechery I leave to mere gluttonous whoremongers like Ben Oliver. What I crave of thee cannot be bought!"

"Aha," smiled Joan, "so 'tis a matter o' strange tastes, is't? I'd not have guessed it by the honest look o' ye, but think not so quickly 'tis out o' the question. Well do I know *There's more ways to the woods than one*, and if't work no great or lasting hurt, why, 'tis but a matter o' price to me, sir. Name me thy game, and I'll fix thee thy fee."

"Joan, Joan, put by this talk!" cried Ebenezer, shaking his head. "Can you not see it tears my heart? What's past is past; I cannot bear to think on't, how much the less hear it from thy sweet lips! Dear girl, I swear to thee now I am a virgin, and as I come to thee pure and undefiled, so in my mind you come to me; whate'er hath gone before, speak not of it. Nay!" he warned, for Joan's mouth dropped open. "Nay, not a word of't, for 'tis over and done. Joan Toast, I *love* thee! Ah, that startles thee! Aye, I swear to Heaven I love thee, and 'twas to declare it I wished thee here. Speak no more of your awful trafficking, for I love thy sweet body unspeakably, and that spirit which it so fairly houses, unimaginably!"

"Nay, Mr. Cooke, 'tis an unbecoming jest ye make, to call thyself virgin," Joan said doubtfully.

"As God is my witness," swore Ebenezer, "I have known no woman carnally to this night, nor ever loved at all."

"But how is that?" Joan demanded. "Why, when I was but a slip of a thing, not yet fourteen and innocent of the world's villainy, I recall I once cried out at table how I had commenced a queer letting of blood, and what was I ill of? And send quick for the leeches! And everyone laughed and made strange jests, but none would tell me what was the cause of't. Then my young bachelor uncle Harold approached me privily, and kissed me upon the lips and stroked my hair, and told me 'twas no common leech I wanted, for that I was letting much blood already; but that anon when I had stopped I should come to him in secret, for he kept in his rooms a great tom leech such as I had ne'er yet been bit by, the virtue of which was, that it would restore by sweet infusions what I had lost. I believed without question all that he had told me, for he was a great favorite o' mine, more brother than uncle to me, and therefore I said naught to anyone, but directly the curse left me went straight to his bedchamber, as he had prescribed. 'Where is the great tom leech?' I asked him. 'I have't ready,' said he, 'but it fears the light and will do its work only in darkness. Make thyself ready,' said he, 'and I'll apply the leech where it must go. 'Very well,' said I, 'but ye must tell me how to ready myself, Harold, for I know naught of leeching.' 'Disrobe thyself,' said he, 'and lie down upon the bed.'

"And so I stripped myself all naked, simple soul that I was, right before his eyes, and lay down upon the bed as he directed—a skinny pup I, as yet unbreasted and unfurred—and he blew out the candle. 'Ah, dear Harold!' I cried. 'Come lie beside me on the bed, I pray, for I fear the bite o' thy great tom leech in the dark!' Harold made me no answer, but shortly joined me upon his bed. 'How is this?' I cried, feeling his skin upon me. 'Do you mean to take the leech as well? Did you too lose blood?' 'Nay,' he laughed, ' 'tis but the manner whereby my leech must be applied. I have't ready for ye, dear girl; are ye ready for't?' 'Nay, dear Harold,' I cried, 'I am fearful! Where will it bite me? How will it hurt?' ' 'Twill bite where it must,' said Harold, 'and 'twill pain ye a mere minute, and then pleasure ye enough.' 'Ah, then,' I sighed, 'let us get by the pain and hasten the pleasure with all speed. But prithee hold my hand, lest I cry out at the creature's bite.' 'Ye shan't cry out,' Harold said then, 'for I shall kiss ye.'

"And straightway he embraced me and kissed my mouth tight shut, and, while we were a-kissing, suddenly I felt the great tom leech his fearful bite, and I was maiden no more! At first I wept, not alone from the pain he'd warned of, but from alarm at what I'd learned o' the leech's nature. But e'en as Harold promised, the pain soon flew, and his great tom leech took bite after bite till near sunup, by which time, though I was by no means weary o' the leeching, my Harold had no more leech to leech with, but only a poor cockroach or simple pismire, not fit for the work, which scurried away at the first light. 'Twas then I learned the queer virtue o' this animal: for just as a fleabite, the more ye scratch it, wants scratching the more, so, once this creature had bit me, I longed for further bites and was forever after poor Harold and his leech, like an opium eater his phial. And though since then I've suffered the bite of every sort and size—none more fearsome or ravenous than my good John's—yet the craving plagues me still, till I shiver at the thought o' the great tom leech!"

"Stop, I beg thee!" Ebenezer pleaded. "I cannot hear more! What, 'Dear Uncle,' you call him, and 'Poor Harold'! Ah, the knave, the scoundrel, to deceive you so, who loved and trusted him! 'Twas no *leechery* he put thee to, but *lechery*, and laid thy maiden body forever in the bed of harlotry! I curse him, and his ilk!"

"Ye say't with relish," smiled Joan, "as one who'd do the like with fire in his eye and sweat on his arse, could he find himself a child fond as I. Nay, Ebenezer, rail not at poor dear Harold, who is these several years under the sod from an ague got swiving ardently in cold chambers. Says I, 'tis but the nature o' the leech to bite and of the leeched to want biting, and 'tis a mystery and astonishment to me, since so many crave leeching and the best leech is so lightly surfeited, how yours hath gone starved, as ye declare, these thirty years! What, are ye a mere arrant sluggard, sir? Or are ye haply o' that queer sort who lust for none but their own sex? 'Tis a thing past grasping!"

"Nor the one nor the other," replied Ebenezer. "I am man in spirit as well as body, and my innocence is not wholly my own choosing. I have ere now been ready enough, but to grind love's grain wants mortar as well as pestle; no man dances the morris dance alone, and till this night no woman e'er looked on me with favor."

"Marry!" laughed Joan. "Doth the ewe chase the ram, or the hen the cock? Doth the field come to the plow for furrowing, or the scabbard to the sword for sheathing? 'Tis all arsy-turvy ye look at the world!"

"That I grant," sighed Ebenezer, "but I know naught of the art of seduction, nor have the patience for't."

"Fogh! There's no great labor to the bedding of women! For the most, all a man need do, I swear, is ask plainly and politely, did he but know it."

"How is that?" exclaimed Ebenezer in astonishment. "Are women then so lecherous?"

"Nay," said Joan. "Think not we crave a swiving pure and simple at any time as do men always—'tis oft a pleasure with us, but rarely a passion. Howbeit, what with men forever panting at us like so many hounds at a salt-bitch, and begging us put by our virtue and give 'em a tumble, and withal despising us for whores and slatterns if we do; or bidding us be faithful to our husbands and yet losing no chance to cuckold their truest friends; or charging us to guard our chastity and yet assaulting it from all quarters in every alleyway, carriage, or sitting room; or being soon bored with us if we show no fire in swiving and yet sermoning us for sinners if we do; inventing morals on the one hand and rape on the other; and in general preaching us to virtue whilst they lure us on to vice —what with the pull and haul of all this, I say, we women are forever at sixes and sevens, all fussed and rattled and torn 'twixt what we ought and what we would, and so entirely confounded, that we never know what we think on the matter or how much license to grant from one minute to the next; so that if a man commence the usual strut, pat, and tweak, we may thrust him from us (if he do not floor us and have at us by main strength); and if he let us quite alone, we are so happy of the respite we dare not make a move; but should e'er a man approach us in all honest friendship, and look upon us as fellow humans and not just a bum and a bosom, from eyes other than a stud-stallion's, and after some courteous talk should propose a cordial swiving as one might a hand of whist (instead of inviting us to whist as lecherously as though to bed)—if, I say, e'er a man should learn to make such a request in such a manner, his bed would break 'neath the weight of grateful women, and he would grow gray ere his time! But in sooth 'twill never happen," Joan concluded, "forasmuch as 'twould mean receiving a partner and not taking a vassal: 'tis not mere sport a man lusts after, 'tis *conquest*—else philanderers were rare as the plague and not common as the pox. Do but ask, Ebenezer, cordially and courteously, as ye would ask a small favor from a good friend, and what ye ask shall rarely be refused. But ye *must* ask, else in our great relief at not being hard pressed for't, we shall pass ye by."

"Indeed," admitted Ebenezer, shaking his head, "it had not struck me ere now, what a sad lot is women's. What beasts we are!"

"Ah, well," sighed Joan, " 'tis small concern o' mine, save when I reflect on't now and again: a whore loses little sleep on such nice questions. So long as a man hath my price in his purse and smells somewhat more sweet than a tanyard and leaves me in peace come morning, I shan't say him nay nor send him off ill-pleased with his purchase. And I love a virgin as a child loves a new pup, to make him stand and beg for't, or lie and play dead. Off your knees, then, and to bed with

63

ye, ere ye take a quartan ague from the draught! There's many a trick I'll teach ye!"

So saying she held out her arms to him, and Ebenezer, breaking at once into sweat and goose bumps from the contest between his ardor and the cold March draughts in which for a quarter hour he'd been kneeling, embraced her fervently.

"Dear God, is't true?" he cried. "What astonishment it is, to be granted all suddenly in fact what one hath yearned for time out of mind in dreams! Dear heart, what a bewilderment! No words come! My arms fail me!"

"Let not thy purse fail thee," Joan remarked, "and for the rest, leave't to me."

"But 'fore God I love thee, Joan Toast!" Ebenezer moaned. "Can it be you think yet of the filthy purse?"

"Do but pay me my five guineas ere ye commence," Joan said, "and then love me 'fore God or man, 'tis all one to me."

"You will drive me to Bedlam with your five guineas!" Ebenezer shouted. "I love thee as never man loved woman, I swear't, and rather would I throttle thee, or suffer myself throttled, than turn my love to mere whoremongering with that accursed five guineas! I will be thy vassal; I will fly with thee down the coasts of earth; I will deliver soul and body into thy hands for very love; but I will not take thee for my whore while breath is in me!"

"Ah, then, 'tis after all a fraud and deceit!" Joan cried, her eyes flashing. "Ye think to gull me with *thee*'s and *thy*'s and your prattle o' love and chastity! I say pay me my fee, Eben Cooke, or I'll leave ye this minute for ever and all; and 'tis many the hour ye'll curse your miserliness, when word of't reaches my Johnny McEvoy!"

"I cannot," Ebenezer said.

"Then know that I despise ye for a knave and fool!" Joan jumped from the bed and snatched up her garments.

"And know that I love thee for my savior and inspiration!" Ebenezer replied. "For ne'er till you came to me this night have I been a man, but a mere dotting oaf and fop; and ne'er till I embraced thee have I been a poet, but a shallow coxcomb and poetaster! With thee, Joan, what deeds could I not accomplish! What verse not write! Nay, e'en should you scorn me in your error and ne'er look on me more, I will love thee nonetheless, and draw power and purpose from my love. For so strong is't, that e'en unrequited it shall sustain and inspire me; but should God grant thee wit to compre-

64

hend and receive it and return it as then you would perforce, why, the world would hear such verses as have ne'er been struck, and our love would stand as model and exemplar to all times! Scorn me, Joan, and I shall be a splendid fool, a Don Quixote tilting for his ignorant Dulcinea; but I here challenge thee—if you've life and fire and wit enough, love me truly as I love thee, and then shall I joust with bona fide giants and bring them low! Love me, and I swear to thee this: I shall be Poet Laureate of England!"

"Methinks thou'rt a Bedlamite already," Joan snapped, hooking up her dress. "As for my ignorance, I had rather be fool than scoundrel, and yet rather scoundrel than madman, and in sooth I believe thou'rt all three in one skin. Mayhap I'm dolt enough not to grasp this grand passion ye make such claim to, but I've mother wit enough to see when I'm hoaxed and cheated. My John shall hear of't."

"Ah Joan, Joan!" Ebenezer pleaded. "Are you then indeed unworthy? For I declare to thee solemnly: no man will e'er offer thee another such love."

"Do but offer me my rightful fee, and I'll say not a word to John: the rest o' your offer ye may put back in your hat."

"So," sighed Ebenezer, still transported, "you *are* unworthy! So be't, if't must: I love thee no less for't, or for the sufferings I shall welcome in thy name!"

"May ye suffer French pox, ye great ass!" Joan replied, and left the room in a heat.

Ebenezer scarcely noted her departure, so full was he of his love; he strode feverishly about the bedchamber, hands clasped behind his back, pondering the depth and force of his new feeling. "Am I waked to the world from a thirty-year sleep?" he asked himself. "Or is't only now I've begun to dream? Surely none awake e'er felt such dizzy power, nor any man in dreams such bursting life! *Hi!* A song!"

He ran to his writing-desk, snatched up his quill, and with little ado penned the following song:

Not Priam *for the ravag'd Town of Troy,*
    Andromache *for her bouncing Baby Boy,*
Ulysses *for his chaste* Penelope,
    Bare the Love, dear Joan, *I bear for Thee!*

But as cold Semele *priz'd* Endymion,
    And Phaedra *sweet* Hippolytus *her Step-Son,*

> *He being Virgin—so, I pray may Ye*
> *Whom I love, love my stainless Chastity.*
>
> *For 'tis no niggard Gift, my Innocence,*
> *But one that, giv'n, defieth Recompense;*
> *No common Jewel pluck'd from glist'ring Hoard,*
> *But one that, taken, ne'er can be restor'd.*
>
> *Preserv'd, my Innocence preserveth Me*
> *From Life, from Time, from Death, from History;*
> *Without it I must breathe Man's mortal Breath:*
> *Commence a Life—and thus commence my Death!*

When he was done composing he wrote at the bottom of the page *Ebenezer Cooke, Gent., Poet and Laureate of England,* just to try the look of it, and, regarding it, was pleased.

" 'Tis now but a question of time," he rejoiced. "Faith, 'tis a rare wise man knows who he is: had I not stood firm with Joan Toast, I might well ne'er have discovered that knowledge! Did I, then, make a choice? Nay, for there was no *I* to make it! 'Twas the choice made *me:* a noble choice, to prize my love o'er my lust, and a noble choice bespeaks a noble chooser. What am I? What am I? *Virgin,* sir! *Poet,* sir! I am a virgin and a poet; less than mortal and more; not a man, but Mankind! I shall regard my innocence as badge of my strength and proof of my calling: let her who's worthy of't take it from me!"

Just then the servant Bertrand tapped softly on the door and entered, candle in hand, before Ebenezer had a chance to speak.

"Should I retire now, sir?" he asked, and added with an enormous wink, "Or will there be more visitors?"

Ebenezer blushed. "Nay, nay, go to bed."

"Very good, sir. Pleasant dreams."

"How's that?"

But Bertrand, with another great wink, closed the door.

"Really," Ebenezer thought, "the fellow *is* presumptuous!" He returned to the poem and reread it several times with a frown.

" 'Tis a gem," he admitted, "but there wants some final touch. . . ."

He scrutinized it line for line; at *Bare the Love, dear* Joan, *I bear for Thee* he paused, furrowed his great brow, pursed his lips, squinted his eyes, tapped his foot and scratched his chin with the feather of his quill.

"Hm," he said.

After some thought, he inked his quill and struck out *Joan*, setting in its place the word *Heart*. Then he reread the whole poem.

" 'Twas the master touch!" he declared with satisfaction. "The piece is perfect."

8

A Colloquy Between Men of Principle, and What Came of It

WHEN HE HAD DONE revising his poem Ebenezer laid it on his night table, undressed, went to bed, and presently resumed the sleep that Joan Toast's visit had interrupted, for the day's events had quite fatigued him. But again his sleep was fitful —this time it was excitement and not despair that bothered him—and, as before, it was short-lived: he had been beneath his quilts no more than an hour before he was waked once again by a loud knocking at the door, which he'd forgot to latch after Joan's departure.

"Who is't?" he called. "Bertrand! Someone's knocking!"

Before he could make a light, or even get up from the bed, the door was opened roughly, and John McEvoy, lantern in hand, strode into the room. He stood beside the bed and held the light close to Ebenezer's face. Bertrand, apparently, was asleep, for to Ebenezer's slight distress he failed to appear.

"My five guineas, if ye please," McEvoy demanded calmly, holding out his other hand.

Ebenezer broke at once into a mighty sweat, but he contrived to ask hoarsely, from the bed, "How is't I owe you money? I cannot recall buying aught of you."

"Ye do but prove your ignorance of the world," declared McEvoy, "for the first principle o' harlotry is, that what a man buys of a whore is not so much her bum but her will and her time; when ye hire my Joan 'tis neither her affair nor mine what use ye make o' her, so long as ye pay yer fee. As't happens, ye chose to talk in lieu of swiving; 'twas a fool's choice, but 'tis your privilege to play the fool if't please ye. Now, sir, my five guineas!"

"Ah, my friend," said Ebenezer, reminding himself grimly of his identity, " 'tis only fair to tell you, if haply Joan did not: I love her wondrously!"

" 'Tis all one, so ye pay your fee," replied McEvoy.

"That I cannot," Ebenezer said. "Your own reasoning in the matter rules it out. For if 'tis true, as you declare, that 'tis the rental of her will and time that makes a woman whore, then to pay you for what of her time she spent here would make her my whore though I did not touch her carnally. And make her my whore I will not—nay, not were I racked for't! I bear you no ill will, John McEvoy, nor must you think me miserly: I've gold enough, and no fear of parting with it."

"Then pay your fee," said McEvoy.

"My dear man," Ebenezer smiled, "will you not take five —nay, *six* guineas from me as an outright gift?"

"Five guineas, as a fee," repeated McEvoy.

"Where's the difference to you, should I call the sum a gift and not a payment? 'Twill fetch no less in the market, I pledge you!"

"If't makes no difference," replied McEvoy, "then call it the fee for Joan Toast's whoring."

"Think not it makes no difference to *me*," Ebenezer said. "To me 'tis *all* the difference! No man makes a whore of the woman he loves, and I love Joan Toast as never man loved woman."

"Out on't!" McEvoy scoffed. "Everything ye say proves ye know naught whatever concerning love. Think not ye love Joan Toast, Mr. Cooke: 'tis your *love* ye love, and that's but to say 'tis yourself and not my Joan. But no matter—love her or swive her, so ye pay your fee. To no man save myself may she be aught but whore; I am a jealous man, sir, and though ye may purchase my Joan's will and time as client, ye mayn't court it as lover."

" 'Sbody, 'tis a passing odd jealousy, I swear't!" Ebenezer exclaimed. "I ne'er have heard its like!"

"Which is to say, ye know naught of love," said McEvoy.

Ebenezer shook his head and declared, "I cannot grasp it. Great heavens, man, this divine creature, this vision of all

68

that's fair in womankind, this Joan Toast—she is your mistress! How is't you can allow men e'en to lay their eyes upon her, much less———"

"Much less much more? How clear it is ye love yourself and not Joan! There's naught o' the divine in Joan, my friend. She's mortal clay and hath her share o' failings like the rest of us. As for this *vision* ye speak of, 'tis the vision ye love, not the woman. 'Twere impossible it could be otherwise, for none o' ye save I e'en knows the woman."

"And yet you play her pimp!"

McEvoy laughed. "I shall tell ye a thing about yourself, Eben Cooke, and haply ye'll recall it now and again: 'tis not simply love ye know naught of, 'tis the *entire great real world!* Your senses fail ye; your busy fancy plays ye false and fills your head with foolish pictures. Things are not as ye see 'em, friend—the world's a tangled skein, and all is knottier than ye take it for. You understand naught o' life: I shan't say more." He drew a document from his pocket and gave it to Ebenezer. "Read it with haste and pay your fee."

Ebenezer unfolded the paper and read it with mounting consternation. It was headed *To Andrew Cooke, 2nd, Gent.,* and commenced thus:

> My dear Sir,
> It is my unhappy duty to bring to your notice certain regrettable matters concerning the behavior of your Son Ebenezer Cooke. . . .

The note went on to declare that Ebenezer was spending his days and nights in the wine- and coffee-houses and the theaters, drinking, whoring, and writing doggerel, and that he was making no effort whatever to find an instructive post for himself as he had been directed. It concluded:

> I bring this lamentable state of affairs to your attention, not alone because it is your right as young Cooke's Father to know them, but also because the young man in question hath added to his other vices, that of luring young women into his bedchamber on promise of generous remuneration, only to default on payment afterwards.
> As agent for one such defrauded young lady, I find myself Mr. Cooke's creditor in the amount of five guineas, which debt he refuses to honor despite the

most reasonable pleas. I feel certain that, as the Gentleman's father, you will be interested in the settlement of this debt either directly, by forwarding me the young lady's fee, or indirectly, by persuading your son to settle it before the matter receives a more general notoriety. Waiting for communication from you upon the business, I am, sir,

Y^r H^{mble} & O^{bt} S^{vt},
John McEvoy

" 'Sblood, 'tis my ruin!" Ebenezer murmured, when he had read it through.

"Aye, if posted," agreed McEvoy. "Do but pay your fee, and 'tis yours to destroy. Else I mean to post it at once."

Ebenezer closed his eyes and sighed.

"Doth the thing so much matter to ye?" smiled McEvoy.

"Aye. And doth it to you?"

"Aye. It must be whore-money."

Ebenezer caught sight of his poem in the lantern-light. His features commenced their customary dance, and then, calming, he turned to face McEvoy.

"It cannot be," he said. "That is my final word on't. Post thy tattling letter if you will."

"I shall," declared McEvoy, and rose to leave.

"And append this to't, if you've a mind to," Ebenezer added. Tearing off the signature *Ebenezer Cooke, Gent., Poet & Laureate of England,* he handed McEvoy the poem.

"Such bravery," smiled his visitor, scanning it. "What is this? *And* Phaedra *sweet* Hippolytus *her Step-Son?* Ye rhyme *Endymion* and *Step-Son?*"

Ebenezer paid his critic no heed. " 'Twill at least belie your charge that I write doggerel," he said.

"Endymion and *Step-Son,"* McEvoy repeated, making a face. "Belie't, ye say? Marry, sir, 'twill confirm it past question! Were I in your boots I'd pay my whore-money and consign letter, *Endymion, Step-Son,* and all to the fire." He returned the poem to Ebenezer. "Will ye not reconsider?"

"Nay."

"Ye'll go to Maryland for a whore?"

"I'd not cross the street for a whore," Ebenezer said firmly, "but I shall cross the ocean for a principle! To you, haply, Joan Toast is a whore; to me she is a principle."

"To me she is a woman," replied McEvoy. "To you she's a hallucination."

"What manner of artist are you," scorned Ebenezer, "that cannot see the monstrous love which fires me?"

"What manner of artist *you*," retorted McEvoy, "that can't see through it? And are ye in sooth a virgin, as Joan Toast swears?"

"And a poet," Ebenezer declared with new serenity. "Now begone, an't please you. Do your worst!"

McEvoy scratched his nose in amusement. "I will," he promised, and went out, leaving his host in total darkness.

Ebenezer had remained in bed throughout the conversation, for at least three reasons: first, he had retired after Joan Toast's departure clothed in no warmer nightshirt than his own fair skin, and, not so much from prudishness as from shyness, he was reluctant to expose himself before another man, even his valet, though not always (as shall be seen) before a woman; second, even had this not been the case, McEvoy had given him little opportunity to get up; and third, it was Ebenezer's ill fortune to be endowed with a nervous system and a rational faculty that operated as independently of each other as two Londoners of wholly various temperament who chance to inhabit the same rooming house, but go blithely each his separate way without thought of his neighbor: no matter how firm his resolve, as regards both Joan Toast and his new-found essences, any strong emotion tended to soak him with sweat, to rob him of muscle if not voice, and to make him sick. Given both the determination and the opportunity, he still could scarcely have accomplished sitting up.

His bedclothes were wet with perspiration; his stomach churned. When McEvoy was gone he sprang out of bed to latch the door against further visitors, but immediately upon standing erect was overcome by nausea and had to run for the commode across the room. As soon as he was able he slipped into his nightshirt and called for Bertrand, who this time appeared almost at once, wigless and gowned. In one hand he held a bare wax candle, in the other its heavy pewter holder.

"The fellow is gone," Ebenezer said. " 'Tis safe to show thyself." Still weak in the knees, he sat at his writing-desk and held his head in his hands.

"Lucky for him he held his temper!" Bertrand said grimly, brandishing his candleholder.

Ebenezer smiled. "Was't thy intent to rap on the wall for silence if he didn't?"

"On his arrogant pate, sir! I stood just without your door the entire while, for fear he'd leap you, and only jumped inside my room when he left, for fear he'd spy me."

"For fear in sooth! Did you not hear my call?"

"I own I did not, sir, and beg your pardon for't. Had he knocked below like any gentleman, he'd ne'er have got by me on *that* errand, I swear! 'Twas your voices waked me, and when I caught the drift of your talk I dared not intrude for fear of presuming, or leave for fear he'd assault you."

"Marry, Bertrand!" Ebenezer said. "Thou'rt the very model of a servant! You heard all, then?"

" 'Twas farthest from my mind to eavesdrop," Bertrand protested, "but I could scarce avoid the substance of't. What a cheat and blackguard the pimp is, to ask five guinea for a tart you spent not two hours with! For five guinea I could fill thy bed with trollops!"

"Nay, 'tis no cheat; McEvoy is as honest a man as I. 'Twas a collision of principles, not a haggle over price." He went to fetch a robe. "Will you make up the fire, Bertrand, and brew tea for both of us? I've small hope of sleep this night."

Bertrand lit the lamp from his candle, put fresh wood in the fireplace, and blew up the embers in the grate.

"How can the wretch harm you?" he asked. " 'Tis unlikely a pimp could press a law-suit!"

"He hath no need of the courts. 'Tis but a matter of telling my father of the affair, and off I go to Maryland."

"For a simple business with a strumpet, sir? Marry, thou'rt not a child, nor Master Andrew any cleric! I beg your pardon for't, sir, but your homeplace is no popish convent, if I may say so! There's much goes on there that Miss Anna and yourself know naught of, nor old Twigg, either, for all her sniffs and snoops."

Ebenezer frowned. "How's that? What in Heav'n do you mean, fellow?"

"Nay, nay, spare your anger; marry, I yield to none in respect for your father, sir! I meant naught by't at all, save that Master Andrew is a natural man, if you follow me, like thee and me; a lusty fellow despite his age, and—no disrespect intended—he's long a widower. A servant sees things now and again, sir."

"A servant sees little and fancies much," Ebenezer said sharply. "Is't your suggestion my father's a whoremonger?"

" 'Sblood, sir, nothing of the sort! He's a great man and an honest, is Master Andrew, and I pride myself on having his confidence these many years. 'Tis no accident he chose *me* to come to London with you, sir: I've managed business of some consequence for him ere now that Mrs. Twigg for all her haughty airs knew naught of."

"See here, Bertrand," Ebenezer demanded with interest, "are you saying you've been my father's pimp?"

"I'll speak no more of't, sir, an it please thee, for it seems thou'rt out of sorts and put an ill construction on my words. All I meant to say in the world was that were I in thy place I'd not pay a farthing for all the scoundrel's letters to your father. The man who says he ne'er hath bought a swiving must needs be either fairy or *castrato*, if he be not a liar, and Master Andrew's none o' the three. Let the rascal say 'tis a vice with thee; I'll swear on oath 'twas the first you've been a-whoring, to my knowledge. No disgrace in that." He gave Ebenezer a cup of tea and stood by the fire to drink his own.

"Perhaps not, even if 'twere true."

"I'm *certain* of't," Bertrand said, gaining confidence. "You had your tart as any man might, and there's an end on't. Her pimp asked more than her worth, and so you sent him packing. I'd advise thee to pay him not a farthing for all his trumpeting, and Master Andrew would agree with me."

"Belike you misheard me through the door, Bertrand," Ebenezer said. "I did not swive the girl."

Bertrand smiled. "Ah, now, 'twas a clever enough stand to take with the pimp, considering he roused you up ere you'd time to think; but 'twill ne'er fool Master Andrew for a minute."

"Nay, 'tis the simple truth! And e'en had I done so I would not pay him a ha'penny for't. I love the girl and shan't buy her for a harlot."

"Now, *that* one hath the touch of greatness in it," Bertrand declared. " 'Tis worthy of the cleverest blade in London! But speaking as your adviser——"

"My adviser! Thou'rt my adviser?"

Bertrand shifted uneasily. "Aye, sir, in a manner of speaking, you understand. As I said before, I pride myself that your father trusts me——"

"Did Father send you to me as a governess? Do you report my doings to him?"

"Nay, nay!" Bertrand said soothingly. "I only meant, as I said before, 'tis clearly no accident he named me and no

73

other to attend ye, sir. I pride myself 'tis a sign of his faith in my judgment. I merely meant 'twas clever to tell the pimp thou're in love with his tart and shan't cheapen her; but if ye repeat the tale to Master Andrew 'twere wise to make clear 'twas but a gambit, so as not to alarm him."

"You don't believe it? Nor that I am a virgin?"

"Thou'rt a great tease, sir! I only question whether thy father would understand raillery."

"I see thou'rt not to be convinced," Ebenezer said, shaking his head. "No matter, I suppose. 'Tis not the business of five guineas will undo me anyhow, but the other."

"Another? Marry, what a rascal!"

"Nay, not another wench; another business. Haply 'twill interest you, as my *adviser*: McEvoy's tattling letter describes my place at Peter Paggen's, that hath not improved these five years."

Bertrand set down his cup. "My dear sir, pay him his rascally guineas."

Ebenezer smiled. "What? Permit the wretch to overcharge me?"

"I've two guinea laid by, sir, in a button box in my chest. 'Tis thine toward the debt. Only let me run to pay him, ere he posts his foul letter."

"Thy charity gladdens me, Bertrand, and thy concern, but the principle is the same. I shan't pay it."

"Marry, sir, then I must off to a Jew for the other three and pay it myself, though he hold liver and lights for collateral. Master Andrew will have my head!"

" 'Twill avail thee naught. 'Tis not five guineas McEvoy wants, but five guineas from my hand as whore-money."

"I'faith, then I'm lost!"

"How so?"

"When Master Andrew learns how ill ye've minded his direction he'll sack me for certain, to punish ye. What comfort hath the adviser? If things go well 'tis the student gets the praise; if ill, 'tis the adviser gets the blame."

" 'Tis in sooth a thankless office," Ebenezer said sympathetically. He yawned and stretched. "Let us sleep out the balance of the night, now. Thy conversation is a marvelous soporific."

Bertrand showed no sign of understanding the remark, but he rose to leave.

"You'll see me sacked, then, ere you pay the debt?"

"I doubt me such a priceless adviser will be sacked," Ebenezer replied. "Belike he'll send thee off with me to Maryland, to advise me."

"Gramercy, sir! Thou'rt jesting!"

"Not at all."

"'Sheart! To perish at the hands of salvages!"

"Ah, as for that, two of us can fight 'em better than one. Good night, now." So saying, he sent Bertrand terrified to his room and attempted to lull himself to sleep. But his fancy was too much occupied with versions of the imminent confrontation of his father and himself—versions the details of which he altered and perfected with an artist's dispassionate care—to allow him more than a restless somnolence.

As it turned out, there was no confrontation at all, though St. Giles was but an easy carriage ride from where he lived. On the evening of the second day after McEvoy's threat, a messenger came to Ebenezer's room (from which, having abandoned Peter Paggen entirely, he had scarcely ventured in two days) with twelve pounds in cash and a brief letter from Andrew:

> My Son: It is truly said, that Children are a certain Care, and but an uncertain Comfort. Suffice it to say, I have learned of your vicious Condition; I shall not sully myself by witnessing it firsthand. You shall on Pain of total and entire Disinheritance and Disownment take Ship for Maryland on the Bark *Poseidon,* sailing from Plimouth for Piscataway on April 1, there to proceed straightway to Cookes poynt and assume Managership of Malden. It is my intention to make a final Sojourn in the Plantations perhaps a Year hence, and I pray that at that Time I shall find a prosperous Malden and a regenerate Son: an Estate worth bequeathing and an Heir worth the Bequest. It is your final Chance.
>
> Your Father

Ebenezer was more numbed than stunned by the letter, for he'd anticipated some such ultimatum.

"Marry, 'tis but a week hence!" he reflected with alarm. The notion of leaving his companions just when, having determined his essence, he felt prepared to begin enjoying them, distressed him quite; whatever fugitive attraction the colonies had held for him fled before the prospect of actually going there.

He showed the letter to Bertrand.

"Ah, 'tis as I thought: thy principles have undone me. I see no summons here to my old post in St. Giles."

"Haply 'twill come yet, Bertrand, by another messenger."

But the servant appeared unconsoled. "I'faith! Back to old Twigg! I had almost rather brave the salvage Indians."

"I would not see thee suffer on my account," Ebenezer declared. "I shall pay your April's wages, and you may start today to seek another post."

The valet seemed scarcely able to believe such generosity. "Bless ye, sir! Thou'rt every inch a gentleman!"

Ebenezer dismissed him and returned to his own problem. What was he to do? During most of that day he anxiously examined various faces of himself in his looking glass; during most of the next he composed stanzas to Gloom and Melancholy, after the manner of *Il Penseroso* (though briefer and, he decided, of a different order of impact); the third he spent abed, getting up only to feed and relieve himself. He refused Bertrand's occasional proffered services. A change came over him: his beard went unshaved, his drawers unchanged, his feet unwashed. How take ship for the wild untutored colonies, now he knew himself a poet and was ready to fire London with his art? And yet how make shift unaided in London, penniless, in defiance of his father and at the expense of his inheritance?

"What am I to do?" he asked himself, lying unkempt in his bed on the fourth day. It was a misty March morning, though a warm and sunny one, and the glaring haze from outside caused his head to ache. The bedclothes were no longer clean, nor was his nightshirt. His late fire was ashed and cold. Eight o'clock passed, and nine, but he could not resolve to get up. Once only, as a mere experiment, he held his breath in order to try whether he could make himself die, for he saw no alternative; but after a half minute he drew air frantically and did not try again. His stomach rumbled, and his sphincters signaled their discomfort. He could think of no reason for rising from the bed, nor any for remaining there. Ten o'clock came and went.

Near noon, running his eyes about the room for the hundredth time that morning, he caught sight of something that had previously escaped him: a scrap of paper on the floor beside his writing-desk. Recognizing it, he climbed out of bed

76

without thinking, fetched it up, and squinted at it in the glare.

Ebenezer Cooke, Gent., Poet & Laureate. . . .

The rest of the epithet was torn off, but despite its loss, or perhaps because of it, Ebenezer was suddenly inspired with such a pleasant resolve that his spirits rose on the instant, driving three days' gloom before them as a March breeze drives away squalls. His spine thrilled; his face flushed. Lighting on a piece of letter paper, he addressed a salutation directly to Charles Calvert, Third Lord Baltimore and Second Lord Proprietary of the Province of Maryland. *Your Excellency*, he wrote, with the same sure hand of some nights before:

It is my Intention to take Ship for Maryland upon the Bark *Poseidon* a few Days hence, for the Purpose of managing my Father's Property, called Cooke's Point, in Dorchester. Y^r L^dshp will do me a great Honour, and Himself no ill Turn it may be, by granting me an Audience before I embark, in order that I might discuss certain Plans of mine, such that I venture will not altogether displease Y^r L^dshp, and in order farther that I might learn, from Him most qualified to say, where in the Province to seek the congenial Company of Men of Breeding and Refinement, with whom to share my leisure Hours in those most civiliz'd Pursuits of Poetry, Music and Conversation, without which Life were a Salvag'ry, and scarce endurable. Respectfully therefore awaiting Y^r L^dshps Reply, I am,

Y^r Most H^mble & O^bt S^vt,
Ebenezer Cooke

And after but a moment's deliberation he appended boldly to his name the single word *Poet*, deeming it a pointless modesty to deny or conceal his very essence.

"By Heav'n!" he exclaimed to himself, looking back on his recent doldrums. "I had near slipped once again into the Abyss! Methinks 'tis a peril I am prone to: 'tis my Nemesis, and marks me off from other men as did the Furies poor Orestes! So be't: at least I know my dread Erinyes for what they are and will henceforth mark their approach betimes.

What is more—thank Joan Toast! I now know how to shield myself from their assault." He consulted his mirror and after some false starts, reflected this reflection: "Life! I must fling myself into Life, escape to't, as Orestes to the temple of Apollo. Action be my sanctuary; Initiative my shield! I shall smite ere I am smitten; clutch Life by his horns! Patron of poets, thy temple be the Entire Great Real World, whereto I run with arms a-stretch: may't guard me from the Pit, and may my Erinyes sink 'neath the vertigo I flee to be transformed to mild Eumenides!"

He then reread his letter.

"Aye," he said, "read and rejoice, Baltimore! 'Tis not every day your province is blessed with a poet. But faith! 'Tis already the twenty-seventh of the month! I must deliver't in person at once."

Thus resolved, Ebenezer called for Bertrand and, finding him not at home, doffed his malodorous nightshirt and proceeded to dress himself. Not bothering to trouble his skin with water, he slipped on his best linen drawers, short ones without stirrups, heavily perfumed, and a clean white dayshirt of good frieze holland, voluminous and soft, with a narrow neckband, full sleeves caught at the wrists with a black satin ribbon, and small, modestly frilled cuffs. Next he pulled on a pair of untrimmed black velvet knee breeches, close in the thighs and full in the seat, and then his knitted white silk hose, which, following the very latest fashion, he left rolled above the knee in order to display the black ribbon garters that held them up. On then with his shoes, a fortnight old, of softest black Spanish leather, square-toed, high-heeled, and buckled, their cupid-bow tongues turned down to flash a fetching red lining. Respectful of both the warmth and the fashion of the day, he left his waistcoat where it hung and donned next a coat of plum-colored serge lined with silver-gray prunella—the great cuffs turned back to show alternate stripes of plum and silver—collarless, tight-shouldered, and full-skirted, which he left unbuttoned from neck to hem to show off shirt and cravat. This latter was of white muslin, the long pendant ends finished in lace, and Ebenezer tied it loosely, twisted the pendants ropewise, and fetched up the ends to pass through the top left buttonhole of his open coat, Steinkirk fashion. Then came his short-sword in its beribboned scabbard, slung low on his left leg from a well-tooled belt, and after it his long, tight-curled white periwig, which he powdered generously and fitted with care on his pate, in its natural state hairless as an egg. Nothing now remained but to top the periwig with his round-crowned, broad-brimmed, feather-edged black beaver, draw on his gauntlet gloves of fawn leather stitched in gold and silver (the cuffs edged in white lace and lined with yellow silk), fetch up his long cane (looped with plum-and-white ribbons like those on his scabbard), and behold the finished product in his looking glass.

"'Sbodikins!" he cried for very joy. "What a rascal! *En garde,* London! Look lively, Life! Have at ye!"

But there was little time to admire the spectacle: Ebenezer hurried out to the street, hired himself the services of barber and bootblack, ate a hearty meal, and took hack at once for the London house of Charles Calvert, Lord Baltimore.

9

Ebenezer's Audience With Lord Baltimore, and His Ingenious Proposal to That Gentleman

To HIS EXTREME DELIGHT and considerable surprise, in a matter of minutes after Ebenezer had presented himself at Lord Baltimore's town house and had sent his message in by a house-servant, word was sent back to him that Charles would receive the visitor in his library, and Ebenezer was ushered not long afterwards into the great man's presence.

Lord Baltimore was seated in an enormous leather chair beside the hearth, and, though he did not rise to greet his visitor, he motioned cordially for Ebenezer to take the chair opposite him. He was an old man, rather small-framed and tight-skinned despite his age, with a prominent nose, a thin white mustache, and large, unusually bright brown eyes; he looked, it occurred to Ebenezer, like an aged and ennobled Henry Burlingame. He was dressed more formally and expensively than Ebenezer, but—as the latter observed at once —not so fashionably: in fact, some ten years behind the times. His wig was a campaigner, full but not extremely long, its tight curls terminating before either shoulder in pendulous corkscrewed dildos; his cravat was of loosely-tied, lace-edged linen; his coat was rose brocade lined with white alamode, looser in the waist and shorter in the skirt than was the current preference, and the unflapped pockets were cut horizontally rather than vertically and set low to the hem. The sleeves reached nearly to the wrists, returned a few inches to show their white linings stitched in silver, and opened at the back with rounded hound's-ear corners. The side vents, cut hip high, were edged with silver buttons and sham buttonholes, and the right shoulder boasted a knot of looped silver ribbons. Beneath the coat were a waistcoat of indigo armozine, which he wore completely buttoned, and silk breeches to match: one saw no more of his shirt than the dainty cuffs of white cobweb lawn. What is more, his garters were hidden under the roll of his hose, and the tongues of his shoes were high and square. He held Ebenezer's letter in his hand and squinted at it in the dim light from the heavily-curtained windows as though re-examining its contents.

"Ebenezer Cooke, is't?" he said by way of commencing the conversation. "Of Cooke's Point, in Dorchester?" His voice, while still in essence forceful, had that uncertain flutter which betrays the onset of senility. Ebenezer bowed slightly in acknowledgment and took the chair indicated by his host.

"Andrew Cooke's son?" asked Charles, peering at his guest. "The same, sir," Ebenezer replied.

"I knew Andrew Cooke in Maryland," reflected Charles. "If memory serves me rightly, 'twas in 1661, the year my father made me Governor of the Province, that I licensed Andrew Cooke to trade there. But I've not seen him for many years and haply wouldn't know him now, or he me." He sighed. "Life's a battle that scars us all, victor and vanquished alike."

"Aye," Ebenezer agreed readily, "but 'tis the stuff of living to fight it, and take't by storm, and your good soldier wears his scars with pride, win or lose, so he got 'em bravely in honest combat."

"I doubt not," murmured Charles, and retreated to the letter. "How's this now," he remarked: *"Ebenezer Cooke, Poet.* What might that mean, pray? Can it be you earn your bread by versifying? Or you're a kind of minstrel, belike, that wanders about the countryside a-begging and reciting? 'Tis a trade I know little of, I confess't."

"Poet I am," answered Ebenezer with a blush, "and no

mean one it may be; but not a penny have I earned by't, nor will I ever. The muse loves him who courts her for herself alone, and scorns the man who'd pimp her for his purse's sake."

"I daresay, I daresay," said Charles. "But is't not customary, when a man tack some bunting to his name to wave like a pendant in the public breeze, that he show thereby his calling and advertise it to the world? Now, did I read here *Ebenezer Cooke, Tinker,* I'd likely hire you to patch my pots; if *Ebenezer Cooke, Physician,* I'd send you the rounds of my household, to purge and tonic the lot; if *Ebenezer Cooke, Gentleman,* or *Esquire,* I'd presume you not for hire, and ring in my man to fetch you brandy. But *Poet,* now: *Ebenezer Cooke, Poet.* What trade is that? How doth one deal with you? What work doth one put you to?"

" 'Tis that very matter I wish to speak of," said Ebenezer, unruffled by the twitting. "Know, sir, that though 'tis no man's living to woo the muse, 'tis yet some men's *calling,* and so 'twas not recklessly I tacked on my name the title *Poet:* 'tis of no moment what I do; poet is what I *am.*"

"As another might sign himself *Gentleman?*" asked Charles.

"Precisely."

"Then 'tis not for hire you sought me out? You crave no employment?"

"Hire I do not seek," Ebenezer declared. "For as the lover craves of his beloved naught save her favor, which to him is reward sufficient, so craves the poet no more from his muse than happy inspiration; and as the fruit of lover's labor is a bedded bride, and the sign of't a crimsoned sheet, so the poet's prize is a well-turned verse, and the sign thereof a printed page. To be sure, if haply the lass bring with her some dowry, 'twill not be scorned, nor will what pence come poetwards from his publishing. Howbeit, these are mere accidents, happy but unsought."

"Why, then," said Charles, fetching two pipes from a rack over the fireplace, "I believe we may call't established that you are not for hire. Let's have a pipe on't, and then pray state your business."

The two men filled and lit their pipes, and Ebenezer returned to his theme.

"*Hire* I care naught for," he repeated, "but as for *employment,* there's another matter quite, and the very sum and substance of my visit. You enquired a moment past, What trade is the poet's, and to what work shall he be put? For answer let me ask you, sir, by'r leave—would the world at large know aught of Agamemnon, or fierce Achilles, or crafty Odysseus, or the cuckold Menelaus, or that entire circus of strutting Greeks and Trojans, had not great Homer rendered 'em to verse? How many battles of greater import are lost in the dust of history, d'you think, for want of a poet to sing 'em to the ages? Full many a Helen blooms one spring and goes to the worm forgot; but let a Homer paint her in the grand cosmetic of his verse, and her beauty boils the blood of twenty centuries! Where lies a Prince's greatness, I ask you? In his feats on the field of battle, or the downy field of love? Why, 'tis but a generation's work to forget 'em for good and all! Nay, I say 'tis not in the deeds his greatness lies, but in their telling. And who's to tell 'em? Not the historian, for be he ne'er so dev'lish accurate, as to how many hoplites had Epaminondas when he whipped the Spartans at Leuctra, or what was the Christian name of Charlemagne's barber, yet nobody reads him but his fellow chroniclers and his students —the one from envy, t'other from necessity. But place deeds and doer in the poet's hands, and what comes of't? Lo, the crook'd nose grows straight, the lean shank fleshes out, French pox becomes a bedsore; shady deeds shed their tarnish, bright grow brighter; and the whole is musicked into tuneful rhyme, arresting conceit, and stirring meter, so's to stick in the head like *Greensleeves* and move the heart like Scripture!"

" 'Tis clear as day," said Charles with a smile, "that the poet is a useful member of a Prince's train."

"And what's true for a prince is true for a principality," Ebenezer went on, stirred by his own eloquence. "What were Greece without Homer, Rome without Virgil, to sing their glories? Heroes die, statues break, empires crumble; but your *Iliad* laughs at time, and a verse from Virgil still rings true as the day 'twas struck. Who renders virtue palatable like the poet, and vice abhorrent, seeing he alone provides both precept and example? Who else bends nature to suit his fancy and paints men better or worse to suit his purpose? What sings like lyric, praises like panegyric, mourns like elegiac, wounds like Hudibrastic verse?"

"Naught, that I can name," said Charles, "and you have quite persuaded me that a man's most useful friend and fearsome foe is the poet. Prithee now, fellow, dispense with farther preamble and deliver me your business plainly."

"Very well," said Ebenezer, planting his cane between his knees and gripping its handle firmly. "Would you say, sir, that Maryland boasts a surfeit of poets?"

"A surfeit of poets?" repeated Charles, and drew thoughtfully upon his pipe. "Well, now, since you ask, I think not. Nay, in good faith I must confess, *entre nous,* there is no surfeit of poets in Maryland. Not a bit of't. Why, I'd wager one might walk the length and breadth of St. Mary's City on a May afternoon and not cross the tracks of a single poet, they're that rare."

"As I reckoned," said Ebenezer. "Would you go so far as to suppose, even, that I might be hard put to't, once I establish myself in Maryland, to find me four or five fellow-planters to match a couplet with, or trade a rhyme?"

" 'Tis not impossible," admitted Charles.

"I guessed as much. And now, sir, if I might: would't be mere gross presumption and vanity for me to suppose, that haply I shall be the absolute first, premier, unprecedented, and genuine original poet to set foot on the soil of *Terra Mariae?* First to pay court to the Maryland Muse?"

" 'Tis not in me to deny," replied Charles, "that should there breathe such a wench as this Maryland Muse, you may well have her maidenhead."

"Faith!" cried Ebenezer joyously. "Only think on't! A province, an entire people—all unsung! What deeds forgot, what gallant men and women lost to time! 'Sblood, it dizzies me! Trees felled, towns raised, a very nation planted in the wilds! Foundings, strugglings, triumphs! Why, 'tis work for a Virgil! Think, m'lord, only think on't: the noble house of Calvert, the Barons Baltimore—builders of nations, bringers of light, fructifiers of the wilderness! A glorious house and history still unmusicked for the world's delight! Marry, 'tis virgin territory!"

"Many's the fine thing to be said of Maryland," Charles agreed. "But to speak plainly, I fear me that virgins are rare as poets there."

"Prithee do not jest!" begged Ebenezer. " 'Twere an epic such as ne'er was penned! The *Marylandiad,* b'm'faith!"

"How's that?" For all his teasing manner, Charles had grown thoughtful in the course of Ebenezer's outburst.

"The *Marylandiad!*" repeated Ebenezer, and declaimed as from a title-page: "An epic to out-epic epics: the history of the princely house of Charles Calvert, Lord Baltimore and Lord Proprietary of the Province of Maryland, relating the

heroic founding of that province! The courage and persever-
ance of her settlers in battling barb'rous nature and fearsome
salvage to wrest a territory from the wild and transform it to
an earthly paradise! The majesty and enlightenment of her
proprietors, who like kingly gardeners fostered the tender
seeds of civilization in their rude soil, and so husbanded and
cultivated them as to bring to fruit a Maryland beauteous beyond description; verdant, fertile, prosperous, and cultured;
peopled with brave men and virtuous women, healthy, handsome, and refined: a Maryland, in short, splendid in her past,
majestic in her present, and glorious in her future, the brightest jewel in the fair crown of England, owned and ruled to
the benefit of both by a family second to none in the recorded history of the universal world—the whole done into
heroic couplets, printed on linen, bound in calf, stamped in
gold"—here Ebenezer bowed with a flourish of his beaver—
"and dedicated to Your Lordship!"

"And signed?" asked Charles.

Ebenezer rose to his feet and beamed upon his host, one
hand on his cane and the other on his hip.

"Signed *Ebenezer Cooke, Gentleman,*" he replied: "*Poet
and Laureate of the Province of Maryland!*"

"Ah," said Charles. "*Poet and Laureate,* now: 'tis a new
bit of bunting you'd add to your name."

"Only think how 'twould redound to Your Lordship's
credit," urged Ebenezer. "The appointment would prove at a
single stroke both the authority and the grace of your rule,
for 'twould give the Province the flavor of a realm and the
refinement of a court to have a bona fide laureate sing her
praises and record in verse her great moments; and as for the
Marylandiad itself, 'twould immortalize the Barons Baltimore, and make Aeneases of 'em all! Moreover, 'twould
paint the Province as she stands today in such glowing colors
as to lure the finest families of England to settle there;
'twould spur the inhabitants to industry and virtue, to keep
the picture true as I paint it; in sum, 'twould work to the
enhancement of both the quality and the value of the colony,
and so proportionately ennoble, empower, and enrich him
who owns and rules her! Is't not a formidable string of
achievements?"

At this Charles burst into such a fit of laughing that he
choked on his pipe smoke, watered at the eyes, and came
near to losing his campaigner; it required the spirited back-

thumping of two body servants, who stood nearby, to restore his composure.

"Oh dear!" he cried at last, daubing at his eyes with a handkerchief. "An achievement indeed, to ennoble and enrich him who rules Maryland! I'm sorry to say, Master Poet, that that fellow already maintains himself a laureate to sing him! There's no ennobling him beyond his present station, and as for enriching him, I venture I've done my share of that and more! Oh dear! Oh dear!"

"How is that?" asked Ebenezer, all bewildered.

"My good man, is't that you were born yesterday? Know you naught of the true state o' the world?"

"Surely 'tis thy province!" exclaimed Ebenezer.

"Surely 'twas my province," corrected Charles with a wry smile, "and the Barons Baltimore were her True and Absolute Lords Proprietary, more often than not, from the day she was chartered till just three years ago. I get my quit-rents yet, and a miserable bit of port-revenue, but for the rest, 'tis King William's province these days, sir, and Queen Mary's, not mine. Why not take your proposal to the Crown?"

"Marry, I knew naught of't!" said Ebenezer. "Might I ask for what cause your Lordship retired from rule? Was't haply your desire to spend quietly the evening of life? Or belike 'twas sheer devotion to the Crown? Egad, what spaciousness of character!"

"Stay, stay," cried Charles, shaking again with mirth, "else I must summon my man again to pound the lights out of me! *Hey! Ha!*" He sighed deeply and beat his chest with the flat of his hand. When he had regained control of himself he said, "I see you are all innocent of Maryland's history, and will plunge into a place not knowing the whys and wherefores of't, or who stands for what. You came to do me a favor, so you declare, and—by Heav'n!—enrich and ennoble me: very well, then, permit me to do you one in return, which may someday haply save you another such wasted hour: by your leave, Mister Cooke, I shall sketch you shortly the history of this Maryland, which, like the gift of a salvage, was first bestowed and then snatched back. Will you hear it?"

" 'Tis my pleasure and honor," answered Ebenezer, who, however, was too crestfallen to relish greatly a lesson in history.

10

A Brief Relation of the Maryland Palatinate,
Its Origins and Struggles for Survival,
as Told to Ebenezer by His Host

" 'Tis truly said," Charles began, *"uneasy lies the head that wears the crown,* inasmuch as *Envy and Covetousness are ne'er satisfied.* Maryland's mine by law and by right, yet her history is the tale of my family's struggle to preserve her, and of the plots of countless knaves to take her from us—chief among them Black Bill Claiborne and a very antichrist named John Coode, who plagues me yet.

"My grandfather, George Calvert, as you may know, was introduced to the court of James I as private secretary to Sir Robert Cecil, and after that great man's death was appointed clerk to the Privy Council and twice Commissioner to Ireland. He was knighted in 1617, and when Sir Thomas Lake was sacked as Secretary of State (owing to the free tongue of his wife), my grandfather was named to replace him, despite the fact that the Duke of Buckingham, James's favorite, wanted the post for his friend Carleton. I have cause to believe that Buckingham took this as an affront and became the first significant enemy to our house.

"What an ill time to be Secretary of State! 'Twas 1619, remember: the Thirty Years' War had just commenced; James had emptied our treasury; we hadn't a single strong ally! 'Twas a choice 'twixt Spain and France, and to choose one was to alienate the other. Buckingham favored Spain, and my grandfather supported him. What could seem wiser, I ask you? Marrying Prince Charles to the Infanta Maria would bind Spain to us forever; Maria's dowry would fill the treasury; and by supporting the King and Buckingham my grandfather would prove his loyalty to the one and shame the resentment of the other! The match was unpopular, to be sure,

86

among the Protestants, and Grandfather was given the odious chore (I think at Buckingham's) of urging defending it to a hostile Parliament. But 'twas the part of wisdom: no man could have guessed the treachery of King Philip and his ambassador Gondomar, who lured us to alienate France, alienate the German Protestant princes, alienate even James's son-in-law Frederick and our own House of Commons, only to break off negotiations at the last minute and leave us virtually helpless!"

"He was a wretch, that Gondomar," Ebenezer agreed politely.

"That, of course, together with his conversion to the Church of Rome, ended Grandfather's public career. Despite the King's entreaties he retired from office, and as reward for his loyalty James named him Baron of Baltimore in the Kingdom of Ireland.

"From then till his death he devoted himself to colonizing America. In 1622 James had patented him the southeastern peninsula of Newfoundland, and my grandfather, deceived by lying reports of the place, put a good part of his fortune into a settlement called Avalon and went to live there himself. But the climate was intolerable. What's more, the French—with whom, thanks to Buckingham's statesmanship, we were at war—were forever snatching our vessels and molesting our fishermen; and as if this were not trouble enough, certain Puritan ministers spread word in the Privy Council that Popish priests were being smuggled into Avalon to undermine the Church of England there. At length my grandfather begged King Charles for a grant farther south, in the dominion of Virginia. The King wrote in reply that Grandfather should abandon his plans and return to England, but ere the letter was received Grandfather had already removed to Jamestown with his family and forty colonists. There he was met by Governor Pott and his Council (including the blackguard William Claiborne), all of 'em hostile as salvages and bent on driving Grandfather away, for fear Charles would grant him the whole of Virginia out from under 'em. They pressed him to swear the oath of supremacy, knowing well that as a good Catholic he would refuse. Not e'en the King had required it of him, but demand it they did, and were like to set bullies and ruffians upon him when he would not swear't."

"Inequity!" said Ebenezer.

"Iniquity!" Charles amended. "So hardly did they use him, he was forced to leave wife and family in Jamestown, and after exploring the coast for a while he returned to England and asked Charles for the Carolina territory. The charter was drawn, but ere 'twas granted who should appear in England but Master Claiborne, who straightway commences to scheme against it. To avoid dispute, Grandfather nobly relinquished Carolina and applied instead for land *north* of Virginia, on both sides of the Bay of Chesapeake. Charles tried in vain to persuade him to live at ease in England and labor no more with grants and colonies, but Grandfather would have none of such idleness and at last prevailed upon the King to make the grant, which he would name *Crescentia,* but which the King called *Terra Mariae,* or Mary-Land, after Henrietta Maria, the Queen."

"Nobly done."

"A charter was writ up then, the like of which for authority and amplitude had ne'er been composed by the Crown of England. It granted to my grandfather all the land from the Potomac River on the south to Latitude Forty on the north, and from the Atlantic west to the meridian of the Potomac's first fountain. To distinguish her above all other regions in the territory, Maryland was named a Province, a county palatine, and over it we Barons Baltimore were made and decreed the true and absolute Lords and Proprietaries. We had the advowsons of churches; we had authority to enact laws and create courts-baron and courts-leet to enforce 'em; we could punish miscreants e'en to the taking of life or member; we could confer dignities and titles——"

"Ah," said Ebenezer.

"—we could fit out armies, make war, levy taxes, patent land, trade abroad, establish towns and ports of entry——"

"Mercy!"

"In short," Charles declared, "for the tribute of two Indian arrows per annum, Maryland was ours in free and common socage, to manage as we please; and what's more 'twas laid down in the charter that peradventure any word, clause, or sentence in't were disputed, it must be read so's most to benefit us!"

"I'faith, it dizzies me!"

"Aye, 'twas a mighty charter. But ere it passed the Great Seal, Grandfather died, worn out at a mere fifty-two years and the charter passed Cecil, my own dear father, who thus in 1632, when he was but twenty-six, became Second Lord Baltimore and First Lord Proprietary of the Province of Maryland. Straightway he set to fitting out vessels and round-ing up colonists, to what a hue and a cry from Bill Claiborne! To what a gnashing of teeth and tearing of hair amongst the members of the old Virginia Company, whose charter had long since been revoked! They would vow in Limehouse that the *Ark* and the *Dove* were fitting out to carry nuns to Spain, and swear in Kensington 'twas to ferry Spanish soldiers Father rigged 'em. So numerous and crafty were his enemies, Father must needs stay behind in London to preserve his rights and trust the voyage to my uncles Leonard and George, who set out from Gravesend for Maryland in October, 1633. But no sooner doth the *Ark* weigh anchor than one of Claiborne's spies, hoping to scuttle us, runs to the Star Chamber and reports we're not cleared through customs, and our crew hath not sworn the oath of allegiance. Secretary Coke sends couriers to Admiral Pennington, in the Straits off Sandwich, and back we're sent to London."

"Connivance!"

"After a month of haranguing, Father cleared away the charges as false and malicious, and off we went again. So's not to give Claiborne farther ammunition, we loaded our Protestants at Gravesend, swore 'em their oath off Tilbury, and then sailed down the Channel to the Isle of Wight to load our Catholics and a brace of Jesuit priests."

"Very clever," Ebenezer said, less certainly.

"Then, by Heav'n, off we sail for Maryland at last, with instructions from Father not to hold our masses in the public view, not to dispute religion with the Protestants, not to anchor under the Virginians' guns at Port Comfort but to lie instead over by Accomac on the Eastern Shore, and not to have aught to do with Captain Claiborne and his people for the first year.

"With the salvages, a nation of Piscataways, we had no quarrel, for they were happy enough to enlist our defense against their enemies and Seneques and Susquehannoughs: 'twas the fiend Claiborne, who caused our trouble! This Claiborne was a factor for Cloberry and Company and Secretary of State for the Dominion by appointment of Charles I, who was easily misled. His main interest was Kent Island, halfway up the Chesapeake, where his trading-post was situated: he'd rather have surrendered an arm than Kent Island, though 'twas clearly within our grant."

"What did he do?" asked Ebenezer.

"Why, says he to himself, Doth not Baltimore's charter grant him the land *hactenus inculta*—'hitherto uncultivated?'

Then he must give up Kent Island, for my traders beat him to't! Thus he pled to the Lords Commissioners for Plantations. But mark you, this accursed *hactenus inculta* was meant as mere description of the land; 'tis the common language of charters, and not intended as a condition of the grant. And truth to tell, Claiborne's traders had not tilled the Island: they bartered their ware for corn to live on as well as furs for Cloberry and Company. The Lords Commissioners disallowed his claim, but give up Kent Island he would not. The Marylanders land in March of 1634—fifty-nine years ago this month—settle at St. Mary's, and inform Claiborne that Kent Island is theirs; he will neither swear allegiance to the Proprietary nor take title to Kent from him, but asks the Virginia Council what to do. You may depend on't he doth not tell 'em of the Lords Commissioners' ruling, and news travels slow from the Privy Council to America; and so they tell him to hold fast, and that he doth, inflaming all whose ears he can catch against my father.

"Uncle Leonard, in St. Mary's, lets Claiborne's year of grace expire and then commands him to acknowledge Father's rights or suffer imprisonment and confiscation of the Island. King Charles orders Governor Harvey of Virginia to protect us from the Indians and allow free trade 'twixt the colonies, and at the same time, being misled by Claiborne's agents to believe Kent Island outside our patent, he orders Father not to molest Claiborne! Now Harvey was a right enough Christian man, willing to live and let live; therefore, our Claiborne had long led a faction aimed at unseating the poor man and driving him from the colony. Thus when Harvey in obeying the King's order declares his readiness to trade with Maryland, the Virginians rise up in a rage against him and declare they'd sooner knock their cattle on the head than sell 'em to us.

"Then 'twas open warfare. Uncle Leonard seizes one of Claiborne's pinnaces in the Patuxent River and arrests her master Thomas Smith for trading with a license from Father. Claiborne arms a shallop and commissions her captain to attack any Maryland vessel he meets. Uncle Leonard sends out two pinnaces to engage him, and after a fight in the Pocomoke River, the shallop surrenders. Two weeks later another Claiborne vessel under command of the same Tom Smith fights it out in Pocomoke Harbor. Poor Governor Harvey by this time is under such fire from his Council that he flies to England for safety.

"Meanwhile Uncle Leonard cuts off the Kent Islanders completely, and the land being altogether *inculta*, they commence to starve. Father points this out to Cloberry and Company, and so persuades them that they pretend no farther title to Kent but send a new attorney to Maryland, with authority to supersede Claiborne. The devil finally yields, asking only that the new man, George Evelyn, not deliver Kent Island to the Marylanders; but Evelyn refuses to promise, and so Claiborne withdraws to London, where he is sued by Cloberry and charged with mutiny by Governor Harvey. Furthermore, Evelyn proceeds to attach all of Claiborne's property in Virginia in the name of Cloberry and Company."

" 'Twas what he deserved," Ebenezer said.

"He saw we'd got the better of him for the nonce, and so he tried a new tack; he buys him Palmer's Island from his cronies the Susquehannoughs, this being in the head of the Chesapeake where their river joins it, and sets him up a new trading-post there, pretending he's outside our patent. Then he petitions Charles to forbid Father from molesting him and further asks—with a plain face, mind!—for a grant to all the land for twelve leagues either side the Susquehannough River, extending southward down the Bay to the ocean and northward to the Grand Lake of Canada!"

"You don't tell me!" cried Ebenezer in alarm, though he hadn't the faintest picture of geography referred to.

"Aye," nodded Charles. "The man was mad! 'Twould have given him a strip of New England twenty-four leagues in breadth and near three hundred in length, plus the entire Chesapeake and three fourths of Maryland! 'Twas his hope to fool the King once more as he'd done in the past, but the Lords Commissioners threw out his petition. Evelyn then acknowledged Father's title to Kent, and Uncle Leonard named him Commander of the Island. He attempted to persuade the Islanders to apply to Father for title to their land and might have won them over, were't not that the rascally Tom Smith is established there, along with Claiborne's brother-in-law. There was naught for't then but to reduce 'em for good and all. Uncle Leonard himself led two expeditions against the islands, reduced them, jailed Claiborne's kin, and confiscated all his property in the Province."

"I trust that chastened the knave!"

"For a time," Charles replied. "He got him an island in the Bahamas in 1638, and we saw none of him for four or five years. As for his kin, we had 'em jailed, but since the Assembly had never yet convened, we had no jury to indict 'em and no court to try 'em in!"

"How did you manage it?" asked Ebenezer. "Pray don't tell me you turned them free!"

"Why, we convened the Assembly as a grand inquest to bring the indictment, then magicked 'em into a court to try the case and find the prisoners guilty. Uncle Leonard then sentences the prisoners to hang, the court becomes an Assembly again and passes his sentence as a bill (since we'd had no law to try the case under), and Uncle Leonard commutes the sentence to insure that no injustice hath been done."

" 'Twas a brilliant maneuver!" Ebenezer declared.

" 'Twas the commencement of our woes," said Charles. "No sooner was the Assembly convened than they demanded the right to enact laws, albeit the charter plainly reserved that right for the Proprietary, requiring only the *assent* of the freemen. Father resisted for a time but had shortly to concede, at least for the nonce, in order to avoid a mutiny. From that day forward the Assembly was at odds with us, and played us false, and lost no chance to diminish our power and aggrandize their own."

He sighed.

"And as if this weren't sufficient harassment, 'twas about this time we learned that the Jesuit missionaries, who had been converting Piscataways by the score, had all the while been taking in return large tracts of land in the name of the Church; and one fine day they declare to us their intent to hold this enormous territory independent of the Proprietary! They knew Father was Catholic and so announced that canon law held full sway in the province, and that by the Papal Bull *In Coena Domini* they and their fraudulent landholdings were exempt from the common law!"

"Ah God!" said Ebenezer.

"What they were ignorant of," Charles continued, "was that Grandfather, ere he turned Catholic, had seen his fill of Jesuitry in Ireland, when James sent him to investigate the discontent there. To nip't in the bud ere the Jesuits snatch the whole Province on the one hand, or the Protestants use the incident as excuse for an anti-Papist insurrection on the other, Father applied to Rome to recall the Jesuits and send him secular priests instead; and after some years of dispute the Propaganda ordered it done.

"Next came Indian trouble. The Susquehannoughs to the north and the Nanticokes on the Eastern Shore had always raided the other tribes now and again, being hunters and not farmers. But after 1640 they took to attacking plantations here and there in the Province, and there was talk of their stirring up our friends the Piscataways to join 'em in a wholesale massacre. Some said 'twas the French behind it all; some alleged 'twas the work of the Jesuits; but I believe 'twas the scheming hand of Bill Claiborne at work."

"Claiborne!" said Ebenezer. "How is that? Did I not mishear you, Claiborne was hid in the Bahamas!"

"So he was. But in 1643, what with the Jesuit trouble, and the Indian trouble, and some dissension in the colony over the civil war 'twixt Charles and the Parliament, Uncle Leonard returned to London to discuss the affairs of the Province with Father, and no sooner did he sail than Claiborne commenced slipping up the Bay in secret, trying to stir up sedition amongst the Kent Islanders. 'Twas about this time one Richard Ingle—a sea-captain, atheist, and traitor—puts into St. Mary's with a merchantman called the *Reformation*, drinks himself drunk, and declares to all and sundry that the King is no king, and that he'd take off the head of any royalist who durst gainsay him!"

"Treason!" Ebenezer exclaimed.

"So said our man Giles Brent, who was Governor against Uncle Leonard's return; he jailed Ingle and confiscated his ship. But as quick as we clap the blackguard in irons he's set loose by order of our own Councilman, Captain Cornwaleys, restored to his ship, and let go free as a fish."

"I am astonished."

"Now, this Cornwaleys was a soldier and had lately led expeditions to make peace with the Nanticokes and drive back the Susquehannoughs. When we impeached him for freeing Ingle, 'twas said in his defense he'd exacted promise from the scoundrel to supply us a barrel of powder and four hundred-weight of shot for the defense of the Province—and sure enough the rascal returns soon after, cursing and assaulting all he meets, and pledges the ammunition as bail against a future trial. But ere we see a ball of't, off he sails again, flaunting clearance and port-dues, and takes his friend Cornwaleys as passenger.

" 'Twas soon clear that Ingle and Claiborne, our two worst enemies, had leagued together to do us in, using the English Civil War as alibi. Claiborne landed at Kent Island, displayed a false parchment, and swore 'twas his commission from the King to command the Island. At the same time, the roundhead Ingle storms St. Mary's with an armed ship and his own false parchment; he reduces the city, drives Uncle Leonard to flee to Virginia, and so with Claiborne's aid claims the whole of Maryland, which for the space of two years suffers total anarchy. He pillages here, plunders there, seizes property, steals the very locks and hinges of every housedoor, and snatches e'en the Great Seal of Maryland itself, it being forty poundsworth of good silver. He does not stick e'en at the house and goods of his savior Cornwaleys but plunders 'em with the rest, and then has Cornwaleys jailed in London as his debtor and traitor to boot! As a final cut he swears to the House of Lords he did it all for conscience's sake, forasmuch as Cornwaleys and the rest of his victims were Papists and malignants!"

"I cannot comprehend it," Ebenezer confessed.

"In 1646 Uncle Leonard mustered a force with the help of Governor Berkeley and recaptured St. Mary's and soon all of Maryland—Kent Island being the last to submit. The Province was ours again, though Uncle Leonard's pains were ill rewarded, for he died a year after."

"Hi!" cried Ebenezer. "What a struggle! I hope with all my heart you were plagued no more by the likes of Claiborne but enjoyed your Province in peace and harmony!"

" 'Twas our due, by Heav'n. But not three years passed ere the pot of faction and sedition boiled again."

"I groan to hear it."

" 'Twas mainly Claiborne, this time in league with Oliver Cromwell and the Protestants, though he'd lately been a swaggering royalist. Some years before, when the Anglicans ran the Puritans out of Virginia, Uncle Leonard had given 'em leave to make a town called Providence on the Severn River, inasmuch as none suffered in Maryland by reason of his faith. But these Protestants despised us Romanists, and would swear no allegiance to Father. When Charles I was beheaded and Charles II driven to exile, Father made no protest but acknowledged Parliament's authority; he e'en saw to't that the Catholic Thomas Greene, Governor after Uncle Leonard died, was replaced by a Protestant and friend of Parliament, William Stone, so's to give the malcontents in Providence no occasion to rebel. His thanks for this wisdom was to have Charles II exiled on the Isle of Jersey, declare him a Roundhead and grant the Maryland government to Sir William Davenant, the poet."

"Davenant!" exclaimed Ebenezer. "Ah, now, 'tis a right

noble vision, the poet-king! Yet do I blush for my craft, that the fellow took a prize so unfairly giv'n."

"He got not far with't, for no sooner did he sail for Maryland than a Parliament cruiser waylaid him in the Channel off Lands End, and that scotched him. Now Virginia, don't you know, was royalist to the end, and when she proclaimed Charles II directly his father was axed, Parliament made ready a fleet to reduce her to submission. Just then, in 1650, our Governor Stone hied him to Virginia on business and deputized his predecessor Thomas Greene to govern till his return. 'Twas a fool's decision, inasmuch as this Greene still smarted at having been replaced. Directly he's deputized he declares with Virginia for Charles II, and for all Governor Stone hastens back and turns the fellow out, the damage is done! The dastard Dick Ingle was still a free man in London, and directly word reached him he flew to the committee in charge of reducing Virginia and caused 'em to add Maryland to the commission. But Father caught wind of't, and ere the fleet sailed he petitioned that Greene's proclamation had been made without his authority or knowledge, and caused the name of Maryland to be stricken from the commission. Thinking that guaranty enough, he retired; straightway sly Bill Claiborne appears and, trusting as always that the committee knew naught of American geography, sees to't the commission is rewrit to include *all the plantations within the Bay of Chesapeake*—which is to say, all of Maryland! What's more, he gets himself appointed as an alternate commissioner of Parliament to sail with the fleet. There were three commissioners—all reasonable gentlemen, if misled—and two alternates: Claiborne and another scoundrel, Richard Bennett, that had taken refuge in our Providence town what time Virginia turned out her Puritans."

"Marry!" cried Ebenezer. "I ne'er have heard of such perfidy!"

"Stay," said Charles. "Not content with being alternates, Claiborne and Bennett see to't two of the commissioners are lost at sea during the passage, and step ashore at Point Comfort with full authority over both Virginia and Maryland!"

"The man's a Machiavel!"

"They reduce Virginia; Bennett appoints himself Governor and Claiborne Secretary of State; then they turn to Maryland, where the rascals in Providence greet 'em with open arms. Good Governor Stone is deposed, Catholics are stripped of their rights wholesale, and all Father's authority is snatched

95

away. As a last stroke, Claiborne and Bennett rouse up the old Virginia Company to petition for wiping Maryland off the map entirely and restoring the ancient boundaries of Virginia! Father pled his case to the Commissioners for Plantations, and while it lay a-cooking he reminded Cromwell that Maryland had stayed loyal to the Commonwealth in the face of her royalist neighbors. Cromwell heard him out, and later, when he dissolved Parliament and named himself Lord Protector, he assured Father of his favor.

"Governor Stone meanwhile had got himself back into office, and Father ordered him to proclaim the Protectorate and declare the commissioners' authority expired. Claiborne and Bennett muster a force of their own and depose Stone again favor of the Puritan William Fuller from Providence. Father appeals to Cromwell, Cromwell sends an order to Bennett and Claiborne to desist, and Father orders Stone to raise a force and march on Fuller in Providence. But Fuller hath more guns, and so he forces Stone's men to surrender on promise of quarter. No sooner doth he have 'em than he murders four of Stone's lieutenants on the spot and throws Stone, grievously wounded, into prison. Fuller's bullies then seize the Great Seal, confiscate and plunder, and drive all Catholic priests out of the Province; Claiborne and his cohorts raise a hue and a cry again to the Commissioners for Plantations; but 'tis all in vain, for at last, in 1658, the Province is restored to Father, and the government delivered to Josias Fendall, whom Father had named to represent him after Stone was jailed."

"Thank Heav'n!" said Ebenezer. *"All's well that ends well!"*

"And ill as ends ill," replied Charles, "for that same year, Fendall turned traitor."

" 'Tis too much!" cried Ebenezer.

" 'Tis plain truth. Some say he was the tool of Fuller and Claiborne; however 'twas, Cromwell being dead and his son a weakling, Fendall persuaded the Assembly to declare themselves independent of the Proprietary, overthrew the whole constitution of the Province, and usurped every trace of Father's authority. 'Twould've been a sorry time for us, had not Charles II been restored to the throne shortly after. Father, Heav'n knows how, made peace with him, and obtained royal letters commanding all to support his government and directing Berkeley of Virginia to aid him. Uncle Philip Calvert was named governor, and the whole conspiracy collapsed."

"Dare I hope your trials ended there?" asked Ebenezer.

"For a time we suffered no more rebellions," Charles admitted. "I came to St. Mary's as governor in 1661, and in 1675, when Father died, I became third Lord Baltimore. During that time our only real troubles were assaults by the Indians and attempts by the Dutch, the Swedes, and others to snatch our land by the old *hactenus inculta* gambit. The Dutch had settled illegally on the Delaware River, and Governor D'Hinoyossa of New Amstel stirred up the Jhonadoes, the Cinagoes, and the Mingoes against us. I considered making war on him, but decided against it for fear King Charles (who had already broken sundry of my charter-privileges) might take the opportunity to seize the whole Delaware territory. I lost it anyhow in 1664, to his brother the Duke of York, and could not raise a word of protest.

"The year I became Lord Baltimore the Cinagoes (what the French call Seneques) descended on the Susquehannoughs, and they in turn overran Maryland and Virginia. The outrages that followed were the excuse for Bacon's Rebellion in Virginia and the cause of much unrest in Maryland. Some time before, in order to harness the malcontents in the Assembly, I had restricted suffrage to the better class of citizens, and held the Assembly in long session to avoid the risk of new elections; but even this failed to quiet things. My enemies intrigued against me from all quarters. Even old Claiborne reappears on the scene, albeit he was well past eighty, and, posing as a royalist again, petitions the King against me —to no avail, happily, and 'twas my indescribable pleasure not long after to hear of the scoundrel's death in Virginia."

" 'Tis my pleasure as well to hear of't now," declared Ebenezer, "for I'd come to fear the knave was immortal!"

"I was accused of everything from Popery to defrauding the King's revenues," Charles went on. "When Nat Bacon turned his private army on Governor Berkeley in Virginia, a pair of rascals named Davis and Pate attempted a like rebellion in Calvert County—urged on, I think, by the turncoats Fuller and Fendall, who ranged privily about the Province. I was in London at the time, but when I heard of the thing, I straightway had my deputy hang the both of 'em. Yet not four years later the traitor Fendall conspires with a new villain to incite a new revolt: This was the false priest John Coode I spoke of, that puts e'en Black Bill Claiborne in the shade. I squelched their game in time and banished Fendall forever, though the conniving Assembly let Coode off free as a bird, to cause more trouble later.

"After this the intrigues and tribulations came in a great rush. In 1681, to settle a private debt, King Charles grants a large area north of Maryland to William Penn—may his Quaker fat be rendered in hell!—and immediately I'm put to't to defend my northern border against his machinations. 'Twas laid out in my charter that Maryland's north boundary is Latitude Forty, and to mark that parallel I had long since caused a blockhouse to be built against the Susquehannoughs. Penn agreed with me that his boundary should run north of the blockhouse, but when his grant appeared no mention at all was made of't. Instead there was a string of nonsense fit to muddle any templar, and to insure his scheme Penn set out a lying surveyor with a crooked sextant to take his observations. The upshot of't was, he declared his southern boundary to be eight miles south of my blockhouse and resorted to every evasion and subterfuge to avoid conferring with me on this outrage. When finally we treed him and proposed a mutual observation, he pled a broken sextant; and when our own instrument showed the line in its true location, he accused me of subverting the King's authority. So concerned was he that the boundary fall where he wished, he proposed a devil's bag of tricks to gain it. Measure north from the Capes, he says, at the short measure of sixty miles to the degree; lower your south border by thirty miles, he says, and snatch land from the Virginians; measure two degrees north from Watkins Point, he says. Then I ask him, 'Why this measuring and land-snatching? Why not take sextant in hand and find the fortieth parallel for good and all?' At last he agrees, but only on condition that should the line fall north of where he wants it, I must sell him the difference at a 'gentleman's price.' "

"I cannot fathom it," Ebenezer admitted. "All this talk of sextants and parallels leaves me faint."

"The truth was," Charles said, "Penn had sworn to his Society for Trade that his grant included the headwaters of the Bay, and he was resolved to have't. When all else failed he fell to plotting with his friend the Duke of York next door, and when to my distress the Duke took the throne as James II, Penn conjures him up that specter of a *hactenus inculta* again and gets himself granted the whole Delaware territory, the which was neither his to take nor James's to grant, but clearly mine.

"Matters reached such a pass that though I feared to leave

98

the Province to my enemies for e'en a minute, I had no recourse but to sail for London in 1684 to fight Penn's intrigues. Now for some time I had been falsely accused of allowing smugglers to defraud the King's port-revenues and of failing to assist the royal tax collectors, and had even paid a fine for't. No sooner do I weigh anchor for London than my kinsman George Talbot in St. Mary's allows a rascally beast of a tax collector to anger him and stabs the knave dead. 'Twas a fool's act, and my enemies seized on't at once. Against all justice they refuse to try him in the Province, but instead deliver him to Effingham, then governor of Virginia —who, by the way, later plotted with the Privy Council to have the whole of Maryland granted to himself!—and 'twas all I could manage to save his neck. Shortly afterwards *another* customs officer is murthered, and though 'twas a private quarrel, my enemies put the two together to color me a traitor to the Crown. Penn, meanwhile, commenced a *quo warranto* suit against my entire charter, and with his friend on the throne I doubt not what would have been the result: as't happened, the folk of England just then pressed their own *quo warranto*, so to speak, against King James, and Penn's game was spoilt, for the nonce, by the revolution."

"I cannot tell how relieved I am to hear it!" Ebenezer declared.

" 'Twas my loss either way," sighed Charles. "When James was on the throne my enemies called me disloyal to him; when he went in exile, and William landed in England, all they cared to remember was that both James and I were Catholics. 'Twas then, at the worst possible time, my fool of a deputy governor sees fit to declare to the Assembly his belief in the divine right of kings and, folly of follies, makes Maryland proclaim officially the birth of James's Catholic son!"

"I tremble for you," Ebenezer said.

"Naturally, the instant William took the throne I sent word to the Maryland Council to proclaim him. But whether from natural causes or, as I suspect, from the malice of my enemies, the messenger died on shipboard and was buried at sea, and his commission with him, so that Maryland remained silent even after Virginia and New England had proclaimed. I sent a second messenger at once, but the harm was done, and those who were not crying 'Papist!' were crying 'Jacobite!' On the heels of this misfortune, in 1689 my enemies in England caused me to be outlawed in Ireland on charges of committing treason there against William in James's behalf—though in sooth I'd never in my life set foot on Irish soil and was at the very moment in England expressly to fight the efforts of James and Penn to snatch Maryland from me! To top all, in March of the same year they spread a rumor over Maryland that a great conspiracy of nine thousand Catholics and Indians have invaded the Province to murther every Protestant in the land: the men sent to Mattapany, at the mouth of the Potomac, are told of massacres at the river's head and, rushing there to save the day, find the settlers arming against such massacres as they've heard of in Mattapany! For all my friends declare 'tis naught but a sleeveless fear and imagination, the whole Province is up in arms against the Catholics."

"Blind! Blind!"

" 'Twas no worse than the anti-Papism here in London," said Charles. "My only pleasure in this dark hour was to see that lying Quaker Penn himself arrested and jailed as a Jesuit!"

"I'faith, it cheers me, too!"

"Naught now remained but for the conspirators to administer the *coupe de grâce*. This they did in July, led by the false priest Coode. He marches on St. Mary's with an armed force, promotes himself to the rank of general, and for all he'd used to be a Catholic himself, shouts *Papist* and *Jesuit* until the whole city surrenders. The President and Council flee to Mattapany, where Coode besieges 'em in the fort till they give up the government to him. Then, calling themselves the Protestant Associators, they beg King William to snatch the government for himself!"

"Surely King William hanged him!" Ebenezer said.

Charles, who had been talking as rapidly and distractedly as though telling a painful rosary, now seemed really to notice his visitor for the first time since commencing the history.

"My dear Poet. . . ." He smiled thinly. "William is at war with King Louis: in the first place, for aught anyone knows the war might spread to America, and he is most eager to gain control of all the colonies against this possibility. In the second place, war is expensive, and my revenues could help to pay his soldiers. In the third place, he holds the crown by virtue of an anti-Papist revolution, and I am a Papist. In the fourth place, the government of Maryland was imploring him to rescue the Province from the oppression of Catholics and Indians——"

"Enough!" cried Ebenezer. "I fear me he snatched it! But by what legal right——"

"Ah, 'twas wondrous legal," said Charles. "William instructed the Attorney General to proceed against my charter by way of *scire facias*, but reflecting afterwards on the time such litigation would require, and the treasury's dire need for food, and the possibility of the Court's finding in my favor, he asks Chief Justice Holt to find him a way to snatch my Maryland with less bother. Holt ponders awhile till he recalls that *jus est id quod principi placet*, and then declares, in all solemnity, that though 'twould be better the charter were forfeited in a proper inquisition, yet since no inquisition hath been held, and since by the King's own word the matter is urgent, he thinks the King might snatch him the government on the instant and do his investigating later."

"Why," said Ebenezer, " 'tis like hanging a man today and trying his crime tomorrow!"

Charles nodded. "In August of 1691 milord Sir Lionel Copley became the first royal governor of the crown colony of Maryland," he concluded. "My rank fell from that of count palatine, with power of life and death over my subjects, to that of common landlord, entitled only to my quit-rents, my port duty of fourteen pence per ton on foreign vessels, and my tobacco duty of one shilling per hogshead. The Commissioners of the Privy Seal, be't said to their credit, disputed Holt's decision, and in fact when the *quo warranto* was instigated the allegations against me fell to pieces for lack of evidence, and no judgment was found. But of course 'twas precisely because he foresaw this that William had leaped ere he looked: you may depend on't he held fast to Maryland, and clasps her yet like a lover his mistress; for *Possession is nine points of the law* in any case, and with a king 'tis parliament, statute book, and courtroom all together! 'Tis said in sooth, *A king's favor is no inheritance;* and *A king promiseth all, and observeth what he will."*

"And," added Ebenezer, *"He who eats the King's goose shall choke on the feathers."*

"How?" Charles demanded angrily. "D'you twit me, fellow? Think thee Maryland was e'er King William's goose?"

"Nay, nay!" Ebenezer protested. "You misread the saying! 'Tis meant to signify merely, that *A great dowry is a bed full of brambles,* don't you know: *A great man and a great river are ill neighbors,* or *A king's bounty is a mixed blessing."*

101

"Enough, I grasp it. So, then, there is your Maryland, fellow. Think you 'tis fit for a *Marylandiad?*"

"I'faith," replied Ebenezer, " 'twere fitter for a Jeremiad! Ne'er have I encountered such a string of plots, cabals, murthers, and machinations in life or literature as this history you relate me!"

Charles smiled. "And doth it haply inspire your pen?"

"Ah God, what a dolt and boor must Your Lordship think me, to burst upon you with grand notions of couplet and eulogy! I swear to you I am sorry for't: I shall leave at once.'

"Stay, stay," said Charles. "I will confess to you, this *Marylandiad* of yours is not without interest to me."

"Nay," Ebenezer said, "you but chide me for punishment."

"I am an old man," Charles declared, "with small time left on earth——"

"Heav'n forbid!"

"Nay, 'tis clear truth," Charles insisted. "The prime of my life, and more, I've laid on the altar of a prosperous, well-governed Maryland, which was given me in trust by my dear father, and him by his, to husband and improve, and which I dreamed of handing on to my son a richer, worthier estate for my having ruled it."

"Marry, I am in tears!"

"And now in my old age I find this shan't be," Charles continued. "Moreover, I am too aged and infirm to make another ocean passage and so must die here in England without laying eyes again upon that land as dear to my heart as the wife of my body, and whose abducting and rape stings me as e'er did Helen's Menelaus."

"I can bear no more!" wept Ebenezer, blowing his nose delicately into his handkerchief.

"I have no authority," Charles concluded, "and so can no longer confer dignities and titles as before. But I declare to you this, Mr. Cooke: hie you to Maryland; put her history out of mind and look you at her peerless virtues. Study them; mark them well! Then, if you can, turn what you see to verse; tune and music it for the world's ears! Rhyme me such a rhyme, Eben Cooke; make me this Maryland, that neither time nor intrigue can rob me of; that I can pass on to my son and my son's son and all the ages of the world! Sing me this song, sir, and by my faith, in the eyes and heart of Charles Calvert and of every Christian lover of Beauty and Justice, thou'rt in sooth Poet and Laureate of the Province! And should e'er it come to pass—what against all hope and expectation I nightly pray for to Holy Mary and all saints—that one day the entire complexion of things alters, and my sweet province is once again restored to her proprietor, then, by Heav'n, I shall confer you the title in fact, lettered on sheepskin, beribboned in satin, signed by myself, and stamped for the world to gape at with the Great Seal of Maryland!"

Ebenezer's heart was too full for words.

"In the meantime," Charles went on, "I shall, if't please you, at least commission you to write the poem. Nay, better, I'll pen thee a draft of the Laureate's commission, and should God e'er grant me back my Maryland, 'twill retroact to this very day."

" 'Sheart! 'Tis past belief!"

Charles had his man fetch him paper, ink, and quill, and with the air of one accustomed to the language of authority, quickly penned the following commission:

> CHARLES ABSOLUTE LORD & PROPRIETARY OF THE PROVINCES OF MARYLAND & AVALON LORD BARON OF BALTIMORE &t To Our Trusty and Welbeloved Our Dear Ebenezer Cooke Esqr of Cookes Poynt Dorset County Greeting Whereas it is our Desire that the Sundrie Excellencies of Our Province of Maryland aforesaid be set down in Verse for Generations to Come and Whereas it is Our Conviction that Your talents Well Equip You for that Task &t We Do Will and Command you upon the Faith which You Owe unto Us that You do compose and construct such an Epical Poem, setting forth the Graciousness of Marylands Inhabitants, Their Good Breeding and Excellent Dwelling-places, the Majesty of her Laws, the Comfort of Her Inns and Ordinaries &t &t and to this Purpose We do Name and Entitle You Poet and Laureat of the Province of Maryland Aforesaid. Witness Ourself at the City of London the twenty-eighth Day of March in the eighteenth Year of Our Dominion over Our said Province of Maryland Annoq Dom 1694

"Out on't!" he cried, handing the finished draft to Ebenezer. " 'Tis done, and I wish you fair passage."

Ebenezer read the commission, flung himself upon his

knees before Lord Baltimore, and pressed that worthy's coat hem to his lips in gratitude. Then, mumbling and stumbling, he pocketed the document, excused himself, and ran from the house into the bustling streets of London.

11

Ebenezer Returns to His Companions, Finds
Them Fewer by One, Leaves Them Fewer
by Another, and Reflects a Reflection

"LOCKET'S!" CRIED EBENEZER to his cabman, and sprang into the hackney with a loose flail of limbs like a mismanaged marionette. With what a suddenness had he scaled the reaches of Parnassus, while his companions blundered in the foothills! Snatching out his commission, he read again the sweet word *Laureat* and the catalogue of Maryland's excellencies.

"Sweet land!" he exclaimed. "Pregnant with song! Thy deliverer approacheth!"

There was a conceit worth saving, he reflected: the word *deliverer*, for instance, with its twin suggestions of midwife and savior. . . . He lamented having no pen nor any paper other than Baltimore's commission, which after kissing he tucked away in his coat.

"I must purchase me a notebook," he decided. " 'Twere a pity such wildflowers should die unplucked. No more may I think merely of my own delight, for a laureate belongs to the world."

Soon the hackney cab reached Locket's, and after rewarding the driver Ebenezer hurried to find his colleagues, whom he'd not seen since the night of the wager. Once inside, however, he assumed a slower, more dignified pace, in keeping with his position, and weaved through the crowded tables to where he spied his friends.

Dick Merriweather noticed him first. " 'Sblood!" he shouted. "Look ye yonder, what comes hither! Am I addled with the sack, or is't Lazarus untombed?"

"How now!" Tom Trent joined in. "Hath the spring wind thawed ye, boy? I feared me you was ossified for good and all."

"Thawed?" said Ben Oliver, and winked. "Nay, Tom, for how could such a lover e'er be chilled? 'Tis my guess he's only now regained his strength from his mighty joust the night of our wager and is back to take all comers."

"Lightly, Ben," reproved Tom Trent, and glanced at John McEvoy beside him, who, however, was entirely absorbed in regarding Ebenezer and seemed not to have heard the remark. " 'Tis unbecoming a good fellow, to hold a grudge o'er such a trifle."

"Nay, nay," Ben insisted. "What more pleasant or instructive, I ask you, than to hear of great deeds from the lips of their doers? Hither with thee, Ebenezer. Take a pot with us and tell us all plainly, as a man amongst men: What think you now of this Joan Toast that you did swive? How is she in the bed, I mean, and what fearsome bargain did you drive for your five guineas, that we've seen none of you this entire week, or her since? Marry, what a man!"

"Curb your evil tongue," Ebenezer said crisply, taking a seat. "You know the story as well as I."

"Hi!" cried Ben. "Such bravery! What, will you say naught by way of explanation or defense when a very trollop scorns you?"

Ebenezer shrugged. " 'Tis near as e'er she'll come to greatness."

"Great Heav'n!" Tom Trent exclaimed. "Who is this stranger with the brave replies? I know the face and I know the voice, but b'm'faith, 'tis not the Eben Cooke of old!"

"Nay," agreed Dick Merriweather, " 'tis some swaggering impostor. The Cooke I knew was e'er a shy fellow, something stiff in the joints, and no great hand at raillery. Know you aught of his whereabouts?" he asked Ebenezer.

"Aye"—Ebenezer smiled—"I know him well, for 'twas I alone saw him die and wrote his elegy."

"And prithee, sir, what carried him off?" inquired Ben Oliver with as much of a sneer as could be salvaged from his late confounding. "Belike 'twas the pain of unrequited love?"

"The truth of the matter is, sirs," Ebenezer replied, "he perished in childbirth the night of the wager and never learned that what he'd been suffering was the pains of labor —the more intense, for that he'd carried the fetus since childhood and was brought to bed of't uncommon late. Howbeit, 'twas the world's good luck he had him an able midwife, who delivered full-grown the man you see before you."

"I'faith!" declared Dick Merriweather. "I have fair lost sight o' you in this Hampton Court Hedge of a conceit! Speak literally, an't please you, if only for a sentence, and lay open plainly what is signified by all this talk of death and midwives and the rest of the allegory."

"I shall," smiled Ebenezer, "but I would Joan Toast were present to hear't, inasmuch as 'twas she who played all innocently the midwife's part. Do fetch her, McEvoy, that all the world may know I bear no ill will towards either of you. Albeit you acted from malice, yet, as the proverb hath it, *Many a thing groweth in the garden, that was not planted there;* or even *A man's fortune may be made by his enviers.* Certain it is, your mischief bore fruit beyond my grandest dreams! You said of me once that I comprehend naught of life, and perchance 'tis true; but you must allow farther that *Fools rush in where wise men fear to tread,* and that *A castle may be taken by storm, that ne'er would fall to siege.* The fact is, I've wondrous news to tell. Will you summon her?"

Ever since Ebenezer's appearance in the winehouse McEvoy had sat quietly, even sullen. Now he got up from his place, growled "Summon her yourself, damn ye!" and left the tavern in a great sulk.

"What ails him?" asked Ebenezer. "The man meant me an injury—doth it chagrin him that it misfired into fortune? 'Twas a civil request; did I know Joan's whereabouts I'd fetch her myself."

"So I doubt not would he," Ben Oliver said.

"What is't you say?"

"Did you not hear it said before," asked Tom Trent, "that nor hide nor hair of your Joan have we seen these three days past?"

"I took it for a twit," said Ebenezer. "She's gone in sooth?"

"Aye," affirmed Dick, "the tart is vanished from sight, and not McEvoy nor any soul else knows aught of't. The last anyone saw of her was the day after the wager. She was in a fearful fret——"

"I'faith," put in Ben, "there was no speaking to the woman!"

106

"We took it for a pout," Dick went on, "forasmuch as you'd—— That is to say——"

"She'd scorned four guineas from a good man," Ben declared in a last effort at contempt, "and got in exchange a penceless preachment from——"

"From Ebenezer Cooke, my friends," Ebenezer finished, unable to hold back the news any longer, "who this very day hath been named by Lord Baltimore to be Poet and Laureate of the entire Province of Maryland! And you've not seen the wench since, you say?"

But none heard the question: they looked at each other and at Ebenezer.

"Egad!"

" 'Sblood!"

"Is't true? Thou'rt Laureate of Maryland?"

"Aye," said Ebenezer, who actually had said only that he'd been *named* Laureate, but deemed it too late, among other things, to clarify the misunderstanding. "I sail a few days hence for America, to manage the estate where I was born, and by command of Lord Baltimore to do the office of Laureate for the colony."

"Have you commission and all?" Tom Trent marveled.

Ebenezer did not hesitate. "The Laureate's commission is in the writing," he explained, "but already I'm commissioned to turn him a poem." He pretended to search his pockets and came up with the document in his coat, which he passed around the table to great effect.

"By Heav'n 'tis true!" Tom said reverently.

"Laureate of Maryland! It staggers me!" said Dick.

"I will confess," said Ben, "I'd ne'er have guessed it possible. But out on't! Here's a pot to you, Master Laureate! Hi there, barman, a pint all around! Come, Tom! Ho, Dick! Let's have a health, now! I hope I may call it," he went on, putting his arm about Ebenezer's shoulders, "for 'tis many a night Eben's taken my twitting in good grace, that would have rankled a meaner spirit. 'Twould be as fair an honor to propose this health t'you, friend, as 'twill be for me to pay for't. Prithee grant me that, and 'twere proof of a grace commensurate to thy talent."

"Your praise flatters me the more," Ebenezer said, "for that I know you—how well!—to be no flatterer. Toast away, and a long life to you!"

The waiter had by this time brought the pints, and the four men raised their glasses.

"Hi there, sots and poetasters!" Ben shouted to the house at large, springing up on the table. "Put by your gossip and drink as worthy a health as e'er was drunk under these rafters!"

"Nay, Ben!" Ebenezer protested, tugging Ben's coat.

"Hear!" cried several patrons, for Ben was a favorite among them.

"Drag off yon skinny fop and raise your glasses!" someone cried.

"Scramble up here," Ben ordered, and Ebenezer was lifted willy-nilly to the table top.

"To the long life, good health, and unfailing talent of Ebenezer Cooke," Ben proposed, and everyone in the room raised his glass, "who while we lesser fry spent our energies braying and strutting, sat aloof and husbanded his own, and crowed him not a crow nor, knowing himself an eagle, cared a bean what barnyard fowl thought of him; and who, therefore, while the rest of us cocks must scratch our dunghills in feeble envy, hath spread his wings and taken flight, for who can tell what eyrie! I give thee Ebenezer Cooke, lads, twitted and teased by all—none more than myself—who this day was made Poet and Laureate of the Province of Maryland!"

A general murmur went round the room, followed by a clamor of polite congratulation that went like wine to Ebenezer's head, for it was the first such experience in his life.

"I thank you," he said thickly to the room. "I can say no more!"

"Hear! Hear!"

"A poem, sir!" someone called.

"Aye, a poem!"

Ebenezer got hold of himself and stayed the clamor with a gesture. "Nay," he said, "the muse is no minstrel, that sings for a pot in the taverns; besides, I've not a line upon me. This is the place for a toast, not for poetry, and 'twill greatly please me do you join my toast to my magnanimous patron Baltimore——"

A few glasses went up, but not many, for anti-Papist feeling was running high in London.

"To the Maryland Muse——" Ebenezer added, perceiving the small response, and got a few more hands for his trouble.

"To Poetry, fairest of the arts"—many additional glasses were raised—"and to every poet and good-fellow in this tavern, which for gay and gifted patrons hath not its like in the hemisphere!"

"Hear!" the crowd saluted, and downed the toast to a man.

It was near midnight when Ebenezer returned at last to his rooms. He called in vain for Bertrand and tipsily commenced undressing, still very full of his success. But whether because of the silence of his room after Locket's, or the unhappy sight of his bed lying still unmade as he'd left it in the morning, the linens all rumpled and soiled from his four days' despair, or some more subtle agency, his gaiety seemed to leave him with his clothes; when at length he had stripped himself of shoes, drawers, shirt, and periwig, and stood shaved, shorn, and mother-naked in the center of his room, his mind was dull, his eyes listless, his stance uncertain. The great success of his first plunge still thrilled him to contemplate, but no longer was it entirely a pleasurable excitement. His stomach felt weak. All that Charles had told him of the history of Maryland came like a bad dream to his memory, and turning out the lamp he hurried to the window for fresh air.

Despite the hour, London bristled in the darkness beneath and all around him, from which came at intervals here a drunkard's shout, there a cabman's curse, the laughter of a streetwalker, the whinny of a horse. A damp spring breeze moved off the Thames and breathed on him: out there on the river, anchors were being weighed and catted, sails unfurled from yards and sheeted home, bearings taken, soundings called, and dark ships run down the tide, out the black Channel, and thence to the boundless ocean, cresting and tossing under the moon. Great restless creatures stirred and glided in the depths; pale gray sea birds wheeled and shrieked down the night wind, or wildly planed against the scud. Could one suppose that somewhere far out under the stars there really lay a Maryland, against whose long sand coasts the black sea foamed? That at that very instant, peradventure, some naked Indian prowled the reedy dunes or stalked his quarry down whispering aisles of the forest?

Ebenezer shuddered, turned from the window, and drew the curtains fast. His stomach was extremely uneasy. He lay down on the bed and tried to sleep, but with no success: the daring of his interview with Charles Calvert, and all that followed on it, kept him tossing and turning long after his muscles had begun to ache and his eyes to burn for sleep. The specters of William Claiborne, Richard Ingle, William Penn, Josias Fendall, and John Coode—their strange and terrible energy, their intrigues and insurrections—chilled and sickened him but refused to be driven from his awareness; and he could not give over remembering and pronouncing his title even after repetition had taken pleasure and sense from the epithet and left it a nightmare string of sounds. His saliva ran freely; he was going to be ill. *Poet and Laureate of the Province of Maryland!* There was no turning back. Out under the night, Maryland and his single mortal destiny awaited him.

"Ah, God!" he wept at last, and sprang from the bed in an icy sweat. Running to the chamber pot he flung off the lid and with a retch heaved into it the wine of his triumph. Once delivered of it, he felt somewhat calmer: he returned to the bed, clasped his knees against his chest to quiet the agitation of his stomach, and so contrived, after countless fretful sighs, a sort of sleep.

PART II: GOING TO MALDEN

1

The Laureate Acquires a Notebook

WHATEVER TREPIDATIONS OR dank night doubts had lately plagued the Laurcate's repose, when the sun rose next morning over London they were burned off with the mist of the Thames. He woke at nine refreshed in body and spirit, and, when he remembered the happenings of the day before and his ncw office, it was with delight.

"Bertrand! You, Bertrand!" he called, springing from the bed. "Are you there, fellow?"

His man appeared at once from the next room.

"Did you sleep well, sir?"

"Like a silly babe. What a morning! It ravishes me!"

"Methought I heard ye taken with the heaves last night."

" 'Sheart, a sour pint, belike, at Locket's," Ebenezer replied lightly, "or a stein of green ale. Fetch my shirt there, will you? There's a good fellow. Egad, what smells as fresh as new-pressed linen or feels as clean?"

" 'Tis a marvel ye threw it off so. Such a groaning and a hollowing!"

"Indeed?" Ebenezer laughed and began to dress with leisurely care. "Nay, not those; my knit cottons today. Hollowing, you say? Some passing nightmare, I doubt not; I've no memory of't. Nothing to fetch surgeon or priest about."

"Priest, sir!" Bertrand exclaimed with a measure of alarm. " 'Tis true, then, what they say?"

"It may be, or it may not. Who are *they,* and what is their story?"

"Some have it, sir," Bertrand replied glibly, "thou'rt in Lord Baltimore's employ, who all the world knows is a famous Papist, and that 'twas only on your conversion to Rome he gave ye your post."

" 'Dslife!" Ebenezer turned to his man incredulously. "What scurrilous libel! How came you to hear it?"

Bertrand blushed. "Begging your pardon, sir, ye may have marked ere now that albeit I am a bachelor, I am not without interest in the ladies, and that, to speak plainly, I and a certain young serving maid belowstairs have what ye might call——"

"An understanding," Ebenezer suggested impatiently. "Do I know it, you scoundrel? D'you think I've not heard the twain of you clipping and tumbling the nights away in your room, when you thought me asleep? I'faith, 'tis enough to wake the dead! If my poor puking cost you an hour's sleep last night, 'tis not the hundredth part of what I owe you! Is't she told you this tale of a cock and a bull?"

"Aye," admitted Bertrand, "but 'twas not of her making."

"Whence came it, then? Get to the point, man! 'Tis a sorry matter when a poet cannot accept an honor without suffering on the instant the slanders of the envious, or make a harmless trope without his man's crying Popery!"

"I crave your pardon, sir," said Bertrand. " 'Twas no accusation, only concern; I thought it my duty to tell ye what your enemies are saying. The fact is, sir, my Betsy, who is a hot-blooded, affectionate lass, hath the bad luck to be married, and that to a lackluster chilly fellow whose only passions are ambition and miserliness, and who, though he'd like a sturdy son to bring home extra wages, is as sparing with caresses as with coins. Such a money-grubber is he that, after a day's work as a clerk's apprentice in the Customs-House, he labors half the night as a fiddler in Locket's to put by an extra crown, with the excuse 'tis a nest egg against the day she finds herself with child. But 'sblood, 'tis such a tax on his time that he scarce sees her from one day to the next and on his strength that he hath not the wherewithal to roger what time he's with her! It seemed a sinful waste to me to see, on the one hand, poor Betsy alone and all a-fidget for want of husbanding, and on the other her husband Ralph a-hoarding money to no purpose, and so like a proper Samaritan I did what I could for the both of 'em: Ralph fiddled and I diddled."

"How's that, you rascal? The both of 'em! Small favor to the husband, to bless him with horns! What a villainy!"

"Ah, on the contrary, sir, if I may say so, 'twas a double boon I did him, for not only did I plough his field, which else had lain fallow, but seeded it as well, and from every sign 'twill be a bumper crop come fall. Look ye, sir, ere ye judge me a monster; the lad knew naught but toil and thankless drudgery before and took no pleasure in't, save the satisfaction of drawing his wage. He came home to a wife who carped and quarreled for lack o' love and was set to leave him for good, which would've been the death of him. Now he works harder than ever, proud as a peacock he's got a son a-building, and his clerking and fiddling have changed from mere labor to royal sport. As for Betsy, that was wont to nag and bark at him before, she's turned sweet as a sugar-tit and jumps to his every whim and fancy; she would not leave him for the Duke o' York. Man and wife are both the happier for't."

"And thou'rt the richer by a mistress that costs you not a farthing to keep," Ebenezer added, "and on whom you may get a household of bastards with impunity!"

Bertrand shrugged, adjusting his master's cravat.

"As't happens, yes," he admitted, "though I hear't said that virtue is its own reward."

"Then 'twas this cuckold of a fiddler started the story?" demanded Ebenezer. "I'll take the wretch to court!"

"Nay, 'twas but gossip he passed on to Betsy last night, who passed it on to me this morning. He had it from the drinkers at Locket's, after all the toasting was done and you were gone."

"Unconscionable envy and malice!" Ebenezer cried. "Do you believe it?"

"Marry, sir, 'tis no concern o' mine what persuasion ye follow. I'll confess I wondered, after Betsy told me, whether all thy hollowing and pitching last night was not a free-for-all 'twixt you and your conscience, or some strange Papish ceremony, for I know they've a bag of 'em for every time o' day. B'm'faith, 'twere mere good business, methinks, to take his superstitious vows for him, if that's the condition for the post. Soon or late, we all must strike our bargains with the world. Everything hath its price, and yours was no dear one, inasmuch as neither milord Baltimore nor any other Jesuit can see what's in your heart. All ye need do is say him his hey-nonny-nonnies whenever he's there to hear 'em; as for the rest of the world, 'tis none o' their concern what office ye hold, or what it cost ye, or who got it for ye. Keep mum on't, draw your pay, and let the Pope and the world go hang."

"Lord, hear the cynic!" said Ebenezer. "My word on't, Bertrand, I struck no bargain with Lord Baltimore, nor dickered and haggled any *quid pro quos.* I'm no more Papist this morning than I was last week, and as for salary, my office pays me not a shilling."

" 'Tis the soundest stand to take," Bertrand nodded knowingly, "if any man questions ye."

" 'Tis the simple truth! And so far from keeping my appointment secret, I mean to declare it to all and sundry—within the bounds of modesty, of course."

"Ah, ye'll regret that!" Bertrand warned. "If ye declare the office, 'tis no use denying ye turned Papist to get it. The world believes what it pleases."

"And doth it relish naught save slander and spite and fantastical allegation?"

" 'Tis not so fantastic a story," Bertrand said, "though mind ye, I don't say 'tis true. *More history's made by secret handshakes than by battles, bills, and proclamations.*"

"Nay!" Ebenezer protested. "Such libels are but the weapon of the mediocre against the talented. Those fops at Locket's slander me to solace themselves! As for your cynical philosophy, that sees a plot in every preferment, methinks 'tis but mere wishful thinking, the mark of a domestical mind, which attributes to the world at large all the drama and dark excitement that it fails to find in its own activity."

" 'Tis all above me, this philosophy," Bertrand said. "I know only what they say."

"Popery indeed! Dear God, I am ill of London! Fetch my traveling wig, Bertrand; I shan't abide another day in this place!"

"Where will ye go, sir?"

"To Plymouth, by the afternoon coach. See to't my chests and trunks are packed and loaded, will you? 'Sheart, how shall I endure e'en another morning in this vicious city?"

"Plymouth so soon, sir?" asked Bertrand.

"The sooner the better. Have you found a place?"

"I fear not, sir. 'Tis a bad season to seek one, my Betsy says, and 'tis not every place I'd take."

"Ah well, no great matter. These rooms are hired till April's end, and thou'rt free to use 'em. Your wage is paid ahead, and I've another crown for you if my bags are on the Plymouth coach betimes."

"I thank ye, sir. I would ye weren't going, I swear't, but ye may depend on't your gear will be stowed on the coach. Marry, I'll not soon find me a civiler master!"

"Thou'rt a good fellow, Bertrand," Ebenezer smiled. "Were't not for my niggard allowance, I'd freight thee to Maryland with me."

"I'faith, I've no stomach for bears and salvages, sir! An't please ye, I'll stay behind and let my Betsy comfort me for losing ye."

"Then good luck to you," said Ebenezer as he left, "and may your son be a strapping fellow. I shan't return here: I mean to waste the whole morning buying a notebook for my voyage. Haply I'll see you at the posthouse."

"Good day then, sir," Bertrand said, "and fare thee well!"

Irksome as was his false friends' slander, it slipped from Ebenezer's mind once he was out of doors. The day was too fair, his spirits too high, for him to brood much over simple envy. "Leave small thoughts to small minds," said he to himself, and so dismissed the matter.

Much more important was the business at hand: choosing and purchasing a notebook. Already his excellent trope of the day before, which he'd wanted to set down for future generations, was gone from his memory; how many others in years gone by had passed briefly through his mind, like lovely women through a room, and gone forever? It must happen no more. Let the poetaster and occasional dabbler-in-letters affect that careless fecundity which sneers at notes and commonplace books: the mature and dedicated artist knows better, hoards every gem he mines from the mother lode of fancy, and at his leisure sifts the diamonds from the lesser stones.

He went to the establishment of one Benjamin Bragg, at the Sign of the Raven in Paternoster Row—a printer, bookseller, and stationer whom he and many of his companions patronized. The shop was a clearinghouse for literary gossip; Bragg himself—a waspish, bright-eyed, honey-voiced little man in his forties of whom it was rumored that he was a Sodomite—knew virtually everyone of literary pretensions in the city, and though he was, after all, but a common tradesman, his favor was much sought after. Ebenezer had been uncomfortable in the place ever since his first introduction to

117

the proprietor and clientele some years before. He had always, until the previous day, been of at least two minds about his own talent, as about everything else—confident on the one hand (From how many hackle-raising ecstasies! From how many transports of inspiration!) that he was blessed with the greatest gift since blind John Milton's and destined to take literature singlehandedly by the breech and stand it upon its periwig; equally certain, on the other (From how many sloughs of gloom, hours of museless vacancy, downright immobilities!) that he was devoid even of talent, to say nothing of genius; a bumbler, a stumbler, a witless poser like many another—and his visits to Bragg's, whose poised habitués reduced him to mumbling ataxia in half an instant, never failed to convert him to the latter opinion, though in other circumstances he could explain away their cleverness to his advantage. In any case, he was in the habit of disguising his great uneasiness with the mask of diffidence, and Bragg rarely noticed him at all.

It was to his considerable satisfaction, therefore, that when this time he entered the establishment and discreetly asked one of the apprentices to show him some notebooks, Bragg himself dismissed the boy and left the short, wigless customer with whom he'd been gossiping in order to serve him personally.

"Dear Mr. Cooke!" he cried. "You *must* accept my felicitations on your distinction!"

"What? Oh, indeed," Ebenezer smiled modestly. "However did you hear of't so soon?"

"So soon!" Bragg warbled. " 'Tis the talk o' London! I had it yesterday from dear Ben Oliver, and today from a score of others. *Laureate of Maryland!* Tell me," he asked, with careful ingenuousness, "was't by Lord Baltimore's appointment, as some say, or by the King's? Ben Oliver declares 'twas from Baltimore and vows he'll turn Quaker and seek the same of William Penn for Pennsylvania!"

" 'Twas Lord Baltimore honored me," Ebenezer replied coolly, "who, though a Romanist, is as civil a gentleman as any I've met and hath a wondrous ear for verse."

"I am certain of't," Bragg agreed, "though I've ne'er met the man. Prithee, sir, how came he to know your work? We're all of us a-flutter to read you, yet search as I may I can't find a poem of yours in print, nor hath anyone I've asked heard so much as a line of your verse. Marry, I'll confess it: we scarce knew you wrote any!"

"A man may love his house and yet not ride on the ridge-
118

pole," Ebenezer observed, "and a man may be no less a poet for not declaiming in every inn and ordinary or printing up his creatures to be peddled like chestnuts on London Bridge."

"Well said!" Bragg chortled, clapped his hands, and bounced on his heels. "Oh, pungently put! 'Twill be repeated at every table in Locket's for a fortnight! Ah, 'slife, masterfully put!" He dabbed his eyes with his handkerchief. "Would you tell me, Mr. Cooke, if't be not too prying a question, whether Lord Baltimore did you this honor in the form of a recommendation for King William and the Governor of Maryland to approve, or whether 'tis still in Baltimore's power to make and fill official posts? There was some debate on the matter here last evening."

"I daresay there was," Ebenezer said. " 'Tis my good fortune I missed it. Is't your suggestion Lord Baltimore would willfully o'erstep his authority and exercise rights he hath no claim to?"

"Oh, Heav'n forbid!" cried Bragg, wide-eyed. " 'Twas a mere civil question, b'm'faith! No slight intended!"

"So be't. Let us have done with questions now, lest I miss the Plymouth coach. Will you show me some notebooks?"

"Indeed, sir, at once! What sort of notebook had you in mind?"

"What sort?" repeated Ebenezer. "Are there sorts of notebooks, then? I knew't not. No matter—any sort will serve, I daresay. 'Tis but to take notes in."

"Long notes, sir, or short ones?"

"How? What a question! How should I know? Both, I suppose!"

"Ah. And will you take these long and short notes at home, sir, or while traveling?"

"I'faith, what difference to you? Both, I should think. A mere silly notebook is all my craving."

"Patience, sir; 'tis only to make certain I sell you naught but fits thy need. *The man who knows what he needs,* they say, *gets what he wants;* but he who knows not his mind is forever at sixes and sevens and blames the blameless world for't."

"Enough wisdom, I beg you," Ebenezer said uncomfortably. "Sell me a notebook fit for long or short notes, both at home and abroad, and have done with't."

"Very well, sir," Bragg said. "Only I must know another wee thing."

"I'faith, 'tis a Cambridge examination! What is't now?"

"Is't thy wont to make these notes always at a desk,

whether at home or abroad, or do you jot 'em down as they strike you, whether strolling, riding, or resting? And if the latter, do you yet ne'er pen 'em in the public view, or is't public be damned, ye'll write where't please you? And if the latter, would you have 'em think you a man whose taste is evidenced by all he owns; who is, you might say, in love with the world? A Geoffrey Chaucer? A Will Shakespeare? Or would you rather they took you for a Stoical fellow, that cares not a fig for this vale of imperfections, but hath his eye fixed always on the Everlasting Beauties of the Spirit: a Plato, I mean, or a Don John Donne? 'Tis most necessary I should know."

Ebenezer smote the counter with his fist. "Damn you, fellow, thou'rt pulling my leg for fair! Is't some wager you've made with yonder gentleman, to have me act the fool for him? Marry, 'twas my retching hate of raillers and hypocrites that drove me here, to spend my final London morn sequestered among the implements of my craft, like a soldier in his armory or a mariner in the ship chandler's; but I find no simple sanctuary even here. By Heav'n, I think not even Nero's lions were allowed in the dungeons where the martyrs prayed and fortified themselves, but had to stay their hunger till the wretches were properly in the arena. Will you deny me that small solace ere I take ship for the wilderness?"

"Forbear, sir; *do* forbear," Bragg pleaded, "and think no ill of yonder gentleman, who is a perfect stranger to me."

"Very well. But explain yourself at once and sell me a common notebook such as a poet might find useful who is as much a Stoic as an Epicurean."

"I crave no more than to do just that," Bragg declared. "But I must know whether you'll have the folio size or the quarto. The folio, I might say, is good for poets, inasmuch as an entire poem can oft be set on facing pages, where you can see it whole."

"Quite sound," Ebenezer acknowledged. "Folio it is."

"On the other hand, the quarto is more readily lugged about, particularly when thou'rt walking or on horseback."

"True, true," Ebenezer admitted.

"In the same way, a cardboard binding is cheap and hath a simple forthright air; but leather is hardier for traveling, more pleasing to behold, and more satisfying to own. What's more, I can give ye unruled sheets, such as free the fancy from mundane restraints, accommodate any size of hand, and make a handsome page when writ; or ruled sheets, which save time, aid writing in carriages or aboard ships, and keep a page neat as a pin. Finally, ye may choose a thin book, easy to carry but soon filled, or a fat one, cumbersome to travel with but able to store years of thought 'twixt single covers. Which shall be the Laureate's notebook?"

" 'Sbodikins! I am wholly fuddled! Eight species of common notebook?"

"Sixteen, sir; sixteen, if I may," Bragg said proudly. "Ye may have

A thin plain cardboard folio,
A thin plain cardboard quarto,
A thin plain leather folio,
A thin ruled cardboard folio,
A fat plain cardboard folio,
A thin plain leather quarto,
A thin ruled cardboard quarto,
A fat plain cardboard quarto,
A thin ruled leather folio,
A fat ruled cardboard folio,
A fat plain leather folio,
A thin ruled leather quarto,
A fat ruled cardboard quarto,
A fat plain leather quarto,
A fat ruled leather folio, or
A fat ruled leather quarto."

"Stop!" cried Ebenezer, shaking his head. " 'Tis the Pit!"

"I may say also I'm expecting some lovely half-moroccos within the week, and if need be I can secure finer or cheaper grades of paper than what I stock."

"Have at thee, Sodomite!" Ebenezer shouted, drawing his shortsword. " 'Tis thy life or mine, for another of thy evil options and I am lost!"

"Peace! Peace!" the printer squealed, and ducked under his serving-counter.

"Peace Peace we'll have do I reach thee," Ebenezer threatened; "nor no mere pair of pieces, either, b'm'faith, but sixteen count!"

"Stay, Master Laureate," urged the short, wigless customer; he came from across the shop, where he'd been listening with interest to the colloquy, and placed his hand on Ebenezer's sword arm. "Calm your wrath, ere't lead ye to blight your office."

"Eh? Ah, to be sure," sighed Ebenezer, and sheathed his sword with some embarrassment. " 'Tis the soldier's task to

121

fight battles, is't not, and the poet's to sing 'em. But marry, who dares call himself a man that will not fight to save his reason?"

"And who dares call himself reasonable," returned the stranger, "that will so be swayed by's passions as to take arms against a feckless shopkeeper? 'Tis thy quandary, do I see't aright, that all these notebooks have their separate virtues, yet none is adequate, inasmuch as your purposes range 'twixt contradictories."

"You have't firmly," Ebenezer admitted.

"Then 'tis by no means this poor knave's fault, d'ye think, that he gives ye options? He's more to be praised than braised for't. Put by your anger, for *Anger begins with folly and ends with repentance;* it makes a rich man hated and a poor man scorned, and so far from solving problems, only multiplies 'em. Follow rather the sweet light of Reason, which like the polestar leads the wise helmsman safe to port through the unruly seas of passion."

"You chasten me, friend," said Ebenezer. "Out with you, Ben Bragg, and never fear: I'm my own man again."

" 'Sheart, thou'rt a spirited fellow for a poet!" Bragg exclaimed, reappearing from under the counter.

"Forgive me."

"There's a good fellow!" said the stranger. *"Anger glances into wise men's breasts, but rests only in the bosoms of fools.* Heed no voice but Reason's."

"Good counsel, I grant thee," Ebenezer said. "But I'll own it passeth my understanding how Solomon himself could reconcile opposites and make a plain book elegant or a fat book thin. Not all the logic of Aquinas could contrive it!"

"Then look past him," said the stranger with a smile, "to Aristotle himself, and where you find opposite extremes, seek always the Golden Mean. Thus Reason dictates: Compromise, Mr. Cooke; compromise. *Adieu.*"

With that the fellow left, before Ebenezer could thank him or even secure his name.

"Who was that gentleman?" he asked Bragg.

" 'Twas one Peter Sayer," Bragg replied, "that just commissioned me to print him some broadsides—more than that I know not."

"No native Londoner, I'll wager. What a wondrous wise fellow!"

"And wears his natural hair!" sighed the printer. "What think ye of his advice?"

" 'Tis worthy a Chief Justice," Ebenezer declared, "and I

mean to carry it out at once. Fetch me a notebook neither too thick nor too thin, too tall nor too small, too simple nor too elegant. 'Twill be Aristotle from start to finish!"

"Your pardon, sir," Bragg protested; "I have already named my whole stock over, and there's not a Golden Mean in the lot. Yet I think ye might purchase a book and alter it to suit."

"How, prithee," Ebenezer asked, looking nervously to the door through which Sayer had made his exit, "when I know no more of bookmaking than doth a bookseller of poetry?"

"Peace, peace!" urged Bragg. "Remember the voice of Reason."

"So be't," Ebenezer said. *"Every man to his trade*, as Reason hath it. Here's a pound for book and alterations. Commence at once, nor let your eye drift e'en for an instant from the polestar of Reason."

"Very good, sir," Bragg replied, pocketing the money. "Now, 'tis but reasonable, is't not, that a long board may be sawn short, but a short board may not be stretched? And a fat book, likewise, may be thinned, but ne'er a thin book fattened?"

"No Christian man can say you nay," Ebenezer agreed.

"So, then," said Bragg, taking a handsome, fat unruled leather folio from the shelf, "we take us a great stout fellow, spread him open thusly, and *compromise* him!" Pressing the notebook flat open upon the counter, he ripped out several handfuls of pages.

"Whoa! Stay!" cried Ebenezer.

"Then," Bragg went on, paying him no heed, "since Reason tells us a fine coat may wear shabby, but ne'er a cheap coat fine, we'll just compromise this morocco here and there ——" He snatched up a letter opener near at hand and commenced to hack and gouge the leather binding.

"Hold, there! I'faith, my notebook!"

"As for the pages," Bragg continued, exchanging the letter opener for goose quill and inkpot, "ye may rule 'em as't please ye, with Reason as the guide: sidewise"—he scratched recklessly across a half-dozen pages—"lengthwise" —he penned hasty verticals on the same pages—"or what ye will!" He scribbled at random through the whole notebook.

" 'Sbody! My pound!"

"Which leaves only the matter of size," Bragg concluded: "He must be smaller than a folio, yet taller than a quarto. Hark ye, now: methinks the voice of Reason orders ——"

"Compromise!" Ebenezer shouted, and brought down his

sword upon the mutilated notebook with such a mighty chop that, had Bragg not just then stepped back to contemplate his creation he'd surely have contemplated his Creator. The covers parted; the binding let go; pages flew in all directions. *"That* for your damned Golden Mean!"

"Madman!" Bragg cried, and ran out into the street. "Oh, dear, help!"

There was no time to lose: Ebenezer sheathed his sword, snatched up the first notebook he spied—which happened to be lying near at hand, over the cash drawer—and fled to the rear of the store, through the print shop (where two apprentices looked up in wonder from their work), and out the back door.

2

The Laureate Departs from London

THOUGH SEVERAL HOURS yet remained before departure time, Ebenezer went from Bragg's directly to the posthouse, ate an early dinner, and sipped ale restlessly while waiting for Bertrand to appear with his trunk. Never had the prospect of going to Maryland seemed so pleasant: he longed to be off! For one thing, after the adventure in Bragg's establishment he was more than ever disgusted with London; for another, he feared that Bragg, to whom he'd mentioned the Plymouth coach, might send men after him, though he was certain his pound was more than adequate payment for both notebooks. And there was another reason: his heart still beat faster when he recalled his swordplay of an hour before, and his face flushed.

"What a gesture!" he thought admiringly. " *'That* for your damned Golden Mean!' Well said and well done! How it terrified the knave, i'faith! A good beginning!" He laid his notebook on the table: it was quarto size, about an inch thick, with cardboard covers and a leather spine. " 'Tis not what I'd have *chosen,*" he reflected without sorrow, "but 'twas manfully got, and 'twill do, 'twill do. Barman!" he called. "Ink and quill, if you please!" The writing materials fetched, he opened the notebook in order to pen a dedication: to his surprise he found already inscribed on the first page *B. Bragg, Printer & Stationer, Sign of the Raven, Paternoster Row, London, 1694,* and on the second and third and fourth such entries as *Bangle & Son, glaziers, for windowglass, 13/4,* and *Jno. Eastbury, msc printing, 1/3/9.*

" 'Sblood! 'Tis Bragg's account book! A common ledger!" Investigating further he found that only the first quarter of the book had been used: the last entry, dated that same day, read *Col. Peter Sayer, broadsides, 2/5/0.* The remaining pages were untouched. "So be't," he smiled, and ripped out the used sheets. "Was't not my aim to keep strict account of my traffic with the muse?" Inking his quill, he wrote across the first page *Ebenezer Cooke, Poet & Laureate of Maryland* and then observed (it being a ledger of the double-entry variety) that his name fell in the *Debit* column and his title in the *Credit.*

"Nay, 'twill never do," he decided, "for to call my office an asset to me is but to call me a liability to my office." He tore out the sheet and reversed the inscription. "Yet *Poet and Laureate Eben Cooke* is as untrue as the other," he reflected, "for while I hope to be a credit to my post, yet surely the post is no liability to me. 'Twere fitter the thing were done sidewise down the credit line, to signify the mutual benefit of title and man." But before he tore out the second sheet it occurred to him that "credit" was meaningless except as credit *to* somebody—and yet anything he entered to receive it became a liability. For a moment he was frantic.

"Stay!" he commanded himself, perspiring. "The fault is not in the nature of the world, but in Bragg's categories. I'll merely paste my commission over the whole title page."

He called for glue, but when he searched his pockets for the commission from Lord Baltimore, he found it not in any of them.

"Agad! 'Tis in the coat I wore last night at Locket's, that Bertrand hath packed away for me!"

He went searching about the posthouse for his man, without success. But in the street outside, where the carriage was being made ready, he was astonished to find no other person than his sister Anna.

"Marry!" he cried, and hurried to embrace her. "People vanish and appear to me of late as in a Drury Lane comedy! How is it thou'rt in London?"

"To see thee off to Plymouth," Anna said. Her voice was no longer girlish, but had a hard, flat tone to it, and one would have put her age closer to thirty-five than twenty-eight years. "Father forbade it but would not come himself, and so I stole away and be damned to him." She stepped back and examined her brother. "Ah faith, thou'rt grown thinner, Eben! I've heard 'twere wise to fatten up for an ocean passage."

"I had but a week to fatten," Ebenezer reminded her. During his sojourn at Paggen's he had seen Anna not more than once a year, and he was greatly moved by the alteration in her appearance.

She lowered her eyes, and he blushed.

"I'm looking for that great cynical servant of mine," he said gaily, turning away. "You've not seen him, I suppose?"

"You mean Bertrand? I sent him off myself not five minutes past, when he'd got all your baggage on the coach."

"Ah, there's a pity. I had promised him a crown for't."

"And I gave it him, from Father's money. He'll be back at St. Giles, I think, for Mrs. Twigg hath a ferment of the blood and is not given long to live."

"Nay! Dear old Twigg! 'Tis a pity to lose her."

They stood about awkwardly. Turning his head to avoid looking her in the eye, Ebenezer caught sight of the wigless fellow of the bookstore, Peter Sayer, standing idly by the corner.

"Did Bertrand tell you aught of my preferment?" he asked cheerfully.

"Aye, he spoke of't. I'm proud." Anna's manner was distracted. "Eben——" She grasped his arm. "Was't true, what that letter said?"

Ebenezer laughed, somewhat nettled at Anna's lack of interest in his laureateship. " 'Twas true I'd got nowhere at Peter Paggen's, in all those years. And 'twas true a woman was in my chamber."

"And did you deceive her?" his sister asked anxiously.

"I did," Ebenezer said. Anna turned away and caught her breath.

"Stay!" he cried. " 'Twas not at all in the way you think. I deceived her inasmuch as she was a whore that came to me to be employed for five guineas; but I took a great love for her and would neither lay nor pay her on those terms."

Anna wiped her eyes and looked at him. "Is't true?"

"Aye," Ebenezer laughed. "Haply you'll judge me not a

126

man for't, Anna, but I swear I am as much a virgin now as the day we were born. What, thou'rt weeping again!"

"But not for sorrow," Anna said, embracing him. "Do you know, Brother, I had come to think since you went to Magdalene College we no longer knew each other—but it may be I was wrong."

Ebenezer was moved by this statement, but a trifle embarrassed when Anna squeezed him more tightly before releasing him. Passersby, including Peter Sayer on the corner, turned their heads to look at them: doubtless they looked like parting lovers. Yet he was ashamed at being embarrassed. He moved closer to the coach, to prevent too gross a misunderstanding, and took his sister's hand, at least partly to forestall further embraces.

"Do you ever think of the past?" Anna asked.

"Aye."

"What times we had! Do you remember how we used to talk for hours after Mrs. Twigg had turned out the lamp?" Tears sprang again to her eyes. "I'faith, I miss you, Eben!"

Ebenezer patted her hand.

"And I thee," he said, sincerely but uncomfortably. "I remember one day when we were thirteen, you were ill in bed with a fever, and so Henry and I went alone to tour Westminster Abbey. 'Twas my first whole day apart from you, and by dinnertime I missed you so sorely I begged Henry to take me home. But we went instead to St. James's Park, and after supper to Dukes Theater in Lincoln's Inn Fields, and 'twas far past midnight ere we reached home. I felt ten years older for the day's adventure and could not see for the life of me how I'd e'er be able to tell you the whole of't. I'd had my first meal away from home, been to my first theater, and tasted my first brandy. We talked of nothing else for weeks but that day, and still I'd remember trifles I'd forgot to tell you. 'Twould give me pain to think of them, and at length I came to regret ever having gone and told Henry so, for't seemed to me you'd ne'er catch up after that day."

"I recall it as if 'twere but last week," Anna said. "How many times I've wondered whether *you'd* forgot it." She sighed. "And I never did catch up! Query as I might, there was no getting the whole story. The awful truth of't was, *I'd not been there to see!*"

Ebenezer interrupted her with a laugh. "Marry, e'en now I recall something of it I forgot to tell you! After supper at some Pall Mall tavern on that day, I waited a half hour alone at the table while Henry went upstairs for one reason or another——" He stopped and blushed scarlet, suddenly realizing, after fifteen years, what in all probability Henry Burlingame had gone upstairs for. Anna, however, to his relief, showed no sign of understanding.

"The wine had gone to my head, and everyone looked odd to me, none less than myself. 'Twas then I composed my first poem, in my head. A little quatrain. Nay, I must confess 'twas no slip of memory: I kept it secret, Heav'n knows why. I can e'en recite it now:

> *Figures, so strange, no* GOD *design'd*
> *To be a Part of Human-kind:*
> *But wanton Nature. . . .*

La, I forget the rest. 'Sheart," he said, resolving happily to record the little verse in his notebook as soon as he boarded the carriage, "and since then what years we've spent apart! What crises and adventures we each have had, that the other knows naught of! 'Tis a pity all the same you had a fever that day!"

Anna shook her head. "I had a secret too, Eben, that Mrs. Twigg knew, and Henry guessed, but never you nor Father. 'Twas no fever I was bedded with, but my first monthly troubles! I'd changed from child to woman that morning, and had the cramp of't as many women do."

Ebenezer pressed her hand, uncertain what to say. It was time to board the coach: footmen and driver were attending last-minute details.

" 'Twill be long ere I see you again," he said. "Belike you'll be a stout matron with half-a-dozen children!"

"Not I," Anna said. " 'Twill be Mrs. Twigg's lot for me, when she dies: an old maid housekeeper."

Ebenezer scoffed. "Thou'rt a catch for the best of men! Could I find your equal I'd be neither virgin nor bachelor for long." He kissed her good-bye, forwarded his respects to his father, and made to board the carriage.

"Stay!" Anna said impulsively.

Ebenezer hesitated, uncertain of her meaning. Anna slipped from her finger a silver seal ring, well known to the poet because it was their only memento of their mother, whom they had never seen; Andrew had bought it during his brief courtship and had presented it to Anna some years past. Equally spaced around the seal were the letters *A N N E B*,

128

for Anne Bowyer, his fiancée, and in the center, overlapped and joined by a single crossbar, was a brace of beflourished *A*'s signifying the connection of Anne and Andrew. The complete seal looked like this:

"Prithee take this ring," Anna entreated, and looked at it musingly. " 'Tis—'tis my wont to alter its significance somewhat . . . but no matter. Here, let me put it on you." She caught up his left hand and slipped the ring onto his little finger. "Pledge me . . ." she began, but did not finish.

Ebenezer laughed, and to terminate the uncomfortable situation pledged that inasmuch as her share of Malden was a large part of her dowry, he would make it flourish.

It was time to leave. He kissed her again and boarded the carriage, taking the seat from which he could wave to her. At the last minute the wigless fellow, Peter Sayer, boarded the coach and took the opposite seat. A footman closed the door and sprang up to his post—apparently there were to be no other passengers. The driver whipped up the horses, Ebenezer waved to the forlorn figure of his twin at the posthouse door, and the carriage pulled away.

" 'Tis no light matter, to leave a woman ye love," Sayer offered. "Is't thy wife, perhaps, or a sweetheart?"

"Neither," sighed Ebenezer. " 'Tis my twin sister, that I shan't see again till Heav'n knows when." He turned to face his companion. "Thou'rt my savior from Ben Bragg's, I believe—Mr. Sayer?"

Sayer's face showed some alarm. "Ah, ye know me?"

"Only by name, from Ben Bragg." He extended his hand. "I am Ebenezer Cooke, bound for Maryland."

Sayer shook hands warily.

"Is Plymouth your home, Mr. Sayer?"

The man searched Ebenezer's face. "Do ye really not know Colonel Peter Sayer?" he asked.

"Why, no." Ebenezer smiled uncertainly. "I'm honored by your company, sir."

"Of Talbot County in Maryland?"

"Maryland! I'faith, what an odd chance!"

"Not so odd," Sayer said, "since the Smoker's Fleet sails on the first. Anyone bound for Plymouth these days is likely bound for the plantations."

"Well, 'twill be a pleasant journey. Is Talbot County near to Dorchester?"

"Really, sir, thou'rt twitting me!" Sayer cried.

"Nay, I swear't; I know naught of Maryland. 'Tis my first visit since the age of four."

Sayer still looked skeptical. "My dear fellow, you and I are neighbors, with only the Great Choptank between us."

"Marry, what a wondrous small world! You must pay me a call sometime, sir: I'll be managing our place on Cooke's Point."

"And writing a deal of verse, did I hear Mr. Bragg aright."

Ebenezer blushed. "Aye, I mean to turn a line or two if I can."

"Nay, put by your modesty, Master Laureate! Bragg told me of the honor Lord Baltimore did ye."

"Ah well, as for that, 'tis likely he got it wrong. My commission is to write a panegyric on Maryland, but I'll not be laureate in fact till the day Baltimore hath the Province for his own again."

"Which day," Sayer said, "you and your Jacobite friends yearn for, I presume?"

"Stay, now!" Ebenezer said, alarmed. "I am as loyal as you."

Sayer smiled for an instant but said in a serious tone, "Yet ye wish King William to lose his province to a Papist?"

"I am a poet," Ebenezer declared, almost adding *and a virgin* from habit; "I know naught of Jacobites and Papists, and care less."

"Nor knew ye aught of Maryland, it seems," Sayer added. "How well do ye know your patron?"

"Not at all, save that he is a great and generous man. I've conversed with him but once, but the history of his province persuades me he was done a pitiful injustice. I'faith, the scoundrels that have fleeced and slandered him! I am confident King William knows not the whole truth."

"But you do?"

"I don't say that. Still and all, a villain is a villain! This fellow Claiborne, that I heard of, and Ingle, and John Coode, that led the latest insurrection——"

"Did he not strike a great blow for the faith, against the Papists?" Sayer demanded.

130

Ebenezer began to grow uncomfortable. "I know not where your sympathies lie, Colonel Sayer; belike thou'rt a colonel in Coode's militia and will clap me in prison the day we step ashore in Maryland——"

"Then were't not the part of prudence to watch thy speech? Mind, I don't say I *am* a friend of Coode's, but for all ye know I may be."

"Aye, 'twere indeed the part of prudence," Ebenezer said, a trifle frightened. "You may say 'tis not always prudent to be just, and I 'tis not always just to be prudent. I am no Roman Catholic, sir, nor antipapist either, and I wonder whether 'tis a matter 'twixt Protestants and Papists in Maryland or 'twixt rascals and men of character, whate'er their faith."

"Such a speech could get thee jailed there," Sayer smiled.

"Then 'tis proof of their injustice," Ebenezer declared, not a little anxiously, "for I'm not on either side. Lord Baltimore strikes me as a man of character, and there's an end on't. It might be I'm mistaken."

Sayer laughed. "Nay, thou'rt not mistaken. I was but trying your loyalty."

"To *whom*, prithee? And what is your conclusion?"

"Thou'rt a Baltimore man."

"Do I go to prison for't?"

"That may be," Sayer smiled, "but not at my hands. I am this very moment under arrest in Maryland for seditious speech against Coode and have been since last June."

"Nay!"

"Aye, along with Charles Carroll, Sir Thomas Lawrence, Edward Randolph, and half a dozen other fine fellows that spoke against the blackguard. I am no Papist either, but Charles Calvert is an old and dear friend of mine. May the day I fear to speak up against poltroons be the last of my life!"

Ebenezer hesitated. "How am I to know 'tis not *now* thou'rt trying me, and not before?"

"Ye can never know," Sayer replied, "especially in Maryland, where friends may change their colors like tree frogs. Why, do ye know, the barrister Bob Goldsborough of Talbot, my friend and neighbor for years, deposed against me to Governor Copley? The last man I'd have thought a turncoat!"

Ebenezer shook his head. *"A man will sell his heart to save his neck*. The picture looks drear enough, i'faith!"

"Yet there's this to say for't," Sayer said, "that it makes the choice a clean one: ye must hold your tongue with all save your conscience or else speak your mind and take the consequences—discretion goes out the window, and so doth compromise."

"Is this the Voice of Reason speaking?" Ebenezer asked.

"Nay, 'tis the Voice of Action. Compromise serves well enough when neither extreme will let ye what ye want: but there are things men must not want. What comfort is a whole skin, pray, when the soul is wounded unto death? 'Twas I wrote Baltimore his first full account of Coode's rebellion, and rather than live under his false Associators I left my house and lands and came to England."

"How is it thou'rt returning? Will you not be clapped in irons?"

"That may be," Sayer said. "Howbeit, I think not. Copley's dead since September, and Baltimore himself had a hand in commissioning Francis Nicholson to replace him. D'ye know Nicholson?"

Ebenezer admitted that he did not.

"Well, he hath his faults—chiefly a great temper and a passion for authority—but his ear's been bent the right way, and he'll have small use for Coode's sort. Ere he got this post he was with Edmund Andros in New England, and 'twas Leisler's rebellion in New York that ran him out—the very model of Coode's rebellion in Maryland. Nay, I fear no harm from Nicholson."

"Nonetheless, 'tis a bold resolve," Ebenezer ventured.

Sayer shrugged. "Life is short; there's time for naught but bold resolves."

Ebenezer started and looked sharply at his companion.

"What is't?"

"Nothing," Ebenezer said. "Only a dear friend of mine was wont to tell me that. I've lost track of him these six or seven years."

"Belike he made some bold resolve himself," Sayer suggested, "though 'tis easier to recommend than do. Did ye heed his counsel?"

Ebenezer nodded. "Hence both my voyage and my laureateship," he said, and since they had a long ride before them he told his traveling-companion the story of his failure at Cambridge, his brief sojourn in London with Burlingame and his long one with Peter Paggen, the wager in the winehouse, and his audience with Lord Baltimore. The motion of the carriage must have loosened his tongue, for he went into considerable detail. When he concluded with his solution to the

132

problem of choosing a notebook and showed him Bragg's ledger, Sayer laughed so hard he had to hold his sides.

"Oh! Ha!" he cried. *"That for your golden mean!* Oh, 'sbodikins! Thou'rt a credit to your tutor, I swear!"

" 'Twas my first act as Laureate," Ebenezer smiled. "I saw it as a kind of crisis."

"Marry, and managed it wondrous well! So here ye sit: virgin and poet! Think ye the twain will dwell 'neath the same roof and not quarrel with each other day and night?"

"On the contrary, they live not only in harmony but in mutual inspiration."

"But what on earth háth a virgin to sing of? What have ye in your ledger there?"

"Naught save my name," Ebenezer admitted. "I had minded to paste my commission there, that Baltimore drafted, but it got packed in my trunk. Yet I've two poems to copy in it from memory, when I can. The one I spoke of already, that I wrote the night of the wager: 'tis on the subject of my innocence."

At his companion's request Ebenezer recited the poem.

"Very good," Sayer said when it was done. "Methinks it puts your notion aptly enough, though I'm no critic. Yet 'tis a mystery to me, what ye'll sing of save your innocence. Prithee recite me the other piece."

"Nay, 'tis but a silly quatrain I wrote as a lad—the first I ever rhymed. And I've but three lines of't in my memory."

"A pity. The Laureate's first song: 'twould fetch a price someday, I'll wager, when thou'rt famous the world o'er. Might ye treat me to the three ye have?"

Ebenezer hesitated. "Thou'rt not baiting me?"

"Nay!" Sayer assured him. " 'Tis a mere natural curiosity, is't not, to wonder how flew the mighty eagle as a fledgling? Do we not admire old Plutarch's tales of young Alcibiades flinging himself before the carter, or Demosthenes shaving half his head, or Caesar taunting the Cilician pirates? And would ye not yourself delight in hearing a childish line of Shakespeare's, or mighty Homer's?"

"I would, right enough," Ebenezer admitted. "But will ye not judge the man by the child? 'Tis the present poem alone, methinks, that matters, not its origins, and it must stand or fall on's own merits, apart from maker and age."

"No doubt, no doubt," Sayer said, waving his hand indifferently, "though this word *merit*'s total mystery to me. What I spoke of was *interest*, and whether 'tis good or bad in

133

itself, certain your *Hymn to Innocence* is of greater interest to one who knows the history of its author than to one who knows not a bean of the circumstances that gave it birth."

"Your argument hath its merits," Ebenezer allowed, not a little impressed to hear such nice reasoning from a tobacco-planter.

Sayer laughed. "A fart for thy *merit!* My argument hath its *interest*, peradventure, to one who knows the arguer, and the history of such debates since Plato's time."

"Yet surely the *Hymn* hath some certain degree of merit, and hath nor more nor less whether he that reads it be a Cambridge don or silly footboy—or for that matter, whether 'tis read or not."

"Belike it doth," Sayer said with a shrug. " 'Tis very like the schoolmen's question, whether a falling tree on a desert isle makes a sound or no, inasmuch as no ear hears it. I've no opinion on't myself, though I'll own the quarrel hath some interest: 'tis an ancient one, with many a mighty implication to't."

"This *interest* is the base of thy vocabulary," Ebenezer remarked, "as *merit* seems to be of mine."

"It at least permits of conversation," Sayer smiled. "Prithee, which gleans more pleasure from thy *Hymn?* The footboy who knows not Priam from Good King Wenceslas, or the don who calls the ancients by their nicknames? The salvage Indian that ne'er heard tell of chastity, or the Christian man who's learned to couple innocence with unpopped maidenheads?"

"Marry!" Ebenezer exclaimed. "Your case hath weight, my friend, but I confess it repels me to own the muse sings clearest to professors! 'Twas not of them I thought when I wrote the piece."

"Nay, ye mistake me," Sayer said. " 'Tis no mere matter of schooling, though none's the worse for a little education. Human experience is what I mean: knowledge of the world, both as stored in books and learnt from the hard text of life. Your poem's a spring of water, Master Laureate—'sheart, for that matter everything we meet is a spring, is't not? That the bigger the cup we bring to't, the more we fetch away, and the more springs we drink from, the bigger grows our cup. If I oppose your notion 'tis that such thinking robs the bank of human experience, wherein I have a considerable deposit. I will not drink with any man who'd have me throw away my cup. In short, sir, though I am neither poet nor critic, nor e'en a common *Artium Baccalaureus*, but only a simple sot-weed planter that hath read a book or two in's time and seen a bit o' the wide world, yet I'm confident your poem means more to me than to you."

"What! That are neither virgin nor poet?"

Sayer nodded. "As for the first, I have been one in my time and look on't now from the vantage-point of experience, which ye do not. For the second, 'tis but a *different* view ye get as author. Nor am I the dullest of readers: I quite appreciate the wordplays in your first quatrain, for instance."

"Wordplays? What wordplays?"

"Why, *chaste Penelope*, for one," Sayer said. "What better pun for a wife plagued twenty years by suitors? 'Twas a clever choice!"

"Thank you," Ebenezer murmured.

"And Andromache's *bouncing* boy," Sayer went on, "that was pitched from the walls of Ilium——"

"Nay, 'tis grotesque!" Ebenezer protested. "I meant no such thing!"

"Not so grotesque. It hath the salt of Shakespeare."

"Do you think so?" Ebenezer reconsidered the phrase in his mind. "Haply it doth at that. Nonetheless you read more out than I put in."

" 'Tis but to admit," Sayer said, "I read more out than *you* read out, which was my claim. Your poem means more to me."

"I'faith, I've not the means to refute you!" Ebenezer declared. "If thou'rt a true sample of my fellow planters, sir, then Maryland must be the muse's playground, and a paradise for poets! Thou'rt indeed the very voice and breath of Reason, and I'm honored to be your neighbor. My cup runneth over."

Sayer smiled. "Belike it wants enlarging?"

" 'Tis larger now than when I left London. Thou'rt no mean teacher."

"For fee, then, if I'm thy tutor, ye may pay me out in verse," Sayer replied. "The three lines that occasioned our debate."

"As you wish," Ebenezer laughed, "though Heav'n only knows what you'll find in 'em! 'Twas once in a Pall Mall tavern, after my first glass of Malaga, I composed them, when all the world looked queer and alien." He cleared his throat:

> *"Figures, so strange, no GOD design'd*
> *To be a Part of Human-kind:*
> *But wanton Nature. . . .*

135

In truth, 'tis but two and a half; I know not whither it went from there, but the message of the whole was simply that we folk were too absurd to do credit to a Sublime Intelligence. No puns or wordplays, that I know of."

" 'Tis a passing cynical opinion for a boy," Sayer said.

" 'Twas just the way I saw things in my cups. Marry, that last line teases my memory!"

Sayer stroked his beard and squinted out the window. A dusty country lad of twelve or thirteen years, wandering idly down the road, stepped aside and waved at them as they passed.

> *"Figures, so strange, no GOD design'd*
> *To be a Part of Human-kind,"*

Sayer recited, and turned to smile mischievously at Ebenezer:

> *"But wanton Nature, void of Rest,*
> *Moulded the brittle Clay in Jest.*

Do I have't right, Eben?"

3

The Laureate Learns the True Identity of Colonel Peter Sayer

"NAY, I'GOD!" Ebenezer blinked, and shook his head, and craned forward as if seeking a message on his companion's face.

"Yes, 'tis I. Shame on you, that you failed to see't, or Anna either."

"But 'sheart, Henry, thou'rt so altered I've still to see't! Wigless, bearded——"

"A man changes in seven years," Burlingame smiled. "I'm forty now, Eben."

"E'en the eyes!" Ebenezer said. "And thy way of speaking!

136

Thy voice itself is different, and thy manner! Are you Sayer feigning Burlingame, or Burlingame disguised as Sayer?"

" 'Tis no disguise, as any that know the real Sayer can testify."

"Yet *I* knew the real Henry Burlingame," Ebenezer said, "and were't not that you knew my quatrain I could not say thou'rt he! I told the poem to none save Henry, and that but once, fifteen years past."

"As I was fetching thee home from St. James's Park," Henry added. " 'Twas past midnight, and the Malaga had oiled thy tongue. Yet you were asleep ere we reached St. Giles, with your head on my shoulder, were you not?"

"Marry, so I was! I had forgot." Ebenezer reached across the carriage and gripped Burlingame's arm. "Ah God, to think I've found you, Henry!"

"Then you do believe 'tis I?"

"Forgive me my doubt; I've ne'er known a man to change so, nor had thought it possible."

Burlingame raised a tutorial finger. "The world can alter a man entirely, Eben, or he can alter himself, down to his very essence. Did you not by your own testimony resolve, not that you *were*, but that you'd *be* virgin and poet from that moment hence? Nay, a man *must* alter willy-nilly in's flight to the grave; he is a river running seawards, that is ne'er the same from hour to hour. What is there in the Maryland Laureate of the boy I fetched from Magdalene College?"

"The less the better!" Ebenezer replied. "Yet I am still Eben Cooke, though haply not the *same* Eben Cooke, as the Thames is Thames however swift she flows."

"Is't not the name alone remains? And was't *Thames* from the day of creation?"

"Marry, Henry, you were ever one for posing riddles! Is't the form, then, makes the man, as the banks make the river, whate'er the name and content? Nay, I see already the objection, that form is not eternal. The man grows stout or hunchbacked with the years, and running water cuts and shapes the banks."

Burlingame nodded. " 'Tis but a change too slow for men to mark, save in retrospect. The crabbed old man recalls his spring, and records tell—or rocks to him who knows their language—where the river ran of old, that now runs such-a-way. 'Tis but a grossness of perception, is't not, that lets us speak of *Thames* and *Tigris*, or even *France* and *England*, but especially *me* and *thee*, as though what went by those names or others in time past hath some connection with the

137

present object? I'faith, for that matter how is't we speak of *objects* if not that our coarse vision fails to note their change? The world's indeed a flux, as Heraclitus declared: the very universe is naught but change and motion."

Ebenezer had attended this discourse with a troubled air, but now he brightened. "Have you not in staring o'er the Precipice missed the Path?" he asked.

"I do not grasp your figure."

"How is't you convinced me thou'rt Henry Burlingame, when name and form alike were changed? How is't we know of changes too nice for our eyes to see?" He laughed, pleased at his acuity. "Nay, this very flux and change you make so much of: how can we speak of it at all, be it ne'er so swift or slow, were't not that we remember how things were before? Thy *memory* served as thy credentials, did it not? 'Tis the house of Identity, the Soul's dwelling place! Thy memory, my memory, the memory of the race: 'tis the constant from which we measure change; the sun. Without it, all were Chaos right enough."

"In sum, then, thou'rt thy memory?"

"Aye," Ebenezer agreed. "Or better, I know not *what* I am, but I know *that* I am, and have been, because of memory. 'Tis the thread that runs through all the beads to make a necklace; or like Ariadne's thread, that she gave to thankless Theseus, it marks my path through the labyrinth of Life, connects me with my starting place."

Burlingame smiled, and Ebenezer observed that his teeth, which had used to be white, were yellow and carious—at least two were missing altogether.

"You make a great thing of this *memory*, Eben."

"I'll own I'd not reflect ere now on its importance. 'Tis food for a sonnet, or two, don't you think?"

Burlingame only shrugged.

"Come, Henry; sure thou'rt not piqued that I have skirted thy pit!"

"Would God you had," Burlingame said. "But I fear me thou'rt seduced by metaphors, as was Descartes of old."

"How is that, pray? Can you refute me?"

"What more refutation need I make of this god *Memory*, than that thou'rt forgetting something?"

"What—" Ebenezer stopped and blushed as he realized the implication of what his friend had said.

"You did not recall sleeping on my shoulder on the way home from Pall Mall," Burlingame reminded him. "This demonstrates the first weakness of your soul-saving thread, which is, that it hath breaks in it. There are three others."

"If that is so," Ebenezer sighed, "I fear for my argument."

"You said 'twas Malaga we drank that night."

"Aye, I've a clear memory of't."

"And I that 'twas Madeira."

Ebenezer laughed. "As for that, I'd trust my memory over yours, inasmuch as 'twas my first wine, and I'd not likely forget the name of't."

"True enough," Burlingame agreed, "if you got it aright in the first place. But I too marked it well as your first glass and well knew Malaga from Madeira, whereas to you the names were new and meaningless, and thus lightly confused."

"That may be, but I am certain 'twas Malaga nonetheless."

"No matter," Burlingame declared. "The fact is, where memories disagree there's oft no means to settle the dispute, and that's the second weakness. The third is, that in large measure we recall whate'er we wish, and forget the rest. 'Twas not until you summoned up this quatrain, for example, that I recalled having slipped upstairs to a whore the while you were composing it. My shame at leaving you thus alone, for one thing, forced it soon out of mind."

"I'faith, my polestar leads me on the rocks!" Ebenezer lamented. "What is the fourth objection to't?"

"That e'en those things it holds, it tends to color," Burlingame replied. " 'Tis as if Theseus at every turn rolled up the thread and laid it out again in a prettier pattern."

"I fear me thy objections are fatal," Ebenezer said. "They are like the four black crows that ate up Gretel's peas, wherewith she'd marked her trail into the forest."

"Nay, these are but weaknesses, not mortal wounds," said Burlingame. "They don't obliterate the path but only obfuscate it, so that try as we might we never can be certain of't." He smiled. "Howbeit, there is yet a fifth, that by's own self could do the job."

" 'Slife, you'd as well uncage the rascal and let us see him plainly."

"My memory served as my credentials, as you told me," Burlingame said. "Blurred, imperfect as it is from careless use, and thine as well, the twain agreed on points enough to satisfy you I am Burlingame, though I could not prove it any other way. But suppose the thread gets lost completely, as't sometimes doth. Suppose I'd had no recollection of my past at all?"

"Then you'd have been Colonel Sayer for all of me," Ebenezer replied. "Or if haply you'd declared yourself my Henry, but knew no more, I'd ne'er have credited your tale. But 'tis a rare occurrence, is't not, this total loss of memory, and rarer yet where no other proof exists of one's identity?"

"No doubt. But suppose again I looked like the man who fetched you to London, and spoke and dressed like him, and e'en was called Burlingame by Trent and Merriweather, and fat Ben Oliver. Moreover, suppose I had before witnesses signed the name as Burlingame was wont to sign it. Then suppose one day I swore I was not Burlingame at all, nor knew aught of his whereabouts, but only a clever actor who had got the knack of aping signatures, and had passed myself as Henry for a lark."

"Thy suppositions dizzy me!" Ebenezer cried.

"However strong your convictions," Burlingame went on, "you'd ne'er have proof that I was he."

"I must own that's true, though it pains me."

"Now another case——"

"Keep thy case, I beg you!" Ebenezer said. "I am cased from head to toe."

"Nay, 'tis to the point. Suppose today I'd claimed to be Burlingame, for all my alteration, and composed a line to fit your quatrain—nay, a whole life story—which did not match your own recollection; and when you questioned it, suppose I'd challenged your own identity, and made *you* out to be the clever impostor. At best you'd have no proof, would you now?"

"I grant I would not," Ebenezer admitted. "Save my own certainty. But it strikes me the burden of proof would rest with you."

"In that case, yes. But I said *at best*. If I had learned aught of your past, however, the discrepancies could be charged to your own poor posing, and if further I produced someone very like you in appearance, 'tis very possible the burden of proof would be on you. And if I brought a few of your friends in on the game, or even old Andrew and your sister, to disclaim you, I'll wager even you would doubt your authenticity."

"Mercy, mercy!" Ebenezer cried. "No more of these tenuous hypotheses, lest I lose my wits! I am satisfied thou'rt Henry; I swear to thee I am Ebenezer, and there's an end on't! Such casuistical speculations lead only to the Pit."

"True enough," Burlingame said good-humoredly. "I

wished only to establish that all assertions of *thee* and *me,* e'en to oneself, are acts of faith, impossible to verify."

"I grant it; I grant it. 'Tis established like the——" He waved his hand uncertainly. "Marry, your discourse hath robbed me of similes: I know of naught immutable and sure!"

" 'Tis the first step on the road to Heaven," Burlingame smiled.

"That may be," Ebenezer said, "or haply 'tis the road to Hell."

Burlingame cocked his eyebrows. " 'Tis the same road, or good Dante is a liar. Thou'rt quite content that I am Burlingame?"

"Quite, I swear't!"

"And thou'rt Ebenezer?"

"I never doubted it; and still thy pupil, as this carriage ride hath shown."

"Good. Another time I'll ask you what *me* and *thee* refer to, but not now."

"No, i'faith, not now, for I've a thousand things to ask of you!"

"And I to tell," Burlingame said. "But so fantastic a tale it is, my first concern is for thy credulity, and thus I deemed necessary all this Sophistical discourse."

Not long afterwards the carriage stopped at Aldershot, for it was well past suppertime, and the travelers had not eaten. Burlingame, therefore, as was his habit, postponed all further conversation on the subject while he and Ebenezer dined on cold capon and potatoes. Afterwards, having been informed by their driver that there would be a two-hour wait for the horses and driver which would take them on to Salisbury, Exeter, and Plymouth, they took seats before the fire, at Burlingame's suggestion, with their pipes and a quart of Bristol sherry. It had grown dark outside; a light rain began to fall. Ebenezer waited impatiently for his friend to begin, but Burlingame, when his pipe was lighted and his glass filled, sighed a comfortable sigh and asked merely, "How fares your father these days, Eben?"

4

The Laureate Hears the Tale of Burlingame's Late Adventures

"FATHER BE DAMNED!" Ebenezer cried. "I know not whether he lives or dies, nor greatly care till I've heard your story!"

"Yet you know who he is, alive or dead, do you not? And in that respect, if not some others, who *you* are."

"Pray let us dismiss old Andrew for the nonce," Ebenezer pleaded, "as he hath dismissed me. Where have you been, and what done and seen? Wherefore the name Peter Sayer, and your wondrous alterations? Commence the tale, and a fig for old Andrew!"

"How dismiss him?" Burlingame asked. " 'Twas he commenced my story, what time he dismissed me."

"What? Is't that nonsense over Anna you refer to? How doth it bear upon your tale?"

"What towering wrath!" Burlingame said. "What murtherous alarm! I'God, the hate he bore me—I am awed by't even yet!"

"I've ne'er excused him for it," Ebenezer said shortly.

"Your privilege, as his son. But I, Eben, I excused him on the instant; forgave him—nay, e'en admired him for't. Had he made to slay me—ah, well, but no matter."

Ebenezer shook his head. " 'Tis past my understanding. But say, must I give up hope of hearing your tale?"

"Thou'rt hearing it," Burlingame declared. " 'Tis the pier whereon the entire history rests; the lute-work that ushers in the song."

"So be't. But I fear me 'twill be a tadpole of a history, whose head is greater than his body. You forgave him, then?"

"More, I loved him for't, and scurried off in shame."

"Yet 'twas a false and vicious charge he charged you!"

Burlingame shrugged. "As for that, 'twas not his justice awed me, but his great concern for his child."

142

"A marvelous concern he bears us, right enough," Ebenezer said. "He will wreck us with his concern! Suppose he'd birched her bloody, as you told me once he threatened: would you not adore and worship such concern?"

"I would kill him for't," Burlingame replied, "but love him none the less."

"Marry, thou'rt come a wondrous way from London, where I left you! Why did you not applaud my resolution to go home with Anna, seeing 'twas pure filial solicitude that prompted it?"

"You mistake me," Burlingame said. "I'd oppose it still, and Anna's bending to his every humor. Were I his son I'd be disowned ere now for flying in the face of his concern; but what a priceless prize it is, Eben! What a wealthy man I'd be, to throw away such treasure! The fellow repines in bed for grief at losing you; he dictates the course of your life to make you worthy of your line! Who grieves for me, prithee, or cares a fig be I fop or philosopher? Who sets me goals to turn my back on, or values to thumb my nose at? In fine, sir, what business have I in the world, what place to flee from, what credentials to despise? Had I a home I'd likely leave it; a family alive or dead I'd likely scorn it, and wander a stranger in alien towns. But what a burden and despair to be a stranger to the world at large, and have no link with history! 'Tis as if I'd sprung *de novo* like a maggot out of meat, or dropped from the sky. Had I the tongue of angels I ne'er could tell you what a loneliness it is!"

"I cannot fathom it," Ebenezer declared. "Is this the man that stood in Thames Street praising Heav'n he knew naught of his forebears?"

" 'Twas a desperate speech"—Burlingame smiled—"like a pauper's diatribe on the sinfulness of wealth. When the twain of you had gone I felt my loneliness as ne'er before, and thought long of Captain Salmon and gentle Melissa that raised me. Do you recall that day in Cambridge when you asked me how I came to be called Henry Burlingame the Third?"

"Aye, and you replied 'twas the name you'd borne from birth."

"I spent some hours grousing in my chamber," Burlingame said, "and at length I came to see this pompous name of mine as the most precious thing I owned. Who bestowed it on me? Wherefore Burlingame *Third*, and not just Burlingame?"

" 'Sheart, I see your meaning!" Ebenezer said. " 'Tis your

name that links you with your forebears; thou'rt not wholly *ex nihilo* after all! 'Tis a kind of clue to the riddle!"

Burlingame nodded. "And did I not profess to be a scholar?" He refilled his glass with Bristol sherry. "Then and there I made myself a vow," he said, "to learn the name and nature of my father, the circumstances of my birth, and haply the place and manner of his death; nor would I value any business higher, but ransack the very planet in my quest till I had found my answer or died a-searching. And search I have—i'faith!—these seven years. 'Tis the one business of my life."

"Then marry, I must hear the tale of't, that I've waited for too long already. Drink off your sherry and commence, nor will I stand for interruption till the tale be done."

"As you wish," Burlingame said. He drank the wine and filled his pipe besides, and told the following story:

"How should a man discover the history of his parentage when he knows not whence he came or how, or even whether the name he bears hath any authenticity? For think not I was blind to't, Eben, that my one hope might be a false one: what evidence had I 'twas not some jest or happenstance, this name of mine, or perchance some other guardians, that nursed me up from infancy till Captain Salmon chanced along? It wants but pluck to vow to build a bridge, yet pluck will never build it. I cast about me for a first step, and betook myself at last to Bristol, where I thought perchance to find some that knew at least my Captain and recalled his orphan ward—and privily, I'll own, I prayed to meet some old and trusted friend of his, or kin, that might know the full story of my origin. 'Twas not unthinkable he might have told the tale, I reasoned, if not broadcast then at least to one or two, unless there was some mighty sin about it."

Ebenezer frowned. "Such as what? The man you've pictured me ne'er could stoop to kidnaping."

Burlingame pursed his lips and raised and let fall his hands. "He had no children, to my knowledge, and the yen for sons can drive a man and woman far. Moreover, 'twould be no great matter to achieve: *Many's the anchor that's dropped at dusk and weighed ere the sun comes up.* Yet 'twas not kidnaping I mainly thought of, though I would not rule it out—more likely, if he came by me improperly, 'twas that he'd got me on some mistress in a port of call."

"Nay," said Ebenezer. "I have indeed read that the sailor is a great philanderer, even at times a bigamist, by reason of his occupation, but Captain Salmon, as I picture him, had neither the youth nor the temper for such folly, the less so far that he was no common sailor, but master of a vessel. 'Twere as unlike such a man to saddle himself with a bastard as 'twould be for Solomon to prattle nonsense or a Jew to strike fair bargains."

Burlingame smiled. "Which is but to say, 'tis not out of the question. Follow Horace if you will when making verse— *flebilis Ino, perfidus Ixion*, and the rest—but think not actual folk are e'er so simple. Many's the Jew hath lost his shirt, and saint that hath in private leaped his houseboy. *A covetous man may be generous on occasion,* and *Even an emmet may seek revenge.* Again, though 'twere unlike Captain Salmon to sow wild oats, 'twere not at all unlike him, if his own plot would not bear, to seek a-purpose a field more fruitful. Melissa may even have pressed him to."

"A wife incite her husband to be unfaithful?"

" 'Twere no breach of faith, methinks, in such a case. Howbeit, no matter: in the first place I thought it most likely he came by me in no such sinister fashion, but simply took him in an orphan babe as any man might who hath a Christian heart; in the second, I cared not a straw for the manner of my getting so I could but discover it and my getter."

"And did you?"

Burlingame shook his head. "I found three or four old people that had known Salmon and remembered his ungrateful charge: one told me, when I revealed my name, 'twas grief at my loss killed the Captain, and grief o'er *his* killed Melissa. I yearn to credit that story, for fear my conscience might accuse me else of fleeing such an awful responsibility; yet there is a temper wont to twist the past into a theaterpiece, mistake the reasonable for the historical, and sit like Rhadamanthus in everlasting judgment. This man, I tell you reluctantly, was of that temper. In any case none knew aught of my origin save that Captain Salmon had fetched me home from somewhere, on his vessel. I asked then, who was the Captain's closest friend, and who Melissa's? And each of the men among them claimed to be the former, and each of the women the latter. Finally I asked whether any remembered who was the mate on Salmon's ship in those days; but Bristol is a busy port, where men change ships from voyage to voyage, and 'tis unlikely they'd have known were't but one year before instead of thirty. Yet as often happens, in asking someone else, I hit on the answer myself, or if not the answer at least a fresh hope: a man called Richard Hill had been first mate on all five voyages I had made with Captain

Salmon, and 'twas my impression, more from their manner with each other than from any plain statement, that he and the Captain were shipmates of some years' standing. 'Twas not *impossible* he'd been mate on that voyage ten years before, though 'twas a long chance; and if indeed he'd been, why, 'twas certain he'd know more than I about the matter. Of course, for aught I knew, this Hill might be long dead, or finding him as hard a matter as finding my father——"

"I grant you, I grant you!" Ebenezer broke in. "Prithee trust me to appreciate your obstacles without enumeration, save such as advance the story, and tell me quickly whether you overcame them. Did you find this Hill fellow? And had he aught to tell you?"

"You must attend the *how* of't," Burlingame said; "else thou'rt as much a Boeotian as he that reads the *Iliad* no farther than the invocation, where the end of't all is plainly told. As't happened, none of my informants recalled for certain this Richard Hill, but two of them, who still were wont to stroll about the wharves, declared there was a Richard Hill in the tobacco fleet. Yet, though he sometimes called at Bristol, they told me he was no Bristolman, nor even an Englishman, but either a Marylander or a Virginian; nor was he a mate, but captain of his own vessel.

"This I took as good news rather than bad. When I had satisfied myself that neither Captain Hill nor farther news of him was to be found in Bristol at that time, I hastened back to London."

"Not to the plantations?" Ebenezer asked, feigning disappointment. " 'Tis unlike you, Henry!"

"Nay, I was ready enough to sail for America," Burlingame replied, "but *'Tis wiser to ask at the carriage-house than to chase off down the road*. London is the very liver and lights of the sot-weed trade; it took but half a day there to learn that Captain Hill was in fact a Marylander, from Anne Arundel County, and master of the ship *Hope*, which lay at that very moment in the Thames with other vessels of the fleet, discharging her cargo. I fairly ran down to the wharf where she lay and with some difficulty (for I had no money) contrived an interview with Captain Hill. But I had no need to ask my great question, for immediately upon hearing my name he enquired whether I was Avery Salmon's boy, that had jumped ship in Liverpool. When we had done shaking our heads at my youthful folly and singing the praises of Captain Salmon (who, however, he told me had died of tumors and not grief), I told him the purpose of my visit and

146

besought him to give me any information he might have on that head.

" 'Why,' he declared, 'I was not Avery's mate in those days, Henry. I know what there is to know of't, and no more.'

" 'And prithee what is that?'

" 'Naught but what ye know already,' said he: 'that ye was fished like a jimmy-crab from the waves of the Chesapeake.' "

"Stay!" Ebenezer cried. "I've ne'er heard you speak of't, Henry!"

" 'Twas as new to me then as to you now," Burlingame said. "I expressed your surprise tenfold and assaulted Captain Hill with questions. When at length I convinced him I was a perfect stranger to the matter, he explained 'twas in the early part of 1654 or '55, to the best of his memory, during a run up the Chesapeake from Piscataway to Kent Island, Captain Salmon's vessel had come upon an empty canoe driven before the wind. The sailors guessed 'twas blown from some salvage Indian and would have taken no further note of it, save that on passing closer they heard strange cries issuing from it. Word was sent to Captain Salmon, who ordered the vessel hove to and sent a boat over to investigate."

"Marry, Henry!" Ebenezer said breathlessly. "Was't you?"

"Aye, a lad of two or three months, stark naked and like to perish of the cold. My hands and feet were bound with rawhide, and on my skin, like a sailor's tattoo, was writ the name *Henry Burlingame III*, in small red letters. They fetched me aboard——"

"Wait, I pray you! I must assimilate these wonders, that you drop as light as a goose-dung! Naked and tattooed, i'faith! Is't still to be seen?"

"Nay, 'tis long since faded."

"But how come you to be there? Surely 'twas some villainy!"

"No man knows," Burlingame said. "The canoe and the thongs wherewith I was bound bespoke salvagery, yet there's not a salvage in the country knows his letters, to my knowledge, and my skin and scalp were whole."

"Agad!" Ebenezer cried. "What creature is't could bear such malice to a silly babe, that not content to do him to death, must do't in such a hard and lingering fashion?"

" 'Tis a mystery to this day. In any case, Captain Salmon had me clapped under coverlets in his own cabin, where for ten days and nights I hung 'twixt here and hereafter, and fed

147

me on fresh goat's milk. At length my fever abated and my health returned; Captain Salmon took a fancy to me and resolved ere his ship returned to Bristol I would be his son. More than this my Captain Hill knew naught, and though 'twas volumes more than erst I'd known, yet so far from laying my curiosity, it but pricked him up the more. I offered then and there to join the *Hope*'s crew for the voyage back to Maryland, where I meant to turn the very marshes inside out for clues."

" 'Twas a desperate resolve, was't not?" Ebenezer smiled. "The more since you knew not whence the canoe had blown, or where the ship o'ertook it."

"It was indeed," Burlingame agreed, "though a desperate resolve may sometimes meet success. In any case, 'twas that or give over my quest. I had a fortnight's time ere the *Hope* sailed, and like a proper scholar I ransacked the records of the Customs-House. My end this time was to search out all the Burlingames in Maryland, for once in the Province I meant to make my way to each, by fair means or foul, and dig for what I sought."

"Well," said Ebenezer, "and did you find any?"

Burlingame shook his head. "To the best of my knowledge not a man or woman of that name lives now in the Province, or hath ever since its founding. Next I resolved to search the records of all the other provinces in like manner, working north and south in turn from Maryland. The task was rendered harder by the many changes in grants and charters over the years, and farther by the fear of civil war, which ever works a wondrous ruin to the custom clerk's faith in his fellow man. I started on Virginia, working back from the current year, but ere I'd got past Cromwell's time my fortnight was run, and off I sailed to Maryland." Burlingame smiled and tapped ashes from his pipe. "Had the wind held bad another fortnight, I'd have found somewhat to fan my hopes enormously. As 'twas, I waited near two years to find it."

"What was that? News of your father?"

"Nay, Eben—of that gentleman I know no more today than I knew then, nor of my mother or myself."

"Ah, 'twere better you'd not told me that," Ebenezer declared, clucking his tongue, "for it spoils the story. What man could pleasure in a quest, or the tale of one, that he knew ere he launched it was in vain?"

"Would you have me forego the rest?" Burlingame asked. "The news was merely of my grandfather, or so I believe— I've come to know somewhat of *that* fellow, at least."

"Ah, thou'rt teasing me, then!"

Burlingame nodded and stood up. "I know no more of my father than before, but 'tis not to say I'm no *nearer* knowing. Howbeit, the tale shall have to keep."

"What! Thou'rt not affronted, Henry?"

"Nay, nay," Burlingame replied. "But I hear our driver harnessing the team in the yard. Stretch your legs a bit, lad, and relieve thyself ere we go."

"But surely you'll take up the tale again?" Ebenezer pleaded.

Burlingame shrugged. " 'Twere better you slept if you can. If not, why then 'tis good to have a tale to wait the dawn with."

At that moment the new driver burst in, cursing the rain, and told the travelers to make ready for departure. Accordingly they went outside, where a high March wind was whipping the light rain into spray.

5

Burlingame's Tale Continued, Till Its Teller Falls Asleep

ONCE SETTLED IN the carriage for the second leg of their journey, Ebenezer and Burlingame tried to sleep, but found the road too rough. Despite their weariness, a half hour of pitching and bouncing persuaded them the attempt was vain, and they gave it up.

"Fie on it," Ebenezer sighed. "Time enough to rest in the grave, as Father says."

"True enough," Burlingame agreed, "though to put it off too long is but to get there the sooner."

At Ebenezer's suggestion they filled and lit their pipes. Then the poet declared, "As for me, I welcome the postponement. Were my bladder full of Lethean dew instead of Bristol sherry, I still could ne'er forget the tale you've told me, nor hope to sleep till I've heard it out."

149

"Thou'rt not bored with it?"

"Bored! Saving only the history of your travels with the gypsies, which you told me years ago in Cambridge, I ne'er have heard such marvels! 'Tis well I know thee a stranger to prevarication, else 'twere hard to credit such amazements."

"Methinks then I had best leave off," Burlingame said, "for no man knows another's heart for certain, and what I've said thus far is but a tuning of the strings, as't were."

"Prithee strike 'em, then, without delay, and trust me to believe you."

"Very well. 'Tis not so deadly long a story, but I must own 'tis a passing tangled one, with much running hither and thither and an army of names to bear in mind."

"*The grapes are no fewer on a tangled vine*," Ebenezer replied, and Burlingame without further prelude resumed his tale:

" 'Twould have pleased Dick Hill well enough," he said, "to keep me in his crew, for a week aboard caused all my sailor's craft, which I'd not rehearsed for over fifteen years, to spring to mind. But once in Maryland I left his vessel and, not wishing to bind myself to one location by teaching, I took a post on Hill's plantation."

"Was't not equally confining?" Ebenezer asked.

"Not for long. I began by keeping his books—for 'tis a rare planter there can do sums properly. Soon I so gained his confidence that he trusted me with the entire management of his sot-weed holdings on the Severn, declaring that though 'twas too considerable a business to let go, yet he had small love for't, and had rather spend his time a-sailoring."

"I'faith, then thou'rt a Maryland sot-weed planter before me! I must hear how you managed it."

"Another time," Burlingame replied, "for here the story makes sail and weighs its anchor. 'Twas 1688, and the provinces were in as great a ferment as England over Papist and Protestant. In Maryland and New England trouble was particularly rife: Baltimore himself and most of the Maryland Council were Catholics, and both the Governor and Lieutenant Governor of New England—Sir Edmund Andros and Francis Nicholson—were also known to be no enemies of King James. The leader of the Maryland rebels was one John Coode——"

"Aye, I had that name from Baltimore," Ebenezer said. "He is the false priest that snatched the government."

"An extraordinary fellow, Eben, I swear't! Haply you'll meet him, for he's still at large. His counterpart in New York was Jacob Leisler, who had designs on Nicholson. Now it happened that winter that Leisler came to Maryland for the purpose of conniving with Coode. Word had just reached us of King William's landing, and 'twas their design to strike together, the one at St. Mary's, the other at New York. To be brief, Captain Hill got wind of't and sent me to New York in January, ere Leisler returned, to warn Nicholson."

"Then Captain Hill is a Papist?"

"No more than you or I," Burlingame replied. " 'Twas not a matter of faith, in Maryland. Old Coode is no more for William than for James: 'tis government itself he loathes, and any kind of order! Leisler's but a fop beside him."

"May I never meet this Coode!" said Ebenezer. "Did you reach New York?"

"Aye, and Nicholson swore like a cannoneer at the news I brought him. He himself had come to Andros in '86 as captain of an Irish Papist troop, and in New York he'd celebrated the birth of James's son; he knew well the rebels marked him for a Romanist and would lose no chance to turn him out. He tried in vain to keep the news suppressed, and inasmuch as Dick Hill had placed me at his service, he sent me on to Boston to warn Andros. I gained the confidence of both men, and at my own request spent the next few months as private messenger betwixt them—my virtue being that I was not a member of their official family and hence could move with ease among the rebels. Nay, I will own I more than once took it upon myself to pass as one of their number, and thus was able on occasion to report their doings to the Governor."

"But thou'rt fearless, Henry!"

"Eh? Ah well, fearless or no, I did the cause of order small good. The rebels seized Andros that spring, as soon as they heard of William's progress, and clapped him in the Boston jail. In New York they spread a tale that Nicholson meant to fire the town, and on the strength of it Leisler mustered force enough to take the garrison."

"What of Nicholson? Did he escape?"

"Aye," said Burlingame. "In June he fled by ship for London, and for all Leisler called him a privateer, he got back safely."

"Safely!" Ebenezer cried. "Was't not a case of frying pan to fire, to flee from Leisler into William's arms?"

Burlingame laughed. "Nay, Eben, Old Nick is not so simple a fool as that, as you shall see betimes."

"Well, what of thee, Henry? Did you make your way back to Maryland?"

"Nay again, for that were a leap to the fire indeed! 'Twas in July that Coode made his play, and by August had the Governor's Council besieged in the Mattapany blockhouse. Nay, I stayed behind in New England—first in New York and then, when Nicholson was safely out, in Boston. My design was to get Sir Edmund Andros out of Castle Island prison."

"B'm'faith!" said Ebenezer. " 'Tis a tale out of Esquemeling!"

"In more ways than one," Burlingame replied with a smile. "There lay in Boston harbor an English frigate, the *Rose*, designed to guard the local craft from pirates. John George, her captain, was friend enough of Andros that the rebels held him hostage, lest he bombard the town for the Governor's release. 'Twas my wish to do exactly that, if need be, and spirit him off to France aboard the *Rose*."

"However did you manage it?"

"I didn't, though 'twas no fault of my plan. I found me a friend of Captain George's named Thomas Pound, a pilot and mapmaker, who was ready for a price to show his loyalty to Andros. The Governor escaped, and five days later we slipped out of the harbor into Massachusetts Bay, put on the guise of pirates, and commenced to harass the fishing fleet."

" 'Sbody!"

" 'Twas our intention so to nettle them that at last they'd send out Captain George in the *Rose* frigate to reduce us; then we'd sail to Rhode Island, pick up Andros, and set our course for France. But ere we'd brought them to such straits, word reached us Andros was already recaptured and on his way to England."

"In any case," Ebenezer said, " 'twas a worthy attempt."

"Belike it was, to start with," Burlingame replied. "But as't turned out, when Tom Pound learned 'twas all for naught, he was in a pickle: he could not sail into Boston harbor lest he be hanged for a pirate; nor could he cross to France for lack of provision. The upshot of it was, we turned to doing in earnest what before we'd feigned."

"Nay, i'God!"

"Aye and we did: turned pirate, and prowled the northern coast for prey."

"But marry, Henry—you were with them?"

" 'Twas that or be thrown to the fishes, Eben. Aye, I fought along with the rest, nor can I say in truth I loathed it, though I felt it wrong. There is a charm in outlawry that the good man little dreams of . . . 'Tis a liquor——"

"I pray you were not long drunk with it!" Ebenezer said. "It seems a perilous brew."

" 'Tis no pap for sucklings, I must own. For full two months Pound robbed and plundered, though he seldom got aught for his pain save salt pork and fresh water. In October he was set on by a Boston sloop off Martha's Vineyard, and every soul aboard killed or wounded. I, thank Heav'n, had made my escape some weeks before, in Virginia, and inasmuch as I'd assumed another name throughout my stay in New England, I little feared detection. I made the best of't back to Maryland and rejoined Dick Hill in Anne Arundel, who'd long since given me up for dead. I was the more anxious to leave Pound for that John Coode knew Captain Hill for an enemy and was sure to work him some injury ere long. Moeover, I had another reason, more selfish, it may be, but no less pressing: I had word that there were Burlingames in Virginia!"

"Nay, 'tis marvelous!" cried Ebenezer. "Kin of thine?"

"That I knew not, nor whether any were yet alive; I had it only that a Burlingame—in sooth a *Henry* Burlingame—was among the very first to settle in that dominion, and I meant to find excuse to go there and make enquiries."

"How ever came you to hear of't, while you sailed willynilly o'er the ocean? 'Tis of the stature of a miracle!"

"No miracle, or 'tis an odd God worked it. The tale is no marvel of brevity, Eben."

"Yet it must be told," Ebenezer insisted.

Burlingame shrugged. " 'Twas while I was with Pound, at the height of his pirating. Our usual prey was small merchantmen and coasting vessels; we would overhaul them, steal what pleased us, and turn 'em loose, offering hurt to none save those who made to resist us. But once when a nor'easter had blown us into Virginian waters we came upon an ancient pinnace at the mouth of the York River, bound up the Chesapeake, which, when we had turned out all her crew for looting, we found to carry three passengers besides: a coarse fellow of fifty years or so; his wife, who was some years younger; and their daughter, a girl not yet turned twenty. She was an uncommon tasty piece, by the look of her, dark-haired and spirited, and her mother not much less. At the sight of them our men put by all thought of plunder, which had in truth been lean, and made to swive the twain of 'em then and there. Captain Pound durst not say them nay, albeit he was

153

himself opposed to violence, for such was their ferocity, having seen nor hide nor hair of woman, as't were, since we sailed from Boston, they'd have mutinied on the spot. And had I made the smallest move to stay them, they'd have flung me in an instant to the fishes!

"In a trice the ruffians stripped 'em and fetched 'em to the rail. 'Tis e'er the pirates' wont to take their captives at the rail, you know, whether bent on't backwards or triced hand to foot o'ertop. A mate of mine saw a maid once forced by thirteen brigands in the former manner, with the taffrail at the small of her back, till at last they broke her spine and heaved her over. 'Tis but to make the thing more cruel, methinks, they do it thus: Captain Hill once told me of an old French rogue he'd met in Martinique, that swore no woman pleased him save when staring at the sharks who'd have her when the rape was done, and that having once tasted such refined delights he ne'er could roger mistresses ashore."

"No more, I pray you!" Ebenezer cried. " 'Tis not a history of the salvagery I crave, but news of the hapless victims."

"Thou'rt overly impatient, then," Burlingame said mildly. "The vilest deed hath a lesson in it for him who craves to learn. Howbeit, where did I leave the women?"

"At the ship's rail, with their virtue *in extremis*."

"Ah, indeed, 'twas a bad hour to be female, for sixteen men lined up to ravage 'em. The husband all the while was begging mercy for himself, with never a word for the women, and the wife resisting with all her strength; but the girl, when she saw the pirates' design, spoke quickly to her mother in French, which none aboard could ken save me, and she made no resistance, but asked the sailors calmly, with a French cast to her voice, which they had more use for, her chastity or a hundred pounds apiece? At first the men ignored her, so taken were they by the sight of her unclothed. But all the way to the rail she pled her case—or rather posed her offer, for her voice was cold and merchantlike. She was of French nobility, she declared, and her mother likewise, and should they meet with injury the entire crew would surely hang for't; but if they were set free unscathed, every man aboard would have a hundred pounds within the week.

"Here I saw a chance to aid them, if I could but stay the pirates' lust a moment. To that end I joined their fondling— even pushed some others aside and forced her to the rail myself, as if to take first place—but then delayed, and when she made again her offer I cried, 'Hold back, mates, and let us hear the wench out ere we caulk her. 'Tis many a tart we

154

could have with a hundred pounds.' I reminded them further of our plan to cross to France when we'd had our fill of pirating, and questioned whether 'twere prudent so to imperil our reception there. My chief intention was to stay them for a time at least and make them reflect, for reflection is a famous foe of violence—'tis a beast indeed who rapes on second thought! So far did the stratagem succeed, the men began to jeer and scoff at the proposal, but made no farther move for the nonce.

"'How is't ye ladies of the court be sailing on such a privy as this?' one asked, and the daughter replied they were not rich, but had only wealth enough to pay their promised ransom and would be paupers after. Another asked profanely of the mother, How was't a noblewoman thought no better of her noble arse than to wed it to that craven lout her husband? This I thought a sharper question, for he was indeed a coarse and common tradesman, by the look of him. But the daughter spoke rapidly in French, and the lady replied, that her husband came from one of Virginia's grandest families. To which the daughter added, 'If you must know, 'twas a marriage of convenience,' and went on to say in effect, that even as her father had bought her mother's honor with his estate, so now she would buy it back from us, for that same estate. The men took this merrily and heaped no end of ridicule upon the husband, who was like to beshit himself with fright upon the deck. They were now of half a mind to swive and half to take the hundred pounds, but scarce knew whether or not to credit the women's story.

"Now you must know that 'twas my wont whenever I met a stranger to enquire of him, Had he ever known a wight by name of Burlingame? And would explain, I had a friend called Henry Burlingame Third, who greatly wished to prove he was no bastard. All the men aboard had got accustomed to't, and made it their jest to speak amongst themselves of Henry Burlingame Third as some grand fellow whom all must know. For this reason, when the lady had made her speech a wag amongst us said, 'If he be a great Virginia gentleman, then surely he must know Sir Henry Burlingame, the noblest Virginian that ever shat on sot-weed.' And he added that if they knew him not they must needs be impostors, and to the rail with 'em. At this methought the game was done, inasmuch as 'twas but a fool's test, to give excuse for swiving. But the maid replied, she did indeed know of a Henry Burlingame of Jamestown, that had come thither with the first settlers and declared himself a knight, and she went on to say, by way of proof, that 'twas much doubted in her circle whether he was in truth of noble origin.

"At this the men were much surprised, none more than myself, and I resolved to risk my life, if need be, to spare theirs so I might query them farther on this head. I declared to the men that all the wench had said of Burlingame was true, and that for my part I believed the whole of her tale and was ready to trade her maidenhead for a hundred pounds. The greater part of the men seemed ready enough to do the same, now their first ardor was cooled—the more for that our pirating ere then had yielded little profit. Captain Pound raised then the question of hostages, and it was resolved that one of their number must remain behind till the ransom was paid, and forfeit life and honor if 'twere not. At this, mother and daughter spoke briefly in French, after which each pleaded to be left as hostage, so that the father might be spared."

" 'Sheart, what solicitude!" Ebenezer cried. "The wretch merited no such affection!"

Burlingame laughed. "So't appeared to all the crew save me, who followed clearly what was said. Know, Eben, that these fine women were bald impostors. The daughter had conceived the ruse and told it to her mother in French. And when the matter of hostages arose, the mother had said 'Pray God they will take Harry, for then we'd be quit of him for fair, and not a penny poorer.' And the maiden's brave reply was, ' 'Tis sure they will take thee or me for swiving, unless we persuade them of his value.' 'Fogh!' had cried the mother. 'The beast hath not the value of *bouc-merde!*'—which is to say, the droppings of a billy goat. To this the maid replied, that such exactly were her sentiments, and the only recourse was to offer themselves and plead for his release, relying on our gullibility.

"The men at first ignored the bait, until I asked the ladies Wherefore their devotion, seeing he was such a craven brute, who had shown no concern for them at all what time we made to swive them, but blubbered only for himself? To which the maid replied, that though 'twas true he cared naught for them and had liefer part with both than lose ten crown, yet they did adore him as foolish women will, and would perish ere they saw him injured. The husband was so entirely astonished by this speech, that at first he could not speak for rage and terror, and ere he could collect himself I declared that clearly he was not to be trusted ashore but must

156

be our hostage, and the ladies sent for the ransom, inasmuch as their devotion to him assured their return. The men were most reluctant to set the wenches free, but Captain Pound saw reason in my argument, and ordered it so. The fellow was sent below in chains, the ladies fetched new clothing from their chests, and a boat was made ready to carry them ashore; but ere it left I got the Captain's ear in secret, and implored him to send me with them to guarantee their return, inasmuch as I could understand their tongue, unknown to them, and would thus be forewarned of any treachery. He was loath to let me go, but at length I prevailed upon him, and rowed off with the ladies in a longboat. The plan was that Pound should go a-pirating for some weeks and come again to the Capes where I would rejoin him at the end of September. Moreover, to quiet the suspicions of the crew, and their envy of my lot, I declared to them aside that I would have the women themselves bring the ransom aboard, which once secured, they could be swived till the rail gave way!"

"Henry!" Ebenezer exclaimed. "Can't be that——"

"Hold on," Burlingame interrupted, "till the tale is done. We were put ashore near Accomac, on Virginia's Eastern Shore, whence we were to start our journey to the ladies' home. 'Twas dark when we landed, for we feared detection, and we resolved to go no farther until dawn, but make a fire upon the beach wherewith to warm ourselves. As we watched the pirates make sail and get under way in the moonlight, both women wept for very joy, and the mother said, in French, 'God bless you, Henrietta; you have rid us of the pirates and your father in a single stroke!' The maid replied, 'Rather bless this fellow with us, who is so wondrous stupid to believe my lies.' 'Indeed,' said the mother. 'Who'd have looked for such a fool 'neath such a handsome skin?' At this they laughed at their boldness, little dreaming I could grasp their every word, and to carry the sport yet farther the maid declared, 'Aye, in sooth he is a pretty fellow, mother, such as you nor I have never spent a night with.' 'Nor would ever,' said the other, 'had we not got shed of Harry. I must own that had he made the threat alone, I'd have let him have his rape and saved our money. Yet I'd not have wished thee touched.' 'Oh la,' the maid replied, 'think not I plan to lose a penny: the handsome wretch will fall asleep anon, and we shall either flee or do him to death. As for my maidenhead, 'tis but a champagne cork to me, which must be popped ere the pleasantries commence.' And looking me in the eye, she said for a tease, 'What say you, fellow: *veux-tu être mon tire-bouchon? Eh? Veux-tu me vriller avant que je te tue?* ' "

"I know not the tongue," said Ebenezer, "but the sound is far from chaste."

"Shame on you, then, that you have not learned it," Burlingame scolded. " 'Tis a marvelous tongue for wooing in. I cannot tell how fetching 'twas to hear such lewdness spoke in such sweet tones. *'Poinçonne-tu mon petit liège'*—— I hear't yet, i'faith, and sweat and shiver! I saw no need to carry the deception farther, and so replied in faultless Paris French, ' 'Twill be an honor, *mademoiselle et madame,* nor need you kill me after, for your joy at leaving those brigands behind doth not exceed my own.' They had like to perish of astonishment and shame on hearing me, the maid especially; but when I explained how I had come to be among the pirates, and what it was I sought, they were soon pacified—nay, cordial, even more than cordial. They could scarce leave off expressing gratitude, and, seeing the cat was out of the bag, we spent the night a-sporting on the sand."

"A pretty tale indeed, if not a virtuous," Ebenezer said. "But did you learn no more of that old Burlingame, for whom you'd saved the ladies?"

"Aye," said Burlingame. "That same night I queried them whether 'twas but a fiction they'd contrived regarding Burlingame. And the maid replied 'twas no fiction at all, that her father was a great pretender to distinction, who, though he was in fact a bastard, was much concerned to glorify his lineage and was forever running hither and thither for ancient records, which his daughter had to search for the family name. 'Twas for just that cause they'd made the trip to Jamestown, where 'mid numerous musty papers she'd found what looked to be some pages of a journal writ by one Henry Burlingame. Howbeit, she gave it but a cursory reading, seeing it made no mention of her family, and recalled only that it spoke of some journey or other from Jamestown; that Captain John Smith was the leader; and that there seemed some ill feeling 'twixt him and the author of the journal. Past that she'd read no more nor could remember aught. 'Twas not long ere I'd had my fill of amorosities—for thirty-five hath no great stamina in such matters—and fell asleep beside the fire. When the sun aroused me in the morning I found the women gone, nor have I seen them since. 'Twas delicacy, methinks, that moved them ere I waked—full many a deed smells sweet at night that stinks in the heat of the sun. What's more, their reputations were secure, for at no time since we'd overhauled their ship had they revealed their names, nor more of where they lived save that 'twas on the Eastern Shore of Maryland."

"And did you make your way thence to Jamestown?"

"Nay, to Anne Arundel County and Captain Hill. I wanted sore to learn whether Coode had harmed him, and too I had not a farthing about me wherewith to eat. 'Twas my design to work awhile for Hill and then pursue my quest, for I will own I was not indifferent toward the politics of the place, and would have welcomed another mission like the one I'd just returned from."

"Thou'rt a glutton for adventure," Ebenezer said.

"Mayhap I am, or better, a glutton for the great world, of which I ne'er can see and learn enough."

"I'll warrant Captain Hill was pleased to see you, and surprised!"

"He was in sooth, for he had heard naught of me since Leisler's rebellion in New York, and feared me dead. He said his position was most perilous, inasmuch as Coode and his men were daily laying waste his enemies' estates, and had spared his either through caprice or uncertainty as to Hill's influence in England. 'Twas Coode's conceit to call himself Masaniello, after the rebel of Naples; Colonel Henry Jowles of Calvert County, his chief lieutenant, played Count Scamburgh; Colonel Ninian Beale the Earl of Argyle; and Kenelm Cheseldyne, the speaker of the Assembly, was Speaker Williams. While they played at court in this manner, and bragged and plundered down in St. Mary's, I spent the winter putting Hill's estate in order. Whene'er 'twas useful I made excursions about the province to the end of fomenting opposition in the several counties, and in the spring, when he got wind of't, Coode resolved to do us in. He trumped up a charge of treasonable speech and dispatched no fewer than forty men to destroy us. They seized the ship *Hope*, which Captain Hill had been at seven hundred pounds' expense to fit out for a voyage, and rifled the estate, and 'twas only our good fortune in escaping to the woods preserved our lives.

"I went at first to sundry other sea-captains, friends of Hill's and enemies of Colonel Coode——"

"*Colonel!*" Ebenezer broke in. "Methought he was a priest!"

"The man is whate'er he chooses to call himself," Burlingame replied. "He owns to no authority save himself, and is a rebel 'gainst man and God alike. In any case, I learned from these men that Francis Nicholson, deposed by Leisler as a Jacobite, was now lieutenant governor of Virginia (which is to say the chief officer, since the governor lives in England), and this by order of King William himself! It seems the King little bothers what a man is called by his enemies, so long as he doth his job well, and in sooth Old Nick is the very devil of a governor for all his faults. These tidings fell sweetly on my ear, inasmuch as Nicholson was the very man who'd best protect us, and Jamestown the very place I wished to go. I had Hill's friends write letters to Nicholson, describing Coode's barbarity and asking asylum for the Captain and his house, and ere June was done we were in Jamestown. 'Masaniello' and his crew begged and threatened Nicholson by turns to get their hands on us, but de'il the good it did him. 'Tis both a fault and a virtue in Virginia, that fugitives from Maryland e'er find haven there."

"But did you find the precious journal-book you sought?" asked Ebenezer. "Or was't but a tale of a cock and a bull the lass on the strand had spun thee? Prithee put me off no farther on the matter; I must know whether such an odyssey bore fruit!"

Burlingame laughed. "Make not such haste to reach the end, Eben; it spoils the pace and mixes the figures. Whoever saw an odyssey bear fruit?"

"Tease no more!" Ebenezer cried.

"Very well, Master Laureate: I did indeed lay hands upon the journal, what of't there was; what's more, I made a copy of it, faithful to the letter save for one or two dull passages that I summarized. I have it here in my coat, and in the morning you shall read it. Suffice it now to say, I am persuaded 'tis a bona fide journal of Sir Henry Burlingame, but whether or no the fellow is my ancestor I've still no proof."

"I'faith, I'm glad you found it, and scarce can wait till dawn! 'Tis good thy tale is not yet done, else 'twere a hard matter to fret away the hours. What wondrous thing befell you next?"

"No more tonight," Burlingame declared. "The road is smoother here, and the night's nigh done. The balance of the tale can wait till Plymouth." So saying, he would hear no protest from Ebenezer, but stretching out his legs as best he could, went to sleep at once. The poet, however, was less fortunate: try as he might, he could not manage even to keep his eyes closed, much less resign himself to sleep, though his head throbbed from weariness. Again his mind was filled with names, the names first heard from Baltimore and now fleshed out by Burlingame's narration, and figures awful in their energy and purpose prowled his fancy—his friend and tutor first among them.

6

Burlingame's Tale Carried Yet Farther; the Laureate Reads from The Privie Journall of Sir Henry Burlingame *and Discourses on the Nature of Innocence*

WHEN AFTER DAWN the travelers stopped for their morning meal at Yeovil, Ebenezer demanded at once to see the document Burlingame had spoken of, but his tutor refused to hear of it until they'd eaten. Then, the sun having come out warm and bright, they retired outside to smoke and stretch their legs, and Burlingame fetched several folded sheets from the pocket of his coat. Atop the first the poet read *The Privie Journall of Sir Henry Burlingame.*

"I should explain the title's mine," said Burlingame. "As you can see, the journal is a fragment, but the journey it describes is writ in John Smith's *Generall Historie.* 'Twas in January of 1607, the first winter of the colony, and they traveled up the Chickahominy River to find the town of Powhatan, Emperor of the Indians. There was much ill feeling against Captain Smith in Jamestown at the time: some were alarmed at his machinations to unseat President Wingfield and President Ratcliffe; others charged him with flaunting the instructions of the London Company, in that he wasted little time searching for gold or for a water passage to the East; others yet were merely hungry, and thought he should arrange for trade with Powhatan. 'Tis plain the voyage up the Chickahominy was a happy expedient, for't promised solution to all these grievances: the Captain would be out of politics for a while, for one thing, and some declared the Chickahominy ran west to the Orient; in any case, 'twas almost certain the Emperor's town lay not many miles upriver. Smith tells in his *Historie* how he was made captive by one of Powhatan's lieutenants, called Opecancanough, and escaped death by means of magical tricks with his compass. He swears next he was carried alone to Powhatan, condemned to death, and saved by intercession of the Emperor's daughter. His version of't I have writ there under the title."

Ebenezer read the brief superscription:

> Being ready with their clubs, to beate out his braines, Pocahontas, the Kings dearest daughter, when no entreaty could prevaile, got his head in her armes, and laid her owne upon his to save him from death; whereat the Emperour was contented he should live to make him hatchets, and her bells, beads, and copper; for they thought him as well of all occupations as themselves.

"I'faith," he said, " 'tis a marvelous rescue!"

" 'Tis a marvelous romance," Burlingame corrected, "for the substance of the *Journall* is, that this Burlingame witnessed the whole proceeding, which was not so wondrous heroic after all. I'll say no more, but leave you to read the piece without delay."

So saying, Burlingame went inside the inn, and Ebenezer, finding a bench in the sun, made himself comfortable and read in the *Journall* as follows:

The Privie Journall of Sir Henry Burlingame

I . . . had divers time caution'd [Smith], that our guide, a rascallie Salvage that had liefer steal y^r purse than look at you, was nowise to be trusted, he being doubtless in the pay of the E^{mpr} [Powhatan]. But he w^d none of this, and when, the River growing too shallowe for our vessels, this same Salvage propos'd we walk overland to the E^{mprs} towne, wch he claim'd was hard bye, our C^{apt} agreed at once, maugre the fact, wch I poynted out to him, that the woods there were thick as any jungle, and we w^d be sett upon with ease by hostile Salvages. The C^{apt} made the usuall rejoynders, that he ever maketh on being shown his ignorance and follie, to witt: that I was a coward, a parasite, a lillie-liver'd infant, and belike an Eunuch into the bargain. This last, he regardeth as the supremest insult he can hurl, for that he him selfe taketh inordinate pride in his virilitie. In sooth, such a devotee of Venus is our C^{apt}, that rare are the times when he doth not boast openlie, and in lewdest terms, of his conquests and feats of love all over the Continent and among the Moors, Turks, and Africkans. He fancieth him selfe a Master of Venereall

Arts, and boasteth to have known carnallie every kind of Woman on Earth, in all of Aretines positions. In addition to wch, he owneth an infamous lott of *eroticka* collected in his travells, items from wch he oft displayeth to certain of us privilie, with all the smuggness of a *Connoisseur*. More of this anon, but I may note here, that judging from our Capts preoccupation with these things, wch oft as not represent unnaturall as well as naturall vices, I wd be no whit surpris'd to learn, that his tastes comprehend more than those of the common libertine . . .

[*The Author here describes, how the party goeth ashore, and is led by their treacherous guide into the hands of the Indians.*]

The Salvages then setting upon us, as had been predicted by men wiser then our Capt, we fought them off as best we cd, with small success, for the quarters were close and our attackers virtuallie atop us. Our leader, for his part, shrewdlie pull'd that Ganelon our Guide before him for a shield, and retreated in all haste, exhorting us the while to fight like men. Happilie, he caught his foot upon a root of cypress, and flew backward off the bank into the mud and ice. The Salvages having by this time captur'd us, leapt upon him, and held him fast on his back, and on our informing them, in response to there querie, Who was our leader? that it was he, there Chief, Opecancanough, and his severall lieutenants, pleas'd them selves openlie, and us privilie, by thereupon making water upon him, each in his turn according to rank.

[*The prisoners, of wch there are five, are carry'd to a clearing, where they are tied one at a time to a sweetgum tree and shot with arrows, till none but Smith and Burlingame remain.*]

. . . coming then to my Capt, they made as if to lay hold of him, to lead him to the same fate suffer'd by the others. A gentleman to the end [Smith] . . . modestlie suggested, that I precede him. Be't said, that in matters of this sort my owne generositie is peer to any mans, and had it prov'd necessarie, I shd stoutlie have declin'd my Capts gesture. Howbeit, Opecancanough pay'd no heed, but him selfe taking the Capt by the arme, pull'd him toward the bloodie tree. At this juncture, the Capt (who afterwards confided to me, he was searching for his Africkan good-luck peece) withdrew from his coat a packet of little colour'd cards, the wch, with seeming innocence, he let fall to the grownd. The Salvages at once became arows'd, and scrabl'd one atop the other, to see who shd retrieve the most. Upon examining them, they found the cards to portray, in vivid colours, Ladies and Gentlemen mother-naked, partaking of sundrie amorosities one with another: in parties of two, three, four, and even five, these persons were shown performing licentious feats,

163

the wch to be perform'd in actuall life w^d want, in addition to uncommon lubricitie, considerable imagination and no small tallent for gymnastick.

One can fancie with what whoops and howls of glee the Salvages receiv'd these works of the pornographers art, for Salvages are a degenerate race, little rais'd above the beastes they hunt, and as such share with white men of the same stamp a love for all that is filthie and salacious. They at least had in their favour, that they had never before seen a white woman cloth'd, much less uncloth'd, and how much less indulging in such anticks as were now reveal'd to them. They laught and shouted, and snatch'd the cards from one another, to see them all.

[They] ask'd [Smith], Whether he had more [of the cards]? Whereat he took the opportunitie to draw from his pocket a small compasse, the wonder of which (for I had seen it before, to my abashment), that not only did it shew the poynts of the compasse, wch marvell alone w^d methinks have suffic'd to awe the Salvages . . . it also, by virtue of tinie paintings on small peeces of glass mounted inside it, treated the deprav'd eye of him who lookt through little peepholes in the sides, to scenes like those of the cards, but more real, for that there devilish creator had a nice facilitie of giving the scenes a sense of depth, so that one had the feeling (pleasant to degenerates) of peering through a keyhole, to witness gentlemen comporting themselves like stallions, and ladies like mares in rutt . . .

Howbeit, the damnable device must needs be held in a certain manner, so that its lenses caught the sun at a proper angle. The Salvages, and Opecancanough in especiall, being quite unable to master this simple trick, it was necessarie they preserve the wretch my C^apts life, in order, presumablie, that he might serve as operator of there Mayfair show for ever. So arows'd were they over there treasures, that maugre what I took to be suggestions on my C^apts part, that only he was needed to perform the miracles of the compasse, the Salvages took both of us along with them to Opecancanoughs town, wch lay, we were told, hard by that of the Emperour . . . entirelie forgetting, in there vicious delight, to fill my stomache with there arrowes . . .

[*The twain are carried to the town of Opecancanough, and thence to Powhatans town, and at length into the presence of the Emperour himself.*]

[This prospect] appear'd to please my C^apt mightilie, for he spoke of naught besides, when indeed he deign'd converse with me at all, but how he had schem'd the most efficacious manner of winning the Emperours favour, as soone as ever he s^hd be presented to that worthie. I . . . warn'd him, more, I confess, toward the saving of my owne skinne, wch I car'd not to loose, then the

164

saving of his, that we were, for aught I cᵈ see, still mere prisoners, and not emissaries of the King, and that as such, I, for one, sʰᵈ be content were I to leave the forthcoming interview with my head yet affix'd to my shoulders, and my bellie free of arrowes, without troubling farther about Emperial favours or bartering agreements. My Cᵃᵖᵗ made me his usuall witless insults for replie. . . .

On being led into the house of this Powhatan, my feares multiply'd, for I sweare he was the evillest-appearing wight I hope to incounter. He seem'd neare sixtie; the browne fleshe of him was dry'd and bewrinkl'd as is the skinne of an apple left overlong in the sunne, and the looke upon his face as sower, as wᵈ be such an apple to the tongue. I sawe in that face no favour . . . His eyes, more then any thing, held me, for despite a certaine hardnesse in them, like old flint, what mark'd them most, so it seem'd to me, was an antick lecherie, such as one remarketh in the eyes of profligates and other dissolute old persons. My Cᵃᵖᵗ, I might say, hath the beginning of such eyes, and at sixtie, it pleaseth me to think, will quite resemble this Powhatan.

The Emperours surroundings, moreover, did beare out my judgement: in addition to his bodie-guard, a goodlie number of Salvage wenches potter'd about the roome, drest like Ladie Eve, only flaunting a bitt of animal-skinne over that part, wᶜʰ the Mother of us all was wont to disguise with a peece of foliage. This one fetch'd her Lord a portion of tobacco; that one lean'd over him to light his pipe with a brand; this one rubb'd his backe with the grease of beare, or some such malodourous decoction . . . and one & all he rewarded with a smart tweake, or like pleasantries, the wᶜʰ, at his advanc'd age, sʰᵈ rightlie have been to him no more than a fond memorie. These the wenches forebore without compleynt . . . in sooth they seem'd to vye for the ancient satyrs attentions, and perform'd there simple duties with all possible voluptuousnesse, as if therebye to rowse there King to acts more fitting a man my age, then a dotard his . . . My Cᵃᵖᵗ observ'd these maids with wondrous interest, and I sawe in his eye more attention, then wᵈ have been requir'd simplie to transfer the scene to his trumpeting *Historie*. For my selfe, I was too occupy'd with the mere holding of my water, wᶜʰ business is chore enough in such a fearsome pass, to care what charmes the heathenish slutts offered there Emperour, or with what lewd behaviour he reply'd. . . .

. . . I must mention here, that Powhatan was seated on a sort of rais'd bedstead, and on the floor before him sat a reallie striking Salvage maid, of perhaps sixteen yeares, who from the richnesse of her costume and the deference pay'd her by the other Salvages, I took to be the Queene. Throughout the banquet that follow'd our entrie into the house, this young ladie scarce took her eyes from us, and though unlike my C^apt, I am a man not given to fooling him selfe as regards his comeliness to the faire sex, I can only say, in sooth, that what was in her eyes exceeded that naturall curiositie, wch one might show on first beholding fair-skinn'd men. Powhatan, I thinke, observ'd this, for his face grew ever more sower as the meale progress'd. For this reason, I avoided the Queenes gaze assiduouslie, so as not farther to prejudice our state. My C^apt, for his part . . . return'd her amourous glances with glances of his owne, of such unmistakeable import, that had I been the Emperour I had struck him dead forthwith. My poore heart trembl'd for the safetie of my head . . .

[*A description followeth of the feast serv'd the two prisoners. It is a Gargantuan affair, but the Author is unable to keep a morsel on his stomach. Smith, on the contrary, gorgeth himself very like a swine in the slaughterhouse.*]

My C^apt . . . took it on him selfe then to make a small speech, the gist of w^ch (for I, too, comprehended somewhat of the heathen gibberish) was, that he had brought with him a singular gifte for the Emperour, but that, unluckilie, it had been remov'd from his person by the Emperours lieutenant (that same infamous Opecancanough, who was the death of our companions earlier). Powhatan forthwith commanded Opecancanough thither, and bade him produce the gifte, if he had it. Albeit he was loath to part with it, Opecancanough fish'd out the wicked compasse before describ'd, and gave it to his Chief, who thereupon caus'd his lieutenant to be birch'd, for that he had intercepted it. This was, certain, a grosse injustice, inasmuch as Opecancanough had had no knowledge that the compasse was meant for Powhatan, as neither had my C^apt, what time to save his skinne he had given the vile machine to Opecancanough. Notwithstanding w^ch, the Salvage was deliver'd out the room, for birching, and I sawe no future good therein for us . . .

Next my C^apt, to my great astonishment, commenc'd to shew to Powhatan the secrets of the compasse, directing its little lenses at the fyre to light the shamefull scenes within. I was certaine our end was at hand, and ready'd my selfe to dye as befitteth a Gentleman, for surelie no man, not even a Salvage, who hath the qualities to raise him selfe to the post of Prince, even over a nation of benighted heathen, c^d but be disgusted by such spectacles, as now lay illumin'd to the Emperours eyes. For the thousandth time, I curs'd my C^apt for a black & arrant fool.

Yet here I reckon'd without the degeneracie of the Salvage, whose bestiall fancie ever delighteth in vilest things. So far from

166

taking umbrage, Powhatan had like to split his lecherous sides on beholding the little painting; he slapt his knees, and slaver'd copiouslie over his wrinkl'd lipps. A long time pass'd ere he c^d remove his eye from the foul peep-hole, and then only to peer therein againe, and againe, each time hollowing with glee.

At length my C^apt made it knowne, the Queene, as well, s^hd receive a gifte. At this pronouncement, I clos'd my eyes and made my peace with God, for knowing sufficient by this time of the nature of my C^apts giftes, and sensing farther the jealousie of the Emperour, I expected momentlie to feel the *tomahawke* at my neck. The Queene, however, seemed greatlie pleas'd at the prospect. As I might have guess'd, my C^apt had reserv'd for her the most impressive gifte of alle. He drew from his inexhaustible pocket a smalle booke of sorts, constructed of a number of little pages bound fast at there tops (this miracle too I had seene at Jamestowne). On everie page a drawing was, of the sort one w^d be loath to shew ones wife, each drawing alter'd only by a little from his neighbour, and the whole in a kind of sequence, so that, s^hd one grasp the lewd booke by the top, and bending it slightlie, allowe the pages to spring rapidlie each after each before the eye, the result was, that the figures thereon assum'd the semblance of life, in that they mov'd to & fro about there sinfull businesse.

Alas! The Queene, it grew cleare, was deprav'd as was her consort. Over & over againe, once having learnt the virtue of the small booke, she set the actors therein to moving, each time laughing alowd at what she sawe . . .

[More food is serv'd, and a sort of Indian liquor, both of wch Smith takes unto himself in quantity. The Author declines, for the same reasons as before. The Queene appoints herself to wait on Smith personally, laving his hands and fetching bunches of wild-turkey feathers wherewith to dry them.]

The while this second feasting was in progresse, I contriv'd to screwe up sufficient courage to observe Powhatan, hoping to reade in his face prognostication of what was to followe. What I sawe did not refresh my spirits . . . The Emperour never took his gaze from the Queene, who in turn, never remov'd hers from my C^apt, with everie indecent promise in her eyes. She was on everie side of him at once, fetching this & carrying that, all her movements exaggerated, and none befitting any save a Drury Lane vestall. My C^apt, whether through his characteristick ignorance, or, what is more likelie, in pursuit of some twisted designe of his owne, reply'd to her coquetries in kind. None of this escap'd the Emperour, who, it seem'd to me, was scarce able to put away his gluttonous repast, for watching them. When then this Powhatan summon'd to his couch three of his evillest-appearing lieutenants, all coal'd & oyl'd & bedaub'd & betassel'd & bedizen'd, and commenc'd with them a long colloquy of heathen grunts & whisperings, the purport whereof was unequivocall, I once againe commended my soule to Gods mercie, for I look'd to met him shortlie face to face. My Capt pay'd no heede, but went on blindlie with his sport.

My . . . feares, it was soon prov'd, were justify'd. The Emperour made a signall, and the three great Salvages lay'd hold of my Capt. Despite his protestations, the wch were lowd enow, he was carry'd up to Powhatans couch, and there forc'd to his knees. The Salvages lay'd his head upon a paire of greate stones, put there for the purpose, and catching up there uglie war-clubbs, had beate out what smalle braines my Capt might make claim to, were it not that at this juncture, the Queene her selfe, to my astonishment, interceded. Running to the altar, she flung her selfe bodilie upon my Capt, and declar'd to Powhatan, that rather wd she loose her owne head, then that they shd dash in his. Were I the Emperour, I owne I shd have done the twain to death, for that so cleare an alliance cd lead but to adulterie ere long. But Powhatan stay'd his bullies; the assemblie was dismist, saving only the Emperour, his Queene, my Capt, & my selfe (who all seem'd to have forgot, thank God), and for the nonce, it appear'd, my heart wd go on beating in my breast . . .

[There follow'd] a speech by the Emperour, wch, as best I grasp'd it, was unusuall as it was improper. Some I grant escap'd me, for that Powhatan spake with great rapiditie and chew'd his wordes withal. But the summe of what I gather'd was, that the Queene was not his Queene at all, neither one amongst his concubines, but his daughter, her name being *Pocahontas*. By this name is signify'd, in there tongue, *the smalle one,* or *she of the smallnesse and impenetrabilitie,* and this, it seem'd, referr'd not to the maidens stature, wch was in sooth but slight, nor to her mind, wch one cd penetrate with passing ease. Rather it reflected, albeit grosslie, a singular physickal short-coming in the childe, to witt: her privitie was that nice, and the tympanum therein so surpassing stowt, as to render it infrangible. This fact greatlie disturb'd the Emperour, for that in his nation the barbarous custom was practic'd, that whensoever a maid be affianc'd, the Salvage, who wisheth to wed her, must needs first fracture that same membrane, whereupon the suitor is adjudg'd a man worthie of his betrothed, and the nuptialls followe. Now Powhatan, we were told, had on sundrie occasions chosen warriors of his people to wedd this Pocahontas, but in everie instance the ceremonie had to be foregone, seeing that labour as they might, none had been able to deflowr her, and in sooth the most had done them selves hurt withal, in there efforts; whereas, the proper thing was, to injure the young lasse, and

168

that as grievouslie as possible, the degree of injurie being reck'd a measure of the mans virilitie. Inasmuch as the Salvages are wont to marrie off there daughters neare twelve yeares of age, it was deem'd a disgracefull thing, the Emperour shd have a daughter sixteene, who was yet a maide.

Continuing this discourse, [Powhatan] said, that whereas his daughter had seen fitt, to save my Capts life, what time it had been the Emperours pleasure to dashe out his braines, then my Capt must needs regard him selfe affianc'd to her, and submit him selfe to that same labour (to witt, essaying the gate to Venus grottoe) as her former suitors. But . . . with this difference, that where, having fail'd, her Salvage beaux had merelie been disgrac'd, and taunted as olde women, my Capt, shd he prove no better, his head wd be lay'd againe upon the stones, and the clubbing of his braines proceed without quarter or respite.

All this Pocahontas heard with greate joye, maugre its nature, wch wd have mortify'd an English ladie; and my Capt, too, accepted readilie (in sooth he had no option in the matter). For my part, I was pleas'd to gaine reprieve once more from the butchers block, albeit a briefe one, for I could not see, since that the Salvages were of large stature, and my Capt so slight of build, how that he shd triumph where they had fail'd, unlesse there were some wondrous disproportion, in both cases, betwixt the size of what in each was visible, and what conceal'd, to the casuall eye. My fate, it seem'd, hung on my Capts, and for that I bade him Godspeed, preferring to heare for ever his endlesse boasting (wch wd surelie followe his successe), then to wett with my braines the Salvage clubbs, wch fate awaited me upon his failure. The carnall joust was set for sunup, in the publick yard of sorts, that fronted the Emperours house, and the entire towne was order'd to be present. This alone, I wot, wd have suffic'd to unstarch an ordinarie man, my selfe included, who am wont to worshipp Venus (after my fashion) in the privacie of darken'd couches; but my Capt appear'd not a whitt ruffl'd, and in sooth seem'd eager to make his essaye publicklie. This, I take it, is apt measure of his swinishnesse, for that whenas a gentleman is forc'd, against his will, to some abominable worke, he will dispatch it with as much expedition, and as little notice, as hc can, whereas the rake & foole will noise the matter about, drawing the eyes of the world to his follie & license, and is never more content, then when he hath an audience to his mischief. . . .

[Here endeth the existing portion of the journal.]

"'Dslife, what a place to end it!" Ebenezer cried when he had finished the manuscript, and hurried to find Burlingame. "Was there no more, Henry?"

"Not another word, I swear't, for I combed the town to find the rest."

"But marry, one must know how matters went—whether this hateful Smith made good his boasts, or thy poor ancestor lost his life."

"Ah well," Burlingame replied, "this much we know, that both escaped, for Smith went on that same year to explore the Chesapeake, and Burlingame at least set down this narrative. What's more, if I be not a bastard he must needs have got himself a wife in later years, for none is mentioned here. I'God, Eben, I cannot tell you how I yearn to know the rest!"

"And I," laughed Ebenezer, "for though belike she was no poet, this Pocahontas was twice the virgin I am!"

To Ebenezer's surprise, Burlingame blushed deeply. "That is not what I meant."

"I know full well you didn't; 'tis your ancestry concerns you. Yet 'tis no vulgar curiosity, this other: the fall of virgins always is instructive, nor doth the world e'er weary of the tale. And the harder the fall, the better."

"Indeed?" Burlingame smiled, regaining his composure. "And prithee tell me, What lesson doth it teach?"

" 'Tis odd that I should be the teacher and you the pupil," Ebenezer said, "yet I will own 'tis a subject close to my heart, and one to which I've given no small attention. My conclusion is, that mankind sees two morals in such tales: the fall of innocence, or the fall of pride. The first sort hath its archetype in Adam; the second in Satan. The first alone hath not the sting of tragedy, as hath the second: the virgin pure and simple, like Pocahontas, is neither good nor vicious for her hymen; she is only envied, as is Adam, by the fallen. They secretly rejoice to see her ravaged, as poor men smile to see a rich man robbed—e'en the virtuous fallen can feel for her no more than abstract pity. The second is the very stuff of drama, for the proud man oft excites our admiration; we live, as't were, by proxy in his triumphs, and are cleansed and taught by proxy in his fall. When we heap obloquy on Satan, is't not ourselves we scold, for that we secretly admire his Heavenly insurrection?"

"That all seems sound," said Burlingame. "It follows, doth it not, that when you profess abhorrence for the Captain, thou'rt but chastising yourself in like manner, or that part of you that wisheth him success?"

" 'Tis unequivocally the case," Ebenezer agreed, "whene'er the critic's of the number of the fallen. For myself, 'twere as if a maid should cheer her ravisher, or my Lord Baltimore support John Coode."

"I think that neither is impossible, but let it go. I will say now, thine own fall, when it comes, must needs be glorious, inasmuch as thou'rt both innocent and proud."

"Wherein lies my pride?" asked Ebenezer, clearly disconcerted by his friend's observation.

"In thy very innocence, which you raise above mere circumstance and make a special virtue. 'Tis a Christain reverence you bear it, I swear!"

"Christian in a sense," Ebenezer replied, "albeit your Christians—St. Paul excepted—pay scant reverence to chastity in men. 'Tis valued as a sign—nay, a double sign, for't harketh back alike to Eve and Mary. Therein lies its difference from the cardinal virtues, which refer to naught beyond themselves: adultery's a mortal sin, proscribed by God's commandment—not so fornication, I believe."

"Then virginity's a secondary virtue, is't not, and less to be admired than faithfulness? I think not even More would gainsay that."

"But recall," Ebenezer insisted, "I said 'twas only in a sense I share the Christians' feeling. Methinks that mankind's virtues are of two main sorts——"

"Aye, that we learn in school," said Burlingame, who seemed prepared to end the colloquy. "*Instrumental* if they lead us to some end, and *terminal* if we love them in themselves. 'Tis schoolmen's cant."

"Nay," said Ebenezer, "that is not what I meant; those terms bear little meaning to the Christian, I believe, who on the one hand hopes by all his virtues to reach Heaven, and yet will swear that virtue is its own reward. What I meant was, that sundry virtues are—I might say *plain*, for want of proper language, and some *significant*. Among the first are honesty in speech and deed, fidelity, respect for mother and father, charity, and the like; the second head's comprised of things like eating fish on Friday, resting on the Sabbath, and coming virgin to the grave or marriage bed, whiche'er the case may be; they all mean naught when taken by themselves, like the strokes and scribbles we call *writing*—their virtue lies in what they stand for. Now the first, whether so designed or not, are matters of public policy, and thus apply to prudent men, be they heathens or believers. The second have small relevance to prudence, being but signs, and differ from faith to faith. The first are social, the second religious; the first are guides for life, the second forms of ceremony; the first practical, the second mysterious or poetic———"

"I grasp the principle," Burlingame said.

"Well then," Ebenezer declared, "it follows that this second sort are *purer,* after a fashion, and in this way not inferior at all, but the reverse."

"La, you have the heart of a Scholastic," Burlingame said disgustedly. "I see no *purity* in 'em, save that all the sense is filtered out—the residue is nonsense."

"As you wish, Henry—I do not mean to argue Christianity but only my virginity, which if senseless is to me not therefore *nonsense,* but *essence.* 'Tis but a sign as with the Christians, that I grant, yet it pointeth not to Eden or to Bethlehem, but to my soul. I prize it not as a virtue, but as the very emblem of my self, and when I call me virgin and poet 'tis not more boast than who should say I'm male and English. Prithee chide me no more on't, and let us end this discourse that pleaseth you so little."

"Nonetheless," Burlingame declared, " 'twill be a fall worth watching when you stumble."

"I do not mean to fall."

Burlingame shrugged. "What climber doth? 'Tis but the more likely in your case, for that you travel as't were asleep —thy friend McEvoy was no dullard there, albeit a callous fellow. Yet haply the fall will open your eyes."

"I would have thought thee more my friend, Henry, but on this head thou'rt brusque as erst in London, when I went with Anna to St. Giles. Have you forgot that day in Cambridge, the pass wherein you found me? Or that malady whereof I spoke but yesterday, that I was wont to suffer in the winehouse? Think you I'd not rejoice," he went on, growing more aroused, "to be in sooth a climber, that stumbling would move men to fear and pity? I do not climb, but merely walk a road, and stumbling ne'er shall fall a mighty fall, but only cease to walk, or drift a wayless ship on every current, or haply just moss over like a stone. I see nor spectacle nor instruction in such a fall."

Burlingame made no more of the matter and apologized to Ebenezer for his curtness. Nonetheless he remained out of sorts, as did the poet, for some hours afterwards, and in fact it was not until a short time before they arrived in Plymouth that they entirely regained their spirits, and Burlingame, at Ebenezer's request, took up again the tale of his adventures, which he'd left at his discovery of the fragmentary journal.

7

Burlingame's Tale Concluded; the Travelers Arrive at Plymouth

"THAT PORTION OF the *Privie Journall* that you read," said Burlingame, "so far from cooling the ardor of my quest, did but enflame it the more, as you might imagine, inasmuch as it said *There was a Henry Burlingame,* yet told me neither that he e'er had progeny, nor that among his children was my father. There was one ground for hope and speculation: namely, that Captain John Smith set out that very summer to explore the Chesapeake, wherein near half a century later I was found floating. Yet nowhere in his *Historie* doth he mention Burlingame, nor is that poor wight listed with the party. I searched the ancient papers of the colony and asked the length and breadth of Jamestown, but no word more could I find on the matter. I made bold to enquire of Nicholson himself whether he knew aught of other records in the Dominion. And he replied he had been there so short time he scarce knew where the privy was, but added, there was a grievous dearth of paper in the provinces, and 'twas no uncommon thing for officers of the government to ransack older records for paper writ on but the *recto,* to the end they might employ the *verso* for themselves. He himself deplored this practice, for he is a man devoted to the cause of learning, but he said there was no cure for't till the provinces erected their own paper mills.

"It seemed to me quite likely my *Journall* had suffered this fate, inasmuch as 'twas writ on a good grade of English paper, and the author had employed the *recto* only. I despaired of e'er discovering the rest, and in the fall of 1690 went with Captain Hill to London. Our intention was to litigate to clear the charges of seditious speech against him, and if possible to undo Colonel Coode and his companions. The moment was propitious, for Coode himself and Kenelm Che-

173

seldyne, his speaker, had also sailed for London and would not have their bullies to defend 'em. I so arranged matters that a number of his enemies appeared in England that same season, and I thought that if we filed a host of depositions against him, we could thereby either work his ruin or at least detain him whilst we plotted farther. To this end I made a secret trip to Maryland ere we sailed, with the design of slipping privily into St. Mary's City and stealing the criminal records of Coode's courts, or bribing them stolen, for no clearer proof could be of his corruption. Howbeit, the man anticipated my plan, as oft he doth: I learned that he and Cheseldyne had carried off the records with 'em.

"In any case we set our plot in motion. No sooner did we dock at London in November than the Lords Commissioners of Trade and Plantations subpoenaed Coode to confront Lord Baltimore before them, to answer that worthy's charges against him. At the same time Colonel Henry Coursey, of Kent County, petitioned against Coode and Cheseldyne, as did John Lillingstone, the rector of St. Paul's Parish in Talbot County, and ten other souls, all known Protestants—for 'twas Coode's chief defense for his rebellion that he was putting down the barbarous Papists. Finally Hill made his own petition, and even our friend Captain Burford of the *Abraham & Francis*, who had helped us flee to Nicholson and whose ship the rogues had lately crossed on, deposed in Plymouth that Coode had in his presence damned Lord Baltimore and vowed to spend the revenues embezzled from the Province.

"For a time it seemed we had him dead to rights, but he is a damned resourceful devil and had a perfect shield for our assaults. The year before, just prior to the rebellion, a wight named John Payne, who collected His Majesty's customs on the Patuxent River, had been shot to death either aboard or near a pleasure-sloop belonging to Major Nicholas Sewall, and Coode had rigged a charge of willful murther against Sewall and four others on the sloop. Nick Sewall was Deputy Governor of Maryland before the rebellion, but more than that, he is Charles Calvert's nephew, the son of Lady Baltimore herself. The rebels had him hostage in St. Mary's, and at any time could turn him over to the court of Neamiah Blackistone, Coode's crony, who would hang him certain. Thus our hands were tied and our plot squelched, the more for that we had not the criminal records for evidence. The Lords Commissioners cleared Captain Hill in December, and Colonel Henry Darnall too, Lord Baltimore's agent, who'd been charged with treasonable speech and inciting the Choptico Indians to slaughter Protestants on the Eastern Shore; but Coode they could not touch, or haply *would* not, at Lord Baltimore's behest.

"I saw no farther usefulness for myself with Captain Hill; he was free to go back to the Severn, and had no more taste for politics. But my interest in John Coode had near replaced my former quest, which seemed a cul-de-sac. The man intrigued me with his cunning and his boldness, his shifting roles as minister and priest, and most of all his motives: he seemed to have no wish for office, and held no post save in the St. Mary's County militia; he plundered more for sport than avarice, and would risk all to make a clever move. The fellow loved intrigue itself, I swear, and would unseat a governor for amusement! At length I vowed to match my wits with his, and to that end offered my services to Lord Baltimore as a sort of agent-at-large in the Maryland business. The Lords Commissioners of Trade and Plantations were kindly disposed towards Baltimore at this time, for they knew full well John Coode was a rascal and King William had no more right than you or I to seize the Province. Therefore when time had come to name a royal governor, they gave milord some say in his selection, and he picked the great dunderhead Sir Lionel Copley, who could not tell a knave from a saint. Now I had caught a rumor that Coode was privy to the Governor's ear, and for simple spite had told him that Francis Nicholson of Virginia was being groomed to take his place, ere Copley had e'en left London. He said this, I was certain, merely to cause friction 'twixt the governors, for he had no love for Nicholson and wanted a weak executive in Maryland who would leave his own hands free. This strategy of his gave me my own, which was to suggest to Baltimore that he should in fact have Nicholson commissioned lieutenant governor of Maryland, since word had it he was to be replaced in Jamestown by none other than Sir Edmund Andros himself; and farther, that he should then name Andros commander-in-chief of the Province, with power to take command in the event of Nicholson's death and Copley's absence. 'Twas a fantastical arrangement, inasmuch as Copley mistrusted Nicholson, Nicholson disliked Andros, and Coode loathed 'em all! My object was, to so mismatch them that their rule would be a farce, to the end that haply someday William might return the reins of government to Baltimore.

"Milord approved the plan, once I had explained it, and, seeing farther I had the confidence both of Andros and of Nicholson, he gave me the post I wished, with one stipulation

175

only, that it be confidential. Nicholson and Andros were commissioned in 1692, and the instant Coode heard it he took fright: he well knew Copley was too thick to see the evidence of his mischief and too weak to harm him if he saw't, and Andros would have work enough in Virginia to absorb him; but Nicholson's neither dull nor weak and knew Coode already for a rascal. Posthaste he wrote instructions to an agent in St. Mary's, to steal the Journal of the 1691 Assembly and destroy it, for there was writ the full tale of his government for all to see. I heard from friends one Benjamin Ricaud had joined the fleet, and knowing him as Coode's messenger, straightway set out after. 'Twas my good luck he boarded the ship *Bailey,* for her master, Peregrine Browne of Cecil County, was a friend of Hill's and Baltimore's, and I knew him well. Moreover, a number of our men were there as well. Between us we contrived to search Ricaud's effects and intercept the letter, which I passed along to Baltimore.

"I resolved at once to sail for Maryland and prevailed on Baltimore to let me go on the very ship with Copley. We had one powerful ally in the government, Sir Thomas Lawrence, who as His Majesty's Secretary to the Province had access to every stamp and paper. 'Twas my design to have him steal the Assembly Journal ere it was destroyed and smuggle it to Nicholson, who would in turn then fetch it here to London for our use. I was the more eager to lay hands on't, for that in that document my separate goals seemed fused: the search for my father and the search for ways to put down Coode were now the selfsame search!"

"How is that?" asked Ebenezer, who had heard the foregoing in wordless amazement. "I do not grasp your meaning in the least."

" 'Twas that note we intercepted," Burlingame replied. "We did not know its import at first sight, for't said no more than *Abington: Such smutt as Capt John Smiths book were best fed to the fire.* 'Abington' we knew was Andrew Abington, a fellow in St. Mary's that Coode had given the post of Collector for the Patuxent after John Payne's murther; but we could not comprehend the rest. At length I bribed Ricaud outright, who was a shifty fellow, and he told us 'John Smiths Book' signified the Journal of the 1691 Assembly, for that 'twas writ on the back of an old manuscript of some sort. For aught I knew it might be but a draft of the *Historie* I'd read in print, but nonetheless I could scarce contain my joy at hearing of it and prayed it might make mention of my namesake. Nor was this the end of my good fortune, for the note itself was writ on aged paper, not unlike that of the *Privie Journall* in Jamestown, and I learned from Ricaud that Coode had traveled often in Virginia and had kin there, and that after the rebellion he'd given Cheseldyne and Blackistone a batch of old papers filched from Jamestown to use in the Assembly and the St. Mary's court. For aught I knew, the rest of the *Privie Journall* might be filed somewhere in Maryland!

"As soon as I arrived in St. Mary's City I made myself known to Sir Thomas Lawrence and laid open Lord Baltimore's strategy. He was to steal the Assembly Journal and pass it on to Nicholson, who would find excuse at once to visit London. In addition I meant to discredit as many as possible of Coode's associates, and to that end persuaded Lawrence to lure them into corruption. Colonel Henry Jowles, for instance, was a member of the Governor's Council and a colonel of militia: we made it easy for him to line his pockets with illegal fees as clerk of Calvert County. Baltimore's friend Charles Carroll, a Papist lawyer in St. Mary's, did the same with Neamiah Blackistone, Coode's own brother-in-law, that was president of the Council and Copley's right-hand man. And the grandest gadfly of 'em all was Edward Randolph, His Majesty's Royal Surveyor, who loved to bait and slander poor old Copley, and spoke openly in favor of King James. Finally we terrified the lot of 'em with stories that the French and the Naked Indians of Canada were making ready for a general slaughter. In June, not a month after we landed, Copley was already complaining of Randolph to the Lords Commissioners of Trade and Plantations; in July Lawrence filched the Journal, but Nicholson whisked it off to London ere I could lay eyes upon it. In October we exposed Colonel Jowles, who was turned out as colonel, councilman, and clerk. In December Copley again complained of Randolph, and swore to the Lords Commissioners that Nicholson was on some sinister errand in London—which letter greatly pleased us, for we meant to use it to advantage when Nicholson himself was governor.

"Thus we harassed old Copley, who scarce knew what was happening till the following February, when the Lords Commissioners charged Blackistone with graft. Then, too late, he saw our plot, and in the spring of last year arrested Carroll, Sir Thomas himself, Edward Randolph, and a host of others, among whom was Peter Sayer of Talbot, the man I was disguised as in Ben Bragg's bookshop. Sir Thomas was jailed, as was Carroll, and impeached into the bargain; Randolph was arrested on the Eastern Shore of Virginia by the Somerset County sheriff, but ere he could get him out of Accomac I sent word of't to Edmund Andros in Williamsburg, who'd been a drinking-friend of Randolph's since the old days in Boston, and Andros fetched him home for safety."

"E'en so, thy cause was damaged, was it not?" asked Ebenezer.

"*My* cause?" Burlingame smiled. " 'Tis thine as well, is't not, since we work for the same employer? Let us say instead our cause was discommoded for a time; we knew well old Copley couldn't hold such men for long, but we wanted them out of prison, not alone for their own comfort but for fear John Coode might turn up in their absence and gain ground with Copley. As't happened our fears were empty, for both the Governor and his wife died in September—methinks they ne'er acclimatized to Maryland. His death suggested to me a wondrous mischief——"

"Great Heavens, Henry, thou'rt a plotting Coode thyself!"

"You recall I said Lord Baltimore had made Andros commander-in-chief of the Province, and his commission gave him full authority in the event of Nicholson's death and Copley's absence. It struck me now that albeit 'twas *Copley* dead and *Nicholson* absent, I could work a grand confusion anyhow, and so I went posthaste to Williamsburg to take the news to Andros and persuade him his commission was in force. He was inclined to doubt it, but he knew me for an agent of Lord Baltimore; what's more, though he made no mention of't, he was not averse to stealing Nicholson's thunder, as't were, by rescuing law and order in Maryland, for he himself had felt the pricks of following Nicholson in Virginia. To be brief, he marched into St. Mary's City, demanded the government of Maryland, dissolved the Assembly, suspended Blackistone, turned Lawrence loose, and took him with his party back to Williamsburg, leaving the Province in the charge of an amiable nobody named Greenberry. 'Twas his design to return again this spring and make Lawrence president of the Council, but whether he hath done it I've yet to learn.

"I could see no immediate employment for myself in the Province after this, and so I crossed come January here to London. I arrived not two weeks past, and learned to my dismay that neither Nicholson nor Baltimore hath the Assembly Journal in his possession for fear of Coode's agents. Instead, Lord Baltimore declares, he hath broken it into three portions for safekeeping and deposited the several portions privily in

178

Maryland, whence I had just come! I begged of him the trustees' names, but he was loath to discover them—not Nicholson himself, it seems, knew more than I on the matter. But a few days past he said he had a mission for me of such importance he could trust it to no other soul; and I replied, surely I was not worthy of such trust, if he dared not name me the keepers of the Journal. Whereat he smiled and said I had him fair; the pieces of the Journal, he confessed, were in the hands of sundry loyal persons of the surname *Smith*, for reasons I'd no need to ask, and he told me their names in greatest confidence. I thanked him and declared I was ready for whatever work he gave me, and he said a young man had called on him that afternoon that was a poet, and he had charged him to write a work in praise of Maryland and the proprietorship—the which, he believed, if nobly done, might profit more than ten intrigues to win him back the Province."

" 'Sheart, what a marvelous small world!" Ebenezer cried. "And how pleased I am to find he sets such store by poetry. But prithee what work was't in this connection, that warranted such concession on his part?"

"He enquired of me, whether I knew the poet Ebenezer Cooke? My heart leaped, for I'd had no word of you or Anna these seven years, but I answered merely I had heard mention of a poet by that name. Then he told me of your visit and proposal, and his commission, and said I should accompany you to Maryland—for that you'd ne'er before been out of England—and act both as your guide and your protector. I leave it to you to imagine with what readiness I took on the task, and straightway sought you out!"

Now the earlier portions of this long narrative had elicited from Ebenezer such a number of *ah's, marry's, 'sheart's,* and *b'm'faith's* that he had come during this last to sit for the most part wordlessly, mouth agape and brows a-pucker in a sort of permanent *i'God!* as one amazement tripped on another's heels. At the end he was moved enough to embrace Burlingame unashamedly—and had, he found, to add bad breath to the host of alterations worked on his friend by this seven-year adventure: it was no doubt a product of the teeth gone carious.

"Ah God," he cried, "if Anna but knew all you've told me! Wherefore this role as Peter Sayer, Henry? Why did you not at least reveal yourself in London ere we left, that she might share my joy at finding you?"

Burlingame sighed, and after a moment replied, "I am wont to go by names other than my own, either borrowed or

179

invented, for sundry reasons stemming from my work. 'Twould do no good for Coode to know my name nor e'en that I exist. What's more, I can confound him and his agents: I posed as Sayer in Bragg's, for instance, and forged his name, merely because Coode thinks the man's in Plymouth with the fleet. In like manner I've pretended to be both friends and enemies of Baltimore, to advance his cause. Once, I shall confess, that time on Perry Browne's ship *Bailey*, I posed as Coode himself to the poor dolt Ben Ricaud, to intercept those letters. The truth is, Eben, no man save Richard Hill, Lord Baltimore, and yourself hath known my name since 1687, when first I commenced to play the game of governments; and the game itself hath made such changes in me, that none who knew me erst would know me now, nor do I mean them to. 'Tis better they think me lost."

"Yet surely Anna——"

" 'Tis but thy first enquiry I've replied to," Burlingame interrupted, raising his forefinger. "For the second, do not forget that many are bound from London for the fleet—Coode's men as well as ours, and haply Coode himself. 'Twould have been foolish, even perilous, to shed my mask in that place. Moreover, there was no time: I scarce caught up with you ere you left, and mark how long I've been discovering myself to you. The fleet had sailed without us."

"Aye, that's true," Ebenezer admitted.

"What's more"—Burlingame laughed—"I'd not yet made my own mind up, whether 'twere wise e'en you should know the truth."

"What! Think you I'd e'er betray thy trust? And could you thus callously deprive me of my only friend? You injure me!"

"As to the first, 'twas just to answer it I posed as Sayer and queried you—the years change any man. Ben Bragg had said thou'rt but an opportunist; nor was your servant more persuaded of your motive, for all he admired you. Again, how could I know your sentiments towards Burlingame? The tale you told to Peter Sayer was your bond; when I had heard it, I revealed myself at once, but had you sung a different tune, 'tis Peter Sayer had been your guide, not Burlingame."

"Enough. I am convinced and cannot tell my joy. Yet your relation shames me for my fearfulness and sloth, as doth your wisdom my poor talent. Thou'rt a Virgil worth a better Dante."

"Oh la," Burlingame scoffed, "you've wit enough, and ear. Besides, the Province is no Hell or Purgatorio, but just a piece o' the great world like England—with the difference, haply, that the soil is vast and new where the sot-weed hath not drained it. What's more, the reins and checks are few and weak; good plants and weeds alike grow tall. Do but recall, if the people there seem strange and rough: a man content with Europe scarce would cross the ocean. The plain fact is, the greatest part are castaways from Europe, or the sons of castaways: rebels, failures, jailbirds and adventurers. Cast such seed on such soil, 'twere fond to seek a crop of dons and courtiers!"

"Yet you speak as one who loves the place," said Ebenezer, "and that alone, for me, is warrant I shall too."

Burlingame shrugged. "Haply so, haply no. There is a freedom there that's both a blessing and a curse. 'Tis more than just political and religious liberty—they come and go from one year to the next. 'Tis philosophic liberty I speak of, that comes from want of history. It makes every man an orphan like myself, that freedom, and can as well demoralize as elevate. But no more: I see the masts and spires of Plymouth yonder. You'll know the Province soon enough and how it strikes you!"

Even as Burlingame spoke the smell of the sea blew into the carriage, stirring Ebenezer to the depths of his being, and when a short while later he saw it for the first time, spread out before him to the far horizon, he shivered twice or thrice all over and came near to passing water.

8

The Laureate Indites a Quatrain and Fouls His Breeches

"REMEMBER," BURLINGAME SAID as the carriage rolled into Plymouth, "I am not Henry Burlingame, nor Peter Sayer either, for the real Sayer's somewhere on the fleet. You'd best not give me any name at all, I think, till I see how lays the land."

Accordingly, as soon as their chests and trunks were put

down they inquired after the *Poseidon* at the wharves and were told it had already joined the fleet.

"What!" cried Ebenezer. "Then we have missed it after all!"

"Nay," Burlingame smiled, " 'tis not unusual. The fleet assembles yonder in the Downs off The Lizard; you can see't from here on a clear day."

Inquiring further he found a shallop doing ferry-service between the Downs and the harbor, and arranged for passage aboard it in the afternoon.

"We'd as well take one last meal ashore," he explained to Ebenezer. "Moreover I must change clothing, for I've resolved to pose as your servant—— What was his name?"

"Bertrand," Ebenezer murmured. "But must you be a servant?"

"Aye, or else invent an entire gentleman as your companion. As Bertrand I can pass unnoticed in your company and hear more news as well of your fellow travelers."

So saying he led the way across the street from the wharves to a tavern advertising itself by two capital letter *C*s, face to face and interlocking, the figure surmounted by a three-lobed crown.

"Here's the King o' the Seas," said Burlingame. "I know it of old. 'Twas here I got my first wee clap, while still a hand on Captain Salmon's ship. A bony Welsh tart gave it me, that had made the best of my inexperience to charge me a clean girl's price, and by the time the fraud came clear I was many a day's sail from Plymouth, bound for Lisbon. The clap soon left me, but I ne'er forgot the wench. When in Lisbon I found a vessel bound for Plymouth and made enquiries amongst the crew, till at length I hit upon a one-eyed Portugee that was like to perish of a miserable clap from Africa, beside which our English sort was but a fleabite. This frightful wight I gave my fine new quadrant to, that Captain Salmon had bought me to practice navigation with, on condition he share his clap with the Welsh whore at the King o' the Seas directly he made port. But no man e'er died of the food here."

It being midmorning, the tavern was deserted except for a young serving maid scrubbing the flagstone floor. She was short and plump, coarse-haired and befreckled, but her eyes had a merry light and her nose a pertness. Leaving Ebenezer to select a table, Burlingame approached her familiarly and engaged her in conversation which, though spoken in voices too low for Ebenezer to hear distinctly, soon had her laughing and wagging a finger.

"The duckling swore she'd naught but fish in the larder," he said when presently he returned, "but when I told her 'twas a laureate she was feeding, that could lay the place low with Hudibrastics, she agreed to stay your pen with roast of beef. 'Twill be here anon."

"You twit me," Ebenezer said modestly.

Burlingame shrugged. "Methinks I'll change costume the while it's fixing."

"But our baggage is on the wharf."

"No matter. Scotch cloth to silk is oft a life-time's journey, but silk to Scotch cloth can be traversed in a minute." He went again to the serving maid, who smiled at his approach, and spoke softly to her, at the same time pinching her smartly. She squealed and, one hand on her hip, pointed laughing to a door beside the fireplace. Burlingame then took her arm as though to lead her along with him; when she drew back he whispered seriously in her ear and whispered again when she gasped and shook her head. She glanced towards Ebenezer, who blushed at once and feigned preoccupation with the set of his cravat; Burlingame whispered a third message that turned her bright eyes coyly, and left the room through the indicated door. The girl lingered for two minutes in the room. Then she took another sharp look at Ebenezer, sniffed, and flounced through the same door.

Though he was not a little embarrassed by the small drama, the poet was pleased enough to be alone for a short while, not only to ponder the wondrous adventures of his friend, but also to take stock of his own position.

"I have been so occupied gaping and gasping at Henry," said he to himself, "I have near forgot who *I* am, and what business I'm embarked upon. Not a line have I writ since London, nor thought at all of logging my journey."

He forthwith spread before him on the table his double-entry ledger, open to that page whereon was transcribed the first quatrain of his official career, and fetching quill and ink from a stand on the wall next the serving-bar, considered what should grace the facing-page.

"I can say naught whate'er of my journey hither, in the *Marylandiad*," he reflected, "for I saw but little of't. Moreover, 'twere fitter I commenced the poem from Plymouth, where most who sail to Maryland take their leave of Albion's rocks; 'twill pitch the reader straightway on his voyage." Pursuing farther this line of thought, he resolved to write his epic *Marylandiad* in the form of an imaginary voyage, thinking thereby to discover to the reader the delights of the Province with the same freshness and surprise wherewith they would discover themselves to the voyager-poet. It was with pleasure and a kind of awe, therefore, that he recalled the name of his ship.

"*Poseidon!*" he thought. "It bodes well, i'faith! A very Virgil for companion, and the Earth-Shaker himself for ferrymaster to this Elysium!"

And turning the happy figure some minutes in his mind, at length he wrote:

> *Let* Ocean *roar his damn'dest Gale:*
> *Our Planks shan't leak; our Masts shan't fail.*
> *With great* Poseidon *at our Side*
> *He seemeth neither wild nor wide.*

At the foot he appended *E.C., G^{ent}, P^t & L^t of M^d*, and beamed with satisfaction. While he was thus engaged, two men came into the tavern and noisily closed the door. They were sailors, by the look of them—but not ordinary seamen —and like enough for twins in manner and appearance: both were short and heavy, red-nosed, squint-eyed, and black-whiskered, and wore their natural hair; both were dressed in black breeches and coats, and sported twin-peaked hats of the same color. Each wore a brace of pistols at his right, stuck down through his sash, and a cutlass at his left, and carried besides a heavy black cane.

"Thou'rt my guest for beer, Captain Scurry," growled one.

"Nay, Captain Slye," growled the other, "for thou'rt mine."

With that, still standing, they both commenced to bang their sticks upon a table for service. "Beer!" one cried, and "Beer!" cried the other, and they glowered, scowled, and grumbled when their cries brought no response. So fearsome was their aspect, and fierce their manner, Ebenezer decided they were pirate captains, but he had not the courage to flee the room.

"*Beer!*" they called again, and again smote the table with their sticks to no avail. Ebenezer buried himself in his notebook, spread out before him on the table, and prayed they'd take no notice of his presence.

" 'Tis my suspicion, Captain Slye," one of them said, "that we must serve ourselves or seek our man with dry throats."

"Then let us draw our beer and have done with't, Captain Scurry," replied the other. "The rascal can't be far away. I shall draw two steins, and haply he'll come in ere we've drunk 'em off."

"Haply, haply," the first allowed. "But 'tis *I* shall draw the steins, for thou'rt my guest."

"The devil on't!" cried the second. " 'Twas I spake first, and thou'rt *my* guest, God damn ye!"

"I'll see thee first in Hell," said Number One. "The treat is mine."

"Mine!" said Number Two, more threateningly.

"Thine in a pig's arse!"

"I shall draw thy beer, Captain Slye," said Number Two, fetching out a pistol, "or draw thy blood."

"And I thine," said Number One, doing likewise, "else thou'rt a banquet for the worms."

"Gentlemen, gentlemen!" Ebenezer cried. "In Heav'n's name hold thy fire!"

Instantly he regretted his words. The two men turned to glare at him, still pointing pistols at each other, and their expressions grew menacing.

" 'Tis none of my affair," he said hastily, for they began moving toward him. "Not the least of my affair, I grant that. What I meant to say was, 'twould be an honor and a pleasure to me to buy for both of you, and draw as well, if you'll but show me how. Nay, no matter, I'll wager I can do't right off, with no instruction, for many's the time in Locket's I've seen it done. Aye," he went on, backing away from them, "there's naught of skill or secret to't but this, to edge the glass against the tap if the keg be wild and let the beer slide gently in; or be't flat, allow the stream some space to fall ere't fill the glass, that striking harder 'twill foam the more——"

"Cease!" commanded Number One, and fetched the table such a clap of the cane that Ebenezer's notebook jumped. "I'God, Captain Slye, did e'er ye hear such claptrap?"

"Nor such impertinence, Captain Scurry," answered the other, "that not content to meddle in our business, the knave would have't all his own."

"Nay, gentlemen, you mistake me!" Ebenezer cried.

"Prithee close thy mouth and sit," said Captain Scurry, pointing with his stick to the poet's chair. Then to his companion he declared, "Ye must excuse me while I put a ball 'twixt this ninny's eyes."

" 'Twill be my pleasure," the other replied, "and then we'll drink in peace." Both pistols now were aimed at Ebenezer.

185

"No guest of mine shall stoop to such trifles," said the first. Ebenezer, standing behind his chair, looked again to the door through which Burlingame and the serving maid had passed.

"My sentiments exactly," growled Captain Slye, "but pray recall who's host, or 'tis *two* pistols I shall fire."

" 'Fore God, good Captains!" Ebenezer croaked, but legs and sphincters both betrayed him; unable to say on, he sank with wondrous odor to his knees and buried his face in the seat of his chair. At that instant the rear door opened.

"Stay, here's the barmaid!" cried Captain Scurry. "Fetch me two beers, lass, while I jettison this stinkard!"

"Beers be damned!" roared Captain Slye, who had a view of the entrance door. "Yonder goes our Laureate, I swear, along the street!"

"I'faith let's at him, then," said the other, "ere he once more slips his mooring!"

Turning their backs on beer and poet alike they hurried out to the street, from which came shortly the sound of pistols and a retreating clamor of curses. But Ebenezer heard them not, for at mention of their quarry he swooned upon the tavern flags.

9

Further Sea-Poetry, Composed in the Stables of the King o' the Seas

WHEN HE REGAINED his senses Ebenezer found himself in the stables of the King o' the Seas, lying in the hay; his friend Burlingame, dressed in Scotch cloth, squatted at his hip and fanned his face with the double-entry ledger.

"I was obliged to fetch you outside," said Henry with a smile, "else you'd have driven away the clients."

"A pox upon the clients!" the poet said weakly. " 'Twas a pair of their clients brought me to this pass!"

"Are you your own man now, or shall I fan thee farther?"

"No farther, prithee, at least from where you stand, or I'll succumb entirely." He moved to sit up, made a sour face, and lay back with a sigh.

"The fault is mine, Eben; had I known aught of your urgency I'd not have lingered such a time in yonder privy. How is't you did not use this hay instead? 'Tis no mean second."

"I cannot make light of't," Ebenezer declared. "The while you sported with the wench, two pirate captains had like to put a ball betwixt my eyes, for no more cause than that I ventured to settle their quarrel!"

"Pirate captains!"

"Aye, I'm certain of't," Ebenezer insisted. "I've read enough in Esquemeling to know a pirate when I see one: ferocious fellows as like as twins; they were dressed all in black, with black beards and walking sticks."

"Why did you not declare your name and office?" Burlingame asked. " 'Tis not likely they'd dare molest you then."

Ebenezer shook his head. "I thank Heav'n I did not, for else my life had ended on the spot. 'Twas the Laureate they sought, Henry, to kill and murther him!"

"Nay! But why?"

"The Lord alone knows why; yet I owe my life solely to some poor wight, that walking past the window they took for me and gave him chase. Pray God they missed him and are gone for good!"

"Belike they are," Burlingame said. *"Pirates,* you say! Well, 'tis not impossible, after all—— But say, thou'rt all beshit."

Ebenezer groaned. "Ignominy! How waddle to the wharf in this condition, to fetch clean breeches?"

"Marry, I said naught o' waddling, sir," said Burlingame, in the tones of a country servant. "Only fetch off thy drawers and breeches now, that me little Dolly maught clean 'em out, and I shall bring ye fresh 'uns."

"Dolly?"

"Aye, Joan Freckles yonder in the King o' the Seas."

Ebenezer blushed. "And yet she is a woman, for all her harlotry, and I the Laureate of Maryland! I cannot have her hear of't."

"Hear of't!" Burlingame laughed. "You've near suffocated her already! Who was it found you on the floor, d'ye think, and helped me fetch you hither? Off with 'em now, Master Laureate, and spare me thy modesty. 'Twas a woman wiped thy bum at birth and another shall in dotage: what matter if

187

one do't between?" And Ebenezer having undone his buttons with reluctance, his friend made bold to give a mighty jerk, and the poet stood exposed.

"La now," chuckled Burlingame. "Thou'rt fairly made, if somewhat fouled."

"I die of shame and cannot even cover myself for filth," the poet complained. "Do make haste, Henry, ere someone find me thus!"

"I shall, for be't man or maid you'd not stay virgin long, I swear, thou'rt that fetching." He laughed again at Ebenezer's misery and gathered up the soiled garments. "*Adieu,* now: thy servant will return anon, if the pirates do not get him. Make shift to clean yourself in the meantime."

"But prithee, how?"

Burlingame shrugged. "Only look about, good sir. *A clever man is never lost for long.*" And off he went across the yard, calling for Dolly to come get his prize.

Ebenezer at once looked about him for some means to remedy his unhappy condition. Straw he rejected at once, though there was enough and to spare of it in the stable: it could not even be clenched in the hand with comfort. Next he considered his fine holland handkerchief and remembered that it was in his breeches pocket.

" 'Tis as well," he judged on second thought, "for it hath a murtherous row of great French buttons."

Nor could he sacrifice his coat, shirt, or stockings, for he lacked on the one hand clothes enough to throw away, and on the other courage enough to give the barmaid further laundry. "A clever man is never lost for long," he repeated to himself, and regarding next the tail of a great bay gelding in a stall behind him, rejected it on the grounds that its altitude and position rendered it at once inaccessible and dangerous. "What doth this teach us," he reflected with pursed lips, "if not that one man's wit is poor indeed? Fools and wild beasts live by mother wit and learn from experience; the wise man learns from the wits and lives of others. Marry, is't for naught that I spent two years at Cambridge, and three times two with Henry in my father's summerhouse? If native wit can't save me, then education shall!"

Accordingly he searched his education for succor, beginning with his memory of history. "Why should men prize the records of the past," he asked, "save as lessons for the present?" Yet though he was no stranger to Herodotus, Thucydides, Polybius, Suetonius, Sallust, and other chroniclers ancient and modern, he could recall in them no precedent for his present plight, and thus no counsel, and had at length to give over the attempt. " 'Tis clear," he concluded, "that History teacheth not a man, but mankind; her muse's pupil is the body politic or its leaders. Nay, more," he reasoned further, shivering a bit in the breeze off the harbor, "the eyes of Clio are like the eyes of snakes, that can see naught but motion: she marks the rise and fall of nations, but of things immutable—eternal verities and timeless problems—she rightly takes no notice, for fear of poaching on Philosophy's preserve."

Next, therefore, he summoned to mind as much as ever he could of Aristotle, Epicurus, Zeno, Augustine, Thomas Aquinas, and the rest, not forgetting his Platonical professors and their one-time friend Descartes; but though they'd no end of interest in whether his plight was real or fancied, and whether it merited concern *sub specie aeternitatis,* and whether his future action with regard to it was already determined or entirely in his hands, yet none advanced specific counsel. "Can it be they all shat syllogisms, that have nor stench nor stain," he wondered, "and naught besides? Or is't that no fear travels past their Reason, to ruin their breeches withal?" The truth of the matter was, he decided, peering across the court in vain for Henry, that philosophy dealt with generalities, categories, and abstractions alone, like More's *eternal spissitude,* and spoke of personal problems only insofar as they illustrated general ones; in any case, to the best of his recollection it held no answer for such homely, practical predicaments as his own.

He did not even consider physics, astronomy, and the other areas of natural philosophy, for the same reason; nor did he crack his memory on the plastic arts, for he knew full well no Phidias or Michelangelo would deign to immortalize a state like his, whatever their attraction for human misery. No, he resolved at last, it was to literature he must turn for help, and should have sooner, for literature alone of all the arts and sciences took as her province the entire range of man's experience and behavior—from cradle to grave and beyond, from emperor to hedge-whore, from the burning of cities to the breaking of wind—and human problems of every magnitude: in literature alone might one find catalogued with equal care the ancestors of Noah, the ships of the Achaians——

"And the bum-swipes of Gargantua!" he exclaimed aloud. "How is't I did not think of them till now?" He reviewed with joy that chapter out of Rabelais wherein the young Gargantua tries his hand, as it were, at sundry swabs and wipers

189

—not in desperation, to be sure, but in a spirit of pure empiricism, to discover the noblest for good and all—and awards the prize at last to the neck of a live white goose; but hens and guineas though there were a-plenty in the yard around the stable, not a goose could Ebenezer spy. "Nor were't fit," he decided a moment later, somewhat crestfallen, "save in a comic or satiric book, to use a silly fowl so hardly, that anon must perish to please our bellies. Good Rabelais surely meant it as a jest." In like manner, though with steadily mounting consternation, he considered what other parallels to his circumstances he could remember from what literature he had read, and rejected each in turn as inapplicable or irrelevant. Literature too, he concluded with heavy heart, availed him not, for though it afforded one a certain sophistication about life and a release from one's single mortal destiny, it did not, except accidentally, afford solutions to practical problems. And after literature, what else remained?

He recalled John McEvoy's accusation that he knew nothing of the entire great real world and the actual people in it. What, in fact, he asked himself, would others do in his place, who *did* know the great real world? But of such knowledgeable folk he knew but two at all well—Burlingame and McEvoy—and it was unthinkable of either that they would ever be in his place. Yet knowledge of the world, he quite understood, went further than personal acquaintance: how fared the savage hordes and heathen peoples of the earth, who never saw a proper bum-swab? The Arabs of the desert, who had no forest leaves nor any paper? Surely they contrived a measure of cleanliness in some wise, else each perforce would live a hermit and the race die out in a single generation. But of all the customs and exotic practices of which he'd heard from Burlingame or read in his youthful books of voyages and travel, only one could he remember that was to the point: the peasant folk of India, Burlingame had once observed to him, ate with their right hands only, inasmuch as the left was customarily used for personal cleanliness.

" 'Tis no solution, but a mere postponement of my difficulties," the poet sighed. "What hope hath he for other aid, whom wit and the world have both betrayed?"

He started, and despite the discomfort of his position, glowed with pleasure when he recognized the couplet. "Whate'er my straits, I still am virgin and poet! *What hope hath he* . . . Would Heav'n I'd ink and quill, to pen him ere he cools!" He resolved in any case to dog-ear a leaf in his notebook as a reminder to set down the couplet later; it was not until the volume was spread open in his hands, and he was leafing through its empty pages, that he saw in it what none of his previous efforts had led him to.

"A propitious omen, b'm'faith!" said he, not a little awed. He regretted having torn out in the London posthouse those sheets in the ledger on which Ben Bragg had kept his accounts, not only because his years with Peter Paggen had soured his taste for the world of *debit* and *credit*, but also because he remembered how scarce was paper in the provinces, and so was loath to waste a single sheet. Indeed, so very reluctant was he, for a moment he seriously considered tearing out instead what few pages he'd already rhymed on: his *Hymn to Chastity*, the little quatrain recalled to him by Burlingame, and his preliminary salute to the ship *Poseidon*. Only the utter impropriety, the virtual sacrilege of the deed, restrained his hand and led him at length to use two fresh and virgin sheets—and then two more—for the work, which, completed with no small labor, owing to the drying effect of the breeze, he turned into an allegory thus: the unused sheets were songs unborn, which yet had power, as it were *in utero*, to cleanse and ennoble him who would in time deliver them —in short, the story of his career to date. Or they were token of his double essence, called forth too late to prevent his shame but able still to cleanse the leavings of his fear. Or again—but his pleasant allegorizing was broken off by the appearance, from the rear of the King o' the Seas, of befreckled Dolly, bringing his drawers and breeches out to dry. Despite his embarrassment he craned his head around the stable entrance and inquired after Burlingame, who had by this time been absent for nearly an hour; but the woman professed to know nothing of his whereabouts.

"Yet 'twas but across the street he went!" Ebenezer protested.

"I know naught of't," Dolly said stubbornly, and turned to go.

"Wait!" the poet called.

"Well?"

He blushed. " 'Tis something chill out here—might you fetch me a blanket from upstairs, or other covering, against my man's return?"

Dolly shook her head. " 'Tis not a service of the house, sir, save to them as stop the night. Your man paid me a shilling for the breeches, but naught was said of blankets."

"Plague take thee!" Ebenezer cried, in his wrath almost forgetting to conceal himself. "Was Midas e'er so greedy as a woman? You'll get thy filthy shilling anon, when my man appears!"

"No penny, no paternoster," the girl said pertly. "I have no warrant he'll appear."

"Thy master shall hear of this impertinence!"

She shrugged, Burlingame-like.

"A toddy, then, i'God, or coffee, ere I take ill! 'Sheart, girl, I am——" He checked himself, remembering the pirate captains. " 'Tis a gentleman that asks you, not a common sailor!"

"Were't King William himself he'd have not a sip on credit at the King o' the Seas."

Ebenezer gave over the attempt. "If I must catch my death in this foul stable," he sighed, "might you at least provide me ink and quill, or is that too no service of the house?"

"Ink and quill are free for all to use," Dolly allowed, and shortly brought them to the stable door.

"Ye must use your own book to scribble in," she declared. "Paper's too dear to throw away."

"And I threatened you with your master! Marry, thou'rt his fortune!"

Alone again, he set on the dog-eared page of his ledger book that aphoristic couplet which had so aided him, and would have tried his hand at further verses, but the discomfort of his situation made creation impossible. The passage of time alarmed him: the sun passed the meridian and began its fall toward the west; soon, surely, it would be time to board the shallop which was to ferry them to the *Poseidon,* and still there was no sign of Burlingame. The wind changed direction, blew more directly off the harbor and into the stable, and chilled the poet through. At length he was obliged to seek shelter in an empty stall nearby, where enough fresh hay was piled to cover his legs and hips when he sat in it. Indeed, after his initial distaste he found himself warm and comfortable enough, if still a trifle apprehensive—as much for Burlingame's welfare as for his own, for he readily imagined his friend's having fallen afoul of the pirate captains. Resolving to cheer himself with happier thoughts (and at the same time fight against the drowsiness that his relative comfort induced at once) he turned again to that page in his notebook which bore the *Poseidon* quatrain. And for all he'd never yet laid eyes upon that vessel, after some deliberation he joined to the first quatrain a second, which called her frankly

A noble Ship, from Deck to Peaks,
Akin to those that Homers *Greeks*

> *Sail'd east to* Troy *in Days of Yore,*
> *As we sail'd now to* MARYLANDS *Shore.*

From here it was small labor to extend the tribute to captain and crew as well, though in truth he'd met no seafaring men in his life save Burlingame and the fearsome pirate captains. Giving himself wholly to the muse, and rejecting quatrains for stanzas of a length befitting the epic, he wrote on:

> *Our Captain, like a briny God,*
> *Beside the Helm did pace and plod,*
> *And shouted Orders at the Sky,*
> *Where doughty Seamen, Mast-top high,*
> *Unfurl'd and furl'd our mighty Sails,*
> *To catch the Winds but miss the Gales.*
> *O noble, salty Tritons* Race,
> *Who brave the wild* Atlantics *Face*
> *And reckless best both Wind and Tide:*
> *God bless thee, Lads, fair* Albions *Pride!*

In a kind of reverie he saw himself actually aboard the *Poseidon*, dry-breeched and warm, his gear safely stowed below. The sky was brilliant. A fresh wind from the east raised whitecaps in the sparkling ocean, threatened to lift his hat and the hats of the cordial gentlemen with whom he stood in converse on the poop, and fanned from red to yellow the coals of good tobacco in their pipes. With what grace did the crewmen race aloft to make sail! To what a chorus did the anchor rise dripping from the bottom of the sea and the mighty ship make way! The gentlemen held their hats, peered down at the wave of foam beneath the sprit and up at the sea birds circling off the yards, squinted their eyes against sun and spray, and laughed in awe at the scrambling sailors. Anon a steward from below politely made a sign, and all the gay company retired to dinner in the Captain's quarters. Ebenezer sat at that worthy's right, and no wit was sharper than his, nor any hunger. But what a feast was laid before them! Dipping his quill again, he wrote:

> *Ye ask, What eat our merry Band*
> *En Route to lovely* MARYLAND?
> *I answer: Ne'er were such Delights*
> *As met our Sea-sharp'd Appetites*
> *E'er serv'd to* Jove *and* Junos *Breed*
> *By* Vulcan *and by* Ganymede.

There was more to be said, but no sweeter was the dream than its articulation, and so thorough his fatigue, he scarce could muster gumption to subscribe the usual *E.C., G^{ent}, P^t & L^t of M^d* before his eyes completely closed, his head nodded forward, and he knew no more.

It seemed but a moment that he slept; yet when roused by the noise of a groom leading a horse into the stable, he observed with alarm that the sun was well along in the western sky: the square of light from the doorway stretched almost to where he sat in the straw. He leaped up, remembered his semi-nudity, and snatched a double handful of straw to cover himself.

"The jakes is there across the yard, sir," the boy said, not visibly surprised, "though I grant 'tis little sweeter than this stable."

"Nay, you mistake me, lad—— But no matter. See you those drawers and breeches on yonder line? 'Twill be a great service to me if you will feel of them, whether they be dry, and if so, fetch them hither with all haste, for I must catch a ferry to the Downs."

The young man did as instructed, and soon Ebenezer was able to leave the stable behind him at last and run with all possible speed to the wharf, searching as he ran for Burlingame or the two pirate captains into whose clutches he feared his friend had fallen. When he reached the wharf, breathless, he found to his dismay that the shallop was already gone and his trunk with it, though Burlingame's remained behind on the pier exactly where it had been placed that morning. His heart sank.

An old mariner sat nearby on a coil of rope belonging to the shallop, smoking a long clay pipe.

"I say, sir, when did the shallop sail?"

"Not half an hour past," the old man said, not troubling to turn his eyes. "Ye can spy her yet."

"Was there a short fellow among the passengers, that wore"—he was ready to describe Burlingame's port-purple coat, but remembered in time his friend's disguise—"that called himself Bertrand Burton, a servant of mine?"

"None that I saw. No servants at all, that I saw."

"But why did you leave this trunk ashore and freight its neighbor?" Ebenezer demanded. "They were to go together to the *Poseidon*."

" 'Twas none o' my doing," said the mariner with a shrug. "Mr. Cooke took his with him when he sailed; the other man sails tonight on a different ship."

"Mr. Cooke!" cried Ebenezer. He was about to protest that he himself was Ebenezer Cooke, Laureate of Maryland, but thought better of it: in the first place, the pirates might still be searching for him—the old mariner, for all he knew, might be in their employ; *Cooke*, moreover, was a surname by no means rare, and the whole thing could well be no more than a temporary confusion.

"Yet, surely," he ended by saying, "the man was not *Ebenezer* Cooke, Laureate of Maryland?"

But the old man nodded. " 'Twas that same gentleman, the poetical wight."

"I'faith!"

"He wore black breeches like your own," the sailor volunteered, "and a purple coat—none o' the cleanest, for all his lofty post."

"Burlingame!" the poet gasped.

"Nay, *Cooke* it was. A sort of poet, crossing on the *Poseidon*."

Ebenezer could not fathom it.

"Then prithee," he asked, with some difficulty and no little apprehension, "who might that second gentleman be, the owner of this trunk here, that sails tonight on a different vessel?"

The old man sucked his pipe. "He'd not the dress of a gentleman," he declared at length, "nor yet a gentleman's face, but rather a brined and weathered look, like any sailor. The others call him *Captain*, and he them likewise."

Ebenezer paled. "Not Captain Slye?" he asked fearfully.

"Aye, now you mention it," the old man said, "there was a Captain Slye among their number."

"And Scurry too?"

"Aye, Slye and Scurry they were, as like as twins. They and the third came seeking the poetical gentleman not five full minutes after he'd sailed, as you've come seeking them. But they went no farther than the nearest house for rum, where 'tis likely you'll find 'em yet."

In spite of himself Ebenezer cried "Heav'n forfend!" and glanced with terror across the street.

The old man shrugged again and spat into the harbor. "Haply there's company more proper than sailors ashore," he allowed, "but more merry— Out on't!" he interrupted himself. "You've but to read the name from off his baggage there, where he wrote it not ten minutes past. I've not the gift of letters myself, else I had thought of't ere now."

Ebenezer examined his friend's trunk at once and found on one handle a bit of lettered pasteboard: *C^apt J^no Coode*.

"Nay!" His legs betrayed him; he was obliged to sit on the trunk or disgrace anew his fresh-dried drawers. "Tell me not 'twas Black John Coode!"

"Black or white, John or Jim, 'twas Coode," the other affirmed: "Captain Slye, Captain Scurry, and Captain Coode. They're yonder in the King o' the Seas."

Suddenly Ebenezer understood all, though his understanding little calmed his fear: Burlingame, after learning from Ebenezer in the stable about the pirates and their quarry, had spied them and perhaps Coode as well in the neighborhood of the tavern and realized that a plot was afoot against his charge—who as Laureate to Lord Baltimore was after all a potent, even a potentially deadly enemy to their seditious schemes, for the exposure of which few better tools existed than the knife-edged Hudibrastic. What nobler course, then, or more in the spirit of faithful guardianship, than to change to his original clothes again, declare himself the Laureate (since, clearly, they knew not their victim's face), and throw them off the scent by apparently embarking, trunk and all, for the *Poseidon?* It was a stratagem worthy of both the courage and the resourcefulness of his friend: an adventure equal to his escape from the pirate Thomas Pound or his interception of the letters from Benjamin Ricaud! Moreover, it had been accomplished at the risk of his own possessions, which Coode seemed now to have appropriated. The poet's heart warmed: the solicitude, the brave self-abnegation of his friend brought moisture to his eyes.

"And to think," thought he, "I was the while misdoubting him from the safety of my horse stall!"

Very well, he resolved: he would show himself worthy of such high regard. "How is't you gave this Coode leave to claim my trunk?" he demanded of the old seafarer, who had returned to his pipe and meditations.

"*Thy* trunk, sir?"

"*My* trunk! Are you blind as well as unlettered, that you failed to see the Laureate and me this morning when we had our trunks put down from the London carriage?"

"Marry, I know naught of't," the old man declared. " 'Tis my Joseph sails the shallop, my son Joseph, and I but mind the berth till he returns."

"And leave your client's trunks to any rogue that claims them? A proper ferryman you are, and your Joseph, b'm'faith! This wretch John Coode deigns not even to counterfeit, but with your aid robs openly in broad daylight, and by's own name! I'll have the sheriff!"

"Nay, prithee, sir!" the other cried. "My boy knew naught of't, I swear, nor did I think to aid a robber! The merry captains strode up bold as brass, sir, and asked for the poetical gentleman, and said 'This chest is Captain Coode's and must be on the *Morpheides*, by sundown, for the Isle of Man.' "

"And stopped thy questions with a guinea, I doubt not?"

"Two bob," the sailor answered humbly. "How might I know the baggage wasn't his?"

" 'Tis compounding the felony in any case," Ebenezer declared. "Is't worth two bob to breathe your last in prison?"

By dint of this and similar threats Ebenezer soon persuaded the old sailor of his error. "Yet how may I know 'tis thine, sir," he nevertheless inquired, "now you've raised the question? Haply 'tis *thou'rt* the thief, and not Captain Coode, and who shall save me then from jail?"

"The trunk is mine in trust alone," the poet replied, "to see it safely to my master."

"Thou'rt a servingman, and chide me so?" The sailor set his whiskered jaw. "Who might your master be, that dresses his man like any St. Paul's fop?"

Ebenezer ignored the slur. "He is that same poetical gentleman who took the first trunk with him—Ebenezer Cooke, the Laureate of Maryland. And 'twill go hard for you and your loutish Joseph should he speak of this nonsense in the right places."

"I'God, then take the accursed box for all of me!" the poor man cried, and promised to send trunk and servant together to the *Poseidon* as soon as the shallop returned. "Yet prithee show me just one proof or token of your post," he begged, "to ease my heart: for how shall I fare at the hands of the three captains, if thou'rt the thief and they the owners?"

"Never fear," Ebenezer said. "I shall show you proof enough in two minutes: page upon page of the Laureate's writing." He had just remembered, with a mixture of concern and relief, that his notebook was yet in the horse stall. But the old man shook his head. "Were't branded on your arse in crimson letters or graven like the Tables of the Law I'd not make *hog* nor *dog* of't."

"Try my patience no more, old man!" the poet warned. "The veriest numskull knows a poem by the look of't, whether he grasp the sense or no. I'll show you verses fit for the ears of the gods, and there's an end to your caviling!" Charging the mariner as sternly as he could to safeguard Burlingame's trunk and to ready the shallop, should it return, for instant sailing, he made his way in a great arc across the street, giving a wide berth to the entrance of the King o' the Seas, traversed again the alleyway leading to the back yard of the ordinary, and with pounding heart re-entered the familiar stable, expecting at any moment to meet the horrendous trio of captains. He hastened to the stall in which he'd composed his nautical verses: there in the straw, where in embarrassment and haste he'd left it, was the precious ledger. He snatched it up. Had that stableboy, perhaps, defaced it, or filched a sheaf of pages? No, it was intact, and in good order.

"And reckless best both Wind and Tide," he quoted from the page, and sighed with pleasure at his own artistry. "It hath the very sound of toss and tempest!"

But there was no time then for such delights; the shallop might be mooring at that very moment, and the villains in the tavern would not drink rum forever. With all possible speed he scanned the remaining stanza of the morning—those seven or eight couplets describing the shipboard feast. He sighed again, tucked the book under his arm, and hurried out of the stable into the courtyard.

"Stay, Master Poet, or thou'rt dead," said a voice behind him, and he whirled about to face a brace of black-garbed fiends from Hell, each with his left hand leaning on an ebon cane and his right aiming a pistol at the poet's chest.

"Doubly dead," the other added.

Ebenezer could not speak.

"Shall I send a ball through his Romish heart, Captain Scurry, and spare ye the powder?"

"Nay, thankee, Captain Slye," replied the other. " 'Twas Captain Coode's desire to see whate'er queer fish might strike the bait, ere we have his gullet. But the pleasure's thine when that hour comes."

"Your servant, Captain Scurry," said Captain Slye. "Inside with ye, Cooke, or my ball's in thy belly."

But Ebenezer could not move. At length, belting their pistols as unnecessary, his fearsome escorts took each an elbow and propelled him, half a-swoon, to the rear door of the ordinary.

"For God's sake spare me!" he croaked, his eyes shut fast.

" 'Tis not that gentleman can do't," said one of his captors. "The man we're fetching ye to is the man to dicker with."

They entered into a kind of pantry or storage room, and one of his captors—the one called Slye—went ahead to open

198

another door, which led into the steamy kitchen of the King o' the Seas.

"Ahoy, John Coode!" he bellowed. "We've caught ye your poet!"

Ebenezer then was given such a push from behind that he slipped on the greasy tiles and fell asprawl beside a round table in the center of the room, directly at the feet of the man who sat there. Everyone laughed: Captain Scurry, who had pushed him; Captain Slye, who stood nearby; some woman whom, since her feet dangled just before his eyes, Ebenezer judged to be sitting in Coode's lap; and Coode himself. Tremblingly the poet looked up and saw that the woman was the fickle Dolly, who sat with her arms about the arch-fiend's neck.

Then, as fearfully as though expecting Lucifer himself, he turned his eyes to John Coode. What he saw was, if rather less horrendous, not a whit less astonishing: the smiling face of Henry Burlingame.

10

The Laureate Suffers Literary Criticism and Boards the Poseidon

"HENRY!"

His friend's smile vanished. He pushed the barmaid off his lap, sprang scowling to his feet, and pulled Ebenezer up by his shirtfront.

"You blockhead!" he said angrily, before the poet could say more. "Who gave ye leave to sneak about the stables? I told ye to scour the docks for that fool poet!"

Ebenezer was too surprised to speak.

"This is my man Henry Cook," Burlingame said to the black captains. "Can ye not tell a poet from a common servant?"

"Your man?" cried Captain Scurry. "T'faith, 'tis the same

199

shitten puppy was annoying us this morning—is't not, Captain Slye?"

"Aye and it is," said Captain Slye. "What's more, he was scribbling in that very book there, that ye claim is the poet's."

Burlingame turned on Ebenezer again, raising his hand. "I've a mind to box thy lazy ears! Idling in a tavern when I ordered ye to the docks! Small wonder the Laureate escaped us! How came ye by the notebook?" he demanded, and when Ebenezer (though he began to comprehend that his friend was protecting him) was unable to think of a reply, added, "I suppose ye found it among our man's baggage on the wharf and marked it a find worth drinking to?"

"Aye," Ebenezer managed to say. "That is—aye."

"Ah God, what a lout!" Burlingame declared to the others. "Every minute at the bottle, and he holds his rum no better than an altar-boy. I suppose ye took ill of't, then"—he sneered at Ebenezer—"and puked out your belly in the stable?"

The poet nodded and, daring finally to trust his voice, he asserted, "I woke but an hour past and ran to the wharf, but the Laureate's trunk was gone. Then I remembered I'd left the notebook in the stable and came to fetch it."

Burlingame threw up his hands to the captains as in despair. "And to you this wretch hath the look of Maryland's Laureate? I am surrounded by fools! Fetch us two drams and something to eat, Dolly," he ordered, "and all of you begone save my precious addlepate here. I've words for him."

Captain Slye and Captain Scurry exited crestfallen, and Dolly, who had attended the whole scene indifferently, went out to pour the drinks. Ebenezer fairly collapsed into a chair and clutched at Burlingame's coat sleeve.

"Dear God!" he whispered. "What is this all about? Why is't you pose as Coode, and why leave me shivering all day in the stable?"

"Softly," Henry warned, looking over his shoulder. " 'Tis a ticklish spot we're in, albeit a useful one. Have faith in me: I shall lay it open plainly when I can."

The barmaid returned with two glasses of rum and a plate of cold veal. "Send Slye and Scurry to the wharf," he directed her, "and tell them I'll be on the *Morpheides* by sundown."

"Can you trust her?" Ebenezer asked when she had gone. "Surely she knows thou'rt not John Coode, after this morning."

Burlingame smiled. "She knows her part. Fall to, now, and I'll tell you yours."

Ebenezer did as advised—he'd had no food all day—and was somewhat calmed by the rum, which, however, made him shudder. Burlingame peered through a crack in the door leading into the main hall of the King o' the Seas, and apparently satisfied that none could overhear, explained his position thus:

"Directly I left you this morning I went straightway to the dock to fetch fresh breeches, pondering all the while what you had told me of the two pirate captains. 'Twas my surmise they were no pirates, the more for that 'twas you they sought —what use would a pirate have for a poet? Yet, from your picture of them, their manner and their quest, I had another thought, no less alarming, which I soon saw to be the truth. Your two black scoundrels were there on the very dock where stood our chests, and I knew them at once for Slye and Scurry, two smugglers that have worked for Coode before. 'Twas clear Coode knew of your appointment and meant you no good, though what his motives were I could but guess; 'twas clear as well your hunters did not know their quarry's face and could be lightly gulled. They were speaking with the lad that sails the shallop; I made bold to crouch behind our trunks and heard the ferryman say that you and your companion were in the King o' the Seas—happily I'd given him no name. Slye said 'twas impossible, inasmuch as but a short time since they'd been in the King o' the Seas, and had run out on seeing their victim in the street but had lost him."

"Aye, just so," Ebenezer said. " 'Tis the last thing I recall. But whom they spied I cannot guess."

"Nor could I. Yet the ferryman held to his story, and at length Slye proposed another search of the tavern. But Scurry protested 'twas time to fetch John Coode from off the fleet."

"Coode aboard the fleet!"

"Aye," Burlingame declared. "This and other things they said gave me to believe that Coode hath sailed disguised from London on the very man-o'-war with the Governor and his company, who joined the fleet this morning. No doubt he fears for his cause, and wished to see first-hand what favor his enemies have with Nicholson. Then, I gathered, Slye and Scurry were to meet him in the Downs and fetch him to their own ship, which sails tonight for the Isle of Man and thence to Maryland."

"I'God, the boldness of the man!" exclaimed the poet.

Burlingame smiled. "You think he's bold? 'Tis no long voyage from London to Plymouth."

"But under Nicholson's very nose! In the company of the very men he'd driven from the Province!"

"Yet as I crouched this while behind our baggage," Burlingame said, "an even bolder notion struck me—— But first I must tell you one other thing I heard. Scurry asked Slye, How would they know their leader in disguise, when they'd seen not even his natural face? And Slye proposed they use a kind of password employed by Coode's men before the revolution, to discover whether a third party was one of their number. Now it happened I knew two passwords very well from the old days when I'd feigned to be a rebel: In one the first man asks his confederate, 'How doth your friend Jim sit his mare these days?' By which is meant, How sure is King James's tenure on the throne? The second then replied, 'I fear me he'll be thrown; he wants a better mare.' And the third man, if he be privy to the game, will say, 'Haply 'tis the mare wants a better rider.' The other was for use when a man wished to make himself known to a party of strangers as a rebel: he would approach them on the street or in a tavern and say 'Have you seen my friend, that wears an orange cravat?' That is to say, the speaker is a friend of the House of Orange. One of the party then cries, 'Marry, will you mark the man!' which is a pun on Queen Mary and King William.

"On hearing their plans," Burlingame went on, "I resolved at once to thwart 'em: my first thought was for you and me to pose as Slye and Scurry, fetch Coode from off the man-o'-war, and in some wise detain him till we learned his plans and why he wanted you."

" 'Swounds! 'Twould never have succeeded!"

"That may be," Burlingame admitted. "In any case, though I'd learned that Slye and Scurry did not know Coode, it did not follow *they* were strangers to *him*—indeed, they are a famous pair of rascals. For that reason I decided to be John Coode again, as once before on Peregrine Browne's ship. I stepped around the trunks and enquired after my friend with the orange cravat."

Ebenezer expressed his astonishment and asked whether, considering that Burlingame wore the dress of a servant and that Coode was supposed to be aboard the man-o'-war, the move were not for all its daring ill-advised. His friend replied that Coode was known to be given to unusual dress—priest's robes, minister's frocks, and various military uniforms, for example—and that it was in fact quite characteristic of him to appear as if from nowhere among his cohorts and disappear similarly, with such unexpectedness that not a few of the more credulous believed him to have occult powers.

"At least they believed me," he said, "once they had composed themselves again, and I gave 'em small chance to question. I feigned displeasure at their tardiness, and fell into a great rage when they said the Laureate had slipped their halter. By the most discreet interrogation (for 'twas necessary to act as if I knew more than they) I was able to piece together an odd tale, which still I cannot fully fathom: Slye and Scurry had come from London with some wight who claimed to be Ebenezer Cooke; on orders from Coode they'd posed as Maryland planters and escorted the false Laureate to Plymouth, where I fancy they meant to put him on the *Morpheides* for some sinister purpose—belike they thought him a spy of Baltimore's. But whoe'er the fellow was he must have smelled the plot, for he slipped their clutches sometime this morning.

"Now, think not I'd forgotten you," he went on; "I feared you'd find some other clothes and show yourself at any moment. Therefore I led Slye and Scurry to a tavern up the street for rum and detained them as long as possible, trying to hatch a plan for sending you a message. Every few minutes I looked down towards the wharf, pretending to seek a servant of mine, and when at last I saw your trunk was gone I guessed you'd gone alone to the *Poseidon*. Anon, when we walked this way again, the old man at the wharf confirmed that Eben Cooke had sailed off in the shallop with his trunk."

Ebenezer shook his head in wonder. "But——"

"Stay, till I finish. We came here then to pass time till evening; I was quite sure of your safety, and planned simply to send a message to you by the shallop-man, so you'd not think I'd betrayed you or fallen into peril. When Dolly told me your notebook was in the stable I swore to Slye and Scurry we'd catch you yet, inasmuch as a poet will go to Hell for his notebook, and stationed them to watch the stall for your return—in fact I planned to send the book along to you anon with my message in it, and used the stratagem merely to rid myself for a time of those twin apes. Imagine my alarm when they fetched you in!"

Ebenezer remembered, with some discomfort, the scene his entrance had interrupted.

" 'Tis too fantastic for words," he declared. "You thought 'twas I had gone, and I 'twas you—I say, the fellow was wearing your coat!"

"What? Impossible!"

"Nay, I'm certain of't. The old man at the dock described it: a soiled port-purple coat and black breeches. 'Twas for that I guessed it to be you."

"Dear God! 'Tis marvelous!" He laughed aloud. "What a comedy!"

Ebenezer confessed his ignorance of the joke.

"Only think on't!" his friend exclaimed. "When Slye and Scurry came looking for their Laureate this morning and made sport of you, not knowing you were he, Dolly and I had gone back yonder in the stable to play: in the first stall we ran to we found some poor wight sleeping, a servingman by the look of him, and 'twas he I traded clothes with on the spot. Right pleased he was to make the trade, too!"

" 'Sheart, you mean it was the false Laureate?"

"Who else, if the man you heard of wore my coat? Belike he'd just fled Slye and Scurry and was hiding from them."

"Then 'twas he they saw go past the window after, which saved my life!"

"No doubt it was; and learning of your trunk he must have made off with't. A daring fellow!"

"He'll not get far," Ebenezer said grimly. "I'll have him off the ship the instant we're aboard."

Burlingame pursed his lips, but said nothing.

"What's wrong, Henry?"

"You plan to sail on the *Poseidon*?" Burlingame asked.

"Of course! What's to prevent our slipping off right now, while Slye and Scurry wait us on their ship?"

"You forget my duty."

Ebenezer raised his eyebrows. "Is't I or you that have forgot?"

"Look here, dear Eben," Burlingame said warmly. "I know not who this impostor is, but I'll warrant he's merely some pitiful London coxcomb out to profit by your fame. Let him be Eben Cooke on the *Poseidon*: haply the Captain will see the imposture and clap him in irons, or maybe Coode will murther or corrupt him, since they're in the same fleet. Even if he carry the fraud to Maryland we can meet him at the wharf with the sheriff, and there's an end to't. Meanwhile your trunk is safely stowed in the ship's hold—he cannot touch it."

"Then 'fore God, Henry, what is't you propose?"

"I know not what John Coode hath up his sleeve," said Burlingame, "nor doth Lord Baltimore nor any man else. 'Tis certain he's alarmed at Nicholson's appointment and fears for his own foul cause; methinks he plans to land before the fleet, but whether to cover all traces of his former mischief or to sow the seeds for more I cannot guess, nor what exactly he plans for you. I mean to carry on my role as Coode and sail to Maryland on the *Morpheides,* with my trusted servant Henry Cook."

"Ah no, Henry! 'Tis absurd!"

Burlingame shrugged and filled his pipe. "We'd steal a march on Coode," he said, "and haply scotch his plot to boot."

He went on to explain that Captains Slye and Scurry were engaged in smuggling tobacco duty-free into England by means of the re-export device; that is, they registered their cargo and paid duty on it at an English port of entry, then reclaimed the duty by re-exporting the tobacco to the nearby Isle of Man—technically a foreign territory—whence it could be run with ease into either England or Ireland. "We could work their ruin as well, by deposing against them the minute we land. What a victory for Lord Baltimore!"

Ebenezer shook his head in awe.

"Well, come now!" his friend cried after a moment. "Surely thou'rt not afraid? Thou'rt not so distraught about this idle impostor?"

"To speak truly, I *am* distraught on his account, Henry. 'Tis not that he improves his state at my expense—had he robbed me, I'd be nothing much alarmed. But he hath robbed me of myself; he hath poached upon my very being! I cannot permit it."

"Oh la," scoffed Burlingame. "Thou'rt talking schoolish rot. What is this coin, thy *self,* and how hath he possessed it?"

Ebenezer reminded his friend of their first coloquy in the carriage from London, wherein he had laid open the nature of his double essence as virgin and poet—that essence the realization of which, after his rendezvous with Joan Toast, had brought him into focus, if not actually into being, and the preservation and assertion of which was therefore his cardinal value.

"Ne'er again shall I flee from myself, or in anywise disguise it," he concluded. " 'Twas just such cowardice caused my shame this morning, and like an omen 'twas only my return to this true self that brought me through. I was cleansed by songs unborn and passed those anxious hours with the muse."

Burlingame confessed his inability to grasp the metaphor, and so the poet explained in simple language that he had used four blank pages of his notebook to clean himself with and had filled another two with sea-poetry.

"I swore then never to betray myself again, Henry: 'twas only my surprise allowed this last deception. Should Slye and Scurry come upon us now, I'd straightway declare my true identity."

"And straightway take a bullet in thy silly head? Thou'rt a fool!"

"I am a poet," Ebenezer replied, mustering his failing courage. "Let him who dares deny it! Besides which, even were there no impostor to confront, 'twould yet be necessary to cross on the *Poseidon:* all my verses name that vessel." He opened his notebook to the morning's work. "Hear this, now:

> *Let* Ocean *roar damn'dest Gale:*
> *Our Planks shan't leak; our Masts shan't fail.*
> *With great* Poseidon *at our Side*
> *He seemeth neither wild nor wide.*

Morpheides would spoil the meter, to say nothing of the conceit."

"The conceit is spoiled already," Burlingame said sourly. "The third line puts you overboard, and the last may be read as well to *Poseidon* as to *Ocean.* As for the meter, there's naught to keep you from preserving the name *Poseidon* though you're sailing on the *Morpheides.*"

"Nay, 'twere not the same," Ebenezer insisted, a little hurt by his friend's hostility. " 'Tis the true and only *Poseidon* I describe:

> *A noble Ship, from Deck to Peaks,*
> *Akin to those that* Homers *Greeks*
> *Sail'd east to* Troy *in Days of Yore,*
> *As we sail'd now to* MARYLANDS *Shore.*"

"Thou'rt sailing west," Burlingame observed, even more sourly. "And the *Poseidon* is a rat's nest."

"Still greater cause for me to board her," the poet declared in an injured tone, "else I might describe her wrongly."

"Fogh! 'Tis a late concern for fact you plead, is't not? Methinks 'twere childsplay for you to make *Poseidon* from the *Morpheides,* if you can make him from a livery stable."

Ebenezer closed his notebook and rose to his feet. "I know not why thou'rt set on injuring me," he said sadly. " 'Tis your

206

prerogative to flout Lord Baltimore's directive, but will you scorn our friendship too, to have your way? 'Tis not as if I'd asked you to go with me—though Heav'n knows I need your guidance! But Coode or no Coode, I will have it out with this impostor and sail to Maryland on the *Poseidon:* if you will pursue your reckless plot at any cost, *adieu,* and pray God we shall meet again at Malden."

Burlingame at this appeared to relent somewhat: though he would not abandon his scheme to sail with Slye and Scurry, he apologized for his acerbity and, finding Ebenezer equally resolved to board the *Poseidon,* he bade him warm, if reluctant, farewell and swore he had no mind to flout his orders from Lord Baltimore.

"Whate'er I do, I do with you in mind," he declared. " 'Tis Coode's plot against you I must thwart. Think not I'll e'er forsake you, Eben: one way or another I'll be your guide and savior."

"Till Malden, then?" Ebenezer asked with great tears in his eyes.

"Till Malden," Burlingame affirmed, and after a final handshake the poet passed through the pantry and out the rear door of the King o' the Seas, in great haste lest the fleet depart without him.

Luckily he found the shallop at its pier, making ready for another trip. Not until he noticed Burlingame's chest among the other freight aboard did he remember that he had posed as a manservant to the Laureate, and repellent as was the idea of maintaining the deception, he realized with a sigh that it would be folly now to reveal his true identity, for the ensuing debate could well cause him to miss the boat.

"Hi, there!" he called, for the old man was slipping off the mooring-lines. "Wait for me!"

"Aha, 'tis the poet's young dandy, is it?" said the man Joseph, who stood in the stern. "We had near left ye high and dry."

Breathing hard from his final sprint along the dock, Ebenezer boarded the shallop. "Stay," he ordered. "Make fast your lines a moment."

"Nonsense!" laughed the sailor. "We're late as't is!"

But Ebenezer declared, to the great disgust of father and son alike, that he had made an error before, which he now sincerely regretted: in his eagerness to serve his master he had mistaken Captain Coode's trunk for the one committed to his charge. He would be happy to pay ferry-freight on it anyway, since they had been at the labor of loading it aboard; but the trunk must be returned to the pier before Captain Coode learned of the matter.

" 'Tis an indulgent master will suffer such a fool to serve him," Joseph observed; but nevertheless, with appropriate grunts and curses the transfer was effected, and upon receipt of an extra shilling apiece by way of gratuity, the ferrymen cast off their lines once more—the old man going along as well this trip, for the wind had risen somewhat since early afternoon. The son, Joseph, pushed off from the bow with a pole, ran up the jib to luff in the breeze, close-hauled and sheeted home the mainsail, and went forward again to belay the jib sheet; his father put the tiller down hard, the sails filled, and the shallop gained way in the direction of the Downs, heeling gently on a larboard tack. The poet's heart shivered with excitement; the salt wind brought the blood to his brow and made his stomach flutter. After some minutes of sailing he was able to see the fleet against the lowering sun: half a hundred barks, snows, ketches, brigs, and full-rigged ships all anchored in a loose cluster around the man-o'-war that would escort them through pirate-waters to the Virginia Capes, whence they would proceed to their separate destinations. On closer view the vessels could be seen bristling with activity: lighters and ferries of every description shuttled from ship to shore and ship to ship with last-minute passengers and cargo; sailors toiled in the rigging bending sails to the spars; officers shouted a-low and aloft.

"Which is the *Poseidon?*" he asked joyously.

"Yonder, off to starboard." The old man pointed with his pipestem to a ship anchored some quarter of a mile away on their right, to windward; the next tack would bring them to her. A ship of perhaps two hundred tons, broad of bow and square of stern, fo'c'sle and poop high over the main deck, fore, main, and mizzen with yards and topmasts all, the *Poseidon* was not greatly different in appearance from the other vessels of her class in the fleet: indeed, if anything she was less prepossessing. To the seasoned eye her frayed halyards, ill-tarred shrouds, rusty chain plates, "Irish pennants," and general slovenliness bespoke old age and careless usage. But to Ebenezer she far outshone her neighbors. "Majestic!" he exclaimed, and scarce could wait to board her. When at last they completed the tack and made fast alongside, he scrambled readily up the ladder—a feat that would as a rule have been beyond him—and saluted the deck officer with a cheery good day.

"May I enquire your name, sir?" asked that worthy.

"Indeed," the poet replied, bowing slightly. "I am Ebenezer Cooke, Poet and Laureate of the Province of Maryland. My passage is already hired."

The officer beckoned to a pair of husky sailors standing nearby, and Ebenezer found both his arms held fast.

"What doth this mean?" he cried. Everyone on the *Poseidon*'s deck turned to watch the scene.

"Let us test whether he can swim as grandly as he lies," the officer said. "Throw the wretch o'er the side, boys."

"Desist!" the poet commanded. "I shall have the Captain flog the lot of you! I am Ebenezer Cooke, I said; by order of Lord Baltimore Poet and Laureate of Maryland!"

"I see," said the officer, smiling uncordially. "And hath His Laureateship anyone to vouch for his identity? Surely the gentlemen and ladies among the passengers must know their Laureate!"

"Of course I can bring proof," said Ebenezer, "though it seems to me 'tis you should bear the burden! I have a friend ashore who——" He stopped, recalling Burlingame's disguise.

"Who will swear to't through his teeth, for all you've bribed him," declared the officer.

"He lies," said the young man Joseph from the shallop, who had climbed aboard behind Ebenezer. "He told me he was a servant of the Laureate's, and now I doubt e'en that. What servant would pretend to be his master, when his master's near at hand?"

"Nay, you mistake me!" Ebenezer protested. "The man who calls himself Ebenezer Cooke is an impostor, I swear't! Fetch the knave out, that I may look him in the eye and curse him for a fraud!"

"He is in his cabin writing verse," the officer replied, "and shan't be bothered." To the sailors he said, "Throw him o'er the side and be damned to him."

"Stay! Stay!" Ebenezer shrieked. He wished with all his heart he were at the King o' the Seas with Burlingame. "I can prove the man's deceiving you! I have a commission from Lord Baltimore himself!"

"Then prithee show it," the officer invited with a smile, "and I shall throw the other wight o'er the side instead."

"Dear God!" the poet groaned, the facts dawning on him. "I have mislaid it! Belike 'tis in my chest somewhere, below."

"Belike it is, since the chest is Mr. Cooke's. In any case 'tis not mislaid, for I have seen it—the Laureate produced it on request by way of voucher. Toss the lout over!"

But Ebenezer, realizing his predicament, fell to his knees on the deck and embraced the officer's legs. "Nay, I pray you, do not drown me! I own I sought to fool you, good masters, but 'twas only a simple prank, a mere April Foolery. I am the Laureate's servant, e'en as this gentleman affirmed, and have the Laureate's notebook here to prove it. Take me to my master, I pray you, and I shall beg his pardon. 'Twas but a simple prank, I swear!"

"What say ye, sir?" asked one of the sailors.

"He may speak truly," the officer allowed, consulting a paper in his hand. "Mr. Cooke hired passage for a servant, but brought none with him from the harbor."

"Methinks he's but a rascally adventurer," said Joseph.

"Nay, I swear't!" cried the poet, remembering that Burlingame had hired berths that morning for Ebenezer and himself in the guise of the servant Bertrand. "I am Bertrand Burton of St. Giles in the Fields, masters—Mr. Cooke's man, and his father's!"

The officer considered the matter for a moment. "Very well, send him below instead, till his master acknowledges him."

For all his misery Ebenezer was relieved: it was his plan to stay aboard at any cost, for once under way, he reasoned, he could press his case until they were persuaded of his true identity and the mysterious stranger's imposture.

"Ah God, I thank thee, sir!"

The sailors led him toward the fo'c'sle.

"Not at all," the officer said with a bow. "In an hour we shall be at sea, and if your master doth not own you, 'twill be a long swim home."

11

Departure from Albion: the Laureate at Sea

THUS IT HAPPENED that not long afterwards, when anchors were weighed and catted, buntlines cast off, sails unfurled, and sheets, halyards, and braces belayed, and the *Poseidon* was sea-borne on a broad reach past The Lizard, Ebenezer was not on hand to witness the spectacle with the gentlemen of the quarter-deck, but lay disconsolate in a fo'c'sle hammock—alone, for the crew was busy above. The officer's last words were frightening enough, to be sure, but he no longer really wished he were back in the King o' the Seas. There was a chance, of course, that the impostor could not be intimidated, but surely as a last resort he'd let the genuine Laureate pose as his servant rather than condemn him to drown; and Ebenezer saw nothing but certain death in Burlingame's scheme. All things considered, then, he believed his course of action was really rather prudent, perhaps the best expedient imaginable under the circumstances; had he acquiesced to it at Burlingame's advice, and were his friend at hand to lend him moral support in the forthcoming interview, he might still have been fearful but he'd not have been disconsolate. The thing that dizzied him, brought sweat to his palms, and shortened his breath was that he alone had elected to board the *Poseidon*, to pose as Bertrand Burton, to declare to the officer his real identity, and finally to repudiate the declaration and risk his life to reach Malden. He heard the rattling of the anchor chain, the scamper of feet on the deck above his head, the shouted commands of the mate, the chanteys of the crew on the lines; he felt the ship heel slightly to larboard and gain steerage-way, and he was disconsolate—very nearly ill again, as in his room that final night in London.

Presently an aged sailor climbed halfway down the companionway into the fo'c'sle—a toothless, hairless, flinty-eyed salt with sunken cheeks, colorless lips, yellow-leather skin, and a great sore along the side of his nose.

"Look alive, laddie!" he chirped from the ladder. "The Captain wants ye on the poop."

Ebenezer sprang readily from the hammock, his notebook still clutched in his hand, and failing to allow for the incline of the deck, crashed heavily against a nearby bulkhead.

"Whoa! 'Sheart!" he muttered.

"Hee hee! Step lively, son!"

"What doth the Captain wish of me?" the poet asked, steadying himself at the foot of the ladder. "Can it be he realizes who I am, and what indignities I suffer?"

"Belike he'll have ye keelhauled," the old man cackled, and fetched Ebenezer a wicked pinch upon his cheek, so sharp it made the tears come. "We've barnacles enough to take the hide off a dog shark. Come along with ye!"

There was nothing for it but to climb the ladder to the main deck and follow his comfortless guide aft to the poop. There stood the Captain, a florid, beardless, portly fellow, jowled and stern as any Calvinist, but with a pink of debauchery in both his eyes, and wet red lips that would have made Arminius frown.

Ebenezer, rubbing his injured cheek, observed a general whispering among the gentlemen on the quarter-deck as he passed, and hung his head. When he stepped up on the ladderway to the poop, the old sailor caught him by the coat and pulled him back.

"Hold, there! The poop deck's not for the likes of you!"

"Good enough, Ned," said the Captain, waving him off.

"What is't you wish, sir?" Ebenezer asked.

"Nothing." The Captain looked down at him with interest. " 'Tis Mr. Cooke, thy master, wants to see ye, not I. D'ye still say thou'rt his man?"

"Aye."

"Ye know what sometimes happens to stowaways?"

Ebenezer glanced at the sky darkening with evening to the east and storm clouds to the west, the whitecapped water and the fast-receding rocks of England. His heart chilled.

"Aye."

"Take him to my cabin," the Captain ordered Ned. "But mind ye knock ere ye enter: Mr. Cooke is busy rhymin verses."

Ebenezer was impressed: he would not himself have dared to request such a privilege. Whoever this impostor was, he had the manner of the rank he claimed!

The sailor led him by the sleeve to a companionway at the after end of the quarter-deck which opened to the captain's quarters under the poop. They descended a short ladder into what appeared to be a chartroom, and old Ned rapped on a door leading aft.

"What is it?" someone inside demanded. The voice was sharp, self-confident, and faintly annoyed: certainly not the voice of a man fearful of exposure. Ebenezer thought again of the dark sea outside and shivered: there was not a chance of reaching shore.

"Begging your pardon, Mr. Cooke," Ned pleaded, clearly intimidated himself. "I have the wretch here that says he is your servant, sir: the one that tried to tell us he was you, sir."

"Aha! Send him in and leave us alone," said the voice, as if relishing the prospect. All thought of victory fled the poet's mind: he resolved to ask no more than mercy from the man —and possibly a promise to return, when they reached Maryland, that commission from Lord Baltimore, which somehow or other the impostor had acquired. And maybe an apology, for it was, after all, a deuced humiliation he was suffering!

Ned opened the door and assisted Ebenezer through with another cruel pinch, this time on the buttock, and an evil laugh. The poet jumped involuntarily; again his eyes watered, and his knees went weak when Ned closed the door behind him. He found himself in a small but handsomely furnished cabin in the extreme rear of the vessel. The floor was carpeted; the Captain's bed, built into one wall, was comfortably clothed in clean linen. A large brass oil lamp, already lit, swung gently from the ceiling and illuminated a great oak table beneath. There was even a glass-fronted bookcase, and oil portraits in the style of Titian, Rubens, and Correggio were fastened with decorative brass bolts around the walls. The impostor, dressed in Burlingame's port-purple coat and sporting a campaigner wig, stood with his back to the poet at the far wall—actually the stern of the ship—staring through small leaded windowpanes at the *Poseidon*'s wake. Satisfied that Ned was gone, Ebenezer rushed around the table and fell to his knees at the other man's feet.

"Dear, dear sir!" he cried, not daring to look up. "Believe me, I've no mind at all to expose your disguise! No mind at all, sir! I know full well how you came by your clothing in the stable of the King o' the Seas and fooled the ferryman Joseph and his father at the wharf—though how in Heav'n you got my Lord Baltimore's commission, that he wrote for me in his own hand not a week past, I cannot fathom."

The impostor, above him, made a small sound and backed away.

"But no matter! Think not I'm wroth, or mean to take revenge! I ask no more than that you let me pose as your servant on this ship, nor shall I breathe a word of't to a soul, you may depend on't! What would it profit you to see me drown? And when we land in Maryland, why, I'll bring no charge against you, but call it quits and think no more of't. Nay, I'll get thee a place at Malden, my estate, or pay your fare to a neighboring province——"

Glancing up at this last to see what effect his plea was having, he stopped and said no more. The blood drained from his face.

"Nay!" He sprang to his feet and leaped at the impostor, who barely escaped to the other side of the round oak table. His campaigner, however, fell to the floor, and the light from the lamp fell full on Bertrand Burton—the real Bertrand, whom Ebenezer had last seen in his room in Pudding Lane when he left it to seek a notebook at the Sign of the Raven.

"I'God! I'God!" He could scarcely speak for rage.

"Prithee, Master Ebenezer, sir——" The voice was Bertrand's voice, formidable no more. Ebenezer lunged again, but the servant kept the table between them.

"You'd watch me drown! Let me crawl to you for mercy!"

"Prithee——"

"Wretch! Only let me lay hands on that craven neck, to wring it like a capon's! We'll see who drinks salt water!"

"Nay, prithee, master! I meant thee no ill, I swear't! I can explain all of it, every part! Dear God, I never dreamed 'twas *you* they'd caught, sir! Think ye I'd see ye suffer, that e'er was such a gentle master? I, that was your blessed father's trusty friend and adviser for years? Why, I'd take a flogging ere I'd let 'em lay a hand on ye, sir!"

"Flogging you shall have right soon, i'faith!" the poet said grimly, reversing his field in vain from clockwise to counterclockwise. "Nor shall that be the worst of't, when I catch you!"

"Do but let me say, sir——"

"Hi! I near had thee then!"

"—'twas through no fault of mine——"

"Ah! You knave, hold still!"

"—but bad rum and a treacherous woman——"

" *'Sheart!* But when I have thee——"

"—and who's really to blame, sir——"

"—I shall flog that purple coat from off thy back——"

"—is your sister Anna's beau!"

The chase ended. Ebenezer leaned across the table into the lamplight, brighter now for the gathering dark outside.

"What is't I heard you say?" he asked carefully.

"I only said, sir, what commenced this whole affair was the pound sterling your sister and her gentleman friend presented me with in the posthouse, when I had fetched your baggage there."

"I shall cut thy lying tongue from out thy head!"

" 'Tis true as Scripture, sir, I swear't!" Bertrand said, still moving warily as Ebenezer moved.

"You saw them there together? Impossible!"

"God smite me dead if I did not, sir: Miss Anna and some gentleman with a beard, that she called Henry."

"Dear Heav'n!" the poet muttered as if to himself. "But you called him her beau, Bertrand?"

"Well, now, no slur intended, sir; oh, no slur intended at all! I meant no more by't than that—ah, sir, you know full well how folks make hasty judgments, and far be't from me ——"

"Cease thy prating! What did you see, that made you call him her beau? No more than cordial conversation?"

" 'Sheart, rather more than that, sir! But think not I'm the sort——"

"I know well thou'rt a thief, a liar, and a cheat," Ebenezer snapped. "What is't you saw that set thy filthy mind to work? Eh?"

"I hardly dare tell, sir; thou'rt in such a rage! Who's to say ye'll not strike me dead, though from first to last I am innocent as a babe?"

"Enough," the poet sighed, "I know the signs of old. You'll drive me mad with your digressions and delays until I guarantee your safety. Very well, I shan't besmirch my hands on you, I promise. Speak plainly, now!"

"They were in each other's arms," the servant said, "and billing and cooing at a mad rate when I came up with your baggage. When Miss Anna had sight of me she blushed and tried to compose herself, yet all the while she and the gentleman spoke to me, they could not for the life of 'em stand still, but must be ever at *sweetmeat* and *honeybee*, and fondle and squeeze—— Are you ill, sir?"

Ebenezer had gone pale; he slumped into the Captain's chair and clutched his head in his hands. " 'Tis nothing."

"Well, as I said, sir, they could not keep their hands——"

"Finish thy story if you must," Ebenezer broke in, "but speak no more of those two, as you prize your wretched life! They paid you, did they?"

"They did in truth, sir, for fetching down your baggage."

"But a pound? 'Tis rather a princely reward for the task."

"Ah, now, sir, I am after all an old and trusted——" He stopped halfway through the sentence, so fierce was the look on Ebenezer's face. "Besides which," he concluded, "now I see how't strikes ye, 'tis likely they wished me to say naught of what I'd seen. I tell ye, sir, 'tis not for much I'd have missed your setting out! Had not Miss Anna and her gentleman insisted that I leave at once——"

215

"Spare me thy devotion," Ebenezer said. "What did you then, and why did you pose as me? Speak fast, ere I fetch the Captain."

" 'Tis a tragic tale, sir, that shames me in the telling. I beg ye keep in mind I'd never have presumed, sir, save that I was distracted and possessed by grief at your arrest and in direst peril of my life."

"My arrest!"

"Aye, sir, in the posthouse. 'Tis a mystery to me yet how thou'rt free, and how you came so rapidly from London."

Ebenezer smacked his hand upon the table. "Speak English, man! Straight English sentences a man can follow!"

"Very well, sir," Bertrand said. "I shall begin at the beginning, if ye'll bear with me." So saying, he took the liberty of sitting at the Captain's table, facing Ebenezer, and with a full complement of moralizing asides and other commentary, delivered himself during the next half hour of the following story:

" 'Twas a double grief I carried from the posthouse in my heart, sir, inasmuch as I had lost the gentlest, kindliest master that ever poor servingman served, and could not even claim the privilege of seeing him off to Plymouth in his coach, and wishing him a last Godspeed. Therefore I sought a double physic for't. With the pound Miss Anna and her—— What I mean to say, sir, I hied me to a winehouse near at hand and drank a deal of rackpunch, that the rogue of a barman had laced with such poisonous molasses rum I near went blind on the spot. Three glasses served to rob me of all judgment, yet such was my pain at losing you I drank off seven, and bought a quart of ratafia besides, for Betsy Birdsall. That is to say, not all the bottled spirits in London could restore my own, and so at length I fled for comfort back to Pudding Lane, to your rooms, sir. Yet well I knew they'd seem so vacant with ye gone, 'twould but increase tenfold my pain to sit alone, and for that cause I stopped belowstairs to summon Betsy Birdsall—ye recall the chambermaid, sir, that had the unnatural husband and the fetching laugh? We climbed the stairs together, and 'sheart! so far from vacant, your rooms were fit to burst with men, sir! A wight named Bragg there was, that looked nor manlier than my Betsy's husband, and a half-a-dozen sheriff's bullies with him; 'twas you they sought, sir, with some false tale of a ledger-book—I ne'er made rhyme nor sense of't!

"Directly they spied me a shout went up, and they were that bent on justice, I feared for Betsy's honor at their hands.

At length I told them, in answer to their queries, my master was at the posthouse, and off they ran to catch ye—— Nay, look not thus, sir! 'Tis not as ye think, I swear't! Not for a moment would I have breathed the truth, had I not known your coach was some time gone—rather would I have suffered death itself, or prison, at their hands! But well I knew 'twas a wild-goose chase they chased, and good riddance!

"We turned to't then, the wench and I, and with her her ratafia and me my rum we lacked no fire to warm the sheets withal, and were that tired when we had done, that though 'twas brightest day we slept some hours in sweat, *sack a sack.* Anon I knew, by certain signs, my mount was fresh and restless for the jumps; yet for a time I feigned to slumber on. (The truth of't is, though the girl and I are twins in will and skill, I've twice her years and half her strength, and more than once have cantered willy-nilly when I yearned to walk.) There were these signs, I say, that I'd have naught of, till Betsy made a moan and dived head foremost 'neath the covers. The cause wherefore I saw at once in opening my eyes, for 'twas not *her* hands were on me after all, but the hands of Mister 'Prentice-Clerk himself, the winehouse fiddler! Aye, I swear't, 'twas that same Ralph Birdsall, Betsy's husband, that erst was wont to leave his field unplowed, but since I seeded it had grown such a jealous farmer he looked to's plot five times a day. He had come home to run another furrow, like as not, and on advice from one below—the cook's boy Tim, that long himself had leched for Betsy—he stole upstairs to find us.

" 'Sblood, 'twas a murtherous moment, sir! I had like to smirch me for very fright, and waited only for knife or ball. Betsy likewise, albeit her head was buried like the ostrich's, showed great alarm: 'twas writ all over her hinder part. Yet Birdsall himself seemed no less racked: he shivered like a yawning cat and drew his breath unnaturally. Nor was't in wrath his hands lay on me, as I soon saw. Great tears coursed down his cheeks, the which were smooth as any girl's; he sniffed and bit his underlip, yet would not speak nor smite me down.

" 'Out on't!' I cried at last. 'Here I lie, and there lies thy wife, right roundly rogered: ye have caught us fair enough. Then make an end on't, sir, or get thee hence!' He then composed himself and said, that though 'twas in his rights to slay the twain of us, yet he had no taste for bloodshed and loved his wife besides. The horns were on his brow, he said, nor could his short-sword poll him. Moreover, he declared that in bedding Betsy I had bedded him, forasmuch as marriage made them one; and on this ground averred, that whate'er Betsy felt for me, he could but feel the same—in short, to the degree I was her lover, I was his as well, and this in the eyes of God Himself!

"Now all this Jesuitry I heard amazed, yet was right glad to remain unpunctured, and I made bold to put him in mind of that ancient and consoling verity, *None save the wittol knows he is no cuckold*. On hearing which, the wretch straightway embraced me, and de'il I had no taste for't, 'twas give him his head or lose my own. Betsy meanwhile, on hearing how the wind blew, soon calmed her shivering hams and, throwing off the covers, cried she had no mind to play Rub-a-dub-dub nor could she fathom how such a bedful of women had ever got her with child. At this Ralph Birdsall gave a mighty start and in a trembling tone enquired, was't he or I had got the child? Whereupon my Betsy cried, ' 'Twas he! 'Twas my sweet Bertrand!' Methought I was betrayed and cursed her for a liar; to Ralph I swore I'd ne'er laid hands on Betsy till a fortnight past, nor swived her till a good week after, whereas the child was three months in her belly if he was a day. 'He lies!' swore Betsy; 'I swear't!' swore I. 'Nay!' swore she. ' 'Tis full six months I've been his whore, that had no husband to wife me! A hundred times hath he climbed and sowed me, till I am full as a full-corned goose of him!' Ralph Birdsall then fetched out his sword, that, clerk or no, he boasted always at his hip. 'The truth!' he cried, and shook all over as with an ague. I still took Betsy for a traitor, and so declared, ' 'Fore God thy wife's a hellish liar, sir, but nonetheless she is no whore. May I fry in Hell if the child is any man's but yours.'

"Alas! What man can say he knows his fellow man? Who'd not have sworn, when at last I quite persuaded Birdsall, 'twould soften his wrath—the more for that 'twas not his horns that galled him? Yet when I'd said my piece and he *Amen'd* it, he drew himself up and scowled a fearsome scowl. '*Whore!*' he cried at Betsy, and with the flat of his sword he fetched her a swingeing clap athwart her seat. Nor stopped he there, but made to run me through, and 'twas only the nimblest of legs that saved my neck. I snatched up my breeches and dashed for the door, with the fiddler in hot career behind, nor durst I stop to cover my shame till I was half a square before him—*Better lose pride than hide*, sir, as they say. As for my tattling Betsy, the last I saw her she was springing hither and yon about the room, sir, hands on her buttocks and hollowing like a hero, nor have I seen her since. The truth of't was, as I guessed later, the babe in Betsy's belly was the fiddler's claim to manhood, so long as he thought himself the father; it took no more than discovering us *rem in rem* to quite undo him. 'Twas only to save me the wench gave out the truth, and 'sblood! I cut my throat to call her false, for albeit the cuckold lost my trail, he'd vowed to hound me to the earth's ends and poll that horn wherewith himself was horned!

"There was naught for it then but I must flee; yet I had but three pound in my breeches, nor dared return for clothes or savings. I summoned a boy who happened through the alley where I hid and sent him with the money for shirt, hose, and shoes; then for an hour I prowled the streets, debating what to do.

"By merest chance my way led to the posthouse, at sight of which I could not but weep to think of your straits, that were but little happier than my own. 'Twas here I hit upon my plan, sir, whereof the substance was, that though 'twas past my power to help ye, yet in your misery ye might ransom me. That is to say, ye'd bought your passage to Maryland and could not sail; who knew but what ye'd bought your seat to Plymouth as well? Think not I planned to cheat thee, sir! 'Twas but to Plymouth I meant to go, to save my life, and vowed to make ye restitution when I could. I did not doubt I could play the poet, though de'il the bit I know of verse, for I've a gift for mime, sir, if I may say so. Aye, many's the hour at St. Giles I've kept the folk in stitches by 'personating old Mrs. Twigg, with her crooked walk and her voice like an ironmonger's! And once in Pudding Lane, sir, I did Ralph Birdsall to such a turn, my Betsy wept a-laughing, nor could contain herself but let fly on the sheets for very mirth. The only rub was, should someone challenge me I'd naught wherewith to prove my case. For that reason, though I need not say how much I loathed to do't, I called for quill and paper in the posthouse, sir, and as best my memory would serve me I writ a copy of your commission, the which ye'd showed me ere ye left——"

At this point, Ebenezer, who had with the greatest difficulty contained his mounting astonishment and wrath as Bertrand's tale unfolded, cried out, "Devil take it, man, is there aught of infamy you'd stop at? Steal passage, take name and rank, and even forge commission! Let me see it!"

" 'Tis but a miserable approximation, sir," the servant said. "I've little wit in the matter of language and had no seal to seal it with." He drew a paper from his coat and proffered it reluctantly. " 'Twould fool no man, I'm certain."

" 'Tis not Lord Baltimore's hand," Ebenezer admitted, scanning the paper. "But i'faith!" he added on reading it. "The wording is the same, from first to last! And you say 'twas done from memory? Recite it for me, then!"

"Marry, sir, I cannot; 'twas some time past."

"The first line, then. Surely you recall the first line of't? No? Then thou'rt an arrant liar!" He flung the paper to the floor. "Where is my commission, that you copied this from?"

" 'Fore God, sir, I do not know."

"And yet you copied from it in the posthouse?"

"Ye force the truth from me, sir," Bertrand said, shamefaced. " 'Twas indeed from the original I copied, and not from memory; neither was it in the posthouse I did the deed, but in your room, sir, the day ye left. The commission was on your writing table, where ye'd forgot it: I found it there as I was packing your trunk, and so moved was I by the grandness of't I made a copy, thinking to show my Betsy what a master I'd lost. The original I put in your trunk and carried to the posthouse."

"Then why this sneak and subterfuge?" the poet demanded. "Why did you not admit it from the start? Thank Heav'n the thing's not lost!"

Bertrand made no reply, but scowled more miserably than ever.

"Well? Surely 'tis in my trunk this instant, is't not? Why did you lie?"

"I put the paper in your trunk, sir," Bertrand said, "on the very top of all, and fetched your baggage to the posthouse; nor thought I more of't till the hour I've told of, when, to save my life, I vowed to 'personate my way to Plymouth. Then I recalled my copy and luckily found it where it had been since the hour I forged it—folded in quarters in my pocket. To try myself I marched into the posthouse, and to the first wight I met I said, 'I'm Ebenezer Cooke, my man, Poet and Laureate of the Province of Maryland: please direct me to the Plymouth coach.' "

"The brass!"

Bertrand shrugged: the Burlingamelike gesture was the more startling performed as it was in Burlingame's port-purple coat. " 'Twas daring enough," he admitted. "The fellow only stared and mumbled something about the coach being gone. I feared he saw through my imposture, and the more when a stout fierce fellow in black came up behind and said,

'Thou'rt the poet Cooke, ye say? Thou'rt a knave and liar, for the poet Cooke they fetched to jail not two hours past.' "

"To jail!" Ebenezer cried. "What is this talk of jail, man, that ye return to here again?"

" 'Twas what I'd feared, sir: that wretch named Bragg, that would have the law on ye for some false matter of a ledger-book. 'Twas only inasmuch as I knew ye were past rescue, as I say, sir, that I presumed to use your passage——"

"Stay! Stay! One moment, now!" Ebenezer protested. "There is a marvelous discrepancy here!"

"A discrepancy, sir?"

"It wants no barrister to see it," the poet said. " 'Twas you set Bragg on my trail, was't not, when you found him in my room? And 'twas only that you knew I'd be long gone, you said. How is't then——"

"Prithee let me finish, sir," Bertrand pleaded, coloring noticeably. "Tales are like tarts, that may be ugly on the face of 'em and yet have a worthwhile end. This man, I say, declared ye were in jail—a fearsome fellow, he was, dressed all in black, with a great black beard, and pistols in his waist. And not far behind him was another, as like as any twin, which, when he joined the first, the man I'd queried took fright and ran. As would have I, but for access of fear."

"They sound like Slye and Scurry!"

"The very same, sir, they called each other: a pair of sharks as may I never meet again! Yet little I knew of 'em then but that they'd challenged me, and so I said straight out, the man who'd gone to jail was an impostor, and jailed for his imposture, and I was the real Ebenezer Cooke. To prove it I displayed my false commission, scarce daring to hope they'd be persuaded. Yet persuaded they were, and even humbled, as I thought; they whispered together for a while and then insisted I ride to Plymouth with them, inasmuch as the regular coach was gone. I took the boon right readily, fearing any minute to see Ralph Birdsall and his sword——"

"And fell into their hands," Ebenezer said with relish. "By Heav'n, 'tis no more than your desert!"

Bertrand shuddered. "Say not so, sir! Hi, what a pair of fiends! No sooner were we on the road than their intent came clear: they were lieutenants of one Colonel Coode of Maryland, that hath designs upon the government, and had been sent by him to waylay Eben Cooke—which quarry fearing bagged by other hunters, they were the more ready to believe me him. What designs they had on you, sir, I could not guess, but certain 'twas not to beg a verse of ye, for they held each

221

a pistol ready, and left no doubt I was their prisoner. 'Twas not till Plymouth I escaped; one of the twain went to see how fared their ship, and the other wandering some yards off to rouse the stableboy at the King o' the Seas, I leaped round a corner and burrowed into a pile of hay, where I hid till they gave o'er the search and went inside for rum."

"Take them no farther," Ebenezer said; "I know the rest of their history. 'Twas in the hay, then, that Burlingame found you?"

"Aye, sir. I heard the sound of people and trembled for my life, the more for that their footsteps came toward me. Anon I felt a great thrashing weight upon me, and thinking I was jumped by Slye or Scurry, I gave a great hollow and grappled as best I could to save my life. 'Twas the barmaid from the tavern I found opposing me—coats high, drawers low, and ripe for rogering—and Miss Anna's beau stood by, laughing mightily at the combat."

"Enough, enough! How is't you did not know each other, if as you say you'd seen him at the posthouse?"

"Not know him? I knew him at once, sir, and he me, and 'twere hard to tell which was the more amazed. Yet he asked me nothing of my business there, but straightway offered to change clothes with me—I daresay he feared my telling tales to his Miss Anna——"

"Enough!" Ebenezer ordered again.

"No harm intended, sir; no injury meant. In any case I was pleased to make the change, not alone in that I had the better of the bargain but also to escape from Slye and Scurry. Yet I went no farther than the door of the King o' the Seas ere they spied me from inside and gave chase; 'twas only by hiding behind some baggage on a pier that I eluded them. Then fancy my amazement, sir, when I saw 'twas your own trunk had saved me, that I'd packed myself not long before! I knew —alas!—ye were not there to claim it and so resolved to carry my poor deception one step farther; to board your ship, sir, with your own commission, and hide till I deemed it safe to go ashore. To that end, so soon as I was safe aboard I unlocked your trunk——"

"What say you?"

"Ye'd left one key with me in London, what time I packed ye. But I found the paper gone, sir."

"Gone! Great heavens, man, whither?"

"Lost, strayed, or stolen, sir," said Bertrand. " 'Twas on the very top I'd laid it, yet now 'twas nowhere in the trunk. I had to use my false commission instead, which happily convinced 'em for all it had no seal. I told the Captain to keep watch for my pursuers. The rest ye know."

Ebenezer paced the cabin wildly, his finger ends pressed against his temples.

"When word came to me that some stranger was aboard that called himself the Laureate, then swore he was the Laureate's man," Bertrand concluded, watching his master anxiously, "I durst not leave this room. If't was Slye or Scurry or Coode himself, I would be murthered on the spot. I had no choice but to stand here, sick at heart, and watch the ship get under way. The officer then said I must inspect ye, and so sure was I of death, I could not turn from the window till I heard your voice. How isn't thou'rt not in jail, sir?"

"Jail!" Ebenezer said with impatience. "I never was in jail!"

"Then who is't took your place? Slye vowed that when he and Scurry searched the posthouse for ye, they heard on every side of a man who'd been arrested not ten minutes before and carried off to jail. None knew what crime he'd done, but all knew his name was Eben Cooke, for the man had strode about declaring name and rank to the world."

"No doubt a second impostor," the poet replied, "bent on whoring my office to his purpose. May he rot in irons for ever and aye! As for you, since 'twas not among your plans to make a voyage, you'll sail no farther——"

"Ye'll have 'em fetch me ashore?" Bertrand went to his knees in gratitude. "Ah marry, what a place in Heav'n is thine, sir! What an injustice I did ye, to fear ye'd not have pity on my case!"

"On the contrary; 'tis perhaps the one injustice you did me not."

"Sir?"

Ebenezer turned away to the stern windows. " 'Twere well to say a prayer before you rise; I mean you'll swim for't."

"Nay! 'Twere the end o'me, sir!"

"As't were of me," Ebenezer said, "had you not owned——"

He stopped short: master and man measured each other for an instant, then sprang together for the false commission on the floor—which laying hold of at the same instant, they soon destroyed in their struggle.

"No matter," Ebenezer said. " 'Twill take but a minute with the twain of us for any fool to judge which is the poet and which the lying knave."

"Think better of't!" Bertrand warned. " 'Tis not my wish to harm ye, sir, but if it comes to that, there'll be no judgment;

223

I've but to send for the man that fetched ye here and swear I know ye not."

"What! You'll threaten me too, that have already set the law upon me, robbed me of name and passage, and well-nigh caused my death? A pretty fellow!"

For all his wrath, however, Ebenezer was not blind to the uncertainty of his position; he spoke no more of summoning an officer to judge between them nor did he further question Bertrand's tale, though several details of it failed to satisfy him. The valet had declared, for example, that only the certainty of his master's departure had allowed him with clear conscience to send Bragg's bullies to the posthouse; yet it was his certainty of Ebenezer's arrest that had allowed him, before entering the posthouse again, to conceive the notion of posing as Laureate. And how could the commission have disappeared, if master and servant owned the only keys to the trunk? And what had the wretch to gain by his lying tale of Anna and Henry together in the posthouse? Or if it were no lie—— But here his reeling fancy failed him.

"You merit no lenience," he said in a calmer tone, "but so far shall I let mercy temper justice, I'll speak no more of casting you astern. Haply 'twill be punishment enough to spend the balance of your years in Maryland, since you fear it so. For the rest, confess and apologize to the whole ship's company at once, and let future merit atone for past defect."

"Thou'rt a Solomon for judgment," Bertrand cried, "and a Christian saint for mercy!"

"Let us go, then, and have done."

"At once, at once, sir," the valet agreed, "if ye think it safe——"

"How should it be otherwise?"

" 'Tis plain, sir," Bertrand explained, "there's more to this post of yours than meets the eye. I know not what passed 'twixt you and Lord Baltimore, nor is't my business to enquire what secret cause ye've sworn to further——" Here Ebenezer let forth such a torrent of abuse that his valet had need to pause before continuing. "All in the world I mean, sir, is that your common garden laureate is not set upon by knaves and murtherers at every corner as I have been, nor is't a mere distaste for rhyme, methinks, that drives this villain Coode to seek ye out. For aught we know he may be on this ship; certain he's aboard the fleet, and Slye and Scurry as well——"

"Nay, not they," Ebenezer said, "but haply Coode." He described Burlingame's stratagem briefly. " 'Twas Henry bought

224

a passage in your name," he explained, "and left the scoundrel stranded with the fleet."

" 'Twill but inflame him more," said Bertrand, "and who knows what confederates might be with him? Belike he hath a spy on every boat!"

" 'Twere not impossible, from what I've heard of him," Ebenezer admitted. "But what's the aim of all this talk? Think you to persuade me into skulking caution and not to tell my office to the world? Is't to weasel out of penance and confession?"

Bertrand protested vigorously against such misconstruction of his motives. "Confess I shall," he declared, "right readily, and mark it light penance for my imposture—which pray recall I practiced for no vicious ends, but to save that part which makes man man. Yet penance ne'er healed wound, sir." He went on to praise the bounteous and forgiving nature of his master and to upbraid himself for repaying kindness with deceit—not forgetting to justify once more his imposture and to review, apropros of nothing, sundry evidences of the high esteem and confidence in which old Andrew held him. At length he concluded by maintaining that what he sought was not mere penance but restitution; some means wherewith to atone for what humiliation and discomfort his wholly innocent imposture had occasioned the noblest master poor servingman ever served.

"And what means is't you have in mind?" the poet asked warily.

"Only to risk my life for yours," the valet said. "Whate'er the cause you serve——"

"Enough, damn you! I serve the cause of Poetry, and no other."

"What I meant, sir, is that whate'er Lord Baltimore—— That is to say——"

" 'Sblood, then say it!"

"Since I have played ye to your hurt," said Bertrand, "let me play ye to your profit. Let me dare the rascal Coode in your name, sir. If he do me in, 'twill be my just desert and your salvation; if not, there's always time for clean confession when we land. What say ye?"

The plan so astonished Ebenezer that he could not at once find language strong enough to scourge the planner for his effrontery, and—alas!—the moment till he found his tongue discovered the scheme's unquestionable merits. The Laureateship was in truth a perilous post—of that he'd proof enough by now, though *why* he'd still small notion; John Coode was undeniably aboard the fleet and doubtless wroth at having been duped; Burlingame, despite his fanciful last assurances, was not on hand to protect him. Finally and most persuasively, the poet still shuddered at his morning's escape from Slye and Scurry at the King o' the Seas; only the appearance of Bertrand in the street had saved his life.

"If 'twill ease your conscience," he said at last, "I cannot say ye nay, at least for the nonce—'twill give me time to write some verse below. But Coode or no Coode, Bertrand, I swear you this: 'tis the last time I'll be any man whate'er save Eben Cooke. D'you hear?"

"Very good, sir," Bertrand nodded. "Shall I send word to the Captain?"

"Word? Ah, yes—that I'm thy Bertrand, a fop that makes pretense to glory. Aye, spread the word!"

12

The Laureate Discourses on Games of Chance and Debates the Relative Gentility of Valets and Poets Laureate. Bertrand Sets Forth the Anatomy of Sophistication and Demonstrates His Thesis

WHEN THE POSEIDON, running before a fresh breeze from the northeast, left Lizard Point behind and in company with the rest of the fleet set her course southwest to the Azores, life on shipboard settled into its wonted order. The passengers had little or nothing to do: aside from the three daily messes and, for those who had the ingredients with them, the intervening teas, the only other event of the normal day was the announcement of the estimated distance traveled during the past twenty-four hours. Among the gentlemen a good deal of money changed hands on this announcement, and since servants, when idle, can become every bit as bored as their masters, they too made bets whenever they could afford to.

The wagering, as a rule, was done at the second mess, since the runs were computed from noon to noon. Upon arising in the morning, every man sought out some member of the crew, to inquire about the progress of the night past; all morning the company watched the wind, and finally made their estimations. At midday the Captain himself mounted the poop, quadrant in hand, and on notice from the first mate that it was twelve o'clock sharp, made the traditional "noon sight" for longitude; retiring then to his quarters he computed latitude by dead reckoning from the compass course and the estimated distance run since the last measured elevation of the polestar before dawn—which crucial figure was itself reckoned from data in the ship's log concerning the direction and velocity of the wind, the height and direction of the seas, and the making, taking in, and setting of the sails, together with the Captain's own knowledge of the direction and velocity of ocean currents in the general area at that particular time of year, and of the ability of each of his officers to get the most out of the men on his watch and the ship itself. Since even under full sail the *Poseidon* rarely made more than six miles per hour and never more than eight—in other words, a fast walk—the daily run could be anything from zero, given a calm (or, given stormy headwinds, even a negative quantity), up to one hundred ninety-two miles—which theoretical maximum, however, she never managed to attain. Having computed latitude and longitude, the Captain was able to plot the *Poseidon*'s estimated position on his chart with parallel rule and dividers and, again allowing for winds, currents, the leeway characteristics of his vessel, and compass variation, he could give the helmsman a corrected course to steer until further notice. Finally he would enter the main cabin for his midday meal with the ladies and gentlemen among his passengers, who in the meantime had pooled their wagers and their estimates and, after announcing the official figure, he would bid the mate search out the closest approximation from among the folded bits of paper and identify the winner of the day.

The basic gamble was the pool—five to ten shillings a head, usually, for the gentlemen and ladies; a shilling or less for the servants—but the more ambitious speculators soon contrived a variety of side bets: a maximum or minimum figure, for example, could be adjusted for virtually any odds desired, or one could gamble on a maximum or minimum differential between each day's run and the next one. As the five days passed and boredom increased, the sport grew more

227

elaborate, the stakes higher: one really imaginative young minister named George Tubman, suspected by the other passengers of being a professional gambler in disguise, devised a sliding odds system for accepting daily bets on the date of raising Flores and Corvo—the westerly islands of the Azores—a system whereby the announcement of each day's run altered the standing odds against each projected date-of-landfall according to principles best known to the clever young man who computed them, and one could in the light of each day's progress make new wagers to reinforce or compensate for the heightened or diminished probability of one's previous wagers on the same event. This system had the advantages of cumulative interest and a tendency towards geometrically increasing stakes, for when a man saw his whole previous speculative investment imperiled by an unusually long or short day's run, he was naturally inclined to cover himself by betting, on what now seemed a more promising date, an amount equal to or exceeding the sum of his prior wagers; and since, of course, each day brought the *Poseidon* closer to a landfall and narrowed the range of speculation, the odds on the most likely dates lowered sharply, with the result that a man might invest five pounds at the going odds on a currently popular date in order to cover ten shillings previously wagered on a now unlikely one, only to find two or three days later that a third, much larger, bet was required to make good the second, or the first and second combined, and so forth. The excitement grew proportionately; even the Captain, though he shook his head at the ruinous size of the stakes, followed the betting with unconcealed interest, and the crew members themselves, who, of course, would not have been permitted to join in the game even if they could have afforded it, adopted favorites among the bettors, gave, or when possible sold, "confidential" information on the ship's progress to interested parties, made private little wagers of their own on which of the passengers would win the most money, and ultimately, in order to protect their own bets, volunteered or accepted bribes to convey false information to bettors other than the one on whom their money was riding.

For his part, Ebenezer wasted little interest at the outset on this activity, to which his attention had been called early in the first week of the voyage. One sparkling April morning Bertrand had approached him where he stood happily in the bow watching seagulls dive for fish, and had asked, in a respectful tone, his general opinion of gambling. In good spirits because of the weather and a commendable breakfast, and pleased to be thus consulted, Ebenezer had explored the subject cheerfully and at length.

"To ask a man what he thinks of gambling is as much as to ask him what he thinks of life," was one of the positions he experimented with. "Doth not the mackerel gamble, each time he rises, that yonder gulls won't snatch him up, and the gulls make wager that they will? Are we not gamblers all, that match wits with the ocean on this ship of wood? Nay, life itself is but a lifelong gamble, is't not? From the moment of conception our life is on the line; every meal, every step, every turning is a dare to death; all men are the fools of chance save the suicide, and even he must wager that there is no Hell to fry in. Who loves life, then, perforce loves gambling, for he is Dame Chance's conquest. Moreover, every gambler is an optimist, for no man wagers who thinks to lose."

Bertrand beamed. "Then ye favor games of chance?"

"Ah, ah," the Laureate cautioned. He cocked his head, waggled a forefinger, and quoted a proverb which unaccountably made him blush: *There are more ways to the woods than one.* It could as well be argued that the gambler is a pessimistic atheist, inasmuch as he counts man's will as naught. To wager is to allow the sovereignty of chance in all events, which is as much as to say, God hath no hand in things."

"Then ye don't look kindly on't after all?"

"Stay, not so fast: one could as readily say the contrary— that your Hobbesian materialist should never be a gambler, for no man gambles that doth not believe in luck, and to believe in luck is to deny blind chance and cold determinism, as well as the materialist order of things. Who says Yea to Luck, in short, had as well say Yea to God, and conversely."

"In Heav'n's name, then!" Bertrand cried, rather less respectfully than at first. "What *do* ye think of gambling—yea or nay?"

But Ebenezer would not be pressed. " 'Tis one of those questions that have many sides," he said blithely, and turned his attention again to the gulls. Contrary to his expectations, his position aboard the *Poseidon* was turning out to be by no means altogether unpleasant. He had contrived to establish himself as being not another common servant but a kind of amanuensis to the Laureate, in which capacity, he was permitted access to the quarter-deck at Bertrand's side and limited converse with the gentlemen; there was no need to conceal his education, since positions of the sort he pretended to were frequently filled by destitute scholars, and by making Bertrand out to be the lofty, taciturn variety of genius, he hoped to be able to speak for him more often than not and thus protect their disguise. Moreover, he could devote as much time as he chose to his notebook and even borrow books from the gentlemen passengers without arousing suspicion; an amanuensis was expected to busy himself with ink, paper, and books, especially when his employer was a poet laureate. In short, it became ever more clear to him as the voyage progressed that his role offered most of the privileges of his true identity and none of the dangers, and he counted the disguise among his happiest inspirations. While the servants relieved their ennui with gambling and gossip about their masters and mistresses, and the ladies and gentlemen with gambling and gossip about one another, Ebenezer passed the hours agreeably in the company of his own work or that of celebrated authors of the past, with whom, since his commission, he felt a strong spiritual kinship.

Indeed, the only thing he really found objectionable, once his initial embarrassment was forgotten and he had grown accustomed to his position, was mealtimes. For one thing, the food was not what he had imagined: the last entry in his notebook, made just before he fell asleep in the stable of the King o' the Seas, had been:

> *Ye ask, What eat our merry Band*
> *En Route to lovely* MARYLAND?
> *I answer: Ne'er were such Delights*
> *As met our Sea-sharp'd Appetites*
> *E'er serv'd to* Jove *and* Junos *Breed*
> *By* Vulcan *and by* Ganymede.

To which, during his very first day as Bertrand's amanuensis, he had appended:

> *The Finest from two Hemispheres,*
> *From roasted Beef to Quarter'd Deers;*
> *The Best of new and antick Worlds,*
> *Fine curry'd Lamb and basted Squirrels.*
> *We wash'd all down with liquid cheer—*
> Barbados *Rum and* English *Beer.*
> *'Twere vain to seek a nobler Feast*
> *In legend'd West or story'd East,*
> *Than this our plenteous Shipboard Store*
> *Provided by* LORD BALTIMORE.

This even though he had in fact seen nothing at either breakfast or dinner more exotic than eggs, fresh veal, and a few indifferently prepared vegetables. But three days sufficed to exhaust the *Poseidon*'s store of every perishable foodstuff; on the fourth appeared instead, to Ebenezer's unhappy surprise, the usual fare of sailors and sea-travelers: a weekly ration of seven pounds of bread or ship biscuit for master and man alike, with butter scarce enough to disguise its tastelessness; half a pound of salt pork and dried peas per man each mess for five days out of the week, and on the other two salt beef instead of pork—except when the weather was too foul for the cook to boil the kettle, in which case every soul aboard made do for the day with a pound of English cheese and dreams of home.

All this, however, was mere disillusionment, the fault not of Lord Baltimore, the captain of the *Poseidon*, or the social order, but merely of Ebenezer's own naïveté or, as he himself felt mildly, not troubling to put it into words, of the nature of Reality, which had failed to measure up to his expectations. In any case, though the food grew no more palatable, he soon became sufficiently inured to it not to feel disappointed between meals. A more considerable objection—which led him one afternoon to profess his discontent to Bertrand—was that he had to eat with the servants after the ladies and gentlemen were finished.

"Think not 'tis the mere ignominy of't," he assured his valet hastily, "though in truth they are an uncouth lot and are forever making sport of me. 'Tis *you* I fear for; that you'll be drawn into talk at the Captain's table and discover yourself for an ass. Thrice daily I wait for news of your disgrace, and despair of carrying the fraud to Maryland!"

"Ah, now, sir, have no fear." They were in the ship's waist, and Bertrand seemed less concerned with Ebenezer's complaint than with watching a young lady who stood with the Captain by the taffrail. "There's no great trick to this *gentleman* business, that I can see; any man could play the part that hath a ready wit and keeps his eyes and ears open."

"Indeed! I'd say so much for *my* disguise, perhaps; they are no fools *you* dine with, though, but men of means and breeding."

But so far from being chastened by this remark, the valet actually challenged it, still watching the maid more than his master while he talked.

"Marry, sir, none knows better than your servant the merits of wealth and birth," he declared benignly. "Yet, may I hang for't if any man was e'er more bright or virtuous for either." He went on to swear by all his experience with fine ladies and gentlemen, both as their servant and as their peer, that no poor scullery maid among Ebenezer's messmates was more a hussy than yonder maiden on the poop, for example, whom he identified as one Miss Lucy Robotham. "For all her fine clothes and fancy speech, sir, she blushed not a blush this noontime when the Captain pinched her 'neath the table, but smartly pinched him back! And not a half hour later, what time I took her hand to help her up the stairway, what did she do if not make a scratching in my palm? A *whore's a whore whate'er her station,*" he concluded, *"and a fool a fool whate'er his wealth."*

Ebenezer did not question the verity of this democratic notion, but he denied its relevance to the problem. " 'Tis not character and mother wit that make your gentleman, Bertrand," he said, adding the name in order to draw his eyes from Miss Robotham. " 'Tis manners and education. By a thousand signs the gentleman knows his peer—a turn of phrase, a choice of wine, a flourish of the quill—and by as many spies the fraud or parvenu. Be you never so practiced at aping 'em, 'tis but a matter of time till they find you out. A slip of the tongue, a slip of the fork: any trifle might betray you."

"Aye," laughed the other, "but for what, prithee?"

"Why, for not a gentleman 'to the manner born,' as't were!" Ebenezer was disturbed by the increasing arrogance of his servant, who had not wanted presumption to begin with. "How shall you answer them book for book, that have no books to your credit? How shall you hold forth on the new plays in London or the state of things on the Continent, that have not been through a university? Your true authentic gentleman is gallant but not a fop, witty but no buffoon, grave but not an owl, informed but not a pedant—in sum, he hath of every quality neither excess nor defect, but the very Golden Mean."

To which the valet rejoined with a wave and a smile, "Haply so, i'faith, haply so!" And might have said more had not Ebenezer, his interest in the matter fanned by his growing irritation, at once resumed his discourse.

"And just as the speech of the gentleman is to the speech of the crowd as is the lark's song to the rooster's but that of the poet like an angel's to the lark's; so the gentleman himself is a prince among men, and the poet should be a prince among gentlemen!"

"Haply so, sir, haply 'tis so," Bertrand said again, and turning now to his master added, "But would ye believe it? So wretched is this memory of mine, that though I wrote out your commission word for word in ink, and saw clear as gospel where it caused a gentleman to be a laureate poet, I cannot summon up the part that makes your laureate be a gentleman! And so miserable are these eyes and ears, they've tricked me into thinking all the poets they e'er laid hold of—such as Masters Oliver, Trent, and Merriweather back in London, to name no farther—that all these rhyming wights have not a Golden Mean between 'em, nor yet a Brass or Kitchencopper! 'Sblood, to speak plainly, they are sober as jackanapes, modest as peacocks, chaste as billy goats, softtongued as magpies, brave as churchmice, and mannerly as cats in heat! Your common, everyday valet, if I may say so, is like to be twice the gentleman your poet e'er could dream of! Nay, he's oft a nicer spirit than the gentleman his master, as all the world knows, and hath not his peer for how wigs should be powdered or guests placed at table. 'Tis he and not your poet, I should say, that is the gentleman's gentleman!"

Ebenezer was too taken aback by this outburst to do more than squint his eyes and cry "Stay!" But Bertrand would not be put off.

"Yet as for that," he went on, " 'tis little stead my gentleman's lore stands me, now I'm a laureate poet! Marry, the ladies and gentlemen I've met, so far from seeing their poet as a gentleman, look on him as a sort of saint, trick ape, court fool, and gypsy soothsayer rolled in one. Your ladies tell me things no Popish priest e'er heard of, fuss over me as o'er a lapdog, and make me signs a gigolo would blush at; they worship and contemn me by turns, as half a god and half a traveling clown. And the gentlemen, i'God! They think me mad or dullwitted out of hand; for who but your madman would turn his hand to verse, save one too numskulled to turn it to money? In short and in sum, sir, they'd call me no poet at all, or a poor one at best, if e'er I should utter e'en a *sensible* remark, to say nothing of a civil—— But think not I'm so fond as that!"

Ebenezer's features roiled, settling finally into a species of frown. Both men were given wholly to the argument now, which had perforce to be conducted in low tones; they faced seawards, their elbows on the rail and their backs to Miss Robotham, who had descended from the high poop to the quarter-deck on the opposite side of the vessel.

"I grant you this," he said, "that a prating coxcomb of a

233

poet may be guilty of boorishness, as a bad valet may be guilty of presumption, and both may be guilty of affectation. I grant you farther that the best poet is never in essence a gentleman——"

"Unlike your best valet," Bertrand put in.

"As for that," Ebenezer said sharply, "your valet that outshines his master in's knowledge of etiquette and fashion is like the rustic that can recite more Scripture than the theologian; his single gift betrays his limitations. The gentleman valet and the gentleman poet have this in common, that their gentlemanliness is for each a mask. But the mask of the valet masks a varlet, while the poet's masks a god!"

"Oh la, sir!"

"Let me finish!" Ebenezer's eyes were bright, his blond brows crooked and beetled. "Who more so than the poet needs every godlike gift? He hath the painter's eye, the musician's ear, the philosopher's mind, the barrister's persuasion; like a god he sees the secret souls of things, the essence 'neath their forms, their priviest connections. Godlike he knows the springs of good and evil: the seed of sainthood in the mind of a murtherer, the worm of lechery in the heart of a nun! Nay, farther: as the poet among gentlemen is as a pearl among polished stones, so must the Laureate be a diamond in the pearls, a prince among poets, their flower and exemplar—even a prince among princes! To him do kings commit their secular immortality, as they commit their souls' to God! Small mystery that the first verse was religious and the earliest poets pagan priests, as some declare, or that Plato calls the source of poetry a *divine* madness like that of seers and sibyls. If your true poet strays from the path of good demeanor, 'tis but the mark of his calling, an access of the muse; yet the laureate, though in truth he hath by necessity the greatest infusion of this madness, must exercise a godlike self-restraint, for he is to men the ambassador and emblem of his art: he is obliged not only to his muse, but to his fellow poets as well."

" 'Tis your wish, then," Bertrand asked finally, "that in all things I play the gentleman?"

"In every way."

"And take their actions as my model?"

"Nothing less."

"Why, then, I must beg some money of ye, sir," he declared with a laugh, and explained that the last ten shillings of his own small savings had that very noon been sacrificed in the distance-run pool, in which as a gentleman he was absolutely obliged to participate.

"Ah, 'twas for that you asked my thoughts on gambling some while past."

"I must confess it," Bertrand said, and reminded his master that as much could be said in favor of gambling as against it. "Besides which, sir, I must keep on with't now I've begun, as well to guard our masks as to make good my losses."

Now, Ebenezer himself had in reserve only what little he'd saved from his years with the merchant Peter Paggen, the whole of which did not exceed forty pounds; but at Bertrand's insistence that no smaller sum would do, he fetched out twenty from his trunk and, returning to the rail where his proxy waited, passed him the money surreptitiously with suitable admonitions and enjoinders.

At this point their conversation was interrupted by that same Miss Robotham earlier aspersed by Bertrand; at a thump on the shoulder they turned to find her standing close behind them, and Ebenezer paled at the thought of what perhaps she'd heard.

"Madam!" he said, whipping off his hat. "Your servant!"

" 'Tis your master I want," the girl said, and turned her back to him. She was a brown-haired, excellently breasted maid of twenty years or so, and though a certain grossness both of manner and complexion showed a rustic, or at least colonial, essence beneath the elegance of her dress, yet it seemed likely to Ebenezer that she was more innocent than concupiscent. In fact, for the first time since describing his plight to Henry in the Plymouth coach, he was reminded of Joan Toast, his delicate concern for whom had precipitated his departure from London: there was some similarity in eyes and skin and forthright manner.

Bertrand, who had made no move to duplicate his master's courtesy, leaned upon the railing and regarded the visitor with a look of crude appraisal. Not daunted in the least, she clasped her hands pertly, bounced a few times on her heels, and said, "I've a literary question for you, Mr. Cooke."

"Aha," said Bertrand, and chucked her under the chin. "What hath a tight young piece like you to do with literature, pray?"

Ebenezer, as alarmed by the request as by his man's vulgarity, made haste to offer his services instead, suggesting that the Laureate should not be bothered with trifling questions.

"Then what's the use of him?" the maid demanded, feigning a pout. Then she pursed her lips, arched her brows, and added merrily, still in Bertrand's direction, "Am I to suffer his lecherous stares for naught? He'll say what poet wrote *Out, out, strumpet Fortune,* and say't this instant, else my father shall know what poet tweaked me noontime where I blush to mention and left me a bruise to show for't!"

"The moral to that," Bertrand said, "is, *Who hath skirts of straw must needs stay clear of fire.*"

"Moral! Thou'rt a proper priest to speak of morals! Enough now: who said *Out, out, strumpet Fortune,* Shakespeare or Marlowe? I've two bob on't with Captain Meech, that thinks him such a scholar."

Alarmed lest his servant give the game away, either by his reply or by his conduct, Ebenezer was about to interrupt with the answer, but Bertrand gave him no opportunity.

"Captain Meech, is't!" he exclaimed, with a teasing frown and a sidelong look. "I'll bet two bob myself that for any bruise o' mine ye've three of his to sit on!"

Miss Robotham and Ebenezer both protested, the latter genuinely.

"No? Take a pound on't, then," Bertrand laughed. "My pound against your shilling. But mind, I must see the proof myself!" He then asked what poet she'd bet on, offering to swear that man had penned the line.

"The Laureate hath not his peer for gallantry," Ebenezer observed with relief to Miss Robotham's youthful back. "And in sooth, if chivalry be served, what matters it that William——"

"Oh no," the girl protested, cutting him off, "I'll have no favors from you, Mister Laureate, for I well know what 'twill cost me in the end! Besides which, I know the answers for a fact, and want no more than to hav't confirmed:

> *Out, out, thou strumpet Fortune! All you gods*
> *In general synod take away her power.*
> *Knock all her spokes and fellies out,*
> *And bowl the round nave down the hill of Heaven,*
> *As low as to the fiends!*"

"Well done, well done!" Ebenezer applauded. "The Player himself pleased Hamlet no more with't than you——"

"Marry, all those knaves and strumpets!" Bertrand exclaimed. "Whoever wrote it is a randy wight, now, ain't he? To speak the truth, young lady, I might have scratched it out myself, for aught I know."

"If you please, ma'am!" Ebenezer cried, aghast at Bertrand's ignorance and the peril of the situation. This time he forced himself between them and took her arm as though to lead her off. "You must forgive my rudeness, but I cannot let you annoy the Laureate farther!"

"Annoy him!" Miss Robotham snatched her arm away. *"Me* annoy *him!"*

"I quite commend your interest in verse, which is rare enough e'en in a London girl," the poet went on, speaking rapidly and glancing about to see if others were watching them, "and 'tis no reflection on your rearing that you presume so on this great man's gallantry, seeing thou'rt from the plantations; yet I must explain——"

"Hear the wretch!" Miss Robotham applied for sympathy first to an imaginary audience and then specifically to Captain Meech, whom she saw approaching from aft. "I ask Mr. Cooke a civil question, and this fellow calls me a mannerless bumpkin!"

"Never mind him," the Captain said good-humoredly, not without a brief scowl at the offender. "Who wins the bet?"

"Oh, everybody knows 'twas Shakespeare wrote it," she said, "but Mr. Cooke's as great a tease as you: he swears 'twas he himself."

"Grand souls are ever wont to speak in epigrams," Ebenezer explained desperately. "Haply it seemed a mere tease on the face of't, but underneath 'tis deep enough a thought: the Laureate means that one great poet feels such kinship with another, in's service of the Muse, 'tis as if Will Shakespeare and Eben Cooke were one and the same man!"

"My loss, then," sighed the Captain, more in reply to Miss Robotham's remark than to Ebenezer's. "Henceforth," he promised Bertrand, "I'l stick to my last and leave learning to the learned."

"Heav'n forbid!" Bertrand laughed. He had paid no heed whatever to Ebenezer's previous alarm. "I lose enough on your seamanship without betting against ye in the pool!"

Captain Meech then declaring with a wink that all his money was in his quarters, Miss Robotham strode off on his arm to collect her winnings.

Bertrand looked after them enviously. "By God, that is a saucy piece!"

" 'Tis all up with us!" Ebenezer groaned, as soon as the couple was out of earshot. "You've spiked our guns for fair!" He turned again to the ocean and buried his face in his hands.

"What? Not a bit of't! Did ye see how she purred when I chucked her chin?"

"You treated her like a two-shilling tart!"

"No more than what she is," Bertrand said. "D'ye think she's playing at cards with Meech right now?"

"But her father is Colonel Robotham of Talbot County, that used to sit on the Maryland Council!"

Bertrand was unimpressed. "I know him well enough. Yet 'tis a queer father will hear his daughter prate of knaves and strumpets, I must say, and recite her smutty verses at the table."

"God save us!" cried the Laureate. "If you don't discover us with your blunders, you'll have us horsewhipped for your behavior! Speak no more of the valet's refinement, i'God; I've seen enough of't, and of his ignorance!"

"Ah now, compose thyself," said Bertrand. " 'Twas the Laureate I was playing, not the valet, or ye'd have seen refinement and to spare. I knew what I was about."

"You knew——"

"As for this same raillery and bookish converse your fine folk set such store by," he went on testily, "any gentleman's gentleman like myself that hath stood off a space and seen it whole can tell ye plainly the object of't, which is: to sound out the other fellow's sentiments on a matter and then declare a cleverer sentiment yourself. The difference here 'twixt simple and witty folk, if the truth be known, is that your plain man cares much for what stand ye take and not a fart for why ye take it, while your smart wight leaves ye whate'er stand ye will, sobeit ye defend it cleverly. Add to which, what any valet can tell ye, most things men speak of have but two sides to their name, and at every rung on the ladder of wit ye hear one held forth as gospel, with the other above and below."

"Ladder of wit! What madness is this?" Ebenezer demanded.

"No madness save the world's, sir. Take your wig question, now, that's such a thing in London: whether to wear a bob or a full-bottom peruke. Your simple tradesman hath no love for fashion and wears a bob on's natural hair the better to labor in; but give him ten pound and a fortnight to idle, he'll off to the shop for a great French shag and a ha'peck of powder, and think him the devil's own fellow! Then get ye a dozen such idlers; the sharpest among 'em will buy him a bob wig with lofty preachments on *the tyranny of fashion*—haven't I heard 'em!—and think him as far o'er his full-bottomed fellows as they o'er the merchants' sons and bob-

238

haired 'prentices. Yet only climb a rung the higher, and it's back to the full-bottom, on a sage that's seen so many crop-wigs feigning sense, he knows 'tis but a pose of practicality and gets him a name for the cleverest of all by showing their sham to the light of day. But a grade o'er him is the bob again, on the pate of some philosopher, and over that the full-bottom, and so on. Or take your French question: the rustical wight is all for England and thinks each Frenchman the Devil himself, but a year in London and he'll sneer at the simple way his farm folk reason. Then comes a man who's traveled that road who says, 'Plague take this foppish shill-I, shall-I! When all's said and done 'tis England to the end!'; and after him your man that's been abroad and vows 'tis not a matter of *shill-I, shall-I* to one who's traveled, for no folk are cleverer than the clever French, 'gainst which your English townsman's but a bumpkin. Next yet's the man who's seen not France alone but every blessed province on the globe; he says 'tis the novice traveler sings such praise for Paris—the man who's seen 'em all comes home to England and carries all's refinement in his heart. But then comes your grand skeptical philosopher, that will not grant right to either side; and after him a grander, that knows no side is right but takes sides anyway for the clever nonsense of't; and after him your worldly saint, that says he's past all talk of wars and kings fore'er, and gets him a great name for virtue. And after him——"

"Enough, I beg you!" Ebenezer cried, "My head spins! For God's sake what's your point?"

"No more than what I said before, sir: that de'il the bit ye've tramped about the world, and bleared your eyes with books, and honed your wits in clever company, whate'er ye *yea* is *nay'd* by the man just a wee bit simpler and again by the fellow just a wee bit brighter, so that clever folk care less for what ye think than why ye think it. 'Tis this that saves me."

But Ebenezer could not see why. " 'Tis that shall scotch you, I should fancy! A fool can parrot a wise man's judgment but never hope to defend it."

"And only a fool would try," said Bertrand, with upraised finger. "Your poet hath no need to."

Ebenezer's features did a dance.

"What I mean, sir," Bertrand explained, "when they come upon me with one of their mighty questions—only yestere'en, for instance, they'd have me say my piece on witchery, whether I believed in it or no—why, all I do is smile me a

239

certain smile and say, 'Why not?' and there's an end on't! The ones that agree are pleased enough, and as for the skeptical fellows, they've no way to tell if I'm a spook-ridden dullard or a breed of mystic twice as wise as they. Your poet need never trouble his head to explain at all: men think he hath a passkey to Dame Truth's bedchamber and smiles at the scholars building ladders in the court. This Civility and Sense ye preach of are his worst enemies; he must pinch the ladies' bosoms and pull the schoolmen's beards. His manner is his whole argument, as't were, and that certain whimsical smile his sole rebuttal."

"No more," Ebenezer said sharply. "I'll hear no more!"

Bertrand smiled his whimsical smile. "Yet surely 'tis the simple truth?"

"There is skin of truth on't, yes," the Laureate granted; "but 'tis like the mask of sense on a madman or a film of ice on a skaters' pond—it only makes what lies beneath more sinister."

Just then the bell was rung for the gentlemen and ladies to come to supper.

" 'Tis our goose that's cooked," Ebenezer said gloomily. "You'll see this hour Miss Robotham marked your ignorance."

"Haply so," said Bertrand with his smile, "but I'd stake your last farthing she thinks I'm a bloody Solomon. We'll know soon enough who's right."

It was, in fact, closer to four hours before the Laureate was able to speak privately with his man again, for long after the servants had themselves finished eating, the fine folk lingered at cards and brandy in the main cabin. Their very merriment, of course—the sounds of which Ebenezer heard clearly where he stood by the foremast, brooding on the moonlit ocean—seemed to indicate that nothing was seriously amiss; nevertheless his exasperation was tempered by relief when finally he saw Bertrand emerge on the quarter-deck with Captain Meech himself, still laughing at some private joke, and fire up his pipe at the smoking-lamp. The poet felt a pang of envy, yet it was not Bertrand's manner alone that disturbed him; the truth was, he found the man's cynical argument as attractive as his own reply and was at bottom satisfied with neither. For that reason, when he asked what had been said at supper concerning the literary wager of the afternoon, he was, if saddened, not surprised by the report.

" 'Twas the talk of the table, right enough, sir." Bertrand puffed and frowned at his pipe. "The Robotham wench told what I'd said and how ye'd glossed it, word for word. To speak plainly, sir, the Colonel, her father, then asked me why I abided so brash a servant, if ye'll pardon me, as presumes to speak for's master. The rest took up the cry, and the young piece said at last, one could know me for a poet by the look of me, and yourself for a *byo-* . . . *beo-* . . . something or other."

"*Boeotian,*" the Laureate said glumly.

"Aye. 'Twas another of her smutty words."

Ebenezer then inquired, not enthusiastically, what answer his man had made.

"What could I say, to end their gossip? I told 'em flat that naught matters in a secretary save his penmanship. The Captain then summoned up old *strumpet Fortune* again, that seems their favorite bawd: he knew the passage through, he said, but had forgot just when 'twas spoke in some play or other he named."

"Ah." Ebenezer closed his eyes almost hopefully. "Then 'tis over and done with us, after all."

"How's that, sir? I didn't bat an eyelash, thankee, but declared 'twas spoke on shipboard an hour past noon, when the post lost his last quid on a short day's run." He pulled again on his pipe and spat with satisfaction at the rolling ocean. "No more was said of't after that."

13

The Laureate, Awash in a Sea of Difficulties,
Resolves to Be Laureate, Not Before Inditing
Final Sea-Couplets

AFTER THE FOREGOING conversations with Bertrand, Ebenezer's dissatisfaction with his position was no longer confined to mealtimes; rather, he took to a general brooding and spiritual malaise. He could write no verse: even the sight of a school of great whales, which in happier times would have set his fancy spinning, now called forth not a single rhyme. At best he had got on indifferently with his messmates; now they sensed his distaste, and resentment added malice to the jokes they made at his expense. When, therefore, after perhaps a week of this solitary discontent, Bertrand confided to him with a happy leer that Lucy Robotham was about to become the Maryland Laureate's mistress, his reaction to the news was anything but hospitable.

"Lay a finger on her," he threatened, "and you'll finish your crossing in leg irons."

"Ah, well, 'tis a little late for *that* advice, sir; the quail is bagged and plucked, and wants but basting on the spit."

"No, I say!" Ebenezer insisted, as much impatient as appalled. "Why must I say it twice? Your gambling runs counter to my better judgment, but fornication—'tis counter to my very essence!"

Bertrand was altogether unruffled by his master's ire. "Not in the least," he said. "A poet without a mistress is a judge without a wig: 'tis the badge of his office, and the Laureate should keep a staff of 'em. My sole concern is to play the poet well, sir."

Ebenezer remained unpersuaded. " 'Tis an overnice concern that makes a whore of the Colonel's daughter!"

Here Bertrand protested that in fact his interest in Lucy Robotham was largely dispassionate: Colonel Robotham, he had learned, was one of the original conspirators with John Coode who had overthrown Lord Baltimore's government in 1689, and, for all he was sailing presently under Governor Nicholson's protection, he might well be still in secret league with the insurrectionists. " 'Twould not surprise me," he declared, "if old Robotham's using the girl for bait. Why else would he watch us carry on so without a word? Aye, by Heav'n, I'll hoist him with his own petard!"

In the face of this new information and his valet's apparent talent for intrigue, Ebenezer's resolve began to weaken: his indignation changed to petulance. "You've a Sophist's gift for painting vice in virtue's color," he said. " 'Tis clear thou'rt out to make the most of my name and office."

"Then I have your leave, sir?"

"I wonder you even trouble to ask it these days."

"Ah, thankee, sir!" Bertrand's voice showed obvious relief. "Thou'rt a gentleman to the marrow and have twice the understanding of any wight on the boat! I knew ye for a fine soul the first I e'er laid eyes on you, when Master Andrew sent me to look to your welfare in London. In every thing——"

"Enough; you sicken me," the poet said. "What is't thou'rt

after now, for God's sake? I know this flattery will cost me dear."

"Patience, I pray ye, sir," Bertrand pleaded in a tone quite other than that of his earlier conversations; he was for the nonce entirely the valet again. After reaffirming at length his faith in Ebenezer's understanding and their mutual interest in preserving their disguise, and asserting as well that they were of one mind as regarded the importance of gentlemanly wagering to that disguise, he confessed that he needed additional subsidizing to maintain appearances, and this at once.

"Dear God!" the Laureate cried. "You've not lost twenty pounds so soon!"

Bertrand nodded confirmation and explained that he'd wagered heavily in side bets on the past day's run in order to recoup his former losses, but that despite his most careful calculations he'd lost by a paltry mile or so to Miss Robotham, who he suspected had access to private information from the Captain.

"Half my savings! And you've gall enough to ask for the rest to throw after it!"

"Far from it, sir," Bertrand declared. "On the contrary, I mean not only to win your money and mine again, but to pay it back fivefold. 'Tis for this as much as anything I need the Robotham wench." The *Poseidon*, he said, was near the end of her second week of southwestering, and the wise money placed the Azores only two or three days distant. So likely was this landfall, in fact, that the bet-covering parson Mr. Tubman demanded a pound for every shilling on those two dates, whereas any date before or afterwards fetched most lucrative odds. Bertrand's plan, then, was to make such a conquest of Miss Robotham that she would turn to his account all her influence with Captain Meech: if his private estimate of the date or landfall was other than the prevailing opinion, Bertrand would place all his money on and around the new date; if the Captain's guess concurred with that of the passengers, Miss Robotham would employ every art and wile to induce him to sail more slowly and raise the islands on some later date.

"Marry, you give me little choice!" Ebenezer said bitterly when his man had finished. "First you make it seem not foolish to take the girl, then you make it downright prudent, and now you make it necessary, albeit you know as well as I at bottom 'tis naught but prurience and luxury. Take the wench, and my money as well! Make me a name for a gambling whoremonger and have done with't!"

Having thus given vent to his feelings, he fetched out his last twenty pounds from the trunk and with great misgivings tendered the sum to Bertrand, appealing a final time to the man's discretion. The servant thanked him as one gentleman might thank another for a trifling loan and went to seek out Lucy Robotham.

Following this transaction the poet's melancholia grew almost feverish. All day he languished in his berth or slouched ungracefully at the rail to stare at the ocean; Bertrand's announcement, delivered next morning with a roll of the eyes, that the seduction of Miss Robotham was an accomplished fact, elicited only a sigh and a shake of his master's head; and when in an attempt at cheerfulness the valet subsequently declared himself ready to have his way with strumpet Fortune, the Laureate's listless reply was *"Who trafficks with strumpets hath a taste for the pox."*

He was, as he himself recognized without emotion, very near a state like that from which he'd been saved once by Burlingame and again, unintentionally, by John McEvoy. What saved him this time was an event actually in keeping with his mood: on the first of the two "wise money" days the fleet encountered its first really severe weather. The wind swung round from north to southwest, increased its velocity, and brought with it a settled storm of five days' duration. The *Poseidon* pitched, yawed, and rolled in the heavy seas; passengers were confined below decks most of the day. The smell of agitated bilgewater permeated the cabins, and even the sailors grew seasick. Ebenezer fell so ill that for days he could scarcely eat at the servants' mess; he left his berth only when nature summoned him either to the ship's rail or to the chamberpot. Yet, though he voiced his misery along with the others, he had not, like them, any fervent wish for calm: to precipitate a cataclysm is one thing, and requires resolution at the least; but to surrender to and embrace an already existing cataclysm wants no more than despair.

He did not see Bertrand again until late in the fifth and final day of the storm, which was also the most severe. All through the lightless day the *Poseidon* had shuddered along under reefed topsails, the wind having shifted to the northeast, and at evening the gale increased. Ebenezer was on the quarter-deck, in his innocence heaving over the windward rail and in his illness oblivious to the unsavory results. Here he was joined by his valet, as usual dressed in his master's clothes, who had come on deck for the same purpose and who set about the work with similar untidiness. For a while they labored elbow to elbow in the growing dark; presently Ebenezer managed to ask, "What odds doth the Reverend Tubman give on living through this night? I'd make no bets on't."

At this Bertrand fell to a perfect fit of retching. "Better for all if the bloody boat goes under!" he replied at last. " 'Tis not a fart to me if I live or die."

"Is this the Laureate I hear?" Ebenezer regarded his man's misery with satisfaction.

"Don't speak the word!" Bertrand moaned and buried his face in his hands. "God curse the day I e'er left London!"

At every new complaint, Ebenezer's stomach grew easier. "But how is this?" he asked sarcastically. "You'd rather be a gelded servingman in London than a gentleman poet with a mistress and a fortune? I cannot fathom it!"

"Would God Ralph Birdsall had untooled me!" Bertrand cried. "Man's cod's a wretched handle that woman leads him 'round with. Oh, the whore! The treacherous whore!"

Now the poet's satisfaction turned to real delight. "Aha, so the cock must crow *Cuckoo!* By Heav'n, the wench doth well to horn you, that make such a sport of horning others!"

"Nay, God, ye must not praise the slut!"

"Not praise her? She hath my praise and my endorsement; she hath my blessing——"

"She hath your money too," said Bertrand, "all forty pound of it." And seeing his master too thunderstruck to speak, he told the tale of his deception. The Robotham girl, he said, had sworn her love for him, and on the strength of it had six days ago, by her own tearful account, mortgaged her honor to the extent of permitting Captain Meech certain liberties with her person, in return wherefore she was able to advise Bertrand to put his money on a date several days later than the favored ones: she had it straight from the Captain that, though Flores was indeed but one day off, a storm was brewing on the south horizon that could set them back a hundred miles with ease. At the same time she cautioned him not to disclose his wager but to give out that he too was betting on the popular dates; she would see to it, she vowed, that the bookmaking minister held his tongue—*True love recks not the cost!* Finally, should the *Poseidon* not raise Flores on the proper day, she had a maid with whom the lookout on the larboard watch had fallen quite in love and for whose favors he would swear to raising the jasper coasts of Heaven.

Thus assured, Bertrand had put his money at fifteen to one on the day to follow this present day—but alas, as he saw too clearly now, the wench had worked a manifold deception!

Her real lover, it appeared, was no other soul than the Reverend Tubman himself, for the sake of whose solvency she had led every poor fool in the group to think her his secret mistress and bet on the selfsame date. Then when the storm arrived on schedule, how they all had cursed and bemoaned their losses, each laughing up his sleeve at his advantage over the rest! But now, on the eve of their triumph; on this very day of our Lord which might well be their last; in short, one hour ago, the larboard lookout had sworn to sighting the mountains of Corvo from his perch in the maintop, and though no other eye save his had seen them, Captain Meech had made the landfall official.

As though to confirm the valet's story, Captain Meech just then appeared on the poop and ordered the ship hove to under reefed fore-topsail—a measure that the gale alone made prudent, whether Corvo lay to leeward or not. Indeed, the mate's command to strike the main and mizzen topsails was behindhand, for while the men were still in the ratlines a gust split all three sails and sprang the mizzenmast as well. The foresail itself was raised instead, double-reefed, to keep the ship from broaching to until a new fore-topsail could be bent to its yard; then the crew hurried to clear the wildly flapping remnants of the mizzen topsail—and none too soon, for at the next strong gust on the weakened spar a mizzen shroud parted with the crack of a pistol shot.

It was at this least fortunate of moments that Ebenezer, sickened anew by the tidings of his ruin, leaned out again over the rail: the fiddle-tight shroud lashed back and smacked him on the transom, and he was horrified to find himself, for an instant, actually in the sea beside the ship! No one saw him go by the board; the officers and crew had their hands full, and Bertrand, unable to look his master in the eye during the confession, still cowered at the rail with his face in his arms. He could not shout for coughing up sea-water, but nothing could have been done to save him even in the unlikely event that anyone heard his cries. In short, it would have been all over with him then and there had not the same wind that formerly returned his heavings to him now blown the top off the next great wave: crest, spray, and senseless poet tumbled back aboard, along with numerous tons of green Atlantic Ocean, and for better or worse the Laureate was safe.

However, he did not regain his consciousness at once. For what could to him have been as well an hour or a year he languished in a species of euphoria, oblivious to his surroundings and to the passage of time, even to the fact that he was safe. It was a dizzy, dreamlike state, for the most part by no means unpleasant, though interrupted now and then by short periods of uncertain struggling accompanied by vague pain. Sometimes he dreamed—not nightmares at all but oddly tranquil visions. Two recurred with some frequency: the first and most mysterious was of twin alabaster mountain cones, tall and smoothly polished; old men were seated on the peaks, and around the bases surged a monstrous activity the nature of which he could not make out. The other was a recapitulation of his accident, in a strangely altered version: he was in the water beside the *Poseidon,* but the day was gloriously bright instead of stormy; the tepid sea was green, glass calm, and not even wet; the ship, though every sail was full, moved not an inch away; not Bertrand, but his sister Anna and his friend Henry Burlingame watched him from the quarterdeck, smiling and waving, and instead of terror it was ecstasy that filled his poet's breast!

When at length he came fully to his senses, the substance of these dreams defied recall, but their tranquility came with him to the waking world. He lay peacefully for a long time with his eyes open, admitting reality a fact at a time into his consciousness. To begin with, he was alive—a certain dizziness, some weakness of the stomach, and pains in his buttocks vouched for that, though he felt them with as much detachment as if the ailing members were not his. He remembered the accident without alarm, but knew neither how it had occurred nor what had saved him. Even the memory that Bertrand had lost all his money, which followed immediately after, failed to ruffle his serenity. Gradually he understood that he was lying in a hammock in the fo'c'sle: he knew the look of the place from his earlier confinement there. The room was shadowy and full of the smells of lamp-oil and tobacco-smoke; he heard occasional short laughs and muttered curses, and the slap of playing-cards; somewhere near at hand a sleeper snored. It was night, then. Last of all he realized that the ship was riding steady as a church, at just the slightest angle of heel: the storm had passed, and also the dangerous period of high seas and no wind that often follows storms at sea: the *Poseidon* was making gentle way.

Though he was loath to leave that pleasant country where his spirit had lately traveled, he presently swung his legs out of the hammock and sat up. In other hammocks all around him men were sleeping, and four sailors played at cards on a table near the center of the room.

"Marry!" one of them cried. "There stirs our sleeping beauty!" The rest turned round with various smiles to look.

"Good evening," Ebenezer said. His voice was weak, and when he stood erect his legs gave way, and the pain in his buttocks recommenced. He grasped a bulkhead for support.

"What is't, lad?" a smiling jack inquired. "Got a gimp?"

At this the party laughed aloud, and though the point of the joke escaped him, Ebenezer smiled as well: the strange serenity he'd waked with made it of no importance that their laughter was doubtless at his expense.

"Belike I took a fall," he said politely. "I hurt a little here and there."

" 'Twere a nine-day wonder if ye didn't!" an old fellow cackled, and Ebenezer recognized that same Ned who'd first delivered him into Bertrand's presence and had pinched him so cruelly into the bargain. The others laughed again, but bade their shipmate be silent.

A third sailor, somewhat less uncouth appearing than the rest, made haste to say, "What Ned means is, small wonder ye've an ache or two where the mizzen shroud struck ye." He indicated a small flask near at hand. "Come have a dram to steady yourself while the mate's on deck."

"I thank you," Ebenezer said, and when he had done shivering from the rum he mildly asked, "How is't I'm here?"

"We found ye senseless on the main deck in the storm," the sailor said. "Ye'd near washed through the scuppers."

"Chips yonder used your berth for planking," old Ned added gleefully, and indicated the sailor who had spoken first —a lean, sturdy fellow in his forties.

"No offense intended, mind," said the carpenter, playing another card. "We was taking water aft, and all my planks was washed by the board. I asked in the 'tween decks which berth to use, and yours was the one they showed me."

"Ah well, I'll not miss their company, I think." On further questioning Ebenezer learned that his unconsciousness had lasted three days and nights, during which time he'd had no food at all. He was ravenously hungry; the cook, rather expecting him to die, had left no rations for him, but the crewmen readily shared their bread and cheese. They showed considerable curiosity about his three-day coma: in particular, had he felt not anything at all? His assurance that he had not seemed greatly to amuse them.

"Out on't, then!" the carpenter declared. " 'Tis over and done with, mate, and if aught's amiss, bear in mind we thought ye a dying man."

248

"Amiss?" Ebenezer did not understand. By this time the rum had warmed his every member, and the edge was off his hunger. In the lantern light the fo'c'sle looked quite cozy. He had not lately met with such hospitality as had been shown him by these uncouth sailors, who doubtless knew not even his pseudonym, to say nothing of his real identity. "If aught's amiss," he asserted warmly, " 'tis that in my muddled state I've made no proper thanks for all your kindness. Would God I'd pence to pay you for't, though I knew 'twas natural goodness moved you and not the landsman's grubby wish for gold. But I'm a pauper."

"Think never a fart of't," one of the men replied. " 'Tis your master's lookout. Drink up, now."

The Laureate smiled at their innocence and took another drink. Should he tell them whom in fact they were so kind to? No, he decided affectionately; let virtue be its own reward. He called to mind tales of kings in humble dress, going forth among their subjects; of Christ himself, who sometimes traveled incognito. Doubtless they would one day learn the truth, from some poem or other that he'd write: then the adventure would become a legend of the fo'c'sles and a telling anecdote in biographies to come.

The sailors' cordial attitude prevailed through the following fortnight, as did the poet's remarkable tranquility. This latter, at least, he came increasingly to understand: the second of his euphoric visions had come back to him, and he saw in it, with a quiet thrill, a mystic affirmation of his calling, such as those once vouchsafed to the saints. What was this ship, after all, but the Ship of Destiny, from which in retribution for his doubts he had been cast? What was the ocean but a Font of Rededication, a moral bath to cleanse him of despair and restore him to the Ship? The message was unequivocal even without the additional, almost frightening miracle that he had unwittingly predicted it! Hence Burlingame's presence on the dream ship, for he it was, in the King o' the Seas (that is to say, *Poseidon!*) who had scoffed at the third line of Ebenezer's quatrain——

> *Let* Ocean *roar his damn'dest Gale:*
> *Our Planks shan't leak; our Masts shan't fail;*
> *With great* Poseidon *by our Side*
> *He seemeth neither wild nor wide.*

——which, he claimed, placed the poet in the ocean. Ebenezer

thought warmly of his friend and teacher, who for all he knew might long since have been found out by Slye and Scurry and sent to a watery grave. Henry had been skeptical of the laureateship, no doubt about it.

"Would God I had him here, to tell this wonder to!"

Since the momentous sighting of Corvo in the Azores, the *Poseidon* had been sailing a due westerly course along the thirty-seventh parallel of latitude, which if all went well would lead her straight to the Virginia Capes. The lengthy storm had scattered the fleet to the four winds, so that not another sail was visible on the horizon; but Captain Meech looked to overhaul the flagship any day, which he reckoned to be ahead of them. Although some time had been lost in making repairs, when Chips completed a masterful scarfing of the damaged spar the *Poseidon* bowled along for days on end in a whole-sail breeze. They were five weeks out of Plymouth; May was upon them, and landfall again on everybody's lips.

During this period Ebenezer seldom left the fo'c'sle: for one thing, it took him a while to regain his strength; for another, he had no desire to see his former messmates again, and anyway his musings kept him pleasantly occupied. Bertrand, of course, he could not avoid some contact with, but their meetings were brief and uncommunicative—the valet was uncertain of his position, and Ebenezer, besides enjoying the man's discomfort, had nothing to say to him. Though he could entertain no more illusions about the ship's magnificence, his admiration for the sailors had increased tenfold. His despair was gone completely: with tranquil joy he watched the dolphins roll along the freeboard and in the wake and, caught up in the general anticipation, he sharpened his quills, got out the volumes of Milton and Samuel Butler that he used as references, and hatched the following couplets to describe the great event that lay ahead: his first glimpse of Maryland.

> *Belike* Ulysses, *wand'ring West*
> *From* Ilions *Sack, in Tatters drest,*
> *And weary'd of his ten-year Roam*
> *O'er wat'ry Wilds of desart Foam,*
> *Beholding* Ithaca *at last*
> *And seeing all his Hardship past,*
> *Did swear 'twas* Heav'ns *own Shore he'd rais'd,*
> *So lovely seem'd it as he gaz'd,*
> *Despite its Rocks and Fearsome Coast.*

How Heav'nlier, then, this Land I boast,
Whose golden Sands and verdant Trees
And Harbours snug, design'd to ease
The Sailors Burthen, greet the Eye
With naught save Loveliness! Nay, try
As best it might, no Poets Song,
Be't e'er so sweet or ne'er so long,
Could tell the Whole of MARYLANDS Charms,
When from the Oceans boundless Harms
The Trav'ler comes unscath'd at last,
And from his Vessels loftiest mast
He first beholds her Beauty!

To which, at the foot of the ledger-sheet, he duly appended
E.C., G^{ent}, P^t & L^t of M^d, and regarded the whole with a
satisfaction such as he had not felt since the night of Joan
Toast's fateful visit. He was impatient to have done with disguises and assume his true position in the Province; his physical condition was better than it had been before the accident,
and his spirits could scarcely have been improved upon. After
considering the merits of several plans, he resolved at length
to end the fraud by announcing his identity and reciting these
latest verses as soon as the *Poseidon* made a landfall: clearly
there was no plot against the Laureate aboard ship, and the
passengers deserved to know the truth about him and Bertrand.

It was not his fortune, however, to carry out this pleasant
scheme. With their journey's end so near at hand, passengers
and crew alike grew daily more festive, and though the sailors were officially forbidden to drink aboard ship, the fo'c'sle
no less than the main cabin became the scene of nightly rev-
els. The crew's hospitality to Ebenezer waxed proportionately: he had no money to invest in their card-games, but he
readily shared their rum and cordiality.

One evening when all had drunk a fair amount of liquor,
old Ned, whose amiable deportment had most surprised the
Laureate, descended the companionway and announced to
the company at large that he had just returned from an interview with Mister Ebenezer Cooke on the main deck. Ebenezer's ears pricked up and his cheeks burned, for the man's
tone implied that he had been sent as some kind of spokesman for the group. The rest avoided looking at him.

"I told 'Squire Cooke how fairly we'd looked to's man,"
Ned continued, smiling unpleasantly at the poet. "I told him
we'd fetched him from death's door and nursed him back to

health again, and shared our bed and board without complaint. Then I asked him if't wouldn't please him to give us somewhat for our pains, seeing we're coming on to landfall——"

"What did he say?" a man asked. Ebenezer's features boiled about: he was disappointed to learn that their generosity had been at least partly venal, but at the same time he recognized his obligation to them and the legitimacy of their claim.

Ned leered at him. "The lying wretch pled poverty! Says he lost his last farthing when we sighted Corvo!"

" 'Tis all too true," Ebenezer declared, in the face of a general protest at Ned's announcement. "He is a profligate fellow and, not content to squander his own money hath wagered mine as well, which is why I could not join your games. But I swear you shall be paid for your kindness, since you set a price on't. Do but copy down your names for me, and I'll dispatch the sum the day I arrive at Malden."

"I'll wager ye will, and lose my money too!" Chips laughed. "A vow like that is lightly sworn!"

"Prithee let me explain——" Ebenezer made up his mind to reveal his identity then and there.

"No explanation needed," said the boatswain, who in most matters spoke for the crewmen on that watch. "When sailors nurse an ailing sailor they want no thanks, but when they share the fo'c'sle with an ailing passenger, they're paid at the voyage's end."

" 'Tis the code o' the sea," Ned affirmed.

"And a fair one," Ebenezer granted. "If you'll but——"

"Stay," the boatswain commanded with a smile, and brought forth a sheet of paper from his pocket. "Your master pleads poverty, and you as well. There's naught for't but ye must sign this paper."

Ebenezer took the document doubtfully and read the rudely penned words.

"What thing is this?" he cried, and looked up to find all the sailors grinning at his wonder.

" 'Tis the code o' the sea, as Ned says," the boatswain answered. "Sign ye that paper and thou'rt a poor jack like the rest of us, that owes his fellows not a fart."

Indeed, the document proclaimed that its signer was a kind of honorary member of the *Poseidon*'s crew and shared the rights, privileges, and obligations of a common seaman, work and pay excepted. Its language, polished by comparison with the penmanship, suggested that the gesture was in fact a tra-

252

ditional means of coping with what Ebenezer had assumed to be a novel predicament, and Captain Meech's signature in one corner bespoke official sanction.

"Then—you want no payment after all?"

The boatswain shook his head. "'Twould be against the code to think of't from a shipmate."

"Why, 'tis an honor!" the poet laughed, his esteem for the men redoubled. "I'll sign my name right gladly!" And fetching out his quill he fixed his proper name and title to the paper.

"Ah, mate," said Chips, who watched behind his shoulder, "what prank is this ye play us for our kindness? Sign thy own name, not thy master's!"

"Is't you've heard before about the code?" Ned asked suspiciously.

"Nay, gentlemen, I mean no prank. 'Tis time you knew the truth." He proceeded then to tell the whole story of his disguise, explaining as briefly as he could what made it necessary. The liquor oiled his tongue: he spoke eloquently and at length, and by way of credentials even recited from memory every couplet in his notebook. "Do but say the word," he concluded. "I'll fetch my valet hence to swear to't. He could not quote a verse from memory and scarce could read 'em off the page."

At first openly incredulous, the men were clearly impressed by the time the poet was finished. No one suggested summoning Bertrand to testify. Their chief reservation, it turned out, was the fact that Ebenezer had been content with a fo'c'sle hammock while his servant enjoyed the favors of Miss Lucy Robotham, and the Laureate turned this quickly to account by reminding them of his hymn to virginity: such behavior as Bertrand's was unthinkable in a man to whom virginity was of the essence.

"'Sbody!" the boatswain cried. "Ye mean to say a poet is like a popish priest, that uses his cod for naught but a bilge-pump?"

"I speak for no poet save myself," Ebenezer replied, and went on to explain, insofar as modesty permitted, the distinction between ecclesiastical celibacy and true virginity. The former, he declared, was no more than a discipline, albeit a highly commendable one in that it turned to nobler work the time and energy commonly spent on lovemaking, spared the votary from dissipating entanglements with mistresses and wives, and was conducive in general to a longer and more productive life; but it was by no means so pure a state as actual virginity, and in point of fact implied no necessary virtue at all—the greatest lecher is celibate in later years, when his powers have fled. Celibacy, in short, was a negative practice almost always adopted either by default or by external authority; virginity, on the other hand, was a positive metaphysical state, the more to be admired since it was self-imposed and had in itself neither instrumental value nor, in the male, physical manifestation of its possession or loss. For him it had not even the posthumous instrumentality of a Christian virtue, since his interest in it was ontological and aesthetic rather than moral. He expatiated freely, more for his own edification than that of the crew, who regarded him with awe.

"Ye mean to sit there and tell us," the boatswain asked soberly in the middle of a sentence, "ye never caulked a fantail in your life? Ye never turned the old fid to part some dockwhore's hemp?"

"Nor shall I ever," the poet said stoutly, and to forestall further prying he returned the proclamation and proposed a drink to his new position. "Think not I count your honor less as Laureate," he assured them. "Let's have a dram on't, and ere the night's done I'll pay my toll with something more sweet than silver." Indeed, he meant to do them no less an honor than to sing their praises for ever and all in verse.

The sailors looked at each other.

"So be't!" old Ned cackled, and the others voiced approval too. "Get some rum in him, mates, 'fore the next watch!"

Ebenezer was given the bottle and bade to drink it all himself. "What's this?" he laughed uncertainly. "A sort of initiation ceremony?"

"Nay, that comes after," said Chips. "The rum's to make ye ready."

Ebenezer declined the preliminaries with a show of readiness for any mock ordeal. "Let's put by the parsley and have at the meat, then; you'll find me game for't!"

This was the signal for a general uproar: the poet's arms were pinioned from both sides; his chair was snatched from under him by one sailor, and before he could recover from his surprise another pressed his face into a pillow that lay in the center of the table, having magically appeared from nowhere. Not given by temperament to horseplay, Ebenezer squirmed with embarrassment; furthermore, both by reason of his office and from simple fear of pain he did not relish the idea of ritual bastinados on his backside, the administering of which he assumed to be the sailors' object.

When to his horror it grew clear, a moment later, that

birching was not their intent at all, no force on earth could keep him silent; though his head was held as fast as were his limbs, he gave a shriek that even the main-top lookout heard.

"Captain Meech will hang you for this!" he cried, when he could muster words.

"Ye think he knows naught o' the code o' the sea?" Ebenezer recognized old Ned's evil cackle behind him. "Ye saw his name on the paper, did ye not?"

And as if to confirm the hopelessness of his position, no sooner had he recommenced his shrieks than the mate on deck thrust his head down the companionway to issue a cheerful ultimatum: "The Captain says belay the hollering or lay the wretch out with a pistol-butt. He's bothering the ladies."

His only threat thus spiked, Ebenezer seemed condemned to suffer the initiation in its ruinous entirety. But a sudden cry went up on deck—Ebenezer, half a-swoon, paid no attention to it—and in an instant every man ran for the companionway, leaving the novice to his own resorts. Weak with outrage, he sent a curse after them. Then he made shift to dress himself and tried as best he could to calm his nerves with thoughts of retribution. Still oblivious to the sound of shouts and running feet above his head, he presently gave voice to a final sea-couplet, the last verse he was to spawn for weeks to come:

"Hell *hath no fouler, filthier Demon:*
Preserve me, LORD, *from English Seamen!"*

Now to the general uproar on deck was added the sound of musket fire and even the great report of a cannon, though the *Poseidon* carried no artillery: whatever was happening could no longer be ignored. Ebenezer went to the companionway, but before he could climb up he was met by Bertrand, in nightgown and cap, who leaped below in a single bound and fell sprawling on the floor.

"Master Ebenezer!" he cried and, spying the poet by the ladderway, rose trembling to his knees. At sight of the man's terror Ebenezer's flesh tingled.

"What is't, man? What ails you?"

"We're all dead men, sir!" Bertrand wailed. " 'Tis all up with us! *Pirates,* sir! Ah, curse the hour I played at Laureate! The devils are boarding us this moment!"

"Nay! Thou'rt drunk!"

"I swear't, sir! 'Tis the plank for all of us!" In the late af-

255

ternoon, he explained, the *Poseidon* had raised another sail to the southeast, which, taking it for some member of the fleet, Captain Meech made haste to overhaul before dark—the man-o'-war that was to see them safely through pirate waters had been out of sight since Corvo, and two ships together were more formidable prey than one alone. But it had taken until just awhile ago to overtake the stranger, and no sooner were they in range than a shot was fired across their bow, and they realized too late that they were trapped. "Would Heav'n I'd stayed to face Ralph Birdsall!" he lamented in conclusion. "Better my cod lost than my life! What shall we do?"

The Laureate had no better answer for this than did his valet, who still crouched trembling on his knees, unable to stand. The shooting had stopped, but there was even more shouting than before, and Ebenezer felt the shock of another hull brushing the *Poseidon*'s. He climbed a little way up the ladder—just enough to peer out.

He saw a chilling sight. The other vessel rode along the *Poseidon*'s starboard beam, made fast to her victim with numerous grappling hooks. It was a shallop, schooner-rigged and smaller than the *Poseidon*, but owing to its proximity and the long weeks during which nothing had been to be seen but open sea on every hand, it looked enormous. Men with pistols or torches in one hand and cutlasses in the other were scrambling over the railings unopposed, the firelight rendering them all the more fearsome, and were herding the *Poseidon*'s crew around the mainmast; it appeared that Captain Meech had deemed it unwise to resist. The Captain himself, together with his fellow officers, could be seen under separate guard farther aft, by the mizzen, and already the passengers were being rousted out from their berths onto the deck, most in nightclothes or underwear. The men cursed and complained; the women swooned, shrieked, or merely wept in anticipation of their fate. Over the pirates' foremast hung the gibbous moon, its light reflecting whitely from the fluttering gaff-topsails; the lower sails, also luffing in the cool night breeze, glowed orange in the torchlight and danced with giant shadows. Ebenezer leaned full against the ladder to keep from falling. To his mind rushed all the horrors he'd read of in Esquemeling: how Roche Brasiliano had used to roast his prisoners on wooden spits, or rub their stripes with lemon juice and pepper; how L'Ollonais had pulled out his victims' tongues with his bare hands and chewed their hearts; how Henry Morgan would squeeze a man's eyeballs out with a tourniquet about the skull, depend him by the thumbs and great toes, or haul him aloft by the privy members.

From behind and below came the sound of Bertrand's lamentations.

"Now belay it, belay it!" one of the pirates was commanding. It was not the passengers' miserable carcasses they had designs on, he declared, but money and stores. If everyone behaved himself properly, no harm would befall them save the loss of their valuables, a few barrels of pork and peas, and three or four seamen, whom the pirates needed to complement their crew; in an hour they could resume their voyage. He then dispatched a contingent of pirates to accompany the male passengers back to their quarters and gather the loot, the women remaining above as hostages to assure a clean picking; another detail he ordered to pillage the hold; and a third, consisting of three armed men, came forward to search the fo'c'sle for additional seamen.

"Quickly!" Ebenezer cried to Bertrand, jumping to the floor. "Put these clothes on and give me my nightgown!" He commenced pulling the valet's clothes off himself as hastily as possible.

"Why?" Bertrand wailed. " 'Tis all over with us either way."

Ebenezer had his clothes off already and began to yank at the nightgown. "We know not what's in store for us," he said grimly. "Belike 'tis the gentlemen they're after, not the poor folk. At any rate 'twere better to see't through honestly: if I'm to die I'll die as Eben Cooke, not Bertrand Burton! Off with this, now!" He gave a final tug, and the gown came off over Bertrand's head and arms. "I'Christ, 'tis beshit!"

"For very fear," the valet admitted, and scrabbled after some clothes.

"Avast there, laddies!" came a voice from the companionway. "Lookee here, mates, 'tis a floating Gomorry!"

Ebenezer, the foul nightdress half over his head, and Bertrand, still naked on all fours, turned to face three grinning pirates, pistols and swords in hand, on the ladder.

"I do despise to spoil your party, sailors," said the leader. He was a ferocious-looking Moor, bull-necked, broken-nosed, rough-bearded, and dark-skinned; a red turbanlike cap sat on his head, and black hair bristled from his open shirt. "But we want your arses on deck."

"Prithee don't mistake me, sir," Ebenezer answered, pulling the skirts of his nightdress down. He drew himself up as calmly as he could and pointed with disdain to Bertrand.

"This fellow here may speak for himself, but I am no sailor: my name is Ebenezer Cooke, and I am Poet Laureate of His Majesty's Province of Maryland!"

14

The Laureate Is Exposed to Two Assassinations of Character, a Piracy, a Near-Deflowering, a Near-Mutiny, a Murder, and an Appalling Colloquy Between Captains of the Sea, All Within the Space of a Few Pages

UNIMPRESSED BY EBENEZER'S DECLARATION, the horrendous Moor and his two confederates hustled their prisoners up to the main deck, the Laureate clad only in his unpleasant nightshirt and Bertrand in a pair of breeches hastily donned. The uproar had by this time subsided to some extent; though the women and servants wept and wailed on every hand, the officers and crew stood sullenly in groups around the mizzen and foremasts, respectively, and the gentlemen, who were returning one by one from the main cabin under the guard of their plunderers, preserved a tight-lipped silence. Thus far no physical harm had been offered either woman or man, and the efficient looting of the *Poseidon* was nearly complete: all that remained of the pirates' stated objectives, as overheard by Ebenezer, was to finish the transfer of provisions and impress three or four seamen into their service.

For robbery Ebenezer cared little, his valet having picked him clean already; it was the prospect of being impressed that terrified him, since he and Bertrand had been captured in the fo'c'sle and neither was wearing the clothes of a gentleman. His fears redoubled when their captors led them toward the foremast.

"Nay, prithee, hear me!" he cried. "I am no seaman at all! My name is Ebenezer Cooke, of Cooke's Point in Maryland! I'm the Laureate Poet!"

The *Poseidon*'s crew, despite the seriousness of their position, grinned and elbowed one another at his approach.

"Thou'rt a laureate liar, Jack," growled one of the pirates, and flung him into the group. But the scene attracted notice, and a pirate officer, who by age and appearance seemed to be the Captain, approached from the waist.

"What is't, Boabdil?" The officer's voice was mild, and his dress, in contrast to the outlandishness of his men's, was modest, even gentlemanly; on shore one would have taken him for an honest planter or shipowner in his fifties, yet the great Moor was clearly alarmed by his approach.

"Naught in the world, Captain. We found these puppies buggered in the fo'c'sle, and the long one there claims he's no sailor."

"Ask my man here!" Ebenezer pleaded, falling on his knees before the Captain. "Ask those wretches yonder if I'm one of them! I swear to you sir, I am a gentleman, the Laureate of Maryland by order of Lord Baltimore!"

In response to the Captain's question Bertrand attested his master's identity and declared his own, and the boatswain volunteered additional confirmation; but old Ned, though no one had asked his opinion, spitefully swore the opposite, and by way of evidence produced, to the poet's horror, the document signed in the fo'c'sle, which proclaimed Ebenezer a member of the crew.

" 'Twere better for all if ye signed them two aboard," he added. "They're able enough seamen, but thieves and rogues to ship with! Don't let 'em fool ye with their carrying-on!"

Seeing their old shipmate's purpose, some of the other men took up the cry, hoping thereby to save themselves from being forced to join the pirates. But the Captain, after examining Ned's document, flung it over the side.

"I know those things," he scoffed. "Besides, 'twas signed by the Laureate of Maryland." He appraised Ebenezer skeptically. "So thou'rt the famous Eben Cooke?"

"I swear't, sir!" Ebenezer's heart pounded; he tingled with admiration for the Captain's astuteness and with wonder that his own fame was already so widespread. But his troubles were not over, for although the pirate seemed virtually persuaded, he ordered both men brought aft for identification by the passengers, whereupon he was perplexed to hear a third version—neither of the men was a sailor, but it was the older, stouter one who was Laureate, and the skinny wretch his amanuensis. Captain Meech agreed, and added that this was not the servant's first presumption to his master's office.

"Ah," the pirate captain said to Bertrand, "thou'rt hiding behind thy servant's skirts, then! Yet how is't the crew maintain the contrary?"

By this time the looting of the *Poseidon* was complete, and everyone's attention turned to the interrogation. Ebenezer despaired of explaining the complicated story of his disguise.

"What matters it to you which is the liar?" Captain Meech inquired from the quarter-deck, where he was being held at pistol-point. "Take their money and begone with ye!"

To which the pirate answered, undisturbed, " 'Tis not the Laureate's money I want—he hath little enough of that, I'll wager." Ebenezer and Bertrand both vouched for the truth of this conjecture. " 'Tis a good valet I'm after, to attend me aboard ship; the Laureate can go to the Devil."

"Ye have found me out," Bertrand said at once. "I'll own I am the Laureate Eben Cooke."

"Wretch!" cried Ebenezer. "Confess thou'rt a lying scoundrel of a servant!"

"Nay, I'll tell the truth," the pirate said, watching both men carefully. " 'Tis the servant can go hang for all o' me; I've orders to hold the Laureate on my ship."

"There is your poet, sir." Bertrand pointed shamelessly to Ebenezer. "A finer master no man ever served."

Ebenezer goggled. "Nay, nay, good masters!" he said at last. " 'Tis not the first time I've presumed, as Captain Meech declared! This man here is the Laureate, in truth!"

"Enough," the pirate commanded, and turned to the turbaned Moor. "Clap 'em both in irons, and let's be off."

Thus amid murmurs from the people on the *Poseidon* the luckless pair were transferred to the shallop, protesting mightily all the way, and having confiscated every firearm and round of ammunition they could find aboard their prey, the pirates gave the ladies a final pinch, clambered over the rail, cast off the grapples, and headed for the open sea, soon putting their outraged victims far behind. The kidnaped seamen—Chips, the boatswain, and a youngster from the starboard watch—were taken to the captain's quarters to sign papers, and the two prisoners confined forward in the rope- and sail-locker, which by addition of a barred door and leg irons made fast to the massive oak knees had been turned into a lightless brig.

Sick with wrath at his valet's treachery though he was, and with apprehension for his fate, Ebenezer was also bewildered by the whole affair and demanded to know the reason for their abduction; but to all such queries their jailer—that same black giant who had first laid hands on them—simply responded, "Captain Pound hath his reasons, mate." It was not until the leg irons were fastened and the brute, in the process of bolting the heavy door, repeated this answer for the fourth or fifth time, that Ebenezer recognized the name.

"Captain *Pound,* did you say? Your captain's name is Pound?"

"Tom Pound it is," the pirate growled, and stayed for no further questions.

"Dear Heav'n!" the poet exclaimed. He and Bertrand were alone in the tiny cell now, and in absolute darkness, the Moor having taken the lamp with him.

"D'ye know the blackguard, sir? Is he a famous pirate? Ah Christ, that I were back in Pudding Lane! I'd hold the wretched thing myself, and let Ralph Birdsall do his worst!"

"Aye, I know of Thomas Pound." Ebenezer's astonishment at the coincidence—if indeed it was one—temporarily gained the better of his wrath. "He's the very pirate Burlingame once sailed with, off New England!"

"Master Burlingame a pirate!" Bertrand exclaimed. "At that, 'tis no surprise to me——"

"Hold thy lying tongue!" snapped Ebenezer. "Thou'rt a pretty knave to criticize my friend, that would throw me to the sharks yourself for tuppence!"

"Nay, prithee, sir," the servant begged, "think not so hard of me. I'll own I played ye false, but 'twas thy life or mine, no paltry tuppence." What's more, he added, Ebenezer had done the same a moment later, when the Captain revealed his true intention.

To this truth the Laureate had no rejoinder, and so for a time both men were silent, each brooding on his separate misery. For beds they had two piles of ragged sailcloth on the floor timbers, which, since their cell was in the extreme bow of the shallop, were not horizontal but curved upwards from keel and cutwater, so that they also formed the walls. The angle, together with the pounding of waves against the bow, would have made sleep impossible for Ebenezer, despite his great fatigue, even without the additional discomforts of fear and excitement. His mind returned to Henry Burlingame, who had sailed under the very brigand who now held them prisoner; perhaps aboard this very ship.

"Would he were here now, to intercede for me!"

He considered revealing his friendship with Burlingame to Captain Pound, but rejected the idea. He had no idea what name Henry had sailed under, for one thing, and his friend's manner of parting company with his shipmates would scarcely raise the value, in the Captain's eyes, of an acquaintanceship with him. Ebenezer recalled the story, told him in the Plymouth coach, of Burlingame's adventure with the mother and daughter whom he'd saved from rape, and who had rewarded him with, among other things, the first real clue to his ancestry. How sorely did he miss Henry Burlingame! He could not even remember with any precision what his dear friend looked like; at best his mental picture was a composite of the very different faces and voices of Burlingame before and after the adventures in America. Bertrand's remark came to his mind again, and brought with it disturbing memories of the valet's encounters with Henry: their meeting in the London posthouse, never mentioned by his friend, and their exchange of clothing in the stable of the King o' the Seas. Why had Bertrand not been surprised to learn of Burlingame's piracy, which had so astonished Ebenezer?

"Why did you speak so ill of Burlingame?" he asked aloud, but in reply heard only the sound of snoring from the other side of the great keel timber between them.

"In such straits as ours the wretch can sleep!" he exclaimed with a mixture of wonder and exasperation, but had not the heart to wake him. And eventually, though he had thought the thing impossible, he too succumbed to sheer exhaustion and, in that unlikeliest of places, slept.

By morning the question had either gone from his mind or lost its importance, for he said nothing of it to his servant. It appeared as the day went on that their treatment at the hands of Captain Pound was not to be altogether merciless: after a breakfast of bread, cheese, and water—not punishment, but the whole crew's morning fare—they were released from their leg irons, given some purloined clothing, and allowed to come on deck, where they found themselves riding an empty expanse of ocean. The Moor, who seemed to be first mate, set them to various simple chores like oakum-picking and holystoning; only at night were they returned to their miserable cell, and never after the first time were they subjected to the leg irons. Captain Pound put his case plainly to them: he was persuaded that one or the other was the Laureate but put no faith in the assertions of either, and meant therefore to hold both in custody. He would say no more regarding the reason for their incarceration than that he was following orders, nor of its probable term than that when so ordered he would release them. In the meantime they had only to look to their behavior, and no injury would be done them.

From all this Ebenezer could not but infer that his captor was in some manner an agent of the archconspirator John Coode, at whose direction he had lain in ambush for the *Poseidon*. The man would stop at nothing to reach his mischievous ends! And how devilish clever, to let the pirates take the blame! The prospects of death or torture no longer imminent, the Laureate allowed himself boundless indignation at being kidnaped—which mighty sentiment, however, he was sufficiently prudent to conceal from the kidnapers—and at the same time could not but commend his foe's respect for the power of the pen.

" 'Tis perfectly clear," he explained to Bertrand in a worldly tone. "Milord Baltimore had more than the muse in mind when he commissioned the *Marylandiad*. He knows what too few princes will admit: that a good poet's worth two friends at court to make or break a cause, though of course the man's too sensible of a poet's feelings to declare such a thing outright. Why else did he send dear Henry to watch after me, d'you think? And why should Coode waylay me, but that he knows my influence as well as Baltimore? I'faith, two formidable antagonists!"

If Bertrand was impressed, he was not a whit consoled. "God pox the twain of 'em!"

"Say not so," his master protested. " 'Tis all very well to keep an open mind on trifles, but this is a plain case of justice against poltroonery, and the man that shrugs compounds the felony."

"Haply so," Bertrand said with a shrug. "I know your Baltimore's a wondrous Papist, but I doubt me he's a saint yet, for all that." When Ebenezer objected, the valet went on to repeat a story he'd heard from Lucy Robotham aboard the *Poseidon*, the substance of which was that Charles Calvert was in the employ of Rome. "He hath struck a dev'lish bargain with the Pope to join the Papists and the salvages against the Protestants and butcher every soul of 'em! Then when he hath made a Romish fortress out of Maryland, the Jesuits will swarm like maggots o'er the landscape, and ere ye can say 'Our Father' the entire country belongs to Rome!"

"Pernicious drivel!" Ebenezer scoffed. "What cause hath Baltimore to do such evil?"

"What cause! The Pope is sworn to beatify him if he Romanizes Maryland, and canonize him if he snatches the whole country! He'll make a bloody saint of him!" It was to prevent exactly this catastrophe, Lucy Robotham had declared, that her father and the rest had joined with Coode to overthrow the Papists in Maryland, coincidentally with the deposition of King James, and to petition William and Mary to assume the government of the Province. "Yet old Coode was ill paid for's labors," Bertrand said, "for no sooner was the house pulled down than the wreckers fell out amongst themselves, and Baltimore contrived to get this fellow Nicholson the post of Governor. He flies King William's colors, but all the world knows he's a Papist at heart: when he fought with James at Hounslow Heath, he said his mass with the rest, and 'twas an Irish Papist troop he took to Boston."

"Dear Father!" Ebenezer cried. "What a sink of calumny this Robotham strumpet was! Nicholson's as honest a man as I!"

"He is the Duke of Bolton's bastard," the valet went on stubbornly. "And ere he took up with the Papists he was aide-de-camp to Colonel Kirke in Africa. They do declare he had a draught of wine from the Colonel's arse at Mequinez, to please the Emperor Muley Ishmael——"

"Stop!"

"Some say 'twas May-wine and others Bristol sherry; Mistress Lucy herself held with the May-winers."

"I'll hear no more!" the poet threatened, but to his every protest Bertrand made the same replies. "There's a lot goes on that your honest wight dreams naught of," or *More history's made in the bedchamber than in the throne room.*

" 'Tis not a fart to me who's right or wrong," he said at last. "This Coode hath ginned us either way, and we'll ne'er set foot on land."

"How is that?" the poet demanded. "I've fared no worse here than aboard the *Poseidon*, and we're only to be held till farther notice."

"No doubt!" the servant said. "But if thou'rt such a cannon as Charles Calvert thinks, is't likely Coode will turn ye loose to blast him? 'Tis a mystery to me we're still alive!"

Ebenezer could not but acknowledge the logic of this position, yet neither could he be immediately terrified by it. Captain Pound was unquestionably formidable, but he was not cruel: although in the incident related by Burlingame he had apparently condoned rape, he seemed to draw the line at murder, and his plundering of the *Poseidon* had been almost gentlemanly. Moreover he was not even avaricious, as pirates go: for weeks on end the shallop cruised with apparent aimlessness from north to south and back again, flying English colors; when a sail appeared on the horizon the pirates gave chase, but upon overhauling the other ship they would salute it amiably, and Captain Pound would inquire, as might the captain of any vessel met at sea, what port the stranger was bound for, and with what cargo. And though the replies were sometimes provocative—"Bark *Adelaide,* a hundred and thirty days out of Falmouth, for Philadelphia with silk and silverware," or "Brig *Pilgrim* out of Jamaica with rum for Boston"—only twice during the three full months of his imprisonment did Ebenezer witness acts of piracy, and these occurred consecutively on the same early August day, in the following manner:

For several days the shallop had ridden hove to, though the weather was fine and nothing could be seen on any quarter. Just after the midday meal on the day referred to the lookout spied a sail to westward, and after observing it for some time through his glass, Captain Pound said, " 'Tis the *Poseidon,* all right. Take 'em below." The three kidnaped sailors were ordered to their quarters in the fo'c'sle, Bertrand was confined to the sail-locker, and Ebenezer, who had labored all morning at the apparently pointless job of shifting cargo in the hold, was sent below to complete the task.

"Poor Captain Meech!" he thought. "This devil hath lain in wait to ruin him!" Though he deplored the idea of piracy in general and wished neither Meech nor his passengers harm, he could not feel pity for the sailors who had done him such an outrage; having witnessed already the ferocity of the pirates, he rather relished the idea of a fight between them and the *Poseidon*'s crew. In any case he had no intention of missing the excitement on deck: during the chase, which lasted no more than an hour, he toiled dutifully in the hold, moving barrels and boxes aft in order (he understood now) to make room for additional loot; but when the grapples were thrown and all but a handful of the pirates crouched at the lee rail ready to board, he climbed to the edge of the after hatch and peered over.

His heart leaped at sight of the familiar vessel: there was the quarterdeck whereon he'd debated with Bertrand the right demeanor for a poet and from which he'd been cast providentially into the sea; there on the poop stood Captain Meech, grim-faced, exhorting his men as before not to jeopardize the passengers' safety by resisting the assault, even though he had mounted a brand new eight-pounder in the bow.

Ebenezer clucked his tongue. "Poor wretch!"

There in the waist the ladies squealed and swooned as before, while the gentlemen, frowning nervously, were led off to their cabins for robbing; there by the foremast the sailors huddled. Ebenezer saw several of his molesters, including Ned, and many new faces as well. The pirates, having been at sea for at least the six weeks since their last encounter, took no pains to disguise their lust for the ladies and the female servants: they addressed them in the lewdest terms; pinched, poked, tweaked, and stroked. Captain Pound had his hands full preventing wholesale assault. He cursed the crew in his quiet hissing voice and threatened them with keelhauling if they did not desist. Even so, the mate himself, black Boabdil, driven nearly berserk by the sight of an adolescent beauty who, perhaps seasick, had been brought up on deck in her nightdress, flung her over his shoulder and made for the railing, clearly intending to have at her in traditional pirate fashion; it took the Captain's pistol at his temple to restrain the Moor's ardor and send him off growling and licking his lips. The girl, happily, had fainted at his first approach, and so was oblivious to her honor's narrow rescue.

So desperate did the situation become that at length the Captain ordered all hands back aboard the shallop, though the pillaging was not entirely finished, and cast off the grapples. He carried with him Captain Meech, two members of the *Poseidon*'s crew, and one of her longboats, giving as his reasons the need for a consultation on the subject of longitude and the possibility that not all of the eight-pounder's ammunition had been confiscated; he would set them free, he declared, as soon as the shallop was out of range. Then he set the still grumbling crew to stowing the fresh provisions in preparation for the formal dividing of the spoils, and retreated with his hostage to the chartroom.

Now Ebenezer had of course abandoned his observation post when the pirates came back aboard, and so dangerous was their mood that before the first barrel of port came down the hatch he hid himself far aft, behind the old cargo, to avoid their wrath. His hiding place was a wide black cranny, perhaps three feet high, that extended on both sides of the keel under the cabins, as far aft as the rudderpost in the stern. Since the space provided access to the steering-cables running from the wheel on deck through blocks to the rudderpost itself, it was provided with a false floor over the bilge, on which the Laureate lay supine and still. Over his head, which was not two feet from the stern, he heard the sound of chairs scraping on the floor, and presently a pair of chuckling voices.

"By Heav'n, the black had like to split her open!" said one, and Ebenezer easily identified Captain Pound. "I thought he'd pitch me to the fishes when I stopped him!"

The other laughed. "He'd ha' spitted her through for all I'd cross him, Tom, I swear't! 'Twere a pity, though, I'll grant ye; she's a gentleman's morsel, not a beef-bull's, and I mean to try her ere we raise Lands End."

Ebenezer was not surprised to hear the voice of Captain Meech, but he was horrified at the intimacy suggested by their conversation.

"Do ye look for trouble?" Meech asked.

"God knows, Jim. Boabdil is a wild one when he sets his cap for coney. They all need a week ashore, or I'm a dead man."

"Well, I've no orders for ye about your poet, but I did bring ye this—they smuggled it aboard at Cedar Point."

There was a pause while Meech brought forth whatever it was he referred to, then a slap as of papers on the table. Ebenezer strained his ears, though every word thus far he had heard distinctly. He forgot completely about the original purpose of his concealment.

"*A Secret Historie of the Voiage Up the Bay of Chesapeake*," Pound read aloud. "What foolery is this?"

"No foolery," Meech laughed. "Old Baltimore would cut your throat for't! Look on the backsides."

The papers rustled. " 'Fore God!"

"Aye." Meech confirmed whatever realization his friend had reached. "They got it off Dick Smith in Calvert County —God knows how! He's Baltimore's surveyor general."

"But what am *I* to do with it?"

"They said Coode himself will come for't in a month or so. This is only a part of the whole Journal, from what I gather; if he can find the rest ere things get settled, then Nicholson can't touch him. Right now the place is a bedlam, Tom: ye should see St. Mary's City! Andros came and went; Lawrence is back in; Henry Jowles hath Ninian Beale's old job; old Robotham's back in, that hath the daughter ye liked—remember Lucy?"

"Aye," said Pound, "from the last time. She hath a birthmark on her arse, you told me."

"Nay, Tom, no birthmark! 'Tis the Great Bear in freckles, I swear't, and the pointers point——"

"No more!" Pound laughed. "I remember where the pole-star was, that all men's needles aimed at. Go on with Maryland, now, ere ye have to leave."

"Marry, what a wench!" Meech said. "Where was I? Did I tell ye about Andros?" He went on to relate that John Coode's brother-in-law, Neamiah Blackistone, so influential under the late Governor Copley, had died in disgrace last February after the Commissioners of the Customs-House, on evidence from the "Burlingame's *Journall* documents" smuggled to Lord Baltimore by Nicholson, had charged him with graft. Sir Edmund Andros of Virginia had returned to St. Mary's in May with Sir Thomas Lawrence, whom Copley had impeached, and made him President of the Council and acting Governor of Maryland—to the rebels' dismay, since it was Lawrence who had smuggled the notorious Assembly Journal of 1691 to Nicholson. Then Nicholson had landed, embraced his good friend Lawrence, and made a Maryland councillor out of Edward Randolph, the Jacobite Royal Surveyor so well known up and down the colonies for his prankish contempt of provincial authorities. But so far from thanking his old superior Andros for governing in his absence, Nicholson had promptly called that government illegal, declared null and void all statutes passed thereunder, and demanded (thus far in vain) that Andros return the five-hundred-pound honorarium awarded him for his services by Lawrence's Council! The insurrectionists, Meech declared, were making the most of this rebuff to turn Andros against Nicholson; their leader Coode still held with impunity the post of sheriff in St. Mary's County and a lieutenant-colonelcy in the county militia under Lawrence himself, and in these capacities drew his salary from the very government he was doing his best to overthrow. Andros had already allowed Coode the services of his "coast-guard" Captain Pound, of course, and in addition had virtually promised Coode asylum in Virginia if, as was feared imminent, Nicholson opened cases against him, his ally Kenelm Cheseldyne of the Assembly, and old Blackistone's widow. The insurrectionists, Meech said further, were engaged both defensively and offensively: they were ransacking the Province for the other portions of the incriminating Journal, which they understood to be cached with various Papists and Jacobites, and at the same time they were inciting the Piscataway Indians to rebel, perhaps in league with other Indian nations.

"Marry, 'tis a perilous game they play!" said Pound. "I'm happy to be at sea!"

"I'm happy to be sailing east to London, Tom; this Coode would burn a province on a bet. Yet he doth pay handsomely."

"Speaking whereof——"

"Aye," Meech said. There was another pause. "They gave me *this* to give ye for holding Cooke, and there's another like it for keeping these papers." Nicholson had learned of the Journal's absence, he explained, and was turning the Province upside down to find it—hence the rebels' decision to remove it from the colony altogether until things settled down. Pound was to cruise in his present latitude for six weeks, or until a ship came out from Coode to fetch the papers. At that time he would receive his fee and, in all likelihood, instructions concerning his prisoners.

"Good enough," said Captain Pound. "Now let me give ye *your* share from the last trip."

"Did ye do well by't, Tom?"

"Not bad," Pound allowed, and added that since the terms of their agreement gave all the cash to the pirates and all the jewels to Meech, who could easily sell them in London, it was to be expected that on westbound trips the pirates would fare as well or better, but on eastbound trips, when many of the passengers would have nothing left but the family jewels, Meech would get the lion's share. The transaction was completed; Meech made ready to depart in the longboat, and Ebenezer, who had heard the entire colloquy in horror and astonishment, prepared to evacuate his hiding-place, the pirates having long since finished loading the hold.

"One more thing," Meech said, and the poet scrambled back to hear. "If Coode hath not found the rest of his Journal by the time he fetches this part, tell him I've a notion where to look for't, but 'twill cost him twenty pounds if he finds it there. Did ye see what's writ on the back of all those pages?"

"You mean this *Voiage Up the Bay of Chesapeake?* What is it?"

Meech explained that Kenelm Cheseldyne had recorded the Journal of the 1691 Assembly on the reverse pages of a bound quarto manuscript provided him by Coode, which happened to be an old diary the rebel had acquired while hiding out in Jamestown. " 'Twas a wight named Smith wrote the diary—damnedest thing ye ever read!—and they all call it 'Smith's book' for safety's sake, the Papists as well as the rebels, though few of 'em e'er laid eyes on't." What would be more natural, then, he asked of Pound, than for Baltimore to distribute the portions for safekeeping to various confederates of the same surname?

Ebenezer began to sweat. Pound, to his great relief, laughed at the conjecture as preposterous, but promised to relay it to Coode's agents for what it was worth.

"Which is twenty pounds," Meech declared merrily. "Come, threaten me to my boat, now, or they'll see our game. I'll be back with the Smoker's Fleet next spring or before."

Ebenezer scrambled out of his cranny, over boxes and barrels, and up the ladder to the hatch, nearly sick with indignation and excitement. He was bursting to tell Bertrand all he'd heard; in the considerable uproar that greeted the appearance of the two captains he was able to climb to the deck and move forward to the fo'c'sle companionway (which led also to his berth in the rope-locker) without attracting undue notice.

The men were indeed in mutinous spirits, ready to make trouble at the slightest excuse. Grudgingly they released the two terrified sailors from the *Poseidon,* whom they had tormented throughout the captains' private conversation; their faces darkened as Meech's longboat, under the barrels of their pistols, struck out for its mother ship on the north horizon.

Ebenezer slipped through the fo'c'sle to his cell—which customarily remained unlocked—and told Bertrand the story of Meech's treachery, Coode's latest intrigues, and the valuable document in the Captain's quarters.

"I must lay hands on those papers!" he exclaimed. "How Coode came by them I can't imagine, but Baltimore shall have them!"

Bertrand shook his head. "Marry, sir, 'tis not thy fight. A poet hath no part in these things."

"Not so," Ebenezer replied. "I vowed to fling myself into the arms of Life, and what is life but the taking of sides? Besides, I've private reasons for wanting that Journal." How pleased would Burlingame be, he reflected happily, to learn that Captain John Smith had a secret diary! Who knew but what these very papers were the key poor Henry so long had sought to unlock the mystery of his parentage?

"I see those reasons plain enough," the valet declared. "The book would fetch a pretty price if ye put it up for bids. But 'twill do ye small good to steal it when we've no more than a fortnight left on earth. Marry, did ye see what spirits the Moor is in? If this Coode doth not kill us, the pirates will."

But the Laureate did not agree. "This faction may be our

salvation, not our doom." He described the delicate atmosphere on deck. " 'Tis Pound that holds us prisoner, not the crew," he said. "They've naught to gain by killing us if they mutiny, but they may well kill him. What's more, they know naught of the Journal. Belike they'll make us members of the crew, and once the turmoil hath subsided I'll find a way to steal the book. Then we can watch our chance to slip ashore. Or better, once we're pirates like the rest we can hide aboard some ship we're sent to plunder; they'd never miss us. Let 'em mutiny, I say; we'll join them!"

As if the last were a command, an instant later a shout went up on deck, followed at once by a brace of pistol-shots. Ebenezer and Bertrand hurried up to declare their allegiance to the mutineers, who they readily assumed had taken charge of the shallop, and indeed they found Boabdil at the helm, grinning at the men assembled in the waist. But instead of lying dead on the deck, Captain Pound stood beside him, arms crossed, a smoking pistol in each hand and a grim smile upon his face, and it was one of the crew, a one-eyed Carolina boy named Patch, who sprawled, face-down and bleeding on the poop companionway.

"We'll put into port when I say so," Pound declared, and returned the pistols to his sash. Two men stepped forward to retrieve their wounded shipmate.

"Over the side with him," the Captain ordered, and despite the fact that he was not yet dead, the Carolinian was tumbled into the ocean.

"The next man I shan't waste a ball on," Pound threatened, and did not even look back to see his victim flounder in the wake.

"Why is the Moor so happy?" Bertrand whispered to Ebenezer. "Ye said he was the wrathfulest of all."

The poet, stunned by his first sight of death, shook his head and swallowed furiously to keep from being ill.

Just then the lookout cried "Sail, ho! Sail to eastward!" The pirates looked to see a three-master heading in their direction, but were too chastened to display any great interest.

"There, now!" laughed Captain Pound, after examining the stranger through his glass. "If Patch had held his peace ten minutes more, he'd not be feeding sea-crabs! D'ye know what ship stands yonder, men?"

They did not, nor did the prospect of robbing it fill them with enthusiasm.

" 'Tis the London ship I've laid for these two weeks,"

Pound declared, "whilst you wretches were conspiring in the fo'c'sle! Did ye ne'er hear tell of a brigantine called the *Cyprian?*"

On hearing this name the crew cheered lustily, again and again. They slapped one another's backs, leaped and danced about the deck, and at the Captain's orders sprang as if possessed to ratlines, sheets, halyards, and brace. Topsails and forestaysail were broken out, the helm was put hard over, and the shallop raced to meet her newest prey head-on.

"What is this *Cyprian*, that changed their minds so lightly?" Bertrand whispered.

"I do not know," his master answered, sorry to see the mutiny come to nothing. "But she hath sprung from the sea like her namesake, and haply we'll have cause to love her. Look sharp for your chance to slip aboard; I hope to steal the Journal if I can."

15

The Rape of the Cyprian; *Also, the Tale of Hicktopeake, King of Accomack, and the Greatest Peril the Laureate Has Fallen Into Thus Far*

IN LESS THAN a quarter of an hour the shallop and the brigantine, sailing smartly on opposite reaches, were within cannon-range of each other. Dozens of the brigantine's passengers were crowded forward to see the shallop, possibly the first vessel they'd met in weeks; they waved hands and kerchiefs in innocent salute. The pirates, every idle hand of whom was similarly occupied, responded with a fearsome cry and fired a round into the water dead ahead of their quarry. It was not until then, when the others screamed and ran for cover, that Ebenezer began to guess in a general way what was afoot: every one of the passengers he could see was female.

"Dear Heav'n!" he breathed.

The captain of the brigantine realized the shallop's intention and came about to run north before the wind, at the same time firing on the attacker; but his defense came too late. Anticipating exactly such a maneuver, Captain Pound had his crew already stationed to follow suit, and the shallop was under way on the new course before the brigantine finished setting her sails. Moreover, although the several square-rigged sails of the brigantine were better for running before the wind than the fore-and-aft rig of her pursuer, the shallop's smaller size and lighter weight more than compensated for the difference. Captain Pound ordered his men not to return the musket- and pistol-fire; instead, taking the helm himself, he cut so close under the brigantine's stern that the name *Cyprian,* on a banner held by carved oak cupids, was plainly legible on her transom. At the very moment when the shallop's bowsprit seemed about to pierce the victim's stern, he veered a few degrees to starboard; the cannoneer in the bow fired a ball point-blank into the brigantine's rudder, and the chase was over. The *Cyprian*'s crew scrambled to take in sail before the helpless vessel capsized. By the time the shallop came about and retraced her course the brigantine was rolling under bare poles in the swell; the crew stood with upraised arms, the first mate ran a white flag up the main halyards, and the captain, hands clasped behind him, waited on the poop for the worst.

The pirates were beside themselves. They thronged to the rail, shouting obscenities and making lewd gestures. It was all Boabdil could do to bring the shallop alongside, so preoccupied were they all with their joy: the Moor himself had stripped off all but his tall red headgear and stood like a nightmare at the helm. At length the grapples were made fast, the sails struck, and the ships lashed together along their beams, so that they rode like mated seabirds on the waves. Then with howls the pirates swarmed over the rails, cursing and stumbling in their haste. The *Cyprian*'s crew backed off in fright, but no one paid them the slightest attention: indeed, Captain Pound had finally to force three of his men at pistol-point to tie them to the masts. The rest had no thought for anything but breaking open the companionway and cabin doors, which the terrified passengers had bolted from inside.

Their savagery made Ebenezer blanch. Beside him where he stood near the shallop's foremast was the oldest member of the pirate crew, Carl, the sailmaker—a wizened, evil-appearing little man in his sixties with a short, dirty beard and no teeth at all—chuckling and shaking his head at the scene.

"Is the ship full of women?" the Laureate asked him.

The old man nodded mirthfully. "She's the whore-boat out o' London." Once or twice a year, he explained, the *Cyprian's* captain took on a load of impoverished ladies who were willing to prostitute themselves for six months in the colonies, where the shortage of women was acute. The girls were transported without charge; the enterprising captain received not only their fares but—in the case of girls with special qualifications such as virginity, respectability, or extreme youth or comeliness—a bonus as well from the brothel-masters who came to Philadelphia from all over the provinces for the purpose of replenishing or augmenting their staffs. As for the girls, some had already been prostitutes in London, others were women rendered desperate by poverty or other circumstances, and some simply hard-reasoning young serving girls bent on reaching America at any cost, who found six months of prostitution more attractive than the customary four-year indenture of the colonial servant.

"Every pirate on the coast keeps his eye out for the *Cyprian* this time o' year," the sailmaker said. "There's better than a hundred wenches behind that door. Lookee there at Boabdill!"

Ebenezer saw the naked Moor push aside his shipmates and raise a huge maul that he had found nearby, probably left on deck by the brigantine's carpenter. With one blow he splintered the door and dived headlong inside, the others close behind him. A moment later the air was split with screams and curses.

Ebenezer's knees trembled. "Poor wretches! Poor wretches!"

"*This!*" scoffed Carl. " 'Tis but a bloody prayer meeting, *this* is! Ye should have shipped with old Tom Tew of Newport, as I did. One time last year we sailed from Libertatia to the coast of Araby, and in the Red Sea we overhauled one o' the Great Mogul's ships with pilgrims bound for Mecca; a hundred gun she carried, but we boarded her without losing a man, and what do ye think we found? *Sixteen hundred virgins*, sir! Not a maidenhead more nor less! Sixteen hundred virgins bound for Mecca, the nicest little Moors ye e'er laid eyes upon, and not above a hundred of us! Took us a day and a night to pop 'em all—Frenchmen, Dutchmen, Portogeezers, Africans, and Englishmen, we were—and ere we had done, the deck looked like a butcher's block. There is not the like o' that day and night in the history of the lickerish world, I swear't! I cut a brace myself, for all I was coming on to sixty

—little brown twins they were, and tight as a timber-hitch, and I've ne'er got up the old fid since!"

He rambled on, but Ebenezer could not bear to hear him out. For one thing, the scene on deck was too arresting for divided attention: the pirates dragged out their victims in ones and twos, a-swoon or awake, at pistol-point or by main strength. He saw women assaulted on the decks, on the stairways, at the railings, everywhere, in every conceivable manner. None was spared, and the prettier prizes were clawed at by two and three at a time. Boabdil appeared with one over each shoulder, kicking and scratching him in vain: as he presented one to Captain Pound on the quarter-deck, the other wriggled free and tried to escape her monstrous fate by scrambling up the mizzen ratlines. The Moor allowed her a fair head start and then climbed slowly in pursuit, calling to her in voluptuous Arabic at every step. Fifty feet up, where any pitch of the hull is materially amplified by the height, the girl's nerve failed: she thrust bare arms and legs through the squares of the rigging and hung for dear life while Boabdil, once he had come up from behind, ravished her unmercifully. Down on the shallop the sailmaker clapped his hands and chortled; Ebenezer, heartsick, turned away.

He saw Bertrand a little distance behind him, watching with undisguised avidity, and recalled his plan. The time was propitious: every member of the shallop's crew except old Carl was busy at his pleasure, and even Captain Pound, who normally stood aloof from all festivities, had found the Moor's trophy too tempting to refuse and had disappeared with her into the brigantine's cabin.

"Look sharp!" he whispered to the valet. "I'm going for the Journal now, and then we'll try to slip aboard the *Cyprian*." And ignoring Bertrand's frightened look, he made his way carefully aft to the doorway of Captain Pound's quarters. It required no searching to find what he sought: the Journal lay in plain view on the table, its loose pages held fast by a fungus-coral paperweight. Ebenezer snatched it up and scanned the first page with pounding heart: a transcription of the Assembly's convening, meaningless to him. But on the *recto*——

"Ah!"

A *Secret Historie of the Voiage Up the Bay of Chesapeake From Jamestowne in Virginia,* he read, *Undertaken in the Yeer of Our Lord 1608 By C^{apt} J^{no} Smith, & Faithfullie Set Down in Its Severall Parts By the Same.* And below, in an antique, almost illegible hand, the narrative commenced, not

275

as a diary at all but as a summary account, probably meant as the initial draft of part of the author's well-known *Generall Historie of Virginia:*

> *Seven souldiers, six gentlemen, Dr Russell the Chirurgeon & my selfe did embark from the towne of Kecoughtan, in Virginia, in June of the present yeer 1608,*

> > *To walk a wayless Way with uncouth Pace,*
> > *W^ch yet no Christian Man did ever trace. . . .*

Much farther than this the poet dared not read at the moment, but he could not refrain from thumbing rapidly through the rest of the manuscript in search of the name *Henry Burlingame.* It did not take long to find: *No sooner was the King asleep,* he read on an early page, *then I straightway made for the doore, and w^d have fulfill'd his everie wish, had not Ld Burlingame prevented me, and catching hold of my arme, declar'd, That he did protest my doing this thing. . . .*

"Burlingame a Lord!" Ebenezer exclaimed to himself, and joyfully thrust the manuscript into his shirt, holding it fast under the waist of his breeches. He peeped out onto the deck. All seemed clear: the only man in a position to spy him was the Moor in the *Cyprian*'s mizzen-rigging, and he was occupied with climbing down for further conquests, leaving his first quite ravaged in the ratlines. The sun was setting; its long last rays lit the scene unnaturally, from the side, with rose and gold.

"Hi' ho, Master Eben!"

The Laureate quailed at the salute; but the voice was Bertrand's.

"Stupid fellow! He'll do me in yet!" He looked for the valet in vain on the shallop's deck: the sailmaker stood alone by the railing.

"Come along, Master Eben! Over here!" The voice came from the direction of the brigantine. Horrified, Ebenezer saw Bertrand standing in the vessel's stern, about to have at a plump lass whom he was bending over the taffrail. Ebenezer signaled frantically for the man to come back, but Bertrand laughed and shook his head. "They've asked us to join 'em!" he called, and turned to his work.

For Ebenezer to slip aboard unnoticed was unthinkable in the face of this defection. All over the *Cyprian* the debauch continued; the hapless women, gilded by the sunlight, had for the most part abandoned hope, and instead of running, submitted to their attackers with pleas for mercy or stricken silence. The poet shuddered and fled to his cell in the rope-locker, determined, since he could not make his escape, to take advantage of the diversion to read through the precious manuscript. He borrowed a lamp from the fo'c'sle, closed the heavy door, took out the Journal, and lay on his bed of tattered sailcloth, where he read as follows:

Seven souldiers, six gentlemen, Dr Russell the Chirurgeon & my selfe did embark from the towne of Kecoughtan, in Virginia, in June of the present yeer 1608,

> To walk a wayless Way with uncouth Pace,
> W^ch yet no Christian Man did ever trace.

We took for the voiage a barge of three tonnes burthen, to the provisioning whereof I earlie set the great Liverpooler Henry Burlingame, that I durst not leave behind to smirch my name with slander & calumnie. Yet scarce had we dropt Kecoughtan to Southward, then I found the wretch had play'd me false; to feed the companie of fifteene men the summer long, he had supply'd one meager sack of weevilie oats and a barricoe of cloudie water! I enquir'd of him, W^d he starve us? Or did he think to make me turn tayle home? W^ch latter hope I knew, he shar'd with all the idle Gentlemen his fellows. Then I set them all to short rations and fishing over the gunwales, albeit I knew no means to cooke a fish in the barge. The truth was, I reckon'd on a landfall within two days, but said naught of it, and what fish they caught I threw back in the Bay. I then commenc'd instructing one & all in the art of sayles & tiller, wch matters the souldiers took to readilie and the Gentlemen complayn'd of—none lowder then Ld Burlingame, that I had a-bayling water from the bilge.

This Burlingame w^d say to his neighbour, What doth the Captain reck it if we perish? What time he getteth in a pickle, we Gentlemen must grubb him out, else some naked Salvage wench flieth down from Heaven to save his neck. By wch he referr'd to Pocahontas, Powhatans daughter, that some months past had rescu'd me, and I saw, he meant to devill me through the voiage.

Next day we rays'd a cape of land, lying due North of Kecoughtan, and the companie rejoyc'd thereat, inasmuch as there bellies all complayn'd of meale & clowdie water. We made straightway to shoar, whereupon we found a pair of fearsome Salvages, arm'd with bone-poynt speares. I made bold to salute them, and was pleas'd to learn, they spake a tongue like Powhatans, to wch Emperour they declar'd them selves subject. The fierce-nesse of these men was in there paynt alone; they were but spearing fish along the shallows. Upon my entreatie, they led us to there town and to there King, that was call'd Hicktopeake.

Then follow'd an adventure, wch I cannot well include among my Histories. I shall set it down upon these privie pages, for that it shews afresh that enmity I spake of, betwixt Ld Burlingame & my selfe, wch led us anon to the verie doore of Death. . . .

"Mercy!" Ebenezer cried, and turned the page.

This Hicktopeake, then, bade us well come to his Kingdom, the wch he did call Accomack, and lay'd before us a sumptuous meale. I observ'd him, while that we ate, and I sweare him to be the comliest, proper, civill Salvage we incounter'd. I din'd well, as is my wont, and also Walter the physician and the souldiers, but our Gentlemen shew'd smalle appetyte for Salvage cookerie. Burlingame, in especiall, shew'd little stomacke, for a man of his corpulencie, and who had been erst so lowd of his bellie. The meale done, Hicktopeake deliver'd him selfe of a smalle speech, again bidding us well come to his towne, and offering to replenishe our supplies ere we left him. It seem'd to me then, he shew'd a curious eagernesse, that we s^hd tarrie somewhile with him, but I learn'd not the cause of it at once.

On my enquiring of him, the extent of his Kingdom? Hicktopeake reply'd onely that it was of considerable breadth, and ran awaye up the countrie, untill that the land grewe wider. This territorie he rul'd conjoyntlie with his Brother, one Debedeavon, called by the Salvages, the Laughing King of Accomack. Debedeavons towne, we learn'd was farther inland, where he liv'd with his Queene in a goodlie house. I ask'd then, Where was Hicktopeakes Queene? meaning no more then a courtesie by my question. But seeing his face grewe all beclowded, I sought to change the topick, and inquir'd, Why was Debedeavon call'd the Laughing King? Whereupon, albeit I knew not why, Hicktopeakes wrath did but increase, so that he was scarce able to contain him selfe. I sawe no frute in farther inquirie, and so held my peace, and smoak'd of the tobacco that was then past round.

Hicktopeake at length regayning somewhat of his controll, he did command my partie to be given lodging for the night, and I consented, for that the skye was lowring, and bade fowle weather. The Gentlemen and my selfe, were given place in Hicktopeakes howse, that for all his being King, was but a single roome of large dimension. All did forthwith set them selves to sleep, save Burlingame, who ever hownds my steps, and sleeps not save when I sleep also. The King & I then smoak'd many pipes beside the fyre, in all silence. I knew well, he was desirous of speaking farther to me, but that after the manner of the Salvages, he tarry'd long ere commencing. For this reason I yearn'd that Burlingame s^hd retyre, that we might speake privilie, but this he w^d not, maugre my hints & suggestions.

At last Hicktopeake spake, and talk'd a great while of trifling things, as is the Salvages wont. Then he said, in substance (for I am here Englishing his speech), Sir, ye doubtlesse mark me a batchelor, for that no wife attendeth me in my house, or at my board, and farther, that upon thy enquirie, Where was my Queene? I mayde thee no replie. Yet in this thou art mistaken. Queene have I in sooth, and of surpassing comelinesse, that I have onely latelie had to wife. Yet wife she is not, for is it not the first requirement of a wife, that she seeke not farther than her wedded spouse, for her felicitie? But my Queene, she findeth me deficient, though I mark my selfe a man in everie wise, and she goeth about unsatisfy'd. And Queene she is not, for is it not the first requirement of a Queene, that she doe naught but what will shewe the greatnesse of her King? But my Queene, from her dissatisfaction with my manlinesse, doth ever seek pleasure in the howses of other men, thereby bringing disgrace upon my head; and stille she goeth unsatisfy'd, by her own pronouncement. Now this is an evill thing, for that not only doth this woman dishonour my selfe, and keep me for ever wearie, but also she fatigueth all the young men of my towne, and old as well. She is even as is the leech, that having tasted bloud, can never drink his fille; or as the owle, that devoureth all the myce of the field, and goeth yet hungrie to her nest. My Brother, Debedeavon, maketh much of this matter, and laugheth at me still (wherefor they call him, the Laughing King). A wife he hath, that he keepeth well satisfy'd, and hence regardeth him selfe my better, as doe his people mine. (Yet is his wife a mowse, and lightlie fill'd, for that oft have I try'd her my own selfe, the while my brother fish'd.) Therefore I aske of thee of the faire skinne this, that ye assaye to please the Queene, or teach her to be pleas'd even with that wᶜʰ she hath alreadie, to the end that peace & honour may reign in my towne, and my Brother mock me no farther. For I judge of thy dress, thy strange vessell, and thy manlie bearing, thou art no common man, but a doer of wonders.

Thus spake this Hicktopeake, and I heard him with amazement, for that most men, that cᵈ not satisfye there wives, were loath to own there deficiencie to another man. Yet I did admire his truthfullnesse & candour, & his generositie, in inviting my selfe to attempt, what he cᵈ not doe. With as much of grace as I cᵈ muster, I accepted Hicktopeakes offer, whereupon he shew'd me a doore of his howse, the wᶜʰ he said, open'd upon the chamber of the Queene. Then he lay'd him selfe down next the fyre and slept, onely fitfullie, as well a man might, that hath granted leave to another to go in unto the wife of his bed.

No sooner was the King asleep, then I straightway made for the doore, and wᵈ have fulfill'd his everie wish, had not Lᵈ Burlingame prevented me, and catching hold of my arme, declar'd, That he did protest my doing this thing. I enquir'd, Why did he protest? seeing that I knew him for no Catholick Saint. Whereto he reply'd, That be that as may, he purpos'd to doe the thing him selfe, for that I had receiv'd the favours of Pocahontas, and had deflowr'd that same maide by scurrilous subterfuge, whereas he had enjoy'd naught of her, nor had layn with woman, since that he set sayle from London. Moreover, he declar'd, That sh^{d} I refuse him this favour (albeit he was in my debt for his scurvie life), he meant to noyse the truth about my egg-plant receipt all over Jamestowne, and London as well.

Hereupon I told him, That he c^{d} plough the Salvage Queene all he chose, I car'd not, and said farther, That were she halfe the Messalina good Hicktopeake made her out, it w^{d} want more man then tenne of Burlingame, to pacifie her. This said, I bow'd him to the doore, and joyn'd my snoaring fellows at the fyre. Yet I went not to sleep my owne selfe, but rested awake & smoak'd tobacco, thinking, That in all probabilitie my nights adventures were not done.

At length Burlingame return'd, much out of humour, and upon my enquiring of him, Was the Queene so lightlie pleas'd? he but broke wind at me, and seeing the King stille slept, call'd her divers kinds of whoore & peddle-bumme. He w^{d}, he said, have gone into her, for that she had receiv'd him with friendlinesse enow, but that when he stoode all readie to doe his carnall work, she had demanded of him, Where was his monie? and he having naught to offer, save a parcell of tobacco, she straightway turn'd upon her bellie, and w^{d} no more of him. Whereon he had left her.

I did laugh greatlie at this tale, and said to him, that he w^{d} ever fare ill in conquests of women, for that he was put off so lightlie. And it was a happie thing, for both our heads, that Powhatan erst had set my selfe to pierce his daughters nether armour, and not him. By way of answer, Burlingame but broke wind againe, and said, That if I wish'd to make good my boasts, the doore was yet unlatch'd, and the Queene yet flatt upon the grownd. For him, he w^{d} nothing farther of the whoore, be she Queen or scullerie maide.

I hi'd me then without losse of time to the Queenes apartment, leaving Burlingame at the fyre to stewe in his owne cowardice. Directlie my eyes grewe us'd to the dark, I made out the Queene her selfe, once more upon her back. She was a passing comelie Salvage, I c^{d} see, with gracious features, shapelie limbs, and a smalle flatt bellie, and her papps & other appurtenancies were such, as to whett any mans lust. Upon her directing me, in Salvage jargon, to doe my wille, I prick'd up like a doggs eare, at smelle of meate. I presented my selfe as C^{apt} J^{no} Smith of Virginia, deeming it a beastlie thing, to swive a woman without first exchanging cordialities. But to this she pay'd no heed at all, onely shew'd me, by certaine movements, she mark'd such pleasantries a waste of time. Therefore I hasten'd to undoe my selfe, and had clipp'd her on the instant, but that she stay'd my ardour; and poynting to that place, the wch she had in Salvage fashion pluck'd bald as a biskett & bedawb'd with puccoon paynt, she demanded first some payment, saying, That she was not wont to bestowe her charms for naught.

This troubl'd me not a whitt, for that I was us'd to dealing with both whoores & Salvages. I fetch'd up my breeches, and withdrewe therefrom a fistfull of bawbles, that ever charme the Salvage eye. These I gave her, but she flung them awaye, and demanded something more. I gave her then a smalle charme, that I had got from a dead Moor, the wch was said to have magick powers, but this neither she deign'd to accept. After that I offer'd the slutt a lewd figure done in ivorie, a smalle coyne inscrib'd in filthie Arabick, and the pledge of twelve yardes of Scotch cloth, to be deliver'd on the next boat from London—all to no availe. She w^d have six lengths of *wompompeag,* she said, or nine of *roanoke,* for her favours, and naught besides, for that her other lovers were wont to pay that summe for her bodie, she being the Queene. I made replye, That I had no Salvage monies on my person, nor meanes of acquiring any, but w^d she grant me satisfaction of my lust, I w^d send her a pound Sterling from James-towne, enough coyn to purchase a bakers dozen tarts in London. But the Queene w^d none of my pound Sterling, and rolling on her bellie, let goe a fart wch had done honour to Elizabeth her selfe. I did declare, That C^apt J^no Smith was not put off so lightlie, and when that she reply'd as before, I vow'd to have my fille of her regardlesse. There is a saying amongst the worldlie French, that when a man cannot eate thrush, he must perforce make doe with crowe. I tarry'd no longer, but straightway work'd upon the Queene that sinne, for wch the Lord rayn'd fyre upon the Cities of the Playne. . . .

When that I had done, I drewe away and waited for the Queene to call her bodie-guards to fetch me, wch I suppos'd she w^d forthwith. For a space she lay a-panting on the grownd, and when at last she had her winde, tooke from her necke tenne strings of *wompompeag,* wch she presentcd me. She then declar'd, That she had got love enow that night, to give her payne till the new moone. So saying, she felle into a swoone-like sleep, and I retir'd to the other roome, to chide Burlingame for his want of fancie. This he took in his wonted ill humour, for that I had the better of him yet againe. . . .

I did sleep late into the daye, and when I woke, found Hick-topeake in his royall chaire, with all his Lieutenants round about. He had bade them be silent, the while I slept; and on my rowsing up came forward, and embrac'd me, and declar'd I sh^d be second in rule over his towne, and have the comeliest Salvage of his tribe to wife, for that I had restor'd his peoples peace. I enquir'd, How was that so? and he made answer, That the Queene had come to him that dawne, and begg'd forgivenesse for her infidelitie, and swore that so satisfy'd was she of me, she never w^d againe goe a-roving from the Kings' bedstead. Onely, he said, he fear'd her resolve might not endure for long; it must needs have been by meanes of some uncommon virilitie I had pleas'd her, and I was leaving his towne anon.

With that I led him aside, and related to him privilie the simple trick I had employ'd, assuring him, that he c^d doe the thing as well as I. For so smalle was the puddle, any frogg seem'd greate therein. Hicktopeake had never heard of such a practice (wch I had learnt from the scurvie Arabs), and he listened in amazement. Naught w^d then suffice but he must put his learning to the test, and so he hi'd him selfe apace from out the roome.

While that he was gone thus a-wooing, I gather'd together my companie, and told them to make readie our vessell, for I design'd to sayle that selfe same morning, to take up the course of our explorations. They did set to at once, all save Burlingame, that grows'd about the shoarline kicking pebbles, and we were neare readie to sayle, when Hicktopeake came out from his howse. He embrac'd me againe, this time more warmlie then before, and begg'd me stay in his towne for ever, as his Prince & successor. So had he woo'd the Queene, he said, she w^d be three days rysing from her bed, and costive the week. But I declin'd his offer, saying, That I had businesse elsewhere to attend. After much debate he did resigne him selfe, and gave me leave to goe, presenting me & my companie with all manner of Salvage gifts, and food & water for our vessell.

Thus at last we did set sayle once more, and headed for the maine, and whatever lay before us. I was a trifle loath to goe, and w^d fain have tarry'd some smalle space, for that Hicktopeake did declare to me his intention, of journeying to the towne of Debedeavon his Brother, and there so ploughing Debedeavons Queene, after the manner he had learnt, as to confound his Brother for ever. Whereupon he, Hicktopeake, s^{hd} be the Laughing King of Accomack. W^{ch} forsooth were worth the witnessing. But the favour of Kings is a slipperie boone, lightlie granted & as lightlie forsworne, and I deem'd it more prudent to absent my selfe betimes, while that I was yet in his good graces, then to linger, and perchance weare out my welcome there in Accomack. . . .

Here ended the narrative, or what fragment of it Meech had brought aboard. Ebenezer read it again, and a third time, hoping to find in it something to connect Henry Burlingame with his luckless namesake in the story. But there was every indication that Captain Smith's antagonist, who Henry hoped would prove to be his ancestor, was not only childless but unmarried, and his future with the company of explorers was far from promising. With a sigh the Laureate assembled the pages of the Journal and concealed it under his sailcloth bed, where no one was likely to find it. Then he extinguished the lantern and sat for some while in the dark. The naked sounds of rape, floating through the shallop's fo'c'sle, conjured pictures clear enough to make him shiver. Together with the story in the manuscript—which was as much a revelation to him as it had been to Hicktopeake—they forced his reverie willy-nilly into a single channel, and before long he found himself physically moved by desire. He could not in honesty assert that his pity for the *Cyprian* girls was unambiguous, or his condemnation of their assault wholehearted; if he had been shocked by the spectacle, he had also been excited by it, and so fascinated that no lesser business than that of the Journal could have summoned him away. Indeed, the sight of the girl trapped in the rigging like a fly in a web, and of Boabdil climbing leisurely to envelop her like a great black spider, had aroused him as its memory aroused him now.

It was abundantly clear to him that the value of his virginity was not a moral value, even as he had explained to Bertrand one day on the *Poseidon*. But the mystic ontological value he had ascribed to it seemed less convincing now than it had seemed then. The recollection of Joan Toast's visit to his room, for example, which was customarily dominated by his speech at her departure or the hymn to virginity composed afterwards, stopped now at the memory of the girl herself, sitting pertly on his bed, and would go no farther. She had leaned forward and embraced him where he knelt before her; her breasts had brushed like cool silk on his forehead; his cheek had lain against the cushion of her stomach; his eyes had lingered close to The Mystery!

From outside came another cry, a hard, high protest that trailed into lamentation. There was an ancient ring to it, an antique sorrow, that put the poet in mind of Philomela, of Lucretia, of the Sabine virgins and the daughters of Troy, of the entire wailing legion of the raped. He went to the companionway, and climbing it looked skyward at the stars. How trifling was the present scene to them, who had watched the numberless wars of men, the sack of nations, and the countless lone assaults in field and alley! Was there a year in time when their light had not been dimmed, somewhere on earth, by the flames of burning cities? That instant when he stepped out on the deck, how many women heard—in England, Spain, and far Cipango—the footfall of the rapist on the stair, or in the path behind? The ranks of women ravished, hundreds and thousands and millions strong, of every age and circumstance—the centuries rang and echoed with their cries; the dirt of the planet was watered with their tears!

The scene aboard the *Cyprian* was considerably less violent now, though by no means tranquil. Around the masts her crew were still tied fast, and watched the festivities in sullen silence; thus far none had been harmed. The pirates, their first lust spent, had broken out the rum and were fast succumbing to it. Already some lay senseless in the scuppers; others sprawled with their prizes on the decks and cabin roofs, taking drinks and liberties by turn, but no longer able to consummate their wooing; still others had lost interest altogether in the women—they danced, sang bawdy songs, or played ombre under lanterns in the balmy air, almost as on any other evening at sea. From the cabins came the sound of more carousing, but not of violence: two girls, it seemed, were being obliged to perform some trick against their will, and Ebenezer heard several women join in the general laughter and encouragement.

"So lightly they accept their fate!" He thought again of the Trojan widows, advised by Hecuba to resign themselves without protest to being concubines and slaves.

The least enviable lot, so far as he could see, was that of seven ladies trussed hip to hip over the *Cyprian*'s starboard rail in classic pirate fashion, so that their heads, and upper bodies hung over the somewhat lower shallop; yet even these, despite the indignity and clear discomfort of their position, were not entirely overwhelmed with misery. One, it is true, appeared to be weeping, though she was not being molested at the moment, and two others stared expressionless at their arms, which were lashed at the wrist to the bottom of the balusters; but the others were actually gossiping with Carl the sailmaker, who smoked his pipe on the shallop's deck before them! At sight of Ebenezer, who came up beside him, they were not in the least abashed.

"Oh dear," said one, feigning alarm, "here comes another!"

"Ah, now, he seems a likely lad," said her neighbor, who was older. "Ye'd not do aught unchivalrous, would ye, son?"

Even as they laughed, a drunken pirate reeled up behind them.

"Ouch!" cried the one to whom he made his presence known. "Tell him, Carl, 'tis not my turn! *Hi!* The wretch takes me for a roast of mutton! Tell him, Carl!"

The sailmaker, by reason of his age, had some authority among his shipmates. "Have at some other, matey," he advised. The pirate obligingly moved to the tearful youngster on the end, who at his first touch gave a cry that pierced Ebenezer to the heart.

"Nay, ye blackguard, don't dare jilt me!" cried the woman first molested. "Come hither to one that knows what's what!"

"Aye, leave the child in peace," another scolded. "I'll show ye how 'tis done in Leicestershire!" Aside to her companions she added, "Pray God 'tis not the Moor!"

"Ye asked for't," said the pirate, and returned to his original choice.

"*Marry,* there's a good fellow!" she cried, pretending pleasure. " *'Sheart,* what a stone-horse, girls!" To her neighbor she said in a stage whisper, " 'Tis not the Moor by half, but Grantham gruel: nine grits and a gallon o' water. *Aie! Gramercy,* sir! *Gramercy!*"

The other three were highly entertained.

"Your friend is yonder in the cabin," Carl said to Ebenezer. "Hop to't if ye've a mind for the ladies, for we shan't tarry here much longer."

"Indeed?" Ebenezer shifted uncomfortably; the women were regarding him with interest. "Perhaps I'd better see what mischief Bertrand is about."

"Ah, 'sbood, he doth not care for us," one of the women said. "He likes his friend better." The rest took up the tease, even the one being wooed, and Ebenezer beat a hasty retreat.

"I cannot fathom it," he said to himself.

Though he had dismissed entirely the notion of stowing away aboard the *Cyprian* and had little or no interest in his valet's present activities, he borrowed courage enough from those two motives to board the brigantine, having first walked aft to escape the women's remarks. He could not deny, however, his intention to stroll back in their direction from the vantage point of the *Cyprian*'s deck, at least out of curiosity. He climbed to the rail and grasped the brigantine's mizzen shrouds to pull himself over. When by chance he happened to look aloft, the moonlight showed him a surprising sight: high in the mizzen-rigging the Moor's first conquest still hung, forgotten by all; her arms and legs stuck through as though in stocks. One could not judge her condition from below: perhaps she maintained her perch out of fear, hoping to escape further assault; or it could be she was a-swoon—her position would keep her from falling. Neither was it impossible that she was dead, from the bite of her great black spider. Assuring himself that only his curiosity wanted satisfying, but in a high state of excitement nonetheless, Ebenezer swung his feet not to the deck of the *Cyprian* but onto the first of the mizzen ratlines, and methodically, in the manner of Boabdil, climbed skyward to the dangling girl. . . .

His ascent caused the shrouds to tremble; the girl stirred, peered downwards, and buried her face with a moan. The poet, positively dizzied with desire, made crooning noises in her direction.

"I shall have at thee, lass! I shall have at thee!"

When he had got but halfway up, however, Captain Pound stepped out from the cabin below, and the Moor ordered all hands back to the shallop. The men responded with loud protests but nevertheless obeyed, taking desperate final liberties as they went. Ebenezer doubled his rate of climb.

"I shall have at thee!"

But Boabdil's voice came up from below. "You in the mizzen-rig! Down with ye, now! Snap to't!"

The girl was literally within reach. "Thou'rt a lucky wench!" he called up boldly.

She looked down at him. In the moonlight, from the present distance, she bore some slight resemblance to Joan Toast, the recollection of whom had fired his original desire. There was a look of horror on her face.

Weak with excitement, Ebenezer called out to her again: "A minute more and I had split thee!"

She hid her face, and he climbed down. A few minutes later the pirates had cast off the grapples and were doing their best to make sail. Looking back over the widening stretch of ocean, Ebenezer saw the women of the *Cyprian* untie their colleagues at the rail and set free the crew. Up in the mizzen-rigging he could still discern the white figure of the girl, his desire for whom, unsatisfied, began already to discommode him. The relief he felt at the accidental rescue of his essence was, though genuine, not nearly so profound a sensation as had been his possession in the rigging, which he could not begin to understand. Surely, he insisted, there was more to it than simple concupiscence: if not, why did the thought of the Moor's attack, for example, make him nearly ill with jealousy? Why had he chosen the girl in the ratlines instead of those along the rail? Why had her resemblance to

Joan Toast (which for that matter he may only have fancied) inflamed rather than cooled his ardor? His whole behavior in the matter was incomprehensible to him.

He turned away and made for his cell in the rope-locker, both to assure himself of the safety of his precious manuscript and in some manner to alleviate, if he could, his growing pain. Even as he lowered himself down the fo'c'sle companionway a sharp, shrill female cry rang out through the darkness from the brigantine's direction, followed by another and a third.

"*Their* turn, now," said someone on the shallop, and a number of the pirates chuckled. The blood rushed from Ebenezer's brain; he swayed on the ladderway and found it necessary to pause a moment, his forehead pressed against an upper rung.

"She's but a whore; a simple whore," he said to himself, and was obliged to repeat the words several times before he could proceed with his descent.

Whether because he thought he had put it away for safekeeping before boarding the *Cyprian* or because he was too drunk on returning to notice its absence, Captain Pound did not disclose the loss of the Journal fragment until after noon of the following day, by which time Ebenezer had found an even better hiding-place for it. Thinking it imprudent to trust his valet too far, he had waited until Bertrand went on deck that morning and had then transferred his prize from under his pallet to a fold in the canvas of a brand new sail which lay at the bottom of a pile of others on a large shelf near at hand. Thus when in the afternoon he and Bertrand stripped to the skin with the rest of the crew and stood by while Boabdil and the Captain combed the ship, he was not alarmed to see them throw aside the rag-beds in his cell: for them to unfold and refold every spare sail on the shelf would have been unthinkable. After a two-hour search failed to discover the manuscript, Captain Pound concluded that someone from the *Cyprian* had sneaked aboard to steal it. All that day and the next the pirates raced to find the brigantine again, until the sight of Cape Henlopen and Delaware Bay put an end to the chase and forced them back to the safety of the open sea.

His loss made the Captain daily more sour and irascible. His suspicion naturally fell heaviest on Ebenezer and Bertrand: though he had no reason to believe that either had prior knowledge of the Journal's presence on the ship and no evidence that either had stolen it—both had been seen aboard the *Cyprian*, for example—he nevertheless confined them to their cell again, out of ill humor. At the same time he had the Moor lay ten stripes on the sailmaker's aged back as punishment for failing to see the thief: the flogging could be heard in the rope-locker, and Ebenezer had to remind himself, uncomfortably, that the manuscript was exceedingly valuable to the cause of order and justice in Maryland. To Bertrand, who had nearly swooned during the search of their quarters, he declared that he had thrown the Journal into the sea for fear of discovery, and that old Carl was after all a pirate whom any judge ashore would doubtless hang.

"Nonetheless," he added resolutely, "should I hear they mean to kill or torture anyone for't, even that loathesome beast Boabdil, I shall confess." Whether he would in fact, he did not care to wonder; he made the vow primarily for Bertrand's sake, to forestall another defection.

"Small difference whether ye do or no," the valet answered. "Our time's nigh up in either case." He was, indeed, perilously disheartened; from the first he had been skeptical of Ebenezer's plan to escape, and even that long chance was precluded by their present confinement. In vain did Ebenezer point out that it was Bertrand who, by his conduct aboard the *Cyprian*, had spoiled their best opportunity to escape: such truths are never consolations.

Their prospects darkened as the day of the shallop's scheduled rendezvous approached. They heard the crew in the fo'c-'sle complain of the Captain's mounting severity: three had been put on short rations for no greater crime than that Pound had overheard them comparing notes on the *Cyprian* women; a fourth, who as spokesman for the group had inquired how soon they would put into some port, had been threatened with keelhauling. Daily the two prisoners feared that he would take it into his head to put them to some form of torture. The one bright happenstance of the entire period, both for the crew and for Ebenezer, was the news that the Moor, whom they had come to resent for executing the Captain's orders, had been blessed by one of his victims on the brigantine with a social disease.

"Whether 'tis French pox or some other I don't know," said the man who had the news, "but he is sore as a boil of't and cannot walk to save him."

Ebenezer readily assumed that it was the girl in the mizzen-rigging who had been infected, for though Boabdil had assuredly not confined his exercise to her, none of the other pirates showed signs of the malady. The disclosure gave him a complexly qualified pleasure: in the first place he was glad to see the Moor thus repaid for the rape, yet he quite understood the oddity of this emotion in the light of his own intentions. Second, the relief he felt at so narrowly escaping contagion himself, like the relief at having his chastity preserved for him, failed to temper his disappointment as he thought it should. And third, the presence of infection suggested that the girl had not been virginal, and this likelihood occasioned in him the following additional and not altogether harmonious feelings: *chagrin* at having somewhat less cause to loathe the Moor and relish his affliction; *disappointment* at what he felt to be a depreciation of his own near-conquest; *alarm* at the implication of this disappointment, which seemed to be that his motives for assaulting the girl were more cruel than even the Moor's, who would not have assumed her to be virginal in the first place; *awe* at the double perversity that though his lust had been engendered at least partially by pity for what he took to be a deflowered maiden, yet he felt in his heart that the pity was nonetheless authentic and would have been heightened, not diminished, during his own attack on her, whereas the revelation that she had not lost her maidenhead to Boabdil materially diminished it; and finally, a sort of overarching *joy* commingled with *relief* at a suspicion that seemed more probable every time he reviewed it—the suspicion that his otherwise not easily accountable possession by desire, contingent as it had been on the assumption of her late deflowering and his consequent pity, was by the very perverseness of that contingency rendered almost innocent, an affair as it were between virgins. This mystic yearning of the pure to join his ravished sister in impurity: was it not, in fact, self-ravishment, and hence a variety of love?

"Very likely," he concluded, and chewed his index fingernail for joy.

How Captain Pound explained his dereliction, the Laureate never learned. The six weeks ran their course; well after dark on the appointed day the prisoners heard another ship saluted by the pirates, and the sound of visitors brought aboard from a longboat. Whatever the nature of the parley, it was brief: after half an hour the guests departed. All hands were ordered aloft, and into the rope-locker came the sounds of the pirates making sail in the gentle breeze. As soon as the shallop gained steerage-way the acting first mate—none other than the boatswain impressed from the *Poseidon*, who had so rapidly and thoroughly adjusted to his new circumstances that Pound appointed him to replace the ailing Moor—

climbed down into the fo'c'sle, unlocked the door of the brig, and ordered the prisoners on deck.

"Aie!" cried Bertrand. " 'Tis the end!"

"What doth this mean?" the Laureate demanded.

" 'Ts the end! 'Tis the end!"

" 'Tis the end o' thy visit," the boatswain grumbled. "I'll say that much."

"Thank Heav'n!" Ebenezer cried. "Is't not as I said, Bertrand?"

"Up with ye, now."

"One moment," the poet insisted. "I beg you for a moment alone, sir, ere I go with you. I must give thanks to my Savior." And without waiting for reply he fell to his knees in an attitude of prayer.

"Ah, well, then——" The boatswain shifted uncertainly, but finally stepped outside the cell. "Only a moment, though; the Captain's in foul spirits."

As soon as he was alone Ebenezer snatched the Journal manuscript from its hiding-place nearby and thrust it into his shirt. Then he joined Bertrand and the boatswain.

"I am ready, friend, and to this cell bid *Adieu* right gladly. Is't a boat hath come for us, or are we so near shore? 'Sblood, how this lifts my heart!"

The boatswain merely grunted and preceded them up the companionway to the deck, where they found a mild and moonless mid-September night. The shallop rode quietly under a brilliant canopy of stars. All hands were congregated amidships, several holding lanterns, and greeted their approach with a general murmur. Ebenezer thought it only fit that he bid them farewell with a bit of verse, since all in all they had, save for the past six weeks, treated him quite unobjectionably: but there was not time to compose, and all he had in stock, so to speak (his notebook having been left behind, to his great sorrow, on the *Poseidon*) was a little poem of welcome to Maryland that he had hatched at sea and committed to memory—unhappily not appropriate to the occasion. He resolved therefore to content himself with a few simple remarks, no less well turned for their brevity, the substance of which would be that while he could not approve of their way of life, he was nonetheless appreciative of their civil regard for himself and his man. Moreover, he would conclude, what a man cannot condone he may yet forgive: *Many a deed that the head reviles finds absolution in the heart;* and while he could not but insist, should they ever be apprehended at their business, that their verdict be just, he could pray nonetheless, and would with his whole heart, that their punishment be merciful.

But it was not his fortune to deliver himself of these observations, for immediately upon reaching the gathering he and Bertrand were set upon by the nearest pirates and held fast by the arms. The group separated into a double column leading to the larboard rail, from the gangway of which, illuminated by the flickering lanterns, the prisoners saw a plank run out some six feet over the sea.

"Nay!" Ebenezer's flesh drew up. "Dear God in Heav'n!"

Captain Pound was not in sight, but somewhere aft his voice said "On with't." The grim-faced pirates drew their cutlasses and held them ready; Ebenezer and Bertrand, at the inboard end of the gauntlet, were faced toward the plank, released, and at the same moment pricked from behind with swords or knives to get them moving.

"From the first, gentlemen, I have been uncertain which of you is Ebenezer Cooke," said Captain Pound. "I know now that the twain of you are impostors. The real Ebenezer Cooke is in St. Mary's City, and hath been these several weeks."

"Nay!" cried the poet, and Bertrand howled. But the ranks of steel blades closed behind them, and they were shortly teetering on the plank. Below them the black sea raced and rustled down the freeboard; Ebenezer saw it sparkle in the flare of lanterns and fell to his knees, the better to clutch at the plank. No time for a parting song like that of Arion, whose music had summoned dolphins to his rescue. In two seconds Bertrand, farther outboard, lost his balance and fell with a screech into the water.

"Jump!" cried several pirates.

"Shoot him!" others urged.

"I'God!" wailed Ebenezer, and allowed himself to tumble from the plank.

16

The Laureate and Bertrand, Left to Drown, Assume Their Niches in the Heavenly Pantheon

FOR BETTER OR WORSE, the Laureate found the water warm; the initial shock of immersion was gone by the time he scrabbled to the surface, and when he opened his eyes he saw the lights of the shallop's stern, already some yards distant, slipping steadily away. But despite the moderate temperature of the water his heart froze. He could scarely comprehend his position: uppermost in his mind was not the imminence of death at all, but that last declaration of Captain Pound's, that the *real* Ebenezer Cooke was in St. Mary's City. Another impostor! What marvelous plot, then, was afoot? There was of course the possibility that Burlingame, so clever at disguises, had arrived safely and found it useful to play the poet, the further to confound Coode. But if he had learned of Ebenezer's capture from passengers on the *Poseidon*, as one would suppose, surely he understood that assuming his identity would jeopardize his friend's life; and if instead he believed his ward and protégé dead, it was hard to imagine him having the heart for imposture. No, more likely it was Coode himself who was responsible. And to what evil purpose would his name be turned? Ebenezer shuddered to think. He kicked off his shoes, the better to stay afloat; the precious manuscript too he reluctantly cast away, and began treading water as gently as possible to conserve his strength.

But for what? The hopelessness of his circumstances began to make itself clear. Already the shallop's lights were small in the distance, obscured by every wave; soon they would be gone entirely, and there were no other lights. For all he knew he was in mid-Atlantic; certainly he was scores of miles from land, and the odds against another ship's passing even within sight by daylight were so great as to be unthinkable. Moreover, the night was young: there could be no fewer than eight hours before dawn, and though the seas were not rough, he could scarcely hope to survive that long.

"I'faith, I am going to die!" he exclaimed to himself. "There is no other possibility!"

This was a thing he had often pondered. Always, in fact—every since his boyhood days in St. Giles, when he and Anna played at saints and Caesars or Henry read them stories of the past—he had been fascinated by the aspect of death. How must the cutpurse feel, or the murderer, when he mounts the stairway to the gibbet? The falling climber, when he sees the rock that will dash out brains and bowels? In the night, between their bedchambers, he and his sister had examined every form of death they knew of and compared their particular pains and horrors. They had even experimented with death: once they pressed the point of a letter knife into their breasts as hard as they dared, but neither had had the courage to draw blood; another time each had tried being throttled by the other, to see who could go the farthest without crying out. But the best game of all was to see who could hold his breath longer; to see, specifically, whether either was brave enough to hold it to the point of unconsciousness. Neither had ever reached that goal, but competition carried their efforts to surprising lengths: they would grow mottled, their eyes would bulge, their jaws clench, and finally would come the explosion of breath that left them weak. There was a terrible excitement about this game; no other came so close to the feel of death, especially if in the last frantic moments one imagined himself buried alive, drowning, or otherwise unable to respire at will.

It is not surprising, therefore, that however unparalleled in his experience, Ebenezer's present straits were by no means novel to his imagination. Even the details of stepping from the plank at night, clawing from the depths for air, and watching the stern lights slip away they had considered, and Ebenezer almost knew ahead of time how the end would feel: water catching the throat and stinging the nose, the convulsive coughing to expel it, and the inevitable reinspiration of air where no air was, the suck of water into the lungs; then vertigo, the monstrous pressure in head and chest, and worst of all the frenzy, the anxiety of the body not to die, that total mindless lust for air which must in the last seconds rend body and soul unspeakably. When he and Anna chose their deaths, drowning—along with burning, slow crushing, and similar protracted agonies—was disqualified at once, and the news that anyone had actually suffered from such an end would thrill them to the point of dizziness. But in his heart the fact of death and all these sensuous anticipations were to Ebenezer like the facts of life and the facts of history and geography, which, owing to his education and natural proclivities, he looked at always from the *storyteller's* point of view: notionally he admitted its finality; vicariously he sported with its horror; but never, never could he really embrace either. That lives are stories, he assumed; that stories end, he allowed—how else could one begin another? But that the teller himself must live a particular tale and die——Unthinkable! Unthinkable!

Even now, when he saw not the slightest grounds for hope and knew that the dread two minutes must be on him soon, his despair was as notional, his horror as vicarious, as if he were in his chamber in St. Giles playing the dying-game, or acting out a story in the summerhouse. Bertrand, he assumed with some envy, had strangled on his water and was done with it; there was no reason why he himself should not get it over with at once. But it was not simply fear that kept him paddling; it was also the same constitutional deficiency that had made him unable to draw his own blood, will himself unconscious, or acknowledge in his heart that there really *had* been a Roman Empire. The shallop was gone. Nothing was to be seen except the stars, or heard except the chuckle of water around his neck, yet his spirit was almost calm.

Presently he heard a thrashing in the sea nearby; his heart pounded. " 'Tis a shark!" he thought, and envied Bertrand more than ever. Here was something that had not occurred to him! Why had he not drowned himself at once? The thing splashed nearer; another wave and they were in the same trough. Even as Ebenezer struck out in the opposite direction, his left leg brushed against the monster.

"Aie!" he shrieked, and "Nay!" cried the other, equally alarmed.

"Dear God!" said Ebenezer, paddling back. "Is't you, Bertrand?"

"Master Eben! Praise be, I thought 'twas a sea-serpent! Thou'rt not drowned?"

They embraced each other and came up sputtering.

"Get on with't, or we shall be yet!" the poet said, as happy as though his valet had brought a boat. Bertrand observed that it was but a matter of time after all, and Ebenezer replied with feeling that death was not so terrible in company as alone.

"What say you," he proposed, in the same spirit wherewith he had used to propose the breath-game to Anna: "shall we have done with't now, together?"

"In any case 'twill not be many minutes," Bertrand said. "My muscles fail me already."

"Look yonder, how the stars are darkened out." Ebenezer pointed to a lightless stretch on the western horizon. "At least we'll not need to weather that storm."

"Not I, 'tis certain." The valet's breath came hard from the exertion of paddling. "Another minute and I'm done."

"Howe'er you've injured me before, friend, I forgive you. We'll go together."

"Ere the moment comes," Bertrand panted, "I've a thing to say, sir——"

"Not *sir!*" cried the poet. "Think you the sea cares who's master and man?"

"—'tis about my gambling on the *Poseidon*," Bertrand continued.

"Long since forgiven! You lost my money: I pray you had good use of't! What need have I of money now?"

"There's more, sir. You recall the Parson Tubman offered odds——"

"Forgiven! What more's to lose, when you had plucked me clean?"

But Bertrand would not be consoled. "What a wretch I felt, sir! I answered to your name, ate at your place, claimed the honors of your post——"

"Speak no more of't!"

"Methought *'Tis he should tumble Lucy on these sheets, not I*, and then I lost your forty pound as well! And you, sir, in a hammock in the fo'c'sle, suffering in my place!"

" 'Tis over and done," Ebenezer said kindly.

"Hear me out, sir! When that fearful storm was done and we were westering, I vowed to myself I'd have ye back that money and more, to pay ye for your hardship. The Parson had got up a new swindle on raising the Virginia Capes, and I took a notion to woo Miss Lucy privily to my cause. Then we would fleece the fleecer!"

" 'Tis a charitable resolve, but you'd naught to use for stakes——"

"Nor did some others that had been gulled," Bertrand replied. "They threatened to take a stick to Tubman for all he was a cleric. But he smelled what was in the wind, and gave 'em a chance to bet again on Maryland. They'd but to pledge some property or other——"

"I'faith!" cried Ebenezer. "His cassock frocked a very Jew!"

"He had the papers drawn like any lawyer: we'd but to sign, and we could wager to the value of the property."

"You signed a pledge?" Ebenezer asked incredulously.

"Aye, sir."

"Dear God! To what?"

"To Malden, sir. I——"

"To Malden!" Such was the poet's amazement he forgot to paddle, and the next wave covered his head. When he could speak again he demanded, "Yet surely 'twas no more than a pound or two?"

"I shan't conceal it, sir; 'twas rather more."

"Ten pounds, then? Twenty? Ha, out with't, fellow! What's forty pounds more to a drowning man? What is't to me if you lost a hundred?"

"My very thought, sir," Bertrand said faintly; his strength was almost gone. " 'Twas e'en for that I told ye, now we're drowning men. Lookee how the dark comes closer! Methinks I hear the sea rising yonder, too, but I shan't be here to feel the rain. Farewell, sir."

"Wait!" Ebenezer cried, and clutched his servant by one arm to help support him.

"I'm done, sir; let me go."

"And I, Bertrand; I shall go with thee! Was't two hundred you lost, pray?"

" 'Twas but a pledge, sir," Bertrand said. "Who's to say I lost a farthing? For aught I know thou'rt a wealthy man this moment."

"What did you pledge, man? Three hundred pounds?"

Bertrand had stopped treading water and would have gone under had not Ebenezer, paddling furiously, held him up with one hand by the shirt front.

"What doth it matter, sir? I pledged it all."

"*All!*"

"The grounds, the manor, the sot-weed in the storehouse —Tubman holds it all."

"Pledge my legacy!"

"Prithee let me drown, sir, if ye won't yourself."

"I shall!" said Ebenezer. "Sweet Malden gone? Then farewell, and God forgive you!"

"Farewell, sir!"

"Stay, I am with thee yet!" Master and man embraced each other. "Farewell! Farewell!"

"Farewell!" Bertrand cried again, and they went under. Immediately both fought free and struggled up for air.

"This will not do!" Ebenezer gasped. "Farewell!"

"Farewell!" said Bertrand. Again they embraced and went under, and again fought free.

"I cannot do't," said Bertrand, "though my muscles scarce can move, they bring me up."

"*Adieu,* then," said the poet grimly. "Thy confession gives me strength to die alone. Farewell!"

"Farewell!"

As before, Ebenezer took a breath before sinking and so could not do more than put his face under. This time, however, his mind was made up: he blew out the air, bade the world a last farewell, and sank in earnest.

A moment later he was up again, but for a different reason.

"The bottom! I felt the bottom, Bertrand! 'Tis not two fathom deep!"

"Nay!" gasped the valet, who had been near submerged himself. "How can that be, in the middle of the ocean? Haply 'twas a whale or other monster."

" 'Twas hard sand bottom!" Ebenezer insisted. He went below again, this time fearlessly, and from a depth of no more than eight feet brought up a fistful of sand for proof.

"Belike a shoal, then," Bertrand said, unimpressed. "As well forty fathom as two; we can't stand up in either. Farewell!"

"Wait! 'Tis no cloud yonder, man, but an ocean isle we've washed to! Those are her cliffs that hide the stars; that sound is the surf against her coast!"

"I cannot reach it."

"You can! 'Tis not two hundred yards to shore, and less to a standing place!" Fearing for his own endurance, he waited no longer for his man to be persuaded, but struck out westwards for the starless sky, and soon heard Bertrand panting and splashing behind. With every stroke his conjecture seemed more likely; the sound of gentle surf grew distant and recognizable, and the dark outline defined itself more sharply.

"If not an isle, at least 'twill be a rock," he called over his shoulder, "and we can wait for passing ships."

After a hundred yards they could swim no farther; happily, Ebenezer found that by standing on tiptoe he could just clear the surface with his chin.

"Very well for you, that are tall," lamented Bertrand, "but I must perish here in sight of land!"

Ebenezer, however, would hear of no such thing: he instructed the valet to float along behind him, hands on the poet's shoulders for support. It was tedious going, especially for Ebenezer, only the balls of whose feet were on the bottom: the weight behind pulled him off balance at every step, and though Bertrand rode clear, his weight held Ebenezer at a constant depth, so that only between waves could he catch his breath. The manner of their progress was thus: in each trough Ebenezer secured his footing and drew a breath; when the wave came he stroked with both arms from his breast and, with his head under, rode perhaps two feet—one of which would be lost in the slight undertow before he regained his footing. Half an hour, during which they covered no more than forty or fifty feet, was enough to exhaust his strength, but by then the water was just shallow enough for the valet to stand as well. It required another thirty minutes to drag themselves over the remaining distance: had there been breakers they might yet have drowned, but the waves were never more than two feet high, and oftener less than one. At last they reached a pebbly beach and, too fatigued for words, crawled on all fours to the base of the nearby cliff, where they lay some while as if a-swoon.

Presently, however, despite the mildness of the night and the protection provided by the cliff against the westerly breeze, they found their resting-place too cold for comfort and had to search for better shelter until their clothes were dry. They made their way northward along the beach and were fortunate enough to find not far away a place where the high sandstone was cut by a wooded ravine debouching onto the shore. Here tall wheatlike weeds grew between the scrub pines and bayberries; the castaways curled together like animals in a nest and knew no more till after dawn.

It was the sand fleas that roused them at last: scores of sand fleas hopped and crawled all over them—attracted, luckily, not by hunger but by the warmth of their bodies—and tickled them awake.

Ebenezer jumped up and looked unbelievingly about. "Dear God!" he laughed. "I had forgot!"

Bertrand too stood up, and the sand fleas—not really parasites at all—hopped madly in search of cover.

"And I," he said, hoarse from exposure. "I dreamt I was in London with my Betsy. God pox those vermin for waking me!"

"But we're alive, at that. 'Tis more than anyone expected."

"Thanks to you, sir!" Bertrand fell to his knees before the

298

poet. " 'Tis a Catholic saint that saves the man who ruined him!"

"Make me no saint today," Ebenezer said, "or you'll have me a Jesuit tomorrow." But he was flattered nonetheless. "No doubt I had better drowned when Father hears the news!"

Bertrand clasped his hands together. "Many's the wrong I've done ye, sir, that I'll pay in Hell for, anon—nor shall I want company in the fire. But I vow ye a vow this instant I'm your slave fore'er, to do with as ye will, and should we e'er be rescued off this island I shall give my life to gaining back your loss."

The Laureate, embarrassed by these protestations, replied, "I dare not ask it, lest you pledge my soul!" and proposed an immediate search for food. The day was bright, and warm for mid-September; they were chilled through from exposure, and upon brushing the sand from themselves found their joints stiff and every muscle sore from the past night's labors. But their clothes were dry except for the side on which they'd slept, and a little stamping of feet and swinging of arms was enough to start the warm blood coursing. They were without hats, wigs, or shoes, but otherwise adequately clothed in the sturdy garb of seamen. Food, however, they had to find, though Ebenezer longed to explore the island at once: their stomachs rumbled, and they had not much strength. To cook their meal was no great problem: Bertrand had with him the little tinderbox he carried in his pocket for smoking purposes, and though the tinder itself was damp, the flint and steel were good as new, and the beach afforded driftwood and dry seaweed. Finding something to cook was another matter. The woods no doubt abounded with small game; gulls, kingfishers, rails, and sandpipers soared and flitted along the beach; and there were certainly fish to be caught in the shallows; but they had no implements to hunt with.

Bertrand despaired afresh. " 'Tis a passing cruel prank fate plays us, to trade a quick death for a slow!" And despite his recent gratitude, the surliness with which he rejected various proposals for improvising weapons betrayed a certain resentment toward Ebenezer for having saved him. Indeed, he shortly abandoned as hopeless the search for means and went to gather firewood, declaring his intention to starve at least in relative comfort. Ebenezer, left to his own resources, resolved to walk some distance down the beach, hoping to find inspiration along the way.

It was a long beach. In fact, the island appeared to be of considerable size, for though the shoreline curved out of sight in both directions, its reappearance farther south suggested a cove or bay, perhaps a succession of them; one could not locate the actual curve of the island's perimeter. Of its body nothing could be seen except the line of stratified cliffs, caved by the sea and weathered to various browns and oranges, and the edge trees of the forest that ran back from the precipice —some with half their roots exposed, some already fallen the sixty or a hundred feet to the beach and polished like pewter by salt air and sand. If one scaled those cliffs, what wonders might one see?

Ebenezer had been at sea nearly half a year in all, yet never had he seen it so calm. There was no ground swell at all: only catspaws riffling here and there, and laps of waves not two hands high. As he walked he noticed minnows darting in the shallows and schools of white perch flipping and rippling a few feet out. Crabs, as well, of a sort he had never seen, slid sideways out to safety as he approached; in the water their shells were olive against the yellow sand, but the carapaces he found along the beach were cooked a reddish-orange by the sun.

"Would God I had a net!"

Around a bend just past the place where they had crawled ashore he saw a startling sight—all along the foreshore, below the line of weed and driftwood that marked high tide, were sheets of white paper; others rolled and curled in the rim of the sea. The thought that there might be people on the island made his face burn, not entirely with joy—in fact, it was a curious relief he felt, small but undeniable, when the papers proved to be the tale of Hicktopeake, Laughing King of Accomack; but he could not as yet say plainly what it was that relieved him. He gathered all the pages he could find, though the ink had run so that only an occasional word was legible: they would, when dry, be good for lighting fires.

He started back with them, thinking idly of John Smith's adventures. Did this curious pleasure stem from the fact that he, like Smith, was in *terra incognita,* or was there more to it? He hoped they would find no Indians, at least, like the fearsome fellows Smith had found spearing fish along the shore. . . .

" 'Sheart!" he cried aloud, and kissed the wondrous Journal.

An hour later their dinner was on the fire: seven respectable perch, half a foot long after cleaning, roasted on a green laurel turnspit, and on a thin piece of shale such as could be picked up anywhere along the cliffs, four crabs, frankly an experiment, fried in their natural juices. The hard-shelled ones could not be speared, but in pursuit of them Bertrand had found these others—similar in appearance but with shells soft as Spanish kid—brooding in clumps of sea-grass near the shore. Nor did they want for water; in a dozen places along the base of the cliff Ebenezer had found natural springs issuing from what looked like layers of hard clay, whence they ran seawards across the beach on the beds of softer clay one encountered every few hundred feet. One had, indeed, to take care in approaching these springs, for the clay beds were slippery and in places treacherously soft, as Ebenezer learned: without warning one could plunge knee-deep into what looked rock-hard on the surface. But the water was clean and sweet from filtering through the stone, and so cold it stung the teeth.

To get full benefit of the sun they did their cooking on the beach. Bertrand, humbled anew by his master's inspiration, attended the meal; Ebenezer made use of a fallen tree nearby for a back rest and was content to chew upon a reed and regard the sputtering crabs.

"Where do ye fancy we are?" inquired the valet, whose curiosity had returned with his good spirits.

"God knows!" the poet said cheerfully. " 'Tis some Atlantic isle, that's sure, and belike not giv'n on the charts, else I doubt me Pound would choose the spot to plank us."

This conjecture pleased the valet mightily. "I have heard tell of the Fortunate Islands, sir; old Twigg at St. Giles was wont to speak of 'em whene'er her gout was paining."

"Well I recall it!" Ebenezer laughed. "Didn't I hear from the cradle how she stood watch all the voyage from Maryland, hoping for a sight of them?"

"Think ye this is the place?"

"I'faith, 'tis fair enough," the poet granted. "But the ocean swarms with isles that man knows naught of. How many times dear Anna and I have pled with Burlingame to tell of them—Grocland, Helluland, Stokafixa, and the rest! How many fond hours I've pored over Zeno the Venetian, Peter Martyr d'Anghiera, and good Hakluyt's books of voyages! E'en at Cambridge, when I had better done other things, I spent whole evenings over ancient maps and manuscripts. 'Twas there at Magdalene, in the antique Book of Lismore, I saw described the Fortunate Islands dear old Mrs. Twigg yearned for, and read how St. Brendan found them. 'Twas there I learned of Markland, too, the wooded isle; and Frisland and Icaria. Who knows which this might be? Haply 'tis Atlantis risen from the sea, or the Sunken Land of Buss old Frobisher found; haply 'tis Bra, whose women have much pain in bearing children, or magic Daculi, the cradle island, where they go for gentler labor."

"It matters naught to me," said Bertrand, "so we be not killed by salvages. 'Tis a thing I've feared for since we stepped ashore. Did ye read what manner of husbands the wenches have?"

"I've shared your fear," Ebenezer admitted. "Some isles are bare of men; others, like famed Cibola, boast wondrous cities. Some are like Estotiland, whose folk are versed in every art and read from books in Latin; some others are like her neighbor Drogio, where Zeno says the salvages eat their captives."

"Pray Heav'n this is not Drogio!"

"We shall climb to the cliff top when we've eaten," Ebenezer said. "If I can see the island whole, I may be able to name it." He went on to explain that, while the location and size of islands varied widely from map to map, there was some agreement among cartographers as to their shape. "If 'tis the form of a great crescent, for example, 'twill of necessity be Mayda; if a small one, 'tis doubtless Tanmare, that Peter Martyr spoke of. A large parallelogram would be Antillia; a smaller one Salvagio. A simple rectangle we shall know for Illa Verde, and a pentagon for Reylla. If we find this isle to be a perfect circle, we must look farther for its inland features: if 'tis cut in twain by a river we shall know it for Brazil, but if instead 'tis a kind of ring or annulus about an inland lake, the which hath sundry islets of its own, then Heav'n hath smiled on us as ne'er on Coronado, for 'twill be Cibola, the Isle of the Seven Golden Cities!"

"'Sheart, may we find it so!" said Bertrand, turning the fish to brown. "'Twere not like folk in a golden city to eat up strangers, d'ye think?"

"Nay, 'tis more likely they'll take us for gods and grant our every pleasure," Ebenezer declared.

"Marry, I hope and pray 'tis the Isle of Seven Cities, then; I shall have three and you the rest, to make up for losing Malden! Doth the book say aught of the women in these towns, whether they be fat or thin, or fair of face?"

"Naught that I can recall," the poet replied.

"I'God, let us make short work of these fish, sir!" Bertrand urged, sliding them from the laurel spit to the clean-washed slates they had found to eat from. "I cannot wait to see my golden towns!"

"Be not o'erhasty, now; this may not be Cibola after all. For aught we know it may lie in the shape of a human hand, in which case our goose is cooked: Hand-of-Satan hath such a shape, and 'tis one of the *Insulae Demonium*—the demons' isles."

This final possibility chastened them sufficiently to do full justice to the perch and soft crabs, which they seasoned with hunger, ate with their fingers, and washed down with clamshellfuls of cold spring water. Then they stuffed an extra soft crab each into their pockets, grease and all, and climbed through the ravine to the top of the cliff, whence to their chagrin they could see no more than open water on one side of them and trees on the other. The sun was still but forty-five degrees above the eastern horizon; there was time for some hours of exploration before they need think of dinner and a shelter for the night.

"What course do ye propose, sir?" Bertrand asked.

"I have a plan," said Ebenezer. "But ere I tell it, what course do *you* propose?"

" 'Tis not for me to say, sir. I'll own I have spoken out of turn before, but that's behind me. Ye have saved my life and forgiven the harm I've done ye; I'll dance to any tune ye call."

Ebenezer acknowledged the propriety of these sentiments, but took issue with them nevertheless. "We are cast here on some God-forsaken isle," he said, "remote from the world of bob-wig and dildo. What sense here hath the title *Poet Laureate,* or the labels *man* and *master?* Thou'rt one man, I another, and there's an end on't."

Bertrand considered this for a moment. "I confess I have my preferences," he said. "If 'twere mine to decide, I'd strike out inland with all haste. Haply we'll find one or two golden cities ere dinnertime."

"We've no certain knowledge this is the Isle of Seven Cities," Ebenezer reminded him, "nor do I relish walking overland without shoes. What *I* propose is that we walk along the shore to learn the length and shape of the island. Haply 'twill identify our find, or show us what manner of people live here, if any. Nay, more, we've paper aplenty here, and charcoal sticks to mark with: we can count our paces to every turn and draw a map as we go."

"That's so," the valet admitted. "But 'twould mean another

303

meal of fish and soft crabs and another night upon the ground. If we make haste inland, haply 'tis golden plates we'll eat from, and sleep in a golden bed, by Heav'n!" His voice grew feverish. "Just fancy us a pair of bloody gods, sir! Wouldn't we get us godlets on their maiden girls and pass the plate come Sunday? 'Tis a better post than Baltimore's paltry sainthood, b'm'faith! I'd not trade places with the Pope!"

"All that may happen yet," Ebenezer said. "On the other hand we might encounter monsters, or salvage Indians that will eat us for dinner. Methinks 'twere wise to scout around somewhat, to get the lay of the land: what do a few days matter to an immortal god?"

The prudence of this plan was undeniable; reluctant as he was to postpone for even a day the joys of being a deity, Bertrand had no mind to be a meal for either cannibals or dragons—both of whose existence he might have been skeptical of in London, but not here—and so agreed to it readily, if not enthusiastically. They made their way down to the beach again, marked their point of departure with a stake to which was tied a strip of rag from Bertrand's shirt, and struck out northward along the shore, Ebenezer counting paces as they walked.

He had not reached two hundred when Bertrand caught his arm.

"Hark!" he whispered. "Listen yonder!"

They stood still. From behind a fallen tree not far ahead, a hackle-raising sound came down on the breeze: it was half a moan, half a tuneless chant, lugubrious and wild.

"Let us flee!" Bertrand whispered. " 'Tis one of those monsters!"

"Nay," Ebenezer said, his skin a-prickle. "That is no beast."

"A hungry salvage, then; come on!"

The cry floated down to them again.

"Methinks 'tis the sound of pain, not of hunger, Bertrand. Some wight lies hurt by yonder log."

"God save him, then!" the valet cried. "If we go near, his friends will leap us from behind and make a meal of us."

"You'll give up your post so lightly?" Ebenezer teased. "What sort of god are you, that will not aid his votaries?"

A third time came the pitiable sound, and though the valet stood too terrified to move, Ebenezer approached the fallen tree and peered over it. A naked black man lay there on the sand, face down, his wrists and ankles bound; his back was striped with the healed scars of floggings, and from myriad cuts and scratches on his legs he bled upon the sand. He was a tall, well-muscled man in the prime of life, but obviously exhausted; his skin was wet, and a spotty trail of blood ran from where he lay to the water's edge. Even as Ebenezer watched him from above, unobserved, he lifted his head with a mighty effort and resumed his cry, chanting in a savage-sounding tongue.

"Come hither!" the poet called to Bertrand, and scrambled over the log. The Negro wrenched over on his side and shrank against the tree trunk, regarding the newcomer wildly. He was a prepossessing fellow with high cheekbones and forehead, massive browbones over his great white eyes, a nose splayed flat against his face, and a scalp shaved nearly bald and scarified—like his cheeks, forehead, and upper arms —in strange designs.

"God in Heaven!" Bertrand cried on seeing him. The black man's eyes rolled in his direction. " 'Tis a regular salvage!"

"His hands are bound behind him, and he's hurt from crawling over the stones."

"Run, then! He'll ne'er catch up with us!"

"On the contrary," said the Laureate, and turning to the black man he said loudly and distinctly, *"Let-me-untie-the-ropes."*

His answer was a string of exotic gibberish; the black man clearly expected them to kill him.

"Nay, nay," Ebenezer protested.

"Prithee do not do't, sir!" said Bertrand. "The wretch will leap on ye the minute he's free! Think ye these salvages know aught of gratitude?"

Ebenezer shrugged. "They could know no less of't than some others. Hath he not been thrown, like us, into the sea to die and made his way by main strength to this shore? *I-am-the-Poet-Laureate-of-Maryland,"* he declared to the black man; *"I-will-not-harm-you."* To illustrate he brandished a stick as though to strike with it, but snapped it over his knee instead and flung it away, shaking his head and smiling. He pointed to Bertrand and himself, flung his arm cordially about the valet's shoulders and said, *"This-man-and-I-are-friends. You"*—he pointed to all three in turn—*"shall-be-our-friend-as-well."*

The man seemed still to be fearful, but his eyes showed more suspicion now than dread. When Ebenezer forcibly moved behind him to release his hands and Bertrand, at his master's insistence, reluctantly went to work on the ropes that bound his feet, the fellow whimpered.

Ebenezer patted his shoulder. "Have no fear, friend."

It took some labor to undo the ropes, for the knots were swollen from the water and pulled tight by the captive's exertions.

"Whose prisoner do ye take him for?" asked Bertrand. "My guess is, he's one of those *human sacrifices* ye told me of, that the folk in golden cities use in lieu of money on the Sabbath."

"That may well be," the poet agreed. "His captors must in sooth be clever men, and no mere salvages, else they ne'er could make such fine stout rope or tie such wondrous hitches in't. Haply they were ferrying him to the slaughter when he escaped; or belike 'twas some sea-god he was meant for. Confound these knots!"

"In any case," said Bertrand, " 'twill scarcely please 'em to learn we set him loose. 'Tis like stealing from the collection plate in church."

"They need not know of't. Besides, we are their rightful gods, are we not? What we do with our offerings is our own affair."

That last, to be sure, he spoke in jest. They loosened the final knots and retreated a few paces for safety's sake, not certain what the man would do.

"We'll run in different directions," Ebenezer said. "When he takes out after me, the other will pursue him from behind."

The black shook off the loosened bonds, still looking warily about, and rose with difficulty to his feet. Then, as if realizing that he was free, he stretched his limbs, grinned mightily, raised his arms to the sun, and delivered a brief harangue, interspersing his address with gestures in their direction.

"Look at the size of him!" Bertrand marveled. "Not e'en Boabdil was so made!"

Ebenezer frowned at mention of the Moor. "Methinks he's speaking to the sun now; belike 'tis a prayer of thanks."

"He is a very percheron stud!"

Then, to their discomfort, the fellow ended his speech and turned to face them; even took a step towards them.

"Run!" cried Bertrand.

But no violence was offered; instead, the black prostrated himself at their feet and with muttered reverences embraced their ankles each in turn; nor would he rise when done, but knelt with forehead on the sand.

" 'Sbody, sir! What doth this signify?"

"I would not say for certain," Ebenezer replied, "but it seems to me you have what erst you wished: This wight hath bid his farewells to the sun and taken us for his gods."

"I'faith," the valet said uncomfortably. "We did not ask for this! What in Heav'n would he have us do?"

"Who knows?" the poet answered. "I never was a god till now. We gave him his life, and so he's ours to bless or bastinado, I suppose." He sighed. "In any case let's bid him rise ere he takes a backache: no god keeps men upon their knees forever."

17

The Laureate Meets the Anacostin King and Learns the True Name of His Ocean Isle

"ONE THING IS CERTAIN," Ebenezer said, when they resumed their exploration of the beach: "we must demand obedience of this fellow, if we're to be his deities. That is the clearest common attribute of gods, for one thing, and the safest policy besides: he may slay the twain of us if he learns we're mortal."

They had raised the black man up and bade him wash his wounds, which happily were no worse than scratches from the shells, and had moreover presented him with the extra soft crabs—cold and linty from their pockets, but edible nonetheless—and stood by while he made short work of them. Their charity provoked a fresh display of prostrate gratitude, which acknowledged, they had squatted with him some while on the sand and tried by words, gestures, and pictures drawn with sticks to hold converse. What was the name of the island? Ebenezer had asked him. What was his name? Where was his town? Who had bound his limbs and flung him into the sea, and for what cause? And Bertrand, not to be outdone, had added queries of his own: How distant from where they sat was the first of the golden cities? What sort of false gods had its citizens, and were the ladies dark or fair?

But though the black man had heard their inquiries with worshipful attention, his eyes had shown more love than understanding; all they could get from him was his name, which —though it was doubtless from no civilized tongue at all— sounded variously to Ebenezer like *Drehpunkter, Dreipunkter, Dreckpächter, Droguepécheur, Droitpacteur, Drupègre, Drêcheporteur,* or even *Despartidor,* and to Bertrand invariably like *Drakepecker.* For that matter it may have been not his name at all but some savage call to worship, since every time they said the word he made a genuflection.

"What shall we do with him?" Bertrand asked. "He shows no mind to go about his business."

"So be't," Ebenezer replied. "Let him help with ours, then. 'Tis readiness to take orders that makes the subject, and readiness to give them that makes the lord. Besides, if we set him labors enough he can plot us no mischief."

They resolved, therefore, to let the big black man accompany them as food- and wood-gatherer, cook, and general factotum; indeed, they were given little choice, for he clearly had no intention of leaving and could if angered have destroyed them both in half a minute. The three set out northward once again, Ebenezer and Bertrand in the lead and Drakepecker a respectful pace or two behind. For an hour or more they trudged over pebbles, soft sand, and beds of red, blue, and egg-white clay, always with the steep unbroken cliff-face on their left and the strangely placid ocean on their right; every turn Bertrand expected to discover a golden city, but it would reveal instead only a small cove or other indentation of the shoreline, which in the main ran still directly north. Then, leg weary and footsore, they stopped to rest beneath the mouth of a natural cave some ten or twelve feet up on the cliff wall. The savage, to whom Ebenezer had entrusted the rude spear with which he'd caught their breakfast, indicated by brandishing it and rubbing his stomach a desire to forage for dinner; upon receiving permission he scrambled like a monkey up the rock-face and disappeared.

Bertrand watched him go and sighed. " 'Tis the last we'll see of Drakepecker; and good riddance, says I."

"What!" Ebenezer smiled. "Thou'rt so soon tired of being God?"

The valet admitted that he was. "I had rather do the work myself than lord it o'er so fearsome a wight as he. This very minute he might be plotting to spit the twain of us on his spear and fry us up for's dinner!"

"I think not," said the poet. "He likes to serve us."

"Ah, sir, no man enjoys his bondage! Think you there'd be a servant in the world, if each man had his choice? 'Tis ill luck, force, and penury that make some men serve others; all three are galling masters."

"What then of habit, and natural predilection?" teased Ebenezer. "Some men are born to serve."

Bertrand considered these for a moment and then said, "Habit's no first cause, but a child of bleak necessity, is't not? Our legs grew calloused to the pirates' shackles, but we wished them off us nonetheless. As for this natural bent to slavery, 'tis a tale hatched by the masters: no slave believes it."

"A moment past you spoke of doing the chores thyself," Ebenezer said, "but never a word of *me* doing them; yet 'twas I proposed we forget our former stations, since the wilderness knows naught of classes."

Bertrand laughed. "Then to my list of yokes add *obligation;* he's no more mild a master."

"Call him *gratitude* or *love* instead," said Ebenezer, "and watch how men rejoice in their indenture! This Drakepecker, as you call him, chose his present bondage when we set him free of a worse, and he may end it by his own leave when he lists. Therefore I fear him not, and look to have him serve us many a day." He then asked the valet how he proposed to lord it over an entire city alone, if one subject shared between them scared him so.

" 'Tis god I want to be, not king," the valet said. "Let others give and take commands, or lead and put down mutinies; I'll stock me a temple with food and drink and sleep all morning in my golden bed! Ten young priestesses I'll have for company, that shall hear confessions and say the prayers in church, and a brace of great eunuchs to take collection and guard the money."

"Sloth and viciousness!"

"Would ye not do the same, or any wight else? Who wants the chore of ruling? 'Tis the *crown* men lust for, not the scepter."

"Who wears the one must wield the other," Ebenezer answered. "The man men bow to is lead sheep in a running flock, that must set their pace or perish."

"Ye'll rule, then, in your city?" Bertrand wanted to know.

"Aye," said Ebenezer. They were sitting side by side, their backs against the cliff, gazing idly out to sea. "And what a government would I establish! 'Twould be an anti-Platonist republic."

"I should hope, sir! What need have you of the Pope, when thou'rt the god?"

"Nay, Bertrand. This Plato spoke of a nation ruled by philosophers, to which no poets might be admitted save those that sing the praises of the government. There is an antique quarrel 'twixt poet and sage."

"Marry, as for that," Bertrand said, " 'tis little different from England or any place else; no prudent king would let a poet attack him. Why did Lord Baltimore employ ye, if not to sing the praises of his government, or John Coode work to your ruin, if not to squelch the poem? Why, this wondrous place ye speak of could as well be Maryland!"

"You miss my point," Ebenezer said uncomfortably. "To forbid a subject for verse is one thing; to prescribe, another. In my town philosophers will all be welcome—so long as they do not start insurrections—but a poet shall be their god, and a poet their king, and poets all their councillors: 'twill be a *poetocracy!* Methinks 'twas this Sir William Davenant had in's mind, what time he sailed in vain to govern Maryland. The poet-king, Bertrand—'tis a thought to conjure with! Nor is't folly, I swear: who better reads the hearts of men, philosopher or poet? Which is in closer harmony with the world?"

He had more to say to Bertrand on the subject, which had been stewing all morning in his fancy, but at this instant a pair of savages fell, as it were, out of the blue and stood before them, spears in hand. They were half-grown boys, no more than ten or twelve years old, dressed in matchcoats and deerskin trousers; their skin was not brown-black like Drakepecker's but copper-brown, the color of the cliffs, and their hair, so far from being short and woolly, fell straight and black below their shoulders. They put on the fiercest look they could manage and aimed their spears at the white men. Bertrand shrieked.

" 'Sheart!" cried Ebenezer, and raised his arm to protect his face. "Drakepecker! Where is Drakepecker!"

"He hath undone us!" Bertrand wailed. "The wretch hath played us false!"

But it was unthinkable that the boys had leaped from the cliff top, and unlikely that they had climbed down without making a sound or dislodging a pebble. It seemed probable to Ebenezer that they had been hiding in the cave, above their heads, waiting their chance to jump. One of them addressed the prisoners sharply in an unknown tongue, signaling them to rise, and pointed to the mouth of the cave.

"Must we climb up?" asked Ebenezer, and for answer felt a spear point prick his ham.

"Tell them we're gods!" Bertrand urged. "They mean to eat us alive!"

The command was repeated; they scrambled up the rocks to the lip of the cave. The boys chattered as though to someone inside, and from the shadow an older, calmer voice answered. The prisoners were forced to enter—bent over, since the roof was never more than five feet high. The inside stank of excrement and other unnameable odors. After a few moments, when their eyes grew accustomed to the dark, they saw a full-grown savage lying naked on a blanket on the floor, which was littered with shells, bones, and crockery pots. At least part of the stench came from his right knee, wrapped in ragged bandages. He raised himself on his elbows, wincing, and scrutinized the prisoners. Then, to their unspeakable surprise, he said "English?"

"I'God!" Ebenezer gasped. "Who are you, sir, that you speak our tongue?"

The savage considered again their matted hair, torn clothing, and bare feet. "You seek Quassapelagh? Did Warren send you for Quassapelagh?" The boys moved closer with their spears.

"We seek no one," the poet said, clearly and loudly. "We are Englishmen, thrown into the sea by pirates to drown; we reached this isle last night, by great good fortune, but we know not where we are."

One of the boys spoke excitedly and brandished his spear, eager to have at them, but the older man silenced him with a word.

"Prithee spare us," Ebenezer pleaded. "We do not know this *Warren* that you speak of, or any soul else hereabouts."

Again the youths made as if to run them through. The injured savage rebuked them more sharply than before and apparently ordered them to stand guard outside, for they evacuated the clammy cave with some show of reluctance.

"They are good boys," the savage said. "They hate the English as much as I, and wish to kill you."

"Then there are English on this island? What is the name of't?" Bertrand was still too frightened to speak, but Ebenezer, despite his recent daydreams of a poet's island, could not contain his joy at the prospect of rejoining his countrymen.

The savage regarded him narrowly. "You do not know where you are?"

"Only that 'tis an ocean isle," the Laureate replied.

"And you know not the name of Quassapelagh, the Anacostin King?"

"Nay."

For some moments their captor continued to search their faces. Then, as though persuaded of their innocence, he lay back on the pallet and stared at the roof of the cave.

"I am Quassapelagh," he declared. "The Anacostin King."

"*King!*" Bertrand exclaimed in a whisper to Ebenezer. "D'ye think he's king of one of our golden towns?"

"This is the land of the Piscataways," Quassapelagh went on. "These are the fields and forests of the Piscataways. That water is the water of the Piscataways; these cliffs are our cliffs. They have belonged to the Piscataways since the beginning of the world. My father was a king in this land, and his father, and his father; and so for a time was I. But Quassapelagh is king no more, nor will my sons and grandsons rule."

"Ask him which way to the nearest golden town," Bertrand whispered, but his master gestured him to silence.

"Why do you lie here in this miserable den?" Ebenezer asked. " 'Tis no fit dwelling for a king, methinks."

"This country is Quassapelagh's no more," the King replied. "Your people have stolen it away. They came in ships, with sword and cannon, and took the fields and forests from my father. They have herded us like animals and driven us off. And when I said, 'This land belongs to the Piscataways,' they turned me into prison. Our emperor, Ochotomaquath, must hide like an animal in the hills, and in his place sits a young whelp Passop, that licketh the English emperor's boots. My people must do his bidding or starve."

"Injustice!" Ebenezer cried. "Did you hear, Bertrand? Who is this *Warren* that so presumes, and makes me feel shame to be an Englishman? Some rogue of a pirate, I'll wager, that hath claimed the island for his own. I'faith!" He clutched at the valet's sleeve. "I recall old Carl, the sailmaker, spoke of a pirate town called Libertatia, on the Isle of Madagascar; pray God 'tis not the same!"

"I know not the Emperor's name," Quassapelagh said, "for he hath but lately come to oppress my nation. This Warren is but a jailer and chief of soldiers——"

At this moment a great commotion began outside the cave.

"Drakepecker!" Bertrand cried.

There at the cave's mouth the great black stood indeed: at his feet, dropped in anger, lay the rude spear improvised by Ebenezer, on which two bloody rabbits were impaled, and in each great hand he held a young sentry by the neck. One he had already by some means disarmed, and before the other could use his weapon to advantage, the fearsome Negro cracked their heads together and flung them to the beach below.

"Bravo!" Ebenezer cheered.

"In here, Drakepecker!" Bertrand called, and leaped to pinion Quassapelagh. "Come hither and crack this rascal's head as well!"

The Negro snatched up his spear and charged into the cave with a roar, plainly intending to add Quassapelagh to his other trophies.

"Stay! *Drakepecker!*" Ebenezer commanded.

"Stick him!" shouted Bertrand, holding Quassapelagh's arms from behind. The savage offered no resistance, but regarded the intruder with stern contempt.

"I forbid it!" said Ebenezer, and grasped the spear.

Bertrand protested: " 'Tis what the wretch designed for us, sir!"

"If so, he showed no sign of't. Release him." When his arms were free Quassapelagh lay back on the blanket and stared impassively at the ceiling. "Those young boys were his sons," Ebenezer said. "Go with Drakepecker and fetch them here, if he hath not killed them." The two men went, Bertrand with considerable misgivings which he did not hesitate to give voice to, and Ebenezer said to Quassapelagh, "Forgive my man for injuring your sons; he thought we were in peril. We mean you no harm at all, sir. You have suffered enough at English hands."

But the savage remained impassive. "Shall I rejoice to find an Englishman with mercy?" He pointed to his evil-smelling knee. "Which is more merciful, a spear in the heart or this poisoned knee, that I cut while fleeing like a rabbit in the night? If my sons are dead, I starve; if they live I die of this poison. Your heart is good: I ask you to kill Quassapelagh."

Presently Bertrand and the Negro returned, marching at the points of their spears the two young boys, who seemed to be suffering only from bruises and sore heads.

"It is enough that my sons live," Quassapelagh said. "Tell your man to kill me now."

"Nay, I've better work for him," Ebenezer said, and to Bertrand he declared, "Drakepecker will remain here with the king and mind his wants while we sound the temper of these English bandits. The boys can lead us to the outskirts of their settlement."

313

"'Tis not mine to argue," Bertrand sighed. "I only hope they've not snatched all the goden towns and set themselves up as gods."

Ebenezer then made clear to the Negro, by means of signs, that he wished him to feed the King and dress the infected knee; to the latter item, presented more as a query than a command, the black man responded with bright affirmative nods and an enthusiastic chatter that suggested acquaintance with some prophylactic or therapeutic measures. Without more ado he removed the dirty dressing and examined the malodorous inflammation with a clearly chirurgical interest. Then, in his own tongue, accompanying his orders with enough gesticulation for clarity, he directed one of the boys to clean and cook the rabbits and sent the other to fetch two crockery pots of water.

"'Sheart!" Bertrand said respectfully. "The wight's a physician as well! 'Tis an honor to be his god, is't not, sir?"

The poet smiled. "Haply he merits a better, Bertrand; he is in sooth a masterly creation."

Before two hours had elapsed, the rabbits were cooked and eaten—along with raw oysters provided by the youths and a kind of parched and powdered corn called *rockahominy,* of which the King had a large jarful—and Quassapelagh's wound had been lanced with his own knife, drained of pus, washed clean, and dressed with some decoction brewed by the Negro out of various roots and herbs which he had gathered in the woods while the rabbits were roasting. Even the savages were impressed by the performance: the boys fingered their lumps with more of awe than of resentment, and Quassapelagh's hard eyes shone.

"If the English are not far distant, I should like to have a look at them ere dark," the Laureate announced. When Quassapelagh replied that they were not above three miles away, he repeated his orders to the Negro, who, kneeling as usual at the sound of his name, acquiesced tearfully to the separation.

"If we find them to be pirates or highwaymen, we'll return at once," Ebenezer told the King.

"The Emperor of the English will not harm you," Quassapelagh said, "nor need you fear for my sons, who are unknown to him. But speak not the name of the Anacostin King to any man unless you wish me dead, and do not return to this cave. Your kindness to Quassapelagh will not be forgotten." He spoke in the native tongue to one of the boys, fetched him a small leather packet from the rear of the cave.

" 'Tis a map of the Seven Cities he means to show us!" Bertrand whispered.

"Take these," said the King, and gave to each of the men a small amulet, carved, it appeared, from the vertebra of a large fish—a hollow, watery-white cylinder of bone perhaps three quarters of an inch in width and half that in diameter, with small projections where the dorsal and ventral ribs had been cut off and the near-translucence characteristic of the bones of fish. Bertrand's face fell. "It seems a small repayment for my life," Quassapelagh said sternly, "but it was for one of these that Warren turned me free."

"This Warren is a fool," grumbled Bertrand.

The King ignored him. "Wear it as a ring upon your finger," he told Ebenezer. "One day when Death is very close, this ring may turn him away."

Ebenezer too was somewhat disappointed by the present, the rude carvings of which could not even be called decorative, but he accepted it politely and, since the outside diameter was too large for comfort, strung it upon a thin rawhide thong and wore it around his neck, under his shirt. Bertrand, on the other hand, stuffed his ungraciously into a pocket of his trousers. Then, it being already late in the afternoon and the beach in shadow from the cliffs, they bade warm goodbyes to the big Negro and Quassapelagh and, with the savage boys as guides, ascended to the forest and struck out more or less north-westward, moving slowly because of their bare feet.

"Thou'rt not o'erjoyed at traveling to our countrymen," Ebenezer observed to Bertrand.

"I'm not o'erjoyed at walking into a pirates' nest, when we could as lightly search for golden towns," the valet admitted. "Nor did we drive a happy bargain with that salvage king, to trade Drakepecker for a pair of fishbones."

" 'Twas not a trade, nor yet a gift," the poet said. "If he was obliged to us for his life, then saving ours discharged his obligation."

But Bertrand was not so easily mollified.

" 'Sbody, sir, I mean nor selfishness nor blasphemy, but 'tis precious rare a valet gets to be a god! Yet I'd scarce commenced to take the measure of the office, as't were, and get the hang of't, ere ye trade off my parishioner for a pitiful pair of fishbones! I wanted but another day or two to god it about, don't ye know, ere we turned old Drakepecker loose."

"Not I," the Laureate said. " 'Tis a post I feel well quit of.

We found him cast up helpless from the sea and left him helpful in a cave; he hath been slave to a god and now is servant to a king. Whither he goes thence is his own affair. We twain did well to start him on his journey—is that not godding it enough? Besides which," he concluded, "you had not the chore of keeping him occupied, as I did, or you'd not complain; I was pleased to find that work to set him to. If we reach our golden cities, my own shall be republican, not theocratic, nor have I any wish to be its ruler. That much Drakepecker hath taught me."

Bertrand smiled. "Ye've been not long a master, thus to speak, sir! D'ye think I mean to fill my head with dogmas and decretals, once I'm in my temple? That is the work of the lesser fry—priests and clerks and all that ilk. A god doth naught but sit and sniff the incense, count his money, and take his pick o' the wenches."

"Methinks your reign in Heaven shan't be long," Ebenezer observed.

"Nor doth it need be," said his valet.

After a while the woods thinned out, and to westward, through the trees, they saw a cleared field of considerable size in which grew orderly green rows of an unfamiliar broadleaved plant. Ebenezer's heart leaped at the sight.

"Look yonder, Bertrand! That is no salvage crop!" He laid hold of one of their guides and pointed to the field. "What do you call that?" he demanded loudly, as if to achieve communication by volume. "What is the name of that? Did the English plant that field?"

The boy caught up the word happily and nodded. "English. English." Then he launched into some further observation, in the course of which Ebenezer heard the word *tobacco*.

"*Tobacco?*" he inquired. "That is tobacco?"

"How can that be?" Bertrand wondered.

" 'Tis not so strange, after all," said the Laureate. "Captain Pound was wont to sail the latitude of the Azores, that ran to the Virginia Capes, and any isle along that parallel would have Virginia's climate, would it not?"

Bertrand then demanded to know why a band of pirates would waste their time on agriculture.

"We have no proof they're pirates," Ebenezer reminded him. "They could as well be sot-weed smugglers, of which Henry Burlingame declares there are a great number, or simply honest planters. 'Tis a thing to hope for, is't not?"

A contrary sentiment showed in Bertrand's face, but before he had a chance to voice it the two boys motioned them to silence. The four moved stealthily through a final grove of trees to where the forest ended at a riverbank on the north and a roadway paved with bare logs on the west. Sounds of activity came to them from a large log structure like a storehouse, obviously the work of white men, that ran from the roadside back into the trees; at their guide's direction they crept up to the rear wall, from which point of vantage, their hearts in their mouths, they could safely peer down the road toward the river.

"I'God!" Ebenezer whispered. The noise they had heard, a rumbling and chanting, was made by several teams of three Negroes each, who, barefoot and naked to the waist, were rolling enormous wooden hogsheads over the road down to a landing at the river's edge and singing as they worked. On a pier that ran out from the shore was a group of bareheaded, shoeless men dressed in bleached and tattered Scotch cloth, who despite their sunburnt faces and generally uncouth appearance were plainly of European and not barbaric origin; they were engaged in nothing more strenuous than leaning against the pilings, smoking pipes, passing round a crockery jug (after each drink from which they wiped their mouths on the tops of their hairy forearms), and watching the Negroes wrestle their burdens into a pair of lighters moored alongside. At sight of them Ebenezer rejoiced; but more marvelous still—so marvelous that the beholding of it brought tears to his eyes—out in mid-channel of the broad river, which must have been nearly two miles wide at that point, a stately, high-pooped, three-masted vessel rode at anchor, loading cargo from the lighters, and from her maintop hung folds of red, white, and blue that could be no other banner but the King's colors.

"These are no brigands, but honest English planters!" Ebenezer laughed. " 'Tis some island of the Indies we have hit on!" And for all the others warned him to be silent, he cried out for joy, burst out onto the roadway, and ran whooping and hallooing to the wharf. The young savages fled into the forest; Bertrand, filled with gloom and consternation, lingered by the warehouse wall to watch.

"Countrymen! Countrymen!" Ebenezer called. The Negroes stopped their song and left their labors to see him go by, and the white men too turned round in surprise at the outcry. It was indeed a most uncommon spectacle: even thinner than usual from the rigors of his months on shipboard, Ebenezer bounded down the log road like a shaggy stork. His feet were bare and blistered, his shirt and breeches shred to rags; bald and beardless at the time of his abduction from the *Poseidon*, he had let his hair grow wild from scalp and chin alike, so that now, though still of no great length, it was entirely matted and ungroomed. Add to this, he was more sunburnt than the planters and at least as dirty, the very picture of a castaway, and his haste was made the more grotesque by the way he clutched both arms across his shirt front, wherein he carried still the curling pages of the Journal.

"Countrymen!" he cried again upon reaching the landing. "Say something quickly, that I may hear what tongue you speak!"

The men exchanged glances; some shifted their positions, and others sucked uneasily on their pipes.

"He is a madman," one suggested, and before he could retreat found himself embraced.

"*Thou'rt English!* Dear God, thou'rt English!"

"Back off, there!"

Ebenezer pointed jubilantly seawards. "Where is that vessel bound, sir, as thou'rt a Christian Englishman?"

"For Portsmouth, with the fleet——"

"Praise Heav'n!" He leaped and clapped his hands and called back to the warehouse, "Bertrand! *Bertrand!* They're honest English gentlemen all! Hither, Bertrand! And prithee, wondrous Englishman," he said, and laid hold of another planter who, owing to the water at his back, could not escape, "what isle is this I have been washed to? Is't Barbados, or the far Antilles?"

"Thy brains are pickled with rum," growled the planter, shaking free.

"The Bermoothes, then!" Ebenezer cried. He fell to his knees and clutched the fellow's trouser legs. "Tell me 'tis Corvo, or some isle I have not heard of!"

" 'Tis not the one nor the other, nor any isle else," the planter said. " 'Tis but poor shitten Maryland, damn your eyes."

18

The Laureate Pays His Fare to Cross a River

"MARYLAND!" Ebenezer released his victim's trousers and looked back toward the woods he'd emerged from, at the fields of green tobacco and the Negroes grinning broadly beside their hogsheads. His face lit up. Still kneeling, as though transfixed, he laid his right hand over his heart and raised his left to the gently rolling hills, behind which the sun was just descending. "Smile, ye gracious hills and sunlit trees!" he commanded. "Thine own sweet singer, thy Laureate, is come to noise thy glory!"

This was a disembarkation-piece he had composed aboard the *Poseidon* some months before, deeming it fit that as Laureate of Maryland he should salute his bailiwick poetically upon first setting foot on it, and intending also to leave no question among his new compatriots that he was poet to the bone. He was therefore not a little piqued to see his initial public declamation received with great hilarity by his audience, who guffawed and snorted, smacked their thighs and held their sides, wet their noses and elbowed their neighbors, and pointed horny fingers at Ebenezer, and broke wind in their uncouth breeches.

The Laureate let go his pose, rose to his feet, arched his great blond eyebrows, pursed his lips, and said, "I'll cast you no more pearls, my friends. Have a care, or I'll see thy masters birch you one and all." He turned his back on them and hurried to the foot of the landing, where Bertrand stood uncomfortably under the scrutiny of several delighted Negroes.

"Put by your dream of seven cities, Bertrand: you stand upon the blessed soil of Maryland!"

"I heard as much," the valet said sourly.

"Is't not a paradise? Look yonder, how the sunset fires those trees!"

"Yet your fellow Marylanders would win no place at Court, I think."

"Nay, who shall blame them for their disrespect?" Ebenezer looked down at his own garb and Bertrand's, and laughed. "What man could see a Laureate Poet here? Besides, they're only simple servants."

" 'Tis an idle master lets 'em drink their afternoons, then," Bertrand said skeptically. "I cannot blame Quassapelagh——"

"La!" the poet warned. "Speak not his name!"

"I merely meant, I see his point of view."

"Only think!" Ebenezer marveled. "He was king of the salvage Indians of Maryland! And Drakepecker——" He looked with awe on the muscular Negroes and frowned.

Bertrand followed the thought, and his eyes welled up with tears. "How could that princely fellow be a slave? Plague take your Maryland!"

"We must not judge o'erhastily," Ebenezer said, but he stroked his beard reflectively.

All through this colloquy the idle Englishmen had wheezed and snickered in the background. One of their number—a wiry, wrinkled old reprobate with clipped ears and a branded palm—now scraped and bowed his way up to them and said with exaggerated accent, "Your Grace must pardon our rudeness. We're at your service, m'lord."

"Be't so," Ebenezer said at once, and giving Bertrand a knowing look he stepped out on the pier to address the group. "Know, my good men, that rude and tattered though I appear, I am Ebenezer Cooke, appointed by the Lord Proprietary to the office of Poet and Laureate of the Province of Maryland; I and my man have suffered imprisonment at the hands of pirates and narrowly escaped a watery grave. I shall not this time report your conduct to your masters, but do henceforth show more respect, if not for me, at least for Poetry!"

This speech they greeted with applause and raucous cheers, which, taking them as a sign of gratitude for his leniency, elicited from the Laureate a benign smile.

"Now," he said, "I know not where in Maryland I stand, but I must go at once to Malden, my plantation on Choptank River. I shall require both transportation and direction, for I know naught of the Province. You, my man," he went on, addressing the old man with the branded palm who had spoken previously. "Will you lead me thither? I'm certain your

320

master shan't object, when he learns the office of your passenger."

"Aye, now, that's certain!" the fellow answered, with a glance at his companions. "But say, now, Master Poet, how will ye pay me for my labor? For we must paddle o'er this river here, and there's nothing floats like gold."

Ebenezer hid his discomfort behind an even haughtier mien. "As't happens, my man, what gold I have is not upon my person. In any case, I daresay your master would forbid you to take money in such a worthy service."

"I'll take my chances there," the old man said. "If ye cannot pay me, ye'll cross as best ye can. Is't possible so great a man hath not a ring or other kind of valuable?"

"Ye may have mine," growled Bertrand. " 'Tis a bona fide salvage relic, that I hear is worth a fortune." He reached into his breeches pocket. "Hi, there, I've lost it through a hole——"

"Out on't!" Ebenezer cried, losing patience with the Marylander. "Not for nothing am I Laureate of this Province! Ferry me across, fellow, and you shall be rewarded with the finest gold e'er mined: the pure coin of poetry!"

The old man cocked his head as though impressed. *"Coin o' poetry,* is it? Ye mean ye'll say me a verse for paddling across the river?"

"Recite?" Ebenezer scoffed. "Nay, man, I shan't recite; I shall *compose!* I shall *extemporize!* Your gold will not be soiled from many hands but be struck gleaming from the mint before your eyes!"

The man scratched one clipped ear. "Well, I don't know. I ne'er heard tell of business done like that."

"Tut," Ebenezer reassured him. " 'Tis done from day to day in Europe, and for weightier matters than a pitiful ferry ride. Doth not Cervantes tell us of a poet in Spain that hired himself a harlot for three hundred sonnets on the theme of Pyramus and Thisbe?"

"Ye do not tell me!" marveled the ferryman. "Three hundred sonnets! And what, pray, might a *sonnet* be?"

Ebenezer smiled at the fellow's ignorance. " 'Tis a verse-form."

"A verse-form, now!"

"Aye. We poets do not merely make poems; we make certain *sorts* of poems. Just as in coins you have farthings and pence and shillings and crowns, in verse you have quatrains and sonnets and villanelles and rondelays."

"Aha!" said the ferryman. "And this *sonnet,* then, is like a shilling? Or a half crown? For I shall ask a crown to paddle ye o'er this river."

"A crown!" the poet cried.

"No less, Your Excellency—the currents and tides, ye know, this time of year."

Ebenezer looked skeptically at the placid river.

"He is a rogue and very Jew," Bertrand said.

"Ah well, no matter, Bertrand." Ebenezer winked at his valet and turned again to the Marylander. "But see here, my man, you must know a sonnet's worth a half pound sterling on the current London market."

"Spare me the last line of't then," said the ferryman, "for I shan't give change."

"Done." To the bystanders, who had watched the bargaining with amusement, he said, "Witness that this fellow hath agreed, on consideration of one sonnet, not including the final line, to ferry Ebenezer Cooke, Poet and Laureate of Maryland, and his man across the——I say, what do you call this river?"

"The Choptank," Ebenezer's boatman answered quickly.

"You don't say! Then Malden must be near at hand!"

"Aye," the old man vowed. " 'Tis just through yonder woods. Ye can walk there lightly once ye cross this river."

"Excellent! Done, then?"

"Done, Your Highness, done!" He held up an unclean finger. "But I shall want my payment in advance."

"Ah, come now!" Ebenezer protested.

"What doth it matter?" whispered Bertrand.

"What warrant have I thou'rt a poet at all?" the man insisted. "Pay me now, or no ferry ride."

Ebenezer sighed. "So be't." And to the group: "A silence, now, an it please you."

Then, pressing a finger to his temple and squinting both his eyes, he struck an attitude of composition, and after a moment declaimed:

> *"Hence, loathed Melancholy,*
> *Of Cerberus and blackest Midnight born*
> *In Stygian cave forlorn*
> *'Mongst horrid shapes, and shrieks, and sights unholy!*
> *Find out some uncouth cell,*
> *Where brooding Darkness spreads his jealous wings,*
> *And the night-Raven sings;*
> *There, under Ebon shades, and low-browed Rocks,*

> As ragged as thy Locks,
>   In dark Cimmerian desert ever dwell."

There was some moments' silence.

"Well, come, my man!" the poet urged. "You have your fare!"

"What? Is that a sonnet?"

"On my honor," Ebenezer assured him. "Minus the final line, to be sure."

"To be sure, to be sure." The boatman tugged at his mutilated ear. "So that is my half-pound sonnet! A great ugly one 'twas, at that, with all those shrieks and hollowings in't."

"What matter? Would you lift your nose at a gold piece if the King had an ugly head? A sonnet's a sonnet."

"Aye, aye, 'tis truth," sighed the ferryman, and shook his head as though outwitted. "Very well, then; yonder's my canoe."

"Let's be off," said the poet, and took his valet's arm triumphantly.

But when he saw the vessel they were to cross in, he came near to letting his ferryman keep the sonnet gratis. "Had I guessed this swine trough was to be our boat, I'd have kept the *dark Cimmerian desert* in my purse."

"Complain no more," the boatman answered. "Had I but known what a grubby pittance was your sonnet, ye'd have swum for all o' me."

Thus understanding each other, ferryman and passengers climbed cautiously aboard the dugout canoe and proceeded out onto the river, which lay as smooth as any looking glass. When well past mid-channel they found the surface still unrippled, the passengers began to suspect that the difficulty of the crossing had been exaggerated.

"I say," asked Bertrand from the bow, "where are those wicked tides and currents, that made this trip so dear?"

"Nowhere save in my fancy," said the ferryman with a grin. "Since ye were paying your passage with a poem, I had as well demand a big one—it cost ye no more."

"Oho!" cried Ebenezer. "So you deceived me! Well, think not thou'rt aught the richer for't, my fellow, for the sonnet was not mine: I had it from one whose talent equals my own——"

But the boatman was not a whit put out by this disclosure. "Last year's gold is as good as this year's," he declared, "and one man's as good as another's. Though ye did play false upon your pledge, I'm nowise poorer for't. A ha' pound's a ha' pound, and a sonnet's a sonnet." Just then the canoe touched the opposite shore of the river. "Here ye be, Master Poet, and the joke's on you."

"Blackguard!" grumbled Bertrand.

Ebenezer smiled. "As you will, sir; as you will." He stepped ashore with Bertrand and waited until the ferryman pushed back onto the river; then he laughed and called to him: "Yet the truth is, Master Numskull, you sit fleeced from nape to shank! Not only is your sonnet not my doing; 'tis not even a sonnet! Good day, sir!" He made ready to flee through the woods to Malden should the ferryman pursue them, but the gentleman merely clucked his tongue, between strokes of his paddle.

"No matter, Master Madman," he called back. " 'Tis not the Choptank River, either. Good night, sir!"

19

The Laureate Attends a Swine-Maiden's Tale

UPON REALIZING THAT the ferryman had marooned him in he knew not what wild woods, Ebenezer set up a considerable hallooing and crying, hoping thereby to attract someone from the opposite shore to rescue him; but the men in Scotch cloth were evidently in on the prank, for they turned away and left the hapless pair to their own devices. Already the light was failing: at length he left off his calling and surveyed the woods around them, which grew more shadowy by the minute.

"Only think on't!" he said. " 'Twas Maryland all along!"

Bertrand kicked disconsolately at a tree stump. "More's the pity, says I. Your Maryland hath not even civil citizens."

"Ah, friend, your heart was set on a golden city, and Maryland hath none. But *Gold is where you find it,* is't not? What treasure is more valuable than this, to reach unscathed our journey's end?"

"I would I'd stayed with Drakepecker on the beach," the

324

valet said. "What good hath come since we discovered where we are? Who knows what beasts we'll find in yonder shadows? Or salvages, that rightly hate an English face?"

"And yet, 'tis Maryland!" Ebenezer sighed happily. "Who knows but what my father, and his father, have crossed this selfsame river and seen those selfsame trees? Think on't, man: we are not far from Malden!"

"And is that such a joyous thought, sir, when for aught we know 'tis no more your estate?"

Ebenezer's face fell. "I'faith, I had forgot your wager!" At thought of it he joined his valet's gloom and sat at the foot of a nearby birch. "We dare not try these woods tonight, at any rate. Build up a fire, and we'll find our way at dawn."

" 'Twill draw the Indians, will it not?" Bertrand asked.

"It might," the poet said glumly. "On the other hand, 'twill keep away the beasts. Do as you please."

Indeed, even as Bertrand commenced striking on the flint from his tinderbox—in which also he had brought from the beach a small supply of dried sea-grass for tinder—the two men heard the grunt of an animal somewhere among the trees not many yards upstream.

"Hark!" Goose flesh pimpled the Laureate's arms, and he jumped to his feet. "Make haste there with the fire!"

The grunt sounded again, accompanied by a rustling of leaves; a moment later another answered from farther away, and then another and another, until the wood was filled with the sound of beasts, advancing in their direction. While Bertrand struck furiously at the flint, Ebenezer called once more across the river for help, but there was no one to hear.

"A spark! I have a spark!" cried Bertrand, and cupped the tinder in his hands to blow up a flame. "Make ready the kindling wood!"

" 'Sheart, we've not got any!" The sound was almost upon them now. "Run for the river!"

Bertrand dropped the seaweed, and they raced headlong into the shallows; nor had they got knee-deep before they heard the animals burst out of the woods behind them and squeal and snuffle on the muddy shore.

"You there!" cried a woman's voice. "Are ye mad or merely drunken?"

"Marry!" said Bertrand. " 'Tis a woman!"

They turned around in surprise and in the last light saw standing on the mud bank a disheveled woman of uncertain age, dressed, like the men on the landing, in bleached and tattered Scotch cloth and carrying a stick with which she drove a number of swine. These latter grumped and rooted along the shore, pausing often to regard the two men balefully.

"Dear Heav'n, the jest's on us!" the poet called back, and did his best to laugh. "My man and I are strangers to the Province, and were left stranded here by some dolt for a prank!"

"Come hither, then," the woman said. "These swine shan't eat ye." To reassure them she drove the nearest hog off with her stick, and the two men waded shorewards.

"I thank you for your kindness," Ebenezer said; "haply 'tis in your power to do me yet another, for I need a lodging for the night. My name is Ebenezer Cooke, Poet and Laureate of the Province of Maryland, and I—nay, madam, fear not for your modesty!" The woman had gasped and turned away as they approached. "Our clothes are wet and ragged, but they cover us yet!" Ebenezer prattled on. "In sooth I'm not the picture of a laureate poet, I know well; 'tis owing to the many trials I've been through, the like of which you'd ne'er believe if I should tell you. But once I reach my manor on the Choptank—*i'God!*"

The woman had turned in his direction and raised her head. Her black hair showed no signs of soap or comb, nor had she plagued her skin overmuch with scrubbing. But what caused Ebenezer to break off in midsentence was the fact that except for her slovenliness and the open sores that even in the shadow were conspicuous on her face and arms, the swine-maiden could have passed for the girl in the *Cyprian's* rigging; and but for a decade's difference in their apparent ages, she bore a certain resemblance to the youthful whore Joan Toast.

"Am I such a sight as that?" the woman asked harshly.

"Nay, nay, forgive me!" Ebenezer begged. " 'Tis quite the contrary: you look in some ways like a girl I knew in London—how long since!"

"Ye do not tell me! Had this wench my lovely clothes and fine complexion, and did ye show a nice concern for her maidenhead?"

"Ah, prithee, speak less sourly!" the Laureate said. "If I said aught to hurt thee, I swear 'twas not intended!"

The maid turned sullenly away. "My master's house lies just round yonder point, a mile or two. Ye can bed there if ye've a mind to." Without waiting for reply she smote the nearest hog upon its ham-butt with her stick, and the procession grunted upstream toward the point.

"She bears some likeness to Joan Toast," Ebenezer whispered to Bertrand.

"As doth a bat to a butterfly," the valet replied contemptuously, "that make their way through the world by the selfsame means."

"Ah, now," the poet protested, and the memory of his adventure on the *Cyprian* made him dizzy; "she's but a swineherd and unclean, yet she hath a certain air. . . ."

" 'Tis that she's windward of us, if ye should ask me."

But Ebenezer would not be discouraged; he caught up to the woman and asked her name.

"Why, 'tis Susan Warren, sir," she said uncordially. "I suppose ye want to hire me for your whore?"

"Dear Heavens, no! 'Twas but an idle pleasantry, I swear! D'you think a laureate poet plays with whores?"

For answer, Susan Warren only sniffed.

"Who is your master, then?" Ebenezer demanded, somewhat less gently. " 'Twill be surpassing pleasant to meet a proper gentleman, for I've met no Marylander yet who was not either a rogue or a simpleton. Yet Lord Baltimore, when he wrote out my commission, made much of the manners and good breeding in his Province and charged me to write of them."

Instead of answering, the swine-maiden, to Ebenezer's considerable surprise, began to weep.

"Why, what is this? Said I aught to affront you?"

The procession halted, and Bertrand came up chuckling from behind. " 'Tis that the lady hath tender feelings, sir. 'Twas boorish of ye not to hire her services."

"Enough!" the poet commanded, and said to Susan Warren, " 'Tis not my wont to traffic in harlotry, ma'am; forgive me if I gave you to think otherwise."

" 'Tis none o' your doing, sir," the woman replied, and resumed her pace along the path. "The truth is that my master's such a rascal, and uses me so ill, e'en to think on't brings the tears."

"And how is that? Doth he beat you, then?"

She shook her head and sniffed. "If 'twere but a birching now and again I'd not complain. The rod's but one among my grievances, nor yet a very great one."

"He doth worse?" Ebenezer exclaimed.

"I'faith, he must be hard pressed for diversion," said the valet, and drew a stern look from his master.

Susan Warren permitted herself another round of wails and tears, after which, heaving a sigh to Heaven and kicking

327

in the bacon a pig that stopped before her to make water in the path, she poured out to the Laureate the whole tale of her tribulations, as follows:

"I was born Susan Smith," she said, "and my mother died a-bearing me. My father had a small shop in London, near Puddle Dock, where he coopered casks and barrels for the ships. One day when I was eighteen and pretty as ye please, I took a stroll down Blackfriars o'er to Ludgate, and was bowed to by a handsome wight that called me *Miss Williams*, and asked to walk along with me. 'Ye may not do't,' I told him, 'nor is my name Miss Williams.' 'How's this?' he cried. 'Thou'rt not Miss Elizabeth Williams from Gracechurch Street?' 'I am not,' said I. 'Then pardon me,' said he, 'thou'rt like as twins.'

" 'Twas clear to me the lad spoke truly, for he was a civil gentleman and blushed at his mistake. He said he was in love with this Miss Williams, but for all she said she loved him she'd have none o' him for her husband, and spoke of some great sin that damned her soul. Yet this Humphrey Warren (that was his name) declared he'd have her to wife with all the sins o' man upon her conscience.

"I saw poor Humphrey often then by Ludgate, for Miss Williams grew less ardent day by day; he told me all his trials on her account, and said we looked so much alike, 'twas as if he spoke to her instead of me. For my part, I envied this Miss Williams not a little, and thought her a great fool to scorn so fine a gentleman. Dear Humphrey was not rich, but he held a decent post in the firm of a Captain Mitchell, that was Miss Williams' older half brother, and had every other virtue that could please a woman's heart.

"Then one day Humphrey came to Father's shop near Puddle Dock, weeping fit to die, and said Miss Williams had done herself to death with poison! I took pity on the man, albeit at heart I had none for Miss Williams, and rejoiced when Humphrey came to see me every day. At length he said, 'Dear Susan, thy likeness to Elizabeth is my curse and my salvation! I weep to see ye, thinking of her dead; yet I cannot think her gone, with her living image every day before me.' And I said, 'I could wish, sir, ye saw somewhat beyond that likeness.'

"This gave him pause, and anon he went to Father, and we two were wed. Yet for all I strove to win my Humphrey's love, I saw 'twas but the image of Miss Williams he made love to. One night when he lay sleeping fast I kissed him, and in his sleep he said, 'God save ye, sweet Elizabeth!' Fool that

I was, I woke him on the instant, and made him choose betwixt the two of us. 'Elizabeth is dead,' I said, 'and I'm alive. Do ye love me, love myself and not my likeness, else I shan't stay in this bed another moment!'

"Ah, God! Had I been but ten years older, or one groatsworth wiser, I'd have held my tongue! What matter what he called me, so he loved me? Why, didn't he call me *Honey* and *Sweetheart* and a flock of names besides, as well as Susan? I cursed my speech the moment 'twas spoke, but the hurt was done. 'Dear Susan!' Humphrey cried. 'Why did ye that? Would God ye had not asked me to choose!'

"All for naught then my begging and weeping; he'd not let me put by my words, but he must choose. And choose he did, though not a word he said of't; for next morn he was too ill to rise, and died not four days after. Thus was I widowed at nineteen years. . . .

"My father had troubles of his own, for his trade was poor, and Humphrey's niggard funeral took his savings. He went into debt to pay for food and stock, and just when the lot was gone, and the creditors were hounding at our door, a man came in to order casks for's vessel, which he said was bound for Maryland at month's end. So pleased was Father to get the work, he bade me brew the man some tea. But at sight o' me the wight turned pale and wept, for all he was a burly bearded sailor!

"'What is't?' said I, that had been like to die of grief myself those many weeks. The captain begged forgiveness and said 'twas my likeness to his dear dead sister caused his tears. In short, we learned he was Captain William Mitchell of Gracechurch Street, the same that was half brother to Elizabeth and my Humphrey's late employer. Had I but known then what vipers hid behind that kindly face, I had turned him out and bolted fast the door! But instead we wept together: I for my Humphrey, Captain Mitchell for his sister, and Father for the miseries of this life, wherein we lose the ones we love and cannot even mourn them fitly, for grubbing to feed the living."

Here Susan had to interrupt her narrative for some moments to give expression to her grief. Tears ran as well down Ebenezer's face, and even Bertrand was no longer hostile, but sighed in sympathy.

"Captain Mitchell then came oft to visit us," she went on, "and Father and I being innocent of the World's wickedness, we took him to our hearts. We had no secret he was not made privy to, though he gave us to know little of himself.

Yet we guessed that he was rich, for he spoke of carrying twenty servants to Maryland, whither he sailed to take some fine post in the government.

"Then when the coopering was done and all the casks hauled over to the dock, Captain Mitchell made my father a strange proposal: he would pay off Father's debts and leave him unencumbered for good and all, if I would sail to Maryland with Mrs. Mitchell and himself. He would treat me as his own dear sister, he declared; nay, more—'twas just that likeness had resolved him, and he meant to call me Elizabeth Williams. I was to be a sister to him, and companion to his ailing wife . . .

"My father wept and thanked him for his kindness, but said he could not live if I were gone, whereupon Captain Mitchell proposed at once that he sell the shop—lock, stock, and barrels—and start a new life in America. Naught would do then but we fetch our books and ledgers, almost a-swoon with joy and gratitude, and he paid our creditors in cash. 'Surely there's some condition to this kindness!' Father cried, and Captain Mitchell said, 'No more than what I stated: Miss Warren is now my sister.'

"Thus was the business done, with my consent. That night, when things were calm again, I felt odd at being Elizabeth Williams, that I had envied and despised, and wondered if I'd spoken in too great haste. Yet 'twas a kind of pleasure too, inasmuch as Humphrey had loved Elizabeth all in vain and now would have his love returned tenfold!

"On shipboard I was placed in Mrs. Mitchell's room, while Father was placed with Captain Mitchell's servants in the 'tween decks. Mrs. Mitchell was bedridden with some strange malady, but she was sweet to me. She called me Elizabeth, and bade me do whate'er her husband asked, because he was a great good man that she could not live without. Two times a day I gave her medicine in little phials that Captain Mitchell took from a wooden chest: if I was late 'twould drive her almost mad, but once she had her phial, she'd off to sleep at once. Captain Mitchell had a great many of these phials, and one morning he made me take one lest I get seasick.

" 'Thankee,' said I, 'but we're eight days out and I've not been seasick yet.' Captain Mitchell then came near and put his arm about my waist, right before Mrs. Mitchell's eyes, and said, 'Sister, ye must do as your brother says.' And Mrs. Mitchell cried, 'Aye, aye, Elizabeth, do as your brother says!'

"He gave a phial to me then, and to pacify them both I did as he bade me, and chewed the brown gum inside. Ah Christ,

330

that the first bitter taste had killed me! 'Twas no medicine I took at all, but itself a malady worse than death :'twas *opium* I ate, sirs, all innocently that day!"

" 'Sheart!" cried Bertrand.

"The wretch!" cried Ebenezer.

" 'Twas opium kept Mrs. Mitchell to her bed and drove her mad when 'twas lacking! 'Twas opium led to my downfall, and my father's, and brought me to this state ye see: a filthy trollop driving swine! God curse the hand that raised the poppy that made the opium I ate that day! Yet I thought 'twas simple medicine, belike a soporific, and bitter as it was, I ate it all. Straightway I drowsed upon my feet, and the room changed sizes; I was on the bed with Mrs. Mitchell, that grasped me by the hand, and the Captain leaning o'er the twain of us. His head had got huge; his eyes were afire. 'Sister Elizabeth! Sister Elizabeth!' he said. . . .

"In my dream I rose up high o'er the ship, hand in hand with Mrs. Mitchell. The sky was blue as sapphire, and the sea beneath us looked like crepe. The ship was a wee thing, clear and bright, and straight on the horizon was the sun. Then the sun was the eye of a man, and Mrs. Mitchell said, 'Lookee yonder, Elizabeth: that man is Christ Almighty, and ye must do what he says, as thou'rt a proper Catholic girl.' We went up near to Christ's great eye, and when He looked to us we stood naked for his judgment.

" 'Sister Elizabeth,' he said to me, 'I shall soon choose ye for a mighty work. I mean to get a child on ye, as my Father did on Mary!' I saw myself next in the habit of a nun, and Mrs. Mitchell called me *Sister Elizabeth, the bride o' Christ.* Then Christ's voice came like a great warm wind behind me, calling, 'Sister! Sister! Sister!' and while that Mrs. Mitchell held me, I was swived.

" 'Twas all clear when I woke, for the face o' Jesus was Captain Mitchell's face: I saw why Elizabeth had turned in shame from Humphrey and killed herself with poison; I saw why Captain Mitchell called me his sister, in his awful wickedness, and why Mrs. Mitchell had to help him in his sin. From that day I was lost, and Captain Mitchell hid no longer his real nature. Again and again they forced the drug upon me, till I was dreaming half the day of Christ my lover. The craving got such hold on me, I'd have killed any man to get my phial. Five pounds apiece he set his fee, till I had borrowed from my father all the money Captain Mitchell had given him, and the poor man went to Maryland a pauper. After that there was naught for't but to sell my services for the future, a month of bondage for every phial: I signed a blank indenture-bond for Captain Mitchell to count the months on, and knew I was his slave and whore for life.

"All through this time I'd not seen Father once, nor did I wish to. Captain Mitchell told him I was ill and that the money was for medicine. When all was gone the poor man near lost his mind; he begged for more money, but Captain Mitchell bade him indent himself to the captain of the ship, who then would sell the indenture-bond in port. My father sold himself at first for two years, then for four, and all the money went to Captain Mitchell for my medicine.

"One day near the end o' the passage Captain Mitchell gave his wife two phials instead of one, and two more after that, until she died before my eyes. Inasmuch as we had no physician, and everyone knew of the lady's illness, she was buried at sea and no questions asked. When we raised St. Mary's City, Father's bond was sold to a Mr. Spurdance on the Eastern Shore, and 'tis the last I've seen o' him in these five years. Captain Mitchell moved into a fine large house in St. Mary's, and no longer did I pose as Elizabeth Williams (save in bed), but was Susan Warren, his indentured servant.

"I was wont to say to myself 'St. Mary's City, St. Mary's City,' and in my opium dreams it was *St. Susan's City,* that I ruled over, and Christ came down and swived me night by night. One morning Mrs. Sissly, the neighbor woman, said, 'Miss Warren, thou'rt with child,' and I said, 'Mrs. Sissly, if I am with child 'twas inspired by no man, but by the Holy Ghost.' But Mrs. Sissly thought 'twas some manservant of the town I'd lain with, and told the tale to Captain Mitchell. He fell into a rage on hearing the news, for all he was the father; he told Martha Webb, the cook, to boil me an egg next morning, and he put a horrid physic in't, and made me eat it all. Then he put a towel round his neck and told Mrs. Webb he had physicked himself, and not to allow any visitors whilst he was a-purging. 'Twas a terrible strong physic, that had me three days purging strongly on the close-stool. It made me ill besides, and scurvied all my body; I broke out in boils and blains, and lost the hair off head and privates. Then the babe in my womb was murthered dead by't, and I knew wherefore he'd given it me to take. . . .

"'What think ye now?' he said. 'Will ye try that trick again?' And I said, 'That child was holy, sir; 'twas fathered on me by Jesus in your person.' And 'Jesus Christ indeed!' said he. 'There is no such person, Sister, nor any Holy

Ghost!' And he said he was astonished that the world had been deluded these many years by a man and a pigeon.

"Now these blasphemies were heard by Mrs. Webb and Mrs. Sissly, that ofttimes listened outside our doors, and being both good Christian women they took the tale to the sheriff. Captain Mitchell was summoned to the next grand jury and charged with fraud, murther, adultery, fornication, blasphemy, and murtherous intent. I did rejoice withal, despite he had the opium and my life would end with his.

"But, alas, I recked without the man's position, and the evil o' Maryland's courts: Captain Mitchell was fined a sniveling five thousand pounds o' sot-weed, whereof one third was remitted by the Governor, while I—that God knows had endured enough—I was sentenced to thirty-nine lashes on my suffering naked back, by the courthouse door, for leading a *lewd course o' life!* They also took my master's post away—not for his wickedness, but for his blasphemies—and freed me from my indenture. But little good that did me, that for my next phial must indent myself again, and take another bastinado at his hands!

"We moved then to this place in Calvert County, and my master plants tobacco. I am more wretched than e'er before, for since the physic robbed my beauty he'll not have me now but once in a passing while. He courts a new girl, only lately come from London, a wee child of a thing that hath the face of Elizabeth Williams and myself, and he treats her like a queen the while I'm set to drive the swine. Yet he gives me still my phials, and I well know why: 'twill not be long ere I hold her for him, while he puts the first opium in her mouth and calls her *Sister Elizabeth*. I shall get no more phials after that: I will fling myself to drown in yon Patuxent and be well out of't, and he will have his new young sister for good and all. . . .

"God curse that man and this province!" the woman cried finally, leaning upon her staff to weep. "Would Christ I had died while yet a maiden girl, in my father's little coopery on the Thames!"

20

The Laureate Attends the Swine-Maiden Herself

EBENEZER AND BERTRAND listened dumb struck to this tale, which done the poet cried, "Out on't, but your master is the Devil himself! Charles, Charles! Where is the majesty of Maryland's law, when a woman is used so ill? I would to Heav'n my baggage were here and not God alone knows where; then would I fetch up my sword, and this Captain Mitchell speak nimbly!"

"Ah nay, ye dare not," Susan warned. "Let fall but a word of what I've said, and we're all dead men."

"In that event," the Laureate said after some reflection, "he shall not have the honor of my visit. Aye, the boor shall learn how decent folk shun such beasts as he!"

"B'm'faith!" commented Bertrand. " 'Tis a fearsome punishment you exact, sir!"

Susan straightway recommenced her weeping. " 'Tis done, then!" she declared. " 'Tis o'er and done!"

"How's that?" the poet inquired. "What's done?"

"I," the maid replied, "for when I saw your face and heard o' your wondrous office, my poor brain hatched a plan. But what I hatched, ye've scotched, and 'tis done for Susan Warren."

"A plan, you say?"

The swine-girl nodded. "To make my escape and be rid o' that antichrist my master."

"Pray lay it open, then, that we might judge it."

"I know," she said, "that some time past, when Captain Mitchell found this newest prey, I guessed my phials would soon become a burthen to him and so, while feigning to eat the whole of the contents, in fact I laid by a little every time and saved it in my snuffbox. Of each phial I ate a grain less and saved a grain more, till now I've near a month's worth in re-

334

serve; and I have farther hid my one good dress, that Mrs. Sissly gave me to be flogged in. Now I have it privily that Father's indenture is run out, and Mr. Spurdance his master hath given him twenty acres of his own to till on the Eastern Shore. If I can flee from this evil house I shall make my way to my father's farm and hide myself till my cure is done; then he and I shall seek passage back to London."

"Brave plans!" said Bertrand, whose sympathy the swine-maid's plight had won entirely. "What can we do to aid ye?"

"Ah, sir!" wept Susan, still addressing Ebenezer. "These brave plans were fond indeed, should I simply strike out on the road. The law goes hard on fleeing servants, and my back thirsts not for farther stripes. What I require to fly this sink o' Hell fore'er is but a sum of silver, that ye would not miss; I have found a boatman that will risk flogging to sail me o'er the Bay, but he demands his fare. Two pounds, my lord!" she cried, and greatly disconcerted the Laureate by falling to her knees before him and embracing his legs. "Two pounds will send me safe to my dear father! Oh, sir, refuse me not! Think of someone ye love in these sad straits—thy sister, or some sweetheart!"

" 'Fore God, I would 'twere in my power to help you," Ebenezer said, "but I am penniless. I've but this trifling ring, here, made of bone——"

He drew it ruefully from his shirt to show his poverty, but at sight of it Susan jumped up and cried, "God save us! Whence came that ring?"

"I may not tell," the poet replied. "Why doth the sight of it alarm you?"

"No matter," said Susan, and clutched at the fishbone ring that hung still on its thong about the poet's neck. "It hath a certain value in the market, and methinks the boatman will accept it for his fare."

But Ebenezer hesitated. " 'Twas a kind of gift," he said. "I am loath to part with't . . ."

"Christ! Christ!" Susan wailed. "Ye will refuse me! Look ye hither, how that fiend abuses me! Will ye send me back for more?"

She raised her tattered skirt above her knees and displayed two legs which, wealed and welted though they were, had not been spoiled by the physic that had uglified the rest of her. Indeed, they were quite fetching legs, the first Ebenezer had seen since that day aboard the *Cyprian*.

"Ah, well, thou'rt still a woman," Bertrand said appreciatively, "and a good wench sits upon her own best argument."

This observation brought fresh tears from Susan and a scathing look from Ebenezer.

"I have seen harlotry enough," she declared, "and the boatman is a man too old to care."

"Indeed?" the valet smiled. "But my master and I are not."

"Hold thy tongue!" the poet commanded. Susan came up to him, and more than ever he was moved by her strange story and her resemblance to Joan Toast.

"Ye'd not see me beat again, would ye, sir?" They were in sight of a house by this time, whose lamplit windows shone across the tobacco-fields. "Yonder there is Captain Mitchell's house; he'll take you in right gladly as his guest, but me he will whip privily 'till he wearies of the sport."

Ebenezer had some difficulty with his voice. "'Twere in sooth a pity," he croaked.

"I shan't allow it," the girl said softly. "If the man I loathe most in the world hath his will o' me whene'er it please him, shall I deny the man who delivers me from all my pain?" She fingered the fishbone ring and smiled. "Nay, 'twere a sin if my savior took not his entire pleasure this very night, ere I fly."

"Prithee, say no farther," Ebenezer answered. "My conscience would not rest were I to stand 'twixt you and your loving father. You shall have the ring." He slipped the rawhide thong over his head and presented her with the ring of Quassapelagh. To his mild annoyance the swine-maiden did not immediately melt with gratitude; indeed, her bearing stiffened as she took the gift, and her smile showed a certain bitterness.

"Done, then," she said, and stuffed the ring and lanyard into a pocket of her dress. They were at the edge of the woods, by a tobacco-field; the moon rising over the mouth of the river whitened their faces and the flanks of the hogs that rooted idly in the green tobacco. Susan stepped into the field, laid her staff on the ground between the rows, and turned to face them with arms akimbo.

"Now, Master Laureate of Maryland," she said, "come swive me in the sot-weed and have done with't."

The poet was shocked. "'Sheart, Mrs. Warren, you misconstrue my gesture!"

"Oh?" She tossed her uncombed hair back from her face. "Anon, then, in the haymow by the barn? Surely thou'rt not the sort that wants a bed!"

Ebenezer stepped forward to protest. "I beg of you, madam——"

" 'Tis not your servant's presence puts ye off, now, is it?"
she said mockingly. "Ye look the type that swives in broad
daylight, let watch who will! Would it please ye better if I
feign a rape?"

"God save us," Bertrand said, "the jade hath spirit! Plague
take the hour I lost my fishbone ring!"

"Enough!" the Laureate cried. "I have no designs upon
your person, Mrs. Warren, nor do I want reward of any sort,
save that you join your father and throw off the vicious craving that hath whored you. To lay with women is contrary to
my vows, and to set a price on charity is an insult to my
principles."

This gave the swine-maid pause; she folded her arms,
turned her head away, and dug a pensive toenail in the dirt.

"My master is a sort of rhyming priest," Bertrand explained quickly. "The bishop, don't you know, of all the
poets. But 'tis a well-known fact the priest's vows are not
binding on his sexton, nor do my master's principles extend
to me——"

"Is't principle that makes your master scorn me?" Susan
interrupted, and though her question was addressed to Bertrand it was Ebenezer she regarded. "Or is't my sorry state
that makes him moral? He'd sing a lustier tune, methinks,
were I free of whip-scars and the smell o' pigs, and young
and sprightly as the girl Joan Toast."

"What name is thus?" cried the poet. "Dear God, I thought
you said *Joan Toast!*"

Susan nodded affirmatively, once more dissolving into
tears. "That is the girl I spoke of, that anon will be my master's newest *sister,* and the death of Susan Warren."

Ebenezer appealed to his valet. " 'Tis too fantastic, Bertrand!"

"I scarce can credit it myself, sir," Bertrand said. "Yet
there is that passing likeness, that her tale explains."

" 'Tis not so strange," the girl said testily. "For all her
sweet airs, this Joan Toast was a simple whore in London not
long since, and many's the man hath known her."

"I forbid you to speak thus!" the Laureate ordered. "I hold
a certain reverence for Joan Toast; she hath a strange deep
home in me, for reasons known to none besides ourselves.
Where is she, for the love of God? We must preserve her
from this Mitchell!"

"How can we?" Bertrand asked. "We've neither weapons
nor money."

Ebenezer grasped the swine-maiden's arm. "You must take

her with you to your father's farm!" he said. "Tell her your tale and explain the peril she is in. Once I arrive at Malden I shall fetch her there——"

"And marry her?" asked Susan with some bitterness. "Or pimp for her instead, and keep your vows?"

The Laureate blushed. " 'Tis not the time for speculations and conjectures!"

"In any case I cannot take her," Susan said. "I've fare for but a single passage."

"We soon can alter that!" Bertrand laughed, and leaped to pinion both her arms. "Snatch back the ring, sir, while I hold her!"

"Pig!" she squealed. "I'll have your eyes out!"

"Nay, Bertrand," Ebenezer said, "let her go."

"This jade?" cried Bertrand, laughing at her attempts to wriggle free. "She's but a hedge-whore, sir! Snatch the ring!"

Ebenezer shook his head sadly. "Hedge-whore or no, I gave it to her in all good faith. Besides, we do not know this boatman, nor where Joan Toast may be. Release her."

Bertrand let go the swine-girl's arms and gave her a pinch. She squealed another curse, picked up her staff, and let fly at him a blow that, had he not jumped clear of it, would have cost him ribs.

"Ye'll call me a hedge-whore!" she said fiercely, and ran him off some way across the field. Ebenezer, much more concerned about Joan Toast than about either of them, set off with a thoughtful frown toward the house.

"Your servant is a lecherous swine," said Susan, catching up to him a moment later. She brushed her hair back with her hand and prodded the pigs. "I beg your pardon for running him off."

"He had it coming," the poet said distractedly.

"And I thank ye for respecting a gift, e'en though 'twas not all charity that moved ye. Ye must think highly of this wench Joan Toast."

"I will do anything to save her," Ebenezer said.

"I think I can arrange it with the boatman," Susan said. "He hath no use for me, but a fresh young tart like Joan hath ways to please the feeblest."

"Nay, I shan't allow it! I shall find some other way. Where is she?"

The swine-girl did not know where Joan Toast lived, but said she called on Captain Mitchell nightly. "This very night he plans to give her opium, with my help. I shall catch her

338

ere she comes in, if ye wish, and send her to some privy place to meet ye."

Ebenezer agreed wholeheartedly to this plan, and though he quailed at the prospect of meeting Captain Mitchell, Susan persuaded him to join the planter at supper. "The Devil himself can play the gentleman," she said. "All men are welcome at the Captain's board, and belike he'll change your rags for something better when he hears your tale. I'll send ye word when Joan Toast is well hid, and lead ye to her ere I set out for my father's."

"Done!" the poet exclaimed, well pleased. "I cannot fathom why she is in Maryland, but I shall rejoice to see her!"

"And prithee, are ye sure she'll feel the same?" the swine-maid teased. "Can any tart believe thou'rt still a virgin?"

"That doth not matter," Ebenezer declared. "No man would think me Laureate, either, in this condition, yet Laureate I am, and virginal as well. Marry, Susan, how I yearn to see that girl! I beg thee not to fail me!"

Susan sniffed acknowledgment and they came up to the house, a large but ill-kept split-log dwelling. It squatted amid the fields of green tobacco and weed-ridden garden crops, and the bare earth round it was malodorous with the stools of many hens.

"Methinks your master hath fallen far," Ebenezer observed, "to be reduced to such a dwelling."

"How's that?" the woman exclaimed. " 'Tis one o' the finest on the river! Far too fine a seat for such a wretch as he!"

Ebenezer made no comment, but wondered briefly whether to cast away certain verses in his head which praised the grace of Maryland's dwellings, or preserve them lest Susan's knowledge prove incomplete. When the swine-girl left him in order to drive her charges back to the barn, he called for Bertrand, who came forth hurling curses after her, and they made their way to the front of the house.

"Pray Heav'n the wench is right about her master," Ebenezer said, and knocked on the door.

"I would not trust the strumpet twenty paces," Bertrand grumbled. "The man could murther us in our sleep."

The door was opened by a fleshy man in his fifties, red-nosed and chop-whiskered, who had nonetheless an air of good breeding about his person.

"Good evening, gentlemen," he said with a slightly mock-

339

ing bow. His clothes were fashionable, if seedy, and the excellent gravity of his voice came partly from cultivation, Ebenezer suspected, and partly from a well liquored larynx. Despite their wretched appearance he was as hospitable as Susan had predicted: he introduced himself as Captain William Mitchell, invited the visitors into the house most cordially, and insisted they stay the night.

"Be ye from jail or college," he declared, "thou'rt welcome here, I swear. Dinner's on its way, and do ye set down yonder with the rest, there's cider to whet your hunger."

Ebenezer thanked his host and launched into an explanation of their plight—which, however, Captain Mitchell pleasantly declined to hear, suggesting instead that it serve to entertain the table. The guests were then led to the diningroom, from which sounds of merriment had all along been issuing, and were introduced to a company of half a dozen planters of the neighborhood, among whom, to his considerable surprise, Ebenezer saw the clip-eared old ferryman and one or two others who had stood that day in Scotch cloth on the landing. They greeted him merrily and without malice.

"We looked for ye to join us, Mister Cooke," one said. "Ye must forgive Jim Keech's little prank."

"To be sure," Ebenezer said, seeing no other position to take. "I'll grant I look more like a beggar than the Poet Laureate of Maryland, but when you've heard what trials my man and I have suffered, you may appreciate our state."

"We shall, I'm sure," the host said soothingly. "Indeed we shall." He then sent Bertrand to eat back in the kitchen and directed Ebenezer to a seat at the dinner table, which made up in quantity what it lacked in elegance. Being very hungry, Ebenezer fell to at once and stuffed himself with pone, milk, hominy, and cider-pap flavored with bacon fat and dulcified with molasses, washing down the whole with hard cider from the cask that stood at hand. He had, in fact, debated for a moment the wisdom of revealing his identity, but since he had already revealed it on impulse to the men on the landing, and since the company showed no trace of hostility, he saw no harm in relating the whole of the story. This he proceeded to do when the meal was finished and all the guests had retired to greasy leather couches in the parlor; he left out only the political aspects of his capture and the adventure with Drakepecker and the Anacostin King, whose safety he feared the tale might jeopardize. His audience attended with great interest, especially when he came to the rape of the *Cyprian*—his tongue inspired by the rum-keg in the parlor,

Ebenezer spoke with eloquence of Boabdil in the mizzen-rigging and the nobly insouciant ladies at the larboard rail—yet when done he saw, to his mild chagrin, small signs of the pity and terror that he thought his tale must evoke in the most callous auditor: instead, the men applauded as if at some performance, and Captain Mitchell, so far from commiserating, requested him to recite a poem or two by way of encore.

"I must decline," the Laureate said, not a little piqued. "This day hath been fatiguing, and my voice is spent."

"Too bad our Timmy is not with us," said Jim Keech of the branded palm. "He'd spin ye one would ferry ye 'cross the Bay!"

"My son Tim's no mean hand at rhymes himself," Captain Mitchell explained to Ebenezer, "but ye might say they're of a somewhat coarser breed."

"He is a laureate too," Jim Keech affirmed with a grin. "He calls himself the Laureate of Lubricity, that he says means simple smut."

"Indeed?" the poet said, more out of politeness than genuine curiosity. "I did not know our host possessed a son."

He was, in fact, preoccupied with thoughts of Joan Toast and the swine-maiden, of whom he'd been reminded by Keech's reference to crossing the Bay. Captain Mitchell apologized to the group for the absence of his popular son, who he declared had gone to do some business in St. Mary's City and was due to return that night or the following day; it was difficult for Ebenezer to realize that this affable country squire before him was the villain of Susan Warren's tale, yet there were the whip-scars on her legs, every bit as cruel as those on Drakepecker's back, and the otherwise unaccountable resemblance between the victims of his passion.

The company now was ignoring him: pipes made after the Indian fashion had been distributed, and the room was filled with smoke and general gossip. Knowing nothing of the crops, fish, rattlesnakes, or personalities under discussion, irritated that his plight had not aroused more sympathy, and weary of the long, eventful day during which he'd been a castaway, a god, a deliverer of kings and maidens in distress, and the Poet Laureate of Maryland, Ebenezer disengaged his attention from their remarks and slipped into a kind of anxious reverie: How would Joan Toast receive him, after all? Where had she gone from his room in Pudding Lane, and how had her fearful dudgeon led her hither? He burned to know, yet feared the answers to these questions. The hour was growing late; soon now, if she were not deceiving him,

Susan Warren should send word of his rendezvous, and the prospect was in no small sense arousing. He recalled the sight of Joan Toast in his room and of the girl he'd meant to assault aboard the *Cyprian*——

"Dear God in Heaven!" his thoughts cried out, and he tingled to the marrow. The connection he'd not seen till then suffused him with remorse and consternation: had Joan Toast somehow got aboard the *Cyprian*? Was it she whom he had stalked with prurient cries, and whom the horrid Moor . . . ?

His features waxed so rampant at this unspeakable possibility that his host at once inquired about his health.

"Nay, sir, I beg pardon," Ebenezer managed to say. " 'Tis but fatigue, I swear't!"

"To bed, then, ere ye die here in the parlor," Captain Mitchell laughed. "I'll show ye where to sleep."

"Nay, prithee——" begged the poet, afraid lest he miss his scheduled assignation.

"Fie on your London manners, Mister Cooke!" the host insisted. "In Maryland when a man is tired, he sleeps. Susan! *Susan*, ye lazy trollop, get thee hither!"

"Ah, well, sir, if 'tis no affront to you or your gracious guests——" The swine-maiden appeared in the doorway of the parlor, answered Ebenezer's glance with a little nod, and turned a sullen glare upon the planters, who greeted her appearance with horny salutations.

"Show Mister Cooke here to a bedchamber," Mitchell ordered, and bade his guest good night.

"D'ye think she'll lay for a sonnet," Jim Keech called after him, "like that Spanish whore ye spoke of?"

"Nay, Keech," another answered. "What use hath Susie of a laureate poet? She hath Bill Mitchell's red boar to sport with!"

If these comments mortified Ebenezer they titillated him as well, and revived the vague ardor that his late conjecture had not entirely douched. The swine-maiden had donned her flogging-dress, which if scarcely more elegant than the other, was at least clean, and to judge by the smell of her she had washed herself as well. As soon as they were on the stairs he caught her arm and whispered "Where is Joan Toast? I cannot wait to see her!"

The woman's imperfect teeth glinted in the light of her candle. "Thou'rt passing ardent for a virgin, Master Laureate! I fear for your vows when ye see her in your chamber. . . ."

"My chamber? Ah, God, Mrs. Warren, 'twas in my chamber I saw her last, as pink and naked as a lover's dream!

You'd not believe how fine her fair skin feels, or how tight and sprightly is her whole small body—ah, stay, not all, at that: how could I forget the fat of her little buttocks, o'ertop the hard young muscle? Or the softness of her breasts, that gently flattened when she lay supine, but hung like apples of Heav'n when she bent o'er me? I shiver at the memory!"

"Marry, thou'rt afire, sir!" Susan said, leading the way down an upstairs hall. "I dare not leave the poor girl in your clutches: ye sound more like a rapist than a priest!"

She said this drily, without any real concern, but the mention of rape was enough to calm the poet's fever. "I beg your pardon for speaking thus, madam: 'tis rum, fatigue, and joy that work my tongue. Prithee recall I never swived this girl, albeit she's everything I say and more. I've no mind to break my vows."

Susan paused outside a door and turned toward him so that the candlelight flickered on her ruined face. "How can ye know she still hath all her beauty?" she said. "I too was pretty once, and not long since. My husband wept with joy to see my body, and did I place his hand just so, his knees would fail him. Today 'twould make him retch."

"Thou'rt too severe," the poet protested.

"D'ye think I cannot see what's in your mind? Ye wish I'd get me gone posthaste, so ye might have appetite for that *heavenly fruit* ye long for. But life leaves its scars on all of us, the pure as well as the wicked, and a pretty girl gets the worst of't. Ye've changed as well, I'll wager, since she saw ye last."

Ebenezer rubbed his matted beard. "I am no courtier, at that," he admitted, "and I stink of dirt and wood smoke. Is there a pail hereabouts to wash in? Ah, fie on it! Let her receive me as she will, I cannot wait to see her! Good night to you, Mrs. Warren, and good luck. A thousand thanks for aiding my dear Joan! *Adieu,* now, and *bon voyage!*" He moved to pass beside her to the door.

"Nay, wait!" she pleaded.

"Not a moment more!" He pushed past her and stepped into the chamber, which, since it looked out on the river, received some small light from the moon but was otherwise entirely dark. "Joan Toast!" he called softly. "Precious girl, where are you? 'Tis Eben Cooke the poet, come to save you!"

The moonlight showed no other person in the chamber, nor was there answer from the shadows roundabout; when the swine-maiden came in tearfully from the hall, her candlelight confirmed his apprehension.

"Where is she?" he demanded, and when she hung her head he shook her roughly by the shoulders. "Have you deceived me too, thankless trollop? Take me to Joan Toast this instant!"

"She is not here," the swine-girl sobbed. She set the candle down and bolted for the hall, but Ebenezer pulled her back and closed the door.

"By Heav'n, I'll have it from thy horrid hide," he said, holding her tightly from behind. "If any harm befalls Joan Toast I'll kill you!" For all his great alarm, he could not but be conscious of Susan Warren's corsetless hips under the cotton, and the breasts that were mashed beneath his arm. His righteous anger thrilled him: his breath came short and he squeezed her until she paused in her struggling to cry aloud. He wrestled her to the bed, possessed with the urge to punish. Not having prior experience at such sport, he first laid awkward thumps about her back, at the same time gruffly crying "Where is Joan Toast?" A moment later he held her flat with one knee in the small of her back and commenced to spank her smartly with the flat of his hand as though she were an errant daughter.

"She's safe!" squalled Susan. "Leave off!"

Ebenezer paused between blows, but held her fast with his knee. "Where is she?"

"She's on her way across the Chesapeake to Dorset County, to wait for ye at Malden," Susan said. "The boatman said he knows the manor well."

"How's that?" Ebenezer released his hold at once and sprang to his feet, but the swine-girl, her face pressed woefully into the quilt, made no move to rise. "Where did she get the fare, and how is it thou'rt not with her?"

"She was penniless," Susan said. "I caught her on her way to borrow money from Captain Mitchell, which had been the end o'her; but devil the bit she'd take the ring for fare, till I told her who had giv'n it me and whither she was to flee. Then she took it right enough, and would see you on the instant, but I bade her make haste to find the boatman ere he sailed."

Tears sprang to Ebenezer's eyes; with one knee on the bed he hugged the girl's back. "God's body, and I struck you for betraying me! Forgive me, Susan, or I shall perish of remorse! We'll find some way to save you yet, I swear't!"

She shook her head. "The girl ye love is a fresh and comely piece, sir, for all she hath played the whore in London; she said she had got her fill o' men that behaved like

344

goats, and had put by her profession ere it ruined her. She scorned ye once when ye would not hire her, and more when ye resolved to stay a virgin; but the farther she reflected on't the nobler ye appeared, and when she learned her pimp had got ye sent to Maryland, she left him straight and followed ye for very love."

"I'God! I'God! For very love!" the Laureate whispered. "But thou'rt a saint to sacrifice thyself for her!"

"Joan Toast was worth the saving," Susan answered. "There's naught o' Susan Warren to preserve, or I'd look to't myself. Let the poor wretch die."

"I shan't allow it!" Ebenezer cried. He sprang to his feet. "Thou'rt too fine!"

Susan sat up on the bed. " 'Tis not long since ye called me a horrid trollop, and methinks ye took some joy in beating me."

"I was a beast to touch you!" Ebenezer said. "Would God you'd give me back my blows tenfold!"

She covered her face with her hands. "I am so ugly!"

"Not so!" the poet lied. "Thou'rt still uncommon fair, I swear't!" He kneeled before her, embarrassed and contrite, yet still aroused, despite himself, from the recent tussle. "I shall confess somewhat to you for proof," he said. "My beating you was doubly wicked, for not only was it undeserved but—ah God, how sinful!—I took pleasure in't, as you charged. Nor was't a righteous pleasure, but a lustful one! The feel and sight of your—of what I felt and saw—it fired my veins with lust. Doth that not prove you have not lost your beauty, Susan?"

The boldness of his speech excited him further, but Susan was not consoled. "It proves my backside's fairer than my face. That's not the praise a woman longs to hear."

The Laureate pressed his forehead against her legs. His own knees ached a little on the floor, and he remembered, with a shiver, that the last time he had knelt beside a bed it was the legs of Joan Toast that he had clung to. "What can I do to show you my esteem?"

" 'Tis not esteem you feel; 'tis simple gratitude."

But Ebenezer ignored this sullen reply, for even while Susan was making it he found an answer as if by inspiration.

"Call't what you will, 'tis great," he said. "You have sacrificed your self-respect to save the girl I love. Very well, then: I shall sacrifice my essence to save your self-respect!"

The swine-maiden looked at him uncomprehendingly.

"Do you understand?" Ebenezer rose to his feet, breathing

345

so hard that his speech came with difficulty. "So great is my esteem—that though I've vowed to keep my innocence forever—'tis thine in token of my gratitude. 'Twill prove you have not lost your power to please a gentleman!" Trembling all over, he laid his hands on her shoulders.

Susan looked up at his flushed face with alarm. "Ye wish to swive me, sir? What will Joan Toast think, that loves ye for a virgin?"

"My chastity means more than life to me," the poet vowed, "else I'd not presume to match it against your sacrifice. My loss is great, but subtle, and leaves no broken hymen as its symbol. No one shall know but thee and me, and I shall never tell. Come, girl," he croaked, waxing hot, "tarry no longer! I itch for the combat!"

But Susan wriggled free and stepped away from him. "Ye'd deceive her, that hath come so far for love! Haply thou'rt already not a virgin, then!"

"'Fore God I am till now," he said, "and if you call this deed deceit, then grant at least 'tis done for noble cause!"

She turned away in tears, but when, summoning every particle of his courage, Ebenezer embraced her from behind, she offered no more protest than to cry, "What shall I think?"

"That thou'rt yet a comely piece!" Astonished at his own temerity, he caressed her. When even then she did not resist, her passivity fired him with encouragement.

"Ho, here," he cried, "to the bed with you!" Dizzy with success, he gave his tongue free rein. "I shall cleave thee with the rhymer's blade, cure thee with the smoke of love, stuff thee with the lardoon of Parnassus, baste and infuse thee with the muse's nectar, and devour thee while thou'rt yet aquiver!"

"Nay, prithee," Susan said, "ye've proved your point!"

"And now shall press and ply it like St. Thomas," Ebenezer said, "till my virgin quill hath writ a very *Summa!*"

"'Twere cruel to feign such passion out of gratitude, and wicked to cheat Joan Toast!" She offered resistance now, but Ebenezer would not release her.

"Then call me cruel and wicked when thou'rt swived!" He pushed her onto the bed.

"'Twill be common rape!" she squealed.

"So be't!"

"Not here, then! 'Sheart, not here!"

"Why not, pray?" asked the poet; he paused with his innocence at the ready.

"Some women take a man without a sound," the swine-girl

346

said, averting her eyes, "but I cannot; whether 'tis a wooing or what have ye, I must hollow like a rutting cat, and flail about."

"So much the better," Ebenezer said.

" 'Twill bring the houschold running—— *Stop*, I warn ye!"

"They are no canting Puritans, methinks—hold still, there!"

"Then swive me, damn your eyes!" Susan cried, and gave up struggling altogether. "Break your vow, cheat Joan Toast, let Captain Mitchell come a-running when I scream! He'll laugh to see't, and beat me later for't, and tell the tale all up and down the Province!"

This possibility gave the Laureate pause. He released his grip on the woman's arms, and she took the opportunity to move aside and sit up.

"I'll throttle you if I must," he said, but the threat was more surly than sincere.

"Ye needn't," Susan grumbled. "Slack off, now, ere ye take a lover's pain, and meet me in the barn anon."

"Get on with't. I'm not so gullible. We'll go together."

But Susan explained that they were sure to be seen leaving the house, and the scandal would be the same.

"I'll go there now," she said, "and you come half an hour behind. Then ye may play the two-backed beast to your heart's content, with none save my swine to hear me."

And on this ambiguous pledge she left, before the poet could catch her.

21

The Laureate Yet Further Attends the Swine-Maiden

A VERY FEW MINUTES after Susan Warren's departure Bertrand entered the Laureate's chamber and found his master pacing furiously about, sighing and smacking his fist into his hand.

"'Sbody, how these scoundrels eat!" the valet said. His voice was thick and his stance unsteady. "'Tis coarse, I'll grant, but copious."

"Methinks you more than quenched your thirst as well," Ebenezer observed uncordially. "What is't you want?"

"Why, nothing that I know of, sir. What I mean, they said I was to sleep here."

"Sleep, then, and be damned to you. There's the bed."

"Ah, sir 'tis thine, not mine. Only let me have that quilt; I'll want no more."

Ebenezer shrugged and went to the window; unfortunately he could not see the barn from there. His valet spread the quilt on the floor, flopped heavily upon it, and sighed a mighty sigh. "'Tis not the same as being god in a golden town," he declared, patting his stomach, "but 'twill do for the nonce, i'faith! I wonder how our Drakepecker fares?" When he saw no answer was forthcoming he sighed once more, turned on his side, and in a trice fell fast asleep.

His master, less tranquil, cracked his knuckles and clucked his tongue, debating what to do. At Susan Warren's first distraction his mad impulse had faltered, and upon her departure from the room it had foundered altogether. He was at sixes and sevens. Twice now he had come within an ace of fornication—worse, of meaningless rape—and his integrity had been preserved by chance, through outside agencies. The girl in the *Cyprian*'s rigging had been assaulted and was helpless; the Warren woman had been assaulted and was coarse and ugly in the face; both were objects not for passion but for pity, and what resemblance they bore to Joan Toast, so far from serving as an excuse for his inexcusable behavior, was further indictment of it. All this he saw clearly, and remembered as well the relief and shame he had felt a fortnight since, after fate had fetched him from the mizzen ratlines. To go now to the barn would be to cheat the girl who, incredibly, had come half around the world for love of a man never smiled on thitherto by any woman save his sister, and to sacrifice besides a good moiety of his essence to a ruined tart between him and whom no love was lost, and who would contemn the deed as much as he. Yet he also saw, and could not fathom, that in his heart the question still lay open.

"'Tis too absurd!" he thought, and flung himself angrily upon the bed where they had grappled. "I shall think of it no more." He regarded Bertrand with envy, but sleep, for him, was out of the question: his fancy burned with images of the swine-maiden suffering his punishments and molestations,

348

confessing with averted eyes how noisily she wooed, and waiting for him at that moment in the barn. On the scales of Prudence one pan lay empty, while Reason's entire weight tipped down the other; what dark force, then, on the scales of Choice, effected counterbalance?

While thus he lay debating, his valet, though asleep, was by no means at rest. His innards commenced to growl and snarl like beagles at a grounded fox; the hominy and cider in him foamed and effervesced; anon there came salutes to the rising moon, and the bedchamber filled with the perfume of ferment. The author of these snored roundly, but his master was not so fortunate; indeed, he had at length to flee the room, ears ringing, head a-spin, and the smart of bumbolts in his eyes. The guests were still carousing in the parlor; Ebenezer gathered from what he could hear that the host's son Timothy had returned and was regaling them with indelicate verses. He slipped out to the front porch unobserved to breathe the cool air moving off the river, and from the waystation soon enough strolled barnwards, deaf to the judgment of his conscience.

The moon shed light to walk by in the yard, but the inside of the barn was black as Chaos. He thought of calling Susan, but decided not to.

"I shall approach in silence, and clip her like a brigand in the dark!"

This was a thrilling fancy: he pricked up at every rustle in the barn, and the cramps of love like hatching chicks bid fair to burst their prisons. What's more, six stealthy paces in the dark were enough to stir his bladder past ignoring; he was obliged to relieve himself then and there before going farther.

"God aideth those that aid themselves," he reflected.

But unlike Onan, who hit no noisier target than the ground, the hapless Laureate chanced to strike a cat, a half-grown tom not three feet distant that had looked like a gray rock in the dark. And like the finger-flick of Descartes' God, which Burlingame once spoke of, this small shot in the dark set an entire universe in motion! The mouser woke with a hiss and flew with splayed claws at the nearest animal—fortunately not Ebenezer but one of Susan's shoats. The young pig squealed, and soon the barn was bleating with the cries of frightened animals. Ebenezer himself was terrified, at first by the animals, whose number and variety he had not suspected, and then lest the din, now amplified by barking dogs outside, arouse the household. When he jumped back, holding up his breeches in one hand, he happened upon a stick leaning against the wall—possibly Susan's staff. He snatched it up, at the same time crying "Susan! Susan!" and laid about him vigorously until the combatants ran off—the shoat into the cow stalls and the cat into a corner whence had come some sound of poultry. A moment later the respite ended: the barn was filled with quacks and squawks; ducks, geese, and chickens beat the air wildly in their effort to flee the cat, and Ebenezer suffered pecks about the head and legs as bird after bird encountered him. This new commotion was too much for the dogs, a pair of raucous spaniels: they bounded in from the yard in pursuit of what they took to be a fox or weasel preying on the poultry, and for all the Laureate thrashed around him with his stick, they ran him from the barn and treed him in a poplar near the closest tobacco-shed. There they held him at bay for some fifteen minutes before trotting off to sleep, their native lack of enthusiasm overcoming their brief ambition.

As yet the poet had seen no sign of Susan Warren, and he began to fear she had deceived him after all. He resolved to descend and try the barn once more, both to verify his suspicions and to take cover from the mosquitoes, which were raising welts all over his face and ankles; but as he was climbing down he heard a noise like a buzz or rattle in the grass. Was it only a common cricket, or was it one of those snakes Mr. Keech had described during supper? The notion of descent lost all its charm, and though he heard the sound no more, and the mosquitoes were no less hungry, he remained a good while longer in the tree, too frightened even to compose an indignant Hudibrastic.

He might, in fact, have still been there at sunup—for on the heels of Fear, like a tart behind her pimp, came the shame he knew would embrace him soon or late, and Shame brought her gaunt-eyed sister-whore Despair—but at length he heard some man at the back of the house say "No more, now, Susan; good night and get ye gone!" Then the house door closed, and a cloaked form crossed the distant yard and entered the barn.

"That scoundrel Mitchell had her in the parlor!" Ebenezer thought, and recalled the coarse familiarity with which the planter had saluted her. "She was accosted as she left and put to some lewd entertainment, and only now hath managed to escape!"

This conjecture, so far from filling him with pity, revived his ardor at once, as had the plight of the *Cyprian* women; quietly and cautiously he slid down from the poplar and stalked through the tall grass to the barn, expecting at any moment to feel the fangs of the viper in his heel. Arriving safely at the doorway, he entered without a sound and saw inside only the faintest of gleams from a shaded lantern.

"Hssst!" he whispered, and *"Hssst!"* came the reply. Ebenezer heard a labored respiration, unmistakably human, just down the wall from where he stood, and so resolved to call no more, but execute his original plan of surprise assault. Very carefully he crept toward his prey, whose location in the pigpen he fixed easily by her heavy breathing and the rustle of restless swine in her vicinity. Only when he judged himself virtually upon her did he croon "Susie, Susie, me doxy, me dove!" at the same time clutching amorously at her form.

Bare legs he felt, and hams, but—

"Heav'n upon earth, what's this?"

"What is't, indeed?" a man's voice cried, and after a short struggle the poet found himself pinned face down in the sour straw of the pen. His would-be victim sat upon his back and held his arms; sows, hogs, and shoats snuffled nervously together at the far end of the enclosure. "Ye thought me your doxy, your dove, now, did ye? What knave are ye, sir?"

"Prithee, let me but explain!" Ebenezer pleaded. "I am Captain Mitchell's guest!"

"Our guest! What way is this to return our hospitality? Ye drink our cider and eat our hominy and then ye think to swive my Portia!"

"Portia? Who is Portia?"

"The same my father calls Susie. I'll wager he put ye up to this!"

The Laureate's heart sank. "Your father! Then thou'rt Tim Mitchell?"

"The same. And which ungrateful wretch are you?"

"I am Ebenezer Cooke, sir, Poet and Laureate of the Province of Maryland——"

"Nay!" said Mitchell, clearly impressed, and to Ebenezer's great surprise he released his hold at once. "Sit up, sir, please, and forgive my rude behavior; 'twas but concern for my Portia's chastity."

"I—I quite forgive you," the poet said. He sat up hastily, wondering at the fellow's words. Tim Mitchell, to judge by his voice, was a man of Ebenezer's age at least; how could he speak of Susan's chastity? "I believe thou'rt having a jest at my expense, Mr. Mitchell, are you not?"

"Or you at mine," the other man sighed. "Ah well, ye've caught us fair, and Portia's life is in your hands."

"Her life! She's here, then, in this pen?"

"Of course, sir; over yonder with the rest. I beg ye not to speak a word to Father!"

"Marry!" the poet cried. "What madness is this, Mister Mitchell? Explain yourself, I beg you!"

The other man sighed. " 'Tis just as well I did, for if ye mean to ruin us, ye will, and if thou'rt a gentleman, perchance ye'll leave us in peace."

"Thou'rt in love with Susan?" Ebenezer asked incredulously.

"Aye and I am," Tim Mitchell replied, "and have been since the day I saw her. Her name is really Portia, Mister Cooke; 'tis Father calls her Susie, after a whore of a mistress he once had. He regards her as his property, sir, and treats her like a beast! Should he learn the truth of our love there would be no end to his wrath!"

Ebenezer's brain spun dizzily. "Dear Mister Mitchell——"

"The blackguard!" Timothy went on, his voice unsteady. "Till he hath got that new wench in his power, he comes out eveningly to poor sweet Portia, whose maidenhead he claimed when she was yet a shoat too young to fend him off."

Ebenezer could not but admire the metaphor of the shoat, and yet there were obvious discrepancies between the accounts of Susan's past. "I do declare," he protested, "this is not——"

"There is no limit to the man's poltroonery," Timothy hissed. "Albeit he is my father, sir, I loathe him like the Devil! Say naught of this, I beg ye, for in his wickedness, did he know aught of our love, he would give her to the lecherous boar in yonder pen, that e'er hath looked on her with lewd intent, and let him take his slavering will o' her."

Ebenezer gasped. "You do not mean to say——"

But even as the truth dawned on him, young Mitchell called "Portia! Hither, Portia! *Soo-ie!*" and an animal shuffled over from the far wall in the dark.

"Lookee there, how gentle!" Tim said proudly.

"Out on't!" the Laureate whispered.

"Think o' her as your own dear sister, sir: would ye consign her to be ravished by a filthy beast?"

"I would not," Ebenezer exclaimed, "and I am affronted by the analogy! In sooth I cannot tell who's beastlier, the buggerman or the boar; 'tis the viciousest vice I e'er encountered!"

Timothy Mitchell's voice reflected more disappointment than intimidation at the outburst. "Ah, sir, no amorous practice is itself a vice—can ye be in sooth a poet and not see that? Adultery, rape, deceit, unfair seduction—'tis *these* are vicious, not the coupling of parts: the sin is not in the act, but in the circumstances."

Ebenezer wished he could see this curious moralist's face. "What you say may well be true, but you speak of men and women——"

"Shame on a poet that harkens so lightly!" Timothy chided. " 'Twas male and female I spoke of, not men and women."

"But such a foul, unnatural jointure!"

Timothy laughed. "Methinks Dame Nature's not so nice as thee, sir. I grant ye that a rabbit-hound in heat seeks out a bitch to mate with, but doth he care a fig be she turnspit or mastiff? Nay, more, by Heav'n, he'll have at any partner, be't his bitch, his brother, or his master's boot! His urge is natural, and hath all nature for its target—with a hound-bitch at the bulls-eye, so to speak. I have seen yonder spaniels humping sheep. . . ."

Ebenezer sighed. "The face of buggery hath yet a sinful leer, for all the paint and powder of your rhetoric. These poor dumb creatures are betrayed by accident, but man hath light enough to see Dame Nature's plan."

"And sense enough to see it hath no object, save to carry on the species," Timothy added. "And wit enough to do for sport what the beasts do willy-nilly. I have no quarrel with women, Master Poet: 'tis many a maid I've loved ere now and doubtless shall again. But just as Scripture tells us that death is the fruit of the Tree of Knowledge, so Boredom, methinks, is the fruit of Wit and Fancy. A new mistress lies upon her back at night in a proper chamber, and her lover is content. But anon this simple pleasure palls, and they set about to refine their sport: from Aretine they learn the joy of sundry stoops and stances; from Boccaccio and the rest they learn to woo by the light o' day, in fields and wine butts and chimney corners; from Catullus and the naughty Greeks they learn *There are more ways to the woods than one,* and more woods than one to be explored by every way. If they have wit and daring there is no end to their discovery, and if they read as well, they have the amorous researches of the race at their disposal: the pleasures of Cathay, of Moors and Turks and Africans, and the cleverest folk of Europe. Is this not the way of't, sir? When men like us become enamored of a woman, we fall in love with every part and aspect; we cannot rest till we know with all our senses every plain and secret

353

part of our beloved, and then we gnash our teeth that we cannot go beneath her skin! I am no great poet like you, sir, but 'twas just this craving I once turned into verse, in this manner:

> Let me taste of thy Tears,
> And the Wax of thine Ears;
> Let me drink of thy Body's own Wine——"

"Eh! 'Sheart! Have done ere you gag me!" Ebenezer cried. *"Thy body's own wine!* Ne'er have I heard such verses!"

"Thou'rt a stranger to Master Barnes, then, the sonneteer? He longed to be the sherry in his mistress's glass, that she might curl him in her tongue, warm her amorous blood with him, and piss him forth anon. . . ."

"There is a certain truth in all of this you tell me," Ebenezer admitted. "I'll grant you farther that were I not resolved to chastity—nay, do not laugh, sir, 'tis true, as I'll explain in time—were I not resolved to chastity, I say, but had me a mistress like the lot of men, I should feel this urge you speak of, to know her in every wise, saving only her 'body's own wine' and such like liquors, that can stay in her distillery for all I'll quaff 'em! There's naught unnatural in this: 'tis but the lover's ancient wish that Plato speaks of, to be one body with his beloved; and with poets in especial 'tis not to be wondered at, forasmuch as *love* and *woman* are so oft the stuff of verse. Yet 'tis no mean leap from Petrarch's Laura, or even Barnes's thirsty wench, to your fat sow Portia here!"

"On the contrary, sir, 'tis no leap at all," Tim said. "You have already pled my case. Your Socrates had Xanthippe to warm his bed, but he took his sport with the young Greek lads as well, did he not? Ye say that women are oft the stuff o' poetry, but in fact 'tis the great wide world the poet sings of: God's whole creation is his mistress, and he hath for her this selfsame love and boundless curiosity. He loves the female body—Heav'n knows!—the little empty space between her thighs he loves, that meet to make sweet friction lower down; and the two small dimples in the small o' her back, that are no strangers to his kiss."

" 'Tis quite established," Ebenezer said, his blood roused up afresh, "the female form is wondrous to behold!"

"But shall it blind ye to the beauty of the male, sir? Not if ye've Plato's eyes, or Shakespeare's. How comely is a well-formed man! That handsome cage of ribs, and the blocky muscles of his calves and thighs; the definition of his hands, ridged and squared with veins and tendons, and more pleasing than a woman's to the eye; the hair of his chest, that the nicest sculptors cannot render; and noblest of all, his manhood in repose! What contrast to the sweet unclutteredness of women! The chiefest fault of the sculpting Greeks, methinks, is that their marble men have the parts of little boys: 'tis pederastic art, and I abhor it. How wondrous, had they carved the living truth, that folk in ancient times were wont to worship—the very mace and orbs of power!"

"I too have admired men on occasion," Ebenezer said grudgingly, "but my flesh recoils at the thought of amorous connection!" His unseen partner's words, in fact, had recalled to him the indignities which he had suffered more than three months earlier in the *Poseidon*'s fo'c'sle.

"Then more's the pity," Tim said lightly, "for there's much to be said of men in verse. Marry, sometimes I wish I had a gift with words, sir, or some poet had my soul: what lines I would make about the bodies of men and women! And the rest of creation as well!" Ebenezer heard him patting Portia. "Great rippling hounds, sleek mares, or golden cows—how can men and women rest content with little pats for such handsome beasts? I, I love them from the last recesses of my soul; my heart aches with passion for their bodies!"

"*Perversity*, Mr. Mitchell!" the Laureate scolded. "You've parted company now with Plato and Shakespeare, and with every other gentleman as well!"

"But not with mankind," Timothy declared. "Europa, Leda, and Pasiphaë are my sisters; my offspring are the Minotaur, and the Gorgons, and the Centaurs, the beast-headed gods of the Egyptians, and all the handsome royalty of the fairy tales, that must be loved in the form of toads and geese and bears. I love the world, sir, and so make love to it! I have sown my seed in men and women, in a dozen sorts of beasts, in the barky boles of trees and the honeyed wombs of flowers; I have dallied on the black breast of the earth, and clipped her fast; I have wooed the waves of the sea, impregnated the four winds, and flung my passion skywards to the stars!"

So exalted was the voice in which this confession was delivered that Ebenezer shrank away, as discreetly as he could, some inches farther from its author, who he began to fear was mad.

"'Tis a most—interesting point of view," he said.

"I was sure 'twould please ye," Timothy said. "'Tis the only way for a poet to look at the world."

"Ah, well, I did not say I share your catholic tastes!"

"Come now, sir!" Timothy laughed. " 'Twas not in your sleep ye came here calling *Susie!*"

Ebenezer made a small mumble of protest; he did not, on the one hand, care to let Timothy believe that the Laureate of Maryland shared his vicious lust for livestock, but on the other hand he was not prepared to reveal the true reason for his presence in the barn.

"Thou'rt too much the gentleman to molest her now," Tim went on. Ebenezer heard him moving closer and retreated another step.

" 'Twas all an error of judgment!" he cried, tingling with shame. "I can explain it all!"

"Wherefore? D'ye think I mean to ruin your name, when ye have spared my Portia? Susan Warren told me all, and I bade her wait for ye; I'll lead ye straight to her, and ye may sport the night away." He caught up before Ebenezer could run and grasped his upper arm.

" 'Tis more than kind," the Laureate said apprehensively, "but I've no wish to go at all. I really am a virgin, I swear't, for all my ill designs on Susan Warren; 'twas some sudden monstrous passion overcame me, that I am most ashamed of now." Again, and bitterly, he remembered his own ill treatment on the *Poseidon*. "Thank Heav'n I was delayed till prudence cooled my ardor, else I'd done myself and her an equal wrong!"

"Then you really are a virgin yet?" Tim asked softly, tightening his grip on the poet's arm. "And ye still mean to remain one, come what may?"

He spoke in a voice altogether different from the one he'd used until then; it raised the Laureate's hackles, and so drained him with surprise that he could not speak.

" 'Twas not easy to believe," the new voice added. "That's why I said I'd take you to the swine-girl."

"I cannot believe my ears!" the poet gasped.

"Nor could I mine, when Mitchell told me of his dinner guest. Shall we trust our eyes any better?"

He removed the lantern shade completely: in the yellow flare, which drew the slow attention of the swine, Ebenezer saw not the bearded, black-haired "Peter Sayer" Burlingame of Plymouth—though this had been incredible enough!—but the well-dressed, smooth-shaven, periwigged tutor of St. Giles in the Fields and London.

22

No Ground Is Gained Towards the Laureate's Ultimate Objective, but Neither Is Any Lost

"Is'T ONCE, or twice, or thrice I am deceived?" the poet exclaimed. "Is't Burlingame that stands before me now, or was't Burlingame I left in Plymouth? Or are the twain of you impostors?"

"The world's a happy climate for imposture," Burlingame admitted with a smile.

"You were so much altered when I saw you last, and now you've altered back to what you were!"

" 'Tis but to say what oft I've said to you ere now, Eben: your true and constant Burlingame lives only in your fancy, as doth the pointed order of the world. In fact you see a Heraclitean flux: whether 'tis we who shift and alter and dissolve; or you whose lens changes color, field, and focus; or both together. The upshot is the same, and you may take it or reject it."

Ebenezer shook his head. "In sooth you are the man I knew in London. Yet I cannot believe Peter Sayer was a fraud!"

Burlingame shrugged, still holding the lantern. "Then say he hath shaved his hair and beard since then, as doth my version of the case, *and no longer affects a tone of voice like this.*" He spoke these last words in the voice Ebenezer remembered from Plymouth. "If you'd live in the world, my friend, you must dance to some other fellow's tune or call your own and try to make the whole world step to't."

"That's why I'm loath to strike out on the floor"—Ebenezer laughed—"though I came very near to't this night."

Henry laid his hand on the poet's shoulder. "I know the story, friend, and the whore hath fleeced you for the nonce. But I'll get your two pounds from her by and by."

"No matter," the poet smiled ruefully. " 'Twas but a worthless ring I gave her, and I bless the hour she foiled my lecherous plan." The mention of it recalled his friend's recent discourse in the dark, and he blushed and laughed again. " 'Twas for a tease you feigned that passion for a pig, and the rest!"

"Not a bit of't," Henry declared. "That is to say, I have no *special* love for her, but she is in sooth a tasty flitch, despite her age, and many's the time——"

"Stay, you tease me yet!"

"Think what you will," said Burlingame. "The fact is, Eben, I share your views on innocence."

So surprised and pleased was Ebenezer to hear this confession that he embraced his friend with both arms; but Burlingame's response was a movement so meaningful that the poet cried out in alarm and retreated at once, shocked and hurt.

"What I mean to say," Henry continued pleasantly, "is that I too once clung to my virginity, and for the selfsame cause you speak of in your poem. Yet anon I lost it, and so committed me to the world; 'twas then I vowed, since I was fallen from grace, I would worship the Serpent that betrayed me, and ere I died would know the taste of every fruit the garden grows! How is't, d'you think, I made a conquest of a saint like Henry More? And splendid Newton, that I drove near mad with love? How did I get my post with Baltimore, and wrap good Francis Nicholson around my finger?"

" 'Sheart, you cannot mean they all are——"

"Nay," said Henry, anticipating the objection. "That is, they scarcely think so. But ere I was twenty I knew more of the world's passions than did Newton of its path in space. No end of *experimenta* lay behind me; I could have writ my own *Principia* of the flesh! When Newton set his weights and wires a-swing, did they know what forces moved them as he chose? No more than Newton knew, and Portia here—to name no others—what wires of nerve and amorous springs I triggered, to cause whate'er reaction I pleased."

The Laureate was sufficiently astonished by these revelations so that before he could assimilate them Henry changed the subject to one more apparently relevant: their separate crossings from Plymouth and their present positions. He had, he declared, successfully deceived Captains Slye and Scurry into believing that he was John Coode, and in that role had accompanied them to Maryland, confirming in the process Coode's leadership of a sizable two-way smuggling operation: under the rebel's direction, numerous shipmasters ran Maryland tobacco duty-free to New York, for example, whence Dutch confederates marketed it illegally in Curaçao, Surinam, or Newfoundland; or they would export it to the Barbados, where it was transferred from hogsheads to innocent-looking boxes and smuggled into England; or they would run it directly to Scotland. On return trips they imported cargoes from foreign ports directly into Maryland by the simpler device of bribing the local collectors with barrels of rum and crates of scarce manufactured goods.

" 'Tis in this wise," he said, "Coode earns a large part of the money for his grand seditious plots, though he doubtless hath other revenues as well." He went on to assert that from all indications the conspirator planned a *coup d'état*, perhaps within a year, various of Slye's and Scurry's remarks left little doubt of that, though they gave no hint of the agency through which the overthrow was to be effected.

"Then how is it thou'rt here and not on Nicholson's doorstep?" asked the Laureate. "We must inform him!"

Burlingame shook his head. "We are not that certain of his own fidelity, Eben, for all his apparent honesty. In any case 'twould scarcely make him more alert for trouble than he is already. But let me finish." He told how he had surreptitiously disembarked from Slye and Scurry's ship at Kecoughtan, in Virginia, lest the real Coode be present at their landing in St. Mary's, and had crossed to Maryland in his present disguise—or guise, if Ebenezer preferred—only a few weeks ago. Inquiring after the *Poseidon* in St. Mary's, he had learned, to his horror, of the Laureate's abduction by pirates.

" 'Sbody, how I did curse myself for not having sailed with you!" he exclaimed. "I could only presume the wretches had done you in, for one cause or another——"

"Prithee, Henry," Ebenezer interrupted, "was't you that posed as Laureate, somewhile after?"

Burlingame nodded. "You must forgive me. 'Twas but your name I used, on a petition: I thought me how you'd died ere you had the chance to serve your cause, and how old Coode would rejoice to hear't. Then Nicholson declared he meant to move the government from St. Mary's to Anne Arundel Town, to take the Papish taint off it, and some men in St. Mary's sent round a petition of protest. I saw Coode's name on't and so affixed yours as well, to confound him."

"Dear friend!" Tears came to Ebenezer's eyes. "That simple act was near the death of me!"

Astonished, Burlingame asked how, but Ebenezer bade him conclude his narration, after which he would tell the story of his own eventful passage from Plymouth to where they now sat in the straw.

"There's little more to tell," Henry said. "They had put your trunk away against the time when 'twill go up for lawful sale, but I contrived to gain possession of your notebook——"

"Thank Heav'n!"

"How many tears I shed upon your poems! I have't in the house this minute, but I little dreamed I'd ever see its owner again."

While still in St. Mary's, he said, he heard that Coode had learned of the grand deception and was so enraged that he had barred Slye and Scurry from the lucrative smuggling run to punish them. In fact, fearful of traps set by the unknown spy, Coode had been obliged to suspend virtually all smuggling operations in the province for a while: His Majesty's tobacco revenues had seldom been so high.

"I knew the blackguard must needs find some new income," Henry went on, "and so I followed him as close as e'er I could. In this wise I discovered Captain Mitchell: he is one of the chiefest agents of sedition, and his house is oft the rebels' meeting place."

"I'm not a whit surprised, from what I've heard," said Ebenezer, and then suddenly blanched. "But i'God, I gave him my name, and told him the entire story of my capture!"

Burlingame shook his head in awe. "So he told me when I came in, and thou'rt the luckiest wight in all of Maryland, I swear. He thought the twain of you mad and took you in for his dinner guests' amusement. Tomorrow he'd have turned you out, and if he dreamed for a minute you were really Eben Cooke, 'twould be the death of you both, I'm certain."

Returning to his story, he told of his investigation of Mitchell, which had produced two useful pieces of information: the man was instrumental in some sinister new scheme of Coode's, and he had one son, Timothy, whom he'd left behind in England four years previously to complete his education, and who was therefore unknown in Maryland.

"I resolved at once to pose as Mitchell's son: I had seen his portrait hanging in the house, and 'twas not so far unlike me that four years of studious drinking couldn't account for the difference. E'en so, for prudence's sake, I forged Coode's name on a letter to Mitchell, which said Son Tim was now in Coode's employ and was coming home to do a job of work for's father. 'Tis e'er Coode's wont to send a cryptic order, and de'il the bit you question what it means! I followed close on the letter and declared myself Tim Mitchell, come from

London. It mattered not a fart then whether the Captain believed me to be his son or Coode's agent: when he questioned me I smiled and turned away, and he questioned me no more. Yet what the plot is, I've yet to learn."

"Mayhap it hath to do with opium," Ebenezer suggested, and to Burlingame's sharp look said in defense, " 'Twas what he ruined the swine-girl with, and murthered his wife as well." Briefly he recounted Susan Warren's tale, including the wondrous coincidence of Joan Toast's presence and Susan's noble sacrifice to save her. All through the little relation, however, Burlingame frowned and shook his head.

"Is't aught short of miraculous?" the poet demanded.

" 'Tis too much so," said Henry. "I've no wish to be o'er-skeptical, Eben, or to disappoint your hopes; the wench herself is ruined with opium, I grant, and it may be all she says is true as Scripture. But yonder by the river stands a pair of gravestones, side by side; the one's marked *Pauline Mitchell* and the other *Elizabeth Williams*. And I swear the name of Joan Toast hath not been mentioned in this house—at least in my hearing. The only wench I've known him to woo is Susie Warren herself, that we all have had our sport with now and again. Nor have I seen a phial of opium hereabouts, albeit he may well feed her privily. Methinks she heard of Joan Toast from your valet—his tongue is loose enough. As for the rest, 'twas but a tale to wring some silver from you; when it failed she feigned that sacrifice you spoke of, in hopes of doing better the second time. Didn't you say she was in the kitchen with your valet all through supper?"

"So she was," Ebenezer admitted. "But it seems to me she ——"

"Ah well," laughed Henry, "thou'rt no more gulled than Susan, in the last account, and if Joan Toast's here we'll find her. But tell me now of your own adventures: i'faith, you've aged five years since last I saw you!"

"With cause enough," sighed Ebenezer, and though he was still preoccupied with thoughts of Joan Toast, he related as briefly as he could the tale of his encounter with Bertrand aboard the *Poseidon,* the loss of his money through the valet's gambling, his ill-treatment at the hands of the crew, and their capture by Thomas Pound. At every new disclosure Burlingame shook his head or murmured sympathy; at the mention of Pound he cried out in amazement—not only at the coincidence, but also at the implication that Coode had enlisted the support of Governor Andros of Virginia, by whom Pound was employed to guard the coast.

361

"And yet 'tis not so strange, at that," he said on second thought. "There's no love lost 'twixt Andros and Nicholson any more. But fancy you in Pound's clutches! Was that great black knave Boabdil still in his crew?"

"First mate," the poet replied with a shudder. "Dear Heav'n, what horrors he wrought aboard the *Cyprian!* The very wench I spoke of, that I climbed to in the mizzen-rigging, he had near split like an oyster. How it pleased me that she gave the fiend a pox!"

"You had near got one yourself," Burlingame reminded him soberly. "And not just once, but twice. Did ye see the rash on Susan Warren's skin?"

"But you yourself——"

"Have had some sport with her," Henry finished. "But I know more sports than one to play with women." Awed, he rubbed his chin. "I have heard before of whore-ships, and thought 'twas a sailors' legend."

Ebenezer went on to tell of the collusion between Pound and Captain Meech of the *Poseidon,* postponing mention of John Smith's secret diary until later, and concluded with the story of their execution, survival, and discovery of Drakepecker and Quassapelagh, the Anacostin King.

"This is astounding!" Henry cried. "Your *Drakepecker* is an African slave, I doubt not, but this Quassapelagh—— D'you know who he is, Eben?"

"A king of the Piscataways, he said."

"Indeed so, and a disaffected one! Last June he murthered an English wight named Lysle and was placed in the charge of Colonel Warren, in Charles County, that was still a loyal friend of Coode's. This Warren set the salvage free one night, for some queer cause or other, and was demoted for't, but they never saw Quassapelagh after that. The story was that he's trying to inflame the Piscataways against Nicholson."

"'Twere a dreadful thing, if true," the Laureate said, "but I must vouch for the man himself, Henry; I would our Maryland planters had half his nobility. Yet stay, tell me this ere I say another word: what have you learned of Sir Henry Burlingame, your ancestor?"

Burlingame sighed. "No more than I knew in Plymouth. Do you recall I said the Journal was parceled out to sundry Papist Smiths? Well, the first of these was Richard Smith, right here in Calvert County, that is Lord Baltimore's surveyor general. As soon as I was established here and had revealed myself to Nicholson, I set out to collect the various portions, so that Coode and all his cohorts could be prosecuted. But when I reached Dick Smith and gave him the Governor's password——"

"He told you Coode had long since got his portion by some ruse," Ebenezer laughed.

"'Tis a thin joke, 'sheart! Dick Smith had tried to help some Papist friends of his by making 'em deputy surveyors, and after Governor Copley died, Coode saw his chance to raise a cry of Popery and turn Smith's property inside out. How did you hear of it?"

Ebenezer withdrew from his pocket the few folded pages of the diary that remained to him. "How should I not learn something of intrigue myself, with such a marvelous tutor? You'll see naught here to read, but these are pages from the document you speak of."

Burlingame snatched them eagerly and held them to the lamplight. "Ah, Christ!" he cried. "There's scarce a word preserved!"

"Not of the Assembly Journal," Ebenezer agreed. He told how he had stolen the papers from Pound and carried them with him off the shallop's plank. "'Tis Maryland's ill luck we've lost the evidence," he concluded, and laughed again at Burlingame's chagrin. "Cheer yourself, Henry! Do you think I'd keep such a prize two minutes ere I read the *recto* through?"

"Praise God! You've learned to tease as well!"

Without more ado, though the night was nearly done, Ebenezer described the secret history of Captain John Smith's voyage up the Chesapeake and narrated, with some embarrassment, the entire tale of Hicktopeake's voracious queen.

"This is too excellent!" cried Henry at the end of it. "We know Sir Henry came alive with Smith from the town of Powhatan and went with him up the Bay. What's more, from all we've heard, each loathed the other and wished him ill, and there's no word of Burlingame in Smith's *Generall Historie* —d'you suppose Smith did him in?"

"Let's hope not, till Sir Henry sired a son," Ebenezer said. "At best he could be no closer than a grandsire to yourself." He then recalled what Meech had proposed to Pound—that if *he* were Baltimore he'd divide the Journal among several colleagues named Smith. "I'd have thought of it sooner were I not near dead for want to sleep; belike Pound made no mention of't, Coode was so wroth with him."

"Or belike he did, to help redeem himself." Burlingame
363

stood up and stretched. "In any case, we'd best go fetch the rest without delay. Let's sleep now for a while, and come morning we'll make our plans."

The Laureate's desire for sleep overcame his trepidations regarding Captain Mitchell, and they returned through the slumbering house to the bed-chamber where he had so nearly lost his chastity some hours earlier. Bertrand was not there.

" 'Twas your Bertrand I saw first," Henry said, "and scarce believed my eyes! When he told me you were here I sent him off to sleep with our servants, so that you and I could talk in peace. In the morning he can go to St. Mary's in a wagon with one of our men and claim your trunk."

"Aye, very good," Ebenezer said, but he had only half heard Henry's words. Not long before, in the barn, he had been oddly disturbed by his friend's mention of Bertrand, without quite knowing why; now he remembered what the valet had told him at their first encounter aboard the *Poseidon*, nearly half a year past: of the several meetings between valet and tutor not reported by Burlingame, and of Burlingame's liaison with Anna—which latter memory, understandably, was most unpleasant in the light of what he had just learned about his friend's amorous practices.

Burlingame set down the shaded lantern and began undressing for bed. "The wisest thing then would be to have him ferry the trunk right across the Bay to Malden. 'Tis but a matter of——"

"Henry!" the Laureate broke in.

"What is't? Why are you so alarmed?" He laughed. "Get on, now, 'tis not long till dawn."

"Where is my commission from Lord Baltimore?"

For a moment Burlingame looked startled; then he smiled. "So, your servant told you I have it?"

"Nay," Ebenezer said sadly. "Only that I had it not."

"Then doubtless he forgot to tell you 'twas from him I had to buy it," Henry said testily, "with a five-pound bribe, and merely to safeguard it till Maryland? How I wish old Slye and Scurry had caught the wretch while 'twas still in his possession! Don't you understand, Eben? That paper was the warrant for its bearer's death! E'en so, your loyal valet made him a fair copy, telling me 'twas but to boast of in London —I little dreamed he'd steal your place on the *Poseidon!*"

He laid his hand on the poet's arm. "Dear boy, 'tis late in the day for quarrels."

But Ebenezer drew away. "Where is the paper hidden?"

Burlingame sighed and climbed into the bed. "In the ocean off Bermuda, forty fathoms deep."

"What?"

" 'Twas the one time Slye and Scurry played me false. I heard them plotting to search my cabin for jewels, that they thought the king of France had given Coode; I had one hour to draw up papers with Coode's name and throw away all others. Nay, don't look so forlorn! I've long since writ you out another, in hopes you were alive."

"But how can you——"

"As his Lordship's agent in such matters," said Burlingame. He got out of bed and with a key from his trousers' pocket unlocked a small chest in one corner of the room. With the aid of the lantern he selected one from a number of papers in the chest and presented it for Ebenezer's inspection. "Doth it please you?"

"Why 'tis the original! Thou'rt teasing me!"

Burlingame shook his head. " 'Tis two weeks old at most; I could do its like again in five minutes."

"I'faith, then, thou'rt the world's best forger of hands!"

"Haply I am, but you do me too much honor in this instance." He smiled: " 'Twas I that penned the original."

"Not so!" cried the poet. "I saw it penned myself!"

Henry nodded. "I well remember. You fooled and fiddled with the ribbons on your scabbard and had like to piss for very joy."

" 'Twas Baltimore himself——"

"You have never seen Charles Calvert," Burlingame said. "Nor hath any stranger lately who comes uncalled for to his door: 'twas one of my duties then to greet such folk and sound them out. When you were announced I begged his lordship to let me disguise myself as him, as was my wont with uncertain guests. 'Twas but a matter of powdering my beard and feigning stiffness in the joints——" He altered his voice to sound exactly like the one that had narrated to Ebenezer the history of the Province. "The voice and hand were childs play to mimic."

Ebenezer could not contain his disappointment; his eyes watered.

"Ah, now, what doth it matter?" Burlingame sat beside him on the bed and placed an arm across his shoulders. " 'Twas for the same reason I posed as Peter Sayer for a while: to feel you out. Besides, Baltimore heard and seconded all I said. Your commission hath his entire blessing, I swear." He gave Ebenezer a squeeze.

"Tell me truly, Henry," the Laureate demanded, moving clear. "What is your relationship with Anna?"

"Ah, friend Bertrand again," Burlingame said calmly. "What do you think it to be, Eben?"

"I think thou'rt secretly in love with her," Ebenezer accused.

"Thou'rt in error, then, for there's nothing secret in't."

"No trysts or secret meetings? No *sweetmeats* and *honeybees?*"

"Dear friend, control yourself!" Henry said firmly. "Your sister doth me the honor of returning my regard and hath the good sense not to invite her brother's and her father's wrath in consequence. As for me, I love her in the same way I love you—no more, no less."

"Aye, and what way is that?" the poet asked. "Must we not add Portia to the list, and Dolly at the King o' the Seas, and Henry More, and *the barky boles of trees?* Why did my father cashier you at St. Giles?"

"Thou'rt overwrought," said Burlingame, still seated on the bed. "Let me calm you."

Tears streamed down Ebenezer's cheeks. "Son of Sodom!" he cried, and sprang upon his tutor. "You've had my sister's maidenhead and now you lust for mine!"

Though both height and initiative were on his side, the Laureate was no match for Burlingame, who was somewhat heavier, a good deal more co-ordinated, and infinitely more practiced in the arts of combat: in less than a minute he had Ebenezer pinned face down on the bed, his arm twisted up behind his back.

"The truth is, Eben," he declared, "I have yearned to have the twain of you since you were twelve, so much I loved you. 'Twas some inkling of this love enraged old Andrew, and he cashiered me. But on my oath, your sister is a virgin yet for all of me. As for yourself, d'you think I could not force you now, if I so chose? Yet I do not, and would not; rape hath its joys, but they are not worth your friendship, or your sister's love."

He released his grip and lay down, turning his back to Ebenezer. The poet, stricken by what he'd learned, made no move to renew the attack or even to change his position.

"Whate'er could come of a love 'twixt me and Anna?" Burlingame asked. "I have nor wealth, nor place, nor even parentage. D'you think I'd waste my seed on sows, if I could sow a child in Anna Cooke? D'you think I'd flit about the world, if I could take her to wife? Methinks your friend

McEvoy spoke the truth, Eben: you know naught of the great real world!"

The Laureate, in fact, at once felt sorry for his friend's predicament, but because he wasn't sure to what extent he ought to be outraged, and because what the disclosures concerning Anna and Lord Baltimore really made him feel was a sort of bitter melancholy, neither his sympathy nor his anger found a voice. He did not see how, in the light of all this, he could endure ever to face Burlingame again, much less sleep in the same bed with him. What could they say to each other now? He felt unspeakably deceived and put upon—a by no means wholly unpleasurable feeling. Face buried in the pillow and eyes wet with pity for himself, he recalled one of the wonderful dreams he had dreamed while senseless in the *Poseidon*'s fo'c'sle: Burlingame and Anna side by side at the vessel's rail, waving to him where he swam in the flat, green, tepid sea. So stirring was the vision that he gave himself over to it entirely; closed his eyes, and let the sea wash warmly by his loins and hams.

23

In His Efforts to Get to the Bottom of
Things the Laureate Comes Within Sight of
Malden, but So Far from Arriving There,
Nearly Falls Into the Stars

IT WAS ALREADY WELL into the morning when the Laureate awoke: the thin fall sunshine struck his eyelids, and he was mortified to understand that for the first time since early childhood he had wet the bed. He dared not move, for fear of waking Burlingame and discovering his shame. How to conceal it? He considered accidentally spilling the water pitcher onto the bed, but rejected the scheme as insufficiently convincing. The only other alternative was to absent himself stealthily from the premises, since he could not in any case have further dealings with his friend, and to strike out on his own for Malden before anyone was awake; but he lacked the daring for such a move in the first place, and also had no way of securing food and transportation for himself and Bertrand.

While considering and rejecting these courses of action he fell asleep again, and this time it was mid-morning when he woke. Burlingame, in the interval, had donned his clothes and left, and on the table with the pitcher and bowl were a piece of soap, a razor, a complete outfit of gentleman's clothing, including shoes, hat, and sword, and—wonder of wonders—the ledger-book acquired from Ben Bragg at the Sign of the Raven! The Laureate rejoiced to behold the gift, and for all his shock and disappointment of the night just past, he could not but feel a certain warmth for his benefactor. He sprang out of bed, stripped off the clammy, verminous rags he'd worn day and night since his capture by the pirates, and scrubbed himself ferociously from top to toe. Then, before shaving, he could not resist rereading the poems in his notebook—especially the hymn to chastity, which, whether Susan Warren had been lying or not, was given a heightened significance by her mention of Joan Toast and by the Laureate's late adventure. As he shaved he repeated the stanzas over and over, with a growing sense of physical and spiritual well-being. It was a splendid morning for rededication—high and clear and fresh as April, despite the season. Off came the beard and on went the clothes, which if not a tailored fit were at least of good quality; except for his sunburned face and hands and his somewhat shaggy hair, he looked and felt more like a Laureate when he was done than he had at any time since leaving London. He could scarcely wait to set out for Malden, more particularly since Joan Toast might well be waiting there for him!

Now his brows contracted, and his features ticked and twitched: there remained still the problem of passing safely out of Captain Mitchell's clutches and of deciding on an attitude toward Burlingame. The first seemed infinitely simpler than the second, which was complicated not only by his uncertainty about how he should react to his friend's disclosures, but also by his embarrassment at wetting the bed, which childishness Henry had almost surely observed, and his gratitude for the gift of clothing. In fact, the more he considered possible attitudes to adopt, the more perplexing seemed the problem, and he ended by returning to the window sill and staring distractedly at the twin gravestones down by the riverbank.

368

After a while he heard someone mount the stairs, and Henry himself thrust his head into the chamber.

"Shake a leg, there, Master Laureate, or you'll miss your breakfast! Hi, what a St. Paul's courtier!"

Ebenezer blushed. "Henry, I must confess——"

"*Shhh,*" warned Burlingame. "The name is Timothy Mitchell, sir." He entered the room and closed the door. "They're waiting belowstairs, so, I must speak quickly. I've sent your man off to fetch your trunk in St. Mary's: he'll get to Malden before us and make things ready for you. Hark, now: there is an Edward Cooke in Dorchester County, a drunken cuckold of a sot-weed planter; two years ago he complained of his wife's adulteries in a petition to Governor Copley and was the butt of so much teasing that he hath drowned himself in drink. I have told Bill Mitchell thou'rt this same poor wretch, that in your cups are given to playing the Laureate, and he believes me. Act sober and shamed this morning, and there's naught to fear. Make haste, now!"

And without allowing the poet time to protest, Henry led him by the arm toward the stairs, still talking in an urgent, quiet voice:

"Your friend the swine-girl hath flown the coop, and Mitchell declares she'll make her way to Cambridge with the silver he thinks you gave her. I'm to take horse at once to find and fetch her; what you must do is beg his pardon and volunteer to aid me in the search by way of making good your sins. We can fetch the rest of the Journal on our way to Malden, and I'll deliver it to Nicholson when I return." They approached the dining-room. " 'Sheart, now, don't forget: I'm Tim Mitchell and thou'rt Edward Cooke of Dorset."

Ebenezer had no opportunity either to assent to or protest the course of events: he found himself propelled into the dining-room, where Captain Mitchell and a few of the previous evening's guests were breakfasting on rum and a meat identified by Burlingame as broiled rasher of infant bear. They regarded Ebenezer, some with amusement and others with a certain rancor, which, however, observing that he was Timothy's friend, they did not express overtly. When the two new arrivals were seated and served, Burlingame announced to the group what he had already told Mitchell—that their distinguished visitor was not Ebenezer Cooke the poet, but Edward Cooke the cuckold. The news occasioned some minutes of ribaldry, following which Ebenezer made a pretty speech of apology for his imposture and other unseemly deportment, and volunteered to aid Timothy in his search for the fugitive servant.

"As't please ye," Captain Mitchell grumbled, and gave some last instructions to Burlingame: "Look ye well on old Ben Spurdance's place, Timmy. 'Tis a den o' thieves and whores, and belike 'tis there she's flown again. She aims to join her sister puddletrotters now that Cambridge court is sitting."

"That I shall," smiled Burlingame.

"Take care ye don't dally by the way, and fetch Miss Susan hither within the week, for I've a word to say to her. I'll have an end to her drunkenness and leave-takings, by Heav'n! Every simpleton that comes through pays her two pounds for a squint at her backside and swallows her cock-and-bull story into the bargain, and 'tis I must bear the cost o' fetching her home again!"

As he spoke he glared at Ebenezer so accusingly that the poet turned crimson, to the merriment of the other guests, and offered further to bear the charge of Timothy's expedition. He was happy enough to leave the table when the lengthy breakfast was done, although he could not contemplate with pleasure the prospect of setting out for the Eastern Shore with Burlingame. Once on the road, alone with him, it would be necessary to come to some sort of terms with the problem put in abeyance by the urgency of their first encounter that morning: what their future relationship was to be. That it could remain what it had been thitherto, and the revelations of the night before go undiscussed, was unthinkable.

Yet when near noontime they set out on their journey— Ebenezer riding an ancient roan mare of Captain Mitchell's and Burlingame a frisky three-year-old gelding of his own— he could think of no gambit for initiating the discussion that he was courageous enough to use, and Burlingame showed no inclination to speak of anything less impersonal than the unseasonably warm day (which he said was called "Indian summer" by the colonials), the occasional planters or Indians whom they encountered on the road, and the purpose of their route.

"Calvert County is just across the Chesapeake from Dorset," he explained. "If we sailed due east from here we'd land very near Cooke's Point. But what we'll do is sail a bit northeastwards to Tom Smith's place in Talbot, just above Dorchester; he's the wight that hath the next piece of the Journal."

"Whate'er you think best," Ebenezer replied, and despite his wish to get matters out in the open, he found himself talking instead about Susan Warren, to whom, he declared, he was grateful for breaking her pledge to him, and whose flight to her father he pleaded with Burlingame not to intercept. Burlingame agreed not to search for the swine-girl at all, and changed the subject to something equally remote from what most occupied the poet's mind. Thus they rode for two or three hours into the afternoon, their horses gaited to a leisurely walk, and with every new idle exchange of remarks it became increasingly difficult for Ebenezer to broach the subject, until by the time they reached their most immediate destination—a boatlanding on the Chesapeake Bay side of Calvert County—he realized that to introduce the matter now would make him appear ridiculous, and with a sigh he vowed to have it out with his former tutor first thing next morning, if not at bedtime that very night.

Burlingame hired a pinnace to ferry them and their animals to Talbot, and they made the ten-mile crossing without incident. As they entered the wide mouth of the Choptank River, which divides the counties of Talbot and Dorchester, Burlingame pointed to a wooded neck of land nearly two miles off to starboard and said, "If I not be far wide of the mark, friend, that point o'er yonder is your own Cooke's Point, and Malden stands somewhere among those trees."

"Dear Heav'n!" cried Ebenezer. "You didn't say we would pass so near! Pray land me there now and join me when your work is done!"

"'Twould be twice imprudent," Henry replied. "For one thing, thou'rt not yet accustomed to dealing with provincial types, as I am; for another, 'twere unseemly that their Lord and Laureate should arrive alone and unescorted, don't you think?"

"Then you must come with me, Henry," Ebenezer pleaded, and the certain surliness in his voice, which throughout the day had been the only token of his tribulation, finally disappeared. "You can get the Journal later, can you not?"

But Burlingame shook his head. "That were no less imprudent, Eben. There are two pieces of the Journal yet to find: the one with Tom Smith in Talbot, the other with a William Smith in Dorset. Tom Smith I know by sight, and where he lives; we can get his part tomorrow and be off to Cambridge. But this William Smith of Dorset is an entire stranger to me: in the time 'twill take to find him, Coode could kill and rob the twain. Besides, in Oxford, where we'll land, there is a barber that shall trim your hair or shave you for a periwig, at my expense."

To such reason and graciousness Ebenezer could offer no objection, though his heart sank as they dropped Cooke's Point astern and turned north up the smaller Tred Avon River to a village called variously Oxford, Thread Haven, and Williamstadt. There they disembarked and paid calls first on the promised barber—whom Ebenezer on a comradely impulse directed to trim his natural hair in the manner of the Province rather than shave it for a periwig—and then to an inn near the wharf, where they dined on cold roast mallard and beer, also at Burlingame's expense. Assuming that they would sleep there as well, the Laureate vowed to review the whole question of Henry's relations with Anna as soon as they retired for the night, in order to determine once and for all how he should feel about it; but Henry himself frustrated this resolve by declaring, after supper, that sufficient daylight remained for them to reach the house of Thomas Smith, and proposing that they lose no time in laying hands upon his portion of the Journal.

"For I swear," he said, wiping his mouth upon his coat sleeve, "so damning is this evidence for Coode, he'll stop at naught to get it, nor scoff at any hint of its location. Let's begone." He rose from the table and started for the horses; not until he was halfway to the door did he look back to see that Ebenezer, instead of following after, still sat before his empty plate, wincing and sighing and ticking his tongue.

"Ah, then," he said, coming back, "thou'rt distraught. Is't that you came so near your estate and did not reach it?"

Ebenezer shook his head in a manner not clearly either affirmative or negative. "That is but a part of't, Henry; you go at such a pace, I have no time to think things through as they deserve! I cannot collect my wits e'en to think of all the questions I would ask, much less explore your answers. How can I know what I must do and where I stand?"

Burlingame laid his arm across the poet's shoulders and smiled. "What is't you describe, my friend, if not man's lot? He is by mindless lust engendered and by mindless wrench expelled, from the Eden of the womb to the motley, mindless world. He is Chance's fool, the toy of aimless Nature—a mayfly flitting down the winds of Chaos!"

"You mistake my meaning," Ebenezer said, lowering his eyes.

Burlingame was undaunted: his eyes glittered. "Not by

much, methinks. Once long ago we sat like this, at an inn near Magdalene College—do you remember? And I said, 'Here we sit upon a blind rock hurtling through a vacuum, racing to the grave.' 'Tis our fate to search, Eben, and do we seek our soul, what we find is a piece of that same black Cosmos whence we sprang and through which we fall: the infinite wind of space . . ."

In fact a night wind had sprung up and was buffeting the inn. Ebenezer shivered and clutched the edge of the table. "But there is so much unanswered and unresolved! It dizzies me!"

"Marry!" laughed Henry. "If you saw it clear enough 'twould not dizzy you: 'twould drive you mad! This inn here seems a little isle in a sea of madness, doth it not? Blind Nature howls without, but here 'tis calm—how dare we leave? Yet lookee round you at these men that dine and play at cards, as if the sky were their mother's womb! They remind me of the chickens I once saw fed to a giant snake in Africa: when the snake struck one of the others squawked and fluttered, but a moment after they were scratching about for corn, or standing on his very back to preen their feathers! How is't these men don't run a-gibbering down the streets, if not that their minds are lulled to sleep?" He pressed the poet's arm. "You know as well as I that human work can be magnificent; but in the face of what's out yonder"—he gestured skywards—" 'tis the industry of Bedlam! Which sees the state of things more clearly: the cock that preens on the python's back, or the lunatic that trembles in his cell?"

Ebenezer sighed. "Yet I fail to see the relevance of this; 'tis not germane at all to what I had——"

"Not germane?" Burlingame exclaimed. " 'Tis the very root and stem of't! Two things alone can save a man from madness." He indicated the other patrons of the inn. "Dull-headedness is one, and far the commoner: the truth that drives men mad must be sought for ere it's found, and it eludes the doltish or myopic hunter. But once 'tis caught and looked on, whether by insight or instruction, the captor's sole expedient is to force his will upon't ere it work his ruin! Why is't you set such store by innocence and rhyming, and I by searching out my father and battling Coode? One must needs make and seize his soul, and then cleave fast to't, or go babbling in the corner; one must choose his gods and devils on the run, quill his own name upon the universe, and declare, ' 'Tis I, and the world stands such-a-way!' One must *assert, assert, assert,* or go screaming mad. What other course remains?"

"One other," Ebenezer said with a blush. " 'Tis the one I flee . . ."

"What? Ah, 'sheart, indeed! The state I found you in at college! How many have I seen like that in Bedlam—wide-eyed, feculent, and blind to the world! Some boil their life into a single gesture and repeat it o'er and o'er; others are so far transfixed, their limbs remain where'er you place 'em; still others take on false identities: Alexander, or the Pope in Rome, or e'en the Poet Laureate of Maryland——"

Ebenezer looked up, uncertain whether it was he or the impostors whom Burlingame referred to.

"The upshot of't is," his friend concluded, "if you'd escape that fate you must embrace me or reject me, and the course we are committed to, despite the shifting lights that we appear in, just as you must embrace your Self as Poet and Virgin, regardless, or discard it for something better." He stood up. "In either case don't seek whole understanding—the search were fruitless, and there is no time for't. Will you come with me now, or stay?"

Ebenezer frowned and squinted. "I'll come," he said finally, and went out with Burlingame to the horses. The night was wild, but not unpleasant: a warm, damp wind roared out of the southwest, churned the river to a froth, bent the pines like whips, and drove a scud across the stars. Both men looked up at the splendid night.

"Forget the word *sky*," Burlingame said off-handedly, swinging up on his gelding, " 'tis a blinder to your eyes. There is no *dome of heaven* yonder."

Ebenezer blinked twice or thrice; with the aid of these instructions, for the first time in his life he saw the night sky. The stars were no longer points on a black hemisphere that hung like a sheltering roof above his head; the relationship between them he saw now in three dimensions, of which the one most deeply felt was depth. The length and breadth of space between the stars seemed trifling by comparison: what struck him now was that some were nearer, others farther out, and others unimaginably remote. Viewed in this manner, the constellations lost their sense entirely; their spurious character revealed itself, as did the false presupposition of the celestial navigator, and Ebenezer felt bereft of orientation. He could no longer think of up and down: the stars were simply *out there,* as well below him as above, and the wind appeared to howl not from the Bay but from the firmament itself, the endless corridors of space.

"Madness!" Henry whispered.

Ebenezer's stomach churned; he swayed in the saddle and covered his eyes. For a swooning moment before he turned away it seemed that he was heels over head on the bottom of the planet, looking *down* on the stars instead of up, and that only by dint of clutching his legs about the roan mare's girth and holding fast to the saddlebow with both his hands did he keep from dropping headlong into those vasty reaches!

24

The Travelers Hear About the Singular Martyrdom of Father Joseph FitzMaurice, S.J.: a Tale Less Relevant in Appearance Than It Will Prove in Fact

IT REQUIRED LESS THAN an hour's windy ride for Ebenezer and Henry Burlingame to reach their destination; they traveled four miles eastward from the village of Oxford and then turned south for a mile or so along a path leading through woods and tobacco-fields to a small log dwelling on Island Creek, which, like the larger Tred Avon River, debouched into the Great Choptank.

" 'Tis an uncommon fellow you'll meet here," Burlingame said as they approached. "He is a kind of Coode himself, but on the side of the angels. A valuable man."

"Thomas Smith?" asked Ebenezer. "I don't believe Charles Calvert told me aught——" He stopped and grimaced. "That is to say, I have ne'er heard tell of him."

"Nay," laughed Henry, "I haply made no mention of him. He is a Jesuit to the marrow, and so 'tis certain Thomas Smith is not his real name. But for all that, he's a great good fellow that loves his beer and horses. Each Friday night he hath a drinking bout with Lillingstone the minister (the same that helped me steal Coode's letters two years past, in Plymouth harbor); 'twas after one such bout they rode a horse into Talbot courthouse and called it Lambeth Palace! Some

375

say this Smith came down from Canada to spy for the French——"

"I'faith, and Baltimore trusts him with the Journal?"

Burlingame shrugged. "They have loyalties larger than France and England, I daresay. At any rate 'tis precious little spying Smith can do hereabouts, and we've ample demonstrations of his spirit: last year he was charged by Governor Copley with seditious speech, along with Colonel Sayer, and barely missed arrest."

The term *larger loyalties* Ebenezer found disquieting, but he was still too much preoccupied with his own problems to ask Burlingame whether it was the cause of Justice or, say, international Roman Catholicism that he referred to. They tethered their horses, and Burlingame rapped three times, slowly and sharply, on the cabin door.

"Yes? Who is't there?"

"Tim Mitchell, friend," said Burlingame.

"Tim Mitchell, is't? I've heard that name." The door opened enough to permit the man inside to raise a lantern, but was still chained fast to the jamb. "What might you want o' me this time of night?"

"I'm fetching a stray horse to her master," Burlingame replied, winking at Ebenezer.

"Is that so, now? 'Tis a deal o' trouble for a small reward, is't not?"

"I'll have my reckoning in Heaven, Father; for the nonce 'twill suffice me that *the man shall have his mare again.*"

Ebenezer had supposed that Burlingame was, for reasons of delicacy, speaking allegorically of Susan Warren's escape, but at the end he recognized the pass phrase of the Jacobites.

"Ha!" cried the man inside, unlatching the door and swinging it wide. "He shall in sooth, if the Society of Jesus hath not wholly lost its skill! Come in, sir, pray come in! I'd not have been so chary if there were not two of you."

Their host, Ebenezer found upon entering the cabin, was by no means as fearsome as his deep-bass voice and the tale of his exploits suggested: he stood not much over five feet tall; his build was slight, and his ruddy face—more Teutonic than Gallic above his clerical collar—had, despite his nearly fifty years, the boyish look that often marks the celibate. The cabin itself was clean and, except for a wine bottle on the table and a row of little casks along the chimneypiece, as austerely furnished as a monk's cell. For all his carousing, the priest appeared to be something of a scholar: the walls were lined with more books than the Laureate had seen in one room since leaving Magdalene, and around the wine bottle were spread other books, copious papers, and writing equipment.

"This young man is Mr. Eben Cooke, from London," Burlingame said. "He is a poet and a friend of mine."

"Indeed, a poet!" Smith shook Ebenezer's hand vigorously. He had the habit—doubtless due in part to his small stature, but suggestive as well of a certain effeminacy—of rising on his toes and widening his clear blue eyes when he spoke. "How uncommonly delightful, sir! And doth he rhyme *ad majorem Dei gloriam,* as he ought?"

Ebenezer could think of no properly witty rejoinder to this tease, but Burlingame said, " 'Tis more *ad majorem Baltimorensi gloriam,* Father: he hath the post of Maryland Laureate from Charles Calvert."

"Better and better!"

"As for his loyalty, have no fear of't."

The priest let go a booming laugh. "I shan't now, Mr. Mitchell; that I shan't, for Satan himself hath his fiendish loyalties! 'Tis the *object* of't I fear, sir, not its presence."

Burlingame urged him to calm his fears, but when he declared the purpose of their visit, producing authorization from Governor Nicholson to collect the precious papers, the Jesuit's face showed still some reservation. "I have my piece o' the Journal hidden, right enough," he said, "and I know you for an agent of our cause. But what proof have we of your friend's fidelity?"

"Methinks my post were proof enough," Ebenezer said.

"Of *allegiance,* aye, but not fidelity. Would you die to advance our cause?"

"He hath come near to that already," Burlingame said, and told their host briefly of the Laureate's adventure with the pirates.

"The saintly look is on him, that I'll grant," said the priest. " 'Tis but a question of what cause he'll be a martyr to, I suppose."

Ebenezer laughed uncomfortably. "Then I'll confess I would not die for Lord Baltimore, much as I favor his cause and loathe John Coode's."

The priest raised his eyebrows. Burlingame said at once, "Now there's a proper answer, sir: a martyr hath his uses when he's dead, but alive he's oft a nuisance to his cause." He assumed a tone of raillery. "That is the reason why there are no Jesuit martyrs."

"In sooth it is, though we can claim one or two. But *nom*

de Dieu, forgive my rudeness! Sit down and have some wine!" He waved them to the table and set about clearing it of papers. "Correspondence from the Society," he explained, observing Ebenezer's curiosity, and showed them some pages of finely-written Latin script. "I dabble in ecclesiastical history, and just now am writing a relation of the Jesuit mission in Maryland, from 1634 to the present day. 'Tis a sixty-year *Iliad* in itself, I swear, and the fortress hath yet to fall!"

"How very interesting," Ebenezer murmured. He was aware that his earlier blundering remark had been ill-taken, and looked for a way to atone for it.

The priest fetched two extra glasses from the sideboard and poured a round of wine from the bottle on the table. "*Jerez,* from the dusty vineyards of Cadiz." He held his glass to the candlelight. "Judas, see how clear! If Oporto is the blood o' Jesus, then here's the very ichor of the *Spiritu sancti.* To your health, sirs."

When the toast was drunk, Burlingame said, "And now, Father, if thou'rt quite persuaded of our loyalty——"

"Yes, yes indeed," the priest said, but poured another round and made no move to get any hidden documents. Instead he shuffled through his papers again, as though preoccupied with them, and said, "The fact of the matter is, the first martyr in America was a Jesuit priest, Father Joseph FitzMaurice—'tis his unknown history I've pieced together here."

Ebenezer pretended to be much impressed, and said by way of further pleasing their host, "You'd think the Society of Jesus would lead the field in saints and martyrs, would you not? The saint and the citizen may share the selfsame moral principles, but your ordinary man will compromise and contradict 'em every turn, while your saint will follow them through the very door of death. What I mean, the normal state of man is irrational, and by how much the Jesuits are known for great logicians, by so much do they approach the condition of saintliness."

"Would Heav'n that argument were sound!" The priest smile ruefully. "But any proper Jesuit can show you 'tis equivocal. You confuse *rational* with *reasonable,* for one thing, and the preachment with the practice for another. The sad fact is, we are the most *reasonable* of orders—which is to say, we oft will compromise our principles to reach our goal. This holy man FitzMaurice, for example——"

"He is with the blessed, I'm sure," Burlingame broke in, "but ere we hear his story, could we not just have a look at——"

"Nay, nay, there's no great rush," Ebenezer protested, interrupting in turn. "We have all night to fetch the Journal, now we're here, and I for one would greatly like to hear the tale. Haply 'twill be worth mention in my *Marylandiad*." He ignored the disgusted look of his friend, whose eagerness he thought was antagonizing their host. "What was the manner of the fellow's death?"

The priest regarded them both with a thoughtful smile. "The truth is, Father FitzMaurice was burnt as a heretic in a proper auto-da-fé."

"You don't tell me!"

Father Smith nodded. "I learned his story in part from the mission records at the Vatican and in part from enquiries made among the Indians hereabouts; the rest I can supply from rumor and conjecture. 'Tis a touching tale, methinks, and shows both the strengths and weaknesses of sainthood, whereof Mr. Mitchell hath made mention."

"A Jesuit inquisitioned and burnt! Out on't, Father, I must hear it from first to last."

It was quite late in the evening by now, and the wind still whistled around the eaves of the cabin. Ebenezer accepted a pipe of tobacco from his host, lit it from the candle flame, and settled back with a great show of comfort; but the effect of his diplomacy was doubtless nullified by Burlingame, who drank off his wine and poured another glassful without waiting to be invited, and who made no attempt to conceal his disapproval of the progress of events.

Father Smith lit a pipe himself and ignored his guest's unseemly conduct. "In the records of the Society of Jesus in Rome," he began, "one can find all the annual letters of the mission in Maryland. Two priests and a coadjutor came hither in the *Ark* and the *Dove* with the first colonists, and another priest and coadjutor followed ere the year was done. In the very first annual letter to Rome——" He fished through the stack of papers before him. "Aye, here's my copy. We read: *Two priests of Ours were assigned this year as companions to a certain gentleman who went to explore unknown lands. They with great courage performed an uncomfortable voyage of about eight months, both much shaken in health, with spells of illness, and gave us no slight hope of reaping ultimately an abundant harvest, in ample and excellent regions.*"

"Is't Maryland they speak of?" Ebenezer asked. "Why don't they use their patron's name? 'Twas a bit ungrateful, don't you think?" He remembered hearing Charles Calvert—

or, rather, Burlingame in disguise—describe the difficulties Governor Leonard Calvert had had with these same early Jesuits.

"Not at all," the priest assured him. "They knew well old Cecil Calvert was a proper Catholic at heart, if something too liberal-minded, but 'twas necessary to use great caution in all things, inasmuch as the forces of antichrist were e'en more in ascendancy then than now, and the Jesuits lived in constant peril. It was their wont to travel incognito, or with an alias, and refer to their benefactors with coded epithets such as *a certain gentleman*. The *certain gentleman* here was George Calvert—not the first Lord Baltimore, but the brother of Cecilius and Leonard. In the same way, Baltimore himself gave out that *Maryland* was called after Queen Henrietta Maria, albeit 'tis named in fact for the Queen of Heaven, as surely as is St. Mary's City."

"Nay, can that be?" Ebenezer was not a little troubled by all this association of the Baltimores with the Jesuits, which brought to his mind the dark plots Bertrand had believed in. "I understood 'twas King Charles called it Maryland, after Baltimore had proposed the name——" He turned to Burlingame, who was staring thoughtfully into the fireplace. "What was the name, Henry? It slips my mind."

"Crescentia," Burlingame replied, and added: "Whether 'twas meant to signify the holy lunar crescent of Mohammed or the carnal crescent sacred to Priapus is a matter still much argued by the scholars."

"Ah, Henry!" Ebenezer blushed for his friend's rudeness.

"No matter," the priest said indulgently. "In any case 'twas but a piece of courtliness on Calvert's part to give out that he had chosen the King's suggestion o'er his own."

"Then pray let's go on with the tale, sir, and I'll not interrupt you farther."

Father Smith replaced the letter on the pile. "The two priests that made the first voyage were called Father John Gravener and Father Andrew White," he said. "Father White's name is genuine—he wrote this fine account here, called *A Briefe Relation of the Voyage Unto Mary-land*. The other name is an alias of Father John Altham. One of these two went with George Calvert on the journey that you just heard spoken of in the letter, which purported to be an expedition into Virginia. Methinks 'twas Father White, for he was as mettlesome a fellow as ever cassock graced. But the other wight, whose name is absent from the letters, was in fact the saint I spoke of: one Father Joseph FitzMaurice, that also called himself Charles FitzJames and Thomas FitzSimmons. The truth of't is, he ne'er returned from the journey."

"But the letter you read declared——"

"I know—to the author's shame. 'Twas doubtless meant to impress his superiors in Rome with the mission's success. Father FitzMaurice was the last of the three priests to come hither in 1634. His was a soul too zealous for God's work in London in those troubled times, which was best done unobtrusively, and 'twas at his superiors' behest he shipped for Maryland. But alas, on his arrival in St. Mary's, Father FitzMaurice found his brothers' work aimed almost wholly at the planters themselves, that were slipping daily nigh to apostasy. He was farther disillusioned by the Piscataways of the place, that so far from being heathen, far outshone their English breathren in devotion to the One True Faith. Father White had made an early convert of their *Tayac,* as is our policy, and anon the entire town of salvages had set to making rosaries of their *roanoke.* 'Tis little wonder that when George Calvert proposed his journey of exploration, Father FitzMaurice straightway offered to accompany him. 'Twas Calvert's declared intent to learn the western boundaries of his brother's county palatine, but his real design was to dicker privily with Captain William Claiborne about the Kent Island question."

"I recall that name," Ebenezer said. "He was the spiritual father of John Coode!"

"As sure as Satan was of Martin Luther," agreed the priest. "Father FitzMaurice saw how scanty were George Calvert's provisions, and so put by a large stock for himself; regardless of the length of the expedition, he planned to live some months among the wildest heathen he could find, and bring new souls to the Supremest Lord Proprietary of All."

"That is good," Ebenezer said appreciatively. "That is well said."

The priest smiled acknowledgment. "He packed one seachest full of bread, cheese, dried unripe corn, beans, and flour; in a second he packed three bottles of communion wine and fifteen of holy water for baptisms; a third carried the sacred vessels and a marble slab to serve for an altar; and a fourth was fitted with rosaries, crucifixes, medallions, and sundry gewgaws and brummagem oddments for appeasement and persuasion of the heathen. The whole was loaded in the pinnace *Dove,* and on the fourth of September they set sail to southwards. Howbeit, ere the afternoon was done the pinnace came about and headed *up* the Chesapeake instead.

When Father FitzMaurice enquired the reason for't, he was told they were simply tacking to windward, and inasmuch as he knew naught of the ways of ships, he had perforce to say no more.

"At sunset they made anchorage in the lee of a large island, which the Piscataway guide called *Monoponson,* but George Calvert called Kent Island. Father FitzMaurice went ashore in the first boat and was chagrined once more, for 'twas settled and planted from shore to shore and abounded with white men, who were heretic and inhospitable enough, but in no wise heathens. Then fancy his disgust when Calvert gave out to the company that this was in fact their destination, and that his real mission was to negotiate Lord Baltimore's disputes with Captain Claiborne!

"Yet when he voiced his pique to Father White, that good man recommended acquiescence. 'We must make a virtue of necessity,' is what he counseled. 'If Claiborne trades with salvages, 'tis logically antecedent there are Indians on this island. Who then can say but what our paths were guided hither for the improvement of these same salvages, and the furtherance of the One True Faith? Were't not in fact impiety, a denial of God's direction, not to remain here and reap our bounty among the heathen?' "

"There is a pretty piece of casuistry," Burlingame remarked.

" 'Twas reasoned closely enough," the priest agreed, "but Father FitzMaurice would have none of't, nor would he rest content ere he found himself amid truly salvage Indians. Such heathen as remained upon the island, said he, were already half converted by the Virginians, though like as not to some rank heresy or other; the true worth of the missionary could be assayed only among the pure and untouched heathen that had ne'er set eyes on white men.

"Father White spoke farther, but to no avail, so incensed was Father FitzMaurice; they retired at length with some of the ship's company, the rest being engaged in carousal ashore. Next day no trace of Father FitzMaurice was to be found, nor of his four small chests, nor of the small boat that had been tethered beside the *Dove.* One message alone he left, by Father White's breviary: *Si pereo, pereo, A.M.D.G.* He ne'er was seen again, and in time the Society gave him up for dead and struck his name from the records. No wight e'er learned whither he rowed, or what his fate was, until I commenced my researches some fifteen years ago: 'twas my good fortune then to converse with one Tacomon, an ancient salvage that once was king of a town at Castlehaven Point, just o'er the Choptank from here, and from him I heard a tale whose hero could be none but Father FitzMaurice. . . .

"As best I understand it, Father FitzMaurice rowed from Kent past Tilghman's Island and eastward into the mouth of the Choptank, and headed shorewards when he saw the salvage town. Inasmuch as he faced his vessel's stern while rowing, the Indians had long since descried him and knew him for a white man, and King Tacomon with sundry of his *Wisoes* went down to greet him on the beach.

"When the stranger stepped ashore, they observed that he wore a strange black gown, and that the image of a bird was painted on his boat. 'Tis these two details I pounced on when I heard them, for the *Dove's* boat carried such an emblem on its stern, and Father FitzMaurice ne'er removed his cassock save to sleep. Moreover, he had four wooden chests aboard the boat, and when he came ashore he fell to his knees in prayer—no doubt to *Maria Stella Maris,* to thank her for his safe deliverance. The salvages showed great interest in all this, and greater still when Father FitzMaurice gave them baubles from his chest. Tacomon sent a man straightway into the town, who soon fetched down a goodly load of furs and all the other salvage folk as well.

"Father FitzMaurice was delighted, I feel certain, at the numbers of the heathen that he would quite reasonably assume had ne'er seen a Christian man before. Picture him handing 'round trinkets with his left hand and blessing their recipients with his right, and all the while, so Tacomon remembered, babbling in a tongue no man among them kenned. They loaded furs into his boat until at length he saw they took him for a trader, whereupon he gave each one a crucifix and doubtless tried to explain, by signs, the Passion of Our Savior.

"Anon this Tacomon, when he had scrutinized the crucifix, gave commands to one of his Wisoes, at the same time pointing to the cross. The man ran once more to the town and came back with a small wooden box, at sight of which all the salvages fell prostrate on the beach. Would not Father Fitz-Maurice guess the box contained some pagan relic sacred to the tribe? I see him rehearsing in his mind the pretty ceremony of casting their idol to the ground, as did Moses on descending from Mount Sinai, and wondering how much holy water 'twould want to baptize the lot.

"But alas for him, his trials were not yet done; the fact of the matter was, his virgin town had been deflowered years before by some trader passing through—and what was worse, by an arrant heretic Virginian! Tacomon fetched no Golden Calf from the box, but a leathern Bible, which was fronted with a woodcut of the Crucifixion. Just opposite (for I saw the book myself) the dedication ran: *To the Most High and Mighty Prince James . . . that the Church of England shall reap good fruit thereby . . . !* The King held the book aloft for all to see, whereon with one accord the assembled Indians sang by rote the Anglican *Te Deum:*

> *We praise thee, O God, we knowledge*
> *thee to be Lord.*
> *All the earth doth worship thee,*
> *the father everlasting . . .*

The poor father must have come near swooning; in any case he snatched two or three crucifixes from Tacomon and his *cawcawaassoughs,* leaped into his boat, and did not pause to cross himself till he was out of arrowshot. As for the Indians, when they saw him shake his fist at them they took it for a fare-thee-well, which they returned with a reprise of their hymn."

"Luckless wretch!" laughed Ebenezer, and even Burlingame could not but smile and remark that the way of the saint is hard.

"When I had learnt this much of his misfortunes," said the priest, "I could not rest till I discovered his end. I made enquiries up and down the Province, but especially in lower Dorchester County, for I guessed that when his first try failed he would row farther south in search of heathen. For a long time my efforts bore no fruit. Then not many years past an Indian was brought to trial in Cambridge court on charges of killing an entire family of white folk, and, happening to have some business in the area, I took it upon myself to shrive the poor man of his sins. He would none of my services and was hanged anon, but in our bootless colloquy I learned, as't were by accident, the fate of Father Fitz-Maurice.

"The name of the salvage was Charley Mattassin. He was from a warlike band of Nanticokes that in time long past had crossed into the marshes of Dorchester and are said to live there yet in fierce seclusion. This Charley was in fact the Tayac's son, and for all he had run off with an English whore, that later was among the souls he murthered, he bore surpassing hatred for the English, which sentiment he owned was learnt from his father the Tayac. He contemned me in especial, when I went to him with holy water and crucifix to baptize and shrive him: he spat upon my cassock and declared his people had once burned a man like me upon à cross! I then enquired, Did he mean an Englishman? For I had heard of no such deed. And he replied, in essence, 'twas not merely an Englishman but a black-robed priest with crucifix and breviary, such as I, who with all his magic water could not cool the fire that burnt him. And what was yet more curious, this priest was Charley's own grandfather, so he declared, and was burnt by Charley's father."

"Out on't, this is incredible!" Ebenezer cried.

The priest agreed. "When I had heard it I put by my holy errand and implored him to tell me more. I shall answer for the Indian's soul to God, but i'faith, a good tale's worth a guilty conscience, is't not? Moreover, I can but think God sent me thither to hear't, for when 'twas done I knew the full and tragic tale of Father FitzMaurice. . . .

"When that sainted wight left Castlehaven, who knows how long he drifted south, or how many were his vain sallies ashore? What force save miracle could keep his craft afloat for hours and days in the lusty Chesapeake, and wash him at last to the wild rogue Nanticokes? As Charley told me, that had the tale by rote from the Tayac his father, some threescore autumns past a fearsome hurricane swept the marsh and washed a strange boat into the Indian town. In the boat, swooned dead away, was a black-frocked Englishman, haply the first they had laid eyes upon, and sundry brass-bound chests."

"Then in sooth 'twas no man else than Father Fitz-Maurice!"

"So said my heart on hearing it," replied the priest, "yet 'twas so wondrous a coincidence I scarce durst believe it. Howbeit, my informant's next words cleared all doubt: there was an old belief among his tribe, he said, that white-skinned men are treacherous as water-vipers, and should be massacred on sight. Yet so unusual was the aspect of this visitor, and so strangely was he brought into their midst, some feared he was an evil spirit bent on working mischief among them; and they feared this the more strongly inasmuch as his cassock looked like the black storm cloud, *and on the transom of his boat was drawn the image of a bird!*

"Anon they overcame their fear, inasmuch as the man seemed helpless, and whilst he lay still a-swoon they fetched him to a lodge and tethered his ankles with rawhide thongs.

Then they broke open his chests and decked themselves with beads and crucifixes. When the prisoner awoke he knelt for a while with lowered head and then addressed them in a tongue they knew naught of. While the elders of the town held council on what to do with him, the younger men gave him food and stood about to watch his antics, which they thought supremely funny. He caught sight of the crucifixes from his chest and for some hours repeated a ritual of gesticulation, which though not a single salvage understood, it so pleased 'em that they practiced the gestures in turn, and passed them on to succeeding generations. E'en Charley Mattassin could recall them, that had learnt them from his father, and for aught I know his tribe performs 'em yet down in the Dorset marshes. Here was the first, as 'twas shown to me—see what you make of't."

Moving out from the table, Father Smith pointed to himself and then in quick succession plucked at his cassock, held up his crucifix, crossed himself, dropped to his knees in simulated prayer, jumped up, and stretched out his arms and raised his eyes in imitation of Christ on the cross.

"Methinks he meant to show he was a priest," said Burlingame.

"Aye!" the Laureate agreed excitedly. " 'Sheart, 'tis like a voice from the grave!"

"Yet not by half so clever as this next," the priest said.

"How's that? The salvages recalled e'en more?"

Father Smith nodded proudly. "That first was mere identification, but *this:* 'tis no less than Christian doctrine, done in signs! First came this——" He held up three fingers, which Ebenezer correctly interpreted as symbolizing the Holy Trinity.

"Then this——" After indicating the first of three, the priest stood on tiptoe and pointed skywards with his right hand, grasping with his left the area of his genitalia.

"Dear me!" laughed Burlingame. "I fear 'tis the Father in Heav'n!"

"No less," beamed the priest. He then raised his index finger beside the forefinger and, in succession, rocked an invisible child in his arms and displayed the crucifix, unequivocally representing the Son. Raising next his ring finger beside the other two, he lay for a moment prostrate on the ground with closed eyes and then, fixing his gaze on the ceiling, rose slowly to his feet, meanwhile flapping his arms like wings to suggest the Ascension and thus the Holy Ghost.

"Marvelous!" the poet applauded.

"Was't past his powers to do the Virgin Birth?" Burlingame inquired.

Father Smith was not at all ruffled. "Faith moveth mountains," he declared. "How can we doubt his prowess in any article of doctrine, when such a subtle mystery as the Unity of the Trinity he dispenses with so lucidly as this?" Holding forth the same three fingers as before, he alternately spread and closed them.

"Bravo!"

"Of course," he said, " 'twas an entire waste of wit, for not a heathen in the house knew what he meant. Methinks they must have rolled about in mirth, and when the poor priest wearied they would prod him with a stick to set him pantomiming farther."

"Surely your informant could not tell you such details," Burlingame said skeptically. "All these things took place before his birth."

"He could not, nor did he need to," Smith replied. "All salvages are much alike, be they Indian, Turk, or unredeemed English, and I know the ways of salvages. For this reason I shall speak henceforth from the martyr's point of view, as't were, adding what I can surmise to the things Charley Mattassin told me. 'Twill make a better tale than otherwise, and do no violence to what scanty facts we have."

He returned to the table and poured a fourth round of *Jerez.*

"Let us say the young men mock him for some hours, aping his gestures and tormenting him with sticks. They become quite curious about the color of his skin: one grasps the priest's hand in his own, chattering to his companions as he compares the hue; another slaps the flesh of his stomach and points to Father FitzMaurice's cassock, wondering whether the stranger hath the same outlandish color from head to foot. The rest deride this notion, to the great indignation of the curious one; he lifts up his muskrat loincloth and voices a second conjecture, so fantastical to his brothers that their eyes brim o'er with glee. They fall to wagering—four, five strings of *wompompeag*—and at length deprive Father FitzMaurice of his weathered clothes, for proof. *Ecce homo!* There he stands, all miserable and a-shiver; his belly is as white as the belly of a rockfish, and though his parts have lain as idle as a Book of Common Prayer in the Vatican, he boasts in sooth a full set nonetheless. The challenger stalks off with his winnings, and the young Tayac, who is not above thirty years of age, gives commands to end the sport."

387

"Ah, now, prithee, wait a moment!" Burlingame protested. "This is made up from the whole cloth!"

"Say, from the Holy Cloth," rejoined the imperturbable Smith, widening his blue eyes at the jest.

"I for one prefer't thus," Ebenezer declared impatiently to his friend. "Let him flesh his bony facts into a tale."

Burlingame shrugged and turned back to the fire.

"The women then bring forth the evening meal," the priest went on. "To Father FitzMaurice, cowering naked on his grass mat in the corner, it seems interminable, but anon 'tis done; the women remain, tobacco is passed round, and a general carouse ensues. The priest looks on, abashed but curious, for albeit he is a Jesuit, he is a man as well, and plans moreover to write a treatise on the practices of the salvage if his life is spared. His presence is for the nonce ignored, and as they disport in their error he wrings his wits to hit upon a means of speaking with them, so to initiate the business of conversion.

"The hour arrives when the young Tayac addresses certain words to all the group, sundry of whom turn round to regard the priest. Two hoary, painted elders leave the hut to fetch back a carven pole, some ten feet long, that bears a skunk pelt at the bottom and a crudely mounted muskrat on the top. All present genuflect before it, and its bearers hold it forth toward Father FitzMaurice. The Tayac points his finger at the muskrat and speaks certain gibberish, whose imperious tone hath need of no translation: 'tis a call for similar obsequies from the priest.

"Father FitzMaurice deems the moment opportune. His nakedness forgot, he springs to his feet and shakes his head to signify refusal. Then he once more holds aloft his crucifix, nods his head in vigorous affirmation, and makes a motion as though to fling the idol down. The Tayac now grows wroth; he repeats the same command in louder tones, and the other folk are still. But Father FitzMaurice stands firm: he raises a finger to indicate that the figure on the crucifix is the true and only God, and goes so far as to spit upon the sacred staff. At once the Tayac strikes him down; the idol-bearers place the butt of their pole upon the back of his neck to pin him fast to the dirt, and the Tayac pronounces a solemn incantation, whereto the others shout assent."

"Unhappy wretch!" sighed Ebenezer. "I fear his martyrdom is at hand."

"Not yet," the priest declared. "Now the hut is cleared at once, and Father FitzMaurice is left trembling in the dirt.

Anon a dozen salvage maidens enter, all bedaubed with puccoon paint; they spread their mats about the floor and to all appearances make ready for the night . . ."

" 'Tis no mystery what will ensue," Burlingame remarked, "if these Nanticokes are like some other Indians."

But Ebenezer, who knew nothing of such matters, implored Father Smith to go on with the tale.

"Father FitzMaurice is abashed tenfold at the presence of the maidens," said the priest, "more especially as he seems the subject of a colloquy among them, carried on in mirthful whispers. He makes a mental note, for his treatise, that salvage maids all share a common chamber, and rejoices when at last the fire burns out and he can clothe his shame with darkness.

"But his solitude doth not live long: he hath told not more than three *Ave Marias* ere an Indian wench, perfumed with grease of bear and covered no more than an Adamite, flings herself upon him and bites him in the neck!"

"I'God!" cried Ebenezer.

"The good man struggles, but the maid hath strength, and besides, his foot is tethered. She lays hands upon the candle of the Carnal Mass, and *mirabile,* the more she trims it, the greater doth it wax! Father FitzMaurice scarce can conjure up his Latin, yet so bent is he on making at least one convert ere he dies, he stammers out a blessing. For reply the heathen licks his ear, whereupon Father FitzMaurice sets to saying *Paternosters* with all haste, more concerned now with the preservation of his own grace than the institution of his ward's. But no sooner is he thus engaged than *zut!* she caps his candle with the snuffer priests must shun, that so far from putting out the fire, only fuels it to a greater heat and brilliance. In sum, where he hath hoped to win a convert, 'tis Father FitzMaurice finds himself converted, in less time than it wants to write a syllogism—and baptized, catechized, received, and given orders into the bargain!"

Burlingame smiled at the Laureate's absorption in the tale. "Doth that strike you closely, Eben?"

"Barbarous!" the poet said with feeling. "To fall so from his vows by no fault of his own! What misery must his noble soul have suffered!"

"Nay, sir," Father Smith declared, "you forget he is the stuff of saints, and a Jesuit as well."

Ebenezer protested that he did not understand.

"He explores the *pros* and *contras* of his case," the priest explained, "and adduces four good arguments to ease his suffering conscience. To begin with, 'tis e'er the wont of prudent missionaries to wink their eyes, at the outset, at any curious customs of the folk they would convert. In the second place, he is promoting the rapport 'twixt him and the heathen that must be established ere conversion can commence. Third, 'tis to his ultimate good he sins, as is shown past cavil by holy precedent: had not the illustrious Augustine, for example, essayed the manifold refinements of the flesh, the better to know and appreciate virtue? And finally, lest these have an air of casuistry, he is tethered and pinioned from head to foot and hath therefore no choice or culpability in the matter. In fine, so far from wailing o'er his plight, he comes to see in it the hand of Providence and joins in the labor with a will. If his harvest be commensurate to his tilling of the ground, so he reflects, he might well be raised to a bishopric by Rome!

"When anon the maid is ploughed and harrowed, Father FitzMaurice finds her place taken by another, whom he loses no chance to prime like the first for her conversion. Ere dawn, with the help of God, he hath persuaded every woman in the hut of the clear superiority of the Faith, and inasmuch as there were in all some half-score visitants, when the last is catechized he falls exhausted into sleep.

"Not long after, he awakes in high spirits: such strides hath he made toward conversion of the women, he feels sure of making progress with the men. Nor do his hopes seem groundless, for anon the Tayac and his cawcawaassoughs appear and order the women from the hut, after which they cut the tether from his foot. 'Bless you, my friends,' he cries. 'You have seen the true and only Way!' And he forgives them for his cruel use at their hands. They fetch him up and lead him from the hut, and he is overwhelmed with joy at what he sees: the hurricane is gone, and through 'its last dark clouds the sun falls on a large wooden cross, erected in the courtyard of the town, and on the priest's four precious sea-chests at its foot. The Tayac points first to Father FitzMaurice's crucifix and then to the larger cross.

" 'This is God's work,' declares the missionary. 'He hath shewed to thee thine error, and in thy simple fashion thou dost Him homage!' He is moved to kneel in grateful prayer to God, whom he thanks both for working His divine will on the minds of the heathen men and for vouchsafing to His lowly priest the wherewithal to work His will upon their unmarried women. Then alas, his prayers are cut short by two strong men, who grasp his arms and lead him to the cross.

390

Father FitzMaurice smiles indulgently on their roughness, but in a trice they bind him fast to the cross by his ankles, arms, and neck, and then pile faggots on the sea-chests at his feet. All in vain he cries for mercy to the gathering crowd. His novitiates of the night just past, when he addresses them, merely cluck their tongues and watch the scene with interest: 'tis the law of their land that when a man is doomed to die he may enjoy the tribe's unmarried girls on the eve of his execution, and they have discharged their obligation!

"Then comes this great soul's noblest moment. The Tayac confronts him for the last time, in one hand the sacred muskrat, in the other a flaming torch, and makes an ultimate demand for his obeisance. Yet though he sees his case is lost, Father FitzMaurice summons up his last reserves of courage and spits on the idol once again."

" 'Tis a marvel he could summon any spit," Burlingame observed.

"At once a shout goes up, and the Tayac flings his torch upon the faggots! The salvages dance and shake their sacred pole at him—for in fact 'tis as a heretic they condemn him —and the flames leap up to singe his puccoon paint. The good man knows that our afflictions are God's blessings in disguise, and so reasons that he was meant not for a missionary after all, but for a martyr. He lifts his eyes to Heaven, and with his final tortured breath he says, 'Forgive them, for they know not what they do. . . .' "

Though he was not religiously inclined, so impressed was Ebenezer by the tale that he murmured "Amen."

" 'Twould perhaps have made his death more easy, if no less warm, had Father FitzMaurice known that even as he roasted there were three white babes a-building in the wombs of his novitiates. Of these, one died a-bearing, another was exposed out in the marsh, and the third, when she was nubile, became the mother of my informant by the old Tayac himself. As for the Jesuit mission, when George Calvert returned at last to St. Mary's City, his negotiations with Claiborne proving bootless, the remaining priests vowed not to report their colleague's defection to Rome until they learned more of his whereabouts. To this end they reported, in the annual letter I read you, that both priests had returned with the expedition. After that time such various rumors were heard of him that they put off reporting his absence indefinitely. New priests came to the Province; God's work went on less zealously but more steadily, and in time the name FitzMaurice was forgot."

He would have said more, but Burlingame interrupted him to ask, "And what is your opinion of him, Father? Was the man a fool or a saint?"

The priest turned his wide blue eyes upon his questioner. "Those are not true alternatives, Mr. Mitchell: he was a fool of God, as hath been many a holy man before him, and the most that can be said is that his way was not the way of the Society. A dead missionary makes no converts, nor doth a live martyr."

"It is truly said," Ebenezer declared: *"There are more ways to the woods than one."*

"Then permit me a nearer question," Burlingame insisted. "Which way is the more congenial to *your* temper?"

Father Smith appeared to consider this question for some moments before replying. He tapped out his pipe and fingered the papers on the table. "Why do you ask?" he inquired at last, though his tone suggested that he knew the reason already. " 'Tis not likely one could gauge his capacity for martyrdom ere the choice was thrust upon him."

To this Burlingame only smiled, but his meaning was unmistakable. Ebenezer blushed with horror.

"The fact of the matter is," the priest went on, "I scarcely dare deliver the Journal into your hands. The ways of Coode are infinitely devious, and your authorization is signed by Nicholson, not Lord Baltimore."

"So that is the stripe of't!" Burlingame laughed mirthlessly. "You don't trust Nicholson, that owes his post to Baltimore?"

The priest shook his head. "Francis Nicholson is no man's tool, my friend. Hath he not struck out already at Governor Andros, that erst was his superior? Doth he not intend to move the capital from St. Mary's to Anne Arundel Town, for no better reason than to show his allegiance to the Protestant King?"

"But dear God!" Burlingame cried. " 'Twas Nicholson stole the Journal in the first place, and smuggled it to Baltimore!"

" 'Tis as I said before of Mister Cooke," Father Smith explained. "All men are loyal, but their objects of allegiance are at best approximate. Thus Father FitzMaurice showed a loyal zeal for service in the Province, as did Fathers White and Altham, but once here, that same zeal led to his defection; no man knew till then 'twas some other goal he strove for. How shall I say it?" He smiled nervously.

"Many travelers ride the Plymouth coach together," Burlingame suggested, "but not all have Maryland for their destination."

"Our Laureate here could not have put it better! If I could see an authorization in Lord Baltimore's hand, with his signature affixed, as I was instructed to demand, then I should deliver up the Journal to John Calvin himself, and there's an end on't."

Fearing the measures his friend might threaten, Ebenezer came near to imploring the priest to trust him personally, as Charles Calvert's poet laureate, if he could not trust Nicholson or Burlingame; but he checked himself upon remembering again, with no little annoyance, that his commission was not authentic, and that even it it were, he could not produce it for inspection.

A new expression came to Burlingame's face: leaning over the table toward their host he drew from his belt a leather-handled, *poignard*like knife, and in the candlelight ran his thumb across its edge.

"I had thought the Governor's note were sufficient persuasion," he said, "but here is logic keen enough to sway the most adamant of Jesuits! Produce the Journal, an it please you!"

Though he had anticipated some sort of threat, Ebenezer was so shaken by this move that he could not even gasp.

Father Smith stared round-eyed at the knife and licked his lips. "I shan't be the first to perish in the service of the Society."

Even to Ebenezer this remark sounded more experimental than defiant. Burlingame smiled. " 'Twas a coward indeed that feared a clean stroke of the dirk! E'en Father FitzMaurice had a harder lot, to say naught of Catherine on her wheel or Lawrence on his griddle: what would it avail me to let you join their company? I'd be no nearer the Journal than I am."

"Then 'tis some torture you have in mind?" Father Smith murmured. "We Christians are no strangers there, either."

"Most especially the Holy Roman Church," Burlingame said cynically, "that hath authored such delights as never Saracen could devise!" Not taking his eyes from the priest, he proceeded to describe, perhaps for Ebenezer's benefit, various persuasions resorted to by the agents of the Inquisition: the strappado, the *aselli*, the *escalera*, the *potro*, the *tablillas*, the rack, the Iron Maiden, the hot brick, the Gehenna, and others. The Laureate was impressed enough by this recital, though it made him feel no easier about the business at hand. Father Smith sat stonily throughout.

"Yet these are all refinements for the connoisseur," Burlingame declared. "Who inflicts them savors his victim's pain as an end, not as a means, and I've nor taste nor time for such a game." Still thumbing the knife blade he left the table—whereat the priest gave a start despite himself—and bolted the cabin door. "I have observed among the Caribbean pirates that they may make a man eat his own two ears for sport, or fornicate his daughter with a short-sword; but when 'tis certain information that they seek, they have recourse to a simpler and wondrous quick expedient." He advanced toward the table, knife in hand. "Since thou'rt a priest, the loss should cause you no regrets; what shall unbind your tongue, sir, is the manner of the losing. 'Tis a blow to lose a treasure in one fell stroke, but how harder to be robbed of't jewel by jewel! Must I say more?"

" 'Sblood, Henry!" Ebenezer cried, jumping to his feet. "I cannot think you mean to do't!"

"Henry, is't?" the priest said thickly. "Thou'rt impostors after all!"

Burlingame frowned at Ebenezer. "I mean to do't, and you shall aid me. Hold him fast till I find rope to bind him!"

Although the priest showed no inclination to resist, Ebenezer could not bring himself to participate in the business. He stood about uncertainly.

"Now that I know you for an agent of John Coode," Father Smith declared, "I am prepared to suffer any pain. You shall not have the Journal from my hands."

When Burlingame growled and advanced another step, the priest snatched a letter-opener from under his papers and retreated to a farther wall, where, instead of assuming a posture of defense, he placed the point of his weapon against his heart. "Stand fast!" he cried, when Burlingame approached. "Another step and I will end my life!"

Burlingame halted. " 'Tis merely bluff."

"Hither, then, and give't the lie!"

"And do you believe your God excuses holy suicide?"

"I know not what He excuses," said the priest. " 'Tis the Church I serve, and I know well they can justify my act."

After a pause Burlingame shrugged, smiled, and replaced the *poignard* in his belt. *"Pourquoi est-ce que je tuerais un homme si loyal à la cause sainte?"*

The priest's expression changed from defiance to incredulousness. "What did you say?"

"J'ai dit, vous avez démontré votre fidélité, et aussi votre sagesse: je ne me confie pas à Nicholson plus que vous. Allons, le Journal!"

This tactic mystified Ebenezer no less than Father Smith. "I cannot follow your French, Henry!" he complained. But instead of translating, Burlingame turned upon him with the *poignard* and backed him against the wall.

"You will understand anon, fool!" Henry cried, and to the still-bewildered priest he ordered, *"Fouillez cet homme pour les armes, et puis apportez le Journal!"*

"What hath possessed you?" the poet demanded. Coming on the heels of all his other doubts about Burlingame, this new turn of events was particularly discomforting.

"Who are you?" asked the priest. "And what credentials can you show?"

"Parlons une langue plus douce," smiled Burlingame. *"Je n'ai pas d'ordres écrits de Baltimore, et je n'en veux pas. Vous admettrez qu'il ne soit pas la source seule de l'autorité? Quant à mes lettres de créance, je les porte toujours sur ma personne."* He unbuttoned his shirt and displayed the letters *MC* carved into the skin of his chest. *"Celles-ci ne sont peu connues à Thomas Smith?"*

"Monsieur Casteene!" exclaimed Father Smith. *"Vous etês Monsieur Casteene?"*

"Ainsi que vous etês Jésuite," Henry said, *"et je peux faire plus que Baltimore ne rêve pour débarrasser ce lieu de protestants anglais. Vivent James et Louis, et apportez-moi le sacré Journal!"*. . . . .

"Oui, Monsieur, tout de suite! Si j'avais connu qui vous etês——"

"Mes soupçons n'ont pas été plus petits que les vôtres, mais ils sont disparus. Cet épouvantail-ci paraît être loyal à Baltimore, mais il n'est pas catholique: s'il fait de la peine, je le tuerai . . ."

"Oui, Monsieur!" said the delighted priest. *"Mais oui, j'apporterai le Journal tout de suite!"* He ran to unlock an iron-bound chest in one corner of the cabin.

"What in the name of Heav'n doth this mean?" cried Ebenezer, in an anguish of doubt.

"What it means," said his companion, "is that I am not this *Henry* you took me for, nor yet the Timothy Mitchell I am called. I am Monsieur Casteene!"

"Who?"

"Your fame hath not spread to London, sir," the priest laughed from the corner. He fetched a sheaf of manuscript from the chest and turned scornfully to the Laureate. "Monsieur Casteene is known throughout the length and breadth of the provinces as the Grand Enemy of the English. He hath

395

been Governor of Canada, and fought both Andros and Nicholson in New York."

"Until my enemies gained favor with King Louis and undid me," the other said bitterly.

"Monsieur Casteene then fled to the Indians," Smith went on. "He lives among them, and hath taken to wife an Indian woman——"

"*Two* Indian women, Father Smith: 'tis a sin God will forgive, in return for the massacre of Schenectady."

"I had heard you were on Colonel Hermann's manor in Cecil County," said the priest. "Is't possible Colonel Hermann too is more than just Lord Baltimore's man?"

"With faith all things are possible; at least he denied my presence, and disclaimed any knowledge of the Naked Indians."

"Then thou'rt traitors, the pair of you!" cried Ebenezer. "Thou'rt a traitor," he said specifically to his companion, "and I took you to be my dear friend Burlingame! How much doth this discrepancy explain!"

The man with the knife laughed a brief, derisive laugh and held out his hand to Father Smith for the Journal. *"Permettez-moi regarder ce livre merveilleux pour lequel j'ai risqué ma vie."*

The priest gave it to him eagerly, whereupon, without hesitation, Burlingame struck him such a blow upon the back of his neck that he fell senseless to the floor.

"I had not thought him such a fool. Find rope to bind him with, Eben, and we shall see what have we here ere we retire."

Further Passages from Captain John Smith's
Secret Historie of the Voiage Up the Bay
of Chesapeake: *Dorchester Discovered, and
How the Captain First Set Foot Upon It*

"COME, BIND HIM UP," Burlingame repeated, spreading the
Journal open on the table. "Already he hath commenced to
stir." But seeing that Ebenezer was still too disorganized to
act, he fetched some rope himself and bound the priest's
hands and feet. "At least help me lift him into a chair!"

Reviving, Father Smith winced and blinked, and then
stared sullenly at the Journal. He found his voice before the
poet did.

"Who are you, then—John Coode?"

Burlingame laughed. "Only Tim Mitchell, as I said at the
outset, and a loyal friend of Baltimore, if not King Louis and
the Pope. Thou'rt a stiff neck poorer for your lack of faith,
my friend." To Ebenezer, whose turbulent features betrayed
his lingering doubts, he explained further that rumors had
been rife in Maryland since 1692 of the legendary Monsieur
Casteene's presence near the Pennsylvania border. Colonel Augustine Hermann of Bohemia Manor in Cecil County had denied the presence of both Casteene and the so-called Stabbern-
owles, or "Naked Indians" of the north, but so great was the
fear of general massacre at the hands of the French and the
Indians—especially in the light of Maryland and Virginia's
persistent refusal to aid the beleaguered Governor Fletcher of
New York and the mutual distrust among all the provincial
governments—that the rumors still persisted, and the most bizarre details of the Casteene legend, such as that of the scarified monogram on his chest, were widely believed. "I
scratched those letters with my dirk this evening in Oxford,"
he concluded, displaying them again in the candlelight. "See

how fresh they are? 'Twas a card I'd not have played in the light of day!"

Ebenezer sat weakly in a chair. "B'm'faith, how you alarmed me! I know you not from one hour to the next!"

"Nor should you try. Pour out a round of this admirable wine and reflect on what I told you at the inn some hours ago." He clapped the priest on the shoulder. " 'Tis an ungrateful guest that binds his host to a chair for the night, but there's naught for't. Besides, 'tis for that cause wherefore you'd die, and not by half so sore a martyrdom as gelding—*n'est-ce pas?*" He laughed at the priest's expression of disgust, and when the wine was poured, the guests commenced to read together the *verso* (which was in fact the original *recto*) of their prize:

Having receiv'd such cordiall use [*so this fragment of the Historie began*] at the hand of those Salvages at Accomack & those at the River of Wighcocomoco, we set out againe for the maine . . .

"That is the town of Hicktopeake he refers to," Ebenezer volunteered, though in truth he was entertaining such a mixture of feelings towards his former tutor that he spoke only out of a sort of shyness. "The Laughing King of whom I told you. The other Indians I know naught of."

"There are two rivers called *Wicomico* in Maryland," Burlingame said thoughtfully. "One near St. Mary's County on the Western Shore and one below Dorchester County. Methinks 'tis the later he intends, if he coasted up the Bay from Accomac."

. . . but for want of fresh water, in two daies had perforce to seeke out land, that we might replenishe our supplie. We found some Isles, all uninhabited & many in number, falling with a high land upon the maine.

"Haply 'twas the Calvert cliffs he chanced on," Ebenezer suggested, recalling his Island of the Seven Cities. "Let's read on."

Upon waying and going ashoar, we chanc'd on a pond of fresh water, but wch was surpassing warme. Howbeit, we were so verie thirstie, that maugre my counsell to the contrarie, to witt, that the water was doubtlesse fowle, naught w^d doe but my companie must fille there barricoes withal, & drinke therefrom, till that there verie gutts did slushe about. This they learn'd to regrett, but of that, more anon.

From Wighcocomoco to this place, all the coast is but low broken Isles of Moras, a myle or two in breadth, & tenne or twelve in length, & foule and stinking by reason of the stagnant waters therein. Add to w^ch, the aire is beclowded with vile meskitoes, that sucke at a mans bloud, as though they had never eate before. It is forsooth no countrie, for any save the Salvage . . .

"That picture doth apply to one place only," laughed Burlingame, who had read the passage aloud. "Do you know it, Father?"

And the priest, his historical curiosity aroused despite his circumstances, nodded stiffly: "The Dorset marches."

"Aye," Burlingame confirmed. "The Hooper Islands, Bloodsworth Island, and South Marsh. There is a morsel for your epic, Ebenezer: the first white man to set foot on Dorset County."

Ebenezer made perfunctory acknowledgment, but pointed out that as yet the Captain had not gone ashore and perhaps would pass the county by. He showed less petulance in his reply to the priest, who professed great interest in the document and chagrin at having been thitherto unaware of its existence, and for his sake read the remainder of it aloud.

"Being thus refresh'd, despite my warnings, in moving over to other Isles, we incounter'd the winde & waters so much increas'd with thunder, lightning, & raine, that for all my souldiers & my selfe reef'd & belay'd the sayles & lines, our mast & sayle went by the board. Such mightie waves overrack'd us in that smalle barge, that with great persuasions I induc'd our Gentlemen to occupie them selves with freeing out the water, in their hatts, for that else we had fownder'd & sunke. We anchor'd, being not neare any place that promis'd safe harbour, and there we sat a miserable two daies, while the gusts did blowe, with little to nourish our selves withal, save the vile water in the barricoes.

"This same water, the wch my men had taken against my warning, prov'd to be foule indeed, for that upon slaking therewith there thirst, all the companie did growe wondrous grip'd of there bowells, and loose of there bladders, & took a weakness of there reins, so that they still had need of making water, & of voiding their several¹ bummes. Little my men did all the day long, & the night, while that we rode thus at anchor, but besmirch them selves. At length, the wether being warm, if squallie, I did order one & all to divest them selves of there breeches, the wch were beshitt past rescue, and cast them to the fishes. This they all did, but with much compleynt, most markedlie from my rivall Burlingame, who looses no opening to sowe the seedes of discontent & faction."

"Thank Heav'n he is still among the party!" Burlingame exclaimed. "I feared old John had done him in after Accomac."

" 'Tis no light matter to choose betwixt the two," Ebenezer remarked. "Captain Smith is undeniably resourceful, and no leader can indulge factiousness save at his peril."

"True enough for you," Burlingame replied curtly. "He's not your ancestor. For me there is no problem in the choice."

"We've no certain knowledge he is *your* ancestor, either," the poet said."When all's said and done, 'tis a marvelous slender chance, is't not?"

This observation so plainly injured Burlingame that Ebenezer at once regretted making it, and apologized.

"No matter." Burlingame waved him away. "Read on."

"Being left then, with there bummes expos'd, I did command, that they set them selves over the gunwales, inasmuch as the Bay of Chesapeake was of greate size, and c^d accommodate them better then our barge. Yet this new command did little ease our plight, for that albeit they dropp'd there matter to the fishes, the aire round about was no lesse foul'd by there joynt labours. Naught c^d our D^r of Physick do to improve them, and I did wish heartilie to be on shoar, where with the sapp of the sweet-gumme tree & sundrie other herbes, wch grewe a-plentie in the woods thereabouts, I c^d have brew'd a decoction, that had bound the lot of them costive for a fortnight. Forsooth, things did worsen yet, for that the sillie men w^d not restrayne there thirst, but still return'd and drank farther of the water, whereon there fluxes & gripes did intensifie apace. Onely two of our number shew'd no sign of the maladie, namelie my selfe, that had not deign'd to drinke of the barricoes, but had instead made my selfe to chewe upon raw fishes, and friend Burlingame, that had drunke enough for three, but that must needs have had a grand hold on his reins, for that he never did besmirch him selfe throughout those foule two daies.

"When the storme at length overblewe us, and the wether again shew'd faire, I did with all haste order, that the sayle be repair'd, and this the companie did with right good will, using of there shirts for clouts. They were most readie to abandon the maine, and sayle for some shoar, albeit they were now naked as Father Adam, so as to put food & cleanlie water into there bellies, and pass off there fluxes at last. For the extremitie of gusts, thunder, rayne, storms, & ill wether, we did call those Straites, wherein we had for so long layn, *Limbo*, but I think, with all the

400

farting and ill businesse that did pass there, we had better call'd them *Purgatorio*.

"After a surpassing clumsie daye of sayling, making smalle headway, for the crewe must continuallie hang there bummies abeame, we fell with a prettie convenient river on the East, called Cuskarawaok . . ."

"That is a word from the Nanticoke tongue," Father Smith interrupted. "In old times it was applied to that same river we call the Nanticoke today."

"I'faith, then!" Burlingame laughed. " 'Tis precious little ground he gained for all those evil days!" He explained to Ebenezer that the Nanticoke River, which marks the boundary between Dorchester and Somerset Counties, empties into Tangier Sound conjointly with the Wicomico, from where, the record seemed to imply, Smith had departed several days previously.

"All that made the day attractive to me [*Ebenezer read on*], for it were otherwise malodourous enow, was, that Burlingames bowells did seem to commence troubling him, for that he did still wander hither to yon in the barge, his face shewing ever more discomfort, and crost & recrost his leggs, and his want of composure was a tastie thing to watch. When that he s^hd finallie let flie, I guess'd it w^d prove a spectacle in sooth, by reason of his greate corpulencie, and the lengthie space he had held fast his reins . . ."

"Cruel man," said Burlingame, "to savor so the wretch's plight! And thou'rt reading with the same ungentle relish, Eben!"

"Beg pardon." Ebenezer smiled. " 'Tis that the wonder of't stirs my interest as I read. I fancy he is about to land on Dorset."

And in a tone somewhat less partial he continued:

"We made straightwaye for shoar ,but c^d by no means land, seeing a great bodie of Salvages appear from the woods, making everie signe of hostilitie. Whenas they sawe what manner of men we were, not having seen the like before, they ran as amaz'd from place to place, divers got into the tops of trees, and they were not sparing of there arrowes, nor the greatest passion they c^d expresse of there anger. Long they shot, we still ryding at Anchor without there reatch making all the signes of friendship we c^d. But this was a hard matter, inasmuch as for everie cheerie wave of the hand I signall'd them, some souldier or Gentlemen in my companie must needs let goe a fart, wch the Salvages did take as an affront, and threwe more arrowes.

"Next day they return'd, all unarm'd, and with everie one a basket, and danc'd in a ring, to drawe us on shoar: but seeing there was naught in them save villainie, we discharg'd a volley of muskets charg'd with pistoll shot, whereat they all lay tumbling on the grownd, creeping some one way, some another, into a greate cluster of reedes hard by, where there companies lay in Ambuscado. We waited, and it seeming they had left the place, we way'd & approach'd the shoar, for that all were eager to quitt for a time our barge. My thought was, to land as quietlie as possible, catch what food & fresh water we might, & then to flie to some more cordiall place. For that reason I did command, that whereas none among my crewe c^d leave off his bumme-shotts, the wch w^d surelie give notice of our coming, then everie man, that felt the need on him, must thrust his buttockes by the board, so far as to the water, and thus immers'd, do what he w^d. But the first to attempt this, one Anas Todkill a souldier, had no sooner wet his hammes, then he was stung athwart the tayle by a greate Sea-Nettle, a sort of white jellie-fish wch doth occur in number in these waters, raysing upon his buttockes a red welt, and causing him payne. Whereafter, it was onely by dint of much intreatie, that I got any other man to do the same. As for Burlingame, the imminence of his coming defecation shew'd over all his face, and he durst not even speake, lest he explod; but the business of the Sea-Nettle did give him such a fright, he wrestl'd with him selfe, to hold on but a minute more, when that we s^hd be ashoar.

"The prowe of our barge striking land (the wch was but reedes & mudd), I flung our anchor as far inland as I c^d, and we did make readie to disembark. As was my wont, I stepp'd up on the spritt, and w^d have leapt ashoar, for that I still reserve the privilege of stepping first on everie new-found grownd, and this place was to be no exception. But Burlingame, in his passion to get off the vessell, to the end of jettisoning his filthie cargoe, did rudelie push me aside, for all I was his Captain and erst his Saviour, and assum'd the place ahead. I was on the instant wroth, at his impertinencie, and w^d have layd hands on him, but that at the same moment a troup of Salvages leapt from some scrubbie growth near by, and snatch'd up the anchor pendant, purposing thereby to pull us high & drie, and capture us & our vessell as well. With this turn of affaires, I was content that Burlingame s^hd remayne in the van, to afford the rest of us the protection of his fatt carcase."

"Ah God," murmured Burlingame, "I fear my ancestor is in a pickle!"

"The proper strategie [*Ebenezer continued*] was to fyre a charge of shot at the heathens to drive them loose, but they were nigh

402

upon us, and I confess we had not a musket loaded, for that I had thought the shoar vacated of Salvages. Then I might well have cut the pendant, and so rid us of them, but I was loath to sacrifice our anchor, that had serv'd us well in the storme just past, and wch we s^hd doubtlesse need againe. Besides w^ch, the Salvages had appear'd on such a sudden, I scarce had time to think aright. In fine, I did not choose either of these courses, but snatch'd our end of the pendant, and handing it back among the crewe, we pull'd in a line against the Salvages, to regayne our anchor & our libertie. The Salvages, luckilie, were unarm'd, hoping to have us ashoar without difficultie, and thus we were not expos'd to there arrowes. Burlingame was too possess'd by feare to aid us, but stood all witlesse on the bow, and c^d nowise step back into the vessell, for that all of us were crowded behind, heaving on the rope.

"The tugg-o'-war that then insued had been a sporting match, wch methinks we had won, were it that naught had interfear'd with the murtherous game. But the Salvages giving out with terrible whoops & hollowings, did so smite with fear this Burlingame, that at last he forewent entire the hold of his reins, and standing yet in our prowe like unto an uglie figure-head, he did let flie the treasure he had been those daies a-hoarding. It was my ill fortune to be hard behind him, and moreover, crowch'd down beneath his mightie bumme, so as to better brace my feet for pulling, and looking up at that instant of time, to see whether Burlingame was yet with us, I was in a trice beshitt, so much so, that I c^d by no meancs see out of my eyes, or speake out of my mowth. Then the Salvages gave a great pull on the pendant, and the deck all bemir'd, I did loose the purchase of my feet, and sayling betwixt Burlingames legs, did end face downe in the mud of the shoar. This same Burlingame thus knock'd from off his ballance, he fell after, and sat him square upon my head.

"Directlie I freed my mowth of turd & mud, I hollow'd for my souldiers to load & fyre upon the Salvages, but those same Salvages did leap straightway upon me, and upon Burlingame as well, and imploying us to sheeld them & as hostages, demanded by signes the surrender of the companie. I order'd them to shoot & be damn'd, but they were loath to fyre, for feare of hitting me, and so we did surrender our selves up to the Salvage, and were led prisoner to his town.

"Thus was it, in a manner not my wont, I first touched the shoar of this scurvie place, whereof an ampler relation doth follow . . ."

The final passages Ebenezer could scarcely read for laughing; even the captive priest could not restrain his mirth. For a moment Burlingame seemed not to realize that the recitation was done, but then he sat up quickly.

"Is that the *end?*"

" 'Tis the end of this portion," Ebenezer sighed, wiping his eyes. "T'faith, such intrepidity! And by what a marvelous means my county was discovered!"

"But God in Heav'n," cried Burlingame, "this is no stopping-place!" He snatched up the Journal to look for himself. "That wretched, hapless man—how I suffer for him! And I tell you, Eben; though I do not share his form, with every new episode I feel more certain Sir Henry is my forefather. I felt it when first I learnt of him from those ladies that I saved, and more so when I read his *Privie Journall*. How much more now, then, that we have him in Dorchester! He is halfway up the Chesapeake, is he not? And 'twas there that Captain Salmon fished me out!"

"It is a curious proximity, forsooth," Ebenezer allowed, "but nearly fifty years divide the two events, if I guess aright. And since we know John Smith returned anon to Jamestown, we've no proof Sir Henry was marooned behind."

"You'd as well prove to this Jesuit that St. Joseph was a cuckold," Burlingame laughed. "I am as sure of my progenitor as he is of Christ's, though the exact line of descent we've yet to learn. 'Sheart, I'd give an arm to hear the finish of that tale!"

These remarks aroused Father Smith's curiosity, and he entreated Burlingame to explain the mystery before departing.

"Think not you'll see us go so soon!" Henry replied, but their attention to the history having dispelled the general ill will among the three, he went on to say that though his name was Timothy Mitchell he was but a foster child of Captain William Mitchell, and had reason to suspect that Sir Henry Burlingame was in some wise his ancestor. He then favored the priest with a full account of his researches and the fruit they had borne thus far, but despite this general cordiality he insisted that Father Smith be released only long enough to relieve himself under careful guard, after which the unfortunate priest was obliged to spend the night bound upright in his chair while the two visitors shared his bed.

Nevertheless, before the candle had been extinguished for half an hour, Ebenezer was the only man in the cabin still awake. Never an easy sleeper, he was additionally distracted this night by the presences of his friend and his unwilling host—specifically because the former (in sleep, it is to be presumed) held his hand in a grip from which the poet was

404

too embarrassed to pull free, and the latter snored; but more generally because he could not as yet reconcile and assimilate all the aspects of Burlingame's character to which he had been exposed, and because Father Smith's apparent connection with the French and Indians, while it did not in itself reflect discredit on Lord Baltimore, nevertheless cast a new and complicated light upon that gentleman's endeavor. Nor were these troublesome reflections the sum of his diversion: never far from his mind was the image of Joan Toast. Despite Burlingame's skepticism, Ebenezer was confident of Susan Warren's veracity; he fully expected to find his beloved waiting for him when he arrived at Malden. When, after such a harrowing odyssey as his—and who knew what peregrinations of poor Joan's?—they were at last reunited on his own estate-to-be, what would ensue? There was fuel to fire a poet's fancy!

In short, he could not sleep, and after an hour's unpleasantness, he summoned courage enough to leave the bed. From the wood-coals on the hearth he lit a new candle, and making free with the sleeping Jesuit's ink and quill, he spread out his ledger-book to ease himself with verse.

But for the sober thoughts that filled his head he could find no fit articulation; what he composed, simply because he had previously entered on the opposite page certain notes upon the subject, was nothing more sublime or apropos than two score couplets having to do with the Salvage Indians of America. The feat afforded him no solace, but at least it wearied him through: when he could hold his eyes open no longer he blew out the candle, and leaving the bed to Burlingame, laid his head upon the ledger-book and slept.

26

The Journey to Cambridge, and the
Laureate's Conversation by the Way

WHEN MORNING CAME, Burlingame freed Father Smith from his bonds and took it upon himself to prepare a breakfast while the priest exercised his aching limbs. All the while, however, he kept the Journal near at hand, and despite the Jesuit's disclaimer of any further intent to stop them, he insisted that the priest be bound again when the meal was finished and they were ready to depart, nor would he listen to Ebenezer's pleas for clemency.

"You infer the rest of mankind from yourself," he chided. "Because *you* would not try farther to obstruct me if you were in his position, you believe he would not either. To which I reply, my reasoning is identical to yours, and *I* would have me back the Journal ere you reached the Choptank River."

"But he will perish! 'Tis as much as murthering him!"

"No such thing," scoffed Burlingame. "If he is a proper priest he will be missed at once by his parishioners, who will seek him out and have him loose ere midday. If not, they will repay neglect with neglect, as his God would have it or rather, his Order."

This last he directed with a smile to Father Smith, who sat impassively in his chair, and added, "We are obliged to you for bed and board, sir, and your unimpeachable *Jerez*. You may look to see John Coode in trouble soon, and know that you have done your part, albeit reluctantly." He ushered Ebenezer to the door. "*Adieu,* Father: when you commence your holy war, spare my friend here, who hath pled in your behalf. As for me, Monsieur Casteene himself could never find me. *Ignatius vobiscum.*"

"*Et vobiscum diabolus,*" replied the priest.

Thus they left, Ebenezer too ashamed to bid their host farewell, and, after saddling their horses, struck out along a road that, so Burlingame declared, curved southward in wide arc to the Choptank River ferry, whence they planned to cross to Cambridge, inquire the whereabouts of William Smith, and then proceed to Malden. It was a magnificent autumn day, brisk and bright, and whatever the Laureate's mood, Burlingame's was clearly buoyant.

"One more portion of Smith's history to find!" he cried as their horses ambled down the road. "Only think on't: I may soon learn who I am!"

"Let us hope this William Smith is less refractory," the poet replied. "One may acquire more guilt in learning who he is than the answer can atone for."

Burlingame rode on some minutes in silence before he tried again to begin conversation.

"Methinks Lord Baltimore was ill-advised on the character

406

of that Jesuit, but a general cannot know all of his lieutenants. There is a saying among the Papists, *Do not judge the
entire priesthood by a priest."*

"There is another from the Gospels," said Ebenezer. *"By
their fruits ye shall know them. . . ."*

"Thou'rt too severe, my friend!" Burlingame showed a
measure of impatience. "Is't that you did not sleep enough
last night?"

The Laureate blushed. "Last night I had in mind some
verses, and wrote them down lest I forget them."

"Indeed! I'm pleased to hear't; you have been too long
away from your muse."

The solicitude in his friend's voice removed, at least for the
time, Ebenezer's perturbation, and, though he suspected that
he was being humored, he smiled and with some shyness said,
"Their subject is the salvage Indian, that I am much impressed by."

"Then out on't, I must hear them!"

After some hesitation Ebenezer consented, not especially
because he thought Burlingame's eagerness was genuine, but
rather because in the welter of conflicting sentiment he expe-
rienced towards his friend, his poetic gift was the only
ground that in his relations with his former tutor he felt he
could stand upon firmly and without abashment. He fished
out his notebook from the large pocket of his coat and, leaving his mare to walk without direction, opened to the freshly
written couplets.

" 'Twas a salvage we saw yesterday morning that prompted
me," he explained, and began to read, his voice jogging with
the steps of his horse:

> *"Scarce had I left the Captains Board*
> *And taking Horse, made Tracks toward*
> *The Chesapeake, when, giving Chase*
> *To flighty Deer, a horrid Face*
> *Came into View: a Salvage 'twas——* }
> *We stay'd our Circumbendibus* }
> *To look on Him, and He on us.* }
> *O'ercoming soon my first Surprize,*
> *I set myself to scrutinize*
> *His Visage wild, his Form exotick*
> *Barb'rous Air, and Dress erotick,*
> *His brawny Shoulders, greas'd and bare*
> *His Member, all devoid of Hair*
> *And swinging free, his painted Skin*

> *And naked Chest, inviting Sin*
> *With Ladies who, their Beauty faded,*
> *Husbands dead, or Pleasures jaded,*
> *Fly from Virtues narrow Way*
> *Into the Forest, there to lay*
> *With Salvages, to their Damnation* }
> *Sinning by their Copulation,*
> *Lewdness, Lust, and Fornication,*
> *All at once . . ."*

"Well writ!" cried Burlingame. "Save for your preachment at the last, 'tis much the same sentiment as my own." He laughed. "I do suspect you had more on your mind last night than just the heathen: all that love-talk makes me yearn for my sweet Portia!"

"Stay," the poet cautioned at once. "Fall not into the vulgar error of the critics, that judge a work ere they know the whole of it. I go on to speculate whence came the Indian."

"Your pardon," Burlingame said. "If the rest is excellent as the first, thou'rt a poet in sooth."

Ebenezer flushed with pleasure and read on, somewhat more forcefully:

> *"Whence came this barb'rous Salvage Race,*
> *That wanders yet 'oer MARYLANDS Face?*
> *Descend they all from those old Sires,*
> *Remarked by* Plato *and such like Liars*
> *From lost* Atlantis, *sunken yet*
> *Beneath the Ocean, cold and wet?*
> *Or is he wiser who ascribes*
> *Their Genesis to those ten Tribes*
> *Of luckless* Jews, *that broke away*
> *From* Israel, *and to this Day*
> *Have left no Traces, Signs, or Clews—*
> *Are Salvages but beardless* Jews?
> *Or are they sprung, as some maintain,*
> *From that same jealous, incestuous* Cain,
> *Who with twin Sister fain had lay'd*
> *And whose own Brother anon he slay'd:*
> *Fleeing then* Jehovah's *Wrath*
> *Did wend his cursed, rambling Path*
> *To* MARYLANDS *Doorsill, there to hide*
> *In penance for his Fratricide,*
> *And hiding, found no liv'lier Sport*
> *Than siring Heathens, tall and short?*
> *Still others hold, these dark-skinn'd Folk*

Escap'd the Deluge all unsoak'd
That carry'd off old Noahs Ark
Upon its long and wat'ry Lark,
And drown'd all Manner of Men save Two:
The Sailors in Old Noahs Crew
(That after all were but a Few),
And this same brawny Salvage Host,
Who, safe behind fair MARYLANDS Coast,
Saw other Mortals sink and die
Whilst they remain'd both high and dry.
Another Faction claims to trace
The Hist'ry of this bare-Bumm'd Race
Back to Mankinds Pucelage,
That Ovid calls the Golden Age:
When kindly Saturn rul'd the Roost.
Their learned Fellows have deduc'd
The Salvage Home to be that Garden
Wherein three Sisters play'd at Warden
Over Heras Golden Grove,
Whose Apples were a Treasure-Trove:
That Orchard robb'd by Hercules,
The Garden of Hesperides;
While other Scholards, no less wise,
Uphold the Earthly Paradise—
Old Adams Home, and Eves to boot,
Wherein they gorg'd forbidden Fruit—
To be the Source and Fountainhead
Of Salvag'ry. Some, better read
In Arthurs Tales, have settl'd on
The Blessed Isles of Avalon,
And others say the fundamental
Flavoring is Oriental,
Or that mayhap ancient Viking,
Finding MARYLAND to his liking,
Stay'd, and father'd red-skinn'd Horsemen:
One Part Salvage, One Part Norsemen.
Others say the grand Ambitions
Of the restless old Phoenicians
Led that hardy Sailor Band
To the Shores of MARYLAND,
In Ships so cramm'd with Man and Beast
No Room remain'd for Judge or Priest:
There, with Lasses and Supplies,
The Men commenc'd to colonize
This foreign Shore in Manner dastard,
All their Offspring being Bastard.
Finally, if any Persons

> *Unpersuaded by these Versions*
> *Of the Salvages Descent*
> *Should ask still for the Truth anent*
> *Their Origins—why, such as these,* }
> *That are so damned hard to please,*
> *I send to* Mephistopheles,
> *Who engender'd in the Fires of* Hell
> *The* Indians, *and* them *as well!"*

"Now, that is all damned clever!" Burlingame exclaimed. "Whether 'twas the hardships of your crossing or a half year's added age, I swear thou'rt twice the poet you were in Plymouth. The lines on Cain I thought especially well-wrought."

" 'Tis kind of you to praise the piece," Ebenezer said. "Haply 'twill be a part of the *Marylandiad*."

"I would I could turn a verse so well. But say, while 'tis fresh in my mind, doth *persons* really rhyme with *versions*, and *folk* with *soak'd?*"

"Indeed yes," the poet replied.

"But would it not be better," Burlingame persisted cordially, "to rhyme *versions* with *dispersions*, say, and *folk* with *soak?* Of course, I am no poet."

"One need not be a hen to judge an egg," Ebenezer allowed. "The fact of't is, the rhymes you name are at once better and worse than mine: better, because they sound more nearly like the words they rhyme with; and worse, because such closeness is not the present fashion. *Dispersion* and *version:* 'tis wanting in character, is't not? But *person* and *version*—there is surprise, there is color, there is wit! In fine, there is a perfect Hudibrastic."

"*Hudibrastic*, is it? I have heard the folk in Locket's speak well of *Hudibras*, but I always thought it tedious myself. What is't you mean by *Hudibrastic?*"

Ebenezer could scarcely believe that Burlingame was really ignorant of Hudibrastic rhyme or anything else, but so pleasant was the reversal of their unusual roles that he found it easy to put by his skepticism.

"A Hudibrastic rhyme," he explained, "is a rhyme that is close, but not just harmonious. Take the noun *wagon:* what would you rhyme with it?"

"Why, now, let's see," Burlingame mused. "Methinks *flagon* would serve, or *dragon*, wouldn't you say?"

"Not at all," smiled Ebenezer. " 'Tis too expected, 'tis what any poetaster might suggest—no offense, you understand."

"None whatever."

"Nay, to *wagon* you must rhyme *bag in,* or *sagging:* almost, you see, but not quite.

> *The Indians call their wat'ry Wagon*
> *Canoe, a Vessel none can brag on.*

Wagon, brag on—do you follow me?"

"I grasp the principle," Burlingame declared, "and I recall such rhymes as that in *Hudibras;* but I doubt me I could e'er apply it."

"Why, of course you can! It wants but courage, Henry. Take *quarrel,* now: *The Man and I commenc'd to quarrel.* What shall we rhyme with it?"

Burlingame pondered the problem for a while. "What would you say to *snarl?*" he ventured at last.

> *"The Man and I commenc'd to quarrel:*
> *I to grumble, he to snarl."*

"The line is good," replied the Laureate, "and bespeaks some wit. But the rhyme is humorless. *Quarrel, snarl*—nay, 'tis too close."

"*Sorrel,* then?" asked Burlingame, apparently warming to the sport.

> *"The Man and I commenc'd to quarrel*
> *Who'd ride the Roan, and who the Sorrel."*

"E'en wittier!" the poet applauded. " 'Tis better than Tom Trent could pen, with Dick Merriweather to help him! But you've still no Hudibrastic. *Quarrel, snarl; quarrel, sorrel.*"

"I yield," said Burlingame.

"Consider this, then:

> *The Man and I commenc'd to quarrel*
> *Anent the Style of our Apparel.*

Quarrel, apparel: That is Hudibrastic."

Burlingame made a wry face. "They clash and jingle!"

"Precisely. The more the clash, the better the couplet."

"Aha, then!" cried the tutor. "What says my Laureate to this?

411

> *The Man and I commenc'd to quarrel*
> *Who'd ride the Roan and who the Dapple."*

"*Quarrel* and *dapple?*" Ebenezer exclaimed.

"Doth it not jangle like the brassy bells of Hades?"

"Nay, 'twill never do!" Ebenezer shook his head firmly. "I had thought you'd caught the essence of't, but the words must needs have *some* proximity if they're to jangle. *Quarrel* and *dapple* are ships in different oceans: they cannot possibly collide, and a collision is what we seek."

"Then try this," Burlingame suggested:

> *"The Man and I commenc'd to quarrel*
> *Whose turn it was to woo the Barrel."*

"*Barrel! Barrel,* you say?" Ebenezer's face grew red. "What is this *barrel?* How would you use it?"

" 'Tis a Hudibrastic," replied Burlingame with a smile. "I'd use it to piss in."

"B'm'faith!" He laughed uncomfortably. " 'Tis the pissingest Hudibrastic ever I've heard!"

"Will you hear more?" asked Burlingame. "I am a diligent student of jangling rhyme."

"Piss on't," the poet declared. "Thy lesson's done!"

"Nay, I am just grasping the spirit of't! Haply I'll take up versifying myself someday, for't seems no backbreaking chore."

"But you know the saying, Henry: *A poet is born, not made.*"

"Out on't!" Burlingame scoffed. "Were you not made Laureate ere you'd penned a proper verse? I'll wager I could rhyme with the cleverest, did I choose to put my nose to't."

"No man knows better than I your various gifts," Ebenezer said in an injured tone. "Yet your true poet may have no other gift than verse."

"Only try me," Burlingame challenged. "Name me some names, and hear me rhyme."

"Very well, but there's more to verse than matching words. You must couple me a line to the line I fling you."

"Fling away thy lines, and see what fish you hook on 'em!"

"Stand fast," warned Ebenezer, "for I'll start you with a hard one: *Then did Sir Knight abandon Dwelling.*"

"That is from *Hudibras,*" Burlingame observed, "but I forgot what Butler rhymed with't. *Dwelling, dwelling*—ah, 'tis no chore at all:

> *Then did Sir Knight abandon Dwelling,*
> *Which scarce repay'd the Work of Selling."*

"Too close," said Ebenezer. "Give us a Hudibrastic."

"Your Hudibrastics will break my jaw! Howbeit, if 'tis a jangle you wish, I shall shudder the ears off you:

> *Then did Sir Knight abandon Dwelling,*
> *Riding like a demon'd Hellion.*

Are you jarred?"

"It fills the gap," Ebenezer admitted. "But the difference 'twixt poet and coxcomb is precisely that the latter stops gaps like a ship fitter caulking seams, merely to keep the boat afloat, while the former doth his work as doth a man with a maid: he fills the gap, but with vigor, finesse, and care; there's beauty and delight as well as utility in his plugging."

" 'Sheart, my friend," Burlingame said, "you go on like the gods themselves! How would a Laureate poet fill this gap, prithee, that yawns like the pit of Hell?"

Ebenezer replied, " 'Twas filled by Sam Butler in this wise —observe the art, now, the collision:

> *Then did Sir Knight abundon Dwelling,*
> *And out he rode a Colonelling."*

"Ah, stay!" cried Burlingame. "This is too much! *A Co-lo-nelling!* 'Tis a fabrication—aye, a Chimaera! *Co-lo-nelling,* is't! Why did not Mister Butler, if he was so enamored of his unnatural word, call it *ker*nelling, as't should be called, and rhyme from there?"

"Why not indeed? What would you rhyme with *kernelling,* Henry?"

" 'Tis naught of a chore to me," Burlingame scoffed. "To rhyme with *kernelling*—— Well, *kernelling*——" he hesitated.

"You see," smiled Ebenezer. "In his inspiration the poet chose a rhyme for *dwelling* that is at once a rhyme and a Hudibrastic, and so avoided your quandary. Yield, now; there is no rhyme for *kernelling.*"

"I yield," Burlingame said with apparent humility. "I can get me the first line—*Then went Sir Knight a kernelling*—but can't rhyme the infernal thing."

The two travelers exchanged glances.

"Out upon't," Ebenezer muttered, "the lesson's done."

But Burlingame was delighted to see his unintentional *coup de maître;* he went on to declaim theatrically from his horse:

> *"Then went Sir Knight a kernelling,*
> *Pursuing all infernal Things,*
> *Inflam'd by* Hopes *eternal Springs*
> *Through Winterings and Vernallings*
> *(As testify his Journallings*
> *And similar Diurnallings,*
> *Not mentioning Nocturnallings) . . ."*

"Desist!" Ebenezer commanded. "Spin me no more of this doggerel, Henry, lest I heave my breakfast upon the highway!"

"Forgive me," Burlingame laughed. "I was inspired."

"You were baiting me," the Laureate said indignantly. "Be not puffed up o'er such trifling achievement, the like of which we poets must better fifty times a page! You have a certain knack for rhyming, clear enough; but think not you can rhyme any word in Mother English, for a poet will name you words that have not their like in the language."

"Ha! Oh! Ha!" Burlingame cried with sudden glee. "I have hatched more! I'God, they crowd my fancy like the shoats to Portia's nipples!

> *Now lend me,* Muse, *supernal Wings*
> *To sing Sir Knights Hibernallings,*
> *His Doublings and his Ternallings,*
> *His Forwardings and Sternallings;*
> *To sing of his Hesternallings,*
> *And also Hodiernallings,*
> *Internal and external Things,*
> *Both brief and diuturnal Things,*
> *And even sempiternal Things,*
> *His dark and his lucernal Things,*
> *Maternal and Paternallings,*
> *Sororal and Fraternal Things,*
> *His blue and red Pimpernellings,*
> *And sundry paraphernal Things——"*

"You do not love me!" Ebenezer said angrily. "I'll hear no more!"

"Nay, I beg you"—Burlingame laughed—"fob me not off so!"

"Sinful pride!" the poet chided, when he had recovered something of his composure.

" 'Twas but in jest, Eben; if it vexed you, I am contrite. 'Tis you who are the teacher now, not I, and you may take what steps you will. In truth you've taught me more than erst I knew."

" 'Tis clear your talent wants snaffle and curb in lieu of the crop," said Ebenezer.

"Will you go on, then?"

Ebenezer considered for a moment and then agreed. "So be't, but no more teasing. I shall administer to you the severest test of the rhymer's art: the slipperiest crag on the rocky face of Parnassus!"

"Administer at will," said Burlingame; "if 'tis a point of rhyme I swear there's none can best me, for I have learnt old Mother English to her very privates. But say, let's make a sport of't, would you mind? Else 'twere much the same to win or lose."

"I've naught to wager," Ebenezer said, "nor should you wager if I had, for the word I mean to speak hath not its like." Then he had a happier thought: "Stay, how far yet is that ferry you spoke of?"

"Some five or six miles hence, I'd guess."

"Then let us wager the ride of our mounts, if you've a mind to. If you cannot rhyme the line I give you, you must walk from here to Cambridge ferry; if you can, 'tis I shall walk. Done?"

"Well wagered," Burlingame said merrily, "and I'll add more: who loses must not merely walk, but walk behind the old Roan there, that ever gets the bumbreezes near midmorning. 'Twill add a spice to the winner's victory!"

"Done," agreed the poet. "Let us on with the trial. I shall muse you a line, and you must rhyme it. Not a Hudibrastic, mind, but a perfect match."

"Is't *mosquito?*" asked Burlingame. "I'll say *incognito.*"

"Nay," the Laureate smiled, "nor is it *literature.*"

" 'Twould be bitter-that's-sure," his tutor laughed.

"Nor *misbehavior.*"

"Thank the Savior!"

"Nor *importunacy.*"

"That were lunacy!"

"Nor *tiddlywinks.*"

" 'Twould gain thee little, methinks!"

"Nor *galligaskin.*"

"Was I askin'?"

"Nor *charlatan.*"

"Thin as tarlatan!"

"Nor *Saracen*."

" 'Twould be embarrassin'!"

"Nor even *autoschediastic*."

"Then it ought to be fantastic!"

"Nor *catoptromancy*."

"That's not so fancy!"

"Nor *procrustean*."

"I should bust thee one!"

"Nor is it *Piccadilly bombast*."

"You'd be sick-o'-filly-bum-blast!"

"Nor *Grandma's visit*."

"Then, man, what is it?"

" 'Tis *month*," Ebenezer said.

"*Month?*" cried Burlingame.

"*Month*," the Laureate repeated. "Rhyme me a word with *month. August is the Year's eighth Month*."

"*Month!*" Burlingame said again. " 'Tis but a single syllable!"

"Marry, then, 'twill be easy," Ebenezer smiled. "*August is the Year's eighth Month*."

"*August is the Year's eighth Month*." Burlingame began to show some alarm as he searched his store of language.

"No lisping, now," Ebenezer warned. "Don't say *Whoe'er denieth it ith a Dunth,* or *Athent thee not, then count it oneth*. That will not do."

Burlingame sighed. "And no Hudibrastics, you say?"

"Nay," Ebenezer confirmed. "You mayn't say *August is the Year's eighth Month, And not the tenth or milli-onth*. Ben Oliver tried that once in Locket's and was disqualified on the instant. I want a clear and natural rhyme."

"Is there aught in the language?" Burlingame cried.

"Nay," the poet declared, "as I warned you ere you took the wager."

Burlingame searched his memory so thoroughly that perspiration beaded his forehead, but after twenty minutes he was obliged to yield.

"I surrender, Eben; you have me pat." Most reluctantly, under his protégé's triumphant smile, he dismounted, and taking his place behind the aged roan, prepared to meet the odious consequences of his gamble.

"In future, Henry," Ebenezer boldly advised, "do not engage with poets in their own preserve. If I may speak with candor, the gift of language is vouchsafed to but a few, and though 'tis no great shame not to have't, 'twere folly to pretend to't when you have it not."

And having delivered himself of this unusual rebuke, Ebenezer began to hum a tune for very satisfaction. At the first slight elevation in the terrain over which they traveled, the roan mare, already wearied, broke wind noisily from the effort of climbing. Burlingame growled a mighty oath and cried out in disgust, "What sort of poor vocabulary is't, that possesses nary noun or verb to match the *onth* in *August is the Year's eighth Month?*"

"Do not rail against the language," Ebenezer began, " 'tis really a most admirable tongue . . ."

He halted, as did Burlingame and the roan. The two men regarded each other warily.

"No matter," Ebenezer ventured. "The trial was done."

"Ah nay, Sir Laureate!" Burlingame laughed. "Mine is done, but thine is but begun! Down with you, now!"

"But *onth*," Ebenezer protested—nevertheless dismounting. " 'Tis not an English word, is't? What doth it signify?"

"Tut," said Burlingame, remounting his young gelding, "we set no such criterion as significance, that I recall. 'To match the *onth* . . .' is what I said: *onth* is the object of *match;* objects of verbs are substantives; substantives are words. Get thee behind yon roan!"

Ebenezer sighed, Burlingame laughed aloud, the roan mare once again broke wind, and on went the travelers toward Cambridge, Burlingame singing lustily:

> *"How wondrous a Vocabulary*
> *Is't, that possesseth nary*
> *Noun nor Verb the Rhyme for which'll*
> *Stump the son of* Captain Mitchell!"

27

The Laureate Asserts That Justice Is Blind, and Armed With This Principle, Settles a Litigation

UPON THEIR ARRIVAL at the Choptank River ferry, Burlingame declared Ebenezer's sentence served; he paid out a shilling apiece for their fares and another shilling for the two horses', and the travelers took their places in the sailing scow for the two-mile run to Cambridge.

Burlingame pointed across the channel to a few scattered buildings, scarcely visible on the farther shore. "Yonder stands the seat of Dorset County. When last your father saw it, 'twas but a planter's landing."

Weary from his ordeal, Ebenezer made no effort to conceal his disappointment. "I knew 'twould be no English Cambridge, but I'll own I had not thought 'twas rude as *that*. What is there in't to sing in epical verse?"

"Who knows what manner of sloven huts the real Troy was composed of, or cares to know?" his friend replied. " 'Tis the genius of the poet to transcend his material; and it wants small eloquence to argue that the meaner the subject, the greater must be the transcension."

To this the Laureate clucked his tongue and said, "Methinks the Jesuit hath the better of you, after all: you made a prisoner of his body, and he a convert of your Reason."

Burlingame bristled at the jibe, for it was not the first Ebenezer had directed at him that day. "It ill becomes you to defend the priest," he scolded in a low voice, so that the ferryman could not hear. " 'Tis not the Pope's cause we serve, but Baltimore's: the cause of Justice."

"True enough," the poet agreed. "Yet who's to say which cause is Justice's? Justice is blind."

"But men are not; and as for Justice, her blindness is the blindness of disinterest, not of innocence."

418

"That I deny," Ebenezer said blithely.

"Thou'rt grown entirely captious!"

"You are near forty, and I but twenty-eight," the Laureate declared, "and in experience thou'rt at least three times my age; but despite my innocence—nay, just *because* of't—I deem myself no less an authority than you on matters of Justice, Truth, and Beauty."

"Outrageous!" cried his friend. "Why is't men pick the oldest and most knowledgeable of their number to judge them, if not that worldliness is the first ingredient of Justice?"

But Ebenezer stuck to his guns. " 'Tis but a vulgar error, like many another."

Burlingame showed more irritation by the minute. "What is the difference 'twixt *innocence* and *ignorance*, pray, save that the one is Latin and the other Greek? In substance they are the same: innocence is ignorance."

"By which you mean," Ebenezer retorted at once, "that innocence of the world is ignorance of't; no man can quarrel with that. Yet the surest thing about Justice, Truth, and Beauty is that they live not in the world, but as transcendent entities, noumenal and pure. 'Tis everywhere remarked how children oft perceive the truth at once, where their elders have been led astray by sophistication. What doth this evidence, if not that innocence hath eyes to see what experience cannot?"

"Fogh!" scoffed Burlingame. "That is mere Cambridge claptrap, such as dear old Henry More did e'er espouse. Thank Heav'n such babes are helpless in society—think how 'twould be to have one for your judge!"

"Haply Justice would live up to her motto for the first time ever," Ebenezer said.

"That she would!" Henry laughed. "She could be pictured holding dice in lieu of scales, for where blind Innocence is judge, the jury is blind Chance! I cannot decide," he added, "whether you maintain your innocence because you hold such notions as this, or hold the notions to justify your innocence."

Ebenezer looked away and frowned as if at the approaching wharf, where considerable activity seemed to be in progress. "Methinks 'twere fitter to ask that of yourself, Henry: a man can cast away his innocence when he list, but not his knowledge."

On this ungenerous note the argument ended, for the ferry had reached its destination. The travelers, mutually disgruntled, stepped up to the wharf, which was built at the juncture of Choptank River and a large creek, and with some difficulty—for the tide was out—led their horses up a steep gangplank after them.

Unprepossessing as it had been from afar, the town of Cambridge was even less impressive at close range. There was, in fact, no town at all: a small log structure visible farther inland Burlingame identified as the Dorchester County Courthouse, which had been built only seven years before. Nearer the river was a kind of inn or ordinary of even more recent construction, and at the foot of the wharf itself was what appeared to be a relatively large warehouse and general merchandise store combined—a building which outdated both town and county as such, and which doubtless had been known to Ebenezer's father as early as 1665. Other than these no buildings could be seen, and there were, apparently, no private houses at all.

Yet at least a score of people were strolling on the wharf and about the warehouse; the sounds of general carouse rang down the roadway from the tavern; and in addition to the numerous small craft moored here and there along the shore, two larger, ocean-going vessels—a bark and a full-rigged ship—lay out in the Choptank channel. The activity, so disproportionate to the size and aspect of the town, Ebenezer learned was owing generally to its role as seat of the county and the convenience of its wharf and warehouse to the surroundiing plantations, and specifically to the fall term of the court, currently in session, which provided a rare diversion for the populace.

The roan mare and the gelding they tethered to a sapling near the creek, and after a light dinner at the ordinary the travelers parted company, rather to the Laureate's relief. Burlingame remained at the inn with the object of hiring lodgings for the night, inquiring the whereabouts of William Smith, and refreshing his thirst; and Ebenezer, left to himself, strolled idly up the road toward the courthouse, preoccupied with his thoughts. Since the day was warm, the courthouse small, and litigation such a popular entertainment among the colonials, the court was sitting out of doors, in a little valley just adjacent to the building. Ebenezer found nearly a hundred of the audience present already, though the court had not yet reconvened; they were engaged in eating, drinking heartily, calling and waving to one another across the natural amphitheater formed by the valley, wrestling playfully on the grass, singing rowdy songs, and otherwise amusing themselves in a manner which the poet deemed scarcely befitting the dig-

420

nity of a courtroom. Notes for tobacco were everywhere being exchanged, and Ebenezer soon realized that virtually all the men were making wagers on the outcome of the trials. The fact astonished him and even stirred vague forebodings in his mind, but he took a seat along the top of the amphitheater nevertheless to witness the session; his interest was aroused by his recent debate with Burlingame, for one thing, and he hoped as well to spawn couplets on the majesty of Maryland's law, as had been suggested by——

" 'Sdeath!" he thought, and winced and sighed: he could not manage to remember that it was Burlingame, not Charles Calvert, who had issued his commission; it was a thought too great and painful to hold fast in his awareness.

After some minutes the crier appeared from the courthouse door and bawled *"Oyez! Oyez! Oyez!"* but advanced no farther than the first hedgerow before a rain of cheerfully-flung twigs and pebbles drove him back. Then entered the judge, *sans* wig and robe of office, whom Ebenezer recognized only because, after pausing to chat with several of the audience and nod his head at their exchanges of tobacconotes, he took his place upon the open-air bench. Next came the jury (Ebenezer approved, uncertainly, their apparent practice of wagering only among themselves) and finally the attorneys for prosecution and defense, sharing a simple tall flagon with the judge. The only principals not present were the plaintiff and the defendant, and as Ebenezer scanned the crowd, conjecturing as to their identities, his eye fell on Susan Warren herself, sitting near the front row with an elderly man whom the poet had never seen before! She had, it appeared, cleaned herself up to some extent, but where before her face had been dirty and her brown hair matted, now she was rouged and powdered to excess, and her hair was done up like a tart's. She had exchanged her tattered Scotch cloth for sleazy satinesco, gaudily printed and open at the bosom, and her manner was in keeping with her dress: her laugh was loud and easily provoked; her eyes roved appraisingly from one man to another the while she talked to her escort; and she emphasized her statements with a hand laid lightly now on her partner's arm, now on his shoulder, now on his knee.

Ebenezer watched her for some time with feelings various and strong: his professions to Burlingame to the contrary notwithstanding, he was piqued as well as grateful that she'd jilted him in Captain Mitchell's barn; he yearned to know what had changed her mind, whether she had rejoined her father (and if so, why she was persisting in this harlotry), and —perhaps most urgently—whether she had news of Joan Toast, and why her story had not corresponded quite with Burlingame's. Moreover, despite his disgust at her brazen appearance and his concern for Joan Toast, he felt unmistakable pangs of jealousy at the sight of Susan's escort—who, however, ignored her coquetries. Ebenezer debated with himself whether to catch her eye and attempt to converse with her—among other things, he did not wholly trust Burlingame's pledge not to apprehend her—but at length he decided not to.

"I am well quit of her," he declared to himself. "As my advances to her plague my conscience, may her desertion of me plague hers. The just thing's to meddle farther neither in her flight nor in her capture, and there's an end on't."

So engrossing were these reflections, the Laureate scarcely remarked that the court was now in session and the dispute waxing hot, until the spectators' shouts drew his attention to the bar. In progress was a change-of-venue case from Kent County, and the testimony, evidently, was going hard against the plaintiff, on whose victory a substantial amount of Dorchester's money must have been riding; the audience was shouting down the attorney for the defendants, a married couple of middle age.

"Be't said again," the lawyer was declaiming, "that the accused, my client Mr. Bradnox—himself a bona fide justice o' the peace, was on the eve in question sitting justly and peaceably at home with Mistress Mary Bradnox his wife, when the plaintiff, Mr. Salter, did appear at his door with rum and playing-cards and did invite the two defendants to make merry. 'Twas then near midnight, and Mrs. Bradnox soon after bade the men good night and retired to her chamber—"

" 'Twas the chamber-pot she run to!" bawled the plaintiff from across the yard, and the audience cried assent. The defense counsel held a whispered colloquy with his client.

"I hereby amend my statement on advisement from Mrs. Bradnox that she did in sooth heed nature's call, but went straight from pot to cot, as't were."

"A lie!" the plaintiff cried again. He was a dark, lean fellow in his forties, uncommonly tall and leathery, and had a small jug at his side from which he drank. "When I went upstairs anon to try her, I found her cross-legged in the window seat with a song upon her lips and my good liquor in her bowels, a-firing farts at the waning moon."

"As the plaintiff Mr. Salter hath confessed," the defense lawyer went on slyly, "he did later leave the festivities, having got my client fuddled, and did climb the stairs to Mrs. Bradnox's chamber, whereto he did force entry and assault my client in dastard fashion—the truth of't is, he swived Mistress Mary from arse to Michaelmas and did thereby cuckold her spouse the Justice!"

"Hear!" cried the spectators.

"Having finished which evil work," the defense continued, "this Salter did return to the parlor, where he ill employed his host's beliquorment to cheat him at a game o' lanterloo, to the tune of several hundred pounds of tobacco, plying him the while with yet more rum to hide the fraud. Whenas my pitiful client grew so light with his load o' drams that he tumbled to the floor, by which fall his nose did bleed much, this same John Salter did spit upon him, make water on him, and otherwise offend the laws of hospitality, telling him finally that he was not two hours a hornèd cuckold. Hearing which, my client did on the instant go wondrous sober and, calling this same Salter blasphemer and turdy scoundrel, did ascend unto his wife's chamber in a fearful choler. Entering therein, he did commence to chastise her for a whore and scurvy peddletwat, with divers other epithets of castigation and admonition, and anon did grab her by the birth and drag her thus from bed to floor in an inhumane manner."

"Shame!" bawled the crowd, and, "To the post with him!" Ebenezer too was shocked, but not nearly so much by this revelation as by the entire preceding narrative of the plaintiff's behavior, the like of which, for brazenness, he had never heard. He wondered, in fact, how it was that Salter was the plaintiff and not the accused in the litigation.

"In the course of which domestic altercation," the defense proceeded, "the plaintiff Mr. Salter entered, and intruding himself betwixt the man and wife my clients, did take the part of Mistress Mary against her wedded spouse, clutching same about the neck and choking him till the Justice's eyes did lose their spark and stared all emptily like pissholes in the snow . . ."

"Hear!"

"Whereupon said Justice Bradnox did leave off his grip upon Mistress Mary's privates and confronted Salter with the latter's peccadilloes, contending that, by virtue of his having swived Mary from pot to pallet, said Salter did forfeit any and all claim to the Justice's esteem and was in fact no proper guest but a gigolo and shitabed hypocrite. To which description the plaintiff did reply by blacking both the Justice's eyes and raising a duck-egg knot upon his pate, declaring the while that Justice Bradnox was deficient in manly virtue——"

"I told him he was manly as a steer," Salter specified, wiping the mouth of the wine-jug with his sleeve, "and useful as a whore in church."

"That was well said," remarked a man sitting next to Ebenezer.

"And he did farther declare," the defense went on, "that Mistress Mary was not worth the trouble to hoist her coats . . ."

" 'Twas like humping Aldersgate," Salter complained.

"Whereto the Justice did reply that, should Salter not close his leprous trap, he the Justice my client would close it for him, and shoot him, knock him upon the head, and break his two legs into the bargain. To which the plaintiff rejoined——"

"Enough!" cried the judge. But then he added, "Thy drivel will have us snoring in a minute. What's the charge, for heaven's sake?"

Salter leaped to his feet at once. "The charge," he said, "is that this blackguard Bradnox never paid me for that liquor —a rundlet in all, give or take a dram—and farther, that whilst I was a-swiving Mary Bradnox from sprit to spanker, certain coins did fall from out my breeches, that were upon a chair, and these same coins the rascals ne'er returned to me."

"Mother of God!" the Laureate whispered.

"What say ye, jurymen?" charged the judge. "Is the defendant guilty, or will ye let the scoundrel go?"

The most Ebenezer could hope for during the minute or so of the jury's deliberation was that the notes being exchanged among them were messages and not tobacco-notes; he was too appalled by the conduct of the court to expect an honest judgment. It came, in fact, as something of a shock to him when the foreman of the jury said, "Your Honor, we find the defendant not guilty."

"Not guilty!" roared the judge, and his protest was echoed by the audience. "Sheriff, arrest those twelve rascals and charge 'em all with contempt o' court! Not guilty! Marry, the man's soul is black as the Ace o' Spades, and that of his short-heeled wife little whiter! Good God, men, will ye bring fair Dorset to wrack and ruin? Nay, I say: the defendant is guilty as charged!"

Ebenezer rose indignantly to his feet, but his objections were swallowed up by the crowd's applause.

"The Court here orders that Tom Bradnox pay o'er to Salter the full price of his rundlet and deliver a like amount to the Court come sunrise next, or stand pilloried till this Court adjourns. Farther, that Mary Bradnox return to the plaintiff double the value of the coins he lost while swiving her from bosom to birthright, or else suffer herself the letter *T* to be burnt in her hand, for thievery. Next case!"

The spectators whistled, slapped one another's shoulders, pinched one another's wives, and collected or settled their wagers. Ebenezer remained on his feet, astonished by the conduct of the court, and searched for the most scathing terms in his vocabulary, for he meant to deliver a public rebuke not only to the plaintiff and the judge, who had been clearly in collusion, but to the audience as well, for their undignified behavior. But before he could compose his reprimand the next litigants had taken the stand, and his attention was distracted by the fact that one of them—apparently the defendant—was Susan Warren's escort, with whom the judge appeared to be on familiar terms.

"What is't ye want here, Ben Spurdance?" asked the judge, and Ebenezer gave a start—the name he seemed to have heard before, doubtless from Susan, but he could not recall in what connection.

"Ye'd better ask *him*," Spurdance grumbled, pointing to a hale old man in the plaintiff's seat.

"Who might *you* be?" the judge demanded of him.

The old man answered, "William Smith, your Honor." Ebenezer started once again.

"What is your lying complaint against old Ben Spurdance?" asked the judge, and at this second mention of the name Ebenezer remembered where he'd heard it before: Captain Mitchell, as they left, had instructed his "son" to search for Susan Warren at the home of one Ben Spurdance, which he had called "a den of thieves and whores."

But he was due for yet a further surprise, for in answer to the Court's question Smith replied that upon his arrival in the Province some four years ago he had of necessity indentured himself to the defendant, having spent all his money en route for medicines to aid his ailing daughter, and that the term of his indenture had just recently expired.

" 'Dslife!" the Laureate marveled. " 'Tis not our man at all, but Susan Warren's poor sainted father that she told me of!" And he wondered angrily why Susan had been consorting with the defendant. William Smith, in the meantime, proceeded to articulate his grievance: he had, he declared,

425

served Spurdance faithfully for the four years of his indenture in the position of cooper and smith, but upon the expiration of his service Spurdance had reneged on the terms of their agreement. Specifically, Spurdance had given over to him only an acre and a half of land—and poor land at that, full of stones and gullies—instead of the twenty called for by the indenture, and had told him he could go hang for all the more he'd get.

"Poor wretch!" Ebenezer commiserated to himself. He was all the more ready now to deliver his harangue, but thought it best to wait until he had the whole tale of Smith's misfortunes.

The defendant then testified that while the plaintiff's speech was substantially correct, he Spurdance had not told Smith to go hang for all the rest he'd get.

"I told the old goat to thrust his acres up his arse and leave me in peace," he declared.

"I'God, he e'en admits his guilt!" thought Ebenezer.

The judge frowned uncordially at the plaintiff. "Are ye trying to lie to the Court, sir?"

"Haply 'twas as he says," admitted Smith, "albeit my memory is he said 'Go hang, for all the more ye'll get!' "

"Well, which was't?" the judge demanded.

" 'Twas *Thrust it,*" Spurdance insisted.

" 'Twas *Go hang,*" Smith maintained.

"Thrust it!" shouted Spurdance.

"Go hang!" cried Smith.

"Thrust it," the judge ordered, rapping for silence. "Your friend here hath a slippery lawyer, Ben," he said to the defendant. "Where's yours?"

Spurdance sniffed in the direction of the prosecuting attorney, a plump little man in a black suit such as Quakers often wore. "I need no liars like Richard Sowter to defend me."

"Call your first witness, then, and let's get on with't."

No one except Ebenezer seemed to see anything unorthodox about hearing the defense before the prosecution, and when he saw Susan Warren take the stand in Spurdance's behalf, his wonder was replaced by sheer astonishment.

Susan's testimony, however, surpassed for incredibility anything else he had heard said that afternoon. She had fled to Maryland, she declared, under the protection of one kindly Captain Mitchell of Calvert County, in order to escape the incestuous demands of a father who lusted after her like a billy-goat! "He did then privily pursue me aboard the ship itself," she went on, "and squandered all his money to bribe

Captain Mitchell. 'Twas his object to make the Captain play the pander and deliver me into his evil hands, that he might ravish me from fo'c'sle to poop deck!"

The spectators, though they had greeted Susan's accession to the stand with lewd remarks, were now in obvious sympathy with her plight; they murmured their approval of the testimony that her father's efforts to corrupt her guardian had been in vain, and that as a consequence he had been obliged to indenture himself to Spurdance.

"Good Ben here took him only as a favor to me," she declared, "and 'twas an ill bargain I bade him strike, for my father scorned his end of't. He proved an idler and a rabble rouser, e'en as I'd feared; Mr. Spurdance gave him the acre and a half out of pure Christian charity, for he owed him not a ship fitter's fart. He is my father, worse luck for me, but 'twould give me joy to see the rascal put to the post, I swear, and have the nastiness flogged from his wretched bones!"

The judge commended Susan warmly and with no further ado dismissed the untrustworthy jury and declared himself ready to find the plaintiff guilty of lying and idleness; but before he could render an official verdict, Ebenezer, who had sprung to his feet and trembled with rage through the latter part of Susan's testimony, now raised himself to his full height on the grassy bank and cried, *"Stop!* I demand that this outrageous proceeding be stopped!"

Susan gasped and turned away; the crowd hooted and threw twigs, but the judge brayed louder and banged his gavel.

"Order! *Order,* damn ye! Now who in the name of Antichrist are *you,* and why are ye obstructing the justice of this court?"

As he turned to dodge a twig, Ebenezer saw Henry Burlingame hurrying toward him around the top edge of the amphitheater and signaling urgently for him to hold his peace. But the Laureate's indignation was not so lightly held in check; in fact, the pertinence of the present situation to what he and Burlingame had been arguing not long before made him even more eager to speak out when he saw his former tutor among the audience.

"I am Ebenezer Cooke, Your Honor, Poet and Laureate of this entire province by grace of Charles, Lord Baltimore, and I strenuously object to the verdict just proposed, as being a travesty of Justice and a smirch on the fair escutcheon of Maryland law!"

"Hear!" cried some of the audience, but others shouted

"Turn the Papist out!" As soon as the declaration was made, Ebenezer saw Burlingame halt in full career, clap a hand to his brow, and then with a shrug sit down where he happened to have stopped.

"Oh la," scoffed the judge, " 'tweren't *that* bad." He winked broadly at the assemblage. " 'Twas the best verdict old Ben Spurdance could afford."

Burlingame's alarm had taken its toll on the Laureate's self-confidence, but it was too late now for him to retreat; uncertainty put new wrath into his voice.

"You know not whom you twit, sir! Poltroons greater and blacker than you have felt the sting of Hudibrastic and been brought low! Now will you render Justice to yon poor wretch the plaintiff, whose inequitable case cries out to Heav'n for remedy, and cause the defendant and that perfidious slattern of a witness to suffer for their calumnies? Or will you bring upon yourself the Laureate's wrath, and with it the wrath of an outraged populace?"

Spurdance, meanwhile, had turned pale, and as the crowd murmured to one another, he went to the bench to whisper in the judge's ear during this last challenge.

"I care not a tinker's turd *who* he is!" the judge swore to Spurdance. "This is my court, and I mean to run it honestly: nobody gets a verdict he hath not paid for!"

"So be't!" the poet shouted over the laughter of the crowd. "If Justice in this province belongs for the nonce to the man that buys her, then in this instance I shall pay the harlot's fee." He glared meaningfully at Susan. "Whate'er this evil Spurdance bribed you I shall raise by half, for the privilege of rendering both verdict and sentence."

"Two hundred pounds o' sot-weed," said the judge.

"Three hundred, then," the Laureate replied.

"I object!" cried Spurdance, greatly alarmed.

"And I!" chimed Susan, whose look of terror brought a proud smile to the poet's lips. William Smith stood up as if to add a third objection, but his little black-suited counsel quickly stopped him and whispered in his ear.

"Objections overruled," snapped the judge. "The case is in your hands, Master Poet. But bear in mind 'tis not allowed to take life or member."

The defendant and Susan showed surprise and consternation over the progress of events, as did Burlingame, who sprang up at the judge's ruling and once again hurried towards Ebenezer. But he was still several hundred feet away, and the Laureate proceeded undisturbed.

"I wish neither," he declared, "only Justice. Spurdance, it appears, did no bodily injury to the plaintiff; therefore none shall be done to him. 'Twas a matter of land-payment, and I shall administer Justice of the nature of the crime. My verdict is that the defendant stands guilty as charged, and my sentence is that the plaintiff be awarded in damages not alone the twenty acres originally due him, but all the property from which the grant was made, saving only the acre and a half now held by the plaintiff. In other words, the defendant shall own the pittance he so grudged to give up, and the plaintiff shall own the hoard from which it came! As for Miss Susan Warren, since it seems by no means uncommon in this court to sentence persons not on trial, I find her guilty of fraud, calumny, defamation, lewdness, whoredom, and filial disaffection, and here decree that she must remain in the custody of her father the plaintiff whilst an enquiry be made into the legality of her indenture to Captain Mitchell. Farther, that at the soonest opportunity her father is to arrange a fit match for her, that under the connubial yoke she might instruct herself in the ways of virtue and piety. These strictures, penalties, and decrees to be executed within the fortnight on pain of increased sentence and imprisonment!"

From across the courtyard came a mocking, almost hysterical laugh, and Burlingame, Spurdance, and Susan Warren all cried out at once, but the judge said, "The Court so rules," and banged the table with his gavel. "And I shall add, sir, that in all my years upon the bench I have ne'er witnessed such a foolish generosity!"

Ebenezer bowed. "I thank you. Yet 'twere better the Justice of the sentence be praised, and not its magnanimity. 'Tis a light matter to be generous with another man's property."

The judge made some reply, but it was lost in the uproar of the crowd, who now lifted Ebenezer upon their shoulders and bore him off to the tavern down the street.

" 'Tis not I you should honor, but blind Justice," the poet said to no one in particular. "Howbeit," he added, " 'tis gratifying to find myself at last among folk not purblind to the dignity of my office. My esteem for Cambridge hath been restored entire."

Indeed there was some murmur of saintliness among the more impressionable of the crowd; one mother held up her infant child for him to kiss, but the Laureate modestly waved the lady away. He glanced about in vain for Burlingame, to savor his reaction to this triumph.

The erstwhile plaintiff William Smith was already at the

inn when they arrived, and at the sight of his benefactor he ordered ale for everyone.

"How can I thank ye, sir?" he cried, embracing Ebenezer. "Thou'rt the Christianest soul in the Province o' Maryland, I swear!"

"Tut, now," the Laureate replied. "I only hope they will not cheat you of't yet."

"'Tis what I fear as well, sir," Smith agreed, and drew a paper from his shirt. "My lawyer hath just now drawn up this paper, which if you'll sign, will seal your sentence fast in any court."

"Then let's have done with't, and to the ale," laughed Ebenezer. He took quill and ink from the barman, signed the document with a flourish, and returned it to Smith, wishing Burlingame, Anna, and his London friends were present to witness this most glorious hour of his life.

"Now," declared Smith, raising his bumper of ale in toast: "To Master Cooke, sirs, our Laureate Poet, that is the grandest gentleman e'er graced Dorset County!"

"Hear!" cried the others.

"And to Mr. Smith," Ebenezer rejoined politely, "that hath no more than just reward for all his trials."

"Hear!"

"Here's to that painted puss his daughter," someone shouted from the mob. "May Heav'n preserve us from her—"

"Nay, rather to Justice," the Laureate broke in, embarrassed by the reference to Susan. "To Justice, Poetry, Maryland—and, if you will, to Malden, whither I am bound."

"Aye, to Malden," Smith affirmed. "And ye must know, sir, once I've sacked that rascal Spurdance for a proper overseer, thou'rt ever welcome there to visit when ye will and be my honored guest however long ye choose." He laughed and winked his eye. "I'faith, sir, should Lord Calvert's false commission pay no wage, I'll hire yourself in Spurdance's stead to manage Malden. Ye could be no worse a one than he, that cheated ye blind without your knowing aught of't."

Ebenezer frowned in horror. "Dear sir, I do not follow you for a moment!"

"As well, 'tis no matter now, lad." Smith grinned and took a fresh glass from the barman. *"Many a truth is spoke in ignorance, and many a wrong set right by chance.* To Malden!" he said to the crowd, and clearly for the Laureate's benefit went on: "Now 'tis mine in title, I shall run it as Ben Spurdance never durst!"

"Hear! Hear! Hear!" they all cried, and quaffed so deeply of ale and enthusiasm that few saw the guest of honor swoon away upon the sawdust floor.

28

If the Laureate Is Adam, Then Burlingame Is the Serpent

WHEN HE RECOVERED his senses Ebenezer found himself on a bench in one corner of the tavern; his feet were elevated on a wooden box, and a wet cloth had been placed across his brow. Remembering why he'd fainted nearly carried him off afresh; he closed his eyes again, and wished he could perish on the instant where he lay rather than face the derision of the crowd and his own shame of the folly of his loss. When at length he dared to look about him, he saw Henry Burlingame sitting alone at the nearest table, smoking a pipe and regarding the carousers at the bar.

"Henry!" the stricken poet called.

Burlingame spun around at once. "Not *Henry,* Eben—Tim Mitchell is my name. I found you laid out on the floor."

Ebenezer sat up and shook his head. "Ah, dear Christ, Henry, what have I done? And in the face of your warnings!"

Burlingame smiled. "You've administered innocent Justice, I should say."

"Twit me not, in the name of Heaven!" He buried his face in his hands. "Would God I'd stayed in London!"

"Did old Andrew grant you power of attorney? If not, you had no right to make the gift."

"He never should have," Ebenezer answered, "but he did. I have signed away his estate, and my whole legacy, to that thieving cooper!"

Burlingame sucked on his pipe. " 'Twas a fool's conveyance, but what's done is done. How doth it feel, to be a pauper like myself?"

Ebenezer could not reply at once. Tears came to his eyes,

and he hung his head. " 'Twas Anna's dowry too, the half of it: I shall make over to her my share of the house in Plumtree Street, and beg her pardon. But whate'er will Father say?"

"Stay, now," said Burlingame, "don't preach the funeral ere the patient is quite dead. What do we know of this William Smith? He made his exit when you fell a-swoon."

"He is a scoundrel, else he'd not have taken such advantage of my innocence."

"That only proves him human, as you shall learn. D'you think he is the William Smith we came for?"

"How could he be, a simple cooper? I had his history from Susan Warren back at Mitchell's."

But Burlingame frowned. "There is more to him than that, and her as well, but God knows what; one schemer hath an eye for others. 'Twould not at all surprise me to learn he is our man, a secret agent of Lord Baltimore's."

"What boots it if he's Governor of the Province?" Ebenezer asked gloomily. "Malden is his in any case."

"Haply so, haply so. Or haply when he learns our mission he will be more reasonable."

Ebenezer brightened at once. "I'God, Henry, do you believe it?"

Burlingame shrugged. "No behavior is impossible in the world. Leave things to me, and I shall learn what I can. You'd best assume thou'rt penniless for the nonce, as well you may be, and say nothing of our hope. Drown your loss in liquor like the lot of men."

By this time the Laureate's resuscitation had been observed by the other patrons of the inn, who so far from deriding him, invited him to drink at their expense.

"Don't they know yet of my loss?" he asked Burlingame.

"Aye, they know. Some knew it from the first, and only later learned 'twas not intended."

"What a ninny they must think me!"

Again Burlingame shrugged. "Less of a saint and more of a man. You'd as well oblige 'em, don't you think?"

Ebenezer started up from the bench, but sank back again in despair. "Nay, great God, how can I stand about and drink when I have thrown away my Malden? 'Tis the pistol I should turn to, not the ale-glass!"

"There is a lesson in your loss," his friend replied, "but 'tis not for me to teach it." He got up from his chair. "Well, now thou'rt landless like myself, will you get drunk as I intend to?"

Still the poet hesitated. "I fear liquor as I fear fevers, drugs, and dreams, that change a man's perspective. A man should see the world as it is, for good or ill."

"That is a boon you've ne'er been vouchsafed yet, my friend. Why hope for't tonight?"

"Unkind!" protested Ebenezer. " 'Tis only that I've ne'er been drunk before."

"Nor ever a placeless pauper," Henry retorted. "But do as you list." He turned his back on Ebenezer and went alone to the bar, where he was welcomed familiarly as Tim Mitchell by the other patrons. And Ebenezer, whose objections had been more cautionary than heartfelt, soon joined him—not alone because his loss was too staggering to look at squarely, but also because he did not feel altogether well. Whether owing to the flatulence of the roan, his alarm at Henry's ill treatment of Father Smith, or—what seemed most likely to him—that same period of "seasoning," endured by all new arrivals to the colonies, to which his mother had succumbed, his stomach had been uneasy since the morning, and his brow a trifle feverish since noon.

"Hi, now!" a planter cried at his approach. "Here comes our Christlike Laureate at last!" There was no malice in his tone at all; his greeting was echoed by the others, who made room for him and went so far as to swear to the barman that they would leave in a body if their new comrade were not given free rum at once.

Their cordiality moistened the poet's eyes. " 'Tis not a proper Laureate you see before you, friends," he began, speaking with some difficulty. "Nay, rather it is the very prince of fools, and yet thou'rt civil to him as to a man of sense. I shan't forget it."

Burlingame looked up with interest at the outset of this speech, but seemed disappointed by its close.

"One folly doth not make a fool," someone replied.

" 'Twas a princely stupid grant," another declared, "and you've a princely misery in exchange for't. Methinks thou'rt quits."

Ebenezer drank off his rum and was given another. "A fortune poorer and a groatsworth wiser?" He shook his head. "I see no bargain in't."

"That is the way of't, nonetheless," said Burlingame, in the accents of Timothy Mitchell. "Unless a man matriculate betimes, Life's college hath a dear tuition. Besides, thou'rt in a venerable position."

"Venerable!" protested the Laureate. "If you mean I'm not

433

the world's initial ass, then I agree, but I see naught in that to venerate!"

"Drink up, and I'll explain." His tutor smiled and, when Ebenezer complied, he said, "What is your lot, if not the lot of man?"

"Haply 'tis the rum beclouds me," Ebenezer interrupted, "for I see nor sense nor rhyme in that remark." He terminated his statement with a belch, to his new-found friends' amusement, and called for another drink.

"I mean 'tis Adam's story thou'rt re-enacting." Henry went on. "Ye set great store upon your innocence, and by reason of't have lost your earthly paradise. Nay, I shall take the conceit e'en farther: not only hath your adventure left ye homeless, but like Adam ye've your first bellyful of knowledge and experience; ye'll pluck easy fruit no more to line your gut with, but earn your bread with guilty sweat, as do the mass of men. Your father, if I know him, will not lose this chance to turn ye out o' the Garden!"

Ebenezer laughed as readily as the others at this analogy, if not so heartily, and mug in hand replied, "Such conceits as that are spirited horses, that if not rid with art will take their riders far afield."

"Ye do not like it?"

"The fault is not in the—— Hi, there!" In gesturing his dissent Ebenezer had splashed a deal of rum on his shirt. "What waste of brew, sirs! Prithee fill me up. There's a Christian Dorsetman!" This time he drank off half a glass before he spoke. "What was I saying, now, good friends?" He frowned at his dripping garment. "From the way the water broke, I judge some mighty thought was in travail: another *Errare humanum est*, for aught you know, or *Fiat justitia ruat caelum*."

"It had to do with horses," said one of the delighted patrons.

"With horses!"

"Aye," another laughed, "ye were in argument with Tim Mitchell here."

"Pray God the jade is windless, then," Ebenezer said. "I am sick to death from our last contest of wit!"

Though none but Burlingame really understood this remark, it was received with hilarity by the planters, who now vied with one another to buy the Laureate drinks.

" 'Twas Master Tim's conceit ye took to task," one said.

"Indeed? Then let him look to't, for just as *Many can pack the cards that cannot play*, so many can turn a rhyme that

434

are not poets. Good rhymes are mere embroidery on the muse's drawers, but metaphor's their very warp and woof—if I may say so."

"Ye never would have ere this night," said Burlingame, who seemed not amused.

"I have't now!" Ebenezer cried; the company smiled and urged him to drink dry his glass before he spoke.

" 'Twas all that likening me to Adam I took issue with." He wiped his mouth on his sleeve and leaned his elbow in a puddle on the bar. "Methinks friend Timothy hath forgot old Adam was a sinner, and that his Original Sin was knowledge and experience. Ere he took his sinful bite he was immortal as the beasts, that learn little from experience and know not death; once glutted with the fruit of Learning's orchard, 'twas his punishment to groan with the heartburn of despair, and to grope his little way in the black foreshadow of his death."

Burlingame shrugged. " 'Twas what I——"

"Stay," the Laureate commanded, "I am not done!" For all Burlingame had urged Ebenezer to drink, he was plainly annoyed by his protégé's alcoholic eloquence; he turned away to his own glass, and the patrons nudged each other with apprehensive mirth.

"What you forgot in your o'erhasty trope," Ebenezer declared; "was just the *sort* of apple Father Adam bit. What knowledge is it, Timmy, that is root and stem of all? What vile experience sows the seeds of death in men? I'faith, how did it slip your mind, that are so big with seed yourself and have broadcast in the furrows of two hemispheres? 'Twas *carnal* knowledge, Tim boy, experience of the flesh, that caused man's fall! If I am Adam, I am Eveless, and Adam Eveless is immortal and unfallen. In fine, sir, my estate is lost, but I am not, and there's an end on't!"

"Your tongue runs over," Burlingame grumbled.

"Behold him, citizens of Dorset!" the poet cried, and pointed more or less at Burlingame with one hand while he tipped back his rum-glass with the other. *"Ecce signum! Finem respice!* If knowledge be sin and death, as Scripture says, there stands a Faustus of the flesh—a very Lucifer!"

"Nay, poet, ye go too far," a planter cautioned. "This is no feckless Quaker thou'rt abusing." Several others echoed his discomfort; some even moved discreetly from the bar to nearby tables, where they could watch without being mistaken for participants.

Whether aware of the change in their attitude or not, Ebenezer went on undaunted. "This man you see here is more knowledgeable than a squad of Oxford dons, and more versed in carnal lore than Aretino! Beside him old Cartesius is a numbskull, Wallenstein a babe, and Rabelais but a mincing Puritan. Behold his cheeks, that wear the ashy hue of Chaos! Behold his brow, deep-furrowed by the history of the race!"

"I prithee stay!" someone entreated him.

"Behold his eyes, sirs, that have read of every unholy deed e'er dreamt of by the tortuous minds of man, and looked on these same deeds done in the flesh! Oh, in particular behold those eyes! Turn round here, Henry—Timothy, I mean!—turn round for us, Timmy, and chill us with those eyes! They are cold and old as a reptile's, friends—in sooth, in sooth, they are the eyes of Eden's serpent, that, nested in the Tree of Knowledge, enthralled the earth's first woman with his winkless stare!"

"Curb thy tongue," warned Burlingame. "Thou'rt prating nonsense!"

But Ebenezer was too far gone in rum and wrath to leave off his tirade. "Oh Lord, good sirs, behold those eyes! How many maids hath that stare rendered helpless, that soon were maids no more! What a deal of innocence have those two hands corrupted!"

"This is Tim Mitchell ye speak to!" a frightened planter said. "How is't ye dare abuse him so?"

"How is't I dare?" the poet repeated. His gaze never left Burlingame, whose face betrayed increasing irritation. He set down his glass, and his eyes filled with tears. "Because he hath with his infamous guile bewitched one innocent flower, most precious to my heart of all, a paragon of gentle chastity, and sought by every foul means to possess her!"

"Stop!" Burlingame commanded.

" 'Tis for this alone he feigns to be my friend and makes game of my innocence but takes no umbrage at my abuse: he still pursues his evil end. Yet I am proud to say his craft thus far hath borne no fruit: this flower's virtue is of hardy stock, and hath not yet succumbed to his vile blandishment. Lookee, how the truth doth gall him! This embodiment of lust—how doth it fret him to see that flower go still unplucked!"

Burlingame sighed and turned grimly to the company. "Since it is your pleasure to noise these privy matters in a public house, young man, and boast so of my talents to these gentlemen, I must insist ye tell the whole unvarnished truth about this flower."

"And what is that?" the Laureate asked, but with some apprehension in his sneer. "You will never know her one tenth as well as I."

"Of that I have no doubt, Master Laureate; yet to hear ye speak of her, these gentlemen must think your flower as thorny as the brier rose, or difficult of access as the lofty edelweiss. Yet ten years and more ago, whilst still a bud, she came to me for plucking and bade me be the first to taste her nectar. These eyes of mine, that ye make much of: how often she hath unfolded all her petals for their delight! And with these hands and this mouth, to say no farther, many and many a time I have brought her to the brink of madness— aye, and made her swoon for joy! A little growth or mole she hath—ye know her so well, I need not mention where— which if ye press it such-a-way——"

Ebenezer had gone white; his features roiled and boiled about. "Stop!" he gasped.

"And her most modest countenance—ye must know even more than I what sweet perversions it conceals! That little language that she speaks without her mouth, and her endless tricks to conjure manliness——"

The company laughed and rolled their eyes at one another. Ebenezer clutched his throat, unable to speak, and buried his face in his arms upon the bar. Though he had stopped drinking, the alcohol still mounted to his head. His palms and forehead sweated, saliva poured into his mouth, and his stomach churned.

"I scarce need mention that most fetching game of all," Burlingame went on relentlessly, "the one she plays when other pleasures fail—have ye remarked it? I mean the game she calls *Heavenly Twins,* or *Abel and Jumella,* but I call *Riding to Gomorrah*—"

"Wretch!" shrieked Ebenezer, and endeavored to fling himself upon his former tutor; but he was held fast by the planters and counseled to keep his wrath in check. His vision swam: his equilibrium left him, and he fell into a fit of retching at the image of what he'd heard. As though from another room he heard Burlingame say, " 'Tis time to fill the pipes. Take him somewhere to sleep his liquor out, and mind ye treat him well, for he's a prize." And then, as two planters bore him from the room: "Sleep ye now, my Laureate; in all thy orifices be my sins remembered!"

29

The Unhappy End of Mynheer Wilhelm Tick, As Related to the Laureate by Mary Mungummory, the Traveling Whore o' Dorset

BY THE TIME EBENEZER had quite slept off the effects of his rum, the sky over Maryland had begun to lighten. During the night—which happened to be the last in September—the Indian summer had given way to more characteristic autumn weather; indeed, the early morning air was positively cold, and it was the chattering of his teeth, and general shivering, that woke the Laureate.

"Dear God!" he cried, and sat up at once. He found himself in a sort of corncrib at one end of a stable, presumably behind the ordinary, his legs and trunk buried in the coarse-grained ears. One at a time his woes revealed themselves: he had lost Malden forever and had surely alienated Burlingame as well—whose shocking declarations, the poet now felt certain, had been invented for their retaliatory and sobering effect.

"I'faith, I had it coming!" he reflected.

He was, moreover, in a wretched state of health: his head throbbed from the rum, the light hurt his eyes, and his stomach was still none too strong. The chill air, in addition, had turned his previous indisposition into a real ague: he sneezed and shivered and ran at the nose, and ached in every joint.

"Lovely treatment for their Laureate!" He resolved to chastise the proprietor of the inn, even sue him if he could find proper grounds, and it was not until he stirred to carry out this resolve that he realized the main cause of his chill: his coat, hat, and breeches were gone, and he lay clothed in hose and drawers only. He could think of nothing to do except appeal for help from the first person to bring a horse out to the stable; in the meantime he was obliged to dig a sort of well into the corncobs, lower himself into it, and pack the rough ears all about him to keep the breeze off.

"Out on't!" he swore after an hour had passed. "Where are the man's customers?"

He attempted to while away the minutes by composing couplets to flay all innkeepers, from that one who had put Joseph and Mary in the stable at Bethlehem to the one who allowed the Laureate of Maryland to sleep in a corncrib—but his heart was not in his work, and he gave it up when he found himself unable to summon a rhyme for *diabolical*. He had not eaten since noon of the previous day: as the sun rose, his stomach rumbled. His sneezing grew more severe, and he had nothing more delicate than a corncob on which to wipe his nose. At length, beginning to fear that he would perish of exposure before anyone came to rescue him, he raised a shout for assistance. Again and again he called, to no avail, until at last a large and blowzy woman of middle age, happening to drive her wagon into the yard, heard his cries, reined in her horse, and came over to the stable.

"Who's in there?" she demanded. "And what in thunder ails ye?" Her voice was loud and husky, and her proportions —more truly seen now she was standing—prodigious. She wore the ubiquitous Scotch cloth of the working Marylander; her face was red-brown and wrinkled, and her grey hair as tangled as an old brier-thicket. So far from showing alarm at Ebenezer's outcries, her eyes narrowed with what seemed to be anticipatory mirth, and her half-toothed mouth already smiled.

"Keep hence!" cried Ebenezer. "Pray come no nearer till I explain! I am Ebenezer Cooke, Poet and Laureate of this province."

"Ye do not tell me! Well, I am Mary Mungummory, that once was called the Traveling Whore o' Dorset, but I don't boast of't. Why is't ye linger in the corncobs, Master Poet? Are ye making verse or making water?"

"God forfend I'd choose such a sanctuary to piss in," the poet replied, "and 'twould want a cleverer wight than I to turn a corncob into art."

The woman chuckled. "Belike thou'rt playing unnatural games, then?"

"From what I've learnt of Marylanders, I'm not surprised that you should think so. Howbeit, 'tis only your assistance I crave."

"Well, now!" Mary laughed immensely and approached the corncrib.

439

"Nay, madam!" Ebenezer pleaded. "You've misconstrued me: I've not a farthing to buy aught of your services."

"De'il have your farthings," the big woman said. "I care naught for farthings till the sun goes down. 'Twill be enough for me to see what a poet looks like." She climbed up into the corncrib, rumbling with amusement.

"Stay hence!" Ebenezer raked desperately at additional ears of corn to cover his shame. " 'Tis but a Christian service I beg of you, madam." Briefly he explained his plight, and ended by imploring Mary to find him some clothing at once, before the ague carried him off.

The whole story vastly entertained her, and to the poet's joy she said, " 'Tis no chore at all, young man: I've a pair or two o' breeches in my wagon, I'm certain." She explained that her sobriquet was the pride of her younger years, when she had traveled by wagon from plantation to plantation to practice her trade. Now that she was old, she had turned to procuring for a living; she and her girls made a monthly circuit of every settlement and large plantation in the county, breaking their schedule only for such events as the semiyearly sessions of the court.

From her wagon she fetched a pair of buckskin trousers, a shirt of the same material, and Indian moccasins, all of which she flung up to Ebenezer.

"Here ye be, sir," she said with a chuckle, and climbed up after. "They belong to a young Abaco gallant name o' Tom Rockahominy, that lives in Gum Swamp. He had to bid us a quick farewell last night when a troop of Wiwash braves moved in. Put 'em on."

"I cannot express my gratitude," Ebenezer said, waiting for her to leave. "Thou'rt almost the first kind soul I've met in Maryland."

"Make haste," the woman urged. "I am dying to see what you brave lads look like, that have love on the brain from one verse to the next."

It was only with the greatest difficulty that Ebenezer persuaded her to vacate the corncrib long enough for him to dress. Indeed, his efforts would have been entirely in vain, so determined was she to satisfy her curiosity, had not his extraordinary modesty amused her even more.

"The plain truth is, madam, I am a virgin, and mean to remain one. No woman in my memory hath ever seen my body."

"Dear mother of God!" Miss Mungummory cried. "I will

pay ye two hundredweight o' tobacco to be the first—that is the price of one o' my girls!"

But the poet declined her offer, and it was with awe as well as mirth that at last she climbed out of the corncrib.

"At least ye might tell me somewhat about it, seeing I did ye a service. Haply Nature played the niggard with ye, and thou'rt ashamed?"

"I am a man like other men," Ebenezer said stiffly, "and I quite appreciate my debt to you, Miss Mungummory. 'Tis merely that I am loath to break my personal vows; else out of gratitude I would engage you in your professional capacity."

"Ah now, sir, such a boast doth not become ye! A man like others ye may well be, but think not thou'rt a match for my professional capacity!" She laughed so hard that it was necessary for her to sit down on the earthen floor of the stable. "I once knew a salvage down the county, had the fearsomest way with him ye ever could imagine. *There* was the man for my professional capacity! Belike ye've heard what happens to a man when they hang him? Well, sir, the day they hanged poor Charley for the murther of my sister—it makes the tears come yet when I recall the picture of him . . ."

"I say now, Miss Mungummory, this is extraordinary!" Ebenezer finished dressing and climbed out of the corncrib. "What was this Indian's name?"

But Mary could not reply at once, for the sight of the poet sent her into new flights of hilarity. He was indeed an uncommon spectacle: the Indian garments were too small for his towering frame, and were rendered doubly bizarre by contrast with his English hose.

"I thought I heard you call him *Charley*," Ebenezer said with as much dignity as he could muster, "and I wondered whether I'd not heard something of him before."

"Oh, everybody knows of Charley Mattassin," Mary said when she caught her breath. "One of the folks he murthered was my sister Katy, the Seagoing Whore o' Dorset."

"Marry, this is fantastic! The wretch murthers your sister, and you speak almost endearingly of him! And what is this about a seagoing whore? 'Sdeath!"

" 'Tis what they called her, and God rest her jealous soul, I bear no malice toward her, for all she turned my Charley's head."

Nothing would do then but she tell Ebenezer the story of her sister's murder at the hands of Charley Mattassin—a story which, despite his impatience to find Burlingame, the Laureate consented to hear, both because he owed his rescue to the teller and because he had recognized the murderer as that same incorrigible Indian who had told Father Thomas Smith of Joseph FitzMaurice's martyrdom. He drew up a wooden box to sit upon and pulled self-consciously at his shirt sleeves as if to stretch them into fit. Mary Mungummory elected to remain seated on the ground, but took the trouble to prop her great back against the wall of the stable before she began her tale.

" 'Tis as true a thing of women as of cats," she asserted, "that whatsoever they are told they may not have, that thing they will move Heav'n and earth to get—particularly where love is concerned. God help the husband that obliges his wife's least whim: he'll be a wittol ere he's two years wed! As one o' your poets hath written:

> When old Man takes young Wife to warm his Bower,
> He finds his Cuckold's Horns among her Dower."

"That is well put," Ebenezer said, "though what connection it might bear to your story I can't say."

"My sister Katy had just such a husband, and schemed his ruin, but was hoist by her own petard." Mary sighed. "Kate was less a sister than a daughter to me. Our mother walked the streets near Newgate Market, and in thirty years o' whoring made but two mistakes: the first was to trust a parson, and the second was to trust a physician."

Ebenezer expressed surprise at such cynicism in so charitable a soul as that of his benefactress. "Is there no one you trust?"

Mary shrugged and said, " 'Tis a question o' what ye'd trust 'em *with*, is't not? In any case I bear 'em no grudge: *When a fox hath a hen within his grasp, he will eat her, and when a man hath a woman in his power, he will swive her.* My mother was a starving orphan girl that begged about the streets for food. Ere she reached thirteen, so many men had tried to force her that she begged the rector of her parish for sanctuary and was admitted to his kitchen as a scullion. This rector was a proper Puritan, and not an evening passed but he called her to his chambers to harangue her on the Labyrinth of the Heart, and Original Sin, and the Canker in the Rose. To bolster her against the carnal wiles of men he devised a set of spiritual exercises, one of which was to uncover himself in her presence and oblige her to grasp him like

442

a sacred relic, at the same time reciting a prayer against temptations of the flesh. He was much concerned for her virginity, and at the same time doubtful of her strength and honesty; for this reason on Sunday nights she was obliged to confess to him every lustful thought that had crossed her mind through the week, after which he would examine whether she still had her maidenhead as she claimed."

"He was a hypocritical wretch!" the poet declared.

"Haply so," Mary said indifferently. "He was a wondrous kind and gentle minister, the pride of his parishioners, and raised my mother as a member of his family. Methinks he saw no evil at all in what he did. When Mother was fifteen, and still a virgin, he had so schooled her to resist the fires of lust that they could sit for hours naked on his couch and exchange every manner of caress, talking all the while of the loftiest and most edifying matters. To do this was his pride and his delight, so Mother said, and the virtuous climax of a saintly week."

Ebenezer shook his head. "The heart's a labyrinth indeed!"

"That it is," Mary agreed with a laugh, "and anon the wight got lost in't! The riper grew his charge, the more concerned grew he for her honor. She was such an eager and accomplished pupil, and he had given her such a wondrous education—what a waste if some blackguard forced her against her will, and the joys of swiving turned her head from virtue! This notion so possessed him that he talked of nothing else, and for all my mother's vows that she loathed no thought like that of fornication, he knew no peace till he devised the most rigorous spiritual exercise of all . . ."

"Ah God, don't tell me——!"

Mary nodded, shaking with mirth. " 'Twas but the natural end of all that went before. One Sabbath night whilst they knelt in prayer he went round behind and made a mighty thrust at her; when she cried out he explained 'twas but her final lesson in shackling fleshly passions, and bade her go on with her prayers as if she were in church. Albeit she was much troubled in spirit, and no silly child despite her innocence, she thought it better to oblige him than to seem ungrateful for all his past kindness; therefore she made no farther protest, but only hoped he would take measures to avoid certain consequences, and began the prayer again. Quick as a wink, on the words *Which art in Heav'n,* he took her maidenhead, and if he'd a mind to commit the sin of Onan for her protection, he had no time, for on the words *Thy kingdom come,* I was conceived."

"I'faith!"

"The prayer went no farther, for in the cold light that all men look through after swiving, the rector knew the error of his ways and turned my mother out. From there 'twas no great step to harlotry, inasmuch as she was trained already to do the tricks of love as lightly as a deacon trims his candles, with no stirrings o' the heart. I was born and raised in the alleys o' Newgate, and ere ever I saw thirteen I had sold my first fruits for two pound sterling to a gentleman of St. Andrew's Undershaft and was walking the streets with Mother. 'Twas this led her to her second mistake, with the physician—"

"I doubt not 'tis a tale well worth the hearing," Ebenezer interrupted, "but I'd liefer you hasten to the matter at hand, else I'll not have time to hear you out."

"As't please ye," Mary chuckled. "I'll say no more than that my sister Katy was the issue of't, as was I of her first, and my mother died a-bearing. I was but fifteen then myself, and obliged to work the night through to feed the twain of us, but I raised Katy like my own daughter, and when she was old enough to stand the gaff but young enough to whet the jaded lust o' the wealthy, I made her a fine first match with a Scottish earl that was stopping in London, and prenticed her into the trade. When we learnt what prices were for women in the Plantations, 'twas I that brought us over and set us up in Maryland, where we plied our business with profit for many a year. Yet so far from feeling thankful for my care, young Kate did e'er abuse and despise me. She was wont to play the lady at every chance, and take my labors as her due, and declare 'twas my fault she was a whore. No man was good enough for Kate, and while 'tis true an air of refinement doth ever raise a harlot's price, she must never be refractory in the bed; but so capricious was dear Katy, she'd ofttimes lure a man to hire her and then throw his money in his face!

"Now there lived a wealthy Dutchman on the Little Choptank River, name of Wilhelm Tick. He was a jolly old widower, round as a ball and canny as a Jew, that had got his fortune raising livestock in lieu o' sot-weed. This Wilhelm had two grown sons named Willi and Peter, the one not worth a farthing and the other not worth a fart, that did naught from day to mortal day but drink Barbados rum and race their horses up and down the roads o' Dorset. They were great blond hulking wights, the pair of 'em, more crafty than bright, and since they knew they were old Wilhelm's only heirs, they were content to let him labor to an early grave whilst they spent a part of their inheritance in advance. 'Tis not marvelous to hear that little Kate was a great favorite with these gentlemen, so like were their tempers; devil the bit I warned her they were cruel and shifty louts, that oft as not drank up her fee before she had a penny of't, she would none o' my advice, and gave 'em their will o' her whene'er they pleased.

" 'Twas not till a year of this had passed that I learned her true plan: old Wilhelm, it turned out, knew well his sons were idle spendthrifts, that cared not to fig for all he'd done for them, and after much debate with himself had vowed to change his entire style of life. He resolved to toil no more to increase his wealth but enjoy what he had ere he died, and spend the balance of his years doing the things men do for pleasure.

"Just about this time Willi and Peter found that Katy would have no more of 'em, for all they bribed and threatened. And albeit none knows to this day how she contrived it, within the month she was the bride of Mynheer Wilhelm Tick himself, that little dreamed what he'd wed! The first the brothers knew of't was when they found her in their house, by Wilhelm's side, and their father said, 'Willi and Peter, this little girl is your new mother. We love each other with all our hearts, and ye must cherish and respect her as ye would your own mother if she were alive.'

"Then they were obliged to bow to Katy and kiss her hand, but as soon as Wilhelm was gone they turned on her, and held her by her arms, and said, 'What have ye told our father, to turn his feeble head? D'ye think to steal his wealth and leave us none? What will he say when we tell him thou'rt a Bridewell whore with lash-marks on your back, and have been swived by every wight in Dorset?' But Katy sniffed at their threats, for she had given Wilhelm to know she was an orphan and a virgin, and had been whipped by her heartless sister for not turning to harlotry. And to protect herself from harm, she threatened in turn that should they make a move to injure or malign her, she would complain to Wilhelm they were out to make him a cuckold. Thus they were obliged to stew in silence whilst their father doted shamefully on Kate, and jumped to please her slightest whim. On their wedding night she used every trick I'd taught her to make a man o' Mynheer Wilhelm, with small success; for unlike Boccaccio's leek——"

"Boccaccio!" cried the Laureate. "How is't you know Boccaccio? 'Tis too marvelous!"

Mary laughed. " 'Tis e'en more marvelous than ye think, as I'll explain anon. Unlike Boccaccio's leek, I was about to say, that hath a white head and a green tail, poor Wilhelm bore more likeness to the hound he called a *dachshund*, whose tail lags many paces behind his head and never can o'erhaul it. But by one means or another, Kate got him briefly starched, and then raised such a hue and cry ye'd have thought she was Pasiphaë being rogered by the bull."

" 'Sbody, madam! First Boccaccio and now Pasiphaë!"

"Old Wilhelm thought he'd got her maidenhead, and the more injury she feigned, the more he puffed with pride. Within the week he declared to Willi and Peter that inasmuch as Katy had brought him his first joy in years, he had altered the terms of his will and testament: one moiety of his estate was to pass to Kate, and the other to be divided between the boys.

"This the wastrels could not abide, more especially since their father had taken to toiling so strenuously in the bed that his health was slipping fast; 'twould not be long ere he perished of the effort, and they would be done out of their legacy. But so like to theirs in craftiness was Katy's disposition, she knew well what they schemed, and laid plans of her own to have the best of 'em."

At this point in her narrative Mary's face lost its perpetual expression of good humor; lowering her head, she worried a pebble on the ground with an oat-straw.

" 'Tis here that Charley Mattassin steps on stage," she said.

"Ah," Ebenezer's face brightened. "The murtherous salvage Indian."

"Ye speak from ignorance," Mary said sharply. "Methinks ye should have learned by now what folly it is to judge ere ye know the facts. Charley Mattassin was my lover, and the dearest lover e'er a woman had."

Ebenezer blushed and apologized.

"Charley Mattassin!" she sighed, and narrowed her downcast eyes. "I scarce know how to make ye see him clear."

"I have heard already he was the son of a salvage king," the poet offered, "and had a wondrous hatred of the English."

Mary nodded. "He was the son of Chicamec, that no white man hath seen and lived to tell it. His people are a kind of Nanticokes that call themselves *Ahatchwhoops;* they live to themselves in the wildest parts of the Dorset marshes, and move their town from place to place."

"Marry! Why doth the Governor not reduce 'em?"

"Because he ne'er could find 'em, for one thing. Besides, their number is small, and they live entirely amongst themselves. 'Tis easier to forget them than to hunt 'em out and kill 'em at the peril of your life and member. These Ahatchwhoops never look for trouble, but when an Englishman falls into their hands they either kill him or make him more wretched than a eunuch."

Ebenezer shuddered at the thought. "'Twas perilous to take one for a lover, was't not?"

Now tears welled up in Mary's eyes. "He was my first and only love, was Charley Mattassin. I was forty years old when I first saw him, and he no younger, but for the both of us 'twas love at first swiving. His father, Chicamec, had sent him on an embassy to another salvage king, Quassapelagh——"

"Quassapelagh!" cried the Laureate, and caught himself on the verge of revealing his connection with that fugitive chief.

"Aye, the famous Anacostin King that lately broke from jail. God alone knows what mischief lay behind the errand, but 'twas Mattassin's first adventure amongst the English. His plan then was to cross the Bay direct in his canoe, but he got no farther than the straits off Tangier Sound ere a squall o' wind drove him onto the Dorset mainland. 'Twas my good fortune I was going my rounds, and chanced to drive along a path beside the straits. Mattassin—he had no English first name then, of course—Mattassin had lost his canoe in the storm and, seeing he was in English country, had vowed to kill the first white man that passed and steal his horse. He hid himself in the bushes by the path, and when my wagon passed he sprang aboard and knocked me from the seat.

"His first thought was to take my scalp, but on reflection he resolved to rape me first." Mary's eyes shone. "D'ye grasp it, Master Poet? I'd been a whore for twenty-eight years, all told. Some twenty thousand times I had been swived—give or take a thousand—and by almost that many different men; there was no sort or size of man I had not known, so I'd have sworn, nor any carnal deed I was not master of. I had been forced too many times to count, by paupers and poltroons, and more than once myself had been employed to rape young men."

"Stay," Ebenezer exclaimed. "That is impossible!"

"Don't tempt me, dear," Mary warned with a smile. "I know your thoughts, but naught's impossible at the end of a pistol." She laughed and wept at once. "I've not told ye yet the best of all: he was not tall, was Charley, but he was a sturdy wight, and strong in the muscles; yet when he set about to do his deed, I saw he had no more to do't with than any pitiful puppy-dog! He was, I swear't, less blest by half than most boys in their cradles, and withal he meant to soil the honor o' Mary Mungummory! 'Tis as if ye took a bodkin to scuttle a frigate!

"So struck was I by the sight of him, 'twas only his tomahawk reined in my mirth, and I'd no more have resisted, than would a plowhorse the assault of a flea. 'Have done with't, Charley,' says I, making up the name for a tease, 'I've two trappers and a sot-weed factor waiting up the path.' Whereupon he set to work, and 'sbody, ere I knew what struck I was hollowing for joy!"

The Laureate frowned. "I am not privy to such matters, but this hath an air of *non sequitur,* or some other of the schoolmen's fallacies."

Mary breathed nostalgically. "I have known scholards aplenty, but no phalluses like this!"

"Nay, Miss Mungummory, you mistake my meaning!"

"And you mine," laughed Mary. "For you must know, sir, the wench that hath been twenty thousand times a harlot is no more a child: she could play Europa's game and be none the worse for't. But just as a blind man, lacking sight, grows wondrous keen of nose and ear, or a deaf-mute learns to hear with his eyes and speak with his hands, so had my Charley, unbeknownst to me, learnt strange and wondrous means to reach his end! Thus had good Mother Nature cleared her debt to him, after the fashion of the proverb: what she had robbed from Peter, she bestowed on Paul."

Ebenezer did not quite see the aptness of the saying, but he understood in substance what she meant.

" 'Tis past my knowledge what arts he practised, and past my power to tell my joy. Suffice it to say, there was enough o' Mother's blood in me that my heart was a castle, and of two hundred men not one had come in sight of't. But my Charley, that had not even a lance to tilt with, in two minutes' time had o'ertopped the breastworks, spanned the moat, hoist the portcullis, had his will of every crenel and machicoulis, and raised the flag o' passion from the merlons of my keep!"

" 'Sheart!" the poet whispered.

" 'Twas some time ere I regained my proper senses, but when I was myself again I laid hold of his hair, summoned all the lusty lore my years had taught me, and so repaid him in his coin that for half an hour he lay nine parts a-swoon. The upshot of't was, he ne'er saw town or father again, and got no closer to Quassapelagh than my wagon, wherein we lived thenceforth like hot-souled gypsies. I played the whore no more, but indented other girls to make my rounds, and clove to Charley like a silly bride."

"How is't he did not lose his hatred of the English?"

Mary chuckled and shook her head. "That is beyond my gifts to say. He was wondrous deep, was Charley, and sharp in the wits: in a month he'd learnt to read and speak our tongue like any gentleman; he made me scour the Province for books, and albeit I could not grasp the half of 'em myself, he always plumbed their meaning at a glance. 'Twas as if he'd thought the selfsame thoughts himself, and better ones. Yet for all they'd arouse him, he would not deign to read 'em himself, but set me to't, albeit 'twas not long ere I'd have to stop and ask him what was meant by such-a-word."

"Indeed!" Ebenezer marveled. " 'Twas thus you learnt to speak of Boccaccio and the Greeks?"

"Aye. How he loved and loathed the lot of 'em, and myself as well! Read him half a tale or half a chapter out o' Euclid, he could spin ye the balance from his head; and if it differed from the text, 'twas the author, like as not, that came off badly. Ofttimes I felt his fancy bore a clutch of worlds, all various, of which the world these books described was one—"

"Which, while 'twas splendid here and there," the Laureate interrupted, "he could not but loathe for having been *the case*."

"That's it!" Mary cried, her eyes bright. "You have laid your finger on its very root and fundament!"

Ebenezer sighed, recalling Burlingame. "I know a man who hath that genius, and that very manner: he loves the world, and comprehends it at first glance—sometimes even sight unseen—yet his love is flavored with contempt, from the selfsame cause, which leads him to make game of what he loves."

Tears ran freely down the harlot's ruddy cheeks. " 'Twas in like manner he looked on me," she said. "He loved me—of that I'm sure—yet for all my bag o' tricks I was merely woman, and but one woman. My Charley's curiosity and imagination knew no such bounds: I often pleased him, but ne'er surprised him; naught could I do that he'd not already dreamt of."

"And would you say," pressed the poet, much aroused, "that this cosmic love I spoke of was as strong in his flesh as in his fancy? What I mean, did he lust for aught that struck

449

his eye, be't man or maid or mandrake root, and yet despise the world for its meagerness of bedfellows?"

"That and more," Mary answered, "for so possessed was he with this same lust and fancy, he e'en despised himself that he could not fancy more! Marry come up, there never was the like of him in the history of the world!"

But Ebenezer covered his face with his hands and shook his head. "There was and is, wondrous as't may seem. My friend and former tutor, that till now I think I'd never fathomed, fits this picture marvelous well! Do you know the man they call Tim Mitchell?"

Mary's expression changed to alarm. "Are ye one o' Mitchell's spies, put here to draw me out?"

Surprised, Ebenezer assured her that he was not, and declared further, observing her great apprehension, "I did not mean that Mitchell was my friend and tutor, but that just as this Charley is so like my friend in every way—save the color of his skin and that defect of his natural parts you spoke of —so this Tim Mitchell, that I met not three days past, doth in some respects remind me of my friend. Past that I know naught o' the man."

"Thou'rt not his agent?"

"I swear not. Why is't you fear him so?"

Mary sniffed and glanced about her. "No matter why. Ye'll learn soon enough if ye take him for a friend." Beyond this she would say no more, and only with considerable entreaty could the poet persuade her even to return to the story, so uneasy had the name *Tim Mitchell* made her.

"What hath your lover Charley to do with Kate and Mynheer Tick?" he asked. " 'Twere cruel to leave so good a tale half-told."

" 'Tis not far to the end of't," Mary grumbled, and with some reluctance picked up the thread of her story. "Kate soon got wind of how my life was changed, and lost no time in seeking out the cause of't. I knew she'd set her cap for Charley directly she laid eyes on him, and so made every effort to avoid her. The plain fact is, 'twas not till he had killed her that I learned he'd been two months her lover."

"Nay!"

"He told me so himself, along with many another thing, before they took him off to jail. Somehow Miss Kate had sought him out, and told him she was my sister. She was fair of face, as I was not, and her body was a sweetmeat, where mine was e'er a nine-course meal. But for all her conniving she was dull and gameless, and a sluggard in the bed, and

450

spiteful, and a snot; and while Charley loved and hated me at once, he could only loathe a bitch like Kate, as even he confessed. In sooth, that is the explanation of't."

Ebenezer nodded. "An hour ago I'd not have grasped your meaning, but it seems no paradox now. Why did he do the awful murthers?"

"They hanged him for the lot of 'em," Mary said, "but Kate was the only one he slew. The rest slew one another, albeit dear Charley was the engineer."

She explained that on becoming Katy's lover, Charley had soon learned how matters stood in the house of Mynheer Tick, and for reasons not immediately clear had taken pains to gain the brothers' confidence—not a difficult achievement, since they were regular patrons of Mary's traveling brothel and knew no more than did its proprietress of his relationship with Kate. He guided them on hunting trips, raced horses with them, and at their invitation was a frequent visitor on the Tick estate, where he would drink and carouse on the lawn with Willi and Peter and slip away at intervals to cuckold Mynheer Wilhelm. It was not long before the brothers made known to him their fear and hatred of their stepmother, and Charley, with a laugh, at once proposed a double murder.

Willi had cried, "Thou'rt not serious!"

To which Charley had replied, " 'Twould be quite easy. Peter could go down to the end of the path that runs through the woods behind the house, and hide himself in the junipers where you were wont to swive Miss Katy in the old days. Then Willi can send Katy down there on some pretext, whereupon Peter leaps upon her and kills her. In the meanwhile, 'twill be simple for Willi to murther old Wilhelm alone in the house. Do't with a knife or tomahawk, and blame the Indians for't."

Willi had applauded the plan at once, but Peter, though he expressed his readiness to scalp Kate, was less enthusiastic on the matter of parricide. "A common whore is no great loss, but can we not leave Father to die naturally, or from grief? He is old, and shan't stand long 'twixt us and wealth."

Charley Mattassin had then replied, "Do as you wish, 'tis your affair; but methinks you'll be no sooner rid of Kate than he will wed the next wench with art enough to fool him."

"Aye," Willi had agreed. "Let's kill him now. He hath no love for us."

At length Peter was obliged to overcome his reluctance, and left the drinking-bout to take up his station at the end of the path, carrying with him his hunting knife. But scarcely had he gone before Willi, the cleverer of the two, began to question the division of responsibility.

" 'Tis nowise fair," he complained to Charley, "that I be given the tasteless task of murthering Father, whilst Peter hath Katy to himself in the junipers and may do his list with her ere he doth her in." And the longer he reflected, the less equitable seemed his lot, until at last, forgetting who had proposed the scheme, he commenced to blame Peter for it.

"Check your wrath," Charley had urged him then. "I planned it thus, and for a purpose: send Katy down to Peter, and then tell Wilhelm they are swiving in the junipers. Two of the three will soon be dead, and you've only to kill the third to have the whole estate yourself."

It did not take long for Willi to see the merits of this plan, and when a cursory search failed to discover his stepmother, he readily acted on the Indian's next advice: "Tell Wilhelm anyhow, and I shall run to warn Peter that his father comes to shoot him. The result will be the same, and in the meantime you can search farther for the whore and take your pleasure on her."

Willi went off beaming towards his father's accounting room, and Charley took a short cut through the marshes to the juniper grove where Peter waited, knife in hand. But so far from warning him of Wilhelm's approach, the Indian said "Mistress Kate is hurrying hither and never looked more fetching. Since you mean to kill her in any case, why not have your will of her first? Drop your breeches, man, and stand in ambuscado."

"Peter needed no urging," Mary Mungummory laughed, "for dull wits do not mean dull desires, and a clotpoll in the classroom may be brilliant in the bed: even as Charley left, the boy lowered his breeches, took cod in hand, and waited for his victim to arrive."

"But where was your sister whilst these machinations were in progress?" Ebenezer demanded.

Mary clucked her tongue. "She was neither innocent nor idle, ye may be sure." In fact, Mary explained, it was Kate, and not Charley, who had conceived the scheme to begin with. She had told him in detail of her fear of the brothers and of her life with Wilhelm—how, unable to aspire to natural intercourse, he obliged her to dance for him lasciviously every night in the accounting room, amid his tobacco-notes and business papers—and she had pledged to marry Charley and make him master of the Tick estate if he would aid her

452

in disposing of the other legatees. Their trysting-place was a thick clump of myrtles some distance down the path behind the house: hither it was that she would slip away any hour of the day or night when she heard her lover's signal—a high-pitched yelp like that of a fox or an Indian cur; here it was that she would linger while he caroused with the brothers, and wait for him to find pretext to join her; and here it was she lay this fateful evening, and watched the scheme unfold. She had seen Peter go down the path to the juniper trees and had even heard Charley urging him to rape before he slew; it was scarcely necessary for Charley to tell her, when immediately afterwards he joined her in the myrtles, that their conspiracy was under way. Moreover, their hopes were additionally confirmed a few moments later, for Wilhelm himself came stalking down the path, a pistol in each hand and anger in his face, clearly in response to Willi's announcement. And when he met his trouserless son, they could hear quite clearly the string of Dutch curses he let fly.

"Wait!" they heard Peter cry. "For the love o' God, don't shoot!"

And Wilhelm, to their disappointment, instead of firing at once, asked, "Where is your mother, Peter?"

"I do not know!"

"Why were ye standing so," Wilhelm had demanded then, "with your breeches in one hand and your shame in the other?"

And it must have been that Wilhelm had come closer as he spoke, and threatened with the pistols, for Peter grunted and then replied, "There ye see, 'twas but to ease nature I came hither!"

"Willi told me ye were swiving Katy from stump to stump," Wilhelm had declared.

"Ah," said Peter. "But I am not doing what Willi said, as any wight can see."

"Then why should Willi send me running hither?" his father wanted to know, and Peter asserted that it was not he but Willi who had designs on Kate and had sent Wilhelm out of the house in order to catch her alone and force her virtue.

"*Ach!*" said Wilhelm, and came crashing back along the path.

All this the two conspirators had clearly heard, and near the end of it, from the direction of the house, had come the voice of Willi calling Katy's name.

"What will happen now?" Katy had whispered to Charley.

" 'Tis time for Willi to give o'er his search for you," the

453

Indian replied. "If all goes well he'll come down the path to murther whoever's left alive, and Peter will come up to do the same."

He could explain no more, for by that time old Wilhelm had come as far as the clump of myrtles, brandishing his pistols and puffing with fatigue. In fact, such toll had his emotions and exertions taken on him, he suddenly stopped still, clutched his heart, and sat down on a gum stump in the middle of the path.

" 'Tis his foolish heart hath failed him!" Katy whispered, and Charley clapped his hand over her mouth just in time to prevent their discovery by Willi, who at that moment came running down the path with his musket at the ready.

"What ails you?" he asked his father.

Wilhelm clutched his son's arm and shook his head. "Why did you send me where no trouble was? Your brother was only pissing, nothing more."

"Fogh," sneered Willi. "Why should he walk a mile into the woods to piss, when for years he hath been doing it in the rosebush?"

"You send me to kill Peter, and Peter to kill you," Wilhelm went on, "and both have designs on my sweet Kate. Either way I lose a son, and belike my wife as well!"

"She is a whore, and you a fool," Willi declared, and let go a musket blast point-blank at his father's chest.

"Now I shall do the same to him," Katy had whispered then, and fetching a loaded pistol from her skirts, had taken aim at Willi. But again Charley had restrained her, for the sound of the shot had brought Peter hurrying from the junipers, and before Willi could get powder and ball into the gun, his brother was upon him with the knife. Over and over they rolled in the dirt, and in a minute Willi lay beside his father with an open throat.

Peter rose and wiped the knife blade on a leaf. "So," he said, and said no more, for Katy shot him in the chest where he stood.

"God be praised!" she had cried aloud when it was done. "I am free of the knaves at last!" And so moved was she by the spectacle of so many dead Dutchmen in the path, she would not leave without mounting the gum stump about which they lay and dancing, for Charley's benefit, the same dance that had served poor Wilhelm for love-making.

"So now you have your heart's desire," Charley had observed.

"And so shall you," Kate had called back from the stump. "Come hither, now, and celebrate our wealth!"

And not content to profane the dead by her dance alone, Katy had insisted that they do then and there on the gum stump what they were wont to do secluded in the myrtles, and had whooped and yelped throughout, Indian-fashion . . .

"Stay!" Ebenezer cried. "You do not mean to tell me——"

"No less," Mary declared. "What's more, he asked her to cry their secret signal-cry when the time came, and he did a thing that he and I had learnt together——a thing we'd vowed no other soul should share . . ."

"I say——" the poet protested, much embarrassed, but Mary raised her hand for silence.

"And when she instantly let out the signal cry, he fetched up his knife . . ."

"Nay! He murthered her then and there?"

Mary nodded. "I'll say no more than this, that what he did is a famous trick of soldiers the world over, Christian and heathen alike, with women of the enemy."

"I shall be ill if you say more," warned Ebenezer.

"There is no more to tell," Mary said. "He walked off and left 'em where they lay, all four together, and for want of heirs the estate passed over to the Crown. The joke of't was, as Charley had known from the first and not told either Kate or the brothers, 'twas not till the next sitting of the Maryland Council that old Wilhelm's plea for denizenship was due to be approved."

"I do not grasp the point."

"That means he died a Dutchman," Mary explained, "and aliens can't will property in the first place: the Crown would have got the estate in any event!" She laughed and got up off the stable floor. " 'Twas his huge enjoyment of this jest that undid Charley. That same night, in all innocence, I proposed to him we do our little secret, and he took such a fit o' laughing in the midst of't that I wept like a bride for the first time in my life! He vowed he was sorry, and by way of apology told the entire story just as you've heard it from me, laughing all the while, nor left out a single detail of't. He knew me inside out, did my sweet salvage: he knew 'twould tear my heart to hear he'd played me false, and doubly to hear 'twas Kate he'd done it with, and triply to hear he'd done her to death; yet he knew as well I must and would forgive him all —nay, he knew at bottom I would love him the more for't when the shock had passed, and he was right! What he *didn't* know, by a hundredth part, was how I prized our little trick, not alone that we'd discovered it together, but because 'twixt a man so ill endowed with manly parts and a woman too versed in men to be impressed by any such endowment, this trick of ours was the entire world o' love. 'Twas as if you and your mistress together had invented swiving, that no soul else on earth had thought of: think how ye'd feel then if she told ye, not that she'd kissed another man, but that she'd taught him all that glorious secret ye'd shared!"

"Really," Ebenezer said, "I——"

"Yes. Thou'rt still a virgin and can't know." Mary sighed. "Then bear't in mind, and one day ye'll see it clear enough. In the meanwhile 'tis enough to say, my Charley's error was to tell me he'd shared that thing with Katy. I'God, I could not speak, or weep another tear! I climbed from the wagon and ran down the road, nor stopped till I reached Cambridge, a day and a half later, and told the Sheriff that the Tick family was murthered, and their murtherer was Charley Mattassin!"

Again the tears coursed down her cheeks.

"They found him waiting in the wagon, little dreaming what I'd done, and packed him off to jail. I never spoke to him after that, but they say he took it as a farther joke that I had played him false, and laughed whene'er he thought of't. They say he still was chuckling when they led him to the gallows, and I saw myself that when the noose snapped tight two wondrous things occurred. The first I told ye at the outset, that what was small in life grew uncommon large in death, as sometimes happens; the other is that he died with that monstrous laugh upon his face, and bore it to the grave! That is the tale."

"I ne'er have heard its like," swore Ebenezer. " 'Tis pathetic and terrible at once, and I am still astonished by the likeness of this Indian to my friend and former tutor! I would venture to say that if your Charley had been born an Englishman he could play this world like a harpsichord, as doth my friend, and that if my friend had been born a salvage Indian, he too could die with just that laugh." He shook his head. "What is behind it? Your Charley and my friend, each in his way, came rootless to the world we know; each hath a wondrous gift for grasping it, e'en a lust for't, and manipulates its folk like puppeteers. My friend hath not yet laughed after Charley's fashion, and God grant he never shall, but the potential for't is there; I see it plainly from your tale. A certain shrug he hath, and a particular mirthless smile. 'Tis as though like Jacob he grapples yet with some dark angel in the desert, the which had got the better of your Charley; and 'tis no angel of the Lord whose votaries have this laugh for their stigma, do you think?"

Mary mused at the stable door: " 'Twas the whole o' God's creation Charley laughed at! I can hear him laugh at Kate when he did our thing to her, and again when she barked, and he put her to the knife; when I ride about my rounds or eat a meal, I hear that laugh, and it colors the world I look at, and sours the food in my belly! Naught remains o' Wilhelm Tick but his wretched ghost, that some say wanders nightly down Tick's Path; and naught remains o' Charley save that laugh. The while I told this tale to you I've heard it. Each night I see him laughing in the hangman's noose, and must needs liquor myself to sleep; yet all in vain, for sleep is but a hot dream of my Charley, and I wake with his voiceless laugh still in my ears. Ah God! Ah God!"

She could speak no more. Ebenezer accompanied her out to her wagon and helped her up to the seat, thanking her once more for her generosity and for telling him the tale.

" 'Twas curiosity alone that pricked me," he remarked with a rueful smile. "I took an interest in your Charley when first I heard of him from Father Smith in Talbot, and could not have said wherefore; but this tale of yours hath touched me in unexpected ways."

Mary picked up the reins and took her whip in hand. "Then ye must pray 'twill touch ye no farther, Master Laureate, for as yet thou'rt still an audience to that laugh."

"What do you mean?"

She leaned toward him, her great face puffed and creased with mirth, and answered in a husky whisper: "Yesterday at court, when ye keelhauled poor Ben Spurdance and signed your whole plantation o'er to that devil William Smith——"

Ebenezer winced at the memory. "I'God, then you were there to see my folly?"

"I was there. What's more, Cooke's Point was erst a station on my route: Ben Spurdance is an old and honest friend and client o' mine, and did your father as good a job as any overseer could. I had as great a wish as Ben to see Bill Smith undone . . ."

The Laureate was aghast. "You mean you saw what I was doing and knew 'twas done in ignorance? Dear Heav'n, why did you not cry out, or stay me ere I signed Smith's wretched paper?"

"I saw the thing coming the instant ye cried out who ye are," Mary replied. "I saw poor Ben grow pale at your speech, and the knave Bill Smith commence to gloat and rub his hands. I could have checked your folly in a moment."

"Withal, I heard no frenzied warnings," Ebenezer said bitterly, "from you or anyone else save Spurdance, his trollop of a witness, and my friend Henry—I mean Timothy Mitchell, that all had other reasons for alarm. The rest of the crowd only whispered among themselves, and I even heard some heartless devil laugh——" He checked himself and frowned incredulously at his benefactor. "Surely 'twas not *you!*"

" 'Twas *my* ruin as well as yours I laughed at, as Tim Mitchell might explain if ye should ask him. 'Tis a disease, little poet, like pox or clap! Where Charley took it, God only knows, but yesterday showed me, for the first time, I've caught it from him!" She snapped the reins to start her horse, and chuckled unpleasantly. "Stay virgin if ye can, lad; take your maidenhead to the tomb, and haply ye shan't ever be infected! *Hup* there!" She whipped up the horse and drove away, her head flung back in mute hilarity.

30

Having Agreed That Naught Is in Men Save Perfidy, Though Not Necessarily That Jus est id quod cliens fecit, the Laureate at Last Lays Eyes on His Estate

MUCH MOVED AND DISCONCERTED, Ebenezer stood for some moments in the courtyard. Disturbing enough had been the insight into Burlingame afforded him by the tale of Mynheer Tick: this final disclosure was almost beyond assimilation!

"I must seek Henry out at once," he resolved, "despite what he hath said of himself and Anna."

When he recalled Burlingame's taunting confessions of the night past, his skin broke into heavy perspiration, his legs gave way, and he was obliged to sit for a time in the dust with chattering teeth. In addition he took a short fit of sneezing, for it was not wholly perturbation that afflicted him: he very definitely was feverish, and his night in the corncrib had given him a cold as well. Many hours had passed since his last meal, yet he had no appetite for breakfast, and when he got to his feet in order to seek out Burlingame and lodge a complaint with the innkeeper regarding the theft of his clothes, the ground swayed under him, and his head pounded. He entered the inn and, oblivious to the stares his unusual appearance drew, went straight to the barman—not the same who had served him on the previous evening.

"By Heav'n!" he cried. " 'Tis the end of religion, when a man cannot sleep safely e'en in a corncrib! Is't a den of thieves you keep? Shall the Lord Proprietor learn that such crimes go unredressed in the inns of his province?"

"Haul in thy sheets, lad," the barman said. " 'Tis not wise to go on so of Lords Proprietors in these times."

Ebenezer scowled with embarrassment: in his dizziness he had forgotten, as he was increasingly wont to do, that Lord Baltimore had no authority in the Province and that he himself had never met that gentleman.

"Some wretch hath filched my clothes," he grumbled. The other patrons at the bar laughed—among them a plump, swarthy little man in a black suit who looked familiar.

"Ah well," the barman said, "that's not uncommon. Belike some wag threw your clothes in the fire for a joke, or took 'em to replace his own as was burnt. No hurt intended."

"As a joke! Marry, but you scoundrels have a nice wit!"

"If't gripe your bowels so, I'll not charge ye for last night's lodging. Fair enough?"

"You'd charge a man money to sleep in that rat's nest? You'll return me my clothes or replace 'em, and that at once, or laureateship be damned, all of Maryland shall feel the sting of my rhymes!"

The barman's expression changed: he regarded Ebenezer with new interest. "Thou'rt Mister Cooke, then, the Laureate of Maryland?"

"No other soul," Ebenezer said.

"The same that signed his property away?" He glanced at the black-suited man, who nodded confirmation.

"Then I have a message for ye, from Timothy Mitchell."

"From Timothy? Where is he? What doth he say?"

The barman fished a folded scrap of paper from his breeches. "He left us late last night, as I understand it, but writ this poem for ye to read."

Ebenezer snatched the paper and read with consternation:

To Ebenezer Cooke, Gentleman,
Poet & Laureate of the Province of Maryland

> *When from the Corn thou hiest thy Bum,*
> *And to the Tavern haply come,*
> *All stiff from chill Octobers Breezes,*
> *Full of Sniffs, and Snots, and Sneezes,*
> *Go not with many a Sigh and Groan*
> *To seek out Colt or fragrant Roan;*
> *For Roan, that seldom us'd to falter,*
> *Hath fairly this time slipt her Halter,*
> *And Colts gone with her, and I as well,*
> *Leaving thee to fry in Hell*
> *With all thy Poses and Buffoonery.*
> *Perchance this Piece of fine Poltroonery*
> *Will teach thee that with mortal Men*
> *'Tis Folly to call any Friend;*
> *For Friendship's but a fragile Farce*
> *'Twixt Man and Man. So kiss my Arse,*
> *Poor Ebenezer, foolish Bard—*
> *And henceforth ne'er relax thy Guard!*
>   *Timothy Mitchell, Esq*

For some moments after reading Henry's parting insults, Ebenezer was dumb struck.

"Friendship a farce 'twixt man and man!" he cried at last. " 'Twixt thee and me. Henry, let us say, for 'twixt me and thee it was no farce! Ah God, deliver me from such another friend!"

The swarthy fellow in the black suit observed these lamentations with amusement and said, "Bad news is't, Mister Cooke?"

"Bad news indeed!" the Laureate groaned. "Yesterday my whole estate; today my clothes, my horse, and my friend lost in a single stroke! I see naught for't but the pistol." Despite his anguish, he recognized the man as the advocate who had pled for William Smith in court.

"By Blaise's wool comb, 'tis a wicked world," the fellow observed.

"Thou'rt no stranger to its evils, methinks!" the poet said.

"Ah now, take no offense at me, friend: St. Windoline's crook, 'twas yourself that worked your ruin, not I! I merely labored for the interests of my client, as every advocate must. Sowter's my name—Richard Sowter, from down the county.

460

What I mean, sir, your advocate's a most pragmatical wight, that looks for justice no farther than his client's deeds. He tweaks Justinian's beard and declares that *jus est id quod cliens fecit*. Besides, the law's but one amongst my interests. Will ye take an ale with me?"

"I thank you," Ebenezer sighed, but declined on the grounds that his last night's liquor was still taking its toll on his head. "Forgive my rudeness, sir: I am most distraught and desperate."

"As well ye might be, by St. Agatha's butchered bosoms! 'Tis a wicked world, and rare ye find some good in't."

" 'Tis a wicked province; that I'll grant."

"Why," Sowter went on, " 'twas just last month, or the one before, a young sprat came to see me, young fellow from down-county, he was, came into the smithy where my office is—I run a smithy on the side, ye know—came in and says to me, 'Mr. Sowter,' he says, 'I need a lawyer.' 'St. Huldrick's crab lice!' says I: 'What have ye done to need a lawyer?' 'Mr. Sowter,' he says, 'I am a young fool, that I am,' he says 'I have lived the spendthrift life, have I, and got myself in debt.' 'Ah well,' says I, 'by Giles's hollow purse, I am no money-lender, son.' 'Nay, sir,' says he, 'the fact of't is, my creditors were pressing hard, and I feared 'twas the pillory for me, so what did I do? I hied me to Morris Boon, the usuring son o' Sodom.' 'Peter's fingers, boy,' says I, 'Ye did not!' 'I did,' says he: 'I went to Morris Boon and I says, *Morris, I need money,* I says. So Morris lent me on his usual terms: that directly my debts are paid I must surrender me to his beasty pleasures.' 'Thou'rt a Mathurin's fool!' cries I. 'That I am,' says the lad. 'Now I've settled all my debts, and Morris is waiting his pleasure.' 'Son,' I says then, 'pray to St. Gildas, for I cannot aid ye.' 'Ye must,' says he. 'I have faith in ye.' 'It wants more than faith,' says I. 'I have more than faith,' says he. 'I've wagered money on ye.' And so I asked him, how was that? And he replied, 'I wagered old Morris ye'd get me out o' my pickle.' 'St. Dymphna protects ye,' says I. 'What did ye wager?' 'If ye get me fairly out,' says he, 'Morris pays me again what he loaned me before, and 'tis yours for saving me. If not, why then Morris vows he'll ravish the twain of us from stump to stopgap.' 'Wretch!' says I. 'Had ye to fetch me thus into thy unclean bargain?'

"But there was no help for't," Sowter sighed. "On the morrow the lad comes back, with Morris the usurer hard upon his heels. 'Preserve me!' says the boy. 'Preserve thyself,' says Morris, and eyes me up and down. 'I want the payment we agreed upon.' But I'd not been idle since the day before, and so I said, 'Hold on, sir, by Appolonia's eye-teeth! Rein your horse! What sum was't ye lent this idler here?' 'Twelve hundredweight o' sot-weed,' says Morris. 'And for what purpose?' 'To pay his debts,' says Morris. 'And under what conditions?' 'That his debts once clear, he's mine whene'er I fancy him this month.' 'Well, then,' says I to the lad, that was like to beshit himself for fear, 'the case is closed, by Lucy's wick dipper: see to't ye never return him his twelve hundredweight.' 'Why is that?' asks the boy, and Morris as well. 'Why, Fridoline's eyeglasses.' says I, 'don't ye see't? If ye do not repay him, your debts aren't clear, and so long as thou'rt encumbered, ye need not go to Morris. The truth is, while thou'rt in debt thou'rt free!'

"St. Wulfgang's gout, sirs, I can tell ye old Morris set up a hollowing at that, for I had swived him fair, and he's a man of his word. He paid the young scamp another twelve hundredweight and sent him off with a curse; but the more he thought of't, the more my trick amused him, till at the end we laughed until we wept. Now then, by Kentigern's salmon, what was I after proving?"

"That naught's in men save perfidy," said Ebenezer. "Yet the lad was not wicked, nor were you in saving him."

"Ha! Little ye know," laughed Sowter. "My actual end was not to save the lad but to fox old Morris, who many a time hath had the better of me. As for the lad, by Wulstan's crozier, he never paid me, but took the tobacco-note himself and doubtless went a-whoring. There is a small good in men." He sighed. "Why, there's a redemptioner this minute in my boat——"

"No more!" cried Ebenezer, clutching his head in his hands. "What use have I for farther tales? The pistol now is all I crave, to end my pain."

"Oh la, St. Roque's hound-bitch!" Sowter scoffed. " 'Tis but the vagrant track o' life, that beds ye now in clover, now in thistles. Make shift to bear't a day at a time, and ten years hence ye'll still be sleeping somewhere, and filling thy bowels with dinner, and rogering some wench from Adrian to St. Yves."

" 'Tis light to advise," said the poet, "but this day itself shall see me starve, for I've naught to buy food with and nowhere to go."

"Cooke's Point is but a few hours' sail downriver. If I came half around the world to find a place, by St. Ethelbert I'd not blow out my brains till I laid eyes on't!"

This suggestion greatly surprised Ebenezer. "My valet awaits me there," he said thoughtfully, "and my—my betrothed as well, I hope. Poor Joan, and loyal Bertrand! What must they think of me!" He gripped Sowter's arm. "D'you think that scoundrel Smith hath turned them out?"

"There, now, by Pieran's millstone!" Sowter said. "Thou'rt angry, and anger's e'er a physic for despair. I know naught o' these folk ye speak of, but I'm sure they'll meet no ill reception at Malden. Bill Smith hath his shortcomings, yet he'd ne'er turn out your guests to starve, much less the Laureate himself. Why, haply your friend Tim Mitchell's there as well, and they're all at a game o' ducks and drakes, or dancing a morris dance!"

Ebenezer shook his head. "Yet e'en this last small joy shall be denied me, for I've not the hire of a boat."

"Why then, by Gudule's lantern, ye must come with me," the lawyer said, and explained that he meant to sail out to Malden that very morning, and the Laureate was welcome to come along as ballast. "I have some business there with Mr. Smith," he said, "and must deliver him a servant that I bought this morning for a song."

Ebenezer murmured some words of gratitude; he was, in fact, scarcely able to attend Sowter's speech, for his fever seemed to mount with every passing minute. When they left the inn and walked toward the wharf nearby, he viewed the scene before him as with a drunkard's eyes.

"—most cantankerous wight ye ever did see," he heard Sowter saying as they reached the wharf. "Swears by Gertrude's mousetrap he's no redemptioner at all, but a servant seller out o' Talbot, that is victim of a monstrous prank."

"I am not a well man," the Laureate remarked. "Really, I feel not well at all."

"I've heard my share o' clever stories from redemptioners," Sowter went on, "but St. Tom's packthread, if this one doth not take the prize! Why, would ye believe it——"

" 'Tis the seasoning, belike," Ebenezer interrupted, though it could not be said with certainty whether he was addressing Sowter or himself.

"Ye'll be all right, with a day in bed," the lawyer said. "What I was about to say—nay, not there: my boat's that small sloop yonder by the post—what I was about to say, this great lout claims his name is——"

"Tom Tayloe!" roared a voice from the sloop. "Tom Tayloe o' Talbot County, damn your eyes, and ye know't as well as I, Dick Sowter!"

"St. Sebastian's pincushion, hear him rave!" chuckled Sowter. "Yet his name is writ on the indenture for all to see: 'tis *John McEvoy*, plain as day, from Puddledock in London."

Ebenezer clutched a piling for support. " 'Tis my delirium!"

"Aye, St. Pernel's ague, thou'rt not thyself," the lawyer admitted.

"Ye know full well I'm not McEvoy!" shouted the man in the boat. "McEvoy was the wretch that duped me!"

Focusing his eyes on the sloop, Ebenezer saw the complainant shackled by one wrist to the gunwale. His hair was red, as was his beard, but even through the swimming eyes of fever Ebenezer saw that he was not the John McEvoy he had feared. He was too old, for one thing—in his forties, at the least—and too fat: a mountain of flesh, twice the size of fat Ben Oliver, he was quite the most corpulent human the poet had beheld.

"That is not John McEvoy," he declared, as Sowter helped him into the sloop.

"There, now, ye blackguard!" the prisoner cried. "E'en this skinny wretch admits it, that ye doubtless bribed to swear me false!" He turned imploringly to Ebenezer. " 'Tis a double injury I've been done, sir: this Sowter knows I'm not McEvoy, but he got the papers cheap and means to carry out the fraud!"

"Tush," Sowter answered, and bade his crewmen, of whom there were two, get the sloop under way. "I'm going below to draw up certain papers," he said to Ebenezer. "Ye may take your ease in the cabin till we raise Cooke's Point."

"I beg ye hear me out," the servant pleaded. "Ye said already ye know I'm not McEvoy: haply ye'll believe this is unjust."

" 'Tis no rare name," Ebenezer murmured, moving toward the cabin. "I'll own the John McEvoy I once knew had your red hair, but he was slight and all befreckled, and a younger man than I."

"That is the one! I'Christ, Sowter, can ye go on now with your monstrous trick? This wight hath drawn the very likeness of the man that sold me!"

"By David's leek, man," Sowter said testily. "Ye may file complaint at court the day thou'rt settled on Cooke's Point, for all o' me. Till then thou'rt John McEvoy, and I've bought your papers honestly. Tell Mr. Cooke your troubles, if he cares to hear 'em."

With that he went below, followed by the prisoner's curses,

but Ebenezer, at the first heel of the vessel, felt more ill than at any other time in his life except aboard the *Poseidon*, in the storm off the Canary Islands, and was obliged to remain in misery at the leeward rail.

"This McEvoy," he managed to say. " 'Tis quite impossible he's the one I know, for mine's in London."

"E'en so was mine, till six weeks past," the fat man said.

"But mine's no servant seller!"

"No more was mine, till late last night: 'tis I that sells redemptioners for my living, but this accursed young Irishman did me in, with Sowter's aid!"

Ebenezer shook his head. " 'Tis unthinkable!" Yet he knew, or believed, that Joan Toast had come to Maryland—for reasons he could only vaguely guess at—and also that at the time of his own departure from London, John McEvoy had had no word of his mistress for some days. "Would God my head were clear, so I might think on't, what it means!"

The prisoner interpreted this as an invitation to tell his tale, and so commenced:

"My name is not McEvoy, but Thomas Tayloe, out of Oxford in Talbot County. Every planter in Talbot knows me—"

"Why do you not complain in court, then," the poet interrupted thickly, "and call them in as witnesses?" He was seated on the deck, too ill to stand.

"Not with Sowter as defendant," Tayloe said. "For all his sainting he is crooked as the courts, and besides, the wretches would lie to spite me." He explained that his trade was selling redemptioners: poor folk in England desirous of traveling to the colonies would, in lieu of boat fare, indenture themselves to an enterprising sea captain, who in turn "redeemed" their indentures to the highest bidders in port—a lucrative speculation, since standard passenger fare for servants was only five pounds sterling, more or less, and the indenture-bonds of artisans, unmarried women, and healthy laborers could be sold for three to five times that amount. Those whom it was inconvenient or insufficiently profitable for the captain to sell directly he "wholesaled" to factors like Tayloe, who would then attempt to resell the hands to planters more removed from the port of call. Tayloe's own specialty, it seemed, was purchasing at an unusually low price servants who were old, infirm, unskilled, troublesome, or otherwise especially difficult for the captain to dispose of, and endeavoring to "retail" them before the expense of feeding them much raised his small investment.

" 'Tis a thankless job," he admitted. "Were't not for me

those pinch-penny planters with their fifty-acre patches would have no hands at all, yet they'll pay six pounds for a palsied old scarecrow and hold me to account for't he is no Samson. And the wretched redemptioners claim I starve 'em, when they know very well I've saved their worthless lives: they're the scum o' the London docks, the half of 'em, and were spirited away drunk by the captain: if I didn't take them off his hands in Oxford, he'd sign 'em on as crewmen for the voyage home, and see to't they fell to the fishes ere the ship was three days out."

" 'Tis a charitable trade you practice, I'm persuaded," Ebenezer said in a dolorous voice.

"Well, sir," he declared, "just yesterday the *Morpheides* moored off Oxford with a troop o' redemptioners——"

"The *Morpheides!* Not Slye and Scurry's ship?"

"No other," Tayloe said. "Gerrard Slye's the grandest speculator in the trade, and Scurry is his equal. They are the only order-captains in the Province. Suppose thou'rt a planter, now, and need you a stonemason for four years' work: ye put your order in with Slye and Scurry, and on the next voyage there's your mason."

"No more: I grasp the principle."

"Well then, 'twas yesterday the *Morpheides* moored, and out we all went to bid for redemptioners. They were fetching 'em up as I boarded, and the crew was passing pots o' rum for us buyers. When they brought this redhaired wight on deck he took one look at the shore, broke away from the deckhands, and sprang o'er the side ere any man could stop him. 'Twas his ill luck to light beside the *Morpheides*'s own boat; the mate and three others hauled him back aboard and clapped him into leg irons with promise of a flogging, and I knew then I'd have him ere the day was out."

"Poor McEvoy!" mumbled the Laureate.

" 'Twas his own doing," Tayloe said. "Would God they'd let the whoreson drown, so I'd not be shackled here in his place!" He sniffed and spat over the gunwale. "In any case, the captains filled their orders for bricklayers, cobblers, boatwrights, and the like, and put up for bids a clutch o' cabinet-makers and carpenters, and a sailmaker that fetched 'em twenty-three pounds sterling. As a rule they'd have peddled off the lassies after that, but in this lot the only ladies were a brace o' forty-year spinsters out to catch husbands, so instead they brought their field hands out, and bid 'em off for twelve to sixteen pound. After the field hands came the ladies, and went for cooks at fourteen pounds apiece. When they were

466

sold, only four souls remained, besides the red-head: three were too feeble for field work and too stupid for anything else, and the fourth was so ravaged with the smallpox, the look of him would retch a goat. 'Twas a lean day, for 'tis my wont to buy a dozen or more, but I dickered with Slye and Scurry till at last I got the five for twenty pounds—that's a pound a head less than 'twould've cost to bring 'em over if they'd eaten twice a day, but Slye and Scurry had so starved 'em they were fit for naught but scarecrows, and had some profit e'en at twenty pound.

"They took the red-head's leg irons off and bade him go peaceably with me or take his cat-o'-nine-tails on the spot. By the time I got the five of them ashore, roped round the ankles, and loaded into the wagon, 'twas late in the afternoon, and I knew 'twould be great good fortune to sell even one by nightfall. 'Twas my plan to stop at the Oxford tavern first, to try if I could sell to a drunkard what he'd ne'er buy sober, and thence move on with the worst o' the lot to Dorset, inasmuch as servant-ships rarely land there, and the planters oft are short o' help. The Irishman set up a hollowing for food, whereat I smote him one across the chops, but for fear they'd band together and turn on me, I said 'twas to fetch 'em a meal I stopped at the tavern, and they'd eat directly I'd done seeking masters for 'em. Inside I found two gentlemen in their cups, each boasting to the company of his wealth, and seized the chance to argue my merchandise. So well did I feed their vanity, each was eager to show how lightly he bought servants; and I was careful to bring their audience out as well. The upshot of it was, when Mr. Preen bought the pox-ridden lout, Mr. Puff needs buy two of the ancient dotards to save face. What's more, they durst not bat an eye at the price I charged, though I'll wager it sobered the twain of 'em on the instant!

"I hurried off then with the other two, ere my gentlemen had breath to regret their folly, and steered my course for Cambridge. McEvoy hollowed louder than before, that I'd not fed him: even Slye and Scurry, he declared, had given him bread and water on occasion. Another smite I smote him, this time with the horsewhip, and told him if I'd not saved him he had been eaten instead of eating. I despaired o' selling either that same night, inasmuch as McEvoy, albeit he was young and passing sturdy, was so plain a troublemaker that no planter in his senses would give a shilling for him, and his companion was a crook-backed little Yorkshireman with a sort of quinsy and no teeth in his head, who looked as if he'd die ere the spring crop was up; but at the Choptank ferry landing I had another stroke o' luck. 'Twas after dark, and the ferry was out, so I took my prizes from the wagon and led 'em a small ways down the beach, towards Bolingbroke Creek, where we could do whate'er we needed ere we crossed. We'd gone no more than forty yards ere I heard a small commotion just ahead, behind a fallen tree, and when I looked to see the cause of't, I found Judge Hammaker o' the Cambridge court, playing the two-backed beast with a wench upon the sand! He feigned a mighty rage at being discovered, and ordered us away, but once I saw who he was and called him by name, and asked after his wife's health, he grew more reasonable. In sooth, 'twas not long ere he confessed he was in great need of a servant, and though his leanings were toward McEvoy, I persuaded him to take the Yorkshireman instead. Nay, more, when he agreed that one old servant is worth two young, I charged him twenty-four pounds for Mr. Crookback—near twice the price of an average sturdy field hand. E'en so he got off lightly: the wench he'd been a-swiving had seemed no stranger to me, albeit the darkness and her circumstances had kept me from placing her; but once I'd crossed to Cambridge with McEvoy and heard o' the day's court cases from the drinkers at the inn, it struck me where I'd seen the tart before. She was Ellie Salter, whose husband hath a tavern in Talbot County—the same John Salter who'd got a change of venue to the Cambridge court in his suit with Justice Bradnox, and had won a judgment from old Hammaker that very afternoon! I scarce need tell ye, had I learnt that tale in time 'tis *two* new servants he'd have bought, and paid a swingeing sixty pounds sterling for the pair!

"Yet I'd done a good day's work, at that; I'd sold four worthless flitches that same evening, where I'd hoped to sell one at most, and had above fifteen hundredweight o' sot-weed for 'em, or sixty-three pounds sterling, forty-seven whereof was profit free and clear. 'Twas cause for celebration, so I thought, and though I meant still to try amongst the drinkers to find a buyer for McEvoy, I drank a deal more rum than is my wont and made me a trip upstairs to one o' Mary Mungummory's girls."

"I knew I'd seen your face before," said Ebenezer. "I am Eben Cooke of Cooke's Point, the same that gave his estate away at yesterday's court. I too drank much last night: the rum was at the good fellows' expense, but the sport, I fear, at mine."

"I place ye now!" cried Tayloe. " 'Twas the change of dress misled me."

Ebenezer told as briefly as he could—for he found it ever more difficult to speak plainly and coherently—how he had been robbed of his clothing in the corncrib and rescued by Mary Mungummory herself; and without going into any detail about McEvoy's responsibility for his presence in the Province, he marveled at the coincidence of the Irishman's proximity throughout the evening.

"Marry," said Tayloe, " 'twould not surprise me to learn 'twas he that stole your clothes, he's that treacherous! Out from the tavern I came, so full o' rum I scarce could walk. Just as you made shift in the corncrib, so I climbed up on the wagon with McEvoy to sleep out the balance of the night, and ere I pulled the blanket over me, that I carried for such occasions, I fetched out my knife and threatened him with it, to carve him into soup-beef if he laid a hand on me. Then I went to sleep, nor knew another thing till dawn this morning, when I woke as Sowter's servant!"

"Dear God! How did that happen?"

Tayloe growled and shook his head. "The rum was at the root of't," he declared. "My error was to lay the knife down by my head, against his leaping me, and I was too drunken to lay it out of his reach. I had him hog-tied, but in some wise he wriggled over without waking me and cut himself free with the knife. 'Tis a marvel and astonishment he didn't murther me outright, but I slept like a whelp in the womb, and in lieu of killing me, Mr. McEvoy picks me clean. Out comes my sixty-three pounds—the most, thank Heav'n, in sot-weed bills that he dare not try to exchange in Talbot or Dorset, but five or six pounds in coin o' the realm—and then out comes the happiest prize of all: my half o' the wretch's indenture-bond! Armed with these, from what I gather, he strides bold as brass into the tavern, bribes him a meal, and rousts up Mary Mungummory's girls for a go-round, spending my silver with both his hands. Then at dawn, whilst I'm still dead asleep o' the rum, he crosses paths with Sowter, and there's the end o' me! Had he struck his foul bargain with any soul else, he'd have got no farther than the calling of his name; but Sowter, though he knows me well for all his feigning, would swear for a shilling that King William was the Pope. They made me out to be McEvoy, and for two pounds sterling Sowter bought the indenture-bond. The first I knew of't was when his bullies came to fetch me and led me off on the end of a rope and shackled me here to the gunwale. I'm indented to four years' labor for the master o' Malden, that I hear is Sowter's crony, and the real McEvoy, that hid out o' sight till I was led off, hath doubtless flown the coop with my cart and horse. Nor can I carry my complaint to court, for the bond says of McEvoy only that he hath red hair and beard and is slight of build: my master will argue my size is proof o' his care for me. What's more 'tis Sowter I must sue, that is an eel to catch in a court o' law, and for every friend who'd swear I am Tom Tayloe, he'd find three ingrates that will vow I'm John McEvoy. Yet e'en if these things were not so, my case would still be heard in the court at Cambridge, and on the bench would be Judge Hammaker himself! In short, I go to Malden in straits as sorry as yours—swived by Richard Sowter from bight to bitter end!"

Ebenezer sighed. " 'Tis a sorry tale in truth," he said, though in fact he rather sympathized with McEvoy and more than a little suspected that the redemption-dealer had got his due. "Yet withal thou'rt something better cased than I——" He was seized with another fit of seasickness, after which he clung weakly to the gunwale. "I have not even health enough to bewail my lot."

"Nor time, by Crispin's last," said Richard Sowter, who had emerged from the sloop's cabin in time to hear this last remark, "for yonder off to larboard is Castlehaven Point, and two points farther down is Cooke's."

Ebenezer groaned. "What tidings those should be! And yet 'tis like a knell of death, for de'il the bit I want to see my home, 'tis mine no more, and once I've seen it my life is done."

"Oh la," said Sowter, "there's always some expedient. Ye may at least console yourself 'twas not rum, wrongheadedness, or the rage o' the mob brought ye low, but simple pride and innocence, such as have ruined many a noble wight before. See that house yonder in the poplars?"

The sloop had cleared Castlehaven Point and was now laid over on a starboard tack due westward into a fresh breeze blowing from the Bay. Ashore off the larboard beam had appeared a large white clapboard manor.

"Not Malden so soon!" cried the poet.

"Nay, St. Clement's anchor, 'tis Castlehaven, and where it stands once stood a very castle of a manor-house called *Edouardine*, that was built to last till the end o' time. *There* is a tale o' costly pride, if the truth of it were known."

Ebenezer remembered the story of the young woman

whom his father had rescued from drowning and who had served as wet nurse for himself and Anna until Andrew's return to England. "Methinks I have heard the name," he said gloomily. "I've not fortitude enough to hear the tale."

"Nor I time to tell it," Sowter replied. He pointed to a wooded spit of land some five or six miles to westward, across the expanse of the river's mouth. "There lies Cooke's Point ahead. Ye'll see Malden in a minute, when we're closer."

"God damn your lying soul, Dick Sowter!" cried Tom Tayloe. "Will ye carry this fraud so far?"

Sowter smiled as if surprised. "St. Cuthbert's beads, sir, I know not what fraud ye speak of. Pardon me whilst I get my papers ready for Mr. Smith."

When he had gone again into the cabin, Tayloe clutched at Ebenezer's deerskin shirt. "Thou'rt ill, are ye not, and want nursing back to health?"

"That I'm ill is clear," Ebenezer answered. "But what need hath a ruined man of health? I mean to have one look at Malden and end my life."

"Nay, man, that were foolish! Ye have been swived out o' your rightful place, as I have been, but thou'rt not disliked amongst the public and the courts. Smith and Sowter have undone ye for the present, yet it wants but time, methinks, and careful thought, to have your manor back."

Ebenezer shook his head. "That is vain hope, and cruel to entertain."

"Not at all!" Tayloe insisted. "There is the Governor to appeal to, and belike thy father hath some influence in court. With time enough, and patience, thou'rt sure to find some trick. Why, I'll wager ye have not even seen a barrister yet, that might match old Sowter's craft with craft of his own."

Ebenezer admitted that he had not. "Yet 'tis a lost cause after all," he sighed. "I've not a penny to subsist on, nor any friend to borrow from, and scarce can walk for fever."

"That is my point exactly," Tayloe said. "Ye know I'm not McEvoy, and have been falsely bonded for a servant, and I've shown ye how hopeless is my case. Once I set foot on Cooke's Point I lose four years o' my life—nay, more; 'twill be no chore for Sowter to have the term drawn out on some pretext, since he knows Judge Hammaker will support him."

"Haply 'tis my illness," said Ebenezer. "I fail to see what connection——"

"If this Smith signs my indenture-bond, I'm lost," Tayloe said desperately. "But if 'twere *you* he bonded . . ."

"I!"

"Pray hear me out!" the fat man pleaded. " 'Twould be the answer to both our problems if you served in my stead. I would be free o' Sowter's clutches, and 'tis the master's obligation to feed, clothe, and house his servants, and nurse 'em when they're ill."

Ebenezer screwed up his features as if to aid him in assimilating the idea. "But to be a servant on my own estate!"

"So much the better. Ye can keep your eyes open for ways to get your due. And once I'm free, d'ye think I'll e'er forget your kindness? I'll move Heav'n and earth in your behalf; notify your father——"

"Nay, not that!" Ebenezer blanched at the thought.

"Governor Nicholson, then," Tayloe amended hastily. "I'll petition Nicholson himself, rouse the folk in Dorset to your cause! They'll ne'er sit idly whilst their Laureate leads a servant's life!"

"But four years a menial——"

"Fogh! 'Twill never last four weeks, once I set to work. 'Tis the master o' Malden ye'll be indented to, not Smith himself, and as soon as Malden's in your hands again, ye may use your bond for a bumswipe."

Ebenezer laughed uneasily. "I cannot say your plan hath not some merits——"

" 'Twill save your life, and mine as well!"

"—and yet I scarce can fancy Sowter's hearing you out, much less agreeing."

"There is the key to't!" Tayloe whispered urgently, and drew the Laureate closer. " 'Twere wise *you* make the plea —and not to Sowter, but to Smith, who hath no reason to be my enemy. One servant should be as good as another to him."

"Yet if 'twere I," Ebenezer mused, recalling again the story of his wet nurse, "I'd be more inclined to hire a healthy servant than an ill."

"Not if the ill is willing," Tayloe corrected, "whilst the healthy shows every sign o' making trouble. Make your bargain with Smith, as if 'twere but your motive to regain your health and redress the great injustice of my case."

Ebenezer smiled bitterly. "He knows me already for a man most interested in justice! And belike 'twill please him to have his erstwhile master for a common servant . . ."

Tayloe made as if to embrace him. "Bless ye, sir! Ye'll do't, then?"

Ebenezer drew back. "I've not consented, mind. But 'tis that or suicide, and so it deserves some thought."

Tayloe caught his hand and kissed it. " 'Sheart, sir, thou'rt a very Christian saint!"

"Which is to say, fit meat for martyring," the Laureate answered, "a morsel for the wide world's lions."

The reappearance of Sowter on deck ended their conversation. "Say what ye will," he declared, not clearly apropos of anything, " 'twas a passing fine property to lose, by Martin's rum pot, and were I in thy shoes I'd do all in my power to retrieve it—e'en if 'twere no more than praying to St. Elian, the recoverer of lost goods."

As he spoke he was gazing narrow-eyed out to sea, so that for a moment Ebenezer feared he'd overheard their plans and was hatching some retaliation. But then he said, "Lookee yonder, lad," and with a sheaf of rolled-up documents pointed westward in the direction of his gaze. Though still some two or three miles from shore, the sloop had beaten close enough on its starboard tack so that individual trees could be distinguished—maples and oaks on the higher ground and loblolly pines near the beach—and a boat dock could be seen extending toward them from a lawn of grass that ran back to a white wooden house of gracious design and ample dimensions.

"Is there a tale to that one too?" Ebenezer asked without interest.

"St. Veronica's sacred snot-rag, boy, thou'rt a better judge than I," the lawyer laughed. " 'Tis Malden."

31

The Laureate Attains Husbandhood at No Expense Whatever of His Innocence

As Sowter's sloop drew nearer to the shore, the estate became visible in more detail, and Ebenezer gazed at it with an ever queasier stomach. The house, to be sure, was somewhat smaller than he had anticipated, and of perishable white-painted clapboards rather than the fieldstone one might wish for; the grounds, too, evidenced little attention to artful land-scaping on the part of his father and indifferent care on the part of the residents. But viewed through the triple lenses of fever, loss, and earliest childhood memories, the place took on a noble aspect.

His first thought, oddly, was of his sister Anna. "Dear Heav'n!" he reflected, and tears made his vision swim. "I have let our ancient home slip through my fingers! God curse such innocence!"

This last ejaculation reminded him of Andrew, and though he shuddered at the thought of his father's wrath when the news reached England, he could not help almost wishing that that rage and punishment were upon him, so more miserable and unconsoling was his present self-contempt. Tayloe's star-tling proposal was rendered more attractive by this notion: not only would it provide him with the subsistence and medi-cal care he needed and a chance, however slim, of regaining the estate; indenturing himself to the "master of Malden" would also be a punishment—indeed, to his essentially poetic and currently feverish fancy, even a kind of atonement—for his misdeeds. His innocence had cost him his estate; very well, then, he would be the servant of his innocence—and perhaps, even, as the term *redemptioner* implied, expiate thereby his folly by undoing the cooper William Smith.

When the sloop made fast to the dock, Sowter left Tayloe shackled to the gunwale and invited Ebenezer to accompany him up to the house.

"'Tis not for me to say how welcome ye'll be, but at the least ye may enquire about your servant and your lady friend, and have a look about."

"Aye, and I must see Smith as well," the Laureate said weakly. "I have a thing to say to him."

"Ah, well, we have some business to attend to, he and I, but after that——Lookee, by Goodman's needle! There he comes to greet us. Hallo, there!"

The cooper waved back from the doorway of the house and walked down the lawn in their direction, accompanied by a woman in a Scotch-cloth gown.

"I'faith!" Ebenezer exclaimed. "Is that the trollop Susan Warren?"

"Mr. Smith's daughter," Sowter reminded him.

As they drew nearer, Susan regarded the Laureate intently; Ebenezer, for his part, was filled with anger and shame, and avoided her eyes.

474

"Well, well," Smith cried, " 'tis Mister Cooke! I did not know ye at first in your new clothes, sir, but thou'rt welcome to Malden for certain and must stay to dinner!"

"Methinks he's ill," Susan said with some concern.

"I am sick unto death," Ebenezer said, and could say no more; he swayed dizzily on his feet, and was obliged to catch Sowter's arm to keep from falling.

"Take him inside," Smith ordered Susan. "Haply Doctor Sowter can give him a pill when we've done our business."

The girl obediently and to the Laureate's embarrassment put his arm across her shoulders and led him toward the house. Except that she seemed to have washed, she was as ragged and unkempt now as when he had first seen her driving Captain Mitchell's swine, and even the brief glimpse of her that his shame permitted was enough to show that her face and neck were even more disfigured than before by marks and welts.

"Where is Joan Toast?" he asked, as soon as he was able. "Hath your wretch of a father mistreated her?"

"She never did arrive," Susan answered shortly. "Belike she misdoubted your intentions: a whore hath little grounds for faith in men."

"And a man for faith in whores! I swear you this, Susan Warren: if you have been party to any injury to that girl, you'll suffer for't!" He wanted to press her further, but aside from his weakness there were two unpleasant considerations that kept him from pursuing the subject: in the first place, Joan might well have learned that the man she sought was suddenly a pauper and thus, in her eyes, no longer worth seeking; in the second, she might have got word of McEvoy's having followed her to Maryland, and gone to join him instead. Therefore, when Susan assured him that if any injury had befallen Joan Toast it was not at her, Susan's, hands, he contented himself with asking after Bertrand, whom Burlingame had dispatched to St. Mary's City to retrieve the Laureate's baggage.

"The trunk ye sent him to fetch is here," the girl replied. " 'Twas sent over by the packet from St. Mary's. But of the man I've seen no trace, nor heard a word."

"Whom Fortune buffets, the whole world beats," sighed Ebenezer. " 'Tis best for both if they've found new ground to graze, for I've naught to keep wife or servant on any more. But withal, their lack of loyalty wounds me to the quick!"

They entered the house, and though the interior showed

475

the same need of attention as the outside, the rooms were spacious and adequately furnished, and the Laureate wept to see them.

"How like a paradise Malden seems to me, now I've lost it!" He found it necessary to sit down, but when Susan made to assist him he waved her away angrily. "Why feign concern for a sick and feckless pauper? I doubt not you've made peace with your father, now he's a gentleman planter—get thee gone and play the great lady on my estate! What, you have a tear for me, do you? *When all's consum'd, repentance comes too late.*"

Susan dabbed immodestly at her eyes with the hem of her threadbare dress. "Thou'rt not the only person injured by your day in court."

"Ha! Your father birched you, did he, for taking the stand against him?"

Susan shook her head sadly. "Things are not as they seem, Mister Cooke——"

"I'God!" Ebenezer clasped his head. "The old refrain! My estate and Anna's dowry is lost, my best friend hath betrayed me and left me to starve, the woman I love hath either met foul play or scorned me for a pauper, I am as good as disowned by my father and near dead of the seasoning, and in my final hours on earth I must abide the wisdom of a thankless strumpet!"

"Haply ye'll understand one day," Susan said. "I have no wish to do ye farther hurt than ye've done yourself already!"

With this remark the woman fled weeping from the room.

"Nay, wait!" the Laureate begged, and despite his illness he set out after her to apologize for his unkind words. He was, however, unable to move with any haste or efficiency, and soon lost her. He wandered through a number of empty rooms, uncertain of his objective, until at last he found himself in what appeared to be the kitchen. Three women, all in the dress of servants, were playing a game of cards around a table; they regarded him uncordially.

"I beg your pardon, ladies," he said, leaning against the doorframe; "I am looking for Mrs. Susan Warren."

"Then thou'rt seeking an early grave," the dealer quipped, and the others laughed merrily. "Get along with ye, now; 'tis too early in the day to bother Susie or any o' the rest of us."

"Forgive me," Ebenezer said hastily. "I had no mind to intrude upon your game."

" 'Tis but a simple hand of lanterloo," said the woman with the cards.

"Simple to misdeal!" cried another, who spoke with a French accent. "What is it that you do? Cheat me?"

"Ye dare call me a cheat!" the first replied. "Thou'rt something brave for one not a fortnight loose o' your serving-papers!"

"Hold thy tongue, *boîte sèche!*" growled the French woman. "I know Captain Scurry swived you for your freight, what time he fetched you off the streets and shipped you hither!"

"No more than Slye did you," cried the dealer, "though God alone knows why a man would swive a sow!"

"I beg your pardon," Ebenezer interrupted. "If you are servants of the house——"

"Non, certainement, I am no servant!"

"The truth is," said the dealer, "Grace here's a hooker."

"A what?" asked the poet.

"A hooker," the woman repeated with a wink. "A *quail,* don't ye know."

"A quail!" the woman named Grace shrieked. "You call me a quail, you—*gaullefretière!*"

"Whore!" shouted the first.

"Bas-cul!" retorted the other.

"Frisker!"

"Consoeur!"

"Trull!"

"Friquenelle!"

"Sow!"

"Usagère!"

"Bawd!"

"Viagère!"

"Strawgirl!"

"Sérane!"

"Tumbler!"

"Poupinette!"

"Mattressback!"

"Brimballeuse!"

"Nannygoat!"

"Chouette!"

"Windowgirl!"

"Wauve!"

"Lowgap!"

"Peaultre!"

"Galleywench!"

"Baque!"

"Drab!"

"Villotière!"
"Fastfanny!"
"Gaure!"
"Ringer!"
"Bringue!"
"Capercock!"
"Ancelle!"
"Nellie!"
"Gallière!"
"Chubcheeker!"
"Chèvre!"
"Nightbird!"
"Paillasse!"
"Rawhide!"
"Capre!"
"Shortheels!"
"Paillarde!"
"Bumbessie!"
"Image!"
"Furrowbutt!"
"Voyagère!"
"Pinkpot!"
"Femme de vie!"
"Rum-and-rut!"
"Fellatrice!"

"Ladies! Ladies!" the Laureate cried, but by this time the cardplayers, including the two disputants, were possessed with mirth, and paid him no heed.

"Coxswain!" shouted the one whose turn it was to play.

"Trottière!" Grace replied.

"Conycatcher!"
"Gourgandine!"
"Tart!"
"Coquatrice!"
"Fluter!"
"Coignée!"
"Cockeye!"
"Pelerine!"
"Crane!"
"Drôllesse!"
"Trotter!"
"Pellice!"
"Fleecer!"
"Toupie!"
"Fatback!"

478

"*Saffrette!*"
"Nightbag!"
"*Reveleuse!*"
"Vagrant!"
"*Postiqueuse!*"
"Arsebender!"
"*Tireuse de vinaigre!*"
"Sally-dally!"
"*Rigobette!*"
"Bitch!"
"*Prêtresse du membre!*"
"Saltflitch!"
"*Sourdite!*"
"Canvasback!"
"*Redresseuse!*"
"Hipflipper!"
"*Personnière!*"
"Hardtonguer!"
"*Ribaulde!*"
"Bedbug!"
"*Posoera!*"
"Hamhocker!"
"*Ricaldex!*"
"Bullseye!"
"*Sac-de-nuit!*"
"Brecchdropper!"
"*Roussecaigne!*"
"Giftbox!"
"*Scaldrine!*"
"Craterbutt!"
"*Tendrière de reins!*"
"Pisspallet!"
"*Presentière!*"
"Narycherry!"
"*Femme de mal recapte!*"
"Poxbox!"
"*Touse!*"
"Flapgap!"
"*Rafatière!*"
"Codhopper!"
"*Courieuse!*"
"Bellylass!"
"*Gondinette!*"
"Trollop!"
"*Esquoceresse!*"

"Peddlesnatch!"
"Folieuse!"
"Backgammon!"
"Gondine!"
"Joygirl!"
"Drue!"
"Prickpocket!"
"Galloise!"

"Dear God in Heav'n, cease!" Ebenezer commanded.

"Nay, by Christ, 'tis a war to the end!" cried the dealer. "Would ye surrender to the French? Why, she's naught but a common meatcooker!"

"And you a *janneton!*" the other replied gleefully.

"Arsievarsie!"
"Fillette de pis!"
"Backscratcher!"
"Demoiselle de morais!"
"Bumpbacon!"
"Gaultière!"
"Full-o'-tricks!"
"Ensaignante!"
"Posthole!"
"Gast!"
"Romp!"
"Court talon!"
"Pigpoke!"
"Folle de corps!"
"Scabber!"
"Gouine!"
"Strumpet!"
"Fille de joie!"
"Gullybum!"
"Drouine!"
"Tess Tuppence!"
"Gaupe!"
"Slattern!"
"Entaille d'amour!"
"Doxy!"
"Accrocheuse!"
"Chippie!"
"Cloistrière!"
"Puddletrotter!"
"Bagasser!"
"Hetaera!"
"Caignardière!"

480

"Pipecleaner!"
"Barathre!"
"Rumper!"
"Cambrouse!"
"Hotpot!"
"Alicaire!"
"Backbender!"
"Champisse!"
"Sink-o'-perdition!"
"Cantonnière!"
"Leasepiece!"
"Ambubaye!"
"Spreadeagle!"
"Bassara!"
"Gutterflopper!"
"Bezoche!"
"Cockatrice!"
"Caille!"
"Sausage-grinder!"
"Bourbeteuse!"
"Cornergirl!"
"Braydone!"
"Codwinker!"
"Bonsoir!"
"Nutcracker!"
"Balances de boucher!"
"Meat-vendor!"
"Femme de péché!"
"Hedgewhore!"
"Lecheresse!"
"Ventrenter!"
"Hollière!"
"Lightheels!"
"Pantonière!"
"Gadder!"
"Gruel!"
"Ragbag!"
"Musequine!"
"Fleshpot!"
"Louve!"
"Lecheress!"
"Martingale!"
"Tollhole!"
"Harrebane!"
"Pillowgut!"

481

"Marane!"

"Chamberpot!"

"Levrière d'amour!"

"Swilltrough!"

"Pannanesse!"

"Potlicker!"

"Linatte coiffée!"

"Bedpan!"

"Hourieuse!"

"Cotwarmer!"

"Moché!"

"Stumpthumper!"

"Maxima!"

"Messalina!"

"Loudière!"

"Slopjar!"

"Manafle!"

"Hussy!"

"Lesbine!"

"Priest-layer!"

"Hore!"

"Harpy!"

"Mandrauna!"

"Diddler!"

"Maraude!"

"Foul-mouthed harridans!" Ebenezer cried, and fled through the first door he encountered. It led him by a shorter route back to his starting place, where William Smith now sat alone, smoking a pipe by the fire. "To what evil state hath Malden sunk, to house such a circle of harpies!"

Smith shook his head sympathetically. "Things are in a sorry pass, thanks to Ben Spurdance. 'Twill take some doing to put my business in order."

"Thy business! Don't you see my plight, man? I am ruined, a pauper, and ill to the death of fever. 'Twas mere mischance I granted you Cooke's Point: a sorry accident made with every generous intent! Let me give you twenty acres—that's your due. Nay, thirty acres—after all, I saved your skin! Now return me Malden, I pray you humbly, and so save mine!"

"Stay, stay," Smith interrupted. "Ye'll not have back your Malden, and there's an end on't. What, shall I make me a poor man again, from a rich?"

"Forty acres, then!" begged Ebenezer. "Take twice your legal due, or 'tis the river for me!"

482

"The entire point's my legal due: our conveyance says so plainly."

Ebenezer fell back in his chair. "Ah God, were I only well, or could I take this swindle to an English court of law!"

"Ye'd get the selfsame answer," Smith retorted. "I beg your pardon, now, friend Cooke; I must inspect a man Dick Sowter hath indented me." He made to leave through the front entrance.

"Wait!" the Laureate cried. "That man was falsely indentured—betrayed, like myself, by's trust in his fellow man! His name is not McEvoy at all, but Thomas Tayloe of Talbot!"

Smith shrugged. "I care not if he calls himself the Pope o' Rome, so he hath a willing back and a small appetite."

"He hath not either," Ebenezer declared, and very briefly explained the circumstance of Tayloe's indenture.

"If what ye say be true, 'tis a great misfortune," Smith allowed. "Howbeit, 'tis his to moan, not mine. And now excuse me——"

"One moment!" Ebenezer managed to walk across the room to face the cooper. "If you will not do justice at your own expense, haply you'll see fit to do't at mine. Turn Tayloe free, and bond me in his stead."

"What folly is this?" exclaimed the cooper.

Ebenezer pointed out, as coherently as he could manage, that he was ill and in need of some days' rest and recuperation, in return wherefore, and his keep, he would be a willing and ready servant in whatever capacity Smith saw fit to employ him—especially clerking and the posting of ledgers, with which he had a good deal of experience. Tayloe, on the other hand, was not only in truth a freeman; he was also a gluttonous sluggard who would surely bear a dangerous, if justifiable resentment towards his master.

"There is sense in all ye say," mused William Smith. "Yet I can starve a glutton and flog a troublemaker, at no expense whatever, whilst a sick man——"

"Dear God!" groaned the poet. "Must I beg you to make me a servant on my own estate? Very well, then——" He knelt in supplication on the floor. "I beseech you to bond me as a servant, for any term you choose! If you refuse, 'tis as much as murthering me outright!"

Smith sucked at his pipe and, finding it cold, relit it with an ember from the fire.

"I am nor poet nor gentleman," he said at last, "but only a simple cooper that hath no wish to lose his goods. Yet I please myself to think I am no fool, nor any child in the ways o' the world, and I know well thou'rt moved by no great virtuous cause to be my servant, but merely to be nursed through your seasoning and then to seek out ways and means to work my ruin . . ."

"I swear to you——"

"Stay, I am not done. I'll not indent you, but I *will* see ye nursed past your seasoning, on one condition."

"Name your terms," Ebenezer said. "I am sick past haggling."

"The fact is, I am looking to make a fit match for my daughter Susan, whose husband died some years past in London. If ye'll contract to wed her this very night, I'll give for her dowry a half-year's board at Malden, with all the care ye need from Dick Sowter, the best physician in Dorset. If ye choose to wed her tomorrow, 'twill be five months' board, and a month less for each day thereafter. Done?"

" 'Sheart, man!" gasped the Laureate. " 'Tis preposterous!"

Smith bowed slightly. "Our business is done, then, and good day t'ye."

"Don't go! 'Tis just—i'God, I must have time to ponder the thing!"

"Take the while I finish this pipe," the cooper smiled. "After that I withdraw my offer."

"You'll drive me mad with choices!" Ebenezer wailed, but as Smith made no reply other than puffing on his pipe, he began to weigh frantically the alternatives, wincing at both.

"What is your choice?" Smith inquired presently, tapping out his pipe on an andiron.

"I have none," Ebenezer sighed. "I shall marry your ruined harlot of a daughter to save my life, and God save me from her pox and her perfidy! But I must see your bargain writ into a contract, and both our names appended."

" 'Tis only fair," the cooper agreed, and set before the Laureate a small table on which were quills, a pot of ink, and a sheaf of documents very like those with which Richard Sowter had pointed out Malden from the sloop. "Here are two copies of a marriage contract that I had Dick Sowter draw against the time I made a match for Susan; I'll risk a fine for not publishing the banns. Sign both, and the thing is sealed: Reverend Sowter can tie the knot at once and fetch ye a pill."

"A preacher as well!" Ebenezer marveled, and was so amused in his near-delirium by this news that he had signed one copy of the contract and was halfway through the second before it occurred to him to wonder how it was that Smith could produce, with such readiness, documents not only contracting the marriage but also providing, on the very terms proposed a few moments before by the cooper, for the bridegroom's convalescence. Even as he raised his pen, struck by the plot this fact implied, Richard Sowter, Susan Warren, and Thomas Tayloe entered from outside, accompanied by no other soul than Henry Burlingame.

"Stop!" cried Susan, when she saw what was in progress. "Don't sign that paper!" She ran toward the table, but Smith snatched up the papers before she got there.

"Too late, my dear, he is three fourths signed already, and 'twill be no chore for Timothy here to forge the rest."

Ebenezer looked from one to the other, his features twitching. "Henry! What plot is this? Have you returned to steal these Indian rags, or haply to sport me with more rhymes?"

"There was a weakness in your court order, Mister Cooke," said Sowter, and took one of the several papers from Smith. "Here where't says *That the same William Smith shall see to his daughter's marriage at the earliest opportunity,* and the rest. St. Winifred's cherry, sir! No man in his senses would marry a whore berid with pox and opium, and belike some rogue of a judge would've hung the order on that clause!"

"But," added Smith, brandishing the contract in his hand, "this paper here mends that hole, I think."

" 'Tis a finer clout than e'er St. Wilfred sewed," Sowter agreed.

"I humbly beg your pardon, Mister Cooke," said Thomas Tayloe. " 'Twas Sowter's notion from the first I should ask ye to take my place. He said 'twas the only price he'd take for me."

"Thou'rt forgiven," Ebenezer said, smiling wildly. "McEvoy sacrified you for *his* liberty, and you me for your own —whom shall I trade for mine? But dear fellow, they have swived you twice o'er: thou'rt not a freeman yet."

"How is that?" Tayloe demanded.

" 'Twas not necessary to indenture Mr. Cooke," Smith said coolly. "Susan, you and Timothy fetch out the witnesses from the kitchen and get the bridegroom ready; Reverend Sowter will marry ye directly we've shown McEvoy to the servants' quarters."

Tayloe at once set up a furious protest, but the two men led him off. Throughout the conversation Burlingame had remained silent, and his face had been impassive when Ebenezer had addressed him as Henry instead of Timothy; as soon as

485

Smith and Sowter were out of sight, however, his manner changed entirely. He rushed to the chair where Ebenezer sat as if a-swoon and gripped his shoulders.

"Eben! Eben! Dear God, wake up and hear me!"

Ebenezer squinted and turned away. "I cannot bear the sight of you."

"Nay, Eben, listen! I've little time to speak ere they return, and must speak fast: Smith is no common cooper, but an agent of Captain Mitchell's, that is in turn Coode's chief lieutenant! There is a wondrous wicked plot afoot to ruin the Province with pox and opium, the better to overthrow it. Great brothels and opium dens have been established, and Malden's to be the chiefest in this county. All this I learned by posing as Tim Mitchell, whose job it is on some pretext to journey through the counties with fresh stores of opium and to supervise the brothels." Since Ebenezer displayed no apparent interest or belief, Burlingame went on to explain, in an urgent voice, that for some time Captain Mitchell had been scheming with Smith to ruin Ben Spurdance (who had been loyal both to the government and to his employer) in order to gain access to the strategically situated Cooke's Point estate. He, Burlingame, on the other hand, had been seeking ways to subvert their scheme, although it was not until the occasion of Susan's escape (which was, to be sure, designed by Captain Mitchell) that he had known for certain the location of the proposed new brothel and the identity of Mitchell's Dorchester agent.

"And 'twas not till we arrived in Cambridge, and Spurdance sought me out whilst you were strolling elsewhere, that I learned Susan was not loyal to the cause she served. They came to me together, in answer to a secret sign I made whereby our agents know one another, and whilst the Salter case was a-hearing, they told me they had found a way to undo Smith by the terms of his indenture, and had influenced Judge Hammaker to their end. We had the wretch near scotched, by Heav'n, with Susan's testimony—but your judgment, of course, foiled our plan."

Ebenezer still made no reply, but tears ran from his squinted eyes and down the gaunt reaches of his face.

" 'Twas thus I dared show little sympathy for your loss," Henry went on. "I befriended Smith at once and left you stranded in the corncrib to keep you out of danger till I'd left with him for Malden and learnt more of his plans and temper. I thought he'd beat poor Susan to a powder for betraying him, but instead he showed her every courtesy; 'twas not till some

minutes past, when Susan told me you were here and I heard
from Sowter the tale of John McEvoy and Tom Tayloe, that I
saw the scoundrel's plot, and for all my haste we arrived too
late to stop you."

"It little matters now," the Laureate said, closing his eyes.
"I shall not live to see my father's wrath, in any case."

"Why can I not refuse to have him?" asked Susan, who
throughout Burlingame's relation had been sitting tearfully on
the floor beside Ebenezer's writing table. " 'Twould foil the
contract and greatly please Mr. Cooke, I'm certain."

Burlingame replied that he doubted the former, since the
contract would demonstrate to the court that Smith had complied with the marriage order as far as was in his power. "As
for the latter, 'tis none of my affair, but I know no other way
to care for Eben just now . . ."

"It doth not matter to me any farther," said Ebenezer.

"Nay, don't despair!" Burlingame shook him by the shoulders to stir him awake. " 'Tis my opinion you should marry
Susan, Eben, and let her nurse you back to health. I know
your thoughts, and how you prize your chastity, but—i-
'faith, there is the answer! Thou'rt obliged to wed, but not to
consummate the marriage; when thou'rt well again, and we
have found a means to undo William Smith, then Susan can
sue for annulment on the grounds thou'rt still a virgin!"

Susan hung her head, but said no more. The voices of
Smith and Sowter, laughing together, could be heard in the
rear of the house, joined in a moment by the raucous voices
of the cardplayers in the kitchen.

"Lookee, Eben," Burlingame said quickly. "I have a pill of
Sowter's here in my pocket—he *is* a physician, for all his
knavery. Take it now to tide you through the wedding, and I
swear we'll see you master of this house ere the year is out!"

Ebenezer shook off his lethargy enough to groan and cover
his face with his hands. "I'Christ, that some god on wires
would sweep down and fetch me off! 'Tis a far different
course I'd follow, could I begin once more at Locket's winehouse!"

"Look alive, there!" William Smith called cheerily, and
strode into the room with Sowter and the three women.
"Stand him up, now, Timothy, and let's have an end on't!"

"Marry come up," cried one of the prostitutes, running to
Susan, "I love a wedding!"

"*Aussi moi*," said Grace, "but always I weep." She drew
out her handkerchief in anticipation.

"Ye'll have to marry him where he sits," Burlingame told

Sowter, using the voice of Timothy Mitchell. "Here, now, Master Bridegroom; chew this pill and make your answers when the time comes. Stand here by your husband, Susie, and hold his hand."

" 'Dslife!" the third prostitute exclaimed with mock alarm. "D'ye think he's man enough to take her head?"

"Curb your wretched tongue," snapped Susan, "ere I tear it from your face!" She grasped Ebenezer's hand and glared at the assemblage. "Get on with it, Richard Sowter, damn your eyes! This man is ill and must be got to bed at once."

The ceremony of marriage commenced. Though he could hear Sowter's voice clearly, and Susan's when she made her sullen responses, Ebenezer could not by any effort contrive to open his eyes, nor could he more than mumble when his turn came to repeat the vows. The pill he chewed was bitter on his tongue, but already, though no more clearheaded than before, he felt somewhat less miserable; indeed, when Sowter said, "I now pronounce ye man and wife," he felt an impulse of sheer lightheartedness.

"Sign the certificate quickly," Smith urged him, "ere ye fall out on the floor."

"I'll steady his hand," Burlingame said, and virtually wrote the Laureate's signature on the paper.

"What is't ye gave him?" Susan demanded, and with her thumb peeled open one of Ebenezer's eyelids.

" 'Twas but to ensure he gets his proper rest, Mrs. Cooke," Burlingame replied.

At the sound of the name Ebenezer opened his mouth to laugh, and though no sound issued forth, he was delighted at the result.

"Opium!" Susan shrieked.

This news the Laureate found even more amusing than did the company, but he had no opportunity for another of the pleasant laughs: the fact is, his chair rose from the floor, passed through the roof of Malden, and shot into the opalescent sky. As for Maryland, it turned blue and flattened into an immense musical surface, which suavely slid northwestwards under seagulls.

32

A Marylandiad *Is Brought to Birth, but Its Deliverer Fares as Badly as in Any Other Chapter*

"TO PARNASSUS!" cried the Laureate with a laugh, and the chair sailed over Thessaly to land between twin mountain cones of polished alabaster. The valley wherein he came to rest swarmed with thousands upon thousands of the world's inhabitants, pressing in the foothills.

"I say," he inquired of one nearby who was in the act of tripping up the fellow just ahead, "which is Parnassus?"

"On the right," the man answered over his shoulder.

" 'Tis as I understood it to be," the poet replied. "But what if I'd come up from the other side? Then right would be left, and left right, would it not? I'm only asking hypothetically," he added, for the stranger frowned.

"Right is right and be damned to ye," the man growled, and disappeared into the crowd.

Certainly from where Ebenezer stood, far removed from both, the twin mountains looked alike, their pink peaks lost in clouds. Beginning at a ridge just a little way up their slopes were rows or circles of various obstacles to the climbers. First he saw a ring of ugly men with clubs, who mashed the climbers' fingers and caused them either to give over the ascent entirely or remain where they were; similar rings were stationed at intervals as far as Ebenezer could see up the mountainside, some armed with hatchets or bodkins instead of clubs. Nor were the areas between these circles free of danger. Here and there, for example, were groups of women who invited the climbers from their objective; beds and couches, set beside tables of food and wine, lulled the weary who lay in them to a slumber deep as death; treadmills there were in abundance, and false signposts that promised the summit but led in fact (as could be clearly observed from the valley) to precipices, deserts, jungles, jails, and lunatic asylums. Countless climbers fell to every sort of obstacle. Those who managed to clear the first line of guards—whether by forcing through with main strength, by creating a diversion to distract attention from themselves, or by tickling, fondling, and otherwise pleasing the clubmen—more often than not fell to the women, the beds, the treadmills, or the false signposts, or if they escaped those as well, to the next ring of guards, and so forth. The lucky few who by some one or combination of these techniques passed safely through the farthest obstacles were applauded mightily by the rest, and it sometimes happened that the very noise of this applause sufficed to make the climber lose his grip on the alabaster and plunge feet foremost into the valley again. Others who neared the summit were felled by rocks from the same hands that had earlier applauded, and still others were not stoned but merely forgotten. Of the very, very few who remained fairly secure, some owed their tenure to the heavy pink mists that obscured them as targets; others to the simple bulk of the peak on which they sat, and others to the grapes and China oranges that they flung upon demand to the crowd below.

The most important thing, of course, was to choose the proper mountain in the first place, but since by no amount of inquiry could he gain any certain information, Ebenezer at length chose arbitrarily and began to climb with the rest; doubtless, he reasoned, one learned as one climbed, and in any case, to reach the summit of either would be accomplishment enough. The first thing he discovered, however, was that the obstacles were much more formidable face to face than when viewed from afar as a non-climber: the ring of clubmen, when he reached them, were uglier and more threatening; the women beyond them, and the couches, more alluring; and the signposts quite authentic in appearance. It was, in fact, all he could do to muster courage enough to lunge at the nearest guards; but no sooner was he poised for the attempt than a voice commanded his chair to raise him to the peak, and without having climbed at all he found himself sitting among a group of solitary men on a pinnacle of the mountain.

He singled out one of the oldest and wisest-looking, who was engaged in paring his toenails. "I say, sir, you'll think me ridiculous to ask, but might you tell me which mountain this is?"

"Ye have me there," the ancient replied. "Sometimes I think

'tis one, sometimes the other." He chuckled and added in a stage whisper: "What doth it matter?"

"How did you get here, if I'm not too bold?" Ebenezer asked further.

"That was no chore at all," the old man said. "I was here when the mountain grew, I and my cronies, and we went up with it. They'll never knock *us* down—but they might raise us so high they can't see us any more."

"They're applauding you down there, you know."

The old man shrugged his shoulders, Burlingame-like. "Ye can't hear 'em so well up here. 'Tis the altitude and the thinness of the air, I've always thought. But I care not a fart one way or the other."

"Well," said Ebenezer. "I surely envy you. What a view you have from here!"

" 'Tis in sooth a pleasant view," the old man admitted. "Ye can see well-nigh the entire picture, and it all looks much alike. Tell ye the truth, I get tired looking. 'Tis more comfortable to sit here than to climb, if comfort's what ye like. Climb if ye feel like cimbing, says I, and don't if ye don't. There's really naught in the world up here but clever music; ye'll take pleasure in't if ye've been reared to like that sort of thing."

"Oh, I always did like music!"

"Really?" asked the old man without interest.

Ebenezer leaned down to look at the strugglers far below.

"Sbody, but aren't they silly-looking!" he exclaimed. "And how ill-mannered, pushing and breaking wind on one another!"

"They've little else to do," the old man observed.

"But there's naught here to climb for: you've said that yourself!"

"Aye, nor aught anywhere else, either. They'd as well climb as sit still and die."

"I'm going to jump!" Ebenezer declared suddenly. "I've no wish to see these things a moment more!"

"No reason why ye oughtn't, nor any why ye ought."

The Laureate made no further move to jump, but sat on the edge of the peak and sighed. " 'Tis all most frightfully empty, is't not?"

"Empty indeed," the old man said, "but there's naught o' good or bad in that. Why sigh?"

"Why not?" asked Ebenezer.

"Why not indeed?" the old man sighed, and Ebenezer found himself in a bed and Richard Sowter bending over him.

"St. Wilgefortis's beard, here is our bridegroom at long last! Doc Sowter's oil-o'-mallow ne'er yet let mortal die!"

"Marsh-mallow my arse," said one of the kitchen-women, who appeared beside the bed. " 'Twas St. Susie's thistle-physic brought him back."

Sowter counted Ebenezer's pulse briefly and then popped a spoonful of some syrup into his mouth.

"What room is this, and why am I in't?"

" 'Tis one o' Bill Smith's guest rooms," Sowter said.

"Opium!" the Laureate cried, and sat up angrily. "I recall it now!"

"Aye, by blear-eyed old St. Otilic, 'twas opium Tim Mitchell gave ye, so ye'd have your rest. But ye was that ill to begin with, it came nigh to fetching ye off."

"He'll be the death of me, by accident or design. Where is he now?"

"Timothy? Ah, he's long gone, back to his father's place in Calvert County."

"False friend!" the poet muttered. He paused a moment and then fell back in anguish on his pillow. "Ah God, it escaped me I was wed! Where is Susan, and what said she of my illness on our wedding night? For I take it 'tis another day . . ."

The kitchen woman laughed. " 'Tis plus three weeks ye've languished 'twixt life and death!"

"As for Mrs. Cooke," Sowter said, "I can't say how she felt, for directly we fetched ye to bed she was gone for Captain Mitchell's in Timothy's keep. Haply he did your labors for ye."

"Back to Mitchell's!"

"Aye, she's legal-bound to drive his swine, ye know."

" 'Tis too much!" Ebenezer cried indignantly. "For all she's a hussy, the Laureate's lady shan't drive swine! Fetch her here!"

"Now, don't ye fret," the woman soothed. "Susie's run away twice already, to see for herself what health ye were in and make ye her wondrous thistle-physic. I doubt not she'll do the same again."

"Three weeks a-swoon! I scarce know what to think!"

"St. Christopher's nightmare, friend, think o' getting well," Sowter suggested cheerfully, "then ye can roger Mistress Susan from matins to vespers, if ye dare. I'll tell your father-in-law thou'rt back to life, but 'twill be some weeks yet ere ye have your health entire. Many a poor soul hath been seasoned to his grave." He gathered up his medical paraphernalia and prepared to leave. "Ah yes, here is a present Timmy Mitchell left ye."

"My notebook!" the Laureate exclaimed; Sowter handed him the familiar green-backed ledger, now warped, worn, and soiled from its peregrinations.

"Aye, ye lost it in the inn at Cambridge, and Tim brought it out when last he came for Susan. He said ye might have verses to write in't whilst ye rest your six months out."

"Ah God, I thought 'twas stolen with my clothes!" He clasped it with much emotion. " 'Tis an old and faithful friend, this ledger-book—my only one!"

When he was left alone he found himself still far too weak in body and spirit for artistic creation, and so he contented himself with reading the products of his past—all of which seemed remote to him now. He could, in fact, identify himself much more readily with the stained and battered notebook than with such couplets as:

> *Ye ask, What eat our merry Band*
> *En Route to lovely* MARYLAND?

which seemed as foreign to him as if they were another man's work. Since he had happened to begin with the most recent entry and thence to work towards the front of the book, the last thing he read was a note for his projected *Marylandiad,* made while his audience with Lord Baltimore (that is to say, Burlingame) was still fresh in his memory: MARYLANDS *Excellencies are peerless,* it read; *her Inhabitants are the most gracious, their Breeding unmatch'd; her Dwelling-places are the grandest; her Inns & Ordinaries the most courteous and comfortable; her Fields the richest; her Courts & Laws the most majestic; her Commerce the most prosperous, & cet., & cet.* The note was subscribed, in Ebenezer's own hand, *E.C., G^{ent}, P^t & L^t of M^d.*

He lay back and closed his eyes; his head throbbed from the small exertion of perusing his work. "I'faith!" he said to himself. "What price this laureateship! Here's naught but scoundrels and perverts, hovels and brothels, corruption and poltroonery! What glory, to be singer of such a sewer!"

The more he reflected upon his vicissitudes, the more his anguish became infused with wrath, until at length, despite his weariness, he ripped from the ledger his entire stock of sea-verses, and using the quill and ink provided by his host he wrote on the virgin paper thus exposed:

> *Condemn'd by Fate, to wayward Curse,*
> *Of Friends unkind, and empty Purse,*
> *Plagues worse than fill'd Pandoras Box,*
> *I took my Leave of Albions Rocks,*
> *With heavy Heart, concern'd that I*
> *Was forc'd my native Soil to fly,*
> *And the old World must bid Good-b'ye.*

No sooner were these lines set down than more came rushing unbidden to his fancy, and though he was not strong enough at the time to write them out, he conceived then and there a momentous project to occupy him during the weeks ahead—which, should he find no means of regaining his estate, might well be his last on earth. He would versify his voyage to Maryland from beginning to end, as he had planned before, but so far from writing a panegyric, he would scourge the Province with the lash of Hudibrastic as a harlot is scourged at the public post, catalogue her every wickedness, and expose her every trap laid for the trusting, the unwary, the innocent!

"Thus might others be instructed by my loss," he reflected grimly. "But stay——" He remembered the details of his abuse at the hands of the *Poseidon*'s crew, the rape of the *Cyprian*, Burlingame's pig, and other indelicate features of his adventure. " 'Twill ne'er be printed."

For some moments he was bitterly discouraged, for this reflection implied a cruel paradox: the very wickedness of one's afflictions can prevent one's avenging them by public exposure. But he soon saw a means to circumvent that difficulty.

"I shall make the piece a fiction! I'll be a tradesman, say —nay, a factor that comes to Maryland on's business, with every good opinion of the country, and is swindled of his goods and property. All my trials I'll reconceive to suit the plot and alter just enough to pass the printer!"

The sequence instantly unfolded in his imagination, and he made a quick prose outline lest it slip away. He could do no more just then; exhausted by the effort, he slept for several hours dreamlessly. However, when he reawakened, the vision was still clear in his mind and what was more, the Hudibrastic couplets wherewith he meant to render it began springing readily to hand. He could scarcely wait to launch into composition: as soon as he was strong enough he left his bed, but only because the writing desk in his chamber was more comfortable to work at; there he spent day after day, and week after week, setting down his long poem. So jealous was he of his

494

time that he rebuffed the curiosity and occasional solicitude of Smith, Sowter, and the kitchen-women; he demanded—and, somewhat to his surprise, received—his meals at his desk, and never left his room except to take health-walks in the late October and November sun. All thoughts of suicide departed from him for the time, as did, on the other hand, all thoughts of regaining his lost estate. He was not disturbed or even curious about the absence of any word from Henry Burlingame. When, a week or ten days after his awakening from coma, his legal wife Susan Warren reappeared at Malden, he thanked her brusquely for her aid in nursing him back to health, but although he understood from the kitchen-women that at Mitchell's and Smith's direction she had become a prostitute exclusively for the Indians, he neither protested her activities or her return to Mitchell on the one hand, nor sought annulment of his marriage on the other.

Malden itself was becoming every day more evidently a gambling house, tavern, brothel, and opium den: Susan brought the brown phials with her from Calvert County, and Mary Mungummory—who, the poet learned, had previously resisted Mitchell's efforts to draw her into his organization—moved in with her entire retinue of doxies and accepted the office of madame of the house. Every night the whole point bustled: planters came from all over Dorset by horse and wagon, and by boat from Talbot County as well, and the house rang with their debauchery. From the mid-county fresh marshes and even the salt marshes of the lower county, twenty and thirty miles to the southeast, Abaco, Wiwash, and Nanticoke Indians came to engage Susan and two of Mary Mungummory's least-favored employees in a tobacco-curing house set aside for the purpose. But Ebenezer walked obviously past the gaming tables, through the rooms of intoxicated, narcotized, and lecherous Marylanders, and across the tobacco fields where knots of solemn Indians moved toward the curing-house. He soon became a figure of fun among the clients, but their jests met with the same indifference with which he rewarded Susan when, upon his entry into a room, she would follow him with troubled and inquiring eyes.

Throughout November he labored at the task of casting into rhyme the sorry episodes of his journey:

> *Freighted with Fools, from Plimouth Sound,*
> *To MARYLAND our Ship was bound;*
> *Where we arriv'd, in dreadful Pain,*
> *Shock'd by the Terrors of the Main . . .*

He recalled his first encounter with the planters in St.
Mary's County, whom he had mistaken for field hands——

> *. . . a numerous Crew,*
> *In Shirts and Drawers of Scotch-cloth blew,*
> *With neither Stocking, Hat, nor Shoe . . .*

—and to their description appended the couplets written long
before under different circumstances, painful now to remember:

> *Figures, so strange, no GOD design'd*
> *To be a Part of Human-kind:*
> *But Wanton Nature, void of Rest,*
> *Moulded the brittle Clay in Jest . . .*

Shifting with masterly nonchalance from tetrametric to
pentametric verses, he next proceeded to flay the inhabitants
of his poetical bailiwick——

> *. . . that Shore where no good Sense is Found,*
> *But Conversation's lost, and Manners drown'd . . .*

—and thereafter to describe in turn, once more in four-footed
lines, his trip across the Patuxent River in a canoe:

> *Cut from a Poplar tree, or Pine,*
> *And fashion'd like a Trough for Swine . . .*

The encounter with Susan's herd of pigs:

> *This put me in a pannick Fright,*
> *Lest I should be devour'd quite . . .*

His lawful wife the swine-maiden herself:

> *. . . by her loose and sluttish Dress,*
> *She rather seem'd a Bedlam-Bess . . .*

His fruitless vigil in the barnyard:

> *Where, riding on a Limb astride,*
> *Night and the Branches did me hide,*
> *And I the De'el and Snake defy'd . . .*

The spectacle of the open-air assizes:

496

> *. . . the Crowds did there resort,*
> *Which Justice made, and Law, their Sport,*
> *In their Sagacious County Court . . .*

The trial:

> *The planting Rabble being met,*
> *Their drunken Worships likewise sat,*
> *Cryer proclaims the Noise shou'd cease,*
> *And streight the Lawyers broke the Peace,*
> *Wrangling for Plaintiff and Defendant,*
> *I thought they ne'er wou'd make an End on't,*
> *With Nonsense, Stuff, and false Quotations*
> *With brazen Lies, and Allegations . . .*

Judge Hammaker himself:

> *. . . who, to the Shame,*
> *Of all the Bench, cou'd write his Name . . .*

His night in the corncrib:

> *I lay me down secur'd from Fray,*
> *And soundly snor'd till break o' Day;*
> *When waking fresh, I sat upright,*
> *And found my Shoes were vanish'd quite,*
> *Hat, Wig, and Stockings, all were fled,*
> *From this extended Indian Bed . . .*

The kitchen-whores at Malden:

> *. . . a jolly Female Crew,*
> *Were deep engag'd at Lanterloo,*
> *In Nightrails white, with dirty Mien,*
> *Such Sights are scarce in England seen:*
> *I thought them first some Witches, bent*
> *On black Designs, in dire Convent;*
> *. . . who, with affected Air,*
> *Had nicely learn'd to Curse and Swear . . .*

His illness:

> *A fiery Pulse beat in my Veins,*
> *From cold I felt resembling Pains;*
> *This cursed Seasoning I remember*
> *Lasted . . . till cold December;*
> *Nor cou'd it then it's Quarter shift,*
> *Until by Carduus turn'd adrift:*

> *And had my doct'ress wanted Skill,*
> *Or Kitch'n-Physick at her Will,*
> *My Father's Son had lost his Lands . . .*

And his exploitation by the versatile Sowter:

> *. . . and ambodexter Quack,*
> *Who learnedly had got the Knack*
> *Of giving Clysters, making Pills,*
> *Of filing Bonds, and forging Wills . . .*

When at last he had recounted the sum of his misfortunes by means of the sot-weed-factor conceit, he imagined himself fleeing to an outbound ship, and so concluded ferociously:

> *Embarqu'd and waiting for a Wind,*
> *I leave this dreadful Curse behind.*
> *May Canniballs transported o'er the Sea*
> *Prey on these Slaves, as they have done on me;*
> *May never Merchant's trading Sails explore*
> *This cruel, this Inhospitable Shoar;*
> *But left abandon'd by the World to starve,*
> *May they sustain the Fate they well deserve:*
> *May they turn Salvage, or as Indians wild,*
> *From Trade, Converse, and Happiness exil'd;*
> *Recreant to Heaven, may they adore the Sun,*
> *And into Pagan Superstitions run*
> *For Vengeance ripe—*
> *May Wrath Divine then lay these Regions wast*
> *Where no Man's Faithful, nor a Woman chast!*

The heat of his sustained creative passion must have either enlarged his talent or softened his critical acumen, for never before had he felt so potent, assured, and poetic as in the composition of this satire. During the first two weeks of December he smoothed and polished it—adjusting an iamb here, tuning the clatter of a Hudibrastic there, until on St. Lucy's day, December 13, he was prepared to deem the piece truly finished. At its head he wrote: *The Sot-Weed Factor: Or, a Voyage to* Maryland. *A Satyr. In which is describ'd, the Laws, Government, Courts and Constitutions of the Country; and also the Buildings, Feasts, Frolicks. Entertainments and Drunken Humours of the Inhabitants of that Port of* America. And at the foot, with grand contempt, he affixed his full title—*Ebenezer Cooke, Gentleman, Poet & Laureat of the Province of Maryland*—in full recognition that with the poem's publication, should he ever send it to a printer, he would forfeit any chance of receiving that title in fact.

Publication, however, did not especially interest him at the moment. He put by his quill and surveyed the thousand and more lines of manuscript in his ledger.

"By Lucy's bloody thorn, 'tis writ!" he sighed, mocking Sowter. "And there's an end on't!"

He had not the slightest idea what would happen next, nor had he just then the smallest worry. To the bone he felt the pleasure of large and sure accomplishment, which is ever one part joy and nine relief. Indeed, he was possessed with an urge to close his eyes and sleep where he sat at his writing desk; but the early winter night had only just darkened—it was, in fact, not an hour since supper—and he felt a contrary desire to celebrate in some small way, not *The Sot-Weed Factor* itself, whose existence was its own festivity, but the end of the labors that had brought it to birth.

"A glass of rum's the thing," he decided, and went downstairs to where the evening's activities were just getting started. His intention was to go to the kitchen, that being the only room at Malden, other than his own chamber, where he could be reasonably confident of his reception; but on his way he encountered William Smith and Richard Sowter, who had become fast friends since the fall.

"How now, by Kenelm's dove!" the latter said on seeing him. "Here is our poet."

"Speak of the devil," Smith observed. "Thou'rt looking hale and pleased this night."

"I am both," Ebenezer admitted, "with little cause for either." The truth was, the mere sight of his undoers had cost him much of the pleasant sense of well-being with which he'd left his finished manuscript. "You were speaking of me?"

"That we were," Smith said. " 'Twas a general discussion on points o' law we were having, and I brought ye in by way of illustration."

"Mr. Smith here raised the question," Sowter joined in, "whether, in a contract made to complete a job o' work within a given time, the instrument becomes null and void directly the job is done or remains in force regardless till the designated time runs out. My answer was, it hangs altogether on the wording of the contract, whether its expiration hath a single or alternative contingency."

Ebenezer smiled uncertainly. "That seems a reasonable reply, but I am no lawyer."

"Nor am I," Smith said, "and so to get a fairer notion of

the thing, I asked him to apply it to that contract drawn 'twixt thee and me, regarding your ill health——"

"Go to the point," Ebenezer said stiffly. "I see your purpose."

"Ah, now, I have no wish to cheat ye of your due," Smith insisted. "It hath been an honor and a pleasure to have the Laureate Poet for house guest, and nurse him back to health. Yet the fact is, as well ye can observe, I've a thriving little hostelry in Malden, and an idle room is to an innkeeper like a fallow field to a sot-weed planter."

"In short, now I'm on my feet once more you wish me gone."

"Calm thy heat," Sowter urged. " 'Tis my opinion, as your physician, thou'rt as well a man as ever braided Catherine's tresses, and I have said farther, as Mr. Smith's attorney, his contract in the matter hath alternative contingencies for expiration; namely, the restoration of your health or six months of bed, board, and proper care."

"Say no more," Ebenezer said, "the rest is clear, and I'll not contest it. If you'll but grant me two small favors—nay, three—you will not see me on the morrow."

"Nay, hear me out——"

"Have no fear of these requests," Ebenezer went on contemptuously. "They'll not interfere in any way with your profit. The first is that you give me a pot of rum, wherewith to celebrate a poem I've written; the second is that you send the poem to a certain London printer, whose address I shall give you; and the third is that you lend me a loaded pistol, to use when the rum is gone."

"A turd upon the pistol," Smith declared. "Thou'rt no good Catholic, methinks, e'en to speak of't, and ye spring too quickly to the worst expedient. I have no wish to turn ye out at all."

"What?"

"St. Dunstan's tongs," Sowter laughed, " 'tis what I tried to tell ye! Mr. Smith must have your chamber for his business, but so far from wishing ye ill, he hath proposed to be your patron, as't were." He explained that the cooper had directed him to draw up a remarkable indenture-bond, to sign which would entitle the poet to free room and board in the servants' quarters indefinitely, and commit him only to a nominal amount of chemical work.

" 'Twill be no more than a paper to write or endorse on occasion," Smith assured him. "The balance of the time is your own, to versify or what ye will."

Ebenezer shrugged. "It matters not to me one way or the other. Draw up your bond, and I shall read it."

"I have't here this minute," Sowter said, producing a document from his coat. " 'Tis a virtual sinecure, I swear!"

The opportunity to compose more poetry was in truth attractive to Ebenezer, though at the moment he had no ideas whatever for future poems. He considered also the possibility that Burlingame's unexplained absence might have to do with some scheme for undoing Smith, though he had come rather to attribute it to another, perhaps, final, desertion. And ultimately, of course, the pistol was always there as a last resort: he could see no great loss in postponing its use for a time. Therefore, after reading it cursorily and finding its provisions to be as Sowter had described, he signed both copies of the four-year indenture with no emotion whatever.

"Now thou'rt my patron," he said to Smith, "haply you'll indulge your protégé with a pot of rum."

"No pot, but an entire rundlet," the cooper answered happily. "And hi! Yonder's your wedded wife, fresh-come from Mitchell's!"

"Ye look well chilled, St. Susie," Sowter laughed. "Warm your arse here by the fire and take a dram with our poet ere ye set to work in the curing-house: your father hath indented him to four years o' rhyming."

"I'll fetch the girls in from the kitchen," Smith declared. "We'll have a celebration ere the night's work starts!"

Susan came into the little parlor and stared at Ebenezer without comment.

" 'Twas that or the pistol," he said. Something in her expression alarmed him, and his tone was defensive. Smith reappeared with two women from the kitchen; when the drams were passed round, the Frenchwoman perched on Sowter's knees and the other on Smith's lap.

"So ye fled your master yet again?" Sowter called merrily to Susan. "I swear by Martin's pox, he keeps a light hold on his wenches!"

"Aye, I fled him," Susan said, not joining in the general mirth.

"And did you find another such fool as I," Ebenezer inquired acidly, "to pay your escape and wait your pleasure in Mitchell's barn?" Whether because her wretched appearance —she was shivering, and both her clothes and her face were more ruined than ever—reminded him that his legal wife was a pig-driver, an opium-eater, and the lowest sort of prostitute, or simply because he had never properly thanked her for nursing him back to health, the strangeness of her manner made him feel guilty for having ignored her during the composition of his poem.

"Aye, I found another. A dotard too old for such schemes, says I, though there's no law yet against dreaming." Despite the levity of her words, both her tone and her expression were grave. "I have more cock in my eye than he hath in his breeches, and I'm not cock-eyed. A bespectacled old fool, he was, with a withered arm."

"Nay!" Ebenezer breathed. "Tell me not he had a withered arm!"

"Aye, and he did."

"Yet surely 'twas his left arm was withered, was't not?"

Susan hesitated, and then in the same voice said, "Nay, as I think on't, 'twas his right: he sat at my left in the wagon whilst I told him the tale of my misfortune, and I recall he was obliged to reach over with his far arm to tweak and abuse me."

Ebenezer felt a sudden nausea. "But he was a peasant, for all that," he insisted.

"Not a bit of't. 'Twas clear from his clothes and carriage he was a gentleman of quality, and he said he had arrived that very day from London."

"I'faith," said one of the kitchen-women, "ye'll find no London gentlemen in the curing-house, Susie; ye should have let him swive ye!"

"Nay, God!" Ebenezer cried, so mournfully that the whole company left off their mirth and regarded him with consternation. " 'Tis *I* he'll swive! That man was Andrew Cooke of Middlesex, my father, come to see how fares his son! The pistol!" He jumped to his feet. "There is no help for't now!"

"Stay!" Smith commanded. "Stop him, Susan!"

" 'Tis the pistol!" the poet cried again, and fled for his chamber before anyone could detain him.

33

The Laureate Departs from His Estate

SUCH WAS HIS agitation that not until he was in his room, still lighted by a candle he had left·burning on the writing table, did the Laureate recall that he had no pistol with which to destroy himself, nor even a short-sword—his own having been stolen along with the rest of his costume in the·corncrib and never returned to him. He heard the company swarming up the stairs from the parlor, and threw himself in despair upon his bed.

The first to reach his door was Susan; she took one look at him and bade the others stay back.

"We'll wait below," Smith grumbled. "But mind, see to't there's no trouble. I shan't have his idle brains all over my house."

All this the poet heard face down in the quilts. Susan closed the door and sat on the edge of his bed.

"Do ye mean to blow your head off?" she inquired.

" 'Tis the final misfortune," he answered. "I have no pistol, nor means to purchase one. Ye'll not be widowed this evening, so it seems."

"Will your father's wrath be so terrible?"

"I'Christ, 'tis past imagining!" Ebenezer groaned. "Yet e'en were he the very soul of mercy, I am too shamed to face him."

Susan sighed. " 'Twill be passing strange, to be the widow of a man that ne'er hath wifed me."

"Nor ever shall!" Ebenezer sat up angrily. "Much you care, with your curing-house salvages and your opium! Marry you my friend Henry Burlingame, that will wife you with your swine—there's a match!"

"The world is strange and full o' wickedness," Susan murmured.

"So at least is this verminous province, whose delights I

was supposed to sing!" He shook his head. "Ah, marry, I have no call to injure you: forgive my words."

"'Tis a hard fall ye've fallen, but prithee speak no more o' pistols," Susan said. "Flee, if ye must, and start again elsewhere."

"Where flee?" cried Ebenezer. "Better the pistol than another day in Maryland!"

"Back to England, I mean: hide yourself till the fleet sails, and thou'rt quit of your father for good and all."

"Very good," the Laureate said bitterly. "And shall I kiss the captain for my freight?"

"Mr. Cooke!" Susan whispered suddenly. She leaned over him and clutched his shoulders. "Nay: Ebenezer! Husband!"

"What's this? What are you doing?"

"Stay, hear me!" Susan urged. "'Tis true I'm but a whore and scurvy night-bag, and ruined by ill-usage. 'Tis true ye'd small choice in the wedding of me, and ye've small cause to love me. But I say again 'tis a strange life, and full o' things ye little dream of: not all is as ye think, my dove!"

"'Sheart!"

"I love ye!" she hissed. "Let's fly together from this sink o' perdition and begin anew in England! There's many a trick a poor man can play in London, and I know the bagful of 'em!"

"But marry," Ebenezer protested, snatching at the gentlest excuse he could think of. "I've not one fare, let alone two!"

Susan was not daunted. "'Tis a peddlepot ye've wed," she declared. "I'd as well turn my shame to our advantage, to rid us o' Maryland forever."

"What is't you intend?"

"I'll hie me to the curing-house anon, and whore the sum."

Ebenezer shook his head. "'Tis a noble plan," he sighed. "Such a whoredom were more a martyrdom, methinks, and merits awe. But I cannot go."

The woman released him. "Not go?"

"Nay, not though I changed my name and face and escaped my father's wrath forever. The living are slaves to memory and conscience, and should we flee together, the first would plague me with thoughts of Father and my sister Anna, while the second——" He paused. "I cannot say it less briefly or cruelly than this: nine months ago I pledged my love to the London girl Joan Toast and offered her my innocence, which she spurned. 'Twas after that I vowed to remain as virginal as a priest and worship the god of poetry. This Joan Toast had a lover, that was her pimp as well, and albeit 'twas on his account my father sent me off to Maryland, and I had every cause to think his mistress loathed me, yet she was ever in my thoughts, and in my most parlous straits thereafter, I never broke my pledge. Think, then, how moved I was to learn that she had followed after me, out of love! I had resolved to wed her, and make her mistress of my estate, and indeed I'd have done no less had all gone well, so much I love her! Now Malden's mine no more, and my Joan is disappeared from sight, and whether 'twas to escape marrying a wretched pauper she flew, or to join her lover McEvoy, still she came hither on my account, as did he. How could I fly with you to London, when I know not how they fare, or whether they live or die?"

Susan commenced weeping. "Am I so horrid beside your Joan? Nay, don't trouble to lie: I know by sight the beauty of her face, and the loathesomeness of mine. Little d'ye dream how jealous I am of her!"

"The world hath used you hardly," Ebenezer said.

"Ye know not half! I am its very sign and emblem!"

"And yet thou'rt generous and valiant, and have saved both Joan Toast and myself from death."

Susan grasped his arm. "What would ye say, if ye learned Joan Toast was in this very house?"

"What!" Ebenezer cried, starting up. "How can that be, and I've not seen her? What is't you say?"

"She is in this house this very moment, and hath been since she fled from Captain Mitchell! Here is proof." She drew from her bosom a necklace of dirty string, on which was threaded the fishbone ring presented to Ebenezer by Quassapelagh, the Anacostin King.

"I'God, the ring I gave you for her fare! Where is she?"

"Stay, Eben," Susan cautioned. "Ye've not heard all ye must before ye see her."

"A fart for't! Don't try to keep me from her!"

" 'Tis by her own instruction," Susan said, and blocked the door to the hallway. "Why is't, d'ye think, she hath not shown herself ere now?"

"Marry, I know not, nor dare I think! But I die to see her!"

" 'Tis only fit, for she hath done no less to see you."

Ebenezer stopped as if smitten by a hammer. Tears sprang to his eyes, and he was obliged to take the nearest seat—which happened to be the one at his writing desk—before he fell.

"Aye, she is dead!" Susan said. "Dead of French pox, opium, and despair! I saw her die, and 'twas not pretty."

"Ah God!" Ebenezer moaned, his features in a turmoil. "Ah God!"

"Ye know already how she was taken with love for ye, and for your innocence, after she had spurned ye in your room; and ye know she turned her back on John McEvoy when he wrote that letter to your father. A dream got hold of her, such as any whore is prone to, to live her life with you in perfect chastity, and it so possessed her that anon she vowed to follow ye to Maryland—the more inasmuch as 'twas on her account ye were sent thither—and she fondly hoped ye'd have her. But she had no money for her freight, and so for all she'd sworn to have no more o' whoring, it seemed she was obliged to swive her fare."

" 'Sheart, how this news wounds me!" Ebenezer cried.

" 'Tis joyous beside the rest," Susan declared. " 'Tis common knowledge that a pretty girl can swive most men round her finger, and any man at all if she hath fancy enough and spirit in her sporting—such is the world, and there's no help for't. 'Twas Joan Toast's plan to find a willing sea-captain, as hath many another lass, who'd let her warm his cabin the first week out in payment for her freight; yet she was so loath to play the whore again, she devised another scheme, the which was far more perilous and unpleasant in every way, but had the single merit that if it did not fail, she'd reach the Maryland shore unswived. She had heard it said along the wharves that whores were as scarce in America as Jews in the College o' Cardinals—so much so, that any lass who wished could cross the ocean free of charge in a certain ship, provided that when she got there she would hire herself to one or other of the whoremasters who met the boat."

Ebenezer groaned. "I dare not let my fancy run ahead!"

"Her new plan was, to sign aboard this vessel, that carried no other passengers but friskers, and so reach America unswived; once ashore, she'd bend her wit to find some means, of escaping her obligation—nor did that prospect much alarm her, for so eager were the provinces for women, and so eager the women for the high fees they could charge, there was no contract or other writ to bind 'em to their pledge."

"This ship," Ebenezer broke in. "I tremble to hear its name, but if she told you, I must know't."

" 'Twas called the *Cyprian*—the same that was attacked by pirates off the Maryland coast and all her women, save one, fetched to the rail and raped!"

"Save one? B'm'faith, then dare I hope——"

"Ye dare not," Susan said. "Joan Toast was the one, in sooth, that was not ravished at the rail, but the reason for't is, she fled aloft to the mizzen-rigging!"

"I'Christ, i'Christ, 'twas her!" Ebenezer cried. "Know, Susan, that these were the pirates of Captain Thomas Pound, the same that some time earlier had taken my valet and myself from the *Poseidon* at John Coode's behest! I know not how much Joan told you, but I must make confession now ere I perish of remorse: I was witness to this very piracy; I saw the *Cyprian* women bound up along the rail; I saw a hapless maid break free and scramble up the mizzen ratlines, though I little dreamed then who she was; I saw the Moor go after her——"

"That Moor!" Susan said with a shudder. "I know him well from her relation, and grow sick and cold at the memory! But hear the story——"

"I am not done with my confession," Ebenezer protested.

"Nor have ye aught to confess, that is not known to me already," Susan said grimly, and resumed her tale. "As soon as the pirates showed their colors, the captain advised the women not to resist but rather to submit with right good will, in hopes that once the pirates had swived their lust away, they'd leave 'em with a whole skin and a floating ship. But two girls hid in the farthest crannies of the bilge: Joan Toast because she'd vowed to stay chaste as a nun, and another girl so ruined with claps and poxes that she had but a few more days to live and wished to go to her grave unraped."

"And there the Moor discovered them! I am ill!"

"There he found 'em," Susan affirmed. " 'Twas what every lass shudders at in dreams: they crouched there in the dark, with the sounds o' lewd attack above their heads, and then the hatchway to the bilge was opened, and the monstrous Moor came in! He had a taper in his hand and in its light they saw his face and his great black body. When he spied the two women he gave a snort and leaped upon the nearest, that happened to be the one not far from death. 'Twas Joan's bad luck as well as his he could not see the wench's pox by candlelight, for anon when he was done and went for Joan, she would have two miseries instead of one to fear."

Ebenezer could only moan and shake his head.

"She made to flee whilst he was going at the sick girl, but he caught her by the ankle and knocked her such a swingeing clout she knew no more till he was carrying her and another up the ladderway to the deck. When she managed to break

507

free and climb the rigging, as ye witnessed, 'twas her last fond hope he would give o'er the chase and take his pleasure with the flossies on the deck; but ere she reached the top the roll and pitch o' the rig so terrified her, she was obliged to stop climbing and thrust her arms and legs through like a fly in a web. 'Twas there the great Moor cracked her till she fainted dead away, and 'twas there she hung till Heaven knows when—ravished, poxed, and seeded with the monster's seed!"

"Ah, no!"

"No less," Susan confirmed. "Albeit 'twas not made plain till some time after, the Moor had got her with child. Yet all this barbarous usage was as naught beside her next misfortune: she had scarce thrown off her swoon and found herself still hanging in the rigging, when she heard another pirate climbing up and calling lewdly to her as he climbed. She resolved to leap into the ocean if 'twas the Moor, but when she turned to look——"

" 'Twas I," Ebenezer wept, "and may I fry in Hell for't! For the first time in my life I was possessed with lust like any rutting goat, and I had no hope of seeing Joan Toast again, that I thought despised me. Great God, 'twas only Pound's departure saved her from another rape, and at the hands of the man she'd suffered all the rest for! To this day I cannot understand that weakness, nor the other, when I made to force *you* at Captain Mitchell's."

"For you 'twas simple lust, that mortal men are prone to," Susan replied, "but to Joan Toast 'twas the end o' the world, for she loved ye as more than mortal. When the *Cyprian* put in at Philadelphia she signed herself to the first whoremaster on the dock, that chanced to be Captain Mitchell o' Calvert County."

"Dear Heav'n, d'you mean to say——"

"I mean to say she was his harlot from the first! The pox she'd got from the Moor soon spread over her in foul eruptions, and no gentleman would hire her; what's more she learned she was with child. Anon she took to opium for respite from her miseries, and thus fell into Mitchell's hands by perpetual indenture, and was set to poxing salvages and sundry menial chores. 'Twas then ye appeared a castaway at Mitchell's, like a figure in a dream, and so ashamed she was of her ruin, and possessed by wrath that ye'd betrayed her, and withal despairing of her future, she vowed to make an end on't, and took her life. 'Twas not the fair Joan Toast o'

508

Locket's that this ring set o'er to Malden, but her awful corse!"

"And I her murtherer!" cried Ebenezer. He sprang up from the chair. "I shall see her grave and end my life as well! Where is her body?"

" 'Tis where it hath been many and many a time since the fall o' the year," Susan said, and laid her hand upon her chest. "Here is the corse of your Joan Toast, before your eyes!"

"Ah, nay, this cannot be!" But the realization that it was had already sent fresh tears down his cheeks. " 'Tis too impossible! Henry—Henry would have known, i'Christ! And Smith, your father——"

"Henry Burlingame hath known me from the night ye came to Mitchell's, and hath preserved the secret at my request."

"But the story of Susan Warren and Elizabeth Williams——"

" 'Tis true, the whole of't, save for one detail: it is the story of the poor girl's plight when I was brought to Mitchell's. 'Twas my likeness to her, and hers to Elizabeth Williams, that had fetched the high price he paid me; soon after he'd enthralled me with his opium, he murthered Susan in a fit o' rage, and buried her as Elizabeth Williams!"

" 'Sheart!"

" 'Twas necessary then," Joan declared, "to hide his crime, for he wanted no attention brought to bear on his business. Therefore he sought out William Smith at Malden and told him the girl had died o' pox; then, to be entirely safe, he promised to make Smith a wealthy whoremaster on condition he avow me as his daughter. The cooper's greed got the better of his sentiment, and of course I had no say in the matter."

"But marry!" Ebenezer cried. "This Mitchell's a greater fiend than his master Coode!"

"I know not who is Mitchell's master, or whether in sooth he hath one, but I know there is some monstrous plot afoot. Mitchell is freighting his opium to every quarter of the Province, and girls like me are set a-purpose to pox the hapless Indians."

The image of this latter, together with the memory of his behavior at Mitchell's and his share of responsibility for her plight in general, were too much for Ebenezer to endure: he was seized with a fit of dry retches that left him lying exhausted across the bed.

" 'Twas merely as a test I mentioned Joan Toast's name, to gauge your feeling for her; and another when I bargained to swive ye for my boat fare: had ye spurned me I'd have marked it to my ugliness, inasmuch as ye'd meant to rape me on the *Cyprian* when I was comelier. Yet when instead ye had at me in the bedchamber 'twas still no flattery, for ye declared ye'd play the virgin yet at Malden with Joan Toast."

"Only let me die for shame!" Ebenezer wailed. "Fetch me a pistol from below and take revenge for all your suffering! Or summon John McEvoy and tell him what you've endured on my account—I shall share his pleasure in murthering me!"

"I have already seen John McEvoy," Joan replied, "in this very house, not six weeks past. He had heard of your loss of Malden and sought me out through Burlingame whilst ye were ill."

"How must he loathe me!"

"E'en ere he'd seen the state I'd come to," Joan said glibly, " 'twas his greatest wish to kill ye."

"Then fetch him in to shoot me, and have done with't!"

"Hear me out." Joan moved to stand over him at the edge of the bed. "I told him we were man and wife, albeit ye were still virginal, and I loved ye yet despite my sore afflictions; and I told him that for your misfortunes, and my own, and his as well, no one of us could be blamed alone, but all must share the guilt. At last I said I love him still, but not as I love my husband, and that if he did ye harm, 'twould but be injuring me as well. Then I sent him away and bade him return no more, for *A woman may have at once three-score o' lovers, but only one beloved at a time*. I have had no news of him since, nor do I wish any."

Ebenezer was too overwhelmed to speak.

"Here is six pounds your father gave me to flee Mitchell with," Joan concluded briskly, laying the money on the counterpane. " 'Tis enough for one fare, and two hours in the curing-house will earn the other. The bark *Pilgrim* sails from Cambridge on the early-morning tide, to join the fleet at Kecoughtan."

"You are too good!" the poet wept. "What can I say or do to show my love?"

"No man can love the wreck ye married," Joan replied. "But if ye truly wish to ease my chore, there is a thing I'd have ye do."

"Anything!" Ebenezer swore, and then realized with horror what she might ask.

"I see your fear upon your face," Joan observed. "Put it by; 'tis not your innocence I crave."

"I swear to you——"

"Pray don't; 'twere a needless perjury. I ask ye but to wear this fishbone ring ye gave me, that hath such a curious value with some planters, and give me to wear in turn your silver seal ring: 'twill make me feel more a wife and less a hedge-whore."

" 'Tis little recompense," Ebenezer said, and though in fact it gave him considerable pain to relinquish the ring his sister had given him, he dared not show his feelings when he pulled it from his finger and Joan slipped the larger fishbone in its place.

"Swear to me thou'rt my husband!" she demanded.

"I swear't to Heav'n! And thou'rt my wife, for ever and aye!"

"Nay, Eben, 'twere too much for me to crave, and you to swear. I dare not hope ye'll even wait."

"May some god strike me dead if I do not! How can you think of't!"

Joan shook her head and turned the silver seal ring on her finger. "I must go to the curing-house now in any case," she said grimly. "The ring will help."

For some time after her departure Ebenezer lay fully dressed across the bed, still overcome by all he'd learned that evening. The candle, freshly lit after supper to illuminate the completion of his poem, had long since burned low and was extinguished by the slight draft from the hallway upon Joan's exit. In one hand he clutched the money she had left him; he fingered the fishbone ring and prayed wordless prayers of gratitude to whatever gods had granted him this means of escaping his father's wrath on the one hand and suicide on the other, and at the same time of discharging, in some measure, his awful obligation to Joan Toast.

"What business hath a poet with the business of the world?" he asked himself rhetorically. "With properties and estates, the tangled quarrels of governments, and the nets of love? They are his subject matter only, and the more he plays a part therein, the less he sees them clearly and entire. This was the great mistake I made in starting: the poet must fling himself into the arms of Life, e'en as I said, and pry into her priviest charms and secrets like a lover, but he must hide his heart away and ne'er surrender it, be cold as the callous gigolo, whose art with women springs from his detachment; or

511

like those holy fathers that wallowed once in sin, the better to hie them to their cells and reject the world with understanding, so the poet must engage himself in whate'er world he's born to, but shake free of't ere it shackle him. He is a keen and artful traveler, that finding himself in alien country apes the dress and manners of them that dwell there, the better to mark their barbarous custom; but a traveler nonetheless, that doth not linger overlong. He may play at love, or learning, or money-getting, or government—aye, even at morals or metaphysic—so long as he recalls 'tis but a game played for the sport of't, and for failure or success alike cares not a fart. I am a poet and no creature else; I shall feel conscience only for my art, and there's an end on't!"

This reflection he had launched by way of justifying his flight with Joan; by the time it assumed the tone of a manifesto, however, a new thought had occurred to him, so abominable that he thrust it from his mind at once, and yet so fascinating in its wickedness that it thrust itself back again and again.

"Ah God, that I should e'en conceive it! And whilst the poor wretch toils and shivers in some salvage's embrace to earn our passage!"

But for all he called the notion unthinkable, it was already thought, and the more he reviled and railed against it, the more tenacious grew its hold upon his fancy. After forty-five minutes or so he found himself saying, " 'Twas nowise her doing that the great Moor split her, and poxed her, and got a black babe in her, for all her opium and whoring, she is the same Joan Toast I love, nor was her character disfigured by Mitchell's purgatives and abuse, that ruined her hair and teeth. 'Twas saintly faith and charity to leave me this money, e'en though 'twas my own father she had it from, and that by fraud. What's more she is my wife: it matters naught in the eyes of Heaven that Richard Sowter may not be empowered to make marriages, or that I wed her under duress and she me under a false name, or that in the eyes of the law she hath committed scores and hundreds of adulteries, while our marriage hath not e'en been consummated! I must wait for her return, and in the event she hath not poxed six pounds-worth of filthy salvages, I must in conscience give Father's money back to her, and suffer his wrath after all—which will be so much the greater for her jilting him! Thus runs our Christian code of honor, and though as poet I'm but a guest, as't were, in Christendom, still a guest is bound to honor the rules of the house."

Yet bound by what, if not the very code in question? As best he could estimate, his time was running short: he rose from the bed, put a heavy coat about his shoulders, and searched out his ledger-book. Though he could not make out the verses in the dark, he sang in his head the fierce conclusion of his satire and hugged the notebook to his breast.

But at the darkened exitway he was flooded with a sweat of shame. "Nay, what am I doing! For all I'm more a poet now than ever in my life (and thus obliged to no soul save my muse nor any institution save my craft), and for all my pledge runs counter to the poet's creed and to the vow made long before to Anna, yet damn it, I have given my word, and sealed it with the rings!"

This was the final anguish. As he tiptoed down the stairs and out the back door of the house, he saw his sister's drawn and hardening features; as he stalked across the dark yard to the stables he recalled her presentation of the ring, and his answering nervous vow to make her dowry flourish. By the time he found some visitor's saddled horse and mounted, the image of Joan Toast had somehow got blurred with that of Burlingame, on the one hand, and his own cause merged in some way with Anna's on the other, so that the two pairs stood in an opposition no less positive for its being, presently at least, not quite identifiable.

A cold December wind swept over Cooke's Point and froze the tears on the poet's cheeks. He pressed his heels into the horse and cried "May some god strike me dead!" but clutched the bank note tightly lest he lose it in the dark.

PART III: MALDEN EARNED

1

The Poet Encounters a Man With Naught
to Lose, and Requires Rescuing

THROUGHOUT THE FROZEN fifteen miles between Cooke's
Point and the wharf at Cambridge, Ebenezer shivered not
from the wind alone, nor again from the simple self-revulsion
that came and went in clonic spasms, and between the sei-
zures of which he could affirm the cardinal value of his art
and the corollary value of his independence; what shook him
mainly was his fear that Joan might follow, or that he would
be recognized, apprehended, and returned to Malden as a fugitive from his late indenture. It was not yet dawn when he
arrived at the county seat: the inn and courthouse were dark,
but in the creek-mouth loomed the *Pilgrim,* her ports and
masthead lanterns lit, and about her decks as well as on the
wharf men toiled by lamplight to fit her out for the turning
of the tide. Now nearly set, the moon hid all but the morning
star; it pleased Ebenezer to imagine that it hung over the meridian of London like the star of old over Bethlehem, guiding
him to the cradle of his destiny.

"There's a figure Henry Burlingame would make mince-
meat of," he reflected, and tethering his horse, made his way
nervously towards the wharf. "I know not whether I am
Magus, Messiah, Lazarus, or the Prodigal."

He had not gone far through the laboring stevedores before a hand fell lightly on his shoulder and someone behind him asked, "Are ye quitting Cooke's Point so soon, Master Laureate?"

Ebenezer spun around to face his captor, but the man he saw, though distantly familiar, was no one whose intentions he could confidently assume to be hostile. It was a dirty, ragged old fellow with much untrimmed beard and no wig, thin as a skeleton, who had been coiling lines nearby.

"Who are you?" he demanded.

The fellow showed great surprise. "Ye do not even know me?" he cried, as though the possibility were too good to be true.

Ebenezer scrutinized him uncomfortably: barring a metamorphosis nothing short of miraculous, the man was not Burlingame, McEvoy, Sowter, Smith, or Andrew Cooke, and neither his dress nor his occupation suggested the county sheriff.

"I do not, nor why you accost me."

"Ah now, fear not, Mister Cooke, sir. I care not whether or wherefore ye sail, nor would it matter if I did: ye can see yourself I'm but a wharf rat, and could not stop ye."

"Then prithee let me go," Ebenezer said. "I must find passage out to yonder ship at once."

"Indeed?" The stevedore smiled a toothless smile and squeezed the poet's arm. "Is Madame Cooke sailing with ye, or doth her business keep her at Malden?"

"Put by your hand and your impertinence this instant," Ebenezer threatened, "or I'll have you sacked!" His voice was angry, but in truth he was terrified at the prospect of apprehension. Already a gentleman standing some distance behind the stevedore was watching them with interest.

"There's little ye can do to injure me," the stevedore sneered. "At my wages 'tis no threat to sack me, and I can't sink lower when I'm already on the bottom. Ye might say I am a man with naught to lose, for I've lost it all ere now."

"That is a pity," Ebenezer began, "but I do not see——"

"Know that not long since I was a gentleman, Master Poet, with horse and dog, wig and waistcoat, and sot-weed fields aplenty in my charge; but now, thanks to you, sir, 'tis a good day when my work so wearies me that I sleep o'er the growling of my gut, and I go in tatters, and harvest naught but vermin, chilblains, and blisters."

Ebenezer frowned incredulously. "Thanks to *me?*" Suddenly he recognized his detainer and tingled with alarm. "Thou'rt Spurdance, my father's overseer!"

"No other soul than he, that was deceived by your father, conspired against by your unholy friend Tim Mitchell, and ruined by yourself!"

"Nay, nay!" Ebenezer protested. "There is more to't than you know!" To his distress he saw the interested gentleman moving nearer. " 'Twas my poor innocence undid you!"

" 'Tis you, not I, that are benighted," insisted the stevedore. "I know ye granted Malden away in ignorance, and I know as well as you Tim Mitchell is not Tim Mitchell, nor Susan Warren Susan Warren. But I know too old Captain Mitchell, for all he was erst a wicked and unnatural rogue till some years past, hath lately been in the power of your friend Tim! 'Tis Tim Mitchell that is the grand high whoremaster, whoe'er he is and whoe'er he works for; 'tis he that oversees the opium trade from New York to Carolina; 'tis he conspires with Monsieur Casteene and the Naked Indians; 'tis he made the contracts with your father and the rest to turn their manors into brothels and opium-houses, now the sotweed market's fallen, and woe betide the honest overseer that will have none of't!" He grasped Ebenezer's other arm as well and crowded him backwards toward the bulkhead. "If he be not ruined by some ninny like yourself, that knows not black from white, he will be sacked by's crooked master; if he make the evil public, all his neighbors will turn on him as one man, lest their pleasures be curtailed, and if he dare make trouble for your nameless friend——"

"Beware the bulkhead, sir!" the approaching gentleman cried, and drew his short-sword.

"I cannot help it!" Ebenezer gasped, observing his peril. "This man——"

"Release him!" the stranger commanded.

Spurdance glanced wildly at the sword. "I've naught to lose, damn ye! This wretch and his devilish ally——"

The stranger smote him across the face with the flat of his sword, and before he could collect himself the point was at his gullet.

"Not another word upon that topic," the stranger said: "neither now nor later, else 'twill be your final word on earth." To the assembled stevedores he said, "This madman assaulted Master Cooke, the Laureate Poet of Maryland! If he's a friend of yours, fetch him out of here before I set the sheriff on him."

Though in all likelihood he had been recognized already, Ebenezer was alarmed at the proclamation of his name. Yet the stranger's manner quite awed the stevedores: two of them helped the injured Spurdance move off toward the inn, and another volunteered to ferry both gentlemen out to the *Pilgrim*.

"I'faith, you've saved my life, sir!" Ebenezer said.

"My honor, Mister Cooke," the stranger replied. He was a short, swarthy, and solidly proportioned man, rather older than the poet; he wore his natural iron-grey hair and a short beard of the same color, and his coat, boots, and breeches, though simply designed, were of expensive-looking material.

"Yonder is the *Pilgrim's* gig," he declared. "I'm Nicholas Lowe of Talbot, bound for St. Mary's City."

But even as he identified himself his face was illuminated by the lantern of a passing stevedore: Ebenezer recognized the bright eyes and unfortunate teeth and gasped.

"Henry!"

"*Nicholas* is the name," Burlingame repeated. "Nicholas Lowe, of Talbot County. Are you traveling alone, sir? I understood you were a married man."

Ebenezer blushed. "I—I must try to explain that, Henry, when there's time. But i'God, 'twas not for my sake you smote Spurdance!"

"No other cause," Burlingame said. "*A man may see his friend need, but he will not see him bleed.* And call me Nicholas, if you will, since Nicholas is my name."

"The things he said of you, and of Father! They dizzy me!"

"Sleeveless poppycock."

But Ebenezer shook his head. "What cause had he to lie? As he himself declared, he'd naught to lose."

" 'Tis not enough for trust that a man hath naught to lose," Burlingame replied, "if by virtue of that fact he hath somewhat to gain."

"Nor that he hath naught to gain," Ebenezer added bitterly, thinking of the attack on Spurdance, "when he hath much to lose."

"Yet remove all prospects for gain and loss alike, and for all your witness hath Truth for his mainsail, his rudder will be Whimsy and his breeze inconstant Chance."

"You'd have me think no man is trustworthy, then?" Ebenezer asked. "Methinks there is a motive in that cynicism!"

"What the saint calls cynicism," Burlingame said with a shrug, "the worldly man calls sense. The fact of't is, *all* men can be trusted, but not with the same things. Just as I might trust a sea-captain with my life, but not with my wife, so I trust Ben Spurdance's intention, but not his information. 'Tis only fools and children, or wretches blind with love like poor Joan Toast, that will trust a man with everything."

Ebenezer's face burned. "You know my shame!"

Burlingame shrugged. " 'Tis mankind's shame, is't not, that we are no angels? What have I learnt, save that thou'rt human, and Joan Toast such a fool as I described?"

"And I another!" the poet wept. "What was't but love for you that all these months hath scaled my eyes to your behavior, plugged my ears to your own admissions and the dire reports of others, and so deranged my reason that I justify your arrantest poltrooneries?"

"You believe that booby of an overseer," Burlingame said scornfully. "Why is't you do not swallow hook and leader as well, and believe those folks who say 'twas I brought Coode and Jacob Leisler together and set off the entire string of revolutions? Why not believe the gentlemen who make me chief lieutenant of the Pope or King Louis, or James the Second, or William Penn, or the Devil himself?"

"I believe no one any longer," Ebenezer replied. "I believe naught in the world save that Baltimore is the very principle of goodness, and Coode the pure embodiment of evil."

"Then I must make your disillusionment complete," his tutor said. "But now let's board our ship, or she'll make way without us." He started for the *Pilgrim*'s gig, but Ebenezer tarried behind. "Come on; what holds you back?"

Ebenezer covered his eyes. "Shame and fear; the same that urge me on!"

"They are the *cantinières* of all great enterprise and must be lived with."

"Nay," Ebenezer said. "This talk hath clipped the wings of my resolve: I cannot fly to England."

"Nor did I mean you to, but to St. Mary's City with me, on pressing business."

Ebenezer shook his head. "Whate'er your business, right or wrong, I am done with't."

Burlingame smiled. "And with your sister Anna as well? 'Tis she I hope to meet in St. Mary's City."

"Anna in Maryland! What new enormity is this?"

"We've not time for't here and now," laughed Burlingame, and led Ebenezer by the arm toward the waiting gig. "See yonder how the *Pilgrim* slacks her pendant? The tide is set to turn."

For a moment longer the poet resisted the familiar, urgent spell of his former tutor, but the news of Anna—though he allowed for its being altogether false—was too astonishing and intriguing to let pass. While they were being ferried out into the creek-mouth he fingered absently at his ring, as always when his thoughts dwelt on his sister, and it was with a little shock of regret that he felt fishbone instead of silver.

"What must Joan be doing now?" he wondered, and slipped the fishbone ring into his pocket lest it elicit questions from Burlingame.

Since he carried no other luggage than his ledger-book, it took but a few minutes for Ebenezer to sign on as a passenger aboard the *Pilgrim*. By the time the sun's rim edged the flat horizon the ship had left Castlehaven Point to larboard and was standing for the open waters of the Chesapeake. Both to warm himself and to avoid seeing Cooke's Point again. Ebenezer insisted that they go below, and demanded at once to hear whatever news Burlingame had of Anna.

"From what you told me in the Cambridge winehouse," he said tiredly, "she is more twin to Joan Toast than to me. Yet if in sooth she hath crossed the ocean, methinks her quest is not so chaste as Joan's. What have you learnt of her, Henry?"

"All in its place," said Burlingame. "To commence, you really must call me Nicholas Lowe. Your friend and tutor Burlingame is no more, but hath perished by his own hand."

"Nay, Henry." Ebenezer waved his hand wearily. "I am surfeited with poses and intrigues, and care not how or wherefore thou'rt disguised."

"This case is different," his friend persisted. "Nick Lowe's my legal name, I swear't. D'you recall what business it was first fetched me to Dorset, other than seeing you to Malden? 'Twas to find a Mr. William Smith, that had in his keeping some fragment of John Smith's secret history."

"Marry, that seems a decade past! You mean to say you got the papers from your friend the cooper, and they proved your name is Nicholas Lowe?"

"Slowly, slowly," Burlingame laughed. " 'Tis rather knottier than that. I've yet to lay my hands upon the papers, but when I first learned they were in Smith's possession, I asked him as if from simple curiosity what befell Sir Henry Burlingame in that final portion of the history, and in particular whether any mention was made in't of his issue. His answer was that as best he could recall, naught happened to Burlingame at all: John Smith contrived in some wise to take the salvage doxy's maidenhead, and both men returned to Jamestown shortly after."

Ebenezer frowned. "What's this of maidenheads? The last I

read was the piece you robbed the Jesuit of, that ended with their capture."

"That is the pity of't," Burlingame replied. "What the cooper hath is not Smith's history at all, but a piece of *The Privie Journall of Sir Henry Burlingame,* that tells of Smith's adventure with Pocahontas. 'Twas the first half of't you read in the carriage to Plymouth. Can you see the double import of this news?"

"I see it means your search was fruitless, unless there are more Smiths in Maryland to threaten with castration."

Burlingame laughed. "You little dream the relevance of your words! But aye, that is one implication of't: so far as I know, Smith's history ends where last we read; the rest either is lost or ne'er was writ, and Sir Henry's name appears no more in the records. When I learned this I called my search a failure, abandoned hope of proving my identity, and resolved to create one from the outside in. I went to Colonel Henry Lowe of Talbot, that once years ago I saved from Tom Pound's pirates and, after explaining who I was, prevailed upon him to save my life in turn by owning me as a son. Thus was Nick Lowe born, from nothing and without travail."

"I must own I scarcely see the need for't," Ebenezer said, "much less how 'twould save your life. But Heav'n knows 'tis not your first mysterious action."

"If you think it mysterious, reflect again on the fact that 'tis not Smith's history the cooper hath, but Sir Henry's *Privie Journall.* Do you recall how I came by the first half of that journal? 'Twas when I stole Coode's letters in England from his courier Ben Ricaud! The *Privie Journall* was John Coode's possession, not Baltimore's!"

In spite of his disinclination to show any great interest in Burlingame's affairs, Ebenezer could not conceal his curiosity at this disclosure.

"At first, after what I'd learned from Ben Spurdance," Burlingame went on, "it seemed no great wonder to me that Coode should trust Bill Smith with the papers, since Smith was Captain Mitchell's chief lieutenant on the Eastern Shore. But the more I reflected on't, the muddier it grew: why was the cooper's name included in the list I'd got from Baltimore, if he was one of Coode's company? And how explain the marvelous coincidence that Coode, as well as Baltimore, entrusted his papers to men of the surname Smith? 'Twas not till some days after your wedding, when I chanced to mention the matter to Spurdance at the Cambridge tavern, I learned that Coode had ne'er given Smith the papers in the first place—the cooper had long since stolen 'em from Ben Spurdance. 'Tis Spurdance is Coode's lieutenant, and 'twas on the strength of this prize that Bill Smith became Baltimore's; in fact, 'twas just this *coup* decided Baltimore to divide his precious Assembly Journal into halves—not thirds, as we supposed—and to entrust it to two other friends of his named Smith. He hath a bent for such theatrics, and the move hath cost him dearly."

"Then Smith is Baltimore's man and Spurdance Coode's?" Ebenezer asked incredulously. "How can that be, when the one is such a thorough-going varlet and the other, for all his temper, an honest man? And how is't an agent of Baltimore's is trafficking in whores and opium for Captain Mitchell—which is to say, for Coode? La, methinks expediency, and not truth, is this tale's warp, and subterfuge its woof, and you've weaved it with the shuttle of intrigue upon the loom of my past credulity! In short, 'tis creatured from the whole cloth, that even I can see doth not hang all in a piece. 'Tis a fabric of contradictories."

"It is indeed," Burlingame conceded, "if approached with the assumptions we both have steered by. But we are like a Swedish navigator I knew once in Barcelona that had dreamed up a clever way of reckoning longitude by the stars and was uncommon accurate in all respects save one: to his dying day he could not remember whether Antares was in Scorpius and Arcturus in the Herdsman, or the reverse. The consequence of't was, he reckoned his longitude by Antares with azimuths he'd sighted from Arcturus, and ran his ship into the Goodwin Sands! In plain language, I knew Mitchell had support from some powerful outside agency whose motive was more sinister than mere profit and, since his traffic is wicked, I assumed from the first that Coode was at the bottom of't. 'Twas not till this matter of Spurdance and Bill Smith that alternatives occurred to me——"

Ebenezer had been slouched wearily in his seat, but now he sat upright. "Surely thou'rt about to tell me Baltimore's involved in Mitchell's traffic!"

Burlingame nodded soberly. "Not merely *involved*, Eben: he is the heart, brains, and hand of't! His plan, no less, is so to enervate the English in America with opium, and friendly towns of salvages with the pox, that anon the several governments will fall to the French and the Naked Indians of Monsieur Casteene. Thereupon the Pope hath pledged himself to intervene and unite all the colonies into one great bailiwick of Romanism, and Baltimore, as reward for his services, will be crowned Emperor of America for his lifetime and a holy Catholic saint upon his death!"

"But 'tis absurd!" Ebenezer protested.

Burlingame shrugged. "That Baltimore stands behind Mitchell I am certain, and viewed through the lens of this knowledge, the entire history of the Province takes on a different aspect: who knows but what old William Claiborne was a hero, along with Penn and Governor Fendall and the rest, and Baltimore the monster all along? All I know of Coode is that he hath worked counter to every government in Maryland: did it e'er occur to you that they all might have been as corrupt as Baltimore himself, and that Coode, like Milton's Satan, might more deserve our sympathy than our censure?"

Ebenezer pressed his palm to his forehead and shuddered. "The prospect staggers me!"

" 'Tis not that the facts are absent, after all—I have been Baltimore's chief intriguer these four years, and am privy to more facts than ever Sallust knew of Catiline. The difficulty is, e'en on the face of 'em the facts are dark—doubly so if you grant, as wise men must, that an ill deed can be done with good intent, and a good with ill; and triply if you hold right and wrong to be like windward and leeward, that vary with standpoint, latitude, circumstance, and time. History, in short, is like those waterholes I have heard of in the wilds of Africa: the most various beasts may drink there side by side with equal nourishment."

"But what is this," Ebenezer asked, "except to say the facts avail one naught in making judgments! Is't not that very notion I affirmed last fall in Cambridge, at the cost of my estate?"

"Not at all," Burlingame replied, "for the court judge dons his values with his robe and wig, that are made for him by the legion of the judged, and the jury hath no other office save to rule on facts. Besides which, they see the litigants face to face and hear their testimony, and so can judge their character; but for all his notoriety I ne'er have met the man who hath seen John Coode face to face, nor, despite his fame and influence and the great trust he hath placed in me, have I myself ever seen Lord Baltimore, any more than you have."

"How can that be?"

Burlingame answered that all his communication with the Lord Proprietary had been through messengers, for Baltimore had confined himself to his chambers on the grounds of illness.

"There is no way to lay eyes upon Baltimore now," he said, "but I have lately sworn myself a solemn vow: if there lives in fact such a creature as this John Coode—that hath been Catholic priest, Church-of-England minister, sheriff, captain, colonel, general, and Heav'n alone knows what else —I shall confront him face to face and learn once for all what cause he stands for! 'Tis to seek him out, and Anna as well, I am en route to St. Mary's City."

At mention of his sister's name all thoughts of Maryland politics vanished from the poet's mind, and he demanded once again to know why she and Andrew had come to the province so long before their scheduled visit.

"Your father's cause will be clear," Burlingame said, "once I've told you that they did not make the voyage together. 'Tis to seek her out he's come, and haply to negotiate with Mitchell. He little dreamt, when last I saw him, that he had no more estate in Maryland—but haply he hath heard the news by now. . . ."

"Then Spurdance's charge is true, that my father is in league with Mitchell!"

"Not yet, to the best of my knowledge, but 'twill be true enough anon. What with the war, the want of foreign markets, the unseasonable weather, the scarcity of ships and hardy plants, the fly, the ground worm, the horn-worm, the house-burn, the frostbite, and the perils of sea and enemies, your sot-weed planter nowadays is in sore straits. Some have sold half their landholdings to clear the rest; some have turned to other crops, scarce worth the work of growing; some have moved to Pennsylvania, where the soil hath not as yet been leached and drained of spirit; and some, that have no love for these alternatives, have turned from planting to more lucrative fields. I have cause to think old Andrew had an audience on this topic with Lord Baltimore ere he sailed, else he'd no reason to come straight from Piscataway to Captain Mitchell's, where Joan and I caught sight of him two days past. 'Twas then we fled together—she to warn you of his presence, I to make my bargain with Colonel Henry Lowe and meet the twain of you here. I could stay no more with Mitchell, not alone because I'd learned my search was hopeless, but also because the real Tim Mitchell, so I have heard, is en route to the Province. What's more, the Jesuit priest Thomas Smith, that we called upon near Oxford, hath complained to Lord Baltimore of my abusing him, and on all sides I was looked at with suspicion."

"But damn it!" Ebenezer cried. "What of my sister? Where is she now, and why hath she come to Maryland?"

"You know the cause as well as I," said Burlingame.

"That she loves you!" Ebenezer groaned. "Ah God, how pleased that news would once have made me! But now I know you for the very essence of carnality, I feel as Mother Ceres must have felt, when Pluto took Proserpine for his bride. And galled—i'faith, it galls me sore to think how she praised my innocence, joined hers to mine there in the London posthouse, and sealed our virgin vows with her silver ring! And all was guile and cruel deceit; you'd long since had her maidenhead in the summer-house, and swived her behind my back in London, and e'en that very day of my departure, ere my business with Ben Bragg was done, the twain of you had billed and cooed all shameless in the public view. Hypocrisy! What lewd delight she must have taken in swearing to me she would be chaste, when even as she swore she still felt your hands upon her, and yearned for one last tumble on your bed! 'Tis clear now why that last farewell discomfited me, and the matter of the rings: she was so taken with rut for you, that stood disguised not ten yards distant, she fancied 'twas you whose hand she toyed with, and the fancy near made her swoon!"

"Enough!" Burlingame ordered. "If you believe this rot in sooth, thou'rt not so much innocent as stupid!"

"You deny it?" the poet cried. "You deny 'twas your lewd connection my father learned of in St. Giles and sacked you for?"

"Nay, not entirely."

"And those foul boasts in the Cambridge tavern!" Ebenezer pressed angrily. "That she hath begged you to have at her, and discovered her secrets to your eyes, and gone mad with joy in your lubricious games—do you deny these now?"

"They are true enough in substance," Burlingame sighed, "but what you fail to see——"

"Then where lies my stupidity, save in esteeming her too much to see 'twas common lust for you that fetched her to our rooms in Thames Street, and that this same monstrous lust hath brought her half round the world to warm your bed?"

"No more, you fool!" exclaimed Burlingame. " 'Tis love in

527

sooth hath driven her hither, or lust, if you prefer; but love
or lust—i'Christ, Eben!—have you not remarked these many
years 'tis *you* that are its object?"

2

A Layman's Pandect of Geminology Compended by Henry Burlingame, Cosmophilist

EBENEZER'S FEATURES contorted wondrously. "Dear Heav'nly
Father, Henry! What have you said?"

Burlingame turned his fist in his palm and frowned at the
deck as he spoke. "Your sister is a driven and fragmented
spirit, friend; the one half of her soul yearns but to fuse itself
with yours, whilst the other half recoils at the thought. 'Tis
neither love nor lust she feels for you, but a prime and massy
urge to *coalescence*, which is deserving less of censure than
of awe. As Aristophanes maintained that male and female are
displaced moieties of an ancient whole, and wooing but their
vain attempt at union, so Anna, I long since concluded, repines willy-nilly for the dark identity that twins share in the
womb, and for the well-nigh fetal closeness of their childhood."

"I shudder at the thought!" Ebenezer whispered.

"As well doth Anna—so much so, that her fancy entertains
it only in disguise—yet no other thought than this impelled
her to me in the summer-house! 'Twas quite in the middle of
a fine May night, the night of your sixteenth birthday, and
though the time for't was some days past, a shower of meteors was flashing from Aquarius. I had lingered late outside
to watch these falling stars and plot their courses on a map
of my own devising; so engrossed was I in the work that
when Anna came up behind——"

"No more!" cried Ebenezer. "You took her maidenhead,
God curse you, and there's an end on't!"

"Quite otherwise," Burlingame replied. "We spent some
hours discussing you, that were asleep in your chamber.

Anna likened you to Phosphor, the morning star, and herself to Hesper, the mortal star of evening, and when I told her those twin stars were one and the same, and not a star at all but the planet Venus, the several portents of this fact near made her swoon! We tarried long in the summer-house that night, and long on many a balmy night thereafter; yet always, I will swear't, I pleased her in no wise save as your proxy."

"I'God, and you think this argues to your credit?"

Burlingame smiled. "There are two facts you've got to swallow, Eben. The first is that I love no part of the world, as you might have guessed, but the entire parti-colored whole, with all her poles and contradictories. Coode and Baltimore alike I am enamored of, whate'er the twain might stand for; and you know what various ground hath held my seed. For this same reason 'twas never you I loved, nor yet your sister Anna, but the twain inseparably, and could lust for neither alone. Whence issues the second fact, which is, that de'il the times her blood waxed warm the while she spoke of you, and de'il the times I kissed her as the symbol for you both, and played the sad games of her invention, yet your sister is a virgin still for aught of me!"

He laughed at Ebenezer's shock and disbelief. "Aye, now, that wants some chewing, doth is not? Think with what relish, as a child, she would play Helen to your Paris, but ever call you *Pollux* by mistake! Recall that day in Thames Street when you chided her for lack of suitors and as a tease proposed me for the post——"

Ebenezer clutched his throat. "Marry!"

"Her reply," Burlingame went on, "was that the search for beaux was fruitless, *inasmuch as the man she loved most had the bad judgment to be her twin!* And reflect, in the light of what I've told you, on this matter of your mother's silver ring, that Anna gave you in the posthouse: did you know she was wont to read the letters *ANNE B* as *ANN* and *EB* conjoined? Can a poet be blind to the meaning of that gift and of the manner of its giving?"

"To contemplate it is to risk the loss of my supper," Ebenezer groaned, "yet I must own there is some sense in all you say——" His face hardened. "Save that she's still a maid! That's too much!"

His friend shrugged. "Believe't or no. We'll find her anon, I pray, and you may get a physician's word for't if you please."

"But what you bragged of in the Cambridge tavern!"

"*Many shuffle the cards that do not play.* I could as easily

529

have had at you in Bill Mitchell's barn, but the truth is, as I said before, 'tis not the one nor the other I crave, but the twain as one. Haply the day will come when Anna's secret lust will get the better of her reason and your own likewise (which, deny't as you may, is plain to me!): if such a day dawn, why then perchance I'll come upon you *sack a sack* as did Catallus on the lovers, and like that nimble poet pin you to your work—nay, skewer you both like twin squabs on a spit!"

The poet shuddered. "This is too much to assimilate, Henry: Coode a hero; my father in Maryland searching for Anna and leagued with the villain Baltimore; Anna herself yet virginal; and you, after all that hath transpired—you wholly innocent and still my friend! And marry come up, you make matters no simpler when you declare my sister's lust to be reciprocal! Such a prurient notion hath never crossed my mind!"

Burlingame raised his eyebrows. "Then you quite deceived your servants at St. Giles. Mrs. Twigg was wont to tell me——"

"She was a foul-fancied harridan!"

"Why, they even had a rhyme, the which——"

"I know their scurrilous rhyme, whate'er it be," Ebenezer said impatiently. "I have heard a dozen such, since I was small. Nor is your wicked imputation foreign to me, if you must know, albeit I'm not a little shocked to hear you share it. Poor Anna and I since birth have breathed in an air of innuendo, the which hath oft and oft caused us to blush and lower our eyes. Since I was ten our father's household hath assumed the worst of us, for no other reason than that we were twins. 'Twas Anna's ill luck her body blossomed at an early age, and e'en her fondest girl friends—e'en that same Meg Bromly who took your letters to her from Thames Street—they all declared her ripening was my work and drove Anna to tears with their whispering! All this, mind, on no grounds whate'er save our twinship, and the fact that unlike many brothers and sisters we never quarreled, but preferred each other's company to the concupiscent world's! I cannot grasp it."

"Then for all thy Cambridge learning," Burlingame laughed, "thou'rt not by half the scholar your sister is! When first I guessed her trouble, long ere she saw't herself, we launched a long and secret enquiry into the subject of twins —their place in legend, religion, and the world. 'Twas my intent by this investigation not so much to cure Anna's itch—

530

which I was not at all persuaded was an ailment—as 'twas to understand it, to see it in's perspective in the tawdry history of the species, and so contrive the most enlightened way to deal with it. I need not say my interest was as heartfelt as her own; her oft-sworn love for me, I could see clearly, was love for you, diverted and transmogrified by virtuous conscience. When she would run to me in the summer-house, 'twas as a jilted maiden runs to a convent and becomes the bride of Christ, and I sorely feared, if her case were not soon physicked, 'twould bereave her altogether of her reason or else drive her to some surrogate not so tender of her honor as was I."

"Dear God!"

"For this reason I led her on," Burlingame continued. "I declared my love for her—half in truth, you understand—and together we explored the misty land of legends, Christian and pagan. Four years we studied—from your fourteenth to your eighteenth year—and all in secret. On the face of't our enquiry was beyond reproach, and I yearned for you to join us, but Anna would have none of't. I'faith, Eben, what a tireless scholar is your sister!" He shook his head in reminiscent awe. "I could not find her volumes enough of voyage and travels, or heathen rites and practices: she would fall on 'em like a lioness on her prey, devour 'em in great bites, and thirst for more! I'd wager my life on't, at seventeen years she was the world's foremost authority on the subject of twins, and is today."

"And I knew naught of't!" Ebenezer shook his head and laughed uncomprehendingly. "But what is there to know of us twins, save that we were conceived in a single swiving?"

"Why, that Gemini is your sign and springtime your season," Burlingame replied.

"It wants no scholarship to hit on that. 'Tis common knowledge."

"As is the fact that springtime—and Maytime in particular —is the season of fertility and the year's first thunderstorms."

"Don't tease!" the poet said irritably. "This day and night have been my life's most miserable, and I am near dead from shock and want of sleep, to say naught of misery. If all your study ploughed up no lore save this, have done with't and let us rest. 'Tis all impertinence."

"On the contrary," Burlingame declared. "So pertinent are our findings, methinks you'd as well give o'er the search for Anna unless you hear 'em: 'tis better to be lost than saved by the wrong Messiah." His manner and tone grew serious.

531

"You know that spring is the season of storms and fertility, but do you know, as doth your sister, that of all the things our rustic forebears feared, the three that most alarmed them were thunder, lightning, and twins? Did you know thou'rt worshipped the whole world over, whether by murther or by godhood, if not both? Through the reverence of the most be-nighted salvage runs this double thread of storms and forni-cation, and the most enlightened sages have seen in you the embodiment of dualism, polarity, and compensation. Thou'rt the Heavenly Twins, the Sons of Thunder, the Dioscuri, the Boanerges; thou'rt the twin principles of male and female, mortal and divine, good and evil, light and darkness. Your tree is the sacred oak, the thunder-tree; your flower is the twin-leaved mistletoe, seat of the oak tree's life, whose twin white berries betoken the celestial semen and are thus em-ployed to rejuvenate the old, fructify the barren, and turn the shy maid's fancies to lusty thoughts of love. Your bird is the red cock Chanticleer, singer of light and love. Your emblems are legion: twin circles represent you, whether suggested by the sun and moon, the wheels of the solar chariot, the two eggs laid by Leda, the nipples of Solomon's bride, the spec-tacles of Love and Knowledge, the testicles of maleness, or the staring eyes of God. Twin acorns represent you, both be-cause they are the thunder-tree's seed and because their two parts fit like male and female. Twin mountains represent you, the breasts of Mother Nature; the Maypole and its ring are danced round in your honor. Your sacred letters are *A, C, H, I, M, O, P, S, W, X,* and *Z*——"

"I'Christ!" Ebenezer broke in. " 'Tis half the alphabet!"

"Each hath its separate import," Burlingame explained, "yet all have common kinship with swiving, storms, and the double face of Nature. Your *A,* for example, is the prime and mightiest letter of the lot—a god in itself, and wor-shipped by heathen the great world round. It represents the forked crotch of man, the source of seed, and also, by's peak and by's cross-line, the union of twain into one, that I'll speak of anon. When you set two *A*'s cheek by jowl you see the holy nippled paps of Mother Earth, as well as the sign of the holy Asvins, the twin charioteers of Eastern lore. Your *C* be-tokens the crescent moon, that in turn is held to resemble man's carnal sword, unsheathed and rising to the fray; two *C*'s entwined are the union of Heaven and Earth, or Christ and his earthly church——"

"In Heav'n's name, Henry, what are these riddles thou'rt flooding me with?"

"Anon, anon," Burlingame said. "Your *H* portrays the same happy union of two into one: 'tis the zodiac sign for Gemini; the bridge 'twixt the twin pillars of light and dark, love and learning, or what have you; 'tis also the eighth letter, and inasmuch as 8 is the mystic mark of redemption (by virtue of its copulating circles), 'tis no surprise that *H* is the emblem of *atonement*—the making of two into one."

"Again this mystery of twos and ones!" the poet protested.

" 'Tis no mystery when you know about *I* and *O*," said Burlingame. "In every land and time folk have maintained that what we see as *two* are the fallen halves of some ancient *one*—that night and day, Heaven and Earth, or man and woman were long since severed by their sinful natures, and that not till Kingdom Come will the fallen twain be a blessed one. 'Tis this lies 'neath the tale of Eve and Adam, and Plato's fable, and the fall of Lucifer, and Heav'n knows how many other lovely lies; 'tis this the Lord Himself refers to, in the second epistle of Pope Clement: He declares His Kingdom shall come *When the two shall be one, and the outside as the inside, and the male with the female.* Thus all men reverence the act of fornication as portraying the fruitful union of opposites: the Heavenly Twins embraced; the Two as One!"

Ebenezer shivered.

"Your *I* and *O* are plainly then discovered," Burlingame said with a smile: "the one is male, the other female; together they are the great god Io of Egypt, the ring on the maidens' merry Maypole, the acorn in its cup, the circumcised prepuce of the Jew, the genital letters P and Q—and the silver seal ring Anna slipped upon your finger in the posthouse!"

"I'God!"

"As for the others, your *M* is the twin mountain breasts I spoke of; *S* is the copulation of twin *C*'s face to face, and is sprung as well from the sacred *Z; W*—the double-*you*, as *M* is the double-*me*—*W,* I say, is a pair of *V*'s *sack a sack:* 'tis thus the sign of the Heavenly Twins of India, called *Virtrahana,* and the third part of the Druids' invocation to their god, the whole of which was I.O.W. X, like A and H, is the joining of Two into One, and as such hath been venerated since long ere the murther of Christ; Z is the zigzag lightning flash of Zeus, or whatever god you please, and is ofttimes flanked, in ancient emblems, by the circles of the Heavenly Twins——"

"Enough!" the poet cried. "This dizzies me! What is the message of't, and what hath it to do with Anna and me?"

"Why, naught in the world," Burlingame responded, "save to show you how deep in the marrow of man runs this fear and reverence for twins, and their connection with coitus and the weather. All over Africa the birth of twins is followed by dances of the lewdest sort: sometimes 'tis thought to prove the mother an adulteress, since husbands generally get one babe at a time; other folk think the mother hath been swived by the Holy Spirit, or that the father hath an inordinate lingam. In sundry isles of the western ocean 'tis common for the salvages to throw coffee beans at the walls of a house where twins are born; they believe that otherwise one must die, inasmuch as twins break the laws of chastity while still embraced in their mother's womb! In divers lands no living twins can be found, for the reason that one is always slain at birth; but murthered or not, they are worshipped in every place, and have been since time out of mind. The old Egyptians had their Taues and Taouis, the twins of Serapeum at Memphis, as well as the sisters Tathautis and Taebis, the ibis-wardens of Thebes; in India reigned Yama and Yami, and the holy Asvins I spoke of earlier, that drew the Heavenly Chariot; the Persians worshipped Ahriman and Ormuz; the ancient myths of the Hebrews tell of Huz and Buz, Huppim and Muppim, Gog and Magog, and Bnē and Baroq, to say naught of Esau and Jacob, Cain and Abel—or as the Mohammedans have it, Cain and Alcimand Abel and Jumella——"

"Ah!" Ebenezer exclaimed.

"Some held," Burlingame went on, "that Lucifer and Michael were twins, as are most gods of Light and Darkness; and for the selfsame cause the old Edessans of Mesopotamia, who erst had worshipped Monim and Aziz, were wont to regard e'en Jesus and Judas as hatched from a single egg!"

"Incredible!"

"No more than that God and Satan themselves——"

"I don't believe it!" Ebenezer protested.

" 'Tis not a question of your belief," laughed Burlingame, "but of the fact that other wights think it true; 'tis but a retelling of the tale of Set and Horus, or Typhon and Osiris, whom some Egyptians took for twins and others merely for rivals. But I was coming to the Greeks . . ."

"You may pass o'er them," sighed the poet. "I know of Castor and Pollux, the sons of light and thunder, and as well of Helen and Clytemnestra, that were hatched with 'em from Leda's eggs."

"Then you must know too of Lynceus and Idas, that slew the Dioscuri; of Amphion and Zethus, that sacked and rebuilt

534

Troy; of Heracles and Iphikles, that are twins in this tale and half-brothers in that, and of Hesper and Phosphor, the morning and evening stars."

"And now you'll go to Rome, I'll wager, and speak of Romulus and Remus?"

"Aye," said Burlingame, "to say naught of Picumnus and Pilumnus, or Mutumnus and Tutumnus. 'Twas the great respect accorded these classic twins that carried them into the Christian Church, which had the good sense to canonize 'em. Hence the Greek and Roman Catholics pray to Saints Romolo and Remo, Saints Kastoulos and Polyeuctes, and e'en St. Dioscoros; the fonder amongst them go yet farther and regard as twins Saints Crispin and Crispian, Florus and Laurus, Marcus and Marcellianus, Protasius and Gervasius——"

"A surfeit!" cried the poet. "There is a surfeit!"

"You have not heard the best," Burlingame insisted. "They will hold Saints John and James to be twins as well, and e'en Saints Jude and Thomas, inasmuch as *Thomas* means 'a twin.' I'll not trouble you with Tryphona and Tryphosa, that Paul salutes in's Epistle to the Romans, but turn instead to the Aryan heroes Baltram and Sintram, or Cautes and Cautopates, and the northern tales of Sieglinde and Siegmunde, the incestuous parents of Siegfried, or Baldur, the Norseman's spirit of Light, and his enemy, dark Loki, that slew him with a branch of mistletoe!"

"'Tis a hemisphere o'erridden with godly twins!" Ebenezer marveled.

Burlingame smiled. "Yet it wants twin hemispheres to make a whole: when Anna and I turned our eyes to westward, we found in the relations of the Spanish and English adventurers no less a profusion of Heavenly Twins, revered by sundry salvages; and the logs of divers voyages to the Pacific and Indian Oceans were no different. Old Cortez, when he raped the glorious Aztecs, found them worshipping Quetzalcoatl and Tezcatlipoca, as their neighbors reverenced Hunhun-ahpu and Vukub-hun-ahpu. Pizarro and his cohorts, had they been curious enough to ask, would have found in the southern pantheon such twins as Pachakamak and Wichoma, Apocatequil and Piquerao, Tamendonaré and Arikuté, Karu and Rairu, Tiri and Karu, Keri and Kame. Why, I myself, enquiring here and there among the Indians of these parts, have learnt from the Algonkians that they reverence Menabozho and Chokanipok, and from the Naked Indians of the north that they pray to Juskeha and Tawiskara. From the Jesuit missionaries I have learnt of a nation called the Zuñi, that worship Ahaiyuta and Matsailema; of another called Navaho, that worship Tobadizini and Nayenezkani; of another called Maidu, that worship Pemsanto and Onkoito; of another called Kwakiutl, that worship Kanigyilak and Nemokois; of another called Awikeno, that worship Mamasalanik and Noakaua—all of them twins. Moreover, there is in far Japan a band of hairy dwarfs that pray to the twins Shi-acha and Mo-acha, and amongst the gods of the southern ocean reign the great Si Adji Donda Hatahutan and his twin sister, Si Topi Radja Na Uasan . . ."

" 'Tis your scheme to drive me mad!"

"That is their name, I swear't."

"No matter! No matter!" Ebenezer shook his head as though to jar his senses into order. "You have proved to the very rocks and clouds that twin-worship is no great rarity in this earth!"

Burlingame nodded. "Sundry pairs of these twins are opposites and sworn enemies—such as Satan and God, Ahriman and Ormuz, or Baldur and Loki—and their fight portrays the struggle of Light with Darkness, the murther of Love by Knowledge, or what have you. Sundry others represent the equivocal state of man, that is half angel and half beast: the first of such pairs is mortal and the second divine. Still others are the gods of fornication, like Mutumnus and Tutumnus, or Picumnus and Pilumnus; if less than gods, they yet may be remembered for incestous lust, like Cain and his Alcima, and even be honored for swiving up a hero, as were Sieglinde and Siegmunde. How Anna loved the Siegfried tales!"

So heavy with revelations was the poet, he could only wave his hand against this remark.

"Yet whether their bond be love or hate or death," Burlingame concluded, "almost always their union is brilliance, totality, apocalypse—a thing to yearn and tremble for! 'Tis this union Anna desires with all her heart, howe'er her mind disguise it; 'tis this hath brought her halfway round the globe to seek you out, and your father to fetch her home if he can find her. 'Tis this your own heart bends to, will-ye, nill-ye, as a flower to the light, to make you one and whole and nourished as ne'er since birth; or as a needle to the lode, to direct you to the harbor of your destiny! And 'tis this I yearn for too, and naught besides: I am Suitor of Totality, Embracer of Contradictories, Husband to all Creation, the Cosmic Lover! Henry More and Isaac Newton are my pimps and *aides-de-chambre;* I have known my great Bride part by splendrous part, and have made love to her *disjecta membra,*

- 536

her sundry brilliant pieces; but I crave the Whole—the tenon in the mortise, the jointure of polarities, the seamless universe —whereof you twain are token, *in coito!* I have no parentage to give me place and aim in Nature's order: very well—I am outside Her, and shall be Her lord and spouse!"

Burlingame was so aroused by his own rhetoric that at the end of his speech he was pacing and gesturing about the cabin, his voice raised to the pitch and volume of an Enthusiast's; even had Ebenezer not been too dismayed for skepticism, he could scarcely have questioned his former tutor's sincerity. But he was stunned, as well with recognition as with appall: he clutched his head and moaned.

Burlingame stopped before him. "Surely you'll not deny your share of guilt?"

The poet shook his head. "I'll not deny that the soul of man is deep and various as the reach of Heav'n," he replied, "or that he hath in germ the sum of poles and possibilities. But I am stricken by what you say of me and Anna!"

"What have I said, but that thou'rt human?"

Ebenezer sighed. " 'Tis quite enough."

By this time the sun was bright in the eastern sky, and the *Pilgrim* stood well down the Bay for Point Lookout and St. Mary's City. The other passengers were awake and stirring about their quarters. At Burlingame's suggestion they fastened their scarves and coats and went on deck, the better to speak in private.

"How is't you know Anna to be in St. Mary's? Why did she not come straight to Malden?"

" 'Tis your man Bertrand's fault," Burlingame answered and, laughing at Ebenezer's bewilderment and surprise, confessed that when he had dispatched Bertrand from Captain Mitchell's to St. Mary's City back in September, he had charged the valet not only to retrieve the Laureate's trunk but if possible to claim it in the guise of the Laureate himself, the better to throw John Coode off the scent while they made their way to Malden. "To this end I rashly loaned him your commission——"

"My commission! Then 'tis true you stole it from me back in England!"

Burlingame shrugged. " 'Twas I authored it, was't not? Besides, would it not have gone worse with you had Pound been certain of your identity? In any case, there was some peril in your man's assignment, and 'twas my thought, if Coode should kill or kidnap him with the paper on his person, he might think you yourself were an impostor—'twould have spun his compass for fair! Howbeit, Bertrand could not rest at fetching your trunk, it seems, but must parade St. Mary's City as the Laureate and declare his post in every inn and tavern."

Thus it was, Burlingame declared, that on reaching the port of St. Mary's some time ago, Anna had been given to think her brother was in the town and had disembarked in quest of him. "I myself heard naught of this until old Andrew came to Captain Mitchell's; he had learnt in London of my whereabouts, and, like you, thinks Anna hath come to be my wife. But he believes thou'rt party to the scheme as well and are pimping us in some wise: when he learns the state of things at Malden, today or tomorrow, he'll assume you've fled with the twain of us to Pennsylvania, where fly all fugitives from responsibility—the more readily, inasmuch as neither Anna nor the false Laureate hath been seen or heard of since she landed." He sucked in the corner of his mouth. " 'Twas my intent to stay with Andrew, disguised as Timothy Mitchell, the better to temper his wrath and learn his connection with Lord Baltimore; but so vain hath been my search for parentage in the world, and so much rancor hath that search engendered, 'twas no longer safe to play that role."

Ebenezer asked what were his tutor's present plans.

"We'll put ashore together at St. Mary's," Burlingame said. "You then enquire in public places for news of Anna or Eben Cooke, and I shall search alone for Coode."

"At once? Is't not more urgent to find my sister ere some harm befall her?"

" 'Tis but two paths to a single end," replied Burlingame. "No man knows more than Coode of what transpires in Maryland, and for aught we know he may have made prisoners of them both. Besides which, if I can win his confidence, he may abet us in regaining your estate. 'Twill be a joy to him, after all, to hear the Laureate of Maryland is his ally!"

"Not so swiftly," Ebenezer protested. "I may be disabused of my faith in Baltimore, but I've sworn no oaths of loyalty to John Coode. In any case, as you well know, I ne'er was Laureate—and even had I been, I'd be no longer. Look at this." He drew the ledger from his coat and showed Burlingame the finished *Marylandiad*, which in view of its antipanegyric tone he had retitled *The Sot-Weed Factor*. "Call't a clumsy piece if you will," he challenged. " 'Tis honest nonetheless, and may spare others my misfortunes."

"What's full of heart may be bare of art," Burlingame as-

serted with interest, "—and vice-versa." He held the ledger open against the rail and read the work closely several times while the *Pilgrim* ran down the Bay to Point Lookout, where the Potomac River meets Chesapeake Bay. Although he made no comments either favorable or unfavorable, when the time came for them to transfer to the lighter for St. Mary's City he insisted that the poem be forwarded aboard the *Pilgrim* to Ben Bragg, at the Sign of the Raven in Paternoster Row.

"But he'll destroy it!" exclaimed the poet. "D'you recall how I came by this ledger back in March?"

"He'll not destroy it," Burlingame assured him. "Bragg is obliged to me in ways I shan't describe."

There was no time to ponder the proposal; with some misgivings Ebenezer allowed his former tutor to entrust *The Sot-Weed Factor* to the bark's captain, who also refunded the balance of his fare to England, and the two men ferried upriver to St. Mary's City.

3

A Colloquy Between Ex-Laureates of Maryland, Relating Duly the Trials of Miss Lucy Robotham and Concluding With an Assertion Not Lightly Matched for Its Implausibility

NOT LONG AFTER HIS arrival in the Province some months previously, Governor Francis Nicholson had declared his intention to move the seat of Maryland's government from St. Mary's City, which was unhappily associated with Lord Baltimore, the Jacobean and Carolingian kings, and the Roman Catholic Church, to Anne Arundel Town on the Severn River, which enjoyed the double merit of a central location on the Chesapeake and an altogether Protestant history. Although the actual transfer of government records and the official change of the capital's name from Anne Arundel Town to Annapolis were not to be effected until the end of February, the consequences of the decision were noticeable already in St. Mary's City: few people were on the streets; the capitol and other public buildings were virtually deserted; and some inns and private houses were abandoned or closed and boarded up.

Before the arched doorway of the Statehouse Burlingame said, " 'Twill hasten our search if we move in separate directions; you enquire at the wharves and taverns hereabouts, and I shall do likewise farther in the town. At dusk we'll meet here and go to supper—God grant your sister will be dining with us too!"

Ebenezer agreed to the proposal and to the wish as well, for though the prospect of confronting Anna, after Burlingame's revelations, was a disconcerting one, yet he feared for her safety alone in the Province.

"But if perchance we find her," he asked with a little smile, "what then?"

"Why, haply Coode will find some way to snatch Cooke's Point from William Smith, and then, when Andrew hath returned in peace to England, the three of us will make our home in Malden. Or haply we'll fly to Pennsylvania, as your father suspects already: Anna, if she'll have me, shall become Mrs. Nicholas Lowe, and you, under a nom de plume, poet laureate to William Penn! 'Tis a wondrous tonic for defeat, to murther an old self and beget a new! But we must hatch our chickens ere we count 'em."

The two then separated, Burlingame heading inland and Ebenezer towards an inn not far from where they stood. Upon entering he found a dozen or more townspeople eating and drinking and could not at once muster courage enough to make his inquiries. He had not the small, prerequisite effrontery of the journalist or canvasser, for one thing; for another, he was still too confounded by events of the immediate past to know clearly how he should feel about his present position. When was it he had finished *The Sot-Weed Factor* in his room at Malden? Only the previous evening, though it seemed a fortnight past; yet since that time he had been given to assimilate no fewer than twelve perfectly astounding facts, each warranting the most careful contemplations and modification of his position, and some requiring immediate and drastic action:

He had become the indentured servant of Malden's master. His father was in Maryland and en route to Cooke's Point.

His wife Susan Warren was in fact his Joan Toast of London.

But she was a slave to opium, a victim of the pox, and a whore to the Indians of Dorchester.

Moreover she had been raped by the Moor Boabdil, and almost by Ebenezer himself.

He had in deserting her committed the most thoroughly and least equivocally dishonorable act of his entire life —indeed, the very first of any magnitude, not counting his thwarted ill intentions aboard the *Cyprian* and at Captain Mitchell's manor.

Lord Baltimore might not at all represent, as he had supposed, the very essence of Good, and Coode the essence of Evil, but vice versa, if Burlingame spoke truly; and Andrew might well be party to an enormously vicious plot.

His tutor Burlingame had been, perhaps, a loyal friend after all, and was inflamed with passion for Ebenezer and Anna as one.

His sister was at that moment somewhere in the Province.

She was a virgin to that day, despite her intimacy with Burlingame.

She loved not Burlingame but her brother, in a way too dark and deep for her cognition.

And he himself had no direction, aim, or prospect whatsoever for the future, but was as orphan in the world as Burlingame, without that gentleman's corporal, financial, intellectual, experiential, or spiritual resources.

With these propositions very nearly unhinging his Reason, how could he approach the strangers and calmly put his question? Even their mildly curious stare upon his entrance set his stomach a-quiver and his face afire. His small resolution vanished; with some of the money entrusted to him by Joan Toast he purchased his first meal since the previous day, and when it was eaten he left the inn. For some minutes he wandered unsystematically through the several rude streets of the town, as though in hopes of glimpsing Anna herself on one of them. Had the season permitted, he would doubtless have continued thus all day, for want of courage refusing to comprehend in what serious straits his sister might well languish, and then at sundown have reported with a sigh to Burlingame that his inquiries had borne no fruit. But the wet wind off St. Mary's River soon chilled him through; he was obliged to take refuge in another nameless public house, the only other tavern he had observed, and order rum to still the chattering of his teeth.

This establishment was, he observed, less elegantly appointed than its competitor: the floor was paved with oyster-shells, the tables were bare of cloths, and in the air hung a compound fragrance of stale smoke, stale beer, and stale seafood. This last smell seemed to come not so much from the tavern's cuisine as from the damp coats of its patrons, who in other respects as well appeared to be fishermen. They paid Ebenezer no notice whatever, but went on with their talk of seines and the weather, or fingered beards and brooded into their glasses. Although their indifference removed any possibility of Ebenezer's interrogating them, at the same time it permitted him to feel less uneasy in their presence; he was able to move his chair nearer the fireplace and was even emboldened, as he sipped his rum, to survey the other customers more closely.

In one corner of the room, he noticed a man sleeping with head, arms, and chest upon the table. Whether liquor, despair, or mere fatigue was the soporific, the poet could not tell, but his heart beat faster at the sight, for though the fellow was no cleaner nor less ragged than his companions, his coat in better days had been not the honest Scotch cloth of the laborer, but plum-colored serge and silver-grey prunella —a very twin to the one Ebenezer had worn to his audience with Lord Baltimore and had packed next day in his trunk to bring to Maryland! That there could be two such coats was most unlikely, for Ebenezer had chosen the goods himself and had them tailored to the style of the moment, which was scarcely to be seen outside London; nevertheless he dared not risk a scene by waking the fellow, and so signaled for more rum instead and asked the waiter who the slumbering chap might be.

"Haply 'tis Governor Nicholson, or King William," the man replied. " 'Tis not my wont to pry into my patrons' lives."

"To be sure, to be sure," Ebenezer persisted, and pressed two shillings into his hand. "But 'tis of some small importance that I know."

The waiter examined the coins and seemed to find them satisfactory. "The fact is," he declared, "nobody knows just who the wight may be, albeit he hires his bed upstairs and eats his meals at yonder table."

"What's this! Ye want two shillings for that news?"

542

The waiter held up an admonitory finger and explained that the sleeping man was no stranger to St. Mary's—indeed, he had frequented the tavern for some months past—but current rumor had it that his declared identity was false.

"He hath given all and sundry to believe his is the Laureate Poet of Maryland, name of Ebenezer Cooke, but either he's the grandest swindler that ever prowled St. Mary's, or else he is afraid of his very shadow."

Ebenezer betrayed such considerable interest in this statement that to hear it glossed set him back another shilling.

"He came to St. Mary's last September or October," the waiter went on, pocketing the money, "though whence or how no man knows truly, since the fleet was come and gone some weeks before. He was dressed in the clothes ye see there, that were splendid then as a St. Paul fop's, and had a wondrous swaggering air, and declared he was the Laureate of Maryland, Eben Cooke."

"I'Christ, the fraud!" Ebenezer exclaimed. "Did no man doubt him?"

"He had his share of hecklers; that he did," the waiter conceded. "Whene'er they asked him for a verse he'd say 'The muse sings not in taverns,' or some such; and when they asked him how he was so lately come from England, he declared he'd been kidnaped by the pirates from Jim Meech's boat *Poseidon* ere the fleet reached the Capes, and was later cast o'erside to drown, but swam ashore and found himself in Maryland. The wags and wits had fun at his expense, but his story was borne out anon by Colonel Robotham himself, the Councillor——"

"Nay!"

The waiter nodded firmly. "The Colonel and his daughter had crossed with him on the *Poseidon* and had seen him kidnaped, along with his servant and three sailors, that have ne'er been heard from since. Some skeptical souls still doubt the fellow's story, for he hath spoke not a line of verse these many months, and to set him in a panic one need only mention his father Andrew's name, or the name of his father-in-law."

"Father-in-law!" Ebenezer rose from his chair. "You mean William Smith, the cooper?"

"I know no cooper named Smith," the waiter laughed, "I mean Colonel Robotham of Talbot, that was persuaded enough to take him for a son-in-law, but hath learned since of another wight that's said to be Eben Cooke! He means to file suit against the impostor, but in the meantime this fellow here so fears him——"

"No more," Ebenezer said grimly. Leaving his fresh glass of rum untouched he strode unhesitatingly to the sleeper's table, and seeing that it was in fact Bertrand Burton who slumbered there, he shook him by the shoulders with both hands.

"Wake up, wretch!"

Bertrand sat up at once, and his alarm at being awakened thus ungently turned to horror when he saw who had been shaking him.

"Base conniver!" Ebenezer whispered fiercely. "What have you done now?"

"Stay, Master Eben!" the valet whispered back, glancing miserably about to judge the peril of his position. But the other patrons, if they had observed the scene at all, were watching with the idlest curiosity and amusement: they showed no signs of understanding the confrontation. "Let's leave this place ere ye speak another word! I've much to tell ye!"

"And I thee," the poet replied unpleasantly. "So thou'rt afraid somewhat for your welfare, Master Laureate?"

"With reason," Bertrand admitted, still glancing about. "But more for your own, sir, and for your sister Anna's!"

Ebenezer gripped the man's wrists. "Curse your heart, man! What do you know of Anna?"

"Not here!" the valet pleaded. "Come to my room upstairs, where we may speak without fear."

" 'Tis yours to fear, not mine," Ebenezer said, but permitted Bertrand to lead the way upstairs. The valet was clothed from wig to slippers, he observed, with articles from his trunk, all now much the worse for wear and want of cleaning; but the man himself, though blear-eyed with sleep and trepidation, had clearly much improved his lot by playing laureate. He was well fleshed out, and dignified even in his dishevelment—unquestionably a more prepossessing figure than his master. By the time they entered Bertrand's room, the only furnishings of which were a bed, a chair, and a pitcher-stand, Ebenezer could scarcely contain his indignation.

But the valet spoke first. "How is't thou'rt here, sir? I thought ye were a prisoner at Malden."

"You knew!" Ebenezer paled. "You knew my wretched state and exploited it!" His anger so weakened him that he was obliged to take the chair.

"Pray hear my side of't," Bertrand begged. " 'Tis true I

played your part at first from vanity, but anon I was obliged to—will-I, nill-I—and since I heard of your imprisonment, my only aim hath been to do ye a service."

"I know thy services!" the poet cried. " 'Twas in my service you gambled away my savings aboard the *Poseidon* and got me a name for seducing the ladies into the bargain!"

But Bertrand, little daunted, insisted on explaining his position more fully. "No man wishes more than I," he declared, "that I had stayed behind in London with my Betsy and let my poor cod take its chances with Ralph Birdsall—*Better a shive lost than the whole loaf,* as they say. But Fate would have it otherwise, and——"

"Put by thy whining preamble," his master ordered, "and get on with thy lying tale."

"What I mean to say, sir, there I was, half round the globe from my heart's desire, abused and left to drown by the cursed pirates, and farther disappointed at the loss of my ocean isle——"

"The loss of your ocean isle!"

"Aye, sir—what I mean is, 'tis not every day a man sees seven golden cities slip through his fingers, as't were, to say nothing of my fair-skinned heathen wenches, that would do whatever dev'lish naughty trick might cross my fancy, and fetch me cakes and small-beer by the hour——"

"Go to, go to, thou'rt slavering!"

"And there was my noble Drakepecker, bless his heart—big and black as a Scotland bull, and man enough to crack the Whore o' Babylon, but withal as meek a parishioner as any god could boast—that ye lightly gave away to nurse an ill-odored salvage——"

" 'Sheart, man, pass o'er the history and commence thy fabrication! I was there!"

With this assertion Bertrand declared he had no quarrel. "The sole aim of my relating it," he said, "is to help ye grasp the pity of my straits what time the swine-girl told us this was Maryland, and I was obliged to fall from Heav'n to Hell, as't were."

"Be't thy pitiful straits or thy craven neck," the poet responded, "I'll do my grasping without thy help. As for the swine-girl——" He hesitated, thought better of announcing his marriage, and demanded instead that the servant begin with his arrival in St. Mary's City nearly three months previously and account for his subsequent behavior in a fashion as brief and clear as such a concatenation of chicaneries might permit.

"My one wish is to do that very thing, sir," Bertrand protested. " 'Tis that first pose alone I beg forgiveness for, and thought to whiten by this preamble—the rest is deserving more of favor than reproof, and I shall lay it open to ye as readily as I did to your poor sister, and would to Master Andrew himself, that first sent me to ye in Pudding Lane for no other purpose in the wide, wicked world——"

"Than what?" Ebenezer cried. "Than stealing my name and office to do a Councillor out of his daughter? May the murrain carry me off if I do not flay an honest English sentence from your hide!"

"—than advising and protecting ye," Bertrand said, and when his master made as if to spring upon him he retreated to the other side of the bed and hastened to tell his story. The revelation that they were in Maryland instead of Cibola, he explained, and consequently that he was no longer a deity but only a common servant, had so filled him with dejection that when on orders from Timothy Mitchell he had gone with another servant to fetch Ebenezer's trunk, he could not resist the temptation to pose as poet laureate, only for the term of the errand. He had therefore declared to his companion that he himself was in reality Ebenezer Cooke and the man at Captain Mitchell's his servant, and that they had exchanged roles temporarily as a precautionary measure. However, he had continued, their reception in the Province had been cordial enough, and the disguise was no longer necessary. They had then fetched the trunk in the name of Ebenezer Cooke, and after securing the night's lodgings for master and man, Bertrand had struck out on his own to make the most of his short-term office.

"All went well," he sighed, "until the hour I left Vansweringen's place, up the street. The sun was still high, and I was somewhat dagged with rum; whilst I stood a moment to take my bearings a fine young lady comes a-weeping up pretty as ye please, throws her arms about my neck, and cries out 'Darling Ebenezer!' 'Twas Lucy Robotham, that same tart that plagued me so on the *Poseidon* and that had thought me long since murthered by the pirates!"

For old times' sake, Bertrand went on, he had bought dinner at Vansweringen's for Miss Robotham, whose father was in St. Mary's to sit with the Council, and when she removed her coat to eat he had observed, to his surprise, that she was pregnant. Upon his interrogating her (Ebenezer winced at the thought) she burst into fresh tears and confessed that on reaching Maryland she had been deceived into marrying the

Reverend Mr. George Tubman, the same whose speculative talents had impoverished half the *Poseidon*'s passengers, and had been by him impregnated in the rectory of Port Tobacco parish, only to learn not long after that their marriage was illegal, the Reverend Mr. Tubman having neglected to divorce his first wife in London. Colonel Robotham had arranged at once for annulment of the marriage and had further applied to the Bishop for proceedings of suspension against both Tubman and the Reverend Mr. Peregrine Cony, who he averred had knowingly licensed his colleague's bigamous union, but the Colonel's influence in the Province had as yet been unable to provide another husband for Lucy or retard the growing signs of her condition, which along with the reputation she had got for promiscuity had all but removed her from the gentlemen's list of eligible maidens.

"I saw then the reason for her joy at finding me alive," the valet said, "and I made a great show of sympathy, albeit I'd not have married her as Bertrand Burton, much less as Eben Cooke! *A house already made,* as the saying goes, *but a wife to make.* Yet I kept my feelings hid, nor showed by word or deed that I had grasped her scurvy trick. On the contrary, I played the gallant Laureate with right good will, the better to learn what else the wench had up her sleeve."

"And so resume where you had left off on the *Poseidon,* I doubt not."

Bertrand raised his finger. "I'll not deny we had some sport ere the day was done," he said righteously. "I had been the De'il's own time 'twixt drinks, as 't were and longed to see again that famous emblem Lucy boasts. 'Tis all in freckles, b'm'faith, and——"

"I know, I know," Ebenezer said impatiently. " 'Tis the likeness of *Ursa Major,* and the rest."

Bertrand clucked his tongue before the memory. "Besides, there is an uncommon pleasure in lasses lately got with child——"

"Nay, i'God, you sicken me!"

"In any case," the valet finished with a shrug, "I reasoned 'twas no more than the doxy's due, that had done ye out o' your money with her crooked odds and wagers."

"I say!" cried Ebenezer. "Speaking of wagers——"

"Say no more," Bertrand interrupted with a smile. "The selfsame query was on *my* mind from the instant I beheld her, and directly the time befitted, I asked her straight who had won that last monster of a ship's pool, wherein I'd wagered the whole o' Cooke's Point to regain the money I had lost before. At first she'd not reply, but when I offer'd her my belt athwart her hams—as I was wont to swat sweet Betsy what times she'd tease—why, then I wrung the truth from her, which was, that she herself, by collusion with Tubman and that whoreson Captain Meech, had won the prize!"

"I' Christ!"

The winnings, Bertrand went on, had then been divided between the three partners, and Tubman had increased his share by the impregnation and marriage (respectively, it now turned out) of Miss Robotham. As soon as the conveyances of property were effected he had disclosed the bigamous nature of the match, hoping thereby to rid himself of the girl; but he had reckoned without the ire of his new father-in-law, who had promptly exposed the business and taken the legal action mentioned earlier.

"But what of the property?" Ebenezer demanded. "Doth Tubman hold title to it yet?"

The valet smiled. "To the most he did, at the time I speak of, and to the most he doth yet, for aught I know to the contrary. But aside from my own wager, all his winnings were in cash or chattels, such as horses, pirogues, and hogsheads o' sot-weed. Cooke's Point was the only proper estate he won——"

"God curse you for wagering it!"

Bertrand raised his eyebrows. "Haply 'twas not such a folly after all, sir. The wretch had ne'er before won such a prize, and more especially as he thought us murthered by the pirates, he was afraid to press his claim, for fear the courts would learn the evil of his ways."

" 'Twould but improve his chances if they did," Ebenezer said, but there was relief in his tone. "An honest wight fares ill in a Maryland court. Go on."

In consequence, Bertrand declared, the Reverend Mr. Tubman had contented himself with what winnings he could collect as gentleman's debts from the bettors themselves, out of court, and in an effort to appease Colonel Robotham's wrath on the occasion of the annulment, had reconveyed to Lucy his note of title to Cooke's Point, not many days prior to her encounter with the note's original author.

"She was as doubtful as Tubman how the courts might rule on't," said the valet. " 'Twas her hope I'd make over the deed to her as a gentleman ought, particularly in the light of her condition, but when I gave no signs of such intent, she could no more than weep and threaten."

His next move, he explained, had been to send the other

servant back to Captain Mitchell as Timothy had directed and make plans to ferry himself and his freight to Malden. However, reckoning that his master would allow for unforeseen delays and complications in securing and transporting the trunk, he had lingered another day in St. Mary's as the guest of Colonel Robotham, and another and another after that, loath to relinquish the charms of office and Lucy's desperate favors. During this period his host and mistress had alternately cajoled and threatened him: their primary goal was to unite by marriage the house of Cooke and Robotham, and solve thereby all their problems with one stroke; alternatively they vowed to carry the matter into court, despite the uncertain legality of their claim, in hopes that with Cooke's Point for dowry even a pregnant tart could find a willing spouse of decent lineage. But since neither party could bargain from a position of clear strength, the argument was confined to subtle hints and equivocal negations, and Bertrand, having dispatched the trunk some days before, had enjoyed a week of such leisurely diversions and delights as most valets taste only in their dreams.

At week's end, however, he had heard from an unimpeachable barman in Vansweringen's that a man called Eben Cooke, on the Eastern Shore, had signed over his whole estate to a common cooper—whether in some saintly spirit of justice, in satisfaction of some dark and sinister obligation or merely in error was much debated—and that, the conveyance being apparently legal, Cooke himself had fallen mortally ill and was being cared for on his lost estate, in return for marrying the cooper's whore of a daughter.

"This news near felled me," the valet said. "No man doubted I was really Eben Cooke—for ye must grant, sir, whate'er thy principles, I've a knack for playing poet—but they expected me to fly to Dorset at once and turn both the cooper and the rascally impostor out. What's more, 'twas terrible to hear what had befallen ye, and more terrible yet to think of ye lying at death's door, as't were, and obliged to marry some unwashed coney of a serving maid——"

Ebenezer held up his hand. "Forego thy wondrous pity," he said. "I'm sure it soured your dinner at the Colonel's and made you a zestless lover for Miss Lucy."

"It did no less," Bertrand admitted. "Though of course I durst not give the slightest outward sign of't."

"Of course not."

Instead, declared Bertrand, he had confessed to Colonel Robotham that the same traitors to the King who had arranged to have him kidnaped and murdered by pirates were attempting to work his ruin in the Province, lest by the power of his pen he expose their seditious plots to the light of day. It was in anticipation of their schemes that he had sent his man before him to reconnoiter in the guise of Laureate—that same amanuensis who had served him thus, unasked, on earlier occasions—little dreaming that the stratagem would so misfire. The Colonel then, eager to oblige his guest in any way he could, offered to intercede at once with Governor Nicholson, who had a perfect hatred even of debate, to say nothing of insurrection; but Bertrand proposed a quite different plan of attack, so agreeable to the Robothams that as one they laid down their euchre-hands and tearfully embraced him.

"I wait in mortal fear to hear it," said the poet.

" 'Twas as simple as it was effective," the valet sighed, "—or so it seemed at the time I hatched it. I proposed to keep the matter *entre nous*——"

"*Entre nous?* Marry, thou'rt learning to scheme in French!"

Bertrand blushed. " 'Tis a word Lucy uses whene'er she means to have profit at some other wight's expense. My plan, I say, was to keep the matter *entre nous* until I knew more of your plight and how I best might aid ye; I saw no merit in discovering my true name and rank to the Robothams, nor in risking my disguise by taking my troubles to the Governor. I declared I'd given ye the power of attorney, the better to carry out your pose at Laureate, and that this power lent the cooper's title to Cooke's Point a certain slender substance, if 'twere contested in a biased court; for albeit the grant was made by a false Laureate (so I told the Colonel), yet the impostor was my legal agent and proxy, empowered to do my business in my name."

"I swear, thou'rt as grand a casuist as Richard Sowter!" Ebenezer said. Bertrand beamed.

" 'Tis but the giblet-sauce and dressing to what followed, sir: on the heels of't I proposed to marry Mistress Lucy on the instant and offered as my reason that, though her claim as such had no more law in't than a bumswipe, yet 'twas prior to any the traitors might shark up; if I was to support it as author of the note, husband of the claimant, and bona fide Laureate o' Maryland, 'twould carry the day in the Devil's own assizes!"

"Marry come up!" the poet exclaimed. "You meant to steal my estate to go with my name and office!"

" 'Twas stolen already," Bertrand reminded him. "I meant to steal it back to its rightful owner, if I could, whereupon I'd declare my actual name, and Lucy Robotham could go hang for all she'd be my legal wife!" The Colonel, he added, had been pleased with this proposal, and Lucy more than pleased; the marriage had been solemnized at once and consummated beyond cavil, and although he had not been able, as he had hoped, to enter on Lucy's note a clause of relinquishment in favor of her husband, nonetheless he considered Cooke's Point saved.

"I am staggered by this duplicity!" Ebenezer said. "Where is this miserable creature you've deceived, and her poor father? How is't thou'rt cowering in this tavern instead of lording it at Malden?"

"Colonel Robotham hath been on business up the country these two months," Bertrand sighed, "and his daughter hath been with him at my behest. I declared she was in danger from the traitors and must stay with her father at least till her confinement; but the truth of't was, I had been living at the Colonel's whole expense and would be revealed an arrant pauper the day he left. 'Twas my good fortune Lucy had a few pounds saved, that she entrusted to my keeping: 'twas just enough to buy my food and drink, and pay the hire of this verminous chamber." In vain, he said, had he endeavored to learn more news of Ebenezer's plight and to set in motion the legal strategy he had devised: his hands were tied for lack of money and influence until the Colonel's return.

"And in any case, the game is o'er," he concluded gloomily. "Colonel Robotham will return next week to Talbot, and if he doth not learn the truth from your father, he must guess it when he sees the state I'm in. Or else Master Andrew himself will search me out here when he learns thou'rt not at Malden—I had ne'er escaped him this last time had your sister not forewarned me he was coming——"

"Where did you find Anna, and where is she now?"

" 'Twas she found me," said Bertrand, "the very day she stepped ashore in Maryland. She came to find you in this room, where all St. Mary's knows the Laureate hath been quartered, and at first I scarcely knew her, she hath aged so."

Ebenezer winced.

"She was as taken aback at sight of me as was I at sight of her. I told her what I knew of your straits, without mentioning my own, and for all I begged her not to rush in recklessly, there was naught for't but she cross the Bay that afternoon, traitors or no, and either nurse ye back to health or be murthered at your graveside."

"Dear, darling Anna!" Ebenezer cried, and blushed when he recalled Burlingame's discourse of the morning. "What happened then?"

"She found passage in a sloop for the Little Choptank River," said Bertrand. "I spoke to her captain later below stairs, and he told me she'd gone ashore at a place called Tobacco Stick, his closest anchorage to Cooke's Point. Neither I nor any soul else, to my knowledge, hath farther news of her than that."

"Merciful God! No farther news?" A thought occurred to him, so monstrous that the gorge rose in his throat: William Smith was most certainly angry over his flight from Malden in violation of his indenture-bond, and Joan Toast more wrathful still at having been abandoned; suppose poor Anna had fallen into their clutches, and they had taken revenge on her for her brother's deeds!

"Heav'n save her!" he gasped to Bertrand, rising weakly from the chair. "They might have forced her into whoredom! This very minute, for aught we know, some greasy planter or great swart salvage——"

"Hi, sir! What is't ye say?" Bertrand ran alarmed to pound his master on the back, who had fallen into a fit of retching.

"Hire us a boat," Ebenezer ordered, as soon as he caught his breath. "We'll set out for Malden this instant, and hang the consequences!" Without mentioning his desertion of Joan Toast, he explained as briefly as he could to the astonished servant the fallen state of Malden, the circumstances of his departure, his rescue by Henry Burlingame, the enormous conspiracy afoot in the Province, and the particular danger awaiting Anna whether or not Andrew arrived before her at Cooke's Point. "I'll tell you more the while we're crossing," he promised. "We daren't lose a minute!"

"I know a captain we might hire," Bertrand ventured, "and I'd as well be murthered by your cooper as by Colonel Robotham when he finds me, but in truth I've no more than a shilling left of Lucy's money . . ."

His anger at the man fired anew by this reminder, Ebenezer was ready to chide him further for his abuse of Lucy Robotham, but brought himself up short with a shiver of mortification. "I've money enough," he grumbled, and offered no explanation of its source.

At the waterside they found the captain Bertrand had in mind, and despite the lateness of the afternoon and the un-

promising weather, that gentleman agreed, for the outrageous
price of three pounds sterling, to carry them to Cooke's
Point in his little fishing boat. As they were about to
step aboard Ebenezer remembered his scheduled rendezvous
at the Statehouse.

"I'faith, I well-nigh forgot——I must leave word for Henry
Burlingame, that hath gone to ask John Coode for aid." He
smiled at Bertrand's surprise. "'Tis too long a tale to tell
now, but I will say this: that Tim Mitchell who sent you
hither was not Captain Mitchell's son at all——'twas Henry
Burlingame."

"Ye cannot mean it!" The valet's face was horror-struck.

"No Christian soul else," the poet affirmed.

"Then ye have more need of prayers than messages," said
Bertrand. "God help us all!"

"What rot is this?"

"Your friend need look no farther than his glass to find
John Coode," the valet declared. "He is John Coode!"

4

The Poet Crosses Chesapeake Bay, but
Not to His Intended Port of Call

"'Tis gospel truth, I swear't!" Bertrand insisted. "There is
no better place for news than a St. Mary's tavern, and I've
had eyes and ears wide open these several months. 'Twas
common knowledge amongst his hirelings that Tim Mitchell
was John Coode in disguise, and now ye've told me your
Master Burlingame was Tim Mitchell——b'm'faith, I should
have guessed ere now! 'Tis in the very stamp and pattern of
the man!"

Ebenezer shook his head. "'Tis an assertion not lightly to
be matched for implausibility." Nevertheless, he showed no
indignation, as he had on other occasions when the valet had
aspersed his former tutor.

"Nay, sir, believe me; 'tis as clear as a schoolboy's sums!

553

Only think: Where did ye first hear of this fiend John Coode?"

"From Lord Baltimore, ere I left," Ebenezer replied. "That is—"

"And when did Coode commence his factions and rebellions in the Province? Was't not the very year Burlingame came hither? And is't not true that whene'er Master Burlingame is in England, he tells ye Coode is there too?"

"But Heav'n forfend——"

"D'ye think Master Burlingame could pass for two minutes as Coode with Slye and Scurry, much less make a three-month crossing in their company? 'Tis past belief!"

"Yet he hath a wondrous talent for disguise," the poet protested.

"Aye and he doth, b'm'faith! From all I've heard from yourself and others, he hath posed as Baltimore, Coode, Colonel Sayer, Tim Mitchell, Bertrand Burton, and Eben Cooke, to mention no more, and hath ne'er been found out yet! But what's the chiefest talent of John Coode, if not the same? Hath he not played priest, minister, general, and what have ye? Is't not his wont to travel always incognito, so that his own lieutenants scarce know his natural face?"

"But he was six years my tutor! I know the man!" Even as he made it, Ebenezer realized the vast untruth of this declaration. Although he continued to shake his head as in disbelief, at their ferryman's suggestion he abandoned the idea of returning to the inn to leave a message, and the fishing sloop made way down the St. Mary's River.

" 'Tis all shifting and confounded!" he complained shortly afterwards, when he and Bertrand had retreated from the weather to a tiny shelter-cabin behind the mast. He was thinking not only of Burlingame and the transvaluation of Lord Baltimore and Coode which his former tutor had argued so persuasively that morning (and which, after Bertrand's announcement, seemed most self-incriminating), but for that matter Bertrand, John McEvoy, and virtually everyone else. "No man is what or whom I take him for!"

"There's much goes on," the valet nodded darkly, "that folk like thee and me know naught of. Things are de'il the bit what they seem."

"Why, i'Christ——" Ebenezer gave himself over to exasperated conjecture. "How do I know 'tis Burlingame I've traveled with in the first place, when he alters everything from face to philosophy every time I re-encounter him? Haply

Burlingame died six years ago, or is Baltimore's prisoner, or Coode's, and all these others are mere impostors!"

" 'Tis not impossible," Bertrand admitted.

"And this war to the death 'twixt Baltimore and Coode!" Ebenezer laughed sharply. "How do we know who's right and who's wrong, or whether 'tis a war at all? What's to keep me from declaring they're in collusion, and all this show of insurrection's but a cloak to hide some dreadful partnership?"

" 'Twould not surprise me in the least, if ye want to know. I've never trusted that Jacobite Baltimore, any more than I've trusted Mr. Burlingame."

"*Jacobite,* you say? 'Sheart, what an innocent rustic thou'rt become! Think you King William's not secretly as much in league with James as he is with Louis and the Pope o' Rome? Is't not a well-known fact that *More history's made by secret handshakes than by all the parliaments in the world?*"

"There's much would surprise an honest man, if he just but knew't," the valet murmured, but he shifted uneasily and stared out at the lowering sky.

"I'faith, thou'rt a greater sage than Socrates, fellow! These sayings of yours should be writ in gold leaf on the entablatures of public buildings, lest any wight forget! What is't but childish innocence keeps the mass o' men persuaded that the church is not supported by the brothel, or that God and Satan do not hold hands in the selfsame cookie-jar?"

"Ah, now, sir, ye go too far!" Bertrand's tone was hushed. "Some things ye know as clear as ye know your name."

Ebenezer laughed again, in the manner of one possessed by fever. "Then you really believe 'tis Eben Cooke thou'rt speaking to? How is't you never guessed I was John Coode?"

"Nay, sir, go to!" the servant pleaded. "Thou'rt undone by thy misfortunes and know not what ye speak! Prithee go to!"

But the poet only leered the more menacingly. "You may fool others by playing some looby of a servingman, but not John Coode! I know thou'rt Ebenezer Cooke, and you'll not escape murthering this time!"

"I'll tell the captain to fetch us back to St. Mary's City at once, sir," Bertrand whined, "and summon a good physician to bleed ye. 'Tis late in the day for a crossing anyhow, and marry, look yonder at the whitecaps on the Bay! Rest and sleep—rest and sleep'll make ye a new man by tomorrow, take my word for't. Only look astern, sir: there's a proper hurricane blowing up! I'll speak to the captain——"

"Nay, man, come back; I'll tease no more." He closed his

eyes and rubbed them with thumb and forefinger. " 'Twas just——Ah well, I had a picture in my mind, that I'd forgot till now, and I thought——" He paused to pinch himself unmercifully on the forearm, grunted at the pain of it, and sighed.

"Please, sir, 'tis a frightful storm coming yonder! This wretched toy will go down like stone!"

"And you think we're really here, then, and can drown? This thing I spoke of, that had just jumped to mind—'twas back in Pudding Lane last March—marry, it seems five years ago! I had been offered a sort of wager with Ben Oliver, an obscene business, and had fled to my room for very mortification——"

" 'Sheart, feel how she rolls and pitches, sir, now we're clear o' land!"

The poet ignored his man's terror. "When I was alone again in my room, I had a perfect fit of shame; I longed to go back and play the man with Joan Toast in the winehouse, but I'd not the courage for't, and in the midst of my brooding I fell asleep there at my writing table."

The roll of the boat threw Bertrand to his knees; his face went white.

" 'Tis all very well, sir, all very well indeed; but I must shout to the captain to turn back! We can fetch Miss Anna another time, when the weather's clear!"

Ebenezer declared they would fetch her now, and went on with his reminiscence. "The thing I just recalled," he said, "was how Joan Toast waked me by knocking on my door, and how I was so amazed to see her, and still so full of sleep, I could not tell to save my life whether 'twas a dream or not. And I remember reasoning clearly 'twas doubtless a cruel dream, for naught so wondrous e'er occurred in natural life. All my joys and tribulations commenced with that knock on the door, and so fantastical are they, I wonder if I am not still in Pudding Lane, still wrapped in sleep, and all this parlous history but a dream."

"Would Heav'n it were, sir!" cried the valet. "Hear that wind, i'Christ, and the sky already dark!"

"I have had dreams that seemed more real," Ebenezer said, "and so hath Anna, many's the time. There was a trick we knew as children: when the lions of Numidia were upon us or we'd fallen from some Carpathian cliff, we'd say, *'Tis but a dream, and now I'll wake*: *'tis but a dream, and now I'll wake*—and sure enough, we'd wake in our beds in St. Giles in the Fields! Why, we were even wont to wonder, when we talked at night betwixt our two bedchambers, whether all of life and the world were not just such a dream; many and many's the time we came nigh to trying our magical chant upon't, and thought we'd wake to a world where no people were, nor Earth and Sun, but only disembodied spirits in the void." He sighed. "But we ne'er durst try——"

"Try't now, sir," Bertrand pleaded, "ere we're drowned past saying charms! I'God, sir, try't now!"

The poet laughed, no longer feverishly. " 'Twould do you no good in any case, Bertrand. The reason we never tried it was that we knew only one of us could be *The Dreamer of the World*—that was our name for't—and we feared that if it worked, and one of us awoke to a strange new cosmos, he'd discover he had no twin save in his dream. . . . What would it profit you if I saved myself and left you here to drown?"

But Bertrand fell to pinching himself ferociously and bawling " *'Tis but a dream, and now I'll wake! 'Tis but a dream, and now I'll wake!*"

His concern for the safety of the boat was justified. The sudden half-gale that had blown up from the southwest was piling seas in the open water of the Chesapeake as formidable as any the poet had seen, except during the storm off Corvo in the Azores, and instead of the *Poseidon*'s two hundred tons and two dozen crewmen, his life was riding this time in a gaff-rigged sloop not forty feet long, manned by one white man and a pair of husky Negroes. Already the light was failing, though it could be no later than five in the afternoon; the prospect of sailing through some fifty miles of those seas in total darkness seemed truly suicidal, and at length, despite the urgency of his desire to find Anna, he asked the Captain—a grizzled gentleman by the name of Cairn—whether they had not better return to St. Mary's.

" 'Tis what I've been trying to do this past half hour," the Captain replied sourly, and explained that even with his jib and topsail struck and his mainsail triple-reefed, he had been unable to sail close-hauled back into the Potomac, which lay to windward; so strong were the frequent gusts that the minimum sail required for tacking was enough to dismast or capsize the sloop. The only alternative had been to drop anchor, and even this, according to the Captain, was but a temporary expedient: had the bottom been good holding ground, the anchor pendant would have parted at the first gust; as it was they were dragging to leeward at a great rate and would soon be beyond the depth of the pendant entirely.

"Yonder's Point Lookout," he said, indicating an obscure

and retreating point of land in the very eye of the wind. "'Tis the last land ye'll see this day, if not forever."

Ebenezer felt cold fear. "'Sbody! D'you mean 'tis over and done with us?"

Captain Cairn cocked his head. "We'll heave to and rig a sea anchor; after that 'tis God's affair."

Thus delivered of his sentiments, he and the Negroes bent a little trysail onto the mainmast to keep the bow to windward and replaced the useless iron grapple with a canvas sea anchor, which, so long as the tide was ebbing towards the ocean, would retard the vessel's northeastern leeway. There was nothing else to be done: when the work was finished the Captain lashed the tiller and took shelter with his passengers in the cabin, which, unfortunately for the crew, had room enough for just three people. Point Lookout very soon vanished, and as if its disappearance had been a signal, darkness closed in immediately, and the wind and rain seemed to increase. The sloop was flung high by each black sea and fell with a slap into the trough behind; the sea anchor, though of value in preventing the boat from broaching to, caused her to nose rather deeply and ship a quantity of water at the bow, which the Negroes were obliged to bail out with a crude wooden bilge pump.

"Poor devils!" Ebenezer sympathized. "Should we not spell them at the pumps and give them some respite in the cabin?"

"No need," the Captain replied. "Three hours shall see the end of't, one way or another, and 'twill keep 'em from freezing in the meantime." What he meant, the poet learned on further interrogating him, was that if the storm did not blow itself out, change direction, or sink them, the present rate and course of their leeway would carry them across the Bay in three hours or so and bring them stern-foremost to the Eastern Shore.

"Then marry come up, we've hope after all, have we not?" Even Bertrand, who had been chattering with cold and fright, displayed some cheer at this announcement.

"Ye've hope o' drowning near shore, at least," the Captain said. "The surf will swamp her in a trice and haply break her up as well."

The valet moaned afresh, and Ebenezer's cheeks and forehead tingled. Yet though the prospect of drowning horrified him no less now than it had when he walked the pirates' plank off Cedar Point, about a dozen miles northwest of their present position, the prospect of death itself, he noted with some awe, held no more terrors. On the contrary: while he would not have chosen to die, especially when Anna's welfare was so uncertain, the thought of no longer having to deal with the lost estate, his father's wrath, and the sundry revelations and characters of Henry Burlingame, for example, was sweet. Delicious Death! Not in broodiest night hours of his growth, when in anguish or fascination he would cease to breathe, hold still his brain, and hear the blood rumble in his ears while he strove dizzily and in vain to suspend the beating of his heart—not even then had cool Oblivion seemed more balmy.

Except to grunt at occasional extraordinary crashes of water or lurches of the boat, no one was much inclined during the period that followed to speak aloud to anyone else. The storm, though uneven in its violence, showed no signs of abating, and could at any moment have swamped or capsized them without warning in a sea too cold and rough for the ablest swimmer to survive more than twenty minutes. Yet thanks to the sea anchor, the indefatigable Negroes at the pump, and an apparent general seaworthiness about the hull, not to mention blind Providence, the vessel remained hove to and afloat through gust after gust, sea after sea—and slipped steadily, if not apparently, to leeward all the while. After a time—which to Ebenezer could as reasonably have been twenty as two hours—the Captain left off stroking his beard and raised his head attentively.

"Hark!" He raised a hand for silence. "D'ye hear that, now?" He threw open the door, stepped onto the deck, and, at the risk of swamping, ordered the Negroes to suspend for a moment both their pumping and the rhythmical chantey with which they paced and lightened their labor. Ebenezer strained his ears, but though the open door amplified the noises of the storm and admitted no small quantity of rain and cold air into the bargain, he could detect no novel sound, nor could he see anything at all.

The Captain bade the crew resume their pumping, without musical accompaniment, and thrust his dripping head into the cabin.

"There's land not far to leeward," he announced. "Ye can hear the surf astern." And upon repeating his cheerless prophecy of some hours before, that one way or another their ordeal would soon be over, he disappeared into the darkness forward.

Then, despite Bertrand's protests that he would rather drown where he sat than outside in the cold and wet. Ebenezer insisted that they too leave the cabin, the better to swim for their lives when the boat went down or broke up in the surf. The rainfall, they found, had considerably diminished, so that the entire length of the boat was visible; but the wind howled as fiercely as ever, blowing the tops from the huge black seas that crashed and shuddered about the hull. And now their new peril was identified, Ebenezer could hear it too —the more profound and rhythmical thundering of invisible breakers to leeward.

Up forward the Captain cut loose the sea anchor, whose efficacy had waned with the run of the tide, and cast the grapple in its place—not with any serious hope of its holding fast on the rockless bottom of the marsh country, but merely to hold his vessel's bow into the wind and delay as long as possible her reaching the breakers. Then he joined his passengers aft and, stroking his beard afresh, listened with them to the ominous rumble astern.

"Why can't we let go the anchor and ride the waves ashore?" the poet inquired. "It seems to me I've read of such a practice."

The Captain shook his head. "Your square stern yaws in a following sea, don't ye know, and wants the proper lift as well: the first good sea would either broach ye to or poop ye." He did not trouble himself to define the latter catastrophe, but advised all hands to divest themselves of boots, coats, wigs, and waistcoats, and to take positions more or less amidships.

"Not I," the valet objected. " 'Tis ten yards the less to swim if I jump here astern."

The Captain shrugged his shoulders and replied, "Stay there, then, and be damned t'ye: we can use your weight to keep her trim. But I'll not answer for't if the whole ship breaks on your idle skull!"

Seeing the flaw in his reasoning, Bertrand grew so ready in the Captain's service that, not content to stop amidships, he moved on the extreme bow of the sloop and might even have attempted the sprit had not one of the Negroes added the complementary caution, perhaps as a tease, that too much weight forward would put the vessel down at the head, already hampered by the drag of the grapple and pendant, and jeopardize her rising to the sea.

"Stay, listen!" the Captain interrupted. "D'ye hear?"

Again they strained their ears. "Naught but the storm and yonder surf, as before," Ebenezer said.

"Aye, but not astern now; 'tis off the larboard quarter!"

Facing aft, he pointed about forty-five degrees to the right, to which invisible location, sure enough, the sound of breakers had moved, although they were apparently much nearer than before.

"What doth it mean?" Ebenezer demanded. "Hath the wind shifted?"

"Not a point," said the Captain. " 'Tis sou'-sou'west, and should have brought us to Hooper's Island square astern. Haply 'tis just some cove or bend o' the shoreline——" He broke off his musing to send one of the Negroes aft, to listen for surf to starboard or astern. But only to eastwards could they hear it, and then east-southeastwards, and then dead southeastwards, as it moved from the quarter to the larboard beam; and though at first its apparent proximity had increased at a fearful rate, now that the sound was abreast of them it grew no louder, while astern the storm raged on as it had in the middle of the Bay. Clearly, whatever land that surf broke on they were leaving to larboard.

" 'Twas the run o' the tide in the sea anchor," Captain Cairn declared thoughtfully. "It hath dragged us something eastwards of our sternway—which is to say, something south of Hooper's Island. My guess is, 'tis Limbo Straits we're in, and yonder surf is a marsh called Bloodsworth Island. If it is in sooth—— I'Christ now, let me think!" He tugged ferociously at his beard, while Ebenezer and Bertrand watched with awe. "No surf astern yet, or to starboard?" he demanded again of the Negroes, and was answered in the negative. The breakers to larboard were still moving slowly forward; now the sound reached them from due south—about four points off the larboard bow—and had diminished somewhat in volume, as had the seas in height.

"Is't our ruin or our salvation?" asked the poet, at the same time endeavoring to remember where it was that he had previously encountered the name of the straits.

"It could be either," said the Captain. "If that be Bloodsworth Island yonder, why, there is a cove in the top of't called Okahanikan, just abeam, where we might run for shelter; or we can drift through Limbo Straits and take our chances with the surf on the Dorset mainland. Ye can see the waves are something smaller now we're past that point o' land; if yonder's Okahanikan and we leave't to windward, ye'll soon see 'em large again as e'er they were before . . ."

"Then prithee let us run for't!" Bertrand begged.

"On the other hand," the Captain concluded, with a great

tug of the whiskers, "if we run for't and it *isn't* Okahanikan, or we miss the deepest part of't, we're as good as run aground and swamped."

"I say let's try it," Ebenezer urged. "As well risk drowning as freeze for certain." Indeed, stripped of his boots and outer garments, he had never been so cold. His great jaw chattered; he hugged himself and pumped his legs on the pitching deck. He recalled an observation made winters before by Burlingame: once when the twins had marveled at a tale of the tropical heat endured by Magellan or some other voyager of the horse latitudes, their tutor had observed that, given a covering of clothes and ample water, the severest heat is simply more or less uncomfortable and can be dealt with, but cold is in its essence inimical to life. The image of equatorial climate has at its center those swarming beds of procreation, the great rain forests; but to think of what lies above the Arctic Circle is to think of Chaos, oblivion, the antithesis of life. Even thus (so Burlingame had declared to his charges) do men speak of the heat of passions, and refer to various sentiments and social relationships approvingly as *warm*, forasmuch as the metabolism of life itself is warm; but fear, contempt, despair, and deepest hatred—not to mention facts, logic, analysis, and formality of dress or manner—however involved they may be in the human experience of living, have forever in the nostrils of the race some effluvium of the grave and are described in mankind's languages by adjectives of cold. In sum (Ebenezer remembered Henry concluding with a smile and raking up the fire in his converted summer-house with the ramrod of a Spanish musket on the wall), hot days may well elicit sweat and curses, but chill winds cut through the greatcoats and farthingales of time, knife to the primal memory of the species, shiver that slumbering beast in the caves of our soul, and whisper "Danger!" in his hairy ear. The surf now was a muffled thunder well forward. The Captain ordered the triple-reefed jib and mainsail up and took the helm himself. The Negroes having their hands full with sheets and gaff-halyards, he stationed both passengers forward, Bertrand to take soundings with a pole (the sloop itself, chine-bottomed, drew less than three feet of water, and the keel only two or three more) and Ebenezer to watch and listen for trouble ahead. The luff of the sails cracked like pistol-fire in the wind, and the heavy boom whipped back and forth over the deck. When the anchor pendant had been shortened until the grapple barely held the bow to windward, the Captain put the helm up hard and close-hauled the jib:

the bow fell off at once to larboard, both sails filled with a snap that heeled the sloop far over and bid fair to take out her mast, and the anchor was desperately weighed. For a moment the fearful forces hung in balance: surely, Ebenezer thought, the ship must capsize or broach to, or the mast let go, or the shrouds, or the chain plates, or the sails. But as the next great wave rolled under, the Captain eased the helm; the bow pointed just a shade nearer the wind's eye, and to the accompaniment of cheers from the crew, the sloop righted herself to a reasonable angle of heel, took the next crest fairly at forty-five degrees, and gained steerageway due southwards on a sluggish starboard tack.

Almost at once they found themselves in comparatively calm water, though the wind howled as furiously as ever; clearly they were in the lee of whatever land they'd raised, and while their troubles were by no means over, they were temporarily relieved of the danger of losing their ship from under them. Moreover, with the island, or whatever, to break the wind, they were able to proceed with greater caution and control: almost at once, on their southerly bearing, Bertrand touched bottom with his pole and bawled the news aft—indeed, the sound of the wind in reeds and trees could be plainly heard in the darkness ahead. The Negroes at once slacked off the sheets, and the sloop was brought over on a broad reach paralleling the apparent shoreline, with just enough way to steer by. For ten minutes the soundings remained constant, at between nine and ten feet of water, and the trees howled steadily off the starboard beam. Then this land-sound became more general—seemed, in fact, almost to enclose them everywhere but astern—and at the first brush of the keel against the bottom, heard and felt by none besides Catain Cairn, he ordered the anchor dropped and came up into the wind.

"Dear Heav'n!" Ebenezer cried. "Can it be we're safe?"

"Only the wittol can know he is no cuckold," said the Captain, repeating a proverb Ebenezer had heard before, "and only a dead man is safe from death." Nevertheless he stroked his beard with obvious relief and admitted that, barring a shift in the direction of the wind, there seemed to be no reason why they could not ride out the night at anchor.

" 'Tis some manner of cove, right enough," he declared when the vessel was properly secured, "else we'd hear more sea astern, instead of trees. Whether Okahanikan or some other we'll learn anon."

There being, incredibly to Ebenezer, nothing further to do

until daybreak, all hands put on the clothes they had discarded some time before and made shift to warm and rest themselves. The chore of standing watch for changes in the weather or other perils was assigned to the exhausted crew until Ebenezer protested that the Negroes had already labored valiantly and prodigiously the whole night through, and volunteered to give up his place in the cabin to them and stand watch with Bertrand in their stead.

"Ye may do as ye please," the Captain replied. "Keep a lookout lest we drag anchor, and take soundings astern if we swing with the tide. For the rest, don't wake me unless the wind comes round and blows into the cove."

Having made these injunctions, he retired, but the Negroes, despite Ebenezer's invitation, made no move to follow after. They had followed the conversation as impassively as if they understood not a word of it, and indeed, judging from their reticence, their difficulties with the English language, and the bashfulness—manifested by averted smiles, great rolls of the eyes, and much shifting of their feet—with which they declined his offer of shelter, the poet concluded that despite their seamanship they were not long out of the jungles. This impression was strengthened not long after, when he commenced his watch with Bertrand: the Negroes spread on the deck between them a spare jibsail, folded once leech to luff, and commencing one at the head and one at the foot rolled themselves up in it against the weather. The adroitness with which they performed this feat gave it an air of outlandish ritual, and when it was done and they lay face to face as snug and immobile as scroll-pins, they entertained themselves for a time with a chuckling, husky-whispered colloquy in some exotic tongue—unintelligible to the Englishmen save for the often-repeated name of their supposed anchorage, *Okahanikan,* and another recurrent word which (though Ebenezer was not so certain on this head) Bertrand declared with much emotion to be *Drakepecker.* So moved was he by this conviction, in fact, that he expressed his determination to inquire at once of the Negroes whether they knew any more than he of Drakepecker's welfare and whereabouts and was restrained only by Ebenezer's reminder that their fellow castaway had been clearly a fugitive of some sort, the less said about whom, the better for his safety. The valet was obliged to grant the prudence of this counsel; reluctantly he took up his watch in the vessel's stern, alee of the cabin, where Ebenezer, on his first circuit of the deck a quarter hour later, found him wrapped in a bit of canvas himself, and already asleep.

" 'Sheart, what a hawk-eyed sentry!" He moved to rouse the man, but checked himself and decided to stand the watch alone so long as all went well. He had, at the hour of their departure from St. Mary's, little but contempt and mild disgust for Bertrand, nor had he now, assuredly, any new cause for affection. That he felt it—or at least the absence of its contraries—not only for the valet but also for Henry Burlingame, he could attribute only to the violence of the storm, and more especially to the purgative ordeal of three hours' dancing on the doormat of extinction.

He strolled forward again. The rain had stopped entirely, and though the wind held strong it came now in quick gusts, the intervals between which were mild. But the best sign of all that the storm had blown its worst was the break-up of the lowering blanket of cloud into a heavy black scud that first opened holes for the gibbous moon to breach, then gave way, broke ranks, and fled across its face before the whips of wind like the ragtag of an army in retreat. For the first time since nightfall, Ebenezer could see beyond the white sprit of the sloop: the inconsistent moon disclosed that they were indeed in a cove, a marshy one of ample dimension. The island into which it made was ample too (so much so, that for all the poet could tell it might as reasonably have been the mainland), entirely flat, and, as best one could discern in that light, entirely marshy, its landscape relieved only by the loblolly pine trees, alive and black or dead and silver, that rose in lean clumps here and there from the marsh grass. It was a prospect by no means picturesque, but under the pale illumination stark and beautiful. Ebenezer even thought it serene, for all its bending to the wild wind, just as he felt the Island of his spirit, though by no means tranquil, to be peculiarly serene despite the buffet of past fortune and the sea of difficulties with which it was beset.

So did he savor this reflection, and the spiritual peace from which it had originated, that for a considerable period he was oblivious to wind, weather, and the passage of time; had the tide swung the ship onto a sand bar, or the wind moved round the compass, the change would have escaped his notice. What aroused him, finally, was a sound from the marsh to larboard; he started, saw that the moon had risen a great way into the sky, and wondered whether to rouse the others. But when the sound came again his fears were allayed: it was a hooting chirrup as of doves or owls, some creature of the marsh as glad as he to see the storm pass over.

"Too-*hoo!*" The call came a third time, louder and more clear, and "Too-*hoo!*" came a clear reply—not from the adjacent marsh but from the deck immediately at Ebenezer's back. He thrilled with alarm, spun about to see what bird had perched on the vessel's rail, and was seized at once by the Negro crewmen, who had noiselessly unrolled themselves from the jibsail. One pinioned his arms and held fast his mouth before he was able to cry out; the other held a rigging-knife against his throat and called out over the side, "Too-*hoo!* Too-*hoo!*"—whereupon, as if materialized spontaneously in the reeds, three canoes slid out of hidden waterways nearby, and half a minute later, to the poet's expressible terror, a party of silent savages was swarming over the rail and creeping with great stealth towards the cabin.

5

Confrontations and Absolutions in Limbo

WHAT WITH EVERY military advantage—arms, numbers, and absolute surprise—the strange war party of Indians was not long in attaining its objective, which seemed to be the capture of the sloop with all hands. Bertrand and the Captain were wakened with spearheads at their throats and brought forward, the former inarticulate with fright, the latter bellowing and sputtering—first at his captors, then at Ebenezer for not sounding some alarm, and finally and most violently, when he grasped the situation, at the treacherous members of his crew.

"I'll see ye drawn to the scaffold and quartered!" he declared, but the Negroes only smiled and turned their eyes as if embarrassed by his threats. The leader of the party spoke sharply in an incomprehensible tongue to one of his lieutenants, who relayed it in another, equally strange language to the Negro sailors, and was answered in the same manner;

during their colloquy Ebenezer observed that, though the boarders were dressed almost identically in deerskin matchcoats and hats of beaver, racoon, or muskrat, nearly half their number were not Indians at all, but Negroes. The Captain remarked this fact as well and began at once to rail at them for fugitives and poltroons, but his audience gave no sign of understanding. Apparently satisfied that there were no more passengers aboard the sloop and no more vessels in the cove, the raiders then bound their captives at wrist and ankle, handed them bodily over the rail, and obliged them to lie face-down, one to a canoe, throughout a brief but circuitous passage into the marsh, which, like the earlier phases of the coup, was executed in total silence. Presently the canoes were secured to a clump of wax myrtles, the ropes around the prisoners' ankles were exchanged for a longer one that tethered them by the neck in a line, and the party proceeded on foot down a path as meandering as the waterway, and so narrow that even single file it was hard to avoid misstepping into the muck on either side.

"This is outrageous!" Ebenezer complained. "I never dreamed such things still happened in 1694, in the very bosom of the Province!"

"Nor I," the Captain replied, from his post in the van of the prisoners. "Nor e'er heard tell of an Indian town on Bloodsworth Island. I'Christ, 'tis naught but marsh from stem to stern, and not dry ground enough to stand on."

"God save us!" Bertrand groaned—his first words since he'd fallen asleep some hours before. "They'll scalp our heads and burn us at the stake!"

"Whatever for?" the poet inquired. "We've done 'em no injury, that I can see."

" 'Tis e'er the salvages' wont," his valet insisted. "Ye've but to run afoul of one in your evening stroll, and *bang!* he'll skin your pate as ye'd skin a peach! Why, 'tis still the talk in Vansweringen's how a wench named Kersley was set upon by Indians in Charles County, year before last: she was crossing a field of sot-weed 'twixt her own house and her father's, with the sun still shining and a babe on her arm besides, but ere she reached her husband's door she had been scalped, stuck with a knife, and swived from whipple to whitsuntide! And again, not far from Bohemia Manor——"

"Be still," the Captain snapped, "ere your own tales beshit ye."

" 'Tis all quite well for you to take your scalping without a

567

word," Bertrand replied undaunted. " 'Twas you steered us hither in the first place——"

"*I!* 'Sblood and 'sbody, sir, 'tis thy good fortune the salvage hath belayed my two hands, else I'd have thy scalp myself!"

"Gentlemen!" Ebenezer interposed. "Our case is grave enough without such talk! 'Twas I that hired the passage; you may hold me answerable for everything if 'twill ease your minds to do so, though it strikes me we'd do better to give over wondering who got us into this pickle and bend our minds instead to getting out."

"Amen," the Captain grunted.

"Still and all," Bertrand said disconsolately, "I must hold Betsy Birdsall to some account, for had she not rescued me last March in such a deuced clever manner, I'd not be trussed up here like a trout on a gill string."

"Really!" the Captain cried. "Thou'rt unhinged!"

"Stay, prithee stay," Ebenezer pleaded. Since the Captain's first sharp words to Bertrand, the poet's brow had been knitting, and his admonitions were made distractedly. Now he asked the Captain, "Was't not the Straits of Limbo we entered yonder cove from, or did I mishear you?"

"That was my guess, sir," the older man said, "unless the tide fetched us down as low as Holland or Kedge's Straits, which I doubt."

"But if not, the name of the strait is Limbo? And is there a river mouth not far hence, with an Indian name?"

"A hatchful of 'em," the Captain replied, not greatly interested, "and they all have salvage names: Honga, Nanticoke, Wicomico, Manokin, Annamessex, Pocomoke——"

"*Wicomico!* Aye, Wicomico—'tis the name Smith mentioned in his *Historie!*"

The Captain muttered something exasperated, and to avoid being thought deranged by fear like his servant, Ebenezer explained in the simplest way possible what he had been grasping for since the first mention of *Limbo Straits* and had recalled only with the help of the word *beshit:* that Captain John Smith of Virginia, almost ninety years previously, had discovered those same straits during his voyage of exploration up the Chesapeake; had, like themselves, encountered a furious storm therein and suffered the additional discomforts of a diarrhetic company; had in consequence of his ordeal bestowed the name *Limbo* on the place; and finally had been made prisoner, with all his party, by a band of warlike Indians—perhaps the grandfathers of their present captors!

"Ye don't tell me," the Captain said. Neither did Bertrand appear to be overwhelmed by the coincidence, for when to his single inquiry, "Prithee, what came of 'em?" his master confessed that he had not the slightest idea, the valet relapsed into gloom.

But once Ebenezer had wrested the *Secret Historie* from his memory he could not but marvel at the parallel between John Smith's experience and their own. Moreover, the existence of the *Historie* itself attested that Smith and at least some of his party had escaped or been freed by their captors. His reflections were interrupted at this point by their arrival at the Indians' town, an assemblage of mean little huts arranged in a thick circle upon an island of relatively high ground. There seemed to be well over a hundred in all, dome-shaped affairs of small logs and thatched twigs; surrounded as they were by the marsh, they resembled nothing so much as a colony of muskrat houses, the more since their occupants were cloaked and capped with fur. The citizenry appeared to be sleeping: except for a single hidden sentry who challenged their approach with a "Too-*hoo!*" from his post in a nearby brush clump, and was answered in kind, the town was as still as one deserted.

"'Tis passing queer," the Captain grumbled. "Never saw an Indian town without a pack o' curs about."

But if the silence of the village was disconcerting, what broke it a few moments later was nothing less than extraordinary: they had passed through the ring of dwellings to a clearing or open court in the center of the town, and during a whispered colloquy between the leader and his black lieutenant there came from a hut not far away a sudden wailing that raised the poet's hackles. Through his fancy, in half a second, passed the various Indian cruelties he had learned of from Henry Burlingame: how they bit the nails from their victims' fingers, twisted the fingers themselves from the hands, drove skewers into the remaining stumps, pulled sinews from the arms, tore out the hair and beard, hung hot hatchets around the neck, and poured hot sand on scalped heads.

"Marry come up!" breathed the Captain, and Bertrand's teeth began to chatter. The wail changed pitch and tone and changed again a moment afterwards, and again, but not until the wailer drew fresh breath and recommenced did the prisoners grasp the nature of the sound.

"Dear God in Heav'n!" Ebenezer gasped. "'Tis someone singing!"

And monstrous unlikelihood through it was, the prisoners

recognized the sound to be in truth the voice of a singing man—a tenor, to be exact. This in itself was wonder enough; far more incongruous was the fact that his words (viewed retrospectively from this understanding) were not in a savage tongue at all, but in clear King's English: *I . . . saw . . . my-y la-a-dy weep* was the line he'd sung, and, having drawn his breath, he continued: *And Sor-row proud . . . to be advanced so . . .*

"B'm'faith, 'tis another Englishman!"

"So much the worse for him," the Captain replied, "but no better for us."

"In those fair eyes," the singer went on, *"in those . . . fair eyes . . ."*

"I wonder he hath the spirit to sing," Bertrand marveled, "or his jailer's leave."

This latter, at least, it seemed he did not have after all, for in the course of his next asseveration—*"Where all perfections keep . . ."*—he broke into an unmelodious cursing, the substance of which was that if the so-and-so salvages couldn't let a poor condemned so-and-so sing a so-and-so song without poking their pigstickers into his so-and-so B-flat, they had better cut his so-and-so throat that instant, and be damned to them.

"I swear," Ebenezer said, "I have heard that voice before!"

"Haply 'tis the ghost of your Captain What-ye-may-call-him," the Captain suggested sourly.

"Nay, i'God——" If he had intended to say more, he was prevented from doing so by the Indians, who, their parley finished, gave a jerk on the neck-tether and led the prisoners toward the very hut which held the disgruntled tenor. At its entrance they were unstrung and refettered individually as for the canoe-passage; throughout the operation Ebenezer squinted his face and shook his head incredulously, and when upon another armed Indian's emerging from the hut the tenor at once began his song afresh, the poet moaned again "I'God!" and trembled all over.

Two men then laid hold of Bertrand, who stood nearest the entrance to the hut, forced him to his knees, and with the assistance of a spearpoint obliged him to crawl through the little doorway, whinnying protests and pleas for clemency. The Captain too, now that imprisonment was at hand, let go a fresh torrent of threats and mariner's oaths, to no avail: down upon his knees he went, and through the dark hole after Bertrand.

"I say!" the original tenant complained, breaking off his

song at the ruckus. "This *is* too much! What is't now? 'Sheart! Did I hear an honest English curse there? Hallo, another!" Ebenezer's turn had come to scramble after. "D'ye mean we've enough for four-man shove-ha'penny? Who might you gentlemen be, to come calling so late in the day?"

"A pair of travelers and an innocent shipmaster," the Captain answered, "blown hither by the storm and betrayed by two black devils of a crew!"

"Ah, there's your crime," the other prisoner said. The hut was dark, so that although in its small interior the Englishmen lay like logs in a woodbox, they could not see their companions even faintly. Their jailer, after receiving instructions from the Indian leader, remained on guard outside, and the raiding party dispersed.

"What crime?" the Captain protested. "I've ne'er laid an angry hand on the rascals since the day I bought 'em!"

" 'Tis enough ye bought 'em," replied the tenor. "More than enough. *I* ne'er bought or sold a black man in my life, nor harmed a red—how could I, i'faith, that's but a runaway redemptioner myself?—but 'twas enough I matched the color of them that did."

"What is this talk of slaves and colors?" Bertrand demanded. "D'ye mean they'll scalp poor hapless servingmen like myself?"

"Worse, friend."

"What could be worse?" the valet cried.

"By'r voice I'd judge ye sing a faltering bass," the other declared. "But if they do the trick they've set their minds to, we'll all be warbling descants within the week."

Of the three new prisoners only Ebenezer grasped the meaning of this prediction; yet though horrified by it, he was too disconcerted, even confounded, by his prior astonishment to interpret the figures for his comparisons. Their host, however, the invisible tenor, did so at once in plainest literal English, to the consternation of Bertrand and the Captain.

"I've not been in this wretched province many months," said he, "but I know well the Governor hath enemies on every side—Jacobites and John Coode Protestants within, Andros to the south, and the Frenchman to the north—so that he lives in daily fear of insurrection or invasion. Yet his greatest peril is one he little dreams of: the complete extermination of every white-skinned human being in Maryland!"

"Fogh!" cried the Captain. "They're but one town against a province!"

"Far from it," the tenor replied. "Few white men know

this town exists, but it hath lain hid here many a year; 'tis the headquarters, as I gather, for a host of mutinous salvage chiefs, and a haven for runaway Negroes. All the disaffected leaders are smuggling in this week for a general council of war, and ourselves, gentlemen, will be eunuched and burnt for their amusement."

At this news Bertrand set up such a howling that their guard thrust in his head, jabbed randomly in the dark with the butt end of his spear, and muttered threats. The tenor replied with cheerful curses and remarked, when the guard withdrew, "I say, there were three of ye came in, but I've heard only two speak out thus far: is the other wight sick, or fallen a-swoon, or what?"

" 'Tis not fright holds my tongue, John McEvoy," the poet said with difficulty. " 'Tis shock and shame!"

The other prisoner gasped. "Nay, i'faith! 'Tis past belief! *Ah! Ah!* Too good! Ah, marry, too wondrous good! Tell me 'tis not really Eben Cooke I hear!"

"It is," Ebenezer admitted, and McEvoy's wild laughter brought new threats from the guard.

"Oh! Ah! Too good! The famous virgin poet and reformer o' London whores! 'Twill be a joy to see you roasting by my side. *Aha! Oh! Oh!"*

"It ill becomes you to rejoice," the poet replied. "You set out a-purpose to ruin my life, but whate'er injury or misfortune you've suffered at my hands hath been no wish of mine at all."

"Marry!" Bertrand exclaimed. "Is't the pimp from Pudding Lane, sir, that tattled to Master Andrew?"

"I take it ye gentlemen know each other," the Captain said, "and have some quarrel betwixt ye?"

"Why, nay," McEvoy answered, "no quarrel at all; 'tis only that I made his fortune—albeit by accident—and out of gratitude he hath wrecked my life, hastened my death, and ruined the woman I love!"

"Yet not a bit of't by design, and scarce even with knowledge," Ebenezer countered, "whereas 'twill please you to know *your* revenge hath surpassed your evillest intentions. I have suffered at the hands of rogues and pirates, been deceived by my closest friend, swindled out of my estate, and obliged to flee forever in disgrace from my father; what's more, in following me here, my sister hath been led into Heav'n knows what peril, while poor Joan Toast——" Here he was overwhelmed with emotion and lost his voice.

"What of her?" snapped McEvoy.

"I will say only what I presume you saw at Malden: that she hath suffered, and suffers yet, inconceivable tribulations and indignities, in consequence of which she is disfigured in form and face and cannot have long to live."

McEvoy groaned. "And ye call me to blame for't, wretch, when 'twas you she followed? I'Christ, if my hands were free to wring your neck!"

"I have a burthen of guilt, indeed," Ebenezer admitted. "Yet but for your tattling to my father you'd ne'er have lost her; or, if you had, 'twould've been to Pudding Lane and not to Maryland. In any case, she'd not have been raped by a giant Moor and infected with the pox, or ruined by opium, or whored out nightly to a barnful of salvages!"

At the pronouncement of each of these misfortunes McEvoy moaned afresh; hot tears coursed from the poet's eyes, ran cold across his temples and into his ears.

"Whate'er thy differences, gentlemen," the Captain put in, " 'tis little to the purpose to air 'em this late in the day. All our sins will soon enough be rendered out, and there's an end on't."

"Aiee!" Bertrand wailed.

"True enough," McEvoy sighed. "The man who won't forgive his neighbor must needs have struck a wondrous bargain with his own conscience."

"The best of us," Ebenezer agreed, "hath certain memories in the night to make him sweat for shame. Once before, in Locket's, I forgave you for your letter to my father; yet 'twas a bragging sort of pardon, inasmuch as what you'd done had seemed to make my fortune. Now I have lost title, fortune, love, honor, and life itself, let me forgive you again, McEvoy, and beg your own forgiveness in return."

The Irishman concurred, but admitted that since Ebenezer had at no time set about deliberately to injure either him or Joan Toast, there was little or nothing to be forgiven.

"Not so, friend—i'Christ, not so!" The poet wept, and related as coherently as he could his trials with Captain Pound, the rape of the *Cyprian*, his bargain with the swine-girl, the loss of his estate, and his obligatory marriage to Joan Toast. In particular he dwelt upon his responsibility in Joan's downfall, her solicitude during his protracted seasoning, and the magnanimity of her plan for their flight to England, until not only himself and McEvoy, but the whole imprisoned company were sniffling and weeping at her goodness.

"For reward," Ebenezer went on, "she asked no more than that I give her my ring for hers, to make her feel less a harlot, and that she be given the honor of providing for me in London——"

"As she did for me," McEvoy reverently interposed.

The Captain sniffled. "She is a Catholic saint of a whore!"

"And to think I spoke so freely to her at Captain Mitchell's," Bertrand marveled, "when we thought her but a scurfy wench of a pig-driver!"

"Stay, sirs," Ebenezer demanded sadly; "you have not heard the beginning of my shame. D'you think, when she made this martyr's proposition, I refused to hear of't, but ordered her off to England on her own six pounds and promised to rejoin her when I could? Or did I, at the very least, go down on my knees before such charity and kiss the hem of her ragged dress? Imagine the very worst of me, sirs: d'you suppose I merely thanked her with great feeling, let her whore up her boat fare from the Indians in the curing-house, and sailed off with her to be her pimp in London?"

"God forgive ye if ye did," the Captain murmured.

"Should God forgive me thrice o'er," said Ebenezer, "I would bear still a weight of guilt sufficient to drag ten men to Hell. The fact is, gentlemen, I accepted the six pounds, sent her off to the curing-house—and fled alone to the bark in Cambridge! What say you to that, McEvoy?"

"Forgiven, forgiven!" cried the Irishman. "And God save us all! Methinks the fire that cooks our flesh will be cool beside the flames that roast our souls!"

Some minutes passed in silence while the company reflected on the story and their fate. Presently, in a calmer voice, Ebenezer asked McEvoy what ill fortune had led him to Bloodsworth Island. The query elicited a number of great sighing curses, after which, and several false starts, McEvoy offered the following explanation:

"I am but two-and-twenty, sirs, as near as one can reckon that hath not the faintest notion of his birth date; but i'faith, I've been an old man all my life! My earliest memory is of singing for ha'pennies by Barking Church, for a legless wretch named Patcher that called himself my father; I was half dead o' cold and like to faint away from hunger—for de'il the crust I'd see of a loaf old Patcher bought with my earnings!—and the reason I recall it, I had to sing myself alive, as't were, or fall down in the snow, yet I durst not unclench my teeth lest they ruin the song with chattering. Old Patcher must needs have been a music-master, for whene'er I strayed a quaver out o' key he'd cane me into tune with his hickory-crutch. Many's the lutist that can play with his eyes closed, but I'll wager 'tis a rare tenor can sing a com-all-ye with his jaws shut fast!

"Yet sing 'em I did, and true as gospel, nor did I e'er lament my plight or rail at Patcher in my mind; in sooth, 'twas not his cruelty made me vow to be shed of him but his mistakes upon the lute he played to accompany my songs! Some winters later, when I was stronger and he weaker, we were working Newgate Market in a blizzard; Patcher's fingers were that benumbed, he played as I might with the toes o' my feet, and the sound so offended my ear, I flew into a passion, snatched up the hickory-crutch, and laid him low with a clout aside the head. So doth the pupil repeat his lesson!"

"You killed him, then?" asked Ebenezer.

"I did not tarry to find out," McEvoy laughed. "I snatched up his lute and fled. But Newgate Market was near deserted, and the weather freezing, and though I begged my way through London for many a year after, singing the songs he taught me and playing on his lute, I ne'er saw old Patcher again. Thus ended my apprenticeship: I joined the ranks of those who get their living from the streets, a journeyman musician and master beggar, and my own man from that day to this."

"Unhappy child!"

McEvoy sniffed. "So speaks the virgin poet."

"Nay, John; for all your trials you were still an innocent amongst the wolves."

"Say rather a whelp amongst his elders, and no mean hand at wolfing. My virginity I lost to the whores that nursed my boyish ailments, but innocence I never lost, nor fear nor faith in God and man—for the reason one cannot lose what he never hath possessed. I played in taverns for my bed and board, and whene'er I wanted money—but 'tis no news to the Laureate that your true artist need not be handsome to please the ladies; his talent serves for face, place, and grace together, and for all he hath been sired by a legless beggar upon a drunken gutter-tart, if his art hath power to stir he may be wined and dined by dukes and spread the knees of young marquesas! In short, when I grew fond of inventing melodies, I invested in the love of wealthy women——"

"Invested!" cried Bertrand, who to this point had expressed no interest in the tale. " 'Tis a rare investment that pays cash dividends on no capital!"

"Nay, don't mistake me," McEvoy said seriously. "*Time* was my capital, the precious mortal time one wastes a-wooing; and my return was time as well—hours bought from singing for my supper, and from doing the hundred mean chores a poor man doth for himself perforce. 'Twas an investment like any other, and I chose it for a proper tradesman's reason: it paid a higher return on my capital than did aught else, in mortal time."

"Yet you must own 'twas something callous," ventured the poet.

"No more than any honest business," McEvoy insisted. "If hearts were injured, why, the wounds were self-inflicted; I promised naught, and kept my promise, and there's an end on't."

"But surely Joan Toast——"

"I have said naught o' Joan Toast," the Irishman reproved. " 'Tis the wives and daughters o' the rich I did my business with, that call their pandering *patronage*, and are much given to fornication in the noble cause of Art. Joan Toast was a penceless guttersnipe like myself—and an artist as well, in her way, only her instruments were different from my own."

"Ha! Well said!" cried Bertrand. Ebenezer made no comment.

"I was eighteen when first I met her: she had been hired to service a certain debauched young peer, whose wife, not to be outdone, hired me to play the same game with herself. The four of us sat down to pheasant and Rhenish, for all the world like two pairs o' newlyweds, which much pleased his lordship's fancy; in sooth, as the wine got hold of him he made a series of lewd proposals, each more unnatural than the one before. And since perversion, like refinement, is an arc, the which, if ye but extend it far enough, returns upon itself, by the evening's end naught tickled the wretch so much as the thought of taking his wife to bed! Joan Toast and I were turned out together, and as we'd done no more than eat a meal to earn our hire, we made a night of't in her little room near Ludgate. E'en then, at seventeen, she was the soul o' worldliness: fresh and full of spirit as a blooded colt, but her eyes were old as lust, and in her gestures was the history of the race. Small wonder his lordship craved her: she was the elixir of her sex, and who swived her swived no woman, but Womankind!

"We stayed some days there in her chamber, sending out for food till our hire was spent; when we went down again together to the street, 'twas with a certain pact between us, that lasted till the night o' your wager with Ben Oliver."

"In plain English," remarked the Captain, "ye was her pimp."

"In plainer," McEvoy replied without hesitation, "we twain were to the arts o' love like the hands o' the lutist to his music: together, at our proper work, we could set Heaven's vaults a-tremble; all else was the common business of survival, to be got o'er by whatever means were most expedient. I'd no more have quarreled with her arrangements than I'd quarrel with the sum o' history, or cavil at the patterns of the stars."

"For all that," Bertrand remarked, "thou'rt no nearer Maryland now than when ye started, and this night shan't last forever."

"Let him tell on," the Captain said. " 'Tis either a tale or the Shuddering Fearfuls in straits like these."

"Aye, John, tell on," Ebenezer encouraged. "How is't you knew Joan Toast had followed me? And how is't you fell into Tom Tayloe's hands?"

"Tayloe! Ye've heard o' Tom Tayloe and me?"

Ebenezer explained the circumstances of his acquaintanceship with the corpulent seller of indentured servants. McEvoy was vastly amused; indeed, he laughed as heartily at the news of Tayloe's indenture to the cooper William Smith as if he were hearing the story in Locket's instead of a prisonhut, and the Captain was moved to observe, "Methinks 'tis *he* should be merry, not you, sir; he hath the better bargain after all!"

"Aye and he hath," Ebenezer agreed. "But e'en were we not here in the very vestibule of death, 'twould ill become us to jest at the man's bad luck."

McEvoy laughed again. "What humanists death hatches out of men! Ye have forgot what a worthless wretch Tom Tayloe was, that preyed on masters and servants alike!"

"A wretch he might have been," the poet allowed, "and deserving of your prank; but his time is no less mortal than our own, and to rob him of four years of't is to carry the jest too far." He sighed. "I'Christ, when I think of the weeks and years I've squandered! Precious mortal time! I begrudge every day I spend not writing verse!"

"And I every night I slept alone in London," Bertrand said fervently.

"As for that," the Captain put in, "what matter if a man lives seven years or seventy? His years are not an eyeblink to eternity, and de'il the way he spends 'em—whether steering ships or scribbling verse, or building towns or burning 'em— he dies like a May fly when his day is done, and the stars go round their courses just the same. Where's the profit and loss

577

o' his labors? He'd as well have stayed abed, or sat his bum on a bench."

Although Ebenezer stirred uneasily at these words, remembering his state of mind at Magdalene College and in his room in Pudding Lane, he nevertheless reaffirmed his belief in the value of human time, arguing from the analogy of precious stones and metals that the value of commodities increases inversely with their supply where demand is constant, and with demand where supply is constant, so that mortal time, being infinitesimal in supply and virtually infinite in demand, was therefore infinitely precious to mortal men.

"Marry come up!" McEvoy cried impatiently. "Ye twain remind me of children I saw once at St. Bartholomew's Fair, queued up to ride in a little red pony cart . . ."

He did not bother to explain his figure, but Ebenezer understood it immediately, or thought he understood it, for he said, "Thou'rt right, McEvoy; there is no argument 'twixt the Captain and myself. I recall the day my sister and I turned five and were allowed an extra hour 'twixt bath and bed. Mrs. Twigg would set her hourglass running there in the nursery; we could do whate'er we wished with the time, but when the sand had run 'twas off to bed and no lingering. I'faith, what a treasure that hour seemed: time for any of a hundred pleasures! We fetched out the cards, to play some game or other—but what silly game was worth such a wondrous hour? I vowed I'd build a castle out of blocks, and Anna set to drawing three soldiers upon a paper—but neither of us could pursue his sport for long, for thinking the other had chosen more wisely, so that anon we made exchange and were no more pleased. We cast about more desperately among our toys and games—whereof any one had sufficed for an hour's diversion earlier in the day—but none would do, and still the glass ran on! Any hour save this most prime and measured we had been pleased enough to do no more than talk, or watch the world at work outside our nursery window, but when I cried 'Heavy, heavy hangs over thy head,' to commence a guessing game, Anna fell straightway to weeping, and I soon joined her. Yet e'en our tears did naught to ease our desperation; indeed, they but heightened it the more, for all the while we wept, our hour was slipping by. Now bedtime, mind, we'd ne'er before looked on as evil, but that sand was like our lifeblood draining from some wound; we sat and wept, and watched it flow, and the upshot of't was, we both fell ill and took to heaving, and Mrs. Twigg fetched us off to bed with our last quarter hour still in the glass."

"Which teaches us——?" questioned McEvoy.

"Which teaches us," Ebenezer responded sadly, "that naught can be inferred to guide our conduct from the fact of our mortality. Nonetheless, if Malden were mine, I'd set Tom Tayloe free."

"But in the meanwhile I may laugh at him all I please," McEvoy added, "which—philosophy be damned—is what I'd do in any case. D'ye want to hear my tale or no?"

Ebenezer declared that he did indeed, although in fact his interest in McEvoy's adventures waned with every speeding minute of the night, and he felt in his heart that his digression had been considerably more germane to their plight.

"Very well, then," the Irishman began; "the fact of't is, I had at first no mind at all to come to Maryland. When Joan Toast left me I knew we were over and done—'tis her wont to give all or naught, as well ye know—yet no folly is too immense for the desperate lover, nor any contrary fact so plain that Hope cannot paint it to his colors. To be brief, I feared she'd follow ye off to Maryland, and in order to intercept her I took lodgings in the posthouse, put on my grandest swagger, and gave out to all and sundry I was Ebenezer Cooke, the Laureate of Maryland . . ."

"'Sheart, another!" Ebenezer cried. "Maryland hath an infestation of laureate poets!"

"'Twas a wild imposture," McEvoy said good-humoredly. "Heav'n knows what I meant to do if Joan Toast sought me out! But in any case my tenure was wondrous brief: I had scarce raised a general toast to the Maryland muse ere a gang of bullies burst in with some tale of a stolen ledger-book, and being told I was Master Eben Cooke the poet, they straightway hauled me off to jail."

"La, now!" laughed Bertrand. "There's a mystery cleared, sirs, that hath plagued me these many months whene'er I thought of't! When *I* came to the posthouse to hide from Ralph Birdsall's knife—that I wish I'd suffered, and been a live eunuch instead of a dead one!—what I mean, when I asked about for the Laureate, I heard he'd been fetched off to prison. 'Twas that very tragedy inspired me to take his place and flee to Plymouth; yet when Master Eben found me on the *Poseidon,* he vowed he'd ne'er been set upon by Ben Bragg's men and thought me a liar. Doth this news not absolve me, sir?"

"No fear of that," replied the poet. " 'Tis too late in the day for aught but general absolution. There are some small *lacunae* yet, as't were, in the text of your pretty tale—but let them go. What did you then, McEvoy? I pray you were not held long for my little theft."

"Only till the following morn," McEvoy said, "when Bragg came round and saw he'd hooked the wrong fish. By then I'd lost my taste for farther nonsense; I resolved to quit my search for Joan and commence the mighty labor of forgetting her. I returned to my old pursuits among the wealthy, but though I had some small success at first, my years with Joan had spoiled me: the ladies felt a small scorn in my rutting, belike, or heard some certain coldness in my voice . . . In any case I was soon unemployed and anon was driven to lute it on the street-corners for my living, by Botolph's Wharf and the Steel Yard, and Newgate Market, where my life began. What I earned I spent on whores, to no avail: when a man hath lain a thousand nights with his beloved and no other, he knows her from crown to sole with all his senses—every muscle, every pore, every sigh; every action of her limbs and heart and mind he knows as he knows his own. Put some other wench beside him in the dark: her mere displacement of the air he feels at once as an alien thing; the simple press of her on the pallet is foreign to his senses; her very breathing startles him, so different in pitch and rhythm! She puts out an ardent hand: his flesh recoils as from some brute-o'-the-forest's paw. They come together: i'Christ, how clumsy!—their arms, that would embrace, knock elbows or can find no place to lie; their legs entangle, that would entwine; their chins and noses will not fit. He would caress her: he pokes her ribs instead, or scratches her with a hangnail. Some amorous word or gesture takes him by surprise: he is unmanned, or like a green recruit, shoots his bolt ere the issue is fairly joined. In short, though he hath been to his beloved a master lutes-man upon his lute, now he finds he hath bestrode a violincello, whereof he knows not gooseneck from f-hole; he hits no string aright, fingers blindly to no purpose, and in the end hath but a headache from his plucking."

The whole company, despite their position, were amused by this apostrophe; but the Irishman resumed his discourse in a sober voice:

"Seeing that whores were not my medicine, I turned to rum and soaked myself to oblivion each night. My hands grew clumsy on the lute, my voice thickened and cracked, my ear went dull, and every night required more rum than the night before; so that anon I could not beg enough to drink on, and had perforce to turn to theft to gain my ends. Then one night—'twas a full three months after your departure—a sailorman gave me a shilling to sing *Joan's Placket Is Torn* for him, and when I had done, declared himself so pleased that he filled me with rum at his own expense. 'Twas my guess he had some queer design—and little I cared, so he let me drink my fill! But I was wrong . . ."

"God help ye, then," the Captain muttered. "I can guess the rest: Ye was spirited off?"

"I fell senseless in some inn near Baynard's Castle," McEvoy said, "and woke fettered in the 'tweendecks of a moving ship. At first I had no notion whither we sailed or to what end I had been kidnaped, but anon some among us, that went unfettered, declared they were redemptioners bound for Maryland and explained 'twas not uncommon for a certain sort of captain to fill out his cargo with wharf rats like myself and the half-dozen others who had waked to find themselves legironed to a ship.

"Presently the first mate made us a speech, whereof the substance was that we were in his debt for being saved from our old profligacy and ferried without charge to a land where we might build our lives anew, and that any man of us who honored this obligation and pledged himself to act accordingly would be freed of his leg iron then and there. All the rest were glad enough to swear whatever lying pledge he pledged 'em, but when I saw that this pious first mate was the very wretch who had undone me the night before, I let fly such a grapeshot of curses that he ruined my mouth with his boot and swore he'd starve me into virtue or into Hell ere the voyage was done.

"Now a man like me, that hath been an orphan beggar all his life and feels neither shame nor poverty, is as free a man as any thou'rt like to find, and 'tis no wonder he grows most jealous of his liberty. 'Tis true I'd been jailed not long since for petty stealing, and once ere that when I posed as Laureate; but both times 'twas my own misdoings brought me to jail, and since by *liberty* is meant one's rights, 'tis no loss of liberty to be justly jailed for crime. Contrariwise, 'tis a gross offence against liberty to be fettered against one's wishes and for no just cause, and the wights who swore that scandalous oath to shed their leg irons, so far from gaining any liberty thereby, did but surrender the dearest liberty of all—the right to rail against injustice."

"There is much wisdom in what you say," Ebenezer remarked, considerably impressed by McEvoy's words and humbled anew, not only by his suspicion that under similar circumstances he would not have displayed such integrity, but

581

also by his conviction—no less disquieting for its present irrelevancy—that McEvoy was far more worthy of Joan Toast than was he, and had been so from the beginning.

"Wise or foolish, 'twas my sentiment in the matter," McEvoy said, "and albeit I tasted the whoreson's leather oft and oft in the days that followed, at least 'twas ne'er by licking his boots I learnt the flavor. He did not quite starve me to death as he had promised, whether because he took such pleasure in kicking me or because he was loath to let me perish unrepentant. I was moved from the 'tweendecks into the hold lest I start a mutiny by my example, and I ne'er saw daylight again till the end of the voyage, when they fetched me up on deck to sell with the rest."

"Whereupon," Ebenezer put in, "if Tayloe told me aright, you straightway leaped into the river and made for your liberty—but they fished you out."

"Aye, and saved my life, for I learned too late I had not strength enough to swim ten strokes. And on reflection it seemed a fair choice to go with Tayloe; I judged his brains to be as swinish as his manner, and guessed 'twould be no great matter to outwit him at the proper moment. I only wish my friend Dick Parker had been less rash—but I've not told ye about Dick Parker, have I? No matter: we swim in an ocean of story, but a tumblerful slakes our thirst. Besides, the night's nigh done, is't not? To conclude, then, gentlemen; I bartered Tom Tayloe for a horse, as Eben hath told—and a foundered jade at that, but worth a score o' servant-brokers —and since I'd learnt I was in Maryland I resolved to ride out privily to Cooke's Point, merely to satisfy myself that Joan was there and happy in her choice." He laughed. "La, what rot is that? I rode out in hopes she'd had her fill of innocence! I knew my wretched case would move her to pity and I prayed she might mistake that pity for love. 'Twas a desperate piece o' wishing and proved false in two respects: her plight, I found, was far more wretched than mine, but neither pox nor opium nor cruelty, nor the face o' death itself —how much less pity!—could turn her from her course once she had set it.

"I did not tarry: Tom Tayloe, I supposed, would turn the country inside out to find the fugitive that gulled him. I resolved to make my way to Virginia, if I could find it, or Carolina, and haply join some crew o' pirates. To this end I joined company with a runaway Negro slave that had been chained with me in the ship's hold—one o' Parker's chief lieutenants, he was, named Bandy Lou, that had learnt a mickle English. 'Twas his idea we make for Bloodsworth Island, which he had heard was a-swarm with fugitives like ourselves. We didn't know they love a white man as the Devil loves holy water, and when we learned it, 'twas all too late: Bandy Lou they welcomed as a brother, but me, for all his pleadings, they trussed up and put aside against the day——"

"Hi there!" the Captain interrupted. "What's that I hear?"

McEvoy left his sentence unfinished, and the prisoners strained to listen. From far off in the marshes came a series of sharp cries, like the cawing of a crow, and the guard outside their hut responded in kind.

"Some new arrivals to the grand Black Mass," McEvoy murmured. "They've been coming in every night this week."

The signal cries were repeated, and then in the distance the prisoners could hear a deep, rhythmical mutter, as of many men rumbling a soft chant as they marched. The sentry outside sprang up and cried to the slumbering village some terse announcement, which effected an immediate stir among the huts. People chattered and bustled about the square; sharp orders were issued; new logs clumped and crackled on the fire; and the chant grew clearer and stronger all the while.

"I'faith, 'tis like no Indian song I've heard before," the Captain whispered.

"Nay, 'tis a black man's chanting, by the pitch and rhythm of't," McEvoy replied. "I heard Dick Parker and Bandy Lou sing the like of't in the ship's hold, and the Africans hereabouts have done the same for the last few nights. 'Sheart, but it makes the hackles rise! 'Tis no good news for us, methinks."

"Why is that?" Ebenezer asked sharply.

"They have been waiting for their two chief men to smuggle across the Bay," McEvoy said. "One is the leader of the blacks, and the other's the strongest of the salvage kings that the Governor hath unseated. That much I know from Bandy Lou, that whispered to me some days back through the wall of this hut. They've ne'er been reckless enough to sing so loud before: I'll wager 'tis their majesties have come to town, and the circus is ready to start."

And indeed, as the new arrivals filed into the common, the villagers took up the chant, cried out wild cries, beat drums to mark the rhythm, and—as best the prisoners could judge from sound alone—commenced some vigorous dance around the fire. Bertrand sucked his breath and moaned, and Ebenezer began to tremble involuntarily in every limb. Not even McEvoy could quite preserve his self-control: he fell to intoning oaths and curses in a hissing whisper, like paternosters recited with teeth on edge.

Only Captain Cairn remained calm. " 'Twere folly to wait for their tortures," he declared soberly. "We're all dead men at the end of the chapter, why should we suffer ten times o'er for their heathen pleasure?"

"What is't you propose?" Ebenezer demanded. "Suicide? Methinks I'd gladly take my own life and have done with't."

"We've no means to do the job ourselves," the Captain said. "But it may be still in our hands to die fast or a piece at a time. If they carry us out bodily there's no hope, but if they string us together by the neck and free our feet to walk, as they did before, we must make a run for't, all together, and pray they'll stop us with spears and arrows."

" 'Twould never work," McEvoy scoffed. "They'd simply overhaul us and fetch us back to their carving-knives."

Bertrand wailed.

"Besides," McEvoy added, "I am a Catholic, albeit no model parishioner, and I shan't destroy myself in any case."

"Then here's a better plan," said the Captain, "that ye may help us in with no harm to your faith. Our hands and feet are bound, but we have still the movement of our knees: let Mr. Cooke's man place his neck 'twixt his master's legs, and me place my neck 'twixt yours, and we twain be throttled without delay to end our miseries. Then do ye the same for Mr. Cooke, when he hath done, and thou'rt left to be murthered as ye wish by the Indians. What say ye to that?"

"I'God!" whispered Ebenezer; yet appalled though he was by the old man's proposal, he could scarcely deny that being strangled was less painful than being emasculated and burnt alive.

As it turned out, he was not obliged to choose; the celebration presently subsided, and day dawned to find the prisoners still unmolested. Too anxious to feel much relief, they regarded one another silently—McEvoy, Ebenezer observed, had lost a quarter of his weight and some of his teeth, and had of necessity grown a beard—nor were they ever again as talkative as they had been that first night. The days passed— two, seven, ten—and though the prisoners were never once permitted out of the hut, they could hear the daily-increasing activity in the town.

"I'faith, 'tis like the Convocation o' Cardinals!" McEvoy declared.

No one mentioned the Captain's proposal again, but it must have been on everyone's mind as it was on Ebenezer's, for when one early morning they heard their guard approached by some manner of delegation, as one man they sucked in their breaths and went rigid.

"Make haste!" the Captain urged. "They've come to fetch us!"

"Then fetch us they shall," McEvoy grumbled. "I'm not a murtherer."

Just then the hide-flap door of the hut was thrown open: cold air rushed in, and the dancing light of the fire, and against the grey-white dawn they could see the stiff black shapes of men.

"You, then, in the name o' God!" The Captain twisted towards Ebenezer, and his voice grew shrill. "I beg ye, sir; throttle me now, this instant, ere they lay hands on us! Here, quickly, for the love o' Christ!"

He wrenched himself across Bertrand toward the poet's trembling knees. Ebenezer had no voice to say him nay; he could only shake his head. But even had he been both willing and able, there was not time to do the deed: the black silhouettes closed in, bent over them; black hands laid hold of their ankles and legs; black voices chuckled and grunted. One by one the terrified white men were dragged outside by the heels.

6

*His Future at Stake, the Poet Reflects on a
Brace of Secular Mysteries*

THE COURTYARD OR COMMON enclosed by the Indian town was patchy with thin, wet snow, which had also whitened the tops of all the mound-shaped dwellings. The air was raw and saturated, but not bitter cold; in fact, a mass of temperate air had moved over the Bay, with the result that a great fog enveloped the island. Swirls of mist swept out of the marsh, given voice by invisible gulls, and were blown with a falling cry toward the straits.

Despite the fog and the early hour, Ebenezer could see a great number of people all about, some in Scotch cloth and English woolens, but most in hides and furs and matchcoats. The women were making small fires near their huts and preparing food for the morning meal; the men, for the most part, were occupied with tobacco and conversation around several larger fires in the common itself, Negroes and Indians together: there was a rustle of general talk, as well as much parleying by signs and gestures. In the center of the court the little watch fire of the night had been so fueled with resinous pine that its blaze, flashing orange upon the fog, seemed more ceremonial than useful. The heat of it had melted the snow in a sizeable circle, about whose perimeter were ranged a solemn score of dignitaries, black and red; and just outside the quadrants of their circle, four separate parties of men were raising twelve-foot posts in hip-deep holes.

When the prisoners were all on their feet, a grinning Negro from the deputation that had fetched them out stepped up to McEvoy and said in English, "No more nights in there, ha?" He rolled his eyes towards the prison-hut.

"Thou'rt a black imp o' Satan," McEvoy grumbled. "I would ye'd jumped to the fishes with Dick Parker!"

The Negro—whom Ebenezer took to be McEvoy's erstwhile companion Bandy Lou—flashed his teeth in amusement and gave sharp orders to his men, who cut the thongs from the prisoners' ankles and led them towards the posts. The poet's knees began to fail; his jailers were obliged to support as well as direct him. The hum of conversation on every side changed to a murmur and died away; except for the crackling fires the common was silent, and dark faces regarded the white men coldly as they passed. The men at the central fire turned round at their approach, and a much-painted elder among them nodded towards the nearest of the posts just being tamped into position.

"You be judged by three kings," the smiling Negro repeated to McEvoy. "Others stay here."

None of the prisoners spoke. It appeared that the dread triumvirate was not at the fireside after all, for the Irishman was led toward a larger specimen of muskrat-house across the common. Ebenezer and Bertrand were bound each to a post by the ankles and wrists; the feel of his position brought the poet near to swooning, so clearly did it recall the legion of martyred men. How many millions had been similarly bound since the race began, and for how many reasons put to the unspeakable pain of fire? But he strove to put by the swoon, in hopes of resummoning it when he would need it more desperately.

The Captain, meanwhile, had been obliged to stand by while the third and fourth posts were being raised and tamped. He stood quietly, head bowed, as though resigned to the horrors ahead; his guards, absorbed in plumbing the massive posts, ignored him. Suddenly he leaped behind and away from them and struck out across the common. A shout went up; men scrambled to their feet, snatched their spears, and hurried after him. Ebenezer craned his neck to watch, expecting to see the old man run through, but the Indians held back. The Captain ran for a gap between two council-fires, and was faced with a wall of spears held at the ready; he hesitated, spun about, and was confronted with a similar wall. This time, as if abandoning some tenuous hope of escape and returning to his original purpose, he thrust out his chest and lunged straight for the spears; but their bearers drew back and merely blocked his way with their arms and shafts. He wheeled again, his arms still bound behind, and hopped in another direction, with the same result. The ranks closed now in a large circle around him, and it being quite clear that he could not escape even to the marsh, they began to laugh at his furious endeavor. Again and again the old man rushed at the spears; at length, unable to screw up his desperate resolve again, the Captain gave a cry and fell. His tormentors dispersed, still chuckling; the guards returned him to the post, now ready to accommodate him, and began piling twigs and branches at the feet of all three.

His skin awash, Ebenezer looked away and saw McEvoy reappear from the royal palace with his smiling escort. The Irishman's face was winced up in a curious expression— whether anger, abhorrence, or fear, Ebenezer could not tell, but he assumed when he saw his companion made fast to the one remaining post that the curious "judgment" had not been a pardon.

However, he was mistaken. "'Tis the Devil's own wonder of a happenstance!" McEvoy cried over to him, in a voice as strange and twisted as his expression. "They fetched me before their three kings for sentencing, and two of 'em were scurfy salvages, but the third was my friend Dick Parker, the wight I was chained in the hold with! I thought he was drowned and forgot, but i'faith, he's the king o' these black heathen! This scoundrel Bandy Lou hath known it these many days and said naught of't; he was Dick Parker's chief lieutenant back in Africa!"

Ebenezer was unable to marvel at this coincidence; indeed, he wondered whether McEvoy had not been deranged by fear. Could a sane man relate such trifles while his pyre was a-building round his feet?

Only then did he observe that though his own pyre was completed, as were those of Bertrand and the senseless Captain, not a twig had been laid at McEvoy's post, nor did the guards seem about to fetch any.

"God help me, Eben!" the Irishman shouted. "They mean to turn me loose! Dick Parker hath spared me!" His eyes ran with tears. "As God is my witness," McEvoy cried on, "I begged and pled for ye, Eben, by whate'er friendship had been 'twixt Dick Parker and myself. Ye was my brother, I told him, and dear as life to me; but the others were for burning the four of us, and 'twas all Dick Parker could manage to spare me. As't is I must watch ye suffer there all this day and tomorrow, till their council's done, and then see ye burnt!"

"The pimp hath bartered our skins to save his own!" Bertrand yelled from his post across the way.

"Nay, I swear't!" McEvoy protested. "Whate'er hath been betwixt us in the past, 'tis all behind us; ye mustn't believe I hold aught against ye, or biased your case with Dick Parker!"

"I believe you," Ebenezer said. He had in fact felt a moment of wrath at McEvoy's news; would he, after all, have left London in the first place had not McEvoy betrayed him? But he soon overcame his anger, for despite the extremity of his position, or perhaps because of it, he was able to see that McEvoy had only been following his principles honestly, as had Ebenezer his own; one could as easily blame old Andrew for reacting so strongly, Joan Toast for occasioning the wager, Ben Oliver for proposing it, Anna for crossing alone to Maryland, Burlingame for—among other things—persuading him to disembark in St. Mary's, or Ebenezer himself, who by any of a hundred thousand acts might have altered the direction of his life. The whole history of his twenty-eight years it was that had brought him to the present place at the present time; and had not this history taken its particular pattern, in large measure, from the influence of all the people with whom he'd ever dealt, and whose lives in turn had been shaped by the influence of countless others? Was he not, in short, bound to his post not merely by the sum of human history, but even by the history of the entire universe, as by a chain of numberless links no one of which was more culpable than any other? It seemed to Ebenezer that he was, and that

McEvoy was not more nor less to blame than was Lord Baltimore, for example, who had colonized Maryland, or the Genoese adventurer who had discovered the New World to the Old.

This conclusion, which the poet reached more by insight than by speculation, was followed by another, whose logic ran thus: The point in space and time whereto the history of the world had brought him would be nothing perilous were it not for the hostility of the Indians and Negroes. But it was their exploitation by the English colonists that had rendered them hostile; that is to say, by a people to whom the accidents of history had given the advantage—Ebenezer did not doubt that his captors, if circumstances were reversed, would do just what the English were doing. To the extent, then, that historical movements are expressions of the will of the people engaged in them, Ebenezer was a just object for his captors' wrath, for he belonged, in a deeper sense than McEvoy had intended in his remark of some nights past, to the class of the exploiters; as an educated gentleman of the western world he had shared in the fruits of his culture's power and must therefore share what guilt that power incurred. Nor was this the end of his responsibility: for if it was the accidents of power and position that made the difference between exploiters and exploited, and not some mysterious specialization of each group's spirit, then it was as "human" for the white man to enslave and dispossess as it was "human" for the black and red to slaughter on the basis of color alone; the savage who would put him to the torch anon was no less his brother than was the trader who had once enslaved that savage. In sum, the poet observed, for his secular Original Sin, though he was to atone for it in person, he would exact a kind of Vicarious Retribution; he had committed a grievous crime against himself, and it was himself who soon would punish the malefactor.

Grasping the pair of insights was the labor of but as many seconds, and though they moved him as had few moments in his spiritual autobiography, all he said to Bertrand and McEvoy was, "In any case, 'tis too late to split the hairs of responsibility. Look yonder."

He indicated with his brows the direction of the hut from which McEvoy had been lately escorted. The eyes of the assemblage had turned that way as well, and their conversation dwindled. The three kings had issued forth to render judgment: as best Ebenezer could distinguish through the mists, one was a strapping Negro, one an equally robust red man,

589

and the third, also an Indian, an aged, decrepit fellow who moved with a great deal of difficulty on the arms of his younger colleagues. All three were dressed elaborately by comparison with their subjects: their garments were fringed, tasseled, and colorfully worked with shell-beads; their faces were striped and circled with puccoon; their necks hung with bear's teeth and cowries; the Indians wore headdresses of beadwork and turkey feathers, while the Negro's was wrought of two bull's horns mounted in fur. The two stalwarts held each in his free hand a bone-tipped javelin; the ancient one bore in his right a sort of scepter or ceremonial staff topped with the pelt of a muskrat, and in his left a sputtering pitch-pine torch.

The pace made their approach more somber. McEvoy regarded them wide-eyed over his shoulder; Bertrand began to make moan. Ebenezer blushed with fear; he pressed his lips fast, but the rest of his features ticked and twitched.

Closest to the triumvirate was McEvoy: they confronted him sternly; the Negro raised his spear and made some sort of pronouncement, which his subjects received with an uncertain murmur, and then the younger of the Indian chiefs apparently repeated it in his tongue, for his statement met with a like response. Ebenezer remarked some displeasure in the old chief's face, and great satisfaction in the countenance of McEvoy's companion Bandy Lou, who stood nearby. The party moved next to the bearded Captain, who had just begun to stir and roll his head. Again some sentence was rendered in two languages with upraised spears: the old chief's smile and the assemblage's shouted approval made its meaning clear, and the poet shuddered.

Next came Bertrand, who turned his head away and squinted shut his eyes. The younger of the Indian kings regarded him coldly; the older with malevolent pleasure as he nodded to something the Negro was leaning to whisper in his ear. All eyes were on the great black king, who in both of the previous instances had passed sentence first; he ended his colloquy with the old man, lifted his javelin, and began his pronouncement even as he raised his eyes to the prisoner's face.

But he stopped in mid-sentence and rushed forward to turn Bertrand's face towards his own. Ebenezer's muscles tightened: since the Negro had retained his spear but let go the old chief's arm most uncourteously, the poet rather expected to see Bertrand run through on the instant for the crime of averting his head. Nor were his fears allayed when the Negro gave a cry, snatched a bone knife from the belt of a nearby lieutenant, and leaped toward the valet with the weapon held back. His fellow chiefs frowned; the nearer spectators drew back in alarm, and their consternation mounted when, instead of ending the prisoner's life or dismembering him where he hung, the black king sliced all the thongs and fetters, kicked away the knee-high faggots, and flung himself prostrate at the reeling prisoner's feet!

"Master Eben!" the valet bawled, drawing back against the post. The old chief barked, and the younger made what appeared to be a sharp query, to which the Negro king replied in the Indian tongue, his voice heavy with emotion. The common had gone silent as a church. The Indian king frowned more severely, summoned lieutenants to support his ancient colleague, and strode as quickly as dignity permitted, not toward Bertrand but toward the much-distraught prisoner who had yet to be confronted with his judgment. He had advanced only a pace or two when Ebenezer recognized—under the war paint, regalia, and newly regained health—the ailing fugitive of the cliffside cave.

"Dear Christ, now I see't!" he cried. "Bertrand! 'Tis Quassapelagh and Drakepecker! Yon *Dick Parker* of McEvoy's is your Drakepecker, and here's Quassapelagh come to save me!"

Indeed, when the Indian had looked well into Ebenezer's face, his eyes lost their sternness, and at his command two guards stepped forward to release the poet's bonds.

"I set you free and beg your pardon," Quassapelagh said gravely. " 'Tis well no harm was done the man who saved my life."

Like Bertrand, Ebenezer was too overwhelmed to speak. His eyes welled with tears; he reeled and laughed hoarsely, shook his head, and looked to McEvoy as though in disbelief. The old chief, meanwhile, had not ceased to rail: he apparently understood no more of these marvels than did his subjects or the other two prisoners. Quassapelagh bowed slightly to Ebenezer, suggested that the poet remain where he was for a few minutes more, and returned to pacify the old man. The Negro king too, whom to everyone's dismay Bertrand had embraced upon realizing his identity, now disengaged himself and joined the council. It was clear from the tenor of their discourse that the old chief objected strenuously to freeing the prisoners; after a few moments Quassapelagh summoned Ebenezer, snatched his left hand, and muttered, "You have the ring Quassapelagh gave you?"

The poet fetched from his pocket the fishbone ring, thanking Providence and Joan Toast that he had exchanged his silver seal for it after all. Quassapelagh first showed the ring to the old chief and then, with some half-defiant proclamation, lifted it high for the crowd to view. At the same time Dick Parker, or Drakepecker, issued orders to Bandy Lou, who stood beaming nearby, and all the prisoners except the Captain were hustled back to the jail-hut before the old man had a chance to launch fresh protests.

"I'faith!" Ebenezer laughed tensely. "What a palace this hut seems now!"

On the common, where the mists had been brightened but not dispelled by the rising sun, there was considerable commotion. Peering between the legs of the guards outside their hut, Ebenezer saw the three leaders move off again towards the building from which they had appeared; the old one, clearly by no means pacified, was now supported by two Indians with headgear similar to his own.

" 'Tis a Holy Writ miracle!" cried McEvoy, his eyes and mouth still wincing with astonishment. "Nay, a miracle atop a miracle! How is't Dick Parker is alive, and knows ye? Marry, he fell on his belly as if your man here was a god!"

"I was no less, thank ye," Bertrand said proudly, "and a better parishioner no god could wish for! Hath he not risen to the top of the heap, though! Did ye see him stand up for me to the old tyrant, as bold as ye please?"

For McEvoy's benefit Ebenezer recounted the story of their freeing Drakepecker from his bonds, discovering the fugitive Quassapelagh ill of a festered wound, and leaving the black man to minister to his needs.

" 'Twas for that he gave us the fishbone rings, albeit he said naught of their meaning. What doth it signify, and how came a poor slave like Drakepecker to be a king?"

McEvoy could throw no light on the meaning of the ring. "As for the wight ye call Drakepecker, though, he is the same I spoke of before, that I called Dick Parker. The boat that spirited me off from London took him aboard in Carolina along with Bandy Lou and two score other slaves, to sell in Maryland. They had all been snatched from some African town not long before, and this Dick Parker was their king. The first mate chained him and Bandy Lou in the hold for the same reason I was there." The Irishman grinned. "Dick Parker was after raising a mutiny; the mate was for murthering him, but the captain thought if they could flog his spirit out, they could use him to keep the others from making trouble. Twice a day they laid the lash on him, and he'd spit on the sailor that tied him to the foremast and spit on the sailor that untied him after. O'er and again I advised him, through Bandy Lou, to put by his pride till he was sold and settled, and then escape and help the others; he'd reply my counsel was the best for Bandy Lou and the other lieutenants, but a king that was bought and sold was no king at all. If I declared no dead king ever won a battle, he'd reply 'twas not in the lion to play the jackal's part, and a dead king could still be a living example to his subjects. He gave orders to Bandy Lou to do as I advised, and the next time they fetched Dick Parker up for flogging he spat on the mate himself. 'Twas then they heaved him o'er the side, bound hand and foot. Half the slaves were sold in Anne Arundel Town next day, and the other half, along with us redemptioners, in Oxford the day after that. How the wight managed to stay afloat I'll never know."

Ebenezer shook his head, remembering the stripes on the Negro's back when they had discovered him on the beach. "So now he's king of the runaway slaves, and Quassapelagh king of the disaffected salvage Indians! Heav'n help the English if they carry out their plan!"

"Devil take 'em, I say," McEvoy replied, "they have it coming." Both he and Bertrand declared their intention to beg or steal passage back to London as soon as possible, so that they might wish the rebels success without wishing their own ill fortune. Ebenezer had not lost sight of his late reflections at the stake; yet though he could sympathize with the plight of the slaves and Indians and affirm the guilt even of white men who, like himself, had condoned that plight merely in effect, by not protesting it, he could by no means relish the idea of a wholesale massacre. On the contrary, with his two near-executions to dulcify it, life tasted uncommonly sweet to the poet just then, and he shuddered at the thought of anyone's being deprived of it.

"We must find a way to save the Captain," he declared. "He hath less reason to be here than any of us, since 'twas neither search nor flight that brought him." And he added, though he quite understood the limitations of the statement, "If he dies, 'tis I must answer for't, inasmuch as I hired him to ferry me to Malden and paid him extra to leave at once despite the weather and the time of day."

Both McEvoy and the valet protested this assumption of responsibility and McEvoy asserted further that though he had every wish for the old man's safety, he was not prepared to sacrifice or even jeopardize his own for it.

"In any case," Bertrand offered, " 'tis too early for tears and cheers alike. If Drakepecker hath his way we may all go free; if not, we may burn yet."

His companions agreed, and they fell to speculating on the office and influence of the ancient Indian who had been so loath to see them freed. McEvoy called in the African named —as best their English speech could approximate—Bandy Lou, who replied to their several questions with a huge, invincible smile whether his information was cheering, distressing, or indifferent.

Who was the old Indian king?

"He is the Tayac Chicamec, King of the Ahatchwhoops, and for four-and-eighty summers an enemy to Englishmen. This is his island."

Upon Ebenezer's inquiring about the division of power between the three kings and the jurisdiction of each, Bandy Lou replied that Quassapelagh was a sort of commander-in-chief of all the disaffected Indians on the western side of the Chesapeake, Chicamec held the same post on the Eastern Shore, and *Drepacca* was the king of the runaway Negroes. He went on to assert very candidly that, while in theory the three were invested with equal authority, it was Quassapelagh, the Anacostin King, who wielded the greatest actual power, not only because the chieftains under him—Ochotomaquath of the Piscataways, Tom Calvert of the Chopticoes, and Maquantah of the Mattawomans, for example—were more numerous, influential, and belligerent than were Chicamec's lieutenants, but also because some of the latter—such as the son of the Emperor Umacokasimmon, Asquas, whom Governor Copley had deposed as leader of the Nanticokes in favor of the complaisant Panquas and Annoughtough—were more disposed to follow the younger, more vigorous Quassapelagh than their aged commander-in-chief. Moreover, the lion's share of *potential* power, according to Bandy Lou, was held by Drepacca, for although there were many more belligerent Indians than runaway Negroes, Quassapelagh's authority was limited necessarily to the Province, and the allegiance of his subjects, except for a small group of Piscataways, was directed primarily to the several tribal chieftains and only indirectly to the Anacostin King himself. Drepacca, on the other hand, had in a very short time become the direct and undisputed leader of every fugitive African in the area and the inspiration of thousands still enslaved; furthermore, he had not the obstacles of tribal geography and rival leadership to contend with: Negroes from various African tribes were

594

distributed indiscriminately among the provinces by the slave market, and Drepacca, so far as anyone knew, was the only royalty among them. In consequence of these facts, together with his quick intelligence (he had learned the Piscataway dialect in three weeks from Quassapelagh), his formidable personal appearance, and the advantage his being neither white nor Indian gave him in negotiations with the French and the northern nations, the sphere of Drepacca's influence grew daily more extensive and might well encompass soon the entire Negro population of America, whose number increased with every ship from the western coast of Africa. One guessed, from the unbounded pride in his voice, that Bandy Lou had already crowned his master Emperor of America. Ebenezer shivered.

"More power to him," McEvoy said grimly. "If Dick Parker's as strong as all that, we've naught to fear from this Tayac Chuckaluck, or Chicken-neck, or whatever. Wouldn't ye say so, Bandy Lou? 'Tis a brace of big men against one little one."

Ah, now, the smiling Negro cautioned, things were not so simple as *that*, for while Chicamec held in truth a great deal less power, actual or potential, than did either of his confederates, he was known to Indians all up and down the provinces as an ancient foe of the white man: he was virtually a legend among them; his name for three decades had been synonymous with uncompromising resistance; and in addition his little town of Ahatchwhoops was the hardest core of armed and organized English-haters in the Province, and his island the safest and most nearly central location anyone knew of for a general headquarters. In short, though but a figurehead, he was an extremely valuable one, and his colleagues deferred to him in all but the most important matters of policy—the more readily since nine tenths of the rebels' power was in their hands.

"I'faith!" cried Bertrand. "D'ye mean they might let him burn us after all?"

"I do hope not," said Bandy Lou agreeably. One of the other guards called to him in dialect from outside, and he added, his smile unchanged in magnitude or character: "Come now, and we shall learn."

7

How the Ahatchwhoops Doe Choose
a King Over Them

FOR THE SECOND TIME that morning, then, Ebenezer, Bertrand, and McEvoy were escorted onto the misty common. Though there was light aplenty now, the sky remained overcast, and the foggy salt marsh scarcely less gloomy than before. The cooking fires were out, the women occupied with various housekeeping chores, and most of the men, presumably, out on the marshes and waterways replenishing the supply of seafood and wildfowl. A few dozen, whom Ebenezer took to be minor chieftains and their lieutenants, still sat with their pipes about the larger council-fires, engaged in debate; it was not difficult to guess, from the stony countenances that followed the prisoners' march across the common, what had been the subject of their discussion.

Less apprehensive than before, the poet was able to look about him with greater interest and detachment. He remarked, for example, that the village was considerably larger than he had estimated: the muskrat-house dwellings numbered more nearly three hundred than one hundred, and work-parties of Negroes were constructing new ones around the whole periphery of the town. Indeed, the supply of high ground was exhausted, and the builders were obliged to resort to various expedients; at one edge of the village was a flat-topped mountain of oystershells—piled up, one gathered, by generations of Ahatchwhoops in the days before building lots were at such a premium—which the Negroes were busily shoveling into the adjacent marsh, both to create new ground and to clear the old; in other places the huts were being erected on low pilings in the marsh itself, a curious combining of African and Indian architectures. Again, the poet observed for the first time the disproportion of sexes in the population: even allowing for the exaggeration of fear, he judged that nearly a thousand men had thronged the common that morning—seven hundred at the very least, of whom surely no more than two hundred had arrived with Quassapelagh and Drepacca—whereas the women, unless great numbers of them had been granted the unlikely privilege of sleeping late into the morning, could be counted more easily in dozens than in hundreds. Yet there seemed to be no shortage of children; indeed, the spaces between the huts fairly swarmed with little savages, whose great number and various pigmentation suggested to Ebenezer not only polyandry but a cultural alliance in spheres more intimate than either politics or architecture.

This time the party did not stop at the stakes, but proceeded directly to the royal hut on the opposite side from the jail. To the old Captain, who regarded them as sullenly from his stake as did the chieftains from their councils, Ebenezer called, "Never fear, old man, we shan't betray you. 'Tis all of us or none."

"In a pig's arse," muttered Bertrand beside him, and McEvoy added flatly, "Ye may stake your own fortunes where ye please, but not McEvoy's. If he dies on my account I'll mourn him sorely, but if I die on his I'll hate his guts." As for the Captain himself, either he did not hear the poet's encouragement, or was too unhinged by fear to comprehend it, or simply discounted it, for his expression remained unchanged.

At the entrance to the royal hut Bandy Lou said with his great smile, "We stop here. You go there," and pointed to the hide-flap doorway. The prisoners hesitated, each reluctant to take the initiative, and then Ebenezer, his jaw clenched tight, pushed the flap aside and led them in.

Except for its size and the more numerous hides which served as rugs and wall-hangings alike, Chicamec's palace was little different from his jail. Along the rear wall stood a line of guards, spears in hand. A small fire burned in a circle of rocks in the center of the floor; behind it, tight-lipped and evil-eyed, sat the wrinkled king himself, flanked by his two unsmiling confederates. The Englishmen faced them uneasily, uncertain whether to sit or remain standing, bow or stand still, speak or be silent. In the absence of Bandy Lou, Ebenezer looked to Quassapelagh for instructions, but it was Drepacca who addressed them, apparently having added a fluency in English to the catalogue of his assets.

"It is the wish of Drepacca," he declared sternly, "that the four white men go free; or that, if one must die, it be the old man; or that, if only one may live, it be one of the two who saved Drepacca's life."

McEvoy scowled; Ebenezer and Bertrand avoided each other's eyes.

"It is the wish of Quassapelagh," Drepacca resumed, "that the old man and the red-haired singer die, and you twain be spared; or that, if only one may live, it be the tall one who still wears the Ring of Brotherhood."

"I say!" McEvoy protested; Bertrand's face fell. A guard lowered his spear to the ready, and the Irishman said no more.

"It is the wish of Chicamec," continued the African king, "that every man of white skin on the face of the earth be deprived of his privy member and put to spear. But he allows the tall one is a brother of Quassapelagh and must be spared." He looked at Bertrand, and though neither his tone nor his expression lost its sternness, he said, "I regret that you have lost Quassapelagh's ring, and that I once knelt to you as a god instead of making you my brother in the manner of my people. But I have told Chicamec that you and the tall one saved my life, and that who kills you must kill Drepacca first. Chicamec has made no answer to this, and so you will go free—mind you do not smile, or he will guess my words and strike you dead at any cost."

To McEvoy he said, "You are my friend and the friend of *Bandalu*, and I would not see you die. But the anger of Chicamec is great, and he grants brotherhood only to those who have saved the life of one of us. You must bid your friends farewell."

"Nay, 'sheart!" McEvoy cried; the guard moved closer, and Chicamec's eyes grew dark. "What I mean," McEvoy continued in a calmer voice, "if thou'rt such a friend as ye claim, and have such a gang as Bandy Lou says ye have behind ye, why is't ye let this bloody old flitch be judge and jury? Turn us all loose, and be damned to him!"

Quassapelagh, whose frown had deepened at the Irishman's choice of words, spoke up in reply. "Quassapelagh and Drepacca are strong, but our strength is not on the island of Chicamec. If the Ahatchwhoops fight the people of Drepacca, our cause will lose a mighty ally and a mighty king. Chicamec will not make war to kill brothers of Drepacca and Quassapelagh, but to kill any other white man, Chicamec will make war. You must die."

"Then so must I!" Ebenezer said suddenly. His brow furrowed and unfurrowed at a great rate, his hands twitched about, and his nose was a thing alive. Quassapelagh and Drepacca turned to him with surprise; Bertrand and McEvoy with incredulity. "Either the four of us will go free, or the four of us will die!" declared the poet. "It is my fault these men are here, and I shan't permit myself to be saved without all three of them." He looked accusingly at Drepacca. "Perhaps Drepacca doth not defend his own, but Eben Cooke doth, friends or no."

"I beg my brother to think again," Quassapelagh said, maintaining his stern composure for Chicamec's benefit. "If I must, I shall strike you senseless to spare your life."

But Ebenezer had apparently foreseen this possibility. "Not a bit of't," he replied at once, his voice exhilarated by the rashness of his move. "Not a bit of't, dear Quassapelagh; the moment you say even one of us must die I'll leap and throttle Chicamec yonder, and his bullies will spear me like a pincushion. Nay, don't warn 'em off, or I'll spring this instant."

"I'faith, Eben!" cried McEvoy. "Save yourself; there's naught else for't!"

"Our friend speaks wisely as well as generously," Drepacca added. "Do not throw four lives away instead of two."

"Say no more on't!" Ebenezer ordered briskly. His face was flushed and his voice uneven, and his heart pounded hot blood through his limbs. "Will ye spare your brother's people or put him to the spear? Yea me or nay me, and have done with't!" He swayed on his feet, arms swinging free, as if ready to make good his threat. Chicamec's glance sent two guards closer with upraised spears. Drepacca and Quassapelagh exchanged flickers of their eyes.

"No answer, brothers?" The poet's voice grew shrill. "*Adieu*, then, Brother Quassapelagh! Good luck to you, and bad luck to your murtherous schemes! *Adieu*, Brother Drepacca, *adieu, adieu!* 'Tis a pity you ne'er met my friend Henry Burlingame: you twain would get on famously!"

He went so far as actually to cock his muscles for the leap across the fire, and paused only because Chicamec caught up the name *Henry Burlingame* and unleashed a torrent of interrogation at Quassapelagh, in which the name was repeated several times.

"Wait, brother!" Quassapelagh called sharply, and attended the rest of his elder colleague's excited query while Ebenezer, the moment of his courage past, reeled and sweated in his stance.

"The Tayac Chicamec believes you spoke a certain name just then, and would have you speak it another time."

"A name? Aye, 'twas Henry Burlingame!" Ebenezer laughed like one deranged and leaned over toward the old king, on whose face was the piercing, great-eyed frown of an osprey or fishhawk. "*Henry Burlingame!*" he shouted again, and tears dropped down his cheeks. "You've heard of him, have you, murtherer? Or is it thou'rt Burlingame in disguise, and here's another of thy famous pranks?" Hysteria brought him to the edge of a swoon; his jaw slacked open, and he was obliged to sit heavily on the ground before he fell.

Another sharp query from Chicamec.

"Who is this Henry Burlingame?" translated the Anacostin King. "A friend of yours?"

Ebenezer nodded affirmatively, unable to speak.

"One of these here?" Quassapelagh asked. "No? In the white man's towns, then?"

The affirmative brought more excited Indian-talk from old Chicamec, in reply to which, when it had been translated for his benefit, Ebenezer explained that Burlingame was his former teacher, a man of some forty summers by his own best guess, made in ignorance of his actual birth date, birthplace, and parentage.

One last inquiry Chicamec made, without recourse to language: his whole frame shaking with consternation, he fetched a charred stick out of the fire, drew with it upon a clean deerhide mat the symbol *III,* and raised his terrible questioning stare to the poet again.

"Ay, that's the one," Ebenezer sighed, too weary in spirit to share the troubled surprise of the others. "Henry Burlingame the Third." And then, "I say, Quassapelagh, how is't he knows my Henry?" For it had only just occurred to him that in all his tutor's years of adventure and intrigue, it had been Burlingame's policy never to employ the name he was raised by. The question was duly translated, but instead of answering directly, the ancient Indian—the malevolence of whose countenance was supplanted altogether by fierce astonishment —directed two guards to fetch a carved and decorated chest from one end of the hut and place it directly before the bewildered poet.

"The Tayac Chicamec bids you open the chest," said Drepacca.

Ebenezer did so, and was surprised to see nothing evidently breathtaking among the contents, which so far as he could discern without rummaging about, consisted of a number of black garments (whose obviously English manufacture led him to observe that the little chest itself, beneath its Indian decoration, was the sort used by seamen and travelers, not by savages), four corked glass bottles of what seemed to be nothing but water, and on top of all what looked like an old octavo notebook, bound in stained and battered calf.

Chicamec spoke through the Anacostin King.

"There is a——" Quassapelagh looked to Drepacca for assistance with the translation.

"*Book,*" the African said. "A book, there on the top."

"Book," Quassapelagh repeated. "Chicamec bids my foolhardy brother open the book and read its signs." And he added in the same translator's tone, "It is the hope of Quassapelagh that my brother will read some charm therein to cure his madness."

The poet picked up the volume as directed, whereupon the line of guards behind Chicamec fell as one man to their knees, as though before some holy relic. But Ebenezer found it to be in fact a species of English manuscript-book, penned in the regular calligraphy of a gentleman, but with ink too crusty and crude to be European. It bore on the front page the unassuming title *How the Ahatchwhoops Doe Choose a King Over Them* and commenced with what appeared on quick scanning to be a description of the Dorchester marshes, perhaps the same island on which the tribe now lived.

" 'Tis most intriguing, I concede," the poet said impatiently to Quassapelagh, "but i'faith, this is no time . . . i'Christ, now . . ." He interrupted himself to reread, incredulously, the opening line—*Being then our armes bownd, and led like kine to the Salvage towne, some miles inland, I had leisure to remark the countrie-side, through wch we travell'd*—and embarrassment, apprehension, and all gave way to recognition.

"John Smith's *Secret Historie!*" he exclaimed. " 'Sheart, then 'twas no coincidence . . ." He was thinking of the Straits of Limbo, but his eyes had moved already to the next passages of the *Historie;* his jaw dropped lower, and his sentence was destined never to be completed, for the substance of the manuscript, and more especially of the Tayac Chicamec's tale that followed after, were as amazing as anything in Ebenezer's life.

For the benefit of his mystified companions he read aloud as follows:

"It doth in sooth transcend the power of my pen, or of my fancie, to relate the aspect of this place, so forsaken & desolate & illappearing withal; a sink-hole it is, all marshie and gone to swamp.

Water standeth hereabouts in lakes & pooles, forsooth there is more water than drie land, but most of the grownd is a mixture of the twain, for that the tyde doth rise & fall, covering & discovering grand flatts of mud thereby, and Isles bearing naught but greene reedes & pine-scrubb. When that the tyde runneth out, smalle pooles remaineth everiewhere, the wch do straightway sower & engender in there slyme more meskitoes, then there are beades in a nunnerie, and each meskitoe hungrie as a priest. Add thereto, the entire countrie is flatt, and most belowe the level of the sea, so that the eye doth see this drearie land-scape endlesslie on everie hand; the aire is wett & noisome to the lights; the grownd giveth way beneathe the foot; and the water is too fowle & brynie to drink. It is forsooth Earths uglie fundament, a place not fitt for any English man, and I here venture, no matter how that the countrie neare to hand, such as our owne Virginia, doth prosper in yeers to come, yet will no person but a Salvage ever inhabit this place through wch we march'd, except he be a bloudie foole, or other manner of ass.

"As for those same Salvages, that had us prisoner (thanks to the idiocie of my Nemesis & rivall Ld Burlingame, that fatt clott-poll, as I have earlier discryb'd), they were a fitt reflection of there countrie, being more smalle in stature & meane in appearance, then those others we had incounter'd. . . ."

Ebenezer looked up uncertainly from his reading, but the faces of Quassapelagh and Drepacca showed no reaction to the words.

"Moreover," *he read on*, "they seem'd less wont to speake, for that, upon my enquiring of them, What nation were they? my captor hard by responded merelie, *Ahatchwhoop*. W^ch signifyeth, in the tongue of Powhatans people, that foule aire, that riseth on a mans stomacke, after he hath eate a surfitt of food, and I c^d not determine, whether my Salvage design'd to answer my querie, or meant thereby an insult, or other like barbaritie; he w^d saye no more. None the less I was pleas'd, that they spoke a tongue resembling Powhatans, for that were I able to converse with them, so much greater was our chance of slipping there halter. For alle there silence, they did use us civillie, and harm'd not any of our companie, while that we march'd. I reflected, that did they meane to kill us, they had done so lightlie upon the shoar whereon we were ambuscado'd, but they did not. Verilie, they c^d be sparing of our lives, onelie to take them anon. But to dye on the morrowe, is better by a daye then to dye now, and therefor I did breathe easier, while keeping still alert for a meanes of escaping injurie at there hands.

"At length we arriv'd at there town, the wch was the rudest I had yet seene, being little save a dozen hovells of sticks & mudd, thrown up on a patch of drie grownd, that rose a hand or two from the swamp. At our approach, eight or tenne more Salvages issu'd from the hutts, ag'd and feeble men in the mayn, and with them the women of the trybe, about 15 in number, and uglie as the Devill. Also, a host of scurvie doggs, that snapp'd & bitt at us from everie quarter.

"One great fatt Salvage there was, who coming from a hutt, did greet the leader of those that led us thither, with a long harangue, the summe whereof, as I did grasp it, was, that he was no whitt pleas'd at our being fetch'd to the towne. Whereto the leader of our captors (a smalle Salvage, but lowd of mowth) reply'd, that the speaker was not yet *Werowance*, wch is to say, King, and ought therefore to hold his peece until that the contest was done. That he had captur'd the white-skinn'd men, our selves, whom he took to be Susquehannocks, to joyn in the contest, the Susquehannocks being greate workers of wonders, and famous warriors. Now, I knewe not what was the contest thus spoken of, nor who was the fatt Salvage, nor yet the smalle one our captor. But I had heard telle, from King Hicktopeake, brother of Debedeavon the Laughing King of Accomack, of those same Susquehannocks, to witt: that they were a great nation far to the North, neare to the head of that vast Baye whereon we sayl'd. That they were much fear'd by the other Salvages, as warriors & feerce hunters. It seem'd to me not a sorrie thing, then, to be mistaken for a Susquehannock by our captors, and so did not trouble my selfe to undeceive them.

"More argument ensu'd, betwixt the Salvages, they being each readie to give commands to the other, and each loath to obey any, so that I wonder'd, Where was there King? For it seem'd to me, these heathen had either two Kings, or none at all. Just then, a Salvage wench did appeare, from out a hutt, and bearing a vessell of water upon her head, did carrie it across to another hutt hard by. She was, I sweare, the comliest Salvage ever I saw, slight of stature, and prettie of face & forme, and being uncloth'd above the waist, her bubbs did lift most fetchinglie what tyme she rais'd her armes to steadie the vessell. At her appearance, the two Salvages gave over there debate, and gaz'd after, as did my selfe & all my partie, for that she was of such surpassing beautie. Directlie she was gone, they fell againe to quarrelling, over where we shd be lodg'd, and under what guard, and wd have leapt upon each other, had I not interfear'd, and speaking in Powhatans tongue, declar'd my selfe Capt Jno Smith of Virginia, and offer'd them, that we returne to our barge, there being no handie place for us to sleep, and make our waye in peece as best we might. We had no wishe, said I, to impose upon there hospitallitie, or trouble them in the matter of bedd & board. This I spoke

603

in jest, knowing full well, we were where we were not by there invitation, but as haplesse prisoners. The Salvages were amaz'd, that I spoke a tongue wch they c^d grasp, and I, in turn, was much surpriz'd, when that the fatt Salvage, so far from shewing displeasure at my proposall, took it up on the instant, and w^d have us begone. But the other w^d have none of it, we must needs staye for the contest on the morrowe. More dispute follow'd, and at last we were put all in a hut, with scarce room to lie flatt, and the smalle Salvage him selfe, with divers of his troup, sat guard.

"My companie, understanding naught of all this discourse, were greatlie out of sorts, and grows'd & compleyn'd much, for that they knewe not what w^d be our fate, or whether we s^hd live or dye. Add to w^ch, we had been taken in the morning, and it was then twylight, but naught had we been given to eate, nor had any of the Salvages eat food, all the daye. Methought this was passing queere, for that the meanest of gaolers is seldom that cruell, that he will not give his charges some thing wherewith to staye there grumbling gutts. Despite w^ch, I was little troubl'd in my owne mind, inasmuch as from what I had learnt, in converse with our captors, our straits were at worst uncertain. Our keepers seem'd scarce to know them selves what to doe with us, and there confusion I mark'd as a good signe, together with the faction & dispute wch I had witness'd. For where faction is amongst the enemie, the battle is halfe won. Therefore I made my men a little speach, intreating them to be of good heart, and comport them selves as men. But my intreaties were in vaine, they wish'd them selves back in Jamestowne, or better in London, and curs'd the voiage that had brought them hither. Burlingame, as I had fore-seen, was lowdest in his compleynts, for all it was he, in my estimation, that by his cowardice had brought us to this passe. I had no love for him, that had done all in his power to thwart me & my explorations, and stir up unrest against me in James-towne. I heartilie wish'd him in London, or at the bottom of the Baye, and told him as much. He onelie glar'd at me, and spoke no more, but I guess'd it was in his mind, s^hd I taunt him farther, to tell the companie some scurvie lie, about Pocahontas & my selfe, as he had oft threaten'd, and so I left him alone. Yet I did reflect, that such a state c^d not persist, but must be remedy'd soon, for that faction doth lead still to mutinie, and without my guid-ance, I was certain all w^d perish at the hands of the Salvages, in there follie & ignorance, ere they regayn'd Jamestowne by them selves.

"Greatlie tyr'd from the dayes adventures, and weak for want of food, they all were soon asleep, maugre there feares & com-pleynts, and left to my selfe, I undertook to ingage our guard, the smalle lowd Salvage, in conversation, purposing to learn more of our fate, and peradventure to gayn his favour, or to promote the faction I had observ'd.

"This tyme my luck was better than theretofore; whether by reason that onelie the twain of us were awake, or that he sought to allie me to his cause, the Salvage spake readilie & cordiallie in answer to my queries. I ask'd him, What was his name? to wch he reply'd, it was *Wepenter*, wch is to say, a cookold, and he was so call'd, for his wyfe being taken from him to the bedd of the old *Werowance*, or King. On farther questioning him, I learn'd that this same King, called *Kekataughtassapooekskunoughmass* (wch is to say, Ninetie Fish), had latelie dy'd, and I guess'd it was this same Wepenter, that in jealousie did murther him. The towne then left without a King, and the old King having no heirs save his single concubyne, the Salvages must needs choose a new Werowance from there number, and this they design'd to doe on the morrowe, by a singular means.

"All the Ahatchwhoops are exceeding smalle in stature, and for that reason doe hugelie envie men of large size, and heavie. They believe, that the more a man can eat, the bigger he will become, and the heavier there King, the more secure will be there towne, against its enemies. Therefore, whenever that a King doth dye with no male heirs, all the Ahatchwhoops doe assemble for a feast, and him who doth prove the grandest glutton thereat, they doe call King over them, and bestowe upon him a new name, signifying the achievement whereby he gayn'd the throne. Thus was the old Werowance calld Kekataughtassapooekskunoughmass, for that he did eate ninetie fish on the daye he became there King. And thus, I guess, the folk were fitlie call'd, Ahatchwhoops, for all the rise of bellicgass, that must attend the feasting.

"Such was there curious custom, and when I had learnt it, my owne plight, and that of my companie, grewe somewhat more cleare, albeit I was not certain yet, Why we were held prisoner? But with more speach, I soon learn'd, that there were in the towne two men, who were desirous of the throne. Of these one was the King's assassin, even that same Wepenter, with whom I spoke, and he wish'd to be King, if onelie to regayne to him selfe his wyfe, the old Kings concubyne, that once gone into by the last King, c^d then lie onelie with the next. Wepenters rivall was that same fatt Salvage, that had erst harangu'd us, and he was call'd *Attonceaumoughhowgh*, or Arrowe-targett, for that he was so fatt, and withall an easie marke to hitt. This Attonce too did lust after Wepenters wyfe, that was call'd *Pokatawertussan*, or Frye-bedd, for the surpassing heate wherewith she did disport in matters of love.

"Now were it a simple contest in gluttonie, betwixt this Attonce & this Wepenter, then Wepenter w^d loose the daye perforce, for that he was but smalle, and Attonce exceeding large of bellie &

appetite. But any Salvage, it was there custom, c^d enter the lists by proxie, if willing proxie he c^d find, and s^hd his champion then win the field, they w^d share the throne & the favours of the Queene, but the proxie w^d have no power to command. Thus had they alter'd antient practice, to the end they c^d believe that the fattest man maketh the best King, and yet avoyd the consequences of there belief.

"It was by virtue of this custom, that Wepenter & his fellowes had lay'd hold of us, that we being strange in appearance, and sayling such a curious vessell, he took us for wonder-workers, and was desirous of choosing from our number one to playe his proxie on the morrowe. He declar'd it was Attonces troup, that had shot arrowes from the shoar to drive us off, what tyme milord Burlingame had leagu'd the Gentlemen behind him, to force us ashoar in quest of bellie-timber. Maugre my contention, that the look of the land was hostile. And Wepenter had call'd us Susquehannocks, merely to frighten his rivall out of appetyte.

"These & many other things I learn'd from this Wepenter, who then read me his conditions, on hearing I was Captain of the companie. To witt: that I was to be his proxie at the approaching feast. That s^hd I best Attonce in the matter of gluttonie, all my companions w^d be freed, and we w^d rule the towne conjoyntlie, and share the bedd of Pokatawertussan. That if, on the contrarie, I was beat by Attonce, then I & all my companie must needs dye forthwith at Attonces hands, for such was the custom amongst the Ahatchwhoops.

"I reply'd, that I was honour'd by his choyce, but poynted out I was slight of girth, and temperate of appetyte, not given to feats of gluttonie. Therefore, if he w^d have a proxie, I suggested he choose not me, but examine our companie, and of there number choose the fattest & most gluttonous of aspect, for his proxie. This Wepenter did on the instant, and regarding all my souldiers & Gentlemen, while that they slept, stopt at length over Burlingame, even as I had design'd, and seeing that greate mountaine of dung, spread out & snoring like unto a swine in the wallow, Wepenter did make me a sign, this was his choyce. I commended his wisdome, and assur'd him, that with such a proxie, his victorie was certain, and he w^d have at Pokatawertussan on the morrow. Thereupon we smoak'd severall pypes of tobacco by the fyre, and talk'd through the night of many an idle thing.

"When that I saw the dawn grow light without the hutt, I did wake Burlingame, ere the rest of the companie arose, and address'd him boastfullie in this wise. That I had deflowr'd Pocahontas before his eyes, and had farther layn with Hicktopeakes Queene, what tyme he had abandon'd her for harlot. He then enquir'd, in a fearsome choler, Wherefore had he to heare these things again? to wch I answer'd that even as I had out-done him

606

in manlinesse on these occasions, so was I about to doe againe, for that there was that morn to be a contest, whereof the winner shd lie at his pleasure with a comelie Salvage wench, the dead Kings concubyne. On hearing these tydings, Burlingame grew much arows'd, and with much cursing & gnashing of teeth, did vilifye me, and at length resorted to his antient threat, even that shd I not stand aside this tyme, and lett him futter the Salvage in my stead, he wd straightwaye noyse about, in Jamestowne & the London Co my employer, the truth anent Pocahontas & Hickto-peakes Queene. I did replye, that I car'd not a whitt for all his threats (albeit in sooth things wd goe hard, did my enemies get wind of his foule storie). Besides wch, I declar'd I had no choyce in the businesse, for that the entyre companie, and the Salvage troup as well, had perforce to enter the lists, it being the wont of these Ahatchwhoops, thus to make a pryze of there comeliest lassies. He enquir'd, What manner of contest was it? and upon my telling him, that he won the mayd, who eat the hugest quantitie of food, he was entyrelie pleas'd, and did sweare, he wd eat twice over what any Salvage cd, & thrice what I or any of our companie might eate. That he was insatiable of appetyte, and had eat no food for two daies, and hence was certain to win the faire mayd. I did rejoyn, that tyme wd prove his boast, but for my selfe, all I car'd was that some one of our companie be victor, and not the great fatt Salvage of yesterdaye, for else we shd all be put to the specre. Moreover, that shd he win the test, and so save all our lives, not onelie wd he enjoye the prettie peece with all my blessing, but I wd let bye-gones be bye-gones, and never againe bragg of my conquests, or his owne deficiencie. Farther, that I wd arrange matters with Pocahantas, that he shd trye her favours, when once we return'd to Jamestowne.

"These words fell sweet on the eares of Burlingame. He did growe doublie hott, for thinking of them. When I recall'd to him then, what was our fate shd Attonce win the daye, he reply'd, that he worry'd not a beane. That he cd eate any Englishman or heathen under the table. And he smack'd his greate stomacke with his hand, whereupon it set up such a clamour, one had guess'd all the feends of Hell therein. These things we spoke in English, that Wepenter might not heare & guesse my ruse.

"Somewhile after, our companie was awake, and the souldiers & Gentlemen compleyning of there bellies, that they had naught to eate. The Salvages did gather without the hutt, and a greate fyre built, and we were led outside by Wepenter, and seated in a half-circle, he behind Burlingame. Across from us satt down Attonce, all fatt and uglie he was, and with him a score of his cohorts, in another half-circle upon the grownd. Came then from a hutt hard by, Pokatawertussan, and sat down betwixt the half-circles, on a kind of rugg, to see who shd be her next bedd-fellowe.

607

She was that same mayde, who on the day just past had quieted all harangue, merelie by raysing her armes & walking bye. Half cladd she was, and bedawb'd with puckoone paynt, after the manner of Salvage wenches, and so surpassing faire & tight withal, I had neare wish'd my selfe greate of gutt, to win her favours. At sight of her, Attonce let goe a mightie hollowing, and Burlingame, like the rest of us save onelie me, all naked, for that our shirts had mended our sayle in the storme, and our breeches flung to the fishes after our siege of fluxes & grypes in Limbo Strait, he was so taken with her, that he shook all over, and slaver'd over his lipps & sundrie chinnes. He whisper'd to me, not to tell the others what we were about, that they w^d not contend with him, and I agreed with a right good will, for that I desir'd no man save Burlingame to win.

"Attonce then commenc'd to slapp his bellie with his hands, to the end he might arowse a grander lust for food, and seeing him, Burlingame did likewise, untill the rumbling of there gutts did eckoe about the swamps like the thunder of vulcanoes. Next Attonce, sitting cross-legged, did bump his buttockes up & down upon the earthe, farther to appetyze him selfe; Burlingame also, that he give his foe no quarter, and the verie grownd shudder'd beneath there awful bummes. Burlingame then blubber'd his lipps & snapt the joynt-bones of his fingers, and Attonce likewise. Attonce op'd & shutt his jawes with greate rapiditie, and also Burlingame. And thus they did goe on, through many a ceremonie, whetting there hungers, whilst our companie sat as amaz'd, not knowing what they witness'd, and the Salvages clapt there hands & daunc'd about, and Pokatawertussan look'd all lustilie from one to the other.

"At length, from everie hutt in the towne, the women and old men brought forth the sundrie dishes of the feast, that had been some daies preparing. To each of us was given a platter of divers foods, and onelie one, wch shew'd, though it was sufficient to fill us with comfort, that none of us were reckon'd as contenders, save onelie Burlingame & Attonce, before whom they set dish after dish. For houres thereafter, while that the rest watch'd in astonishment, the two gluttons match'd dish for dish, and herewith is the summe of what they eat:

Of *keskowghnoughmass,* the yellowe-belly'd sunne-fish, tenne apiece.

Of *copatone,* the sturgeon, one apiece.

Of *pummahumpnoughmass,* fry'd star-fish, three apiece.

Of *pawpeconoughmass,* pype-fishes, four apiece, dry'd.

Of boyl'd froggs, divers apiece, assorted bulles, greenes, trees, & spring peepers.

Of blowfish, two apiece, frizzl'd & blow'd.

Of terrapin, a tortoise, one apiece, stew'd.

Also oysters, crabbs, trowt, croakers, rock-fish, flownders, clamms, maninose, & such other sea-food as the greate Baye doth give up. They next did eate:

Of mallard, canvas-backe, & buffle-head ducks, morsels & mix'd peeces in like amounts.

Of hooded mergansers, one apiece, on picks as is there wont.

Of pypers, one apiece, dry'd & pouder'd.

Of *cohunk*, a taystie goose, half apiece.

Of snypes, one apiece, bagg'd.

Of black & white warblers, one apiece, throttl'd.

Of rubie-throated humming-birds, two apiece, scalded, pickl'd, & intensify'd.

Of gross-beeks, one apiece, bill'd & crack'd.

Of browne creepers, one apiece, hitt.

Of long-bill'd marsh wrenns, a bird, one apiece, growsl'd & disembowell'd.

Of catt birds, one apiece, dyc'd & fetch'd.

Of growse, a legg apiece, smother'd naturall.

Also divers eggs, and bitts & bytes of turkie and what all. The fowles done, they turn'd to meat, and eat:

Of marsh ratts, one apiece, fry'd.

Of *raccoon*, half a one apiece, grutted.

Of dogg, equall portions, a sort of spaniell it was.

Of venison, one pryme apiece, dry'd.

Of beare-cubb, a rasher each, roasted.

Of catamount, a haunch & griskin apiece, spitted & turn'd.

Of batts, two apiece, boyl'd, *de gustibus* & cet.

No rabbitts. While that they eat of these severall meats, there were serv'd to them vegetables, to the number of five: beanes, *rocka-hominy* (wch is to say, parch'd & pouder'd mayze), eggplant (that the French call *aubergine*), wild ryce, & a sallet of greene reedes, that was call'd *Attaskus*. Also berries of divers sorts, but no frutes, and the whole wash'd downe with glue-broth and greate draughts of *Sawwehonesuckhanna*, wch signifyeth, bloud-water, a mild spirits they distill out in the swamp.

"The while this wondrous feast was being eat, Wepenter did pownd & stryke Burlingame upon the backe & bellie, to settle his stomacke, and Attonces aides did likewise him smite. After that each course was done, they did both ope there mowths wide, and Wepenter thrust his finger downe Burlingames crawe, & Attonce his owne likewise, or else have recourse to a syrup call'd *hipocoacanah*, so that they did vomitt what was eat, and cleare the holds for more. The Salvages did leap & daunce the while, and Pokatawertussan twist & wrythe for verie lust upon the rugg, at two such manlie men.

"When at last this Attonce did get him selfe to his redd berries, wch was the final dish, that the Salvages had prepar'd, and he did put one in his mawe, and drop out two therefrom, for want of room, his lieutenant smote him one last blow upon the gutt, whereat Attonce did let flie a tooling fart and dy'd upon the instant where he sat. And was too stuff'd, to fall over. Then did the Salvages on our side crie out, *Ahatchwhoop, Ahatchwhoop*, signifying, that Attonce was disqualify'd from farther competition. But albeit he was dead, our Burlingame was not yet victor, for that the twain had eat to a draw as far as to there final berrie. It wanted onelie for Burlingame to take but a single swallow more, and our lives were sav'd. We hollow'd at him, we cry'd & intreated, but Burlingame onelie sat still, his eyes rownd, his face greene, his cheeks blown out, his mowth fill'd with berries, and for all our exhortation, c^d not eat another bite. Here I leapt up from where I sat, and snatching the last boyl'd batt out of the caldron, pry'd open his jaws & thrust it in. Then held shutt his mowth, and delivering him a stout rapp on the head, did cause him to swallow it down.

"So clearlie then was Burlingame the victor, that Wepenter sprang upon him, and rubb'd his nose against Burlingames, and fetch'd him a loving patt upon the bellie. Whereat Burlingame did heave up what he had eat, and so befowl'd Wepenter therewith, the Salvage must needs hie him selfe to the river-shoar & wash. All the people then declar'd Burlingame Werowance, or King, but he was too ill to grasp there words.

"It being by this tyme nightfall, for that the feast had lasted all the daie, Burlingame was carry'd in state to the old Kings hutt, and there install'd, not able to move, and Pokatawertussan follow'd after, all a tremble. Wepenter meanwhile, did exact allegiance from those Ahatchwhoops, that had been with Attonce, and bade them fetch awaye the dead mans carcase, and wch still sat, for buriall. I told my companie, that we were free men, and w^d make sayle on the morrow, at wch tydings they shew'd good humour, though they grasp'd little of what had pass'd.

"When that the sunne rose, we wak'd, and taking provisions a plentie, the gift of Wepenter, made readie to return to our barge, and pick up the broken thread of our journie. This Wepenter was in fine good spirits, and upon my asking, Wherefore? he reply'd, that neare midnight, while that he slept, Pokatawertussan had come to his hutt, albeit she was by custom bound to lye the first night with the proxie. I wonder'd thereat, and Burlingame joyning us at the last minute, even as we left downe the path to the shoar, I ask'd him, Had Pokatawertussan earn'd her name? Whereupon he curs'd me ardentlie, and said, That the last boyl'd Batt had so undone him, he knew not where he was the whole night long. That he had not been able even to see any Salvage trollop, how much the less doe a mans work upon her. He was surpassing wroth with me, for having thrust the Batt upon him, and maugre my protestation, that I had spar'd the lott of us therebye, he vow'd afresh to tell his tatling tale on me, and write letters to the London Co, & cet. . . . I responded, that I had made a pact with him, that shd he win, he cd doe whatsoever he wd, and turning, led my companie downe the path. Burlingame follow'd, in all innocence, till that, to his surprize, the Salvages lay'd hands on him, and maugre his whoops and hollowings, bore him back to the Kings hutt, to reign over them with Wepenter for ever.

"My souldiers and Gentlemen much alarm'd thereat, I made them a speach, that they shd be of good hearte. That the Salvages had demanded Burlingame as tribute for our libertie, and being so few & unarm'd, we had naught for it, but deliver him up & go in peece, onelie bearing his memorie for ever in our heartes. This counsell at length prevayl'd, albeit the companie shew'd great sadnesse, more especiallie the Gentlemen thereof, and we wav'd to Wepenter as we went downe to the barge. For the favour of Princes, even amongst the Salvages, is a slipperie boone, lightlie granted, and as lightlie withdrawn, and we wish'd onelie to retayne it, untill that we were safe againe in our barge, and awaye from this scurvie, barbarous countrie. Whither (God wot) I shall never return, nor yet (God grant) any other Englishman.

"And may He smyte me dead here where I sit, in the sternsheets of our trustie barge, if any word of these adventures passe my lipps, or those of my Companie (the wch I have this daye sworn to silence), or ever appeare in my greate *Generall Historie*, for:
> *When one must needs Companions leave for dead,*
> *'Tis well the Tale thereof were left unread."*

8

The Fate of Father Joseph FitzMaurice, S.J., Is Further Illuminated, and Itself Illumines Mysteries More Tenebrous and Pregnant

WHEN EBENEZER LOOKED UP, still agape, from the couplet at the foot of the *Secret Historie*, Chicamec commanded him, through Drepacca, to return the volume to the chest, and the guards, who had knelt throughout the lengthy reading, rose to their feet and carried the chest back to its corner. Both Bertrand and McEvoy were surprised to hear the name *Burlingame* in the manuscript, but knowing nothing of the current Henry Burlingame's past or the contents of the manuscripts relative to this one—and having the sentence of death upon their heads—they were more bewildered than astonished by the narrative. Ebenezer, on the other hand, was bursting with curiosity, but before he could formulate a proper question, the old chief demanded to hear again the poet's description of his former tutor.

"What is his aspect?" Quassapelagh translated. "Tell of his skin and the rest."

"I'faith——" Ebenezer frowned in recollection. "His skin is not so fair as McEvoy's, yonder, nor yet so dark as Bertrand's; 'tis near in hue to my own, I'd venture. As for his face—i'Christ, he hath so many—let me say only that in stature he is slighter than any of us, a quite short fellow, in fact, but his want of height is the less apparent forasmuch as he hath a deep chest and good shoulders, and his neck and limbs are stout. Ah, yes, and his eyes—they are dark, and have at times the glitter of a serpent's."

Chicamec nodded with satisfaction to hear these things; his next question caused the Anacostin King to narrow his eyes, and Drepacca to smile the briefest of royal smiles.

"The Tayac Chicamec desires to know about your friend . . ." He searched for words, and the old chief, as though to assist him, held up one of his little fingers grasped at the second joint. Quassepelagh went on determinedly, "He wishes to know about the part——"

"They call it the privy member," offered Drepacca.

Quassapelagh did not acknowledge the assistance but relied on it to make his message clear. "Whether it is of that small size, nor ever is moved by love to manly proportion?"

Ebenezer blushed and replied that, quite to the contrary, Burlingame was to be censured more for excess than for defect of carnal resources; that he was, in fact, the embodiment of lust, a man the catalogue of whose conquests surpassed all reasonable bounds in respect not only of length, but as well of manner and object.

The Tayac received this news without surprise or disappointment and merely inquired more particularly whether Ebenezer himself had been present at any of these deplorable activities.

"Of course not," the poet said, a little annoyed, for he found the whole inquiry as uncomfortable as it was distasteful.

But surely the brother of Quassapelagh had observed with his own eyes the instrument of his teacher's lechery?

"I have not, nor do I wish to! What is the end of these questions?"

Drepacca listened to his elder colleague and then declared to Ebenezer, "This man of whom you speak is Henry Burlingame Three; the fat Englishman of the book"—he pointed toward the chest in the corner—"is Henry Burlingame One, the father of the father of your friend."

"In truth?. 'Sheart, 'twas what Henry hoped for from the first, but ne'er could prove!" He laughed ironically. "What joy it is, to gladden a friend's heart with news like this! But when Henry was my friend I'd naught to give him; now I have these wondrous tidings and no friend to give them to, for——" He was about to say that Burlingame had betrayed not only him but the cause of justice; he checked himself upon reflecting that, to say the least, he was no longer certain whether justice lay with Baltimore or John Coode, assuming the real existence of those gentlemen, and whether in fact it was Burlingame or Reality that had betrayed him, or the reverse, or simply he who had betrayed himself in some deep wise. "The truth of't is," he declared instead, and realized the truth of his proposition as he articulated it, "my friend hath passed into realms of complexity beyond my compass, and I have lost him."

This sentiment proved incapable of translation, even by the knowledgeable Drepacca, who first interpreted it to mean that Burlingame was dead.

"No matter"—the poet smiled—"I love him still and yearn to tell him what I've found. But stay—we have the grandsire and grandson, it appears, but what came between? And how is't Henry was found floating in yonder Bay? Ask the Tayac Chicamec who was Burlingame Two, and what came of him."

Drepacca had no need to relay the question, for at the words *Burlingame Two* old Chicamec, who had been listening intently, grunted and nodded his head.

"*Henry Burlingame Two.*" He pronounced the words clearly, with no trace of Indian accent, and tapped his thumb against his shrunken chest. "Henry Burlingame Two."

Even as Ebenezer protested his incredulity, he saw in the high cheekbones and bright reptilian eyes the ghost of a resemblance to his friend. "Ah, nay!" he cried. "Say rather he is the son of Andrew Cooke; tell me his name is Ebenezer, the Laureate of Maryland—'twere as easy to believe! Nay, gentlemen: 'tis beyond the Bounds; outside the Pale!"

Be that as may, Chicamec replied in effect, he was the father of Henry Burlingame III, whom he himself had set afloat to drown. He went on to tell a most surprising tale for which Quassapelagh, clearly his favorite, provided a running translation, deferring with reluctance to Drepacca at the more difficult passages:

"The Tayac Chicamec is a mighty foe of white men!" he began. "Woe betide the white-skinned traveler who sets foot on this island while even one Ahatchwhoop dwells here! For the Ahatchwhoops will not be sold into slavery like the people of Drepacca, nor traffick for English guns and English spirits like the people of Annoughtough and Panquas, nor yet flee their homes and hunting-places——"

"Like the people of Quassapelagh," Drepacca obliged.

"Rather will they put to the torch every white man who stumbles into their midst, and lead the great war-party that shall drive the English Devils into the sea, or else die fighting here upon their island, under the white man's guns!"

Here Ebenezer interrupted. "You must ask the Tayac Chicamec the reason for his wrath, Quassapelagh: I judge from yonder journal-book that his people have suffered small harm from the English these four-score years. He hath not one tenth the grievance of Quassapelagh or Drepacca, yet he shews ten times their spleen."

"My brother asks a barbed question," said Quassapelagh with a smile. "I shall put it to the Tayac Chicamec without the barbs."

He did so, and with the typical indirection of the savage, Chicamec ordered the chest brought out again in lieu of immediate reply. This time he took out the journal himself —the guards knelt down at once and lowered their eyes—and held it grimly at arm's length.

"This is *The Book of English Devils,*" he said through Quassapelagh. "Its tale you know: how my godlike father, the Tayac Henry Burlingame One, did best the great Atton-ceaumoughhough as champion for Wepenter, and drove off the English Devils from our land."

"Nay, one moment——" the poet protested, but thought better of it at once. "I mean to say, he was in sooth a mighty man."

"He drove out the English Devils upon their ship," Chicamec resumed, "and then pursued them himself along the shore, for it was his vow that he would follow them to their next encampment and there destroy the lot. He crossed to the northern mainland by canoe and ran all day along the shore of the marshy Honga, up whose reaches the unwary Devils sailed. And when these Devils put ashore to make their camp, then did the Tayac Burlingame spring to kill them, with no weapon save his hands. But Wepenter had mistrusted the courage and godlike prowess of the white-skinned Werowance and had followed after with a war-party, and for this sin the gods bound fast my father's limbs with invisible thongs, so that the Devils slew Wepenter and divers others, and made good their escape before my father could destroy them. But in their haste they left behind this book, in which was writ the Tayac Burlingame's mighty deeds, and he preserved it to remind all future ages of Ahatchwhoops that the English are the seed of those same Devils, and must be slain on sight.

"Now you must know that my heavenly father was a man of no common parts in carnal matters; but as the storm-god stores his strength for many moons and then in a night lays waste the countryside, so the Tayac Henry Burlingame One had a——"

"A member," Drepacca offered, for the second time that day.

"It was no greater than a puppy's, nor more useful, nor did he go into the Queen Pokatawertussan for three full nights after the Feast. But on the fourth, so say our legends, he summoned her to the bed, and performed the Rites of the Holy Eggplant, after which he got a child in her so mightily, she ne'er left her bed again, and died in bringing me forth!

"For twenty-six summers thereafter," Chicamec's tale continued, "the Ahatchwhoops lived in peace under my father's rule. Our fishermen brought us stories of English Devils far to the south, and divers times we saw their great white ships go up the Bay, yet never did they put ashore on our island or the nearby mainland. And great was my father's wrath against them: when my mother the Queen Pokatawertussan was in travail, he vowed to her he'd slay their child ere its cord was cut, if it was born white. And he named me Henry Burlingame Two, but called me by an Ahatchwhoop name, *Chicamec*. Every day he would read *The Book of English Devils,* and farther inflame the Ahatchwhoops to murther any white man who fell into their hands. In my twenty-sixth year he died, and with his last breath told our people that the

Tayac Chicamec would guard their town against the English Devils, and he swore me to a mighty oath, that I would slay any white-skinned man who came among us, even from the wombs of my wife and concubines.

"Loud were the wails of the Ahatchwhoops upon his passing, and when I became Werowance in his stead, I prayed for a sign of favor from the gods. At once a terrible storm crashed all about us and blew hither a medicine-man from amongst the English Devils, all senseless and half drowned— by which sign we knew the gods favored my reign and my cause. Lest any of our number doubt he was a Devil and take him for a human like ourselves, I held forth our totem for him to reverence, and being a Devil, he spat upon it. Thereupon we offered him the privileges of the damned and burnt him next day in yonder court, as you all—save the brother of Quassapelagh—shall burn."

"Stay, prithee!" cried Ebenezer, whose mind had been wrestling with dates and recollections. "Captain Smith made his voyage in 1608, and you murthered this English Devil in your twenty-sixth year: I say, Quassapelagh, ask him whether that chest yonder did not belong to this medicine-man he speaks of . . ."

The question was translated and answered affirmatively.

"I'faith, then—one more question: hath the Tayac Chicamec any other sons besides my friend Henry Burlingame?" He strove to recall the tales he'd heard from the Jesuit Thomas Smith and from Mary Mungummory. "Hath he a son now dead called Charley . . . *Moccasin? Mackinack?* Nay, not that . . . 'twas *Mattassin,* I believe."

At mention of this name Chicamec's face went hard, and his reply, according to Quassapelagh, was, "The Tayac Chicamec hath no sons."

Ebenezer was sorely disappointed. "Ah well, no matter, then; 'tis only a curious coincidence of events."

"Quassapelagh's brother doth mistake us," Drepacca put in pleasantly. "The Anacostin King hath Englished Chicamec's words, but not his meaning." He turned to Ebenezer. "In truth the Tayac Chicamec hath sons, but they both deserted him to live among the English, and he hath disowned them. One was the man you mentioned, whose name I shan't repeat: he slew a family of English and was hanged."

"Then I'm right!" the poet exulted. "This medicine-man was a Jesuit missionary, and yonder are his soutanes and holy-water! And 'sbody——" His imagination leaped to new connections. "Doth it not follow that Burlingame is half-brother to this murthering Mattassin?"

No one else in the hut, of course, was in a position to appreciate these revelations. The second mention of Charley Mattassin's name elicited strong rebuke from Chicamec.

"Methinks you should be proud of him," Ebenezer ventured. " 'Tis true his victims were Dutch and not English, but they were white-skinned in any case."

"Take care, Brother," warned Quassapelagh. "I shall tell the Tayac Chicamec that you apologize for calling Mattassin his son."

This done, the old chief went on with his story, and for the first time an emotion other than wrath and malevolence could be noticed in his tone:

"For many summers the Tayac Chicamec had denied himself the joys of a wife and sons," Quassapelagh translated. "His heavenly father Henry Burlingame One had given him to know that his seed was mixed, and had farther sworn him to destroy any white-skinned issue; therefore, to spare himself the pain of putting a child of his own to the spear, he chose to live and die without the solace of a family.

"Now it happened that the medicine-man English Devil had lain with divers women of the Ahatchwhoops on the night before he died—as is the privilege of a man condemned, except he be a prisoner of war like yourself—and had got three of them with child. The issue of the third was a daughter, more red than her father and more white than her mother, and the Ahatchwhoops took the child and made to drown her in the Chesapeake; but the Tayac Chicamec stayed their hands, observing to them that the skin of the girl-child was of the same hue as his own. He took her to his empty hut and raised her as his daughter, and this was a mighty sin against the gods, but the Tayac Chicamec knew it not.

"Thus it was that the child of the Devil was reared as a princess amongst the Ahatchwhoops, and grew more beautiful to behold with every circuit of the seasons, so that all the young men of the town became her suitors and applied to the Tayac Chicamec for her hand. But evil spirits put a torch to the Tayac's heart, and albeit he was then in his forty-fourth summer, and she in her fifteenth, he was possessed with love for her and desired her for his own. The fire mounted to his head, and caused him to believe that inasmuch as the blood of the Princess was mixed in the same manner as his own, he could father sons upon her whose skins would have the color of their parents'. To this end he sent away the suitors and revealed to the Princess that albeit he had raised her as his own, she was not in fact the daughter of his loins, and he meant to have her for his Queen. Greatly did the girl protest, whether because she had some favorite amongst the young men of the town or because she was wont to think of the Tayac Chicamec as her father; but such is the power of the vengeful gods, her tears were merely fuel for the Tayac's passion, and he who had lived long years without a wife grew so——"

Drepacca too had to reflect for a moment before he could supply an English approximation. *"Enthralled?* Nay, not as a slave . . . to be helpless, but not as one in shackles . . ."

"Driven?" Ebenezer suggested quickly. *"Exalted? O'ermastered?"* Chicamec's nostrils flared with impatience at the delay.

"He was *driven* with lust," Quassapelagh declared. "So much so, that he shook in every limb like a beast in season. Now the Secret of the Sacred Eggplant, whereby Queen Pokatawertussan was destroyed, had perished with her heavenly spouse, but the Tayac Chicamec had no need of it, being a man in all his parts. When the maid sought to move his pity by kneeling at his feet, he could no longer wait to make her his Queen. Nay, he climbed her then and there, and in the night that followed filled her with his seed!"

Although Quassapelagh had remained impassive as he translated, Chicamec's voice had grown excited; his breath was coming faster, and his old eyes shone. Now he paused, and his face and tone grew stern again.

"In the morning, unknown to all, she was with child, and the Tayac made her his Queen. The evil spirit that had possessed him now left his head at last, and all the while her belly grew he did not touch her again, for shame, and trembled lest she bear a white-skinned boy for him to slay. But strange and far-reaching is the vengeance of the gods! She bore him a fine dark son, a very prince among Ahatchwhoops, a man-child perfect in every wise save one, which the Tayac observed at once the boy had . . ."

"Inherited."

". . . had inherited from his grandsire Henry Burlingame One—the single defect of that lordly man; and it was clear, his grandsire's Secret of the Holy Eggplant being lost, this boy would ne'er be able to carry on the royal line. For that reason he was not called Henry Burlingame Three, but *Mattassinemarough,* which is to say, Man of Copper; and for this reason as well, albeit the lust was gone out of him, the Tayac Chicamec durst force his Queen a second time, and plied her with seed the night through to get another son on her. And again he trembled lest she bring forth a white child for him to slay, and did not go into her the while her belly rose beneath her coats. As before, the Queen was brought to bed of a son, this one neither dark as the dark Ahatchwhoops nor white as the English Devils, but the flawless golden image of his father, save for one thing: like his brother Mattassin he had not the veriest shadow of that which makes men men, and since none but God imparts to men the Mysteries of the Eggplant, this boy could never in a hundred summers get grandsons for the Tayac Chicamec. Thus he was not called Henry Burlingame Three, but *Cohunkowprets*, which is to say, Bill-o'-the-Goose, forasmuch as his mother the Queen, on first beholding his want of manliness, declared *A goose hath pecked him;* and farther, *She would that goose had spared the son and dined upon the father.*

"But the Tayac Chicamec waited for the Queen to gather her strength, and a third time drove her with the seed that brings forth men; and until the harvest he trembled like an aspen in the storm. But the third son of his loins was neither dark like Mattassinemarough, nor yet golden like Cohunkowprets, but white as an English sail from head to foot, and his eyes not black but blue as the Chesapeake! He was his grandsire born again, e'en to that defect shared by his brothers, and albeit the gods might have seen fit to impart to the boy the Eggplant Secret, as they had imparted it to his divine grandsire, there was naught for it but the Tayac Chicamec must fulfill his awful vow and slay the boy for an English Devil.

"Mark how the sinner pays thrice o'er! When the Tayac Chicamec declared to the town that the white-skinned child must die, the Queen snatched up a spear, flung herself upon it, and perished rather than witness the new babe's slaying or bear another child to take its place. But the Tayac Chicamec fetched the white-skinned prince alone to the waterside to drown him, and his heart was heavy. The Queen was dead, that he thrice had ravished in vain, nor durst he get children on the concubines who would share his bed thenceforth, but sow his murtherous seed in the empty air. And at last he was not able to drown the child: instead he painted with red ochre on its chest the signs he had learnt from his father and *The Book of English Devils:* HENRY BURLINGAME III; then he laid the boy in the bottom of a canoe and sent him down the mighty Chesapeake on the tide. And he prayed to the spirit of the Tayac Henry Burlingame One to spare the child from drowning and impart to him the Magic of the Eggplant, that he might further the royal bloodline—even if amongst the English Devils."

"I'God!" Ebenezer marveled. Yet though he remembered Mary Mungummory's tale of her singular love affair with Charley Mattassin—a tale which not till now could he fully appreciate—and also certain startling assertions of Henry's —for example, that he had never made actual "love" to Anna—nonetheless he found this "certain defect" of Chicamec's offspring most difficult to reconcile with the staggering sexuality of his friend.

"The Tayac Chicamec enquires of Quassapelagh's brother," Drepacca said, "whether the man you call Henry Burlingame Three hath many sons in his house?"

Ebenezer was on the verge of a negative reply, but he suddenly changed his mind and said instead, "Henry Burlingame Three was still a young man when he tutored me, but albeit I know where he dwells, I've not seen him these several years. Yet I know him for a famous lover of women, and 'tis quite likely he hath a tribe of sons and daughters." In fact there had occurred to him the dim suggestion of a plan to save his companions as well as himself; not so rash as before, he pondered and revised it as Chicamec, evidently disappointed by the reply, concluded his narration through the medium of Quassapelagh.

"In the years that followed, the Tayac Chicamec raised his other sons to manhood, dark-skinned Mattassin and golden Cohunkowprets; and for all their sore defect they grew strong and straight as two pine trees of their country, bold as the bears who raid the hunter's camp, cunning as the raccoons, tireless as the hawks of the air, and steadfast—steadfast as the snapping-turtle, foe to waterfowl, that will lose his life ere he loose his jaws, and e'en when his head is severed, bite on in death!"

The old chief's voice had rung with pride until this final attribution, which evidently gave him pain. Now the furrows of his face winced deeper, and he spoke more broodingly.

"Who knows what deeds the gods regard as crimes," Quassapelagh translated, "until they take revenge? Was't so grave a sin to raise the daughter of the English Devil in the Tayac's house and get sons upon her when she came of age? Or was't a fresh sin that he vowed to slay his white-skinned child, and

620

drove the Queen to fall upon a spear? If either be sin, is not the other its atonement? Or was his new crime that he spared the boy at last, and he hath lived? One thing alone is given man to know: whate'er his sins, they must perforce be grievous, for terrible is the punishment he suffers, and unending! 'Twas not enough the Tayac flung his third son to the waves, and lost his Queen, and saw his line doomed to perish from the land; nay, he must lose all—lose e'en his stalwart, seedless sons that did so please him with their strength, and that he hoped would lead the Ahatchwhoops in their war against the Devils! Mattassin and Cohunkowprets! Did he not school them day by day to hate the English? Did he not rehearse them in *The Book of English Devils* and recount the warlike passions of their grandsire? And they were not hot-blooded boys, or dogs in season, that blind with lust will mount a bitch or a bulrush basket, whiche'er falls into their path; nay, they were grown men of two-score summers, canny fellows, sound in judgment, and sore they loathed the English as did their father! None were more ready than they to league our cause with the cause of the Piscataways and Nanticokes; when the first black slave escaped to this island 'twas Mattassin himself bade him welcome and made this town a haven for all who fled the English; and 'twas not the Tayac Chicamec that first hit on the plan of joining forces with the man Casteene and the naked warriors of the north to drive the English to the sea—'twas golden Cohunkowprets: wifeless, childless, and athirst for battle! Piscataways, Nanticokes, Chopticoes, Mattawomans—all men envied the Ahatchwhoops, that boasted such a pair of mighty chieftains; and Chicamec, too old to leave the island for the first great meeting of our leaders—was he not proud to send Mattassin in his stead?"

The Tayac Chicamec paused, overcome with bitter memory, and Ebenezer tactfully observed that he was familiar with the subsequent course of Mattassin's life. At the same time, since the information might have some bearing on his nebulous plan, he professed great curiosity about the other son, Cohunkowprets: surely he too had not been hanged for murdering English Devils?

"They have not hanged him," Chicamec said through Quassapelagh, and at no time thitherto had his malice so contorted every feature. "Their crime against Cohunkowprets is more heinous ten times o'er than their crime against Mattassin. Beautiful, golden son! Him too the Tayac Chicamec dispatched, but one full moon ago, upon an errand of great importance: to go north with Drepacca and make treaties with the man Casteene; him too the gods saw fit to lure from his goal, and in the same wise, despite the sternest counsels of Drepacca . . ."

He had previously spoken of the Negro element in the town as one would speak of a blessing by no means unalloyed, and had mentioned his allies' envy of his sons. It now became clear to Ebenezer that Chicamec's partiality to Quassapelagh was not only, as it were, skin deep: it masked a deep distrust of the Africans, and especially of Drepacca, and dated, apparently, from his embassy to Monsieur Casteene. Indeed, the poet went so far as to speculate that Chicamec held Drepacca in some way responsible for Cohunkowprets' defection.

"In short," Quassapelagh went on, "King Drepacca was obliged to leave Cohunkowprets on the mainland near the Little Choptank, with the white-skinned woman he lusted after, and the Tayac Chicamec hath not seen his son these many days."

"A wondrous likeness of misfortune," Ebenezer sympathized, "and a shame in itself! But what is this heinous crime the Tayac speaks of?"

"I had best answer that myself," Quassapelagh replied, "and not rouse farther the Tayac Chicamec's wrath. Rumor hath it that Cohunkowprets hath taken an English name and married an English wife; he lives amongst the English in an English house, speaks their tongue, and wears their clothes. He is no longer an Ahatchwhoop in any wise, but looks upon his people with contempt, and for aught we know may betray us to the English king."

At this point Chicamec, who had held his peace impatiently for some moments, began to speak again, and Quassapelagh was obliged to resume the labors of translation.

"Behold him now, the Tayac Chicamec," he said, "his body enfeebled by the cares of four-score summers, his island peopled with strangers and ringed round by English Devils, his ancient dream of battle in the charge of outland kings; his honor mired and smirched by faithless sons, and his royal line doomed to perish in his person! The brother of Quassapelagh must tell his friends these things if they ask him for what cause they lose their *members* and go to the torch; the brother of Quassapelagh must seek out the man called Henry Burlingame Three and tell him these things, and tell him farther to flee the land at once—with his sons, if he hath any;

for already the Tayac Chicamec hath defied the gods to save him, but now every English Devil in the countryside must die!"

9

At Least One of the Pregnant Mysteries Is Brought to Bed, With Full Measure of Travail, but Not as Yet Delivered to the Light

EBENEZER HAD NOW NO doubts as to the main lines of his plan. He spoke at once, before his imagination drowned him in alternatives and fears.

"This errand that the Tayac Chicamec sets me, dear Quassapelagh—is it a condition of my freedom?"

The latter phrase required some moments, and Drepacca's assistance, for translation, and occasioned some further moments of discussion in Indian language. Finally Drepacca ventured, "Nothing is a true condition that cannot be enforced. We agree, however, that if you are in sooth a brother of Quassapelagh, you will not shirk this errand."

Ebenezer steeled his nerve. "If the Tayac Chicamec murthers my three friends, I will carry no message to Henry Burlingame Three, for the reason that I shall die with them here. Tell this to him."

"My brother——" Quassapelagh protested, but Drepacca translated the declaration. Chicamec's eyes flashed anger.

"Howbeit," the poet continued, "if the Tayac Chicamec sees fit to concur with the merciful opinion of his wise and powerful fellow kings and set the four of us free, I pledge him this: I will go to Henry Burlingame Three and tell him the story of his royal birth and the father who saved his life; moreover I will *bring him here*, to this island, to see the Tayac Chicamec. He knows the tongues of Piscataway and Nanticoke; father and son can converse alone, without interpreters."

All these things filled Quassapelagh and Drepacca with sur-

623

prise; they translated in fits and starts and exchanged impassive glances. Lest they distort his message through astonishment or apprehension, however, Ebenezer rose to his feet and delivered it at close range, in a clear deliberate voice, to the aged king himself, accompanying the English words with unmistakable emphases and gestures: "*I*—bring *Henry Burlingame Three*—*here*—to *Chicamec*. *Chicamec* and *Henry Burlingame Three*—*talk*—*talk*—*talk*. *No Quassapelagh*. *No Drepacca*. *Chicamec* and *Henry Burlingame Three*—*talk*. And just to demonstrate my good faith, sirs: *I* will tell *Henry Burlingame Three* to *look*—*look*—*look* for his brother *Cohunkowprets*. *Henry Burlingame Three* will find *Cohunkowprets* and *talk*—*talk*—*talk*, and haply he'll show him the error of his ways. How would that strike you, old fellow? *Chicamec* here; *Cohunkowprets* here; *Henry Burlingame Three* right here!"

Whether he understood the conditions or not, Chicamec grasped enough of the proposal to make him chatter feverishly at Quassapelagh.

"I thought 'twould not displease you," Ebenezer said grimly, and resumed his seat. "But tell him 'tis all four of us or none," he added to Quassapelagh. Now that his bid was made he nearly swooned at the boldness of it. Bertrand and John McEvoy, who had heard the lengthy tales in despair, came alive again, their faces squinted with suspense.

Some debate ensued, by the sound of it not sharply controversial, and at the end Quassapelagh said, "My brother will not lightly be cured of his foolhardiness when he learns it hath succeeded."

"I'Christ! Do you mean we're free?"

"The Tayac Chicamec yearns to behold his long-lost son," Drepacca declared, in the same stern tone used by Quassapelagh, "and albeit he hath disowned his son Cohunkowprets, he counts an errant son as better than no son at all, and so will entertain entreaties for his pardon. The brother of Quassapelagh will be carried by canoe across the straits and given one full moon to make good his pledge; the others will remain here as hostages. If at the end of that time he hath produced neither Cohunkowprets nor Henry Burlingame Three, the hostages will die."

The faces of the Englishmen fell.

"Ah, nay!" the poet objected. "If the Tayac Chicamec hath no faith in me, let him slay me; if he trusts me, why, there is no need of hostages."

Chicamec smiled upon receiving this protest and countered

624

that if the brother of Quassapelagh made his promises in good faith, he need not fear for the safety of the hostages.

"Very well," Ebenezer said desperately. "But one companion, at least, you must permit me, if you mean to limit my time. Suppose I lose my way on the mainland, where I'm a stranger? Suppose Henry Burlingame Three is not at home, and I must seek him elsewhere, or suppose he insists we find Cohunkowprets before we return here? Two men travel faster than one on an errand like this."

Quassapelagh frowned. "There is reason in what you say. Two hostages, then, instead of three."

"And your servant, my savior Bertrand, for your companion," Drepacca added, "lest your time run out."

"Aye," Bertrand cried, speaking up at last, "I swear I am a very bloodhound for finding folk, and this fellow Burlingame is e'en indebted to me for some small favors."

Chicamec nudged and scolded until the bargaining was translated for his approval; then he frowned, but did not openly protest the new amendment.

Ebenezer laid a hand on his valet's arm and addressed Drepacca. "This man hath been some time my servant, and was my father's before in England. He hath divers times betrayed or otherwise deceived me, yet for the sake more of expediency than of malice, and I bear him no ill will for't. But he is given to presumptuousness and fear, and succumbs to opportunity like a toper to strong drink; I dare not trust this errand to his hands."

Bertrand was aghast, but before he could muster more than a faint *B'm'faith,* Ebenezer was pointing to McEvoy and had proceeded with his statement.

"This man here was once my enemy, and whatever injury I have done him accidentally, he hath repaid threefold a-purpose. Yet all he did, he did on principle, nor e'er hath stooped to dissembling or other fraud. Moreover he is the soul of courage and resourcefulness, and our differences are behind us. I choose this man to go with me."

On this proposal neither Chicamec nor Quassapelagh ventured a judgment; by tacit consent the decision was left to Drepacca, as the man whose interest in the case was greatest, and after considering Ebenezer and the dumfounded McEvoy carefully with his eyes, the African king nodded approval. It was decided that the prisoners should return to their quarters until the midday meal, whereafter the two fortunates would be ferried across Limbo Straits to the mainland of Dorchester County; the remaining pair would be preserved from any injury or molestation for one lunar month and set free at any time before that term if either Burlingame or a repentant Cohunkowprets appeared on the island.

" 'Tis but a hoax and treachery!" Bertrand complained to Ebenezer. "Is this my reward for all I've suffered on your account? Ye'll murther your only friend to save that lying pimp McEvoy?" Tears of self-commiseration welled in his eyes.

"Nay, friend," Ebenezer answered, putting his arm about Bertrand's shoulders as the guards escorted them from the royal hut. "If 'twere a ruse I should choose you, but 'tis not, I swear. I mean to ransom all of us, as I pledged."

"Ah, 'tis easy for you to make grand vows, that will live in any case! How will ye find Burlingame, or this other salvage, that ye ne'er laid eyes upon? And e'en should ye stumble on 'em in yonder marsh across the straits, d'ye think they'll give themselves up to these imps o' Hell? But 'tis no worry of yours, what happens to the man who once saved your life!"

Ebenezer could not, as a matter of fact, recall any such salvation, but he let the claim stand unchallenged. "Prithee don't mistrust me, Bertrand; if I can't make good my pledge in the time allowed, you'll see me trussed beside you on yonder stakes."

The valet snorted. "I doubt it not, thou'rt so prone to folly! But we shan't see McEvoy there, ye may wager."

Seeing that he would not be consoled, Ebenezer said no more. They paused at the center of the common while the guards freed Captain Cairn from his post. Unstrung by fatigue, cramped muscles, and incredulity, the old man could not stand unaided; Ebenezer and McEvoy bore him to the prison-hut. And whether because the ordeal had impaired his understanding or because the reprieve was too gross an anticlimax for rejoicing, he displayed no emotion at all when McEvoy told him the news.

Nor did McEvoy himself make any comment until some two hours later, when he and Ebenezer had bid farewell to the listless Captain and the still-acrimonious valet and had been ferried to a marshy point of land north of the island, the southernmost extremity of Dorset, where Limbo Straits joined the Chesapeake to a broad and choppy sound. There the two were put ashore at what appeared to be a long-abandoned wharf, and were left to make the best of their way on foot.

"We're in luck," the Irishman said soberly. "This is the very road Bandy Lou and I came down to reach the island. 'Tis half a hundred miles from here to Cambridge, but ye can't mistake the path, and there's farms and trappers' cabins along the way."

"Thank Heav'n for that," Ebenezer replied; "we've no time to lose. 'Tis more likely Burlingame's in St. Mary's than in Cambridge, but haply we'll find this Cohunkowprets by the way, if we enquire enough."

They walked up the muddy road for a while in silence, engaged in separate reflections. The afternoon was warm for late December. On every hand the salt marsh and open water extended flat to the horizon: brown marsh grass and cattails rustled in the wet west wind; rails and pipers picked for food along the flats, and from nests in the silvered limbs of salt-cured pines, ospreys and eagles rose and hung.

Ebenezer did not fail to observe that his companion's spirit was in some way troubled, and assumed, not without a certain satisfaction, that McEvoy's problem had to do with the proper way of expressing his gratitude and obligation. Indeed, Ebenezer's own spirit was far from tranquil; he reacted against the boldness of his stratagem, for one thing, now that he was committed to it: with no food, no money, no means of transportation, and no more than a general notion of their quarry's whereabouts, how could they dream of succeeding in their quest? Moreover, now that he was out of immediate peril all his former problems and anxieties reasserted themselves: the loss of his estate, his desertion of Joan Toast, his father's wrath, his sister's safety . . . Despair stretched brown about him like the marsh, unrelieved to his fancy's far horizons.

McEvoy had found a walking stick in the path; now he swung and bobbed a cattail with it.

"Marry come up!" he swore. "I am unmanned in any case!"

"Eh?" Ebenezer looked over in surprise. "How's that?"

McEvoy scowled and slashed. "Ye saved my life, that's how it is, and I'm eternally beholden for't! What's worse, ye'd every cause to hate me. But ye save my life instead!" He was unable to raise his eyes to Ebenezer's. "I'faith, how can a man live with't? If the salvages had gelded me, at least I could have hollowed like a hero and died soon after; here ye've gelded me nonetheless, but I must grovel and sing your praises for't, and live a steer's life till Heav'n knows when!"

"But that's absurd!" the blushing poet protested. " 'Twas a practical expedient; not a favor."

McEvoy shook his head. "Ye've no need to go on thus; 'tis my conscience makes me grovel, not you, and the more you protest I'm not beholden, the deeper I sink in the Slough of Obligation. *I must love ye*, says my conscience, and that

627

voice makes me despise ye, and that despisal makes me farther loathe myself for crass ingratitude."

"Ah, prithee, don't whip yourself so! Put by these thoughts!"

"There I sink, another hand's-breadth in the Mire!" McEvoy grumbled, keeping his eyes averted. "If only ye'd call for gratitude o'ermuch, I might hate ye and have done with't! As't is, I am fair snared, a fawning *castrato*."

Up to this point the poet had been more embarrassed than annoyed, for McEvoy's confession made him realize that he had in fact enjoyed, most unchristianly, a feeling of moral superiority to his comrade in consequence of having saved the fellow's life. But now his embarrassment was supplanted by irritation, perhaps directed at himself as much as at McEvoy; he too fetched up a walking stick, and laid low a brace of cattails on his side of the path.

"Henry Burlingame once told me," he said coldly, "that in ethical philosophy the schoolmen speak of moralities of motive and moralities of deed. By which they mean, a wight may do a good deed for a bad reason, or an ill deed with good intentions." He unstrung another cattail and slashed at a fourth. "Now, 'tis e'er the wont of simple folk to prize the deed and o'erlook the motive, and of learned folk to discount the deed and lay open the soul of the doer. Burlingame declared the difference 'twixt sour pessimist and proper gentleman lies just here: that the one will judge good deeds by a morality of motive and ill by a morality of deed, and so condemn the twain together, whereas your gentleman doth the reverse, and hath always grounds to pardon his wayward fellows."

" 'Tis all profound, I'm sure," McEvoy began, "but how it bears upon——"

"Hear me out," Ebenezer broke in. "The point of't is, methinks I see two pathways from this silly mire you wallow in. The first is to appraise whate'er I say and do from a morality of motive, and you'll find grounds for more contempt than gratitude: I chose you in lieu of Bertrand purely for revenge, to make you roast in the fire of conscience and to even the score for Bertrand's past offenses; I urge you not to thank me overmuch, to the end of driving you to thank me all the more . . ."

McEvoy sighed. "D'ye think I've not clutched at that broomstraw already?"

"Aha. And to no avail? Thou'rt still unmanned by gratitude?" *Swish* went the stick, and another cattail dangled from its stalk. "Then here's your other pathway, friend: turn your morality of motive upon yourself, and see that behind this false predicament lies simple cowardice."

The Irishman looked up for the first time, his eyes flashing. "What drivel is this?"

"Aye, *cowardice*," Ebenezer declared. "Why is't you make no move to second my pledge to Chicamec? Forget this casuistry of who's obliged to whom and mortgage your life along with mine! Bind yourself to come hither with me one month from now, when our quest hath borne no fruit, and we'll commend ourselves together to Chicamec's mercies! How doth that strike you, eh? A fart for these airy little members of the soul; lay your flesh-and-blood privates on the line, as I have, and we're quit for all eternity!" He laughed and slashed triumphantly with his stick. "How's that for a pathway, John McEvoy? I'Christ, 'tis a *grande avenue*, a *camino real*, a very boulevard; at one end lies your Slough of False Integrity—to call it by its name on the Map of Truth —and at the other stands the storied Town . . . where Responsibility rears her golden towers . . ." He faltered; for a moment his voice lost the irony with which he had strung out the figure, but he quickly recovered it. "There, now; take a stroll in *that* direction, and if you vow thou'rt still a gelding, why then sing descant and be damned to you!"

McEvoy made no reply, but it was clear he felt the sting of the poet's challenge: the anger went out of his face, and he put his stick to the homely chore of helping him walk. As for Ebenezer, his outburst had raised his pulse, respiration, and temperature; his step took on a spring; exhilaration narrowed his eyes and buzzed in his fancy; he opened his coat to dry the perspiration and unstrung a phalanx of cattails with one smite.

As the weak winter daylight failed they began to look about for lodging. To expect an inn in such desolate countryside would have been idle; they turned their attention to a barn far up the road and agreed that they were not likely to find better quarters before dark. Ebenezer's position was that they should ask the owner's permission to sleep in the hayloft, on the chance he might have room for them in the house; McEvoy held out for stealing unnoticed into the hay, on the grounds that the planter might send them packing if they asked for his consent. Their debate on the relative merits of these strategies was interrupted by the approach of a wagon from behind them, the first traffic they had encountered all afternoon.

"Whoa, there, Aphrodite; *whoa,* girl! Climb up here lads, and rest your feet a spell!"

From a distance the driver had seemed to be a man, but now they saw it to be a dumpy, leather-faced woman in the hat and deerskin coat of a fur-trapper. The light was poor, but even in the dark Ebenezer would have known her at once.

"I'God, what chance is this?" He laughed incredulously and stepped close to convince himself. "Is't Mary Mungummory I see?"

"No other soul," Mary answered cheerily. "Get up with ye now, and tell me whither thou'rt bound."

They climbed to the wagon-seat readily, glad to rest their legs, and McEvoy named their destination and intent.

Mary shook her head. "Well, lads, 'tis your own affair where ye sleep, but take care; 'tis a cruel and cranky wight owns yonder barn. Thou'rt free to sleep back in the wagon, if ye wish to; I've no end o' quilts and coverlets back there, and nobody to use 'em till we reach Church Creek. *Giddap,* Aphrodite!"

She whipped up her white mare, and they proceeded up the road.

"Mary Mungummory!" Ebenezer cried again. " 'Tis a proper miracle! How is't thou'rt here in this Avernus of a marsh?"

" 'Tis the fundament o' Dorset, right enough," the woman admitted, "but it's on my regular route nonetheless. Just now I'm out o' girls," she explained to McEvoy, who plainly did not know what to make of her, "but there's one in Church Creek I've heard is ripe for whoring."

"Ah Mary!" laughed Ebenezer, still astonished. "Thou'rt the person I've yearned all day to see, and you have forgot me! What news I have to tell you!"

"There's many a lad yearns to see this wagon down the lane," Mary observed, but peered at her passenger more closely. "Why, praise God, now! Is't Eben Cooke the poet? I declare it is, and your poor wife told me ye'd flown to England!"

McEvoy frowned, and the poet blushed with shame. "You've seen Joan?"

Mary clucked her tongue. "I saw her this very week, near dead o' pox and opium—to say naught o' her broken heart. Didn't I tell her to come in the wagon with me and let me give her a cure? Not that there's aught can save her now, but 'twould keep the salvages off her, at the least. Ah, Mister Cooke, ye did wrong by that girl, that asked such a trifle of

630

ye. Are ye bound for Malden, to take your medicine like a man?"

"I—I am," Ebenezer said miserably, "just as soon as I'm free to. There's much I must tell you, Mary, as we go along . . . But i'faith, I've lost my manners! John McEvoy, this is Mary Mungummory."

"The Traveling Whore o' Dorset," Mary added proudly, shaking hands in the masculine fashion with McEvoy.

"So she calls herself," Ebenezer declared, "but she is the most Christian lady in the Province, I swear." He then introduced McEvoy as an old and dear friend from London, and though he could scarcely wait to tell Mary about the coming Indian uprising, her late lover Charley Mattassin's brothers, and the urgent mission to which he was committed, his curiosity and bad conscience led him first to inquire further about the state of things at Malden.

Mary cocked her head and clucked her tongue again. "There's much hath changed since ye ran off: all manner o' queer goings-on, that nor Joan Toast nor any soul else seems to know the sense of—myself included, that left my girls and bade Bill Smith *adieu* as soon as Tim Mitchell disappeared."

"Is my father there, do you know? Andrew Cooke? And what of the cooper?"

"There's a wight that calls himself Andrew Cooke, all right," Mary said. "Whether he's your father is past Joan's proving, and mine, that ne'er laid eyes on him in England. He is a hard-hearted wretch in my case, I swear! Bill Smith's there too, and still hath title to the place, albeit I hear there's every sort o' law-suits on the fire. But i'Christ, I'll say no more; there's much afoot, that ye'll learn of better for yourself." She chuckled. "What a stir 'twill make when you walk in!"

"One question more," begged Ebenezer. "I must know whether my sister Anna is there with Father."

"Ye mean to say ye *do* have a sister?" Mary glanced at him thoughtfully and urged the mare on through the twilight.

"You have news of her? Where is she?"

"Nay," Mary answered, "I've not heard aught of her. The truth is, this wight that calls himself your father told Bill Smith's lawyer—ye recall that blaspheming thief Dick Sowter?—told Sowter ye was the only heir to Cooke's Point: no brothers or sisters. Then when some fellow recollected ye was born twins, he changed his story and swore the other twin died o' the Plague."

"This is fantastic!" Ebenezer pressed the woman for a description of this Andrew Cooke; the detail of the withered right arm convinced him it was his father, but she could shed no light on the strange assertions.

"Ye'll see what's what soon enough, I'll wager," she repeated. By this time their intended lodging was far behind them, and marshy ground began to appear once more not far from the road. A cold wind sprang up in the gathering darkness.

"Marry, I've much to tell you!" the poet cried with new enthusiasm. "I scarce know where to commence!"

"Why, then, think it out tonight and start fresh in the morning," Mary replied. With her whip she pointed to a lighted window in the distance. "Yonder's where we'll stop: 'tis an old friend o' mine lives there."

"I'God, don't put me off! If aught I said distressed you, prithee forgive me for't; but what I have to say concerns you as well as me."

"Indeed, sir? How might that be?"

Ebenezer hesitated. "Well—did you know Charley Mattassin had a brother?"

She regarded him pensively. "Aye, a salvage down on Bloodsworth Island. What do ye know of him?"

Ebenezer laughed distractedly. "There's so much to tell! Stay, now—did you know he had *two* brothers, and Henry Burlingame—that is to say, Tim Mitchell, that I said had the same strange character as your Charley—— I'm all entangled! Tell me this, Mary: when did you last see Tim Mitchell, and where is he now?"

Full of wonder, Mary replied that she had not seen Tim Mitchell for weeks, even months; it was rumored, in fact, that he had not been Captain Mitchell's son at all, but an impostor of some sort, the agent of certain powerful and unidentified interests hostile to the equally powerful and unidentified syndicate in which Captain Mitchell was a major figure. Tim's disappearance had been the occasion for great alarm and mutual suspicion among Captain Mitchell, William Smith, and the other operatives in the organization, but for Mary herself, by her own admission, it had been a stroke of good fortune, for he had been a hard taskmaster for her girls at Malden.

"Then you don't know where he is?" Ebenezer interrupted. "I must find him within a fortnight, or I and three companions will die—nay, I'll explain in time. Know, Mary, that the man you called Tim Mitchell is really Henry Burlingame the Third, son of the Tayac Chicamec of the Ahatchwhoops and brother to Charley Mattassin and Cohunkowprets, whom we must find also or perish! All we know of him is that he was sent on a mission by his father, as was Mattassin before him, and like Mattassin he was detained by some English Calypso——" He smiled in order to indicate to Mary that he had not betrayed her confidence to McEvoy. "This was some days or weeks ago, I gather, and the Tayac hath not seen him since. I hoped you might have heard rumors in the County of a half-breed salvage turned proper Englishman."

"Dear Heav'n!" Mary threw back her head and closed her eyes. "Did ye say he plays the Englishman, Mister Cooke?"

"That is the story as Chicamec heard it. The man took an English name, an English wife, and an English house."

"What did ye say was his English name?" Mary's voice was husky; her face quite white.

"I've no idea. *Cohunkowprets,* so we're told, means Bill-of-the-Goose. What ails you, Mary? Have you seen him, then?"

Mary turned Aphrodite stiffly into the lane of the lighted cabin, and the occupant stepped outside with a lantern to meet them.

"Nay, Mister Cooke, I've not seen him, but I have heard tell of a half-breed named Rumbly: Billy Rumbly——"

"You have? Marry come up, John, this sainted lady will save me once again!" He squeezed her plump arm, but instead of her usual meaty laugh she gave a groan and shrank from his cordiality.

"What in the name of Heaven is wrong with you, Mary?" he demanded. Already their host for the night recognized the sailcloth-covered wagon and called his greetings down the lane.

"No time to tell ye now," the woman muttered. "I'll spin the tale for ye tomorrow morning on our way to Church Creek—that's where this Billy Rumbly's said to live, and I was bound for his place ere ever I met ye yonder on the road."

"Bound for there——" Ebenezer's laugh rang over the marsh. "D'you hear that, John? This woman's an angel of God, I swear! Not only hath she heard of Lord Cohunkowprets; she means to pay him a call!"

Mary shook her head slowly. "Go to, go to, Mister Cooke. Go to." They were close enough to the lantern of their host for Ebenezer to see the consternation on her face, and though he could not imagine what so alarmed her, his heart turned cold.

"D'ye not recall who I am, and what business I have in Church Creek? I am the Traveling Whore o' Dorset, Mister Cooke, and the trollop I lately got wind of, that may wish to join my traveling company—*Whoa,* Aphrodite! Whoa, girl!—I have a notion—just a notion, mind ye now—this tart may be your sister . . ."

10

The Englishing of Billy Rumbly Is Related, Purely from Hearsay, by the Traveling Whore o' Dorset

SUPPLICATE, CAJOLE, AND THREATEN as he might, Ebenezer could not prevail upon Mary Mungummory to speak farther on the subject of Anna's whereabouts and circumstances. She saluted their host, a buck-skinned, thin-grinned, begrizzled old hermit of a fur-trapper, and would not hear the poet's desperate expostulations.

The old fellow held up his lantern and was clearly pleased at what its light disclosed, for he sprang about like a frog, croaking for joy.

"Mary Mungummory! I swear 'tis old Mary at that!"

Mary grunted. "Did ye look to see Helen o' Troy in the Dorset marsh this time of the night?" She talked over-loudly, as one would to a man partially deaf. Her voice was rough with affection, and whether he grasped the allusion or not, the old man hopped and snorted appreciatively. He climbed up onto the side of the wagon and peeked inside as Mary drove Aphrodite up to his cabin.

"Don't strain your eyes, ye old lecher," she shouted. "The cupboard's bare till I reach Church Creek." She changed the subject quickly. "These here are friends o' mine, Harvey, down on their luck. If ye'll stand dinner and lodging for the three of us, I'll make it up to ye next time around."

"What fiddle is this?" Harvey cried. "D'ye think I'd not ha' took after ye, had ye not turned in my lane? I looked at the moon three nights ago, and I thought: 'tis time Mary's wagon came by." He sprang off the wagon the instant it stopped at his cabin. "Come inside and thaw, now; there's partridge and duck a-plenty, and cider to drown the lot o' ye!"

"We thank ye," McEvoy said loudly. Ebenezer was too distraught to acknowledge the man's charity with more than a nod; when their host ran ahead to open the cabin door, the poet whispered a final fierce entreaty to Mary to relieve his tortured fancy with explanation.

"There's no more Christian man in Dorset than Harvey Russecks," she declared, ignoring him. "And few with less cause to feel kindness for his fellow creatures. He's a brother to Sir Harry Russecks in Church Creek."

Her tone implied that this last assertion was intended to be revealing, but to Ebenezer, yawning and shivering with frustration as they entered the rude log cabin, it meant nothing at all.

"I'll just spit us a brace o' partridge on the fire," Harvey declared. "Haply ye'll pass the cider-jug round, Mary; old Harvey's got no cups to offer ye gentlemen." He fussed about like a new bride, and soon two birds were roasting over the pine logs in the fireplace. There was only one chair in the cabin, but the wood floor boasted two black-bear pelts, as warm and easy a seat as one could ask.

"If ye don't know the miller Harry Russecks," Mary went on, "thou'rt among the blest." She addressed herself to Ebenezer; when the poet looked away, wincing at the irrelevancy of her discourse, she flared her nostrils and turned to McEvoy instead. "This Harry Russecks is the lyingest, cheatingest, braggingest bully ye'll e'er mischance upon; thinks he's a London peer, doth the wretch, and browbeats his neighbors to call him 'Sir Harry' all the while he gives 'em short weight on their flour and meal. Truth is, he's no more a nobleman than his brother Harvey here, that's the son of a common house-servant and not ashamed to own it. 'Tis *Mrs.* Russecks is an orphan child o' the peerage—the miller's wife, and as fine a woman as her husband is the contrary. The bitter part is, her father was the gentleman that the miller's father served, but fortune used her so ill their positions turned arsy-turvy: she was a starving orphan and Harry a prosperous miller, and he married her a-purpose to tickle his vanity."

"Ye don't say!" McEvoy shook his head in polite wonder and glanced uncomfortably from Ebenezer to their host, who pottered about, oblivious to the narrative.

"He can't hear me, never fear," Mary assured him. "Poor

devil had both his ears boxed till the drums cracked, as I hear, and ye can lightly guess who boxed 'em."

"The miller?" McEvoy asked.

Mary pressed her lips and nodded. "Both brothers grew up with the lady I mentioned, and the story hath it they both were in love with her from the first, but Harvey was too shy and respectful o' place to do aught but wet-dream of her, e'en when she was a-beggaring, while Harry's lust was public as the moon. 'Twas when Harry wed her that Harvey took to living here in the marsh, and some years after, when he scolded Sir Harry for abusing the girl and putting on airs, the bully boxed his ears and well-nigh ground him into cornmeal."

The Irishman clucked his tongue.

"How she came to be orphaned is a story in itself," Mary went on doggedly. "She's a lady o' spirit, is Roxie Russecks, and don't think she comes fawning at the great lout's beck and call! Why, I could tell ye one or two things she had contrived——"

"No more!" Ebenezer cried, clutching his ears. Even the hard-of-hearing trapper turned round. "I thank you humbly for your hospitality!" Ebenezer shouted to him. "And I've no wish to appear ungracious or ungrateful for't! But Miss Mungummory here hath news of my long-lost sister, and I shall perish of anxiety if she keeps it from me any longer."

Harvey looked questioningly at Mary. "What is't ails the wight?"

"He's not the only poor wretch on tenterhooks," Mary snapped. "He hath news of his own close to my heart, but the tales are long and mazy, and here's no place to spin 'em out. Let him wait till we're on the road."

But the trapper joined his protests to Ebenezer's.

"No pleasure pleasures me as doth a well-spun tale, be't sad or merry, shallow or deep! If the subject's privy business, or unpleasant, who cares a fig? The road to Heaven's beset with thistles, and methinks there's many a cow-pat on't. As for length, fie, fie!" He raised a horny finger. "A bad tale's long though it want but an eyeblink for the telling, and a good tale short though it take from St. Swithin's to Michaelmas to have done with't. Ha! And the plot is tangled, d'ye say? Is't more knotful or bewildered than the skein o' life, that a good tale tangles the better to unsnarl? Nay, out with your story, now, and yours as well, sir, and shame on both o' ye thou'rt not commenced already! Spin and tangle till the Dogstar sets i' the Bay; a tale well wrought is the gossip o' the gods, that see the heart and point o' life on earth; the web o' the world; the Warp and the Woof . . . I'Christ, I do love a story, sirs!"

Even Mary was plainly impressed by her old friend's eloquence, and though her scowl only darkened as he concluded, it was the scowl no longer of recalcitrance but of grudging assent, and she agreed that tales would be told when the partridge was finished.

"The fact of't is," she said loudly to Harvey, "you may have as much to say as any of us. 'Tis the half-breed Rumbly we're interested in, amongst other matters. Master Cooke here can start us off, that hath some mysterious business with the wight, and then we'll each add what we can. But not till the birds are done."

Harvey Russecks's face brightened at the name *Billy Rumbly*, and squinted a bit at the mention of Ebenezer's surname. "Thou'rt the poet chap that gave away his property?"

"The same," Ebenezer replied, no longer embarrassed by this identification. "You all may wait for your dinners if you wish; since I'm to start, I'll start right now, listen who will, and tell you why not only my life but the life of every white-skinned person in the Province may depend on my finding a salvage called Cohunkowprets, within the month, and persuading him to listen to humane reasoning." He proceeded to tell them about the capture of his party on Bloodsworth Island; the grand conspiracy of fugitive Negroes and disaffected Maryland Indians; his relationship with Drepacca and Quassapelagh, and the peculiar status of the Tayac Chicamec in the triumvirate. As briefly as the complexity of the subject permitted he described the history of Chicamec's antagonism towards the English, the ironic fates of his three sons, and the consequent insecurity of his present position in the conspiracy. Mary Mungummory and Harvey Russecks hung astonished on the tale; had not McEvoy been already familiar with the greater portion of it and thus able to devote his attention at times to other matters, the two partridges would have burned untended on the spit.

"Marry sir, do I have't aright?" he asked incredulously. "Ye must deliver Cohunkowprets or the other wight to Bloodsworth Island within the month, or else the salvages will burn the two hostages?"

"They'll burn the three of us," Ebenezer affirmed. " 'Tis my fault they're on Bloodsworth Island."

Both his listeners glanced questioningly at McEvoy, who lowered his eyes to the food and said—in a voice surely too

637

low for the trapper to catch—"I owe Mister Cooke my life; that's true enough. God knows whether I'm hero enough not to renege on the debt."

"The fact is," Ebenezer concluded, "we're all of us like to lose our scalps anon, when the war commences, and there's reason to think 'twill commence when this same month of mine expires. They seemed quite indifferent whether I spread the news of their plot; 'tis as if they feel our militia's not a match for them."

"They're right enough there," declared their host. "Copley and Nicholson both refused help to New York, e'en when the Schenectady folk were murthered, and 'tis folly to look for help from Andros in Virginia or the Quaker William Penn: they'd like naught better than to see us butchered by the salvages and Negroes, for all they might be next at the block themselves." He shook his head. "The worst of't is, an honest man can't hate the wretches for't. When a poor wight's driven from his rightful place, and pushed, and pushed—to say naught o' being clapped in hobbles and sold off the block like a dray-horse—i'faith, 'tis only natural he'll fight the man that's pushing him, if he hath any spirit left in him. I've no great wish to lose my scalp, sirs, but I swear I'm half on the Indians' side o' the question."

"As am I," Mary agreed.

"And I," said Ebenezer; "not alone because there's justice in their cause, but because there's a deal of the salvage in all of us. But as you say, 'twere better to keep one's scalp than lose it. 'Tis for that reason I must find Chicamec's sons: Burlingame I know is a very Siren for persuasion, and this Cohunkowprets, if he hath in sooth embraced the English cause . . . my plan is to apply to his new loyalties, if I can contrive it; send him back to the Ahatchwhoops as a penitent prodigal; let him assume his place as prince of the bloody realm, where he can do his best to influence Quassapelagh and Drepacca, and haply forestall the massacre. 'Tis a chancy gambit, but desperate cases want desperate physic; and until Mary, or the twain of you, tell your tales, I know naught of Cohunkowprets save that he deserted his people to woo some English woman, just as his brother Mattassin before him——" He stopped and blushed. "Forgive me, Mary."

The woman waved his apology away and sighed a corpulent sigh. "Naught to forgive, Mister Cooke. I feel no shame at loving Charley Mattassin, nor any regret nor anger at his end. If I could believe his brother was like him—— Nay no matter! We'll learn soon enough, and in any case——" She paused, and a little tremor shook her. "I'm minded of some old scoundrels Charley read about in his Homer and his Virgil, and the two of us were wont to chuckle at—their names are gone, but one was the father of Achilles and the other of Aeneas——"

Ebenezer supplied the names *Peleus* and *Anchises;* he was surprised anew at the extent, not only of the Indian's late forays into Western culture but also of Mary's pertinent recollections, and McEvoy, who knew nothing of the curious relationship, was flabbergast.

"Those were the wights," Mary affirmed. "Each had bumped his bacon with a goddess, and the twain of 'em were ruined for life by't. No doubt 'twas a bargain at the price, but there are bargains a soul can't afford but once. D'ye see my point?"

They did—Ebenezer and the trapper in any case—and Mary went on.

"Now mind, I'm not saying this Billy Rumbly is Mattassin's brother: I've ne'er laid eyes on him, as Harvey hath, and Charley ne'er spoke overmuch about his family. But what I've heard o' the wretch and his English woman I can fathom to the core. There's something in't of what Mister Cooke declared just now—that there's a piece o' the salvage in us all. 'Tis that and more: the dark of 'em hath somewhat to do with't, I know. What drives so many planters' ladies to raise their skirts for some great buck of a slave, like the Queen in *The Thousand and One Nights?* Methinks 'tis an itch for all we lose as proper citizens—something in us pines for the black and lawless Pit."

She had been looking at the pine logs on the fire; now she straightened her shoulders, rubbed her nose vigorously as if it itched, and sniffed self-consciously. "But that's no tale, is it, Harvey?"

"Not a bit of't," Harvey replied. " 'Tis a great mistake for a taleteller to philosophize and tell us what his story means; haply it doth not mean what he thinks at all." But the trapper was clearly impressed by Mary's analysis, as were Ebenezer and McEvoy.

" 'Tis what *I* thought of, in any case," she said good-naturedly, "when Roxie Russecks told me about Billy Rumbly and the Church Creek Virgin."

Ebenezer bit his lip, and Mary hurried into the story.

"Just a fortnight ago or thereabouts this woman came to Church Creek, all alone, with no baggage or chattels save what little she could carry, and went from house to house looking for lodgings. She was a spinster of thirty or so, so I hear't, and declared she was new out of England; gave her name as Miss Bromly of London."

"Dear Heav'n!" Ebenezer cried. "I know that girl! She was our neighbor when we lived on Plumtree Street!" He laughed aloud with sharp relief. "Aye, there's the answer! She spoke of me, and ye took her for my sister! What business hath Miss Bromly in Maryland?"

"Hear me out," Mary answered darkly. "As I say, she gave her name as Miss Meg Bromly, but when folk asked her what her business was in Church Creek, and how long she meant to hire lodgings, she had no ready reply. Some took her for a runaway redemptioner; others thought she was the mistress o' some planter, that meant to keep her in Church Creek; others yet believed she was got in the family way and either turned out by her father or sent to the country for her confinement —albeit she showed no signs of't in the waist. 'Tis rare to find a maiden lady of thirty years anywhere, but especially in the Plantations, and rarer yet to find one traveling alone, without servants or proper baggage, and not e'en able to state her business plainly. Add to this, she was nowise ugly or deformed, and spoke as civil as any lady—she could have had her choice o' husbands for the asking, I daresay—'tis small wonder the ladies she applied to, whate'er their views, all took her for a bad woman, either a whore already or a whore-to-be, and had naught to do with her. As for the men, they slavered and drooled after her like boars to a salt young sow, and if any doubted she was a whore, they doubted no more when she took rooms at Russecks's inn: 'tis no inn, really, but a common store and tavern that blackguard of a miller owns—Harvey's brother. There's an upstairs to't, no more than a loft walled off into stalls with pallets; 'tis where my girls set up shop when we're in the neighborhood, ere we go on to Cambridge and Cooke's Point.

"Well, she stood them off as haughty as ye please, but they reckoned she was holding out for a higher price. Finally they asked her to name her hire, whereupon she drew a little pistol from her coat and replied, she'd charge a man his life just to lay hands on her, and King William himself couldn't buy her maidenhead. With that she went up into the loft, and no man in the room durst follow her. Thenceforth they called her the Virgin o' Church Creek, merely for a tease, inasmuch as they all believed she was the mistress of Governor Nicholson, or John Coode, or some other important man. She came and went whene'er she pleased, and no man touched her. Now and again she'd make enquiries of 'em, whether they knew aught of the state o' things at Malden, on Cooke's Point, and o' course they knew Malden to be the fleshpot o' Dorset County, so they took her all the more surely for a fashionable whore.

" 'Twas only a few days later, so Roxie told me, this half-breed Indian buck came into Church Creek. As a rule, the salvages travel in pairs when they come to town, but this wight was alone; he strode into Russecks's store as bold as ye please, put a coin on the table, and called for rum!"

"Ah, that can't be Cohunkowprets, can it, John?" Ebenezer asked McEvoy. "I doubt he knew English enough to order rum."

But McEvoy was not so certain. "He might have learned from Dick Parker, ye know; Dick Parker himself learned decent English in two or three months."

"And Charley Mattassin in less time yet," Mary added, and continued her narration. "This salvage was so fierce-looking, Harry Russecks gave him his rum with no argument, and he drank it off like water. 'Twas plain he'd never tasted liquor before, for he gagged and choked on't, but when 'twas down he called for another to follow the first. (All this is my Charley to the letter, Mister Cooke—bold as brass and bound to learn all in a single gulp.) By this time the men saw a chance for some sport with him. They poured him his rum and asked his name, which he gave as Bill-o'-the-Goose——"

"That's it!" Ebenezer and McEvoy cried out at once.

"The Tayac Chicamec told us *Cohunkowprets* means *Goosebeak*," Ebenezer explained. "Why he bears the name I shan't tell here, only that——" He blushed. "I shall say this, Mary, you declared his manner resembled Mattassin's; know then, that save for the lighter hue of his skin, Bill-o'-the-Goose is the likeness of his brother in every particular of his person."

Mary's eyes filled with tears. " 'Sheart, then he is in sooth poor Charley's brother!" She shook her head. "How clear I see it in his behavior, now I know it to be so! Why, marry come up, 'tis Charley and I all over again, after a fashion!"

Bill-o'-the-Goose, she went on tearfully to say, had not got into his second glass of rum before Miss Bromly, the Church Creek Virgin, happening to pass through the room on her way outdoors from her quarters, encountered him face to face. Until that moment she had preserved through all their catcalls and lubricities the iciest demeanor; but by the testimony of every man present in Russecks's tavern, when she beheld the Indian she drew back, shrieked out some unintelligible name, and tottered for some moments on the verge of a swoon; yet when a patron made to assist her she regained her composure as quickly as she had lost it, drove the Samaritan back by reaching under her cape—where the whole town knew she carried her famous pistol—and made her exit with a tight-lipped threat to the company. Bill-o'-the-Goose, like all the others, had stared after her and was the first to speak when she was gone.

"Bill-o'-the-Goose no longer wishes to be Bill-o'-the-Goose," he had declared. "You tell Bill-o'-the-Goose what ordeals he must brave to be an English Devil."

These, Mary Mungummory swore, were his very words as reported to her. Everyone agreed on the context of his statement; they remembered it so exactly because Bill-o'-the-Goose had had difficulty finding an English word for the initiation rites to which, in many Indian nations, young men were subjected as prerequisites to official manhood. A trapper present had at length supplied the word *ordeal*, to the great delight of the company when they grasped the Indian's meaning.

"Ye say ye want to become an Englishman?" one of them had asked gleefully.

"Yes."

"An *English Devil*, ye say?" had asked another.

"Yes."

"And ye want to know what tests a salvage has to pass ere we look on him as our brother?" demanded the miller.

"Yes."

The men had exchanged glances then and found unanimous design in one another's eyes. By tacit agreement the miller had proceeded with the sport.

"Well now," he had said thoughtfully, "first off ye must show yourself a man o' means; we want no ne'er-do-wells about—unless they're pretty as the Virgin, eh, gentlemen?"

The Indian had been unable to follow this speech, but when he was made to understand that they wished him to show his money he produced five pounds in assorted English currency —acquired no man knew where—and a quantity of *wompompeag*, all of which the miller Russecks had promptly pocketed.

"Now, then, ye must have a proper English name, mustn't he, lads?"

It was short work for the men to change *Bill-o'-the-Goose* into *Billy*, but the problem of a fitting surname required much debate. Some, impressed by the stench of the bear-grease with which their victim was larded, held out for *Billy Goat*; others, with his naïveté in mind, preferred *William Goose*. While they deliberated, Bill-o'-the-Goose drank down his rum—with less difficulty than before—and was commanded to take another on the grounds that a proper subject of Their Majesties should be able to put away half a rundlet of Barbados without ill effect. It was this third drink, and the solemnity with which the Indian, already gripping the table-edge to steady himself, had raised his glass like a ceremonial grail, that had inspired the miller with a third suggestion.

"He hath the makings of a proper rummy, hath our Bill," he had remarked, and added when the Indian gave up just then—in the manner of all the Ahatchwhoops—a raucous, unstifled belch: "Hi, there, he's rumbly with the spirit already!"

And since no man present cared to defend his own preference in the matter against the miller's, Bill-o'-the-Goose's new English name became *Billy Rumbly*, and was bestowed on him with much blasphemous mumbo-jumbo and a baptism of cider vinegar.

"Then they shaved off his hair," Mary said, and Ebenezer guessed that in earlier tellings of the story her voice had been marked by nothing like its present bitterness; "shaved it off to the scalp, poured another glass o' rum in his guts, and told him no civil English gentleman e'er reeked o' bear-fat. There was naught fur't, they declared, but he must hie himself down to the creek—in mid-December, mind—strip off his clothes, wade out to his neck, and swab himself sweet with a horse-brush they provided. 'Twas the miller's idea, o' course —*br-r-r*, how I loathe the bully!—and they packed Billy off to crown their pranks, never dreaming they'd see him again; if he didn't freeze or drown, they reckoned, he'd be shocked fair sober by the creek and skulk away home."

In fact, however, she said, they laughed not half an hour at their wit before the butt of it reappeared, returned the horse-brush, and called for more rum: his skin was rubbed raw, but every trace of the bear-grease was gone, and his liquor as well, and he showed no sign of chill or other discomfort. While they marveled, Billy pressed them to set him his next ordeal, and by unhappy coincidence Miss Bromly chose this moment to re-enter the tavern from wherever she had been, cross the room in disdainful silence, and disappear up the stairway to her loft. Even so, nothing further might have come of it, it was Billy who undid himself by demanding to know whose woman she was.

643

"Why, Billy Rumbly, that's the Church Creek Virgin," the miller had answered. "She's nobody's woman but her own, is that piece yonder."

"Now she is Billy Rumbly's woman," the Indian had declared, and had drawn a knife from his belt. "How doth an English Devil take a wife? What man must I fight? Where is the Tayac to give her to me?"

Not until then had the men drawn their breath at the vistas of new sport that lay before them. Not surprisingly, it was Harry Russecks who had spoken first.

"Ye say—ye claim the Church Creek Virgin for your wife?"

At once Billy had moved on him with the knife. "Is she your woman? Do you speak for her?"

"Now, now," the miller had soothed, "put up your knife, Billy Rumbly, and behave like a decent Englishman, or she'll have naught of ye. So she's to be Mrs. Billy Rumbly, is she? Well, now!" And after repeating his earlier assertion, that Miss Bromly had none to answer to but her own good conscience, Russecks declared his huge satisfaction with the match, a sentiment echoed by the company to a man.

"But don't ye know, Billy Rumbly," he had continued, " 'tis not just any Englishman *deserves* a lass like the Virgin Bromly. Ye know the—what-d'ye-call-'em, Sam? *Ordeals:* that's the rascal!—ye know the ordeals of an English bridegroom, don't ye, lad?"

As all had hoped, Billy Rumbly confessed his entire ignorance of English nuptial rites and was enlightened at once by Russecks, who spoke in a solemn and supremely confidential tone:

"In the first place, ye dare not approach an English virgin with marriage in mind till ye have at least a dozen o' drams to fire your passion. They loathe a sober lover like the pox, do our London lassies! In the second place ye must say nary a word: one word, mind ye, and your betrothal's at an end! D'ye follow me, Billy Rumbly? 'Tis a custom with us English Devils, don't ye know, to see to't no shitten pup-dogs get our women. No talk, then; ye must come upon her privily, like a hunter on a doe—i'Christ, won't she love ye for't if ye can catch her in *ambuscado* and take her maidenhead ere she knows what wight hath climbed her! For there's the trick, old Billy, old Buck: our laws declare a man must take his bride as a terrier takes his bitch, will-she, nill-she, and the more she fights and hollows, the more she honors ye in the rape! Is't not the law o' the land I'm reading him, friends?"

Now the others had entertained nothing more serious than a prank, so they all claimed afterwards to their wives; their only thought was to have some sport with a drunken Indian at the expense of the high-and-mighty Miss Bromly. But whether because they dared not gainsay Sir Harry or because his plan was altogether too attractive to resist, they affirmed, with little nods and murmurs, that such indeed were the customs of the English. As Billy took to himself the requisite rum, they told themselves and subsequently their wives that a man with twelve drams of Barbados in his bowels was no more dangerous than a eunuch to any woman's honor; when he had done they made way solemnly for Sir Harry, who with final hushed injunctions led him reeling to the stairway and watched him tiptoe up in drunken stealth.

"Marry, and to think," groaned Mary, interrupting her narrative, " 'twas Mattassin's golden likeness they made a fool of! 'Tis like—oh, God!—'tis as if ye made a pisspot o' the Holy Grail!"

" 'Twas a heartless prank," Ebenezer agreed, "but not alone for Bill-o'-the-Goose! 'Tis poor Meg Bromly I fear for."

"Let's get on with't," their host suggested. "I've heard what I've heard, but there's many a change been rung on the tale of Billy Rumbly these few days. Gets so a wight collects 'em, like tusk-shells on a string."

" 'Twas Roxie Russecks I heard it from," Mary said, "as honest a gossip as ever spread the news, and she had it from Sir Harry not five minutes after it happened. Henrietta heard the shot all the way from the mill and ran outside to see whence it came—for all Sir Harry wallops her just for showing her face at the window. But when she saw folks running to her father's tavern-shop she had perforce to fetch her mother to get the news, and the Indian was gone in a trail o' blood when Roxie got there . . ."

"The shot!" Ebenezer broke in. "Did you say Miss Bromly shot him?"

Mary raised a fat forefinger. "I said the poor salvage was wounded and gone, with his own sweet blood to mark his path: that's all I said."

"But who else——"

"When Roxie got to the tavern," she pressed on, "there was blood on the ground, blood on the gallery, blood all over the floor. The men were fair sobered, ye may wager, but too shamed to look her in the eye; as for Harry, that was braying like a jackass at his prank, she could get no sense from him at all. 'I'Christ, i'Christ!' was all he'd say. 'Did ye see the fool a-hopping and a-croaking like a new-gelt frog?' Then off he'd bray and say no more."

"Miss Bromly!" Ebenezer demanded. "I must know what happened to Miss Bromly! Was't she that shot the poor wretch?"

" 'Twas the Church Creek Virgin," Mary said tersely. "The truth is, she had reckoned from the first that if Sir Harry himself did not try for her maidenhead one day or another, he'd send some drunken lecher to try it for him; hence the pistol, always charged and ready to fire. 'Twas in her coat whene'er she set foot down the stairway, and while she slept, she kept it hid beneath her pallet, whence she could snatch it at the first step on the stairs. The trouble was, even a drunken salvage is still a salvage to the core; Billy Rumbly crept upstairs with no more noise than a Wiwash hunter stalking game, and the first she knew of her danger was when he laid his knife against her throat!"

McEvoy clucked his tongue. "How did she manage to fetch the pistol?"

"There's the rub of't." Mary smiled. "The walls were broached beyond defense, and naught was left to her but to open the gates, surrender the castle, and take vengeance against the invader whilst he plundered."

"Ah God!" cried Ebenezer. "D'you mean the poor girl lost her honor after all?"

"Not yet, though every man thought so, as I did when I heard the tale from Roxie, and wondered how Billy Rumbly was not unstarched by the rum. But ye forget, Mr. Cooke, what we know now: he is Mattassin's brother, and by your own statement shares my Charley's one defect: he carries his manhood not under breeches but in his fancy, where rum is more a virtue than a burthen." Mary shivered again. "Nay, now I think on't, 'tis all in what ye mean by the word: no brother o' Charley's could ever take her in the usual way, and belike she hath her maidenhead yet; but I know well he was at her *honor* from the first instant, and since she was obliged to let him fetch her to the pallet, ye may be sure her precious *honor* was well tattered by the time she got there. Then, of course, she snatched out her pistol and aimed to murther him. Howbeit, her shot was low, from what I gather; it cut him inside the thigh and sent him packing like a wounded rabbit. E'en then Sir Harry couldn't end his wretched game: he must chase after poor Billy Rumbly all the way outside and hollow 'Ye wasn't man enough, damn ye, Bill! Try her again in a fortnight!' "

"But Miss Bromly . . ." said the poet.

"That's the end o' my tale," Mary said firmly, "till Harvey tells his part of't: when Roxie learned the nature of her husband's prank she flew upstairs to look after Miss Bromly and found her lying like a lass well-ravished upon the pallet, with the pistol still a-smoking in her hand. And for all her erstwhile lordly airs, she ran to Roxie like a child to its mother, weeping and a-hollowing enough for two, and declared that albeit she was virgin as ever, the salvage had taken a host of liberties with her person, insomuch that she was like to perish of shame. 'Tis not surprising Roxie disbelieved her—as did I when I heard of't anon—and said, 'Now, now, Miss Bromly, what's done is done, and feigning shan't undo it; thou'rt no virgin now, if in sooth ye were before, but I'm convinced thou'rt no trollop either. Come live with me and my daughter at the mill,' she said, 'and we'll teach ye how a woman can have sport at no cost whate'er to her purse, her pride, or her precious reputation.' "

"Ah, Mary," cautioned their host, who must have been reading her lips, "don't tell tales, now."

Mary replied that Mr. Cooke she knew to be a perfect gentleman, and since McEvoy knew none of the parties involved, she saw no harm in quoting Mrs. Russecks's speech. "Ye know full well she's *my* dearest friend as well as yours, Harvey, and I love Henrietta like a daughter. These gentlemen have heard already what a beast Sir Harry is; 'twere as well they knew this much more to go with't—that Roxie and Henrietta have the spirit and wit to pull the wool o'er the great swine's eyes at every turn."

The trapper was still not entirely pacified, but Ebenezer, though the mixed metaphor made him wince, acknowledged the unknown women's right to their peccadilloes, in order to bring Mary back to her story.

"Aye, Miss Bromly," Mary sighed, "that Roxie tells me I might persuade now to learn my trade."

Ebenezer could not restrain his bitterness. "Is that your notion of a grand and charitable woman, that takes a poor girl in to make a whore of her? Unhappy Miss Bromly! Methinks your Mrs. Russecks is no better than her husband!"

"Gently, gently, Mr. Cooke," Mary said calmly. "Ye forget 'tis not to Sir Harry's mill I'm bound to fetch her, but to the house of her English husband, Mr. Rumbly . . ."

"I'God!"

"Let me finish, now. The girl was that distracted by her rape, or whate'er ye choose to call it, she commenced to gibber like a bedlamite. Her name was not *Meg Bromly* at all, she declared, but *Anna Cooke o' Cooke's Point,* the sister o' the Laureate Poet, and the salvage that attacked her was no salvage at all, but her childhood tutor——"

"Marry, I see it!" cried the poet. "She hath been Anna's friend and mine since we were children in Plumtree Street; some business hath brought her to Maryland, and she had planned to call on me at Malden until she heard of my disgrace and Father's wrath. Aye, 'tis clear! She durst not go near the infamous place, but took lodgings in Church Creek while she made enquiries about me. I'faith, another lost soul upon my conscience! Poor, poor Miss Bromly; how Anna would fly to aid you if she knew!"

As a matter of fact, Ebenezer's feelings were mixed: he was unspeakably relieved to think that the Church Creek Virgin had not been his sister, but distressed at the same time, not only because it had been his sister's friend but also because this fact rendered Anna lost as ever. Now he blanched, for a new thought struck him.

"Nay, 'tis worse yet! Why would Miss Bromly be in Maryland at all, if not as Anna's companion? Aye, 'sheart, they traveled together—what could be more likely?—and when they heard how things fared at Malden, or when my father caught up with Anna and made her stay with him, Miss Bromly took it upon herself to seek me out. That's it, I'm certain: either Joan Toast made no mention of me, or they disbelieved her! 'Sheart, 'sheart, miserable girl! How many more will be brought low on my account? And now, whether 'tis that she seeks pity by desperate subterfuge or that the shock of rape hath deranged her, she calls herself by her best friend's name, and thinks 'tis Henry Burlingame hath undone her!"

" 'Tis a fact she sometimes calls her husband *Henry,*" Mary allowed. "Roxie said as much."

"Stay, now," McEvoy said. "Ye left the wench in her loftroom, a-babbling to the Russecks woman, and now she's wife to the wight that leaped her, and that she pistoled! Ye've o'erskipped some piece o' the tale, lass, have ye not?"

"That I have, sir," Mary nodded, "for 'tis Harvey's to tell. When the girl had done a-gibbering she fell a-swoon in Roxie's arms and was fetched senseless to Henrietta's chamber in the millhouse. For three days Roxie nursed her like an ailing child, and on the fourth she disappeared. No man hath laid eyes on her from that day to this save Harvey here . . ."

648

11

*The Tale of Billy Rumbly Is Concluded by
an Eye-Witness to His Englishing. Mary
Mungummory Poses the Question, Does
Essential Savagery Lurk Beneath the Skin of
Civilization, or Does Essential Civilization
Lurk Beneath the Skin of Savagery?—but
Does Not Answer It*

MARY FINISHED SPEAKING and looked expectantly at Harvey
Russecks, as did Ebenezer and John McEvoy. But because
her last remark had been delivered in a voice lower than that
with which she had told the story and had been directed specifically to McEvoy, the trapper missed it and smiled vacantly
back at them.

"Tell 'em, Harvey," she prompted. "What happened whilst
the Church Creek Virgin was a-swoon at Roxie's, and the rest
of it?"

"Aye, that's true," Harvey laughed, not yet conceiving exactly what she said. Ebenezer concluded that the older man's
mind must have been wandering, for he had caught up the
earlier remark about Mrs. Russecks at once. " 'Twas when I
went out on the trap line in the morning—ice all over the
marsh, don't ye know, and muskrats frozen in the snares—I
spied a campfire down the line and walked over to't to thaw
my finger-joints; there lay this salvage with the bloody
breeches, his head all shaved and his body cold as death.
'Twas my first thought he was dead, and another two hours
had proved me right; but I felt some life in his veins beat yet
and resolved to fetch him here and do what I could for him.
The wound I found no great matter, for all the blood; I
washed and bound it, and forced some hot broth on the fellow directly he could open his mouth. B'm'faith, what a stout
wretch he proved! As nigh as the very latch-string to death's

649

doorway, and an hour later he had his senses again, if not his strength. When I'd won his trust he told me his tale as best he grasped it, and inasmuch as I'd heard o' the Church Creek Virgin and knew my brother's humor besides, it wanted small philosophy to guess the rest.

"I told him he'd been the butt of a low prank (the which he saw plainly when I explained it) and offered to ask for the five pounds sterling Harry had robbed him of; he thanked me kindly, in the plainest English I e'er heard salvage speak, and declared the whole of't was mine for rescuing him, if I could get it. Now ye dare not refuse a salvage's gift, lest he think thou'rt insulting him, and so I declared I'd take two shillings for my trouble and deliver the rest to him. All the while we spoke he had been casting his eyes about the room, and anon he asked me, Would I sell him my house? and Would five pounds purchase it? I replied 'twas not worth it by half, but I'd no mind to sell, and as he showed such eagerness to live in an English cabin I told him of an old one I owned near Tobacco Stick Bay, not far from Church Creek, that was falling to ruin for lack o' tenants, and declared he could live in't without rent if he'd trouble himself to repair it. Ye might think that an odd piece o' charity on such short acquaintance, but this half-breed had an air about him—I've not the words for't, sirs. 'Twas as if . . . d'ye know those stories o' kings and princes that prowl the streets in Scotch cloth? Or Old Nick posing as a mortal man to bargain for souls? He was uncommon quick in his mind, was this salvage, and gave me to feel that had he been reared English from the cradle he'd have been another Cromwell, or what ye will. 'Tis no mystery to me Miss Bromly took him for her tutor in disguise; with a fortnight's practice he could pass for a don of Oxford, I am sure of't, and two years hence for a sunburnt Aristotle! There's many a man I have no use for, gentlemen, and it struck me from the first this salvage would play me false if need be, to gain his ends; but he had that power of attraction —how doth a man speak of it? Will-ye, nill-ye, ye felt that if his purpose and yours weren't one, ye had your own short-sightedness to blame for't, and if he sold ye short, 'twas that your stuff was the stuff o' pawns and not o' heroes. To this hour he hath done me no injury, but that day I was driven to forgive him in advance, in my heart, for aught he might do me!"

"Ah," Ebenezer said.

"In any case, he slept here that night, and next morning I found him gone. My first thought was, he had set out to revenge himself on my brother——" The trapper blushed, but his eyes narrowed. "God forgive me or not, as't please Him: I made no move to warn Harry of his danger, but went out to my line o' traps as usual. There was a frost that morning, I remember, and over by Raccoon Creek, on a stretch o' high ground betwixt the fresh marsh and the salt, I commenced to see bear tracks along the path, and even a bear stool so fresh 'twas not e'en froze, but lay a-steaming in the path. Not long after, near the end o' the line, I saw moccasin-prints with the bear tracks, and inasmuch as they were not half an hour old, I took the trouble to follow 'em out.

"Anon the trail led me to a little stand o' hardwoods, and I could hear Mr. Bear a-grumbling up ahead. I had no weapon on me save my skinning-knife, and so I crept toward the sound as quiet as I could manage. 'Twas no great trick to find him, he was growling so; I came on a little clearing and there he was, a fat black rascal that hadn't bedded down for the winter. He was a male, not quite full-grown—on his hind legs he would've stood as high as your shoulder—and he was worrying a rotten piece o' log to get the grubs on't. I'd just commenced to wonder where the salvage had got to, when a hand came down on my shoulder, and there stood Billy Rumbly himself, looking wise and cheerful as ye please. He led me farther down wind and out of earshot and told me he meant to kill the bear unless I laid a claim on't.

"'Why, Billy,' says I, ''tis not likely I'll take on a bear with a skinning-knife so long as I'm sober, and I'd urge no fellow man to try such tricks.' For I saw he had no weapons on him save his two hands. But he only smiled and declared he'd show me a trick he'd learnt from some western salvages, that were said to use it as a test o' courage when two men quarreled o'er some squaw's favors. I judged 'twould be worth the watching, nor was I mistaken—nay, i'Christ, 'twas the oddest piece o' hunting I'll behold in my life!

"The first thing he did was find two straight saplings, one no thicker than your thumb and the other twice as thick, and snapped 'em off low in a certain way so that the break was a hand's-breadth long. I offered him my knife to point 'em, but he declared 'twas a breach o' the rules to use a knife or any weapon thrown from the hands, and made the best of't by peeling back splinters from the break. One sapling he made a rough spear from by stripping off the branches, and the other he broke off short for a kind of dagger; then we crept to the clearing, where Mr. Bear was scratching his back against a tree, and for all the frost had scarce commenced to melt,

Billy fetched off all his clothes, picked up his sticks, and stepped into the clearing dressed in naught but the rag-strip bandage on his thigh."

Ebenezer observed that Mary had set her jaw and closed her eyes.

"The bear left off scratching and watched him make some salvage sort o' prayer. But when Billy moved toward him he ambled off round the edge of the clearing. Billy set out at a run, hollowing some gibberish or other, but instead o' turning on him or running down the path, the bear made for a stout young oak near the middle o' the clearing and commenced to climb. I stepped out and called 'Bad luck, Billy,' for I never doubted the chase was done; but the bear was scarce off the ground ere Billy was climbing after him, pole in hand and dagger 'twixt his teeth, and never a care how the rough bark flayed him as he climbed! At the first branches, twice your height, the bear stopped to look down, and grumbled and waved his forepaw. Billy shinnied up close and poked as best as he could without a proper purchase, but he got no more than a growl for his pains. I offered to fetch him a longer pole, and learned 'twas a breach o' his murtherous rules to take help from any wight soever or change weapons once ye've touched the bear—I'll own I felt then, and feel yet, he was hatching these customs as he went along, but he followed 'em like Holy Orders.

"In lieu of changing weapons, he changed his plan o' battle and commenced to jab at the bear's face, taking care the brute didn't catch the pole in his teeth or strike it out o' his hand. I guessed 'twas his object to drive the bear farther up the trunk and gain the branches for himself, where he could do more damage with his spear, but instead the animal moved around the trunk to protect his face, and hung his great hindquarters over Billy's head. Yet so far from giving o'er the bout or scrambling away, Billy seemed as pleased as if 'twas just what he'd designed: he gave a whoop and thrust his pole as far as ever, where I need not mention! The bear gave a squeal and tried to get at the spear with his forepaws, but Billy thrust deeper; he climbed a little distance up the trunk and was undone the more by slipping back, and at length he fell, with such a hollowing as ye never heard. In that same instant Billy was on him; he drove the short stake in his throat and sprang away ere I myself had grasped the fact that the bear was down.

"By the time I found a tree o' my own to hide behind, the bear was on his feet and thrashing after the pole, that stuck out behind. All the while, Billy stood empty-handed in plain view, not three yards off, and goaded the bear to attack him; when he did, Billy led him five times round the oak tree, and the poor brute fell down dead."

"Marry!" said McEvoy. " 'Tis as brave a trick as I've heard of!"

"And as gory," Ebenezer added, speaking loudly for the trapper's benefit. " 'Tis a wondrous tale, Mr. Russecks, and yet—you must pardon my rudeness—I cannot but wonder what this feat hath to do with my poor friend Miss Bromly."

"Nay, friend, there's naught to pardon," Harvey replied. "I wondered the same myself, the while I watched, why it was he had set out half mended to match his strength with a bear's, when all the evening past he had talked o' naught save the laws and customs o' the English. He had been that eager and quick a scholar, ye'd have thought he was training for a place in Court—but look at him now, astride o' his kill to drink the hot blood ere the beast's fair dead! The very type and essence of the salvage!

"But I had not long to wonder. When Billy had drunk his fill he went to the creek and washed his body from top to toe, for the tree-bark had cut him as raw as a keelhauled sailor, and he was dirty and a-sweat besides. E'en now the rules he'd set himself were in force; he would have none o' my skinning-knife, but commenced to flay the carcass with an oyster-shell from the creek, and albeit he allowed me to make a fire, he stayed naked as Adam till his work was done. 'Twere a half-day's labor to flay out such a beast with a wretched shell, and I feared he'd catch his death ere the chore was done; but he made me a gift o' both hide and meat, declaring he craved nor the one nor the other, and flayed no more o' the carcass than was required to lay back a deal o' fat. This he gouged by the gobbet onto a foot-square piece o' the pelt, the which he had reserved for himself, and then skewered o'er the fire till it commenced to render. His object, I saw, was to lard himself with bear-grease from heel to hair, as is the wont of salvages from time to time, and as he worked I began to fear that betwixt this bear-hunt and the happenings of the day before, there was a certain dark connection. Nor was I wide o' the mark, for when he was greased as a griskin and reeking like Old Ned's lamp, he gorged himself on the balance o' the fat and then took up his oystershell and gelded the bear——"

Ebenezer and McEvoy expressed their bewilderment, but Mary, who had been so withdrawn throughout that one wondered whether she was entranced or asleep, now opened her eyes and sighed a knowing, compassionate sigh. " 'Twas what I expected, and less than I hoped for, Harvey. And Roxie is mistaken—'twere a waste o' time for me to see her, don't ye think? Ah well, in any case the story's clear."

"Haply 'tis clear to you," complained the poet, "but I grasp naught of 't."

" 'Tis no deep mystery," the trapper declared. "What the bull hath always signed to civil folk, the male bear signifies to the salvage Indian. But not only do they look on him as the emblem o' virility; they hold farther that his carcass is great medicine in matters o' love. Hence the manner of his killing, that Billy had explained before, and hence that larding with his hibernation-fat, the which they say feeds the fires o' love as it warms the bear in winter months. As for the other, 'tis widely believed in the salvage nations that if a man lay hold of a buck-bear's privates, bind 'em up in a pouch o' the un-cured pelt, and belt 'em so with a bearhide thong that they hang before his own, then his potency will be multiplied by the bear's, and Heav'n help the first poor wench that crosses his path! I asked him, 'Is't the Church Creek girl thou'rt bound for?' And albeit he would not answer me directly, he smiled a dev'lish smile and said 'twould please him if I'd pay him a call some day or two hence, when he and Mrs. Rumbly had found my cabin on Tobacco Stick Bay and set up house-keeping! By's speech ye'd take him for a merry English gen-tleman; yet there he stood like the living spirit o' salvage lust! Much as I feared for the poor girl's honor, I pled with Billy Rumbly to move with caution, inasmuch as I supposed she'd be on her guard to shoot him dead. But he said, 'No English pistol e'er killed a bear,' and went his way."

"Now 'tis plain," McEvoy said. "He carried her off and keeps her hid in the cabin ye spoke of! How is't the sheriff hath made no move to find her?"

" 'Tis also plain thou'rt innocent of provincial justice," Ebe-nezer put in bitterly. "Only the virtuous run afoul of Mary-land law."

"Nay, now, ye put your case too strongly," said the trap-per. "Our courts are sound as England's in principle; but 'tis a wild and lawless bailiwick they deal with—frauds and pi-rates and whores and adventurers, jailbirds and the spawn of jailbirds. I don't wonder the courts go wrong, or a judge or two sells justice o'er the bar; at least the judges and courts are there, and we'll make their judgments honest when we've the power to make 'em stick—which is to say, when the spirit o' the folk at large is curbed and snaffled."

Ebenezer's cheeks tingled, not alone because he felt that he had in fact overstated his indictment: his day in the Cambridge court still rankled in his memory, and the price of it drew sweat from all his pores; but his wholesale rancor had got to be something of a disposition, and he had been alarmed to recognize, as the trapper spoke, that he fell into it of late, on mention of certain subjects, more from habit than from honest wrath. So grossly had Maryland used him, he had vowed to smirch her name in verse to his children's children's children; could such outrages dwindle to the like of actors' cues? It was by no progress of reason that he reached this question, but by a kind of insight that glowed in his mind as the blush glowed in his face. By its troubled light, in no more time than was required for him to murmur, "I daresay" to Harvey Russecks, he beheld the homeless ghosts of a thousand joys and sorrows meant to live in the public heart till the end of time: feast days, fast days, monuments and rites, all dedicated to glories and disasters of a magnitude that dwarfed his own, and all forgotten, or rotely observed by a gentry numb to the emotions that established them. A disquieting vision, and no less so to the poet was his response to it. Not long since, he would have gnashed his spiritual teeth at the futility of endeavor in such a world. Not improbably he would have railed at human fickleness in allegorical couplets: the Heart, he would have declared, is a faithless Widow: at the deathbed of her noble Spouse (whether Triumph or Tragedy) she pledges herself forever to his memory, but scarcely has she donned her Weeds before some importuning Problem has his way with her; and in the years that follow, for all her ceremonious visits to the tomb, she shares her bed with a parade of mean Vicissitudes, not one of them worthy even of her notice. Now, however, though such fickleness still stung his sensibilities (which is to say his vanity, since he identified himself with the late Husband), he was not sure but what it had about it a double rightness: "Time *passes* for the living," it seemed to say, "and alters things. Only for the dead do circumstances never change." And this observation implied a judgment on the past, its relation to and importance in the present; a judgment to which he currently half assented. But only half!

The trapper resumed. " 'Twas just a few days later I saw Billy again, coming out of Trinity Church—aye, I swear't, just a Sunday since! He was knee-hosed and periwigged like any gentleman, not a trace o' bear-grease on him, and for all some folk misdoubted what to make of him, the rector and he

655

shook hands at the door and spoke their little pleasantries cordial as ye please! When I drew nigh I heard him chatting with a brace- o' sot-weed planters in better English periods than ye'll hear in the Governor's Council. His companions were two of the same that had tricked him before, but ye'd ne'er have guessed it from their manner: the one was inviting him to join the church, and the other was arguing with him about next year's sot-weed market.

" 'This here's Mr. Rumbly,' they said to me, 'as decent a Christian gentleman as ever shat on sot-weed.' At sight o' me Billy smiled and bowed, and said, 'I've already had the honor, thankee, gentlemen: Mr. Russecks was generous enough to lend me one of his cabins against the day I raise a house of my own.' We twain shook hands most warmly, and, do ye know, I was the envy of no fewer than half a dozen souls round about, so jealous were they grown already of his favor! Billy declared he had a call or two to pay, after which he wished I'd take dinner at his cabin, and when he'd strolled off, his courtiers gathered round me like fops round a new-dubbed knight. From them I learned that the Church Creek Virgin had set out one day from Roxanne's house and disappeared, nor was heard from after till the day Billy Rumbly came to town, dressed in English clothes, and declared she was his bride. Some said he had made a prisoner of her, and told stories of seeing him torture her over the hearth fire, but others that had spied on him declared she could leave the cabin when she pleased and stayed with him of her own will. To them that took the liberty of calling for a proper Christian wedding, he replied that naught would please him more, but his wife was content with the Indian ceremony he'd performed himself and would have no other, nor would he oblige her against her will.

"In any case, albeit 'twas but a short time since that first appearance, and there was still some talk against him here and there, Billy seemed to have won the heart of every woman in Church Creek and the respect of nearly all the men. He hath great plans for improving everything from the sot-weed market to the penal code, as I hear't, and albeit no man would speak out and say't—me being a Russecks, ye know—'twas clear they looked to Billy to stand up to my brother Harry soon or late. They have changed allegiance well-nigh to a man; Billy's too strong and full o' plans, and Sir Harry too jealous of his power, for the twain not to come to grips. What's more, rumor hath it 'twas Harry drove Miss Bromly to run off, from trying to have his way with her, and everyone reasoned Billy would have satisfaction of the wretch when the right time came.

"On our way to the cabin—I forgot to tell ye I was the first wight he'd invited into his house and was envied the more for't—on the way out there I told Billy frankly what I'd heard of him and asked him to sort out fact from fancy, but he was so full of his own questions about everything under the sun, he made me no proper answer. Why could not the tobacco-planters form a guild, he wanted to know, to bargain with the Lords Commissioners of Trade and Plantations? Who was Palestrina, and did I think a man of forty was too old to learn the harpischord? Why did Copernicus suppose the sun stood still, when it and its planets might be moving together through space? If a Christian ascetic comes to take pleasure in mortifying the appetites, must he not gratify them to mortify them, and mortify them to gratify them, and did this not fetch him to a standstill?"

Mary Mungummory shook her head. "So like my Charley, rest his soul! Had the De'il's own packsack o' questions, and no man's answers pleased him!"

Ebenezer pressed the trapper for tidings of Miss Bromly. " 'Tis e'er the lot of the innocent in the world, to fly to the wolf for succor from the lion! Innocence is like youth," he declared sadly, "which is given us only to expend and takes its very meaning from its loss."

" 'Tis that makes it precious, is't not?" asked McEvoy with a smile.

"Nay," Mary countered, " 'tis that proves its vanity, to my way o' thinking."

" 'Tis beyond me what it proves," Ebenezer said. "I know only that the case is so."

Russecks then went on to say that he had found the cabin (which already he had ceased to think of as his own) in excellent repair, its windows newly equipped with real glass panes and the grounds around it clear of brush. In the dooryard stood a recently constructed sundial, perhaps the only one in the area, and atop one gable was a platform used by its builder for readier observation of the stars and planets.

"He'd mentioned along the way that he'd shot a young buck the night before and was waiting till Monday, like a proper Christian, to butcher it, but when we rode around the cabin I spied a salvage woman up to her elbows in the bloody carcass, cleaving off steaks and rump-roasts. She was dressed in dirty deerskin like the old *squaws* wear; her hair was coarse and tangled, and her brown skin greasy as a bacon-flitch. Her back was turned to us as we rode in, and she paid us no heed at all. 'Twas on my mind to twit Billy for her industry—tell him 'twas a merry bit o' Jesuitry, don't ye know, setting heathens to break the Sabbath for him—but ere ever I got the words out he addressed her in the salvage tongue, and I saw when she faced round 'twas no Indian woman at all. I could only gather, she was the famous Church Creek Virgin!"

Ebenezer and McEvoy registered their astonishment.

"I'faith, sirs," Russecks proceeded, "it doth give a civil man pause when first he lays eyes upon a salvage, for't carries him back to view the low origin of his history: yet by how much rarer is the spectacle of one of his kind fallen back to the salvage condition, by so much more confounding is't to behold, for it must drive home to him how strait and treacherous is the climb to politeness and refinement—so much so, that one breath of inattention, as't were, may send the climber a-plummet to his former state. And in the civillest among us, don't ye know—in Mister Cooke the poet there, or who ye will—this precious cultivation—'sheart, sirs, on sight of one like Billy Rumbly's wife . . . !" He paused and started over. "What I mean, sirs, 'tis like the cultivation of our fields, so't seems to me: 'tis all order and purpose—and wondrous fruits doth it bring forth!—yet 'tis but a scratch, is't not, on the face of unplumbable deeps? Two turns o' the spade cuts through't to the untouched earth, and under that lies a thousand miles o' changeless rock, and deeper yet lie the raging fires at the core o' the world!

"The sensible man, I say, is bound to reflect on these things when he sees one of his own gone salvage like the Church Creek Virgin. She was dressed in Indian garb, as I said before, and pig-dirty from head to foot. She'd browned her skin with dye, so't appeared, and basted it with bear-fat, which with the dirt and deer-blood gave her a splendid salvage stink, e'en in the cold out-o'-doors. Never a glance did she cast to me, but stared always at Billy like a good retriever, and at his command she gave o'er hacking the buck and plodded off with two steaks to broil for dinner."

The interior of the cabin, Russecks went on to say, he had found as clean as the housekeeper was not, who in the heat from the fireplace grew redolent as a tan yard; throughout the afternoon, when dinner was done, she had sat stolidly on the hearthrug, Indian fashion, grinding meal in an earthenware mortar, and had spoken only in grunts and monosyllables when Billy addressed her. Yet though her manner and condition were slavelike, at no time had the trapper observed anything suggestive of coercion or intimidation.

"In sum," he said, "she was an English lass no longer, but a simple salvage *squaw*. 'Tis my guess he sought her out in his bear-grease and magical loin-pouch and did such deeds o' salvage love and ravishment that she gave o'er the reins of her mind for good and all."

"Thou'rt off the mark," Mary said flatly. " 'Tis that he made such a conquest with his amorous lore, the girl renounced her Englishness on the spot for ever and aye. I *know* 'tis thus."

"Ah, but I loathe the monster nonetheless!" Ebenezer said. "E'en granting our innocence was given us to lose, still and all—any, rather *therefore*—its whole meaning is in the terms of its surrender, is't not? To have it wrested will-ye, nill-ye, ravished away——" He tried to envision the struggle: he fancied himself in the position of Miss Bromly, forced upon her back among the cold briars of the forest; the knife was at his neck, his coats were flung high, the wind bit his thighs and private parts; and over him, naked and greased, hung a swart, ferocious savage with the face and herpetonic eyes of Henry Burlingame. "God damn him for't! How the wretch must gloat in his victory!"

"How's that?" Russecks showed some surprise. "Gloat, ye say? Ah, well, now, he didn't gloat, ye know. Nay, friend, ye forget Billy Rumbly hath climbed a far greater distance than the lass hath sunk; aye, e'en higher by far than the station she left, I'll wager! Such a civil, proper gentleman as he could ne'er take pleasure in such a victory; yet 'twas the conquest, as I see't, that raised him up. The fact is, sirs, his wife is a constant shame to him: he entreats her to clean herself and dress like an English lady; he yearns to join the Church and have a Christian wedding; naught would please him more than to set sail tonight for Rome, or an English university. But she will none of't; she wallows in her filth and salvage ways, and poor Billy is too much the man of honor now either to desert her or to force her against her will!"

Mary Mungummory shook her head. "How well I know her heart and his as well! I wonder again what I wonder nightly as I watch the circus in my wagon: is man a salvage at heart, skinned o'er with Manners? Or is salvagery but a faint taint in the natural man's gentility, which erupts now and again like pimples on an angel's arse?"

For Ebenezer, at least, absorbed in recollection of certain

violences in his past, the question was by no means without pertinence and interest; neither he nor the other men, however, ventured a response.

12

The Travelers Having Proceeded
Northward to Church Creek, McEvoy
Out-Nobles a Nobleman, and the Poet
Finds Himself Knighted Willy-Nilly

SOON AFTER HARVEY RUSSECKS had concluded his story the company retired for the night on corn-husk mattresses provided by the host, which, with a plentiful supply of blankets from Mary's wagon, afforded Ebenezer and McEvoy the most comfortable night's lodging they had enjoyed for some time. The poet, however, was kept sleepless for hours by thoughts of Miss Bromly, his sister, the gravity of his mission, and the story he had just heard. Next morning as they breakfasted on platters of fried eggs and muskrat—a dish they found more pleasing to the tongue than to the eye—he declared, "I had cause enough before to find this Cohunkowprets, or Billy Rumbly, for he may be the means of sparing my conscience the burthen of two English lives; but now I've heard what state Miss Bromly hath fallen to, purely out of loyalty to my sister, 'tis more urgent than ever I seek the fellow out and try to save her. One ruined life the more on my account, and I'll go mad with responsibility!"

"Nay, friend," McEvoy urged, "I respect your sentiments, Heav'n knows, but think better of't! Thou'rt bound to save our hostages from Chicamec at any cost to yourself, so ye declared, and ye've shamed me into the same tomfoolish honor: d'ye think this Rumbly fellow's likely to oblige us if he sees thou'rt after wooing his wife away? And if he turns his back on us—i'faith!—'twill not be two, but two hundred thousand lives ye may answer for; with Dick Parker and that other wight to general 'em, not all the militia in America can put down the slaves and Indians!"

"I tremble to think of't," said Mary Mungummory from her station at the cook-fire. "Don't forget, Mr. Cooke, whate'er foul play brought the girl to her present pass, 'tis of her own will she stays there." Suddenly she gave an irritated sigh and called on an imaginary tribunal to witness the poet's wrongheadedness. "Marry, sirs, the world's about to explode, and he concerns himself with one poor slut's misfortunes!"

Ebenezer smiled. "Who's to say which end of the glass is the right to look through? One night when Burlingame and I were watching the stars from St. Giles in the Fields, I remarked that men's problems, like earth's mountains, amounted to naught from the aspect of eternity and the boundless heavens and Henry answered, 'Quite so, Eben: but down here where we live they are mountainous enough, and no mistake!' In any case, I mean to do what I can for Miss Bromly. I've no mind to prosecute Billy Rumbly for rape— 'twere a vain ambition in a Maryland court!—and he'll not object to my solicitude, if I have his case aright from Mr. Russecks."

It was still early when they bade the trapper good-bye and set out in Mary's wagon for Church Creek; though the journey took five hours, the sun was scarcely past the meridian when they arrived at the little settlement.

"Yonder's an inn," McEvoy said; he indicated a neat frame structure some distance ahead.

"Aye, there we'll go, like it or not," Mary said, " 'tis Sir Harry's place." She explained that Harry Russecks flew into a dangerous temper when visitors to the town failed to appear before him and state their business. "He knows mine well enough, and ye twain need say no more than that I'm ferrying ye to Cambridge on business for the Governor."

"I say, he is a high-handed rascal!" Ebenezer cried. "What right hath he to pry into everyone's affairs?"

"Ah, well," Mary replied, "for one thing, he can carry five hundred-weight o' grain upon his back, so they say, and break a man's neck as ye'd break a barleystraw. For another, he owns the inn, the mill over yonder on the creek, and half the planters hereabouts." The mill, she went on to say, like most in the Province, had been built originally at Lord Baltimore's order and financed in part with funds from the provincial treasury; hence the government maintained an interest in its operation. Harry Russecks was aware of this fact, but St. Mary's City being so far removed from Church Creek, and the Governor's Council having so many pressing problems to engage its attention and such feeble machinery of enforcement, he did not scruple to exploit his monopoly in every way. What with charging extortionate fees for grinding, and regularly purloining a capful of grain out of each bushel, he had early become a man of means; subsequently he had built the inn and taken to making loans on acreage collateral to the tobacco-planters in the area, so that, regardless of the market, he made large profits every year. If the tobacco price was good, his loans were repaid with interest, his milling fees went up, and his tavern was filled with celebrating planters; if the market fell, he increased his landholdings with forfeited collateral, ground grain as always for his neighbors' daily bread, and sold the planters rum to drown their sorrows in. It was not surprising, then, that he was presently the wealthiest man in the area and one of the wealthiest in the Province: such was the power of his position in Church Creek that he had secured to be his wife the only truly noble lady for miles around, by what arrangements the townsfolk could only conjecture; one and all were obliged to address him by his false title even as he robbed them at the mill, to leap clear whenever he brandished the sword which he affected, even at the grindstones, as an emblem of his rank, and in general to submit without protest to his poltroonery.

"Sir Harry respects naught in the world save patents o' nobility," she concluded, "nor fears any man in the Province —save a brace o' commissioners from St. Mary's, that some folk think have been dispatched to inspect the mills and ferries."

Drawing up before the inn they saw upon its sign a curious armorial device in bold colors: on a field *azure*, between flanches *sable* with annulets *or* (or roundlets square-pierced to look like millstones), a fleur-de-lis *gules* beset from alow and aloft by hard crabs armed *natural*. Their examination of it was cut short by a great commotion within the place it advertised: there was a crash of crockery, a woman shrieked, "Ow! Ow" a man's voice cried, and another roared out "I'll crack thy skull, John Hanker! *Arrah!* Hold still, dammee, whilst I fetch ye a good one!" From the door burst a young colonial, clutching his bare head in both hands and running for his life. At his heels pumped a shaggy bull of a man, black-haired, open-shirted, squint-eyed and mottled; in his right hand he waved a sword (no gentleman's rapier, but a Henry Morgan cutlass fit to quarter oxen with) and in his left he clutched by the arm a distraught young woman—the

662

same, they soon heard, whose shriek had announced the scene. Had his pursuer not been thus encumbered, the young man would have lost more than just his periwig; even with this handicap the wild-haired swordsman—whom Ebenezer understood to be the miller Russecks himself—came within an ace of adding homicide to the catalogue of his sins.

"Yah! Run, Hanker!" he bellowed, giving over his pursuit. "Come to Church Creek again, I grind ye to hogswill!"

" 'Twas only in sport, Father!" cried the girl. "Don't go on so!" Now that the crisis was past she seemed more embarrassed than alarmed.

" 'Sheart!" McEvoy murmured to Ebenezer. "There's a handsome lass!"

The miller turned on her. "I know thy sports! D'ye think I didn't see where he laid his drunken paw, and you smiling him farther? *All dogs pant after the salt bitch!* Dammee if I don't unsalt ye, and thy quean of a mother into the bargain!" With the flat of his cutlass he caught her a swat upon the rump.

"Aiee!" she protested. "Thou'rt a devil out o' Hell!"

"And thee a goose out o' Winchester!" Again he swung, and clapped her smartly along the leg. Ebenezer flushed, and McEvoy sprang to his feet as though ready to leap to the damsel's aid from his perch on the wagon seat. But though the girl protested loudly at her punishment, her complaints were anything but abject.

"Ow! I swear to Christ I'll murther ye in your sleep!"

"Not till I've done basting ye, ye shan't!"

The third blow was aimed where the first had struck, but by dint of wrenching about and biting the miller's wrist, the girl caught it on her hip and broke free as well.

"Hi! Now try and clout me, damn your eyes!" She did not run off at once, but lingered a moment to taunt him from a distance. "Look at him wave his sword, that he bought to beat helpless women with! A great ass is what he is!"

"And thee a whore!"

"And thee a cuckold! La, what a time we'll have, when Billy-Boy takes the scalp off ye!"

The miller roared and charged towards her, but the girl scampered off and led him in a circle around the wagon. When he gave up after a few moments, apparently resigned from past experience to her nimbleness, she halted as well, bright-eyed and panting. Her nostrils tightened; her chin dimpled with scorn. She spat in his direction.

"Buffoon!" With a toss of ash-blond curls she turned her

back on him and marched down the street towards the mill; her father sashed his weapon with a grunt and trudged after, but in the manner of a skulking bodyguard rather than that of an assailant.

"Henrietta Russecks," Mary chuckled. "Ain't she the lively one, though?"

But the men were appalled by the scene. It was some moments before Ebenezer could find voice for his indignation, and then he railed at length against the miller's spectacular ungallantry. McEvoy expressed even greater outrage, and added for good measure a panegyric on the young lady.

"Mother o' God, what spirit, Eben! How she gave the great bully as good as she got! Nor quailed for an instant! Nor shed a tear for his bloody bastinadoes! I here swear to Heav'n I'll see her free o' that beast, if I must murther him myself!"

Ebenezer showed some surprise at his companion's vehemence, and McEvoy blushed.

"Think what ye will," he grumbled, "and be damned t'ye! She hath the face o' Helen and the soul of Agamemnon, hath that girl! Fire and fancy, what Ben Oliver was wont to call the chiefest female virtues; oh, 'tis a rare, rare thing!"

"Best not toy with Henrietta," Mary warned cordially. "Ye saw what befell young Hanker yonder, for no more'n a pat. La, the rector o' Trinity Church himself couldn't court Sir Harry's daughter without a patent out o' peerage."

McEvoy sniffed and furrowed up in thought.

They decided to go directly to the mill, where, in addition to announcing their presence to Russecks, Mary could consult the miller's wife for further news of Billy Rumbly and his bride. On the way, for McEvoy's benefit, she chattered on about Henrietta: the girl was four-and-twenty and of the same lively temper as her mother, who had been a famous beauty in her youth and could still turn the head of any young man with an eye for pulchritude seasoned by experience. It was well past time for the daughter to be wed, but so jealous was the miller of the title he had appropriated from his wife, he would permit Henrietta no husband from among the youth of the place; he held out for a suitor of noble birth. And though with every passing year the task of chaperonage grew more difficult—especially since Mrs. Russecks, so far from sharing her husband's sympathies, not only allied herself with Henrietta in the cause of love but was prepared to join her daughter in any amorous adventure they could contrive.

"Yet for all their ingenuity and the wiles of a score of would-be lovers, Sir Harry hath managed to keep his eye on 'em day and night. When he's at the inn, they are his barmaids, more often than not; when he's at the mill, they are his grist-girls. They even sleep all in a room, with Sir Harry's cutlass hanging ready at the bedpost. Only once in all these years have the pair of 'em got free of him—and marry, 'twas a fortnight folk still talk about!"

When they were still a hundred feet from the mill—which from the look of it served also as the family house—Harry Russecks stepped outside and glared at them, arms akimbo. At the same time they saw in an upstairs window the figures of two women regarding them with interest. Mary Mungummory returned their wave, but Ebenezer shivered.

"And ye say he fears these mill commissioners like the plague?" McEvoy mused. Suddenly he laid his hand on Mary's arm. "I say, thou'rt a good sort, Mary; will ye aid me in a little lark? And you as well, Eben? I owe ye my life already; will ye stand me farther credit?" All he wished to do, he explained to his skeptical companions, was give the boorish miller a draught of his own prescription; if he failed, none would be the worse for it, and if he succeeded——

"I'Christ, but let's put it to the test!" he said hurriedly, for they were almost within earshot of the miller. "State thy own affairs as always, Mary, and say ye know no more of us than that ye picked us up along the road after the storm. Nay, more: ye suspect there is more to us than meets the eye, inasmuch as we've been uncommon secretive from the first, and chary o' stating our names and business."

" 'Twill ne'er succeed, lad," Mary warned, but her eyes twinkled already at prospect of a prank.

"Prithee, John," Ebenezer whispered, "we've no time for frivolous adventures! Think of Bertrand and Captain Cairn——"
He could protest no more for fear of being overheard, and McEvoy's expression was resolute. The Irishman's sudden interest in the miller's daughter struck him not only as a conventional impropriety and a breach of their solemn trust, but also as a sort of infidelity to Joan Toast, despite the fact that Joan had clearly abandoned McEvoy for himself, and that he himself had been unfaithful to her in a sense by far less honorable than the sexual. He held his peace and waited miserably to see what would develop.

"Afternoon, Sir Harry!" Mary called, and clambered down from the wagon. "Just passing through, and came to pay my respect to Roxie."

The miller ignored her. "Who are they?"

"Them?" Mary glanced back in surprise, as if just noticing her passengers. "Ah, *them* ye mean! They're two wights I found near Limbo Straits after the storm." In a voice just audible to the poet she added, "Said they had business in Church Creek, but they'd not say what. Is Roxie in?"

"Aye, but ye'll not see her," the miller declared, still glaring at the two men. "Thou'rt no fit company for a lady, e'en though she be a bitch o' perdition. Get on with ye!"

"Just as ye say." She waited as McEvoy climbed down, followed by Ebenezer. "If ye have any business farther north," she told them with a wink, " 'twould be no chore for me to ferry ye. I'll be yonder by the inn till tomorrow or next day."

"Most charitable of ye, madame," said McEvoy with a short bow. "And I thank ye for service both to ourselves and to His Majesty. 'Twill not be long till we reward ye more tangibly."

"Who are ye?" Russecks demanded. "What's your business in Church Creek?"

McEvoy turned, and so far from being intimidated, he surveyed the miller from head to toe with exaggerated suspicion.

"Speak up, dammee!"

Ebenezer saw the black beard commence to twitch in anger and was tempted to end the hoax before it was irrevocably launched, but before he could muster his courage McEvoy spoke.

"Did I hear this lady address you as *Sir Harry?*"

"Ye did, save ye be deaf as well as cock-proud."

McEvoy looked accusingly at Mary. "Is't some strange humor of thine, madame, or a prank betwixt the twain o' ye, to pretend this glowering oaf is Sir Harry Russecks?"

From above, where the ladies had opened the casement to listen, came a gasp and a titter; even staunch Mary was taken aback by the Irishman's daring.

"How?" shouted the miller. "Doth he say I'm not Sir Harry?" His hand flew to the hilt of his cutlass.

"Nay, Ben, don't draw!" McEvoy cried to Ebenezer, who trembled nearby. "What, ye left your short-sword in the wagon?" He threw back his head and laughed; everyone, the miller and his women included, stood dumfounded.

" 'Tis well for thee, little miller," McEvoy said grimly, and went so far as to tweak the fellow's beard. "My friend Sir Benjamin had pricked thy gizzard in a trice, as he hath pricked two hundred like ye in the service of His Majesty.

Now take us to Sir Harry, and no more impertinence, else I'll bid him flog the flour out o' thy hide."

"If ye please, sir," Mary broke in, plainly relishing the miller's discomfiture: "This *is* Sir Harry Russecks, on my life, sir, flour or no—yonder's his wife and daughter, sir, that will swear to't."

The ladies at the window merrily confirmed the fact, but McEvoy feigned some lingering doubt.

"If thou'rt Sir Harry Russecks, how is't thou'rt got up as a clownish laborer in the mill?"

"What's that ye say? Why, don't ye know, sirs——" He appealed to Mary for aid.

"Why, 'tis Sir Harry's little whim, sir," Mary declared. " 'Tis the mill first earned his bread, ere he married Mrs. Russecks, and he's not one to forget his humble birth, is good Sir Harry."

"Aye, aye, that's it; she hath hit the mark fair." For all his relief at the explanation, Russecks appeared not entirely happy with the reference to his birth. "Did ye—did I hear ye say thou'rt in the King's employ, sirs?"

"In a manner o' speaking, aye," McEvoy declared. "But I'd as well tell ye plainly at the outset, our commission went down with crew and pinnace in the storm, and till a new one comes from St. Mary's ye have the right to bar us from the premises an it please ye."

The miller's eyes widened. "Thou'rt Nicholson's commissioners?"

McEvoy refused either to affirm or deny the identification, declaring that until his authority was legal he thought the wisest course would be to speak no further of it.

"In any case," he said in a tone less stern, "'tis not alone on Nicholson's business I travel. My name's McEvoy—Trade and Plantations when I'm home in London—Sir Jonathan at Whitehall is my father."

"Ye don't tell me!" marveled the miller, not yet entirely free of suspicion. "I can't say I have the pleasure o' knowing a Sir Jonathan McEvoy at Whitehall."

"To our discredit, I'm sure." McEvoy made a slight bow. "But I shan't lose hope that Mrs. Russecks may redeem us by acquaintance with the name."

This thrust evoked another response from the upstairs window; when McEvoy raised his eyes to the ladies, Mrs. Russecks (who Ebenezer saw was indeed the full-blown beauty Mary claimed her to be) nodded archly, and smiling Henrietta made an eager curtsy.

McEvoy gestured towards Ebenezer. "This formidable fellow is my friend Sir Benjamin Oliver, that thanks to his wondrous eye and stout right arm is belike the youngest member o' the peerage. Ladies, I give ye Sir Benjamin: a lion on the battlefield and a lambkin in the drawing-room!"

Ebenezer blushed both at the imposture and the characterization, but bowed automatically to the ladies.

"The fact is," McEvoy went on, "Sir Benjamin's father is visiting the plantations on business of his own, and I'm showing my bashful friend here the countryside. Needless to say, he hath heard of Mrs. Russecks's family in England."

"Ye do not say!" The miller wiped his nose proudly with a forefinger. "Heard o' Mrs. Russecks's family in England! Oh Roxie, did ye hear what the gentleman said? Our family's the talk o' the English peerage! Come down here!"

Mrs. Russecks lost no time in greeting the visitors at the door.

"This here's my wife Roxanne," the miller said proudly. "The noblest damned lady on the Eastern Shore."

"Enchanté," McEvoy said, and to Ebenezer's horror, embraced the woman in a loverlike fashion and kissed her ardently.

"Out upon't!" cried the miller, drawing his sword. "I say, dammee, give o'er! What in thunder d'ye do there, 'pon my soul?"

McEvoy released his bewildered partner, feigning annoyance and surprise. "Whate'er is thy husband alarmed at, Madame? Can it be he's ignorant of the Whitehall Salute? Have ye not schooled him in the customs o' the court?"

Mrs. Russecks, still taken aback by the sudden embrace, managed to confess the possibility that she herself might be out of touch with the very latest fashions in behavior at Whitehall.

"I'll have his lewd head!" the miller threatened, raising the sword.

"My dear friend," McEvoy said, serene and patronizing, "at court 'tis the practice for every proper gentleman to embrace a lady thus on first meeting her; only a bumpkin or a cad would insult her with a sniveling bow." He went on to declare, before Russecks could object, that while he quite appreciated the difficulty provincial gentlemen must have in keeping up with London society, he considered it therefore of the first importance that they maintain an open mind and a humble willingness to be instructed.

"Now put away your sword, that no gentleman should

raise without cause, and be so kind as to present us to your daughter."

Russecks hesitated, clearly torn between his desire to keep up with the fashions of the court and his reluctance to deliver Henrietta into the visitors' embraces. But his wife took the matter out of his hands.

"Henrietta, bestir thyself!" she scolded through the doorway. "The gentlemen will think thou'rt uncivil!"

The girl appeared at once from behind the jamb, curtsied to both men, and prettily presented herself to McEvoy for her Whitehall Salute, which the Irishman executed with even more *élan* than before. At the same time Mrs. Russecks went up to Ebenezer and said, "We're *most* delighted to have the privilege, Sir Benjamin," so that he was obliged to do the same whether he would or no, and again with the eager-eyed, ash-blond daughter who came after, still flushed from McEvoy's kiss, while the miller looked on in helpless consternation.

Mary Mungummory beamed. "I'll just be yonder at the inn if there's aught ye should want o' me," she called.

"Then ye may stable your horse right now and pay me her day's keep in advance," Russecks said crossly.

Mary did as she was told and left, but not before Ebenezer observed an exchange of glances between her and Mrs. Russecks. At a moment when her husband was boasting to McEvoy that he collected a day's stabling charge on every horse brought into Church Creek for more than half a day, Mrs. Russecks had looked at Mary as if to ask, "Can it be that this brash young man has actually deceived my husband?" and further, "Do I dare believe his intentions are what they seem?" Mary's response had been a wink so large and lecherous as to set the poet tingling with apprehension.

13

*His Majesty's Provincial Wind- and
Water-Mill Commissioners, With Separate
Ends in View, Have Recourse on Separate
Occasions to Allegory*

McEvoy now expressed a desire to be shown the operation
of the mill, explaining that though Heaven knew he himself
had seen enough of them in the past several weeks, his friend
Sir Benjamin, who had been raised in London, might find the
device amusing.

"Aye, indeed so, young sirs," Russecks agreed. " 'Twill be
a pleasure to show ye! Roxanne, you and Henrietta begone,
now, whilst I take the gentlemen through my mill."

"Oh prithee, Father," Henrietta protested, " 'twill be a lark
for us to go with ye! We're not afraid to climb ladders with
the gentlemen, are we, Mother?"

"Nay, dammee!" cried the miller. "Get ye gone, ere I raise
a welt athwart thy——"

"Not another word," McEvoy said firmly. " 'Tis the mark
of a well-born lady to crave a bit of adventure now and again,
don't ye think? My arm, Miss Henrietta, an it please ye." The
girl took his arm at once, and Mrs. Russecks Ebenezer's, and
any further expostulations from the miller McEvoy prevented
by a series of pointed questions about the establishment.

"How is't a gentleman stoops to milling?" he wanted to
know as they entered the building.

"Ah, well, sir——" Russecks laughed uncomfortably.
" 'Tis as Mary said—Miss Mungummory yonder, what I
mean—ye might say I run it purely for the sport of't, don't
ye know. 'Tis beneath my station, I grant ye, but a man
wants something to fill his time, I always say."

"Hm."

Walking behind them, Ebenezer saw the Irishman reach
boldly around Henrietta's back with the arm opposite Russecks and give the girl a sportive poke in the ribs. He

blanched, but Mrs. Russecks, who saw the movement as plainly as had he, only squeezed his arm and smiled. As for Henrietta, she showed surprise but not a trace of indignation at the cavalier advance; when her escort repeated it—simultaneously asking the miller why, if his work was in the nature of an avocation, he charged such wondrously profitable fees for doing it—she was hard put to stifle her mirth. She caught his hand; he promptly and unabashedly scratched her palm, and Mrs. Russecks, instead of unleashing maternal wrath upon the seducer as the poet expected, sighed and dug her nails into the flexor of his arm.

"Stay," McEvoy said, cutting into the miller's explanation that what revenue came from the mill was turned to community improvements such as his inn and the tobacco storehouse he was constructing farther down the creek. "I've an urgent private question, if ye please."

With a mischievous expression he whispered loudly into Russecks's ear that he sorely needed to know whether the improvements of the place included a jakes, and if so, where a man might find it in a hurry.

"Why, marry, out in the back, sir," the astonished miller answered, "or thou'rt free to piss in the millrace, e'en as I do. What I mean——"

"Enough: ye quite overwhelm me with hospitality. I'll use your millrace and fore'er be in your debt. *Adieu*, all; on with the tour! I'll o'ertake ye presently."

Thus abruptly he left them, followed by the ladies' marveling eyes; when he returned a few minutes later he clapped Russecks on the back, called him a poet and philosopher for having hit on that wondrous virtue in a millrace, and with the other hand treated Henrietta to a surreptitious carnival of tweaks, pats, pokes, and pinches, so that she seemed ever on the verge of swooning from mirth, titillation, and the effort it required to betray nothing to her father.

"Isn't he the bold one?" Mrs. Russecks whispered to Ebenezer. The poet was mortified to observe the lady's respiration quicken, and guessed she envied her daughter's having drawn the more adventurous partner. But for all his desire to question Mrs. Russecks closely on the matter of Miss Bromly, he had no taste for adulterous flirtation, nor would have even had the circumstances been less perilous and less remote from their pressing business with Billy Rumbly. His body stiffened, and when Mrs. Russecks, aping Henrietta's behavior with McEvoy, slipped a playful hand into his breeches pocket as they moved single file along a catwalk near the grain hopper, his blood ran cold. He was immensely relieved when they came out at the rear of the mill, facing the stable.

"There now, sirs," Harry Russecks said, "ye'll agree there's not a better-kept mill in the Province, will ye not, nor a better run?"

"As to the first, ye may not be far wide o' the mark," McEvoy allowed. "As to the second—but stay, I vowed I'd have none o' business till my papers reach me. I will say, 'twas fine sport to poke about in there; I have toured many a Maryland mill, but none so pleasurably."

The miller spat proudly. "D'ye hear that, Roxie? Ha'n't I always held 'twas no disgrace for a gentleman to know his way around a mill?"

McEvoy went on, turning his eyes brazenly to Henrietta. "I was taken in particular by a handsome hopper I spied whilst we were climbing to the loft. From what I could see, 'twas scarce broke in."

Ebenezer's heart sank, and even Henrietta blushed at the figure, but the miller seemed not to grasp it, for he cried, "Now there's a sharp-eyed fellow, 'pon my word! I made that hopper myself, sir, not long since, and I'm passing proud of't. 'Tis a pity ye didn't just run a hand in, to get the beauty of the lap-joints."

"A pity in sooth," McEvoy agreed. "Ye may bank on't I'll not miss the chance again."

Emboldened by the possibilities of the metaphor, Henrietta insisted that no mere stroke of the hand could disclose the real excellence of the device, which lay in the way it performed its intended function; only by running his own grist through would Mr. McEvoy ever truly appreciate it. The Irishman joyfully replied that nothing would please him more, although he'd heard complaints from local planters about the fee.

"They're liars, all!" cried Russecks. "Let 'em try to find the likes o' that machinery in the county ere they grouse and tattle!"

Here Mrs. Russecks joined the conversation in support of her husband. "That little hopper's not the only marvel o' the place. Haply you were too distracted to remark them, Mr. McEvoy, but the millstones themselves are most unusual."

"Aye, that's a fact, sir," Russecks said eagerly. "Ye might have seen 'em plainly from the ladderway. They've been in daily use for near two-score years, have those millstones, and they're better every year."

Mrs. Russecks declared that Sir Benjamin had been better

situated than Mr. McEvoy to view these marvels, and added that their ever-increasing excellence only demonstrated the truth of an axiom in the trade: *The older the millstones, the finer the grind.*

"To be sure," Henrietta put in tartly, "it wants an uncommon shaft to fit such stones; the one Father's using is nigh worn out."

Ebenezer set his teeth. He looked about for a means of ending the *double-entendre*, and noticed that the stall where Mary had put Aphrodite was empty.

"I say, Miss Mungummory's mare is gone; can it be she drove on without us?"

"Nay, she'd never leave so soon," Mrs. Russecks said. "We'd not had time to talk yet."

The miller declared there was nothing to be concerned about, but McEvoy insisted on seeking out Mary at the inn to make certain the mare had not strayed. Very soon he returned with Mary in tow, making a great show of anger and alarm.

"Really, Sir Harry!" he cried. "Is't your practice to let folks' horses wander loose, after you've extorted your gouging fee from 'em?"

For a moment the miller forgot his role: his face darkened, and his hand went to his sword. "Gently there, young pup, or I'll soon——"

"Where is that horse, sir?" McEvoy pressed. "Sir Benjamin and I owe this lady our lives for bringing us out o' the marsh in her wagon, as I've already apprised Governor Nicholson. D'ye think we'll stand by and see her lose her mare from your negligence?"

"Ah, my poor Aphrodite!" Mary lamented.

"*My* negligence!" the miller shouted.

"Aye, thine, as proprietor of the stables. Draw your sword, fellow, if ye dare! 'Twill be no cowering planter ye face, but one o' King William's deadliest."

"Nay, go to, gentlemen, go to!" the miller pleaded. "D'ye think I turned the mare loose a-purpose? Ye were in plain sight o' me all the while!"

Ebenezer suddenly understood what had happened, and his heart sank.

"I made no such charge," McEvoy said. "Nonetheless, thou'rt answerable for the horse. A true gentleman would ne'er permit the thing to happen, much less weasel out of 't. Am I right, Mrs. Russecks?"

Though she seemed not quite to understand the Irishman's

motives, Mrs. Russecks agreed that caring for the property of his guests is a first concern of the proper gentleman. For a moment Russecks seemed about to strike her.

"Dammee, sirs, nobody's more a gentleman than I am! I'm the biggest bloody gentleman in Church Creek!"

"Then find Aphrodite," McEvoy snapped, "or ye'll answer to the Governor himself."

"Find her! Marry, lad, that nag could be halfway to Cambridge by now!"

" 'Tis a consideration as would ne'er deter your honest gentleman, I believe."

"Please, sir!" Mrs. Russecks took McEvoy's arm. "Don't be hard on my husband in St. Mary's! Do but take a pot of tea with us, you and Sir Benjamin, and I'm sure he'll have the mare back ere sunset."

"Ere sunset!" Russecks cried. "I've not said I'd go chasing after the beast to begin with! What I mean—— God's blood, then, I'll find the cursed animal! But I must have help."

"I'll search with ye," Mary volunteered at once. "I know Aphrodite's ways, and I'll ne'er rest easy till we track her down."

Now the miller was by no means pleased by this arrangement, but though his face plainly registered reluctance, he permitted Mary to lead him off towards a woods behind the stable. Ebenezer watched them go with fainting spirit.

"Methinks I'll help them search," he ventured.

McEvoy laughed. "Nay, ladies, tell me truly: is Sir Benjamin England's greatest coward or her greatest tease? I know for a fact he hath fathered a regiment o' bastards, but to hear the scoundrel ye'd take him for a virgin."

"Stay, John; 'tis time to end disguises."

"Time enough," McEvoy agreed quickly, but instead of revealing their true identities and stations, he confessed that he himself had set Miss Mungummory's mare a-wandering, what time he'd feigned a visit to the millrace; he'd already freely said as much to Mary, who, by no means disturbed at the news, had told him Aphrodite would go at once to a certain farm not far away, where she'd often been stabled, and had offered to lead Harry Russecks on a two-hour chase before they found her.

"There's a queen among women," Mrs. Russecks declared. "So, then, gentlemen: let us go to our tea, since my husband hath such nice feeling for responsibility." She took Ebenezer's arm; McEvoy had already encircled Henrietta's waist and drawn her to his side.

"Really, Mrs. Russecks," the poet said desperately, "there *is* a pressing business I wish to discuss with you——"

"There, now, Mr. McEvoy!" the miller's wife teased. "Your friend is as importunate as yourself! Marry, in *my* youth men were more subtle—for better or worse."

"Nay, you refuse to understand!" Ebenezer protested. "I'm not what you think I am at all!"

"So I begin to grasp, young rascal!"

"Pray, hear me——"

"Peace, Sir Benjamin," McEvoy laughed, but Ebenezer saw alarm in his eyes. "Thou'rt embarrassing Henrietta with your forwardness. Out on't, Madame Russecks, methinks we'd best forego the tea, to spare your lovely daughter farther blushes; by'r leave, I'll ask her to take me once again through the mill, to inspect more closely what I only glimpsed before."

To this bald proposition Mrs. Russecks only replied, "I'm not disposed to keep a man from His Majesty's business, sir; yet if on the grounds of your commission you decide to try the machinery as well as inspect it, I ask you to bear in mind two things . . ."

"Anything, madame: 'tis thine to command."

"First, then, albeit we have your statement for't that you've inspected many a mill before, you must remember that this one is unaccustomed to inspection. 'Tis very dear to me, e'en precious, sir; for all my husband claims it as his own, 'tis not o' his making at all, but came to him with my dowry, as't were. Moreover, we've our reputation to think of, and albeit 'tis a perfectly harmless thing thou'rt commissioned to, if 'twere generally known what thou'rt about, certain ill-minded gossips would make a scandal of't. In sum, inspect and try what ye will, Mr. McEvoy, but be gentle and discreet as becomes an officer of the King."

McEvoy bowed, "I pledge my life on't, lady."

"And you, Henrietta," Mrs. Russecks said more sternly. "Bear in mind that the mill is a perilous place for novices."

"Methinks I know my way around it well enough, Mother!"

"Very well, but mind your step and stay alert for trouble."

With this advice the couple left, and Mrs. Russecks turned to Ebenezer with a proud smile.

"Fetch me into the house, Sir Benjamin, and we'll attend to the pressing business that so distracts you."

Ebenezer sighed; it *was* chilly outside, and he was blind neither to Mrs. Russecks's beauty nor to her flattering invitation. Nevertheless, as soon as they were seated in her parlor

675

he declared that he was not Sir Benjamin Oliver nor any other knight, and that neither he nor his companion were traveling in any official capacity.

"As for my actual identity, I am ashamed of't, but I'll tell it readily——"

"Indeed you shan't!" Mrs. Russecks commanded, with some heat. "Methinks thou'rt younger in the ways of the world than becomes thy years! Do you take me for a whore, sir, that swives all comers in the stews?"

"Prithee, nay, ma'am!"

"You've seen what a gross, unmannered bully is my husband," she went on sharply. "Once in my youth I grew to despise the race of men, and to loathe in myself those things that aroused their lust and mine: 'twas in contempt of life I married Harry Russecks, so that every time he forced me like a slavering brute of the woods, he'd strengthen twice over my opinion of his sex."

"Mercy, ma'am! I scarce know what to think! Many's the time I've pitied woman's lot, and reviled men's coarseness; yet a man is nine parts nature's slave in such matters, methinks, and in any case I assure you not all men are so coarse as your husband." He stopped, covered with confusion by the unintended insult. "What I mean to say——"

"No matter." Mrs. Russecks's face softened; she smiled and laid her hand upon Ebenezer's. "What you just told me, I knew in my heart all along, and soon saw the folly of my marriage. Yet I was and still am victim of another folly, that I got like a family illness from my father: I was too proud to renounce a grand course once I'd embarked on't, e'en though I saw 'twould lead to naught but pain and revulsion. In lieu of admitting my blunder and leaving the Province, I resolved to make the best of't; I vowed I'd lose no opportunity to redeem myself for scorning good men along with bad. That, sir, explains your presence here, and what you no doubt took to be immodest encouragement on our part—I feel more pity for Henrietta than for myself, inasmuch as 'twas none of her choice to live with such a jealous and vigilant despot. Yet albeit I own we've behaved like tarts, sir, I beg you remember that we're not: 'twas to a knight I opened my door and e'en good Guinevere played harlot for a knight! To tell me now thou'rt only Ben the factor's son, or Slim Bill Bones the sailor —'twere less than delicate, Sir Benjamin, were it not?"

While speaking she played distractedly with Ebenezer's hand, stroking down each bony finger-top with her index nail; at the end she raised her excellent brown eyes, furrowed her brows in whimsical appeal and smiled a little crooked smile. Ebenezer's cheeks burned; his nose and eyebrows jerked and twitched.

"Dear lady——" It was time to make a move; he must embrace her at once, or throw himself upon his knees to protest his ardor—but though the feelings so at odds within his breast were strangely different from those he'd known in other passionate impasses, he was unable to bring himself to do what the moment called for. "I beg you, madam: take no offense——"

Mrs. Russecks drew back. Bewilderment was followed at once in her expression by disbelief, which gave way in its turn to wrath.

"Prithee, don't misunderstand——"

"'Tis not likely I shall, d'ye think?" she said furiously. "Or will you tell me thou'rt a Christian saint disguised, that hath such a nice regard for husband's honor!"

"He is a boor," Ebenezer assured her. "What horns he wears, he hath more than earned by's callous——"

"Then the truth is plain," she snapped. "Your friend stole the filly and left you to ride the foundered jade!"

"Nay, madam, b'm'faith! I've no wish to change places with McEvoy, believe me!"

"Hear the wretch! He finds the pair of us sour to's taste, nor scruples to tell us so to our faces! And you call my husband callous?"

Up to this point Ebenezer had spoken gently, even timidly, in his fear of wounding the lady's pride. But among the curious new emotions that possessed him was a strange self-assurance, such as he'd never felt before in a woman's presence. He scarcely bothered to wonder where he had acquired it, but on the strength of it caught her hand, held it fast against her efforts to wrench free, and pressed it against his chest.

"Feel my heart!" he ordered. "Is that the pulse of a Christian saint? Can you believe I sit here coldly?"

Mrs. Russecks made no reply; an uncertain, irritated disdain took the place of her initial anger.

Ebenezer spoke on, still clasping her hand. "Thou'rt no child, Mrs. Russecks; surely you can see you have possessed me with desire! Nay, only twice in my life have I burned so, and both times—i'Christ, the memory scalds me with remorse!—both times I came within an ace of committing rape upon the woman I loved! And 'sblood, thou'rt handsome—by far the comeliest lady I've seen in Maryland! Thou'rt the masterwork whereof your Henrietta's but a copy!"

677

In the face of these protestations, the miller's wife could maintain but a pouting remnant of her ire. "What is't unmans you then?" She could not restrain a smile, or Ebenezer a blush, when even as she spoke she noticed that he was in a condition far from unmanly. "Or better, since I see for a fact thou'rt ardent, what holds you back? Is't fear of my husband?"

Ebenezer shook his head.

"Then where's the rub?" Her voice began to show fresh irritation. "Is't that ye fear I'm poxed like many another strumpet? 'Tis a wondrous prudent ravisher, i'faith, that asks his victims for a bill o' health!"

"Stay, you slander yourself, madam! I swear to Heav'n this is the rarest opportunity of my life: who wins thy favors wins a splendid prize; the world must regard him with awe and envy! 'Twere a rare, a singular pleasure to accept so sweet a gift; 'tis a rare and singular pain to say you nay, and would be e'en if my rejection were no insult——" He paused and smiled. "Dear lady, you little dream the whole and special nature your appeal bears for me!"

His manner was so cordial, his compliment so curious, that Mrs. Russecks's face softened again. Once more she demanded an explanation, and even threatened in a vague way to denounce the poet to her husband as an impostor if he would not be candid with her, but her tone was more coaxing than annoyed.

"You upbraid yourself for having been forward," Ebenezer said, "and declare I contemn you for't; yet the truth is, lady, thou'rt but the more my conqueror for seizing the initiative. I admire your grace, I savor your beauty, but beyond both——How can I phrase it? Methinks you've tact and wisdom enough to deal with my own blundering innocence, which else would make a fiasco of our adventure . . ."

"Ah, now, Sir Benjamin, this is no ravisher I hear speaking!"

"Nay, hear me out! I'll not disclose my name, if you must have it so, but there's a thing you must know. 'Tis a thing I'd hide from one less gentle, lest she wound me with't; but you, lady—ah, belike 'tis folly, but I've an image of you surprised, charmed, e'en delighted at the fact—yet infinitely tender and, above all, *appreciative*. Aye, supremely appreciative, as I should be if——" Bemused by the picture in his mind, Ebenezer would have detailed it further, but the miller's wife cut him short, declaring candidly that her curiosity was now a match for her ardor, and should he deny her satisfaction of the one as well as the other, he must watch her perish upon the spot and suffer the consequences.

"Heav'n forfend." The poet laughed, still marveling at the ease with which he could speak. "The simple truth of't is, my dear Mrs. Russecks, for all my twenty-eight years of age, I am as innocent as a nursling, and have vowed to remain so."

His prediction regarding the effect of this announcement on the miller's wife was in some measure borne out: she studied his face for evidence of insincerity, and apparently finding none, asked in a chastened voice, "Do you mean to tell me—and thou'rt no priest?"

"Not of the Roman or any other church," Ebenezer declared. He went on to explain to her how at the outset, being a shy ungainly fellow, he had come to regard his innocence as a virtue rather from necessity; how not a year past (though it seemed decades!) he had elevated it, along with a certain artistic bent of his, to a style of life, even identifying it with the essence of his being; and how through a year of the most frightful tribulation, and at a staggering expense not only of property but perhaps of human lives, he had managed to preserve it intact. It had been some while since he'd been obliged to consider seriously the matter of his innocence, and though to enlarge upon its virtues and shudder verbally at the prospect of its loss had become second nature for him, he was surprised to find himself dissociated emotionally from his panegyric; standing off, as it were, and listening critically. Indeed, when Mrs. Russecks asked with sharp interest for an explanation of this wondrous *innocence*, he was obliged to admit, both to her and to himself, that he could call himself innocent no longer except with regard to physical love.

But the lady was not yet satisfied. "Do you mean you've no notion of what your friend and Henrietta have been about this last half hour?"

Ebenezer blushed, not alone at the reference to the other couple, but also at the realization (which he readily confessed to Mrs. Russecks) that even in the physical sense his innocence had come to be limited to the mere technical fact of his virginity—which fact itself (though he would not elaborate further) was not so unqualified as he might wish.

"The truth of't is, then," Mrs. Russecks persisted, "this precious Innocence you cling to hath been picked at and pecked at till you've scarce a tit-bit of't left."

"I must own that is the case, more's the pity."

"And doth that wretched tatter mean so much?"

Ebenezer sighed. The critical listener in his soul had posed that very question not many moments earlier, during his speech, and had observed by way of answer a startling fact: his loss of the quality of innocence, it suddenly seemed, had been accompanied by a diminution of the value that he placed on it; although he still sang its praises from witless force of habit, he had been astonished to remark, in these moments of dispassionate appraisal, what slight emotion he truly felt now at the thought of losing it altogether. Thus his sigh, and the slight smile with which he replied, "In sooth I have grown indifferent to't, lady. Nay, more: I am right weary of innocence."

"La, then speak no farther!" Her voice was husky, her eyes bright; she held out both her hands for him to take. "Hither with thee, and an end to innocence!"

But though he took her hands to show her that his own were a-tremble with desire and appreciation, Ebenezer would not embrace her.

"What I prized before hath all but lost its point," he said gently, "and when I think that soon or late 'twill come, this end you speak of, as sure as death will come, and belike in circumstances by no means so pleasurable as these, why, then I wonder: What moral doth the story hold? Is't that the universe is vain? The chaste and consecrated a hollow madness? Or is't that what the world lacks we must ourselves supply? My brave assault on Maryland—this knight-errantry of Innocence and Art—sure, I see now 'twas an edifice raised not e'en on sand, but on the black and vasty zephyrs of the Pit. Wherefore a voice in me cries, 'Down with't, then!' while another stands in awe before the enterprise; sees in the vanity of't all nobleness allowed to fallen men. 'Tis no mere castle in the air, this second voice says, but a temple of the mind, Athene's shrine, where the Intellect seeks refuge from Furies more terrific than e'er beset Orestes——"

"Enough!" Mrs. Russecks protested, but not incordially. "Since 'tis plain you'll have none of me, I withdraw my invitation. But don't expect me to fathom this talk of Pits and Castles: speak your piece in Church Creek English, else I'll never know in what wise I'm insulted!"

Ebenezer shook his head. "Here's nobility in sooth, that is rendered gracious by rejection! And here's a paradox, for this same grace that lends me courage to make clear my resolve, at the same time deals it a nigh-to-mortal blow!"

"Go to; 'tis a plain account I crave, not flattery."

Thus assured, Ebenezer declared that although to present her then and there with the final vestige of his innocence would be a privilege as well as a joy, he was resolved to deny himself a pleasure which, however sublime, would be devoid of a right *significance*.

"When erst I entered the lists of Life," he said, "Virginity was a silken standard that I waved, all bright and newly stitched. 'Tis weatherblast and run now, and so rent by the shocks of combat e'en its bearer might mistake it for a boot rag. Notwithstanding which, 'tis a banner still, and hath earned this final dignity of standards: since I must lose it, I'll not abandon it by the way, but surrender it with honor in the field."

The poet himself was not displeased by this conceit, which he judged to be acceptably free from insult as well as lucid and sincere. Whether the miller's wife shared his good opinion, however, he never did learn, for even as he prepared to question her she sprang up white-faced from the couch, having heard an instant before he did the sound of running footfalls up the path.

"Pray God to spare you for the day of that surrender," she said, in a voice quite shaken with fright. "Here is my husband at the door!"

14

Oblivion Is Attained Twice by the Miller's Wife, Once by the Miller Himself, and Not at All by the Poet, Who Likens Life to a Shameless Playwright

MRS. RUSSECKS'S FRIGHT, so out of keeping with her character, provoked such terror in Ebenezer that at sight of the miller rushing in with sword held high, he came near to suffering again the misfortune he had suffered at the King o' the Seas in Plymouth.

"Mercy, my dear!" Mrs. Russecks cried, running to her husband. "Whatever is the matter?"

"Go to, don't I'll have thy whoring head along with his!"

He endeavored to push her aside in order to get at the

cowering poet, but she clung to him like a vine upon an oak, so that he could only hobble across the parlor.

"Stay, Harry, thou'rt mistaken!" she pleaded. "What're thy suspicions, God smite me dead if there hath been aught 'twixt this man and me!"

" 'Tis *I* shall smite!" the miller cried. "Commissioner or no, there's guilt writ plain athwart his ugly face!"

"As Heav'n is my witness, sir!" Ebenezer pleaded, "Madame Russecks and I were merely conversing!" But however true the letter of his protest, his face indeed belied it. He leaped for safety as the miller swung.

"Hold still, dammee!"

The miller paused to fetch his wife so considerable a swat with the back of his free hand that she gave a cry and fell to the floor. "Now we'll see thy liquorous innards!"

Ebenezer strove to keep the parlor table between himself and dismemberment.

"Let him go!" Mrs. Russecks shrieked. " 'Tis the other one you must find, ere he swive Henrietta!"

These words undoubtedly saved the poet's life, for Harry Russecks had flung over the table with one hand and driven him into a corner. But the mention of Henrietta, whom he had apparently forgotten, drove the miller nearly mad with rage; he turned on his wife, and for an instant Ebenezer was certain she would suffer the fate he had temporarily been spared.

"He fetched her into the woods," Mrs. Russecks said quickly, "and vowed he'd murther her if Sir Benjamin or myself so much as blinked eye at him!"

Like a wounded boar at scent of his injurer, the miller gave a sort of squealing grunt and charged outdoors.

"Make haste to the mill!" Mrs. Russecks cried to Ebenezer. "Bid Henrietta slip into the woods where Harry and I can find her, and you and your friend hide yourselves in Mary's wagon!"

The poet jumped to follow her instructions, but upon stepping outside, just a few seconds behind the miller, they saw the plan foiled before their eyes. Mary Mungummory, leading the lost Aphrodite, had run puffing and panting into the dooryard just as the miller charged out again; at the same moment, though Ebenezer could not see them from the front steps of the house, either McEvoy or Henrietta or both must have peered out from the mill to see what the commotion was about, for although Russecks was headed in the general direction of the woods, Mary, knowing nothing of the ruse, dropped Aphrodite's halter and ran as best she could toward the mill, calling "Go back! Here comes Sir Harry!" The miller wheeled about and lumbered after. A scream came from the mill and was answered by another from Mrs. Russecks, who ran a few steps as though to intercept her husband and then, stumbling or swooning, fell to the ground.

Ebenezer found himself running also, but with no idea at all what to do. He was still somewhat closer to the mill door than was Russecks and could doubtless have headed him off, but with no weapons of his own such a course would have been suicidal as well as ineffective. Yet neither could he simply stand by or look to his own escape while McEvoy, and perhaps the girl too, were done to death. Therefore he simply trotted without object into the yard, and when Russecks charged past without a glance, he turned and followed a safe ten yards behind.

Mary, meanwhile, had disappeared, but as soon as Russecks entered the mill (whence issued at once fresh screams from Henrietta) she trundled from around the corner, most distraught.

"God's blood, Mister Cooke, I did all a body could, but the farther we went, the more jealous he grew, till he swore he'd go no farther for the King himself! Nay, don't go in, sir; 'tis your life! Ah, Christ, yonder lies Roxie, done to death!"

She hurried off to the fallen Mrs. Russecks, whom she supposed to have been run through and Ebenezer, ignoring her advice, proceeded quickly into the mill. Already Russecks had started up the ladder that led to the catwalk and grain hopper; McEvoy was scrambling from the upper rungs of the second ladder, which led from the hopper to the loft; and near the edge of the loft itself stood pretty Henrietta, incriminated by the petticoats in which she stood and screamed.

"Ha! Ye'll run no farther!" the miller shouted from the platform, and Ebenezer realized that the lovers were trapped.

"Throw down the ladder!" he cried to McEvoy. The Irishman heard him and leaped to follow his counsel just as Russecks began to climb. But although the ladder was neither nailed nor tied in place, its stringers had been wedged between two protruding floor-joists of the loft, too tightly for McEvoy to free them by hand from his position. The miller climbed with difficulty to the second rung, the third, and the fourth, holding the cutlass in his hand and watching his quarry's struggle.

Now on the platform himself, Ebenezer watched with fainting heart. "Throw something down, John! Knock him off!"

McEvoy looked wildly about the loft for a missile and came up with nothing more formidable than a piece of cypress studding, perhaps three feet long and three inches on a side. For a moment he stood poised to hurl it; Russecks halted his climb and waited to dodge the blow, growling and jeering. Then, thinking better of it, McEvoy fitted one end of the stud behind the topmost rung of the ladder, and using the edge of the loft for a fulcrum, pulled back upon the other with all his weight. There was a loud crack; Ebenezer caught his breath; but apparently neither rung nor lever had broken, for McEvoy placed a foot against each stringer-top for mechanical advantage and heaved back again. Another crack: Ebenezer saw the ladder move out an inch or so, and the miller, uncertain whether to rush for the top or climb down before he fell, gripped the sides more tightly and cursed. The new angle of the lever afforded McEvoy less of a purchase and tended to lift as well as push the ladder, but Henrietta sprang to his assistance, and on the third try their effort succeeded in freeing the ladder from the joists. Its slight inclination kept it from falling backwards at once, and in the moment required for McEvoy to pull it over sideways, the miller jumped safely to the platform.

McEvoy laughed. *"Love conquers all,* Your Majesty! Murther us now, sir!"

Russecks picked himself up and shook his sword at the loft. "Well done, dammee; what keeps me down will keep ye up, and we shall see how soon ye choke on your damned love! *There's many a keep taken by siege that hath withstood the worst assaults!"*

Ebenezer had observed all this from the far end of the same platform on which the miller now stood. That his own position was far from safe did not occur to him; his whole attention was directed to the lovers, and when he recalled that McEvoy knew nothing of Mrs. Russecks's abduction-story, his sudden vision of a stratagem blinded him to more prudent considerations.

"Prithee, sir!" he cried to the miller, in a voice loud enough for them to hear and be advised by. "Don't tempt his anger, I beg you, while he hath your daughter in his clutches! Howe'er he hath wronged you, 'tis better he go free than that he murther Henrietta before your eyes, or work lewd tortures on her as desperate men are wont——"

He got no farther; whether Russecks had heard his earlier suggestions to McEvoy or now noticed his presence for the first time, he was clearly of the same mind no longer about the poet's innocence. He turned on him, brandishing the cutlass, and said, *"Who gives a man horns must beware of a goring!"*

Ebenezer lost no time fleeing down the nearby ladder to the ground and racing for the front doorway, where he saw Mary and the miller's wife anxiously looking on. But however distraught, Mrs. Russecks still had her wits about her; before Ebenezer reached the door she ran in towards the fallen ladder.

"Now, Henrietta! Climb down while he chases Sir Benjamin!"

Her order was so public and premature, its object must have been merely to divert her husband. If so, it succeeded at once: the miller stopped half across the platform and glared from her to the loft.

"I'll quarter the lot o' ye!"

Ebenezer spied against the wall a hooked iron rod, like a fireplace poker, and snatching it up, hastened to Mrs. Russecks's defense.

"Go to the inn," he ordered Mary, "fetch all the folk this wretch hath bullied!"

"Bravo!" McEvoy shouted from the loft. "Let him run ye round the millstones, Eben, till I scramble down; 'tis one against all the rest of us, and I've a sickle here to match his bloody meat-axe!"

So saying he hurled his piece of studding at the miller, tucked the newfound sickle into his belt, and swung his legs around one of two wooden pillars supporting the loft, ready to climb down at the first opportunity. Mary disappeared on her errand, and Mrs. Russecks, with a wary eye on her husband, struggled to raise the fallen ladder. Russecks himself, though untouched by McEvoy's missile, seemed driven to the verge of apoplexy by his own wrath. After some moments of indecision he fixed his attention upon Ebenezer, who trembled at the hatred in his face.

" 'Twill not be two against one for long!" He advanced two steps towards the end of the platform and then, seeing Ebenezer prepare to flee, turned back to the middle and commenced to climb the railing. It was evidently his intention either to jump or to climb down upon the millstones themselves in order to prevent Ebenezer from playing the part of Hector around the walls of Troy.

"Ah, nay!" Mrs. Russecks cried at once, and before her husband could let go the railing she sprang to pull the lever that engaged the millstone shaft with that of the waterwheel outside. The great top stone rumbled and turned, and Russecks jerked himself up, his footing removed from under him.

"God dammee!" he bellowed almost tearfully. "God dammee one and all!"

Holding on with his free hand, he threw his leg back over the rail to regain the platform and was undone: as he swung himself over, the great scabbard at his inside hip caught momentarily between the rails; to free it he drew back his abdomen and endeavored to hold on with the finger ends of his cutlass-hand. They slipped at once, and being either unwilling or unable to let go his sword and snatch for a new grip, he tumbled backwards. Both women screamed, and Ebenezer's nerves tingled. The fall was short, the attitude deadly: Russecks's bootheels were still at the level of the platform when his head struck the millstone below.

"Smite him!" McEvoy called to Ebenezer. But there was no need to, for the miller's head and shoulders rolled off the stone and he lay senseless on the ground. Henrietta waxed hysterical; her mother, on the other hand, screamed no more after the first time, but calmly pushed the clutch-lever to disengage the stone and only then inquired of Ebenezer, "Is he dead?"

The poet made a gingerly examination. The back of the miller's head was bloody where it had struck, but he was respiring still.

"He seems alive, but knocked quite senseless."

Mary Mungummory peered cautiously through the doorway. "Heav'n be praised, the blackguard's dead! Not a coward would come to help, for all he hath abused 'em, and Master Poet hath turned the trick himself!"

"Nay," said McEvoy, on the ground at last, "he tricked himself, did Sir Harry, and he's not dead yet." He took up the cutlass and held it to the miller's throat. "With your permission, Mrs. Russecks . . ."

But though the miller's wife showed no emotion whatever regarding his accident, she would not permit a *coup de grâce*. "Fetch down my daughter, sir, an it please you, and we'll put my husband to bed."

All the company showed surprise, and all but Ebenezer indignation as well.

"The scoundrel might come to his senses any minute and have at us again!" McEvoy protested.

"I trust you and Sir Benjamin will be well out of Church Creek ere he comes to."

"What of thyself, lady?" Ebenezer asked.

"And Henrietta!" McEvoy protested.

Mrs. Russecks replied that for all his threats, her husband would do no worse than beat the two of them, and they had lived through many such beatings before.

" 'Tis all very fine if ye've a taste for birch," McEvoy said shortly, "but the devil shan't lay a finger on Henrietta! I'll fetch her out o' the county if need be!"

"Henrietta may stay or leave as she pleases," Mrs. Russecks declared.

Mary Mungummory regarded the witless miller and shook her head. "I cannot fathom ye, Roxanne! I'd have swore ye'd rejoice to see the beast dead, as every soul else in Church Creek would! Sure, thou'rt not o' that queer sort that lust after floggings, are ye? Or haply thou'rt of such soft stuff e'en a wounded viper moves ye to pity?"

Mrs. Russecks waved an irritated hand at her friend. "I loathe him, Mary. He is the grossest of men and the cruellest; he hath made a torture of my life, and poor Henrietta's. I wed him knowing full well 'twould be so, and God hath fitly punished me for that sin; 'tis not for me to terminate the punishment."

Ebenezer was moved by this speech, but at the risk of offending her he ventured to point out that she had not scrupled to commit adultery in the past.

"What doth that serve to prove," she demanded sharply, "save that mortals sometimes stray from the path of saints? 'Tis true I've played him false with pleasure; 'tis likewise true I rejoiced to see him fall (albeit 'twas not my motive when I pulled the lever), and would rejoice thrice o'er to see him in the grave. But 'twill ne'er be I that puts him there or gives any soul leave to murther him."

Mary sniffed: " 'Sheart, is this Roxie Russecks I hear, or Mary Magdalene? At least don't nurse the scoundrel back to health, if ye've any love left for the rest o' mankind."

But Mrs. Russecks stood firm and ordered Henrietta—now properly attired and rescued from the loft—to help her carry the still-senseless miller to his chamber. The girl looked uncertainly to McEvoy, whose eyes challenged her, and refused to obey.

"I pray ye'll forgive me, Mother, but I shan't lift a finger to save him. I hope he dies."

Her mother frowned for just an instant; on second thought

she smiled and declared that if Henrietta intended to "place herself under the protection" of Mr. McEvoy, the two of them could depart immediately with her blessing and should do so before Russecks regained consciousness; then, to the surprise of Ebenezer and McEvoy, she added something in rapid, murmuring French, of which the poet caught only the noun *dispense de bans* and the adverb *bientôt*. Henrietta blushed like a virgin and replied first in clearer French that while she had reason to believe McEvoy actually admired her *à la point de fiançailles*, she had no intention of becoming his mistress until she had further knowledge of his station in life. "For the present," she continued in English, "I mean to stay here with you and share your misfortunes, but dammee if I'll do aught to hasten their coming!"

"Well spoken!" Mary applauded. "No more will I, Roxie."

"Nor I," McEvoy joined in. "Neither will I run off like a mouse ere the cat awakes. I mean to stand guard outside his chamber with this sword, if ye will permit me—or on the edge o' yonder woods if ye will not—and the hour he lays a wrathful hand on Henrietta shall be his last on earth, if it be not mine."

" 'Tis past my strength to carry him alone," Mrs. Russecks entreated Ebenezer. "I beg you to help me, sir."

Feeling partly responsible for the miller's condition, Ebenezer agreed. The brief exchange in French had set his mind strangely abuzz, so that he scarcely heard the protests of the others until Mary happened to say, as they left the mill, "Whence sprang this nice concern for the devil's health, Roxie? There was a time you abandoned him right readily to be murthered!"

" 'Twas that time taught me my lesson," Mrs. Russecks replied, "else I'd ne'er have ransomed him. If they had thrown him to the sharks, methinks I'd have ended my own life as well."

A number of villagers had gathered between the inn and the mill to learn the outcome of the fight; on catching sight of the vanquished miller they sent up a cheer, whereupon Mrs. Russecks dispatched Mary to warn them that their joy was in some measure premature. The rest of the party entered the house; Henrietta and McEvoy remained in the parlor, while Mrs. Russecks and the poet carried their burden to the master's bedroom. The miller showed no signs at all of recovering from his coma, even when his wife set to work washing and bandaging his injury.

"I shall bind up his head and fetch him a physician," she

sighed. "If he lives, he lives; if he dies, he dies. In any case I am your debtor for humoring my wishes." She paused noticing the poet's distracted countenance. "Is something amiss, sir?"

"Only my curiosity," Ebenezer answered. "If you fancy yourself in my debt, dear lady, prithee discharge it by allowing me one bold question: were you and your daughter once captured by a pirate named Thomas Pound?"

The woman's alarm made clear the answer. She looked with new eyes at Ebenezer and marveled as though to herself, "Aye, but why did it not occur to me before? Your weathered clothes and story of a shipwreck——! But 'tis nigh six years ago you captured us, 'twixt Jamestown and St. Mary's —howe'er could you recall it?"

"Nay, madam, I am no pirate," Ebenezer laughed, "nor ever was; else 'twere not likely I'd be yet a virgin, do you think?"

Mrs. Russecks colored. "Yet surely our shame is not the talk of England, and thou'rt not a native of the Province. How is't you know the story?"

" 'Tis more famous than you imagine," the poet teased. "I swear to you I heard it from my tutor, in the coach to Plymouth."

"Nay, sir, don't shame me farther! Speak the truth!"

Ebenezer assured her that he had done just that. "This tutor is an odd and formidable fellow, that hath been equally at home in Tom Pound's fo'c'sle and Isaac Newton's study; to this hour I know not whether he is at heart a fiend or a philosopher. 'Tis in search of him and his salvage brother I came hither, for reasons so momentous I tremble to tell them, and so urgent—ah well, you shall judge for yourself anon, when I explain. This man, dear lady, you were once of wondrous service to, albeit you knew it not, and in consideration of that service he saved your life and honor from the pirates. Have you e'er heard tell of Henry Burlingame?"

Mrs. Russecks crimsoned further; looking to assure herself that neither her husband nor the couple in the parlor had overheard, she closed the bedroom door. Ebenezer apologized for his ungallantry and begged forgiveness on grounds of the great urgency of his mission, adding that Henry Burlingame (which, he gave her to understand, was actually the name of her saviour and *quondam* lover) had surely not told the story to anyone else, and that he had expressed nothing but the fondest and most chivalrous opinions of both Mrs. Russecks and her daughter. The miller's wife glanced uneasily toward the door.

"Let me assure you farther," Ebenezer said. "You need not be anxious after Henrietta's honor: McEvoy knows naught of this."

"Methinks he hath learned already she is no virgin, for all that's worth," Mrs. Russecks said candidly. "But I must tell you, Mister—*Benjamin*—albeit 'tis an empty point of honor and bespeaks no merit for us whatsoever, thy tutor is a most uncommon sort of lover, such as I've ne'er heard tell of before or since, and 'tis quite likely you have a wrong conception of our adventure . . ."

Ebenezer lowered his eyes in embarrassment and admitted that he had indeed been misled on that matter—and not alone with regard to the two ladies present—until quite recently, when the curious truth about Burlingame had been discovered to him.

"I'God, lady, such a deal I have to tell you! Burlingame's quest, that you yourself played no small role in! My own enormous errand, wherein you may play yet another role! What a shameless, marvelous dramatist is Life, that daily plots coincidences e'en Chaucer would not dare, and ventures complications too knotty for Boccacce!"

Mrs. Russecks concurred with this sentiment and expressed her readiness to hear the full story once she'd had a private word with Henrietta to spare her daughter unnecessary alarm. "Methinks my husband will not soon be dangerous, and whate'er this weighty quest of thine, I'm sure it can wait till morning. 'Twill make a pleasant evening's telling, Sir Benjamin."

"Ah, then, may we not have done with pseudonyms at last?" He boldly put his arm about Mrs. Russecks's waist. "I am no more Sir Benjamin Oliver than McEvoy is His Majesty's Commissioner of Provincial Wind- and Water-Mills; did you not hear Mary call me 'Mister Poet?'"

He felt the miller's wife stiffen and removed his arm, assuming that she was not pleased by the familiarity; to cover his embarrassment he pretended that it was his vocation which disturbed her. "Ah, now, is a poet less attractive than a knight? What if peradventure he bore a pompous title, like *Laureate of Maryland?*"

Mrs. Russecks averted her eyes. "You replace one disguise with another," she said tersely.

"Nay, I swear't! I am Ebenezer Cooke, that once pretended to the title *Laureate of Maryland.*"

The miller's wife seemed not so much skeptical as angry. "Why do you lie to me? I happen to know for a certainty that the Laureate of Maryland is living in Malden this minute with his father, and doth not resemble you in any particular."

Ebenezer laughed, though somewhat disconcerted by her manner. " 'Tis no surprise to me if certain evil men have hired a brace of new impostors; their motives still appall me, but I've grown used to their methods. But look me straight in the face, my dear Roxanne: I swear by all that's dear to me, I am Ebenezer Cooke of St. Giles in the Fields and Malden."

Mrs. Russecks turned to him a drained, incredulous face. "Dear Heav'n, what if we——" She turned to the door, laid her hand upon the knob, and swooned to the floor as senseless as her husband.

15

*In Pursuit of His Manifold Objectives the
Poet Meets an Unsavaged Savage Husband
and an Unenglished English Wife*

HENRIETTA AND McEVOY came quickly at Ebenezer's summons, and with the assistance of Mary Mungummory Mrs. Russecks was put to bed in Henrietta's room. When, a little later, she was revived by salts of ammonia, she demanded, through Mary, that Ebenezer leave her house immediately and never return.

"Thou'rt a sly deceiver, Eben!" McEvoy teased, though he was as mystified by the demand as were the others. "What is't ye tried to do in the chamber yonder?"

"I swear to Heav'n I have done naught!" the poet protested. "Prithee, Mary, tell her I shall go instantly, but I *must* know in what wise I offended her, and crave her pardon for't!"

Mary delivered the message and came back to report that Mrs. Russecks would neither explain her demand nor give ear to any apologies. "She said 'The man hath done naught

691

amiss, but I cannot bear him in my house'—her very words! De'il take me if I've e'er seen the like of't, have you, Henrietta?"

The girl agreed that such passionate unreasonableness was quite out of character for her mother.

Ebenezer sighed. "Ah well, then I must leave at once and find a bed somewhere. Prithee think no ill of me, Miss Russecks, and do endeavor to learn what lies behind all this, for I shan't rest easy till I've heard and redressed it." In the morning, he went on to say, he would find some means of traveling to Tobacco Stick Bay; whether his double mission there met success or failure, he would soon return to Church Creek, where he profoundly hoped to find Mrs. Russecks relenting enough, if not to forgive, at least to explain his *faux pas*. "You had best remain here," he told McEvoy. "If the twain of us go, Billy Rumbly might think he's being threatened."

"Did you say *Billy Rumbly*?" Henrietta asked.

"He did," Mary affirmed, "but ye must swallow your curiosity till Mr. McEvoy and I can tell ye the tale." To Ebenezer she said, " 'Tis you must forgive poor Roxie, Mr. Cooke; this wretched afternoon hath o'erwrought her. As for tomorrow, ye must allow me to take ye in the wagon. I greatly wish to see this Billy Rumbly my own self, for what reasons I scarce need say, and 'tis not impossible I may be able to help persuade him to our cause."

Ebenezer gratefully accepted both her offer and a loan of two pounds sterling, his own resources being exhausted. He charged Mary to inform him at once of any change in Mrs. Russecks's attitude or the miller's condition, and departed. He walked alone to the inn, much troubled in spirit, and was received almost as a hero by a number of villagers who lingered there for news from the mill. Ebenezer's announcement that as yet Russecks showed no improvement was greeted with ill-disguised rejoicing, and the innkeeper himself, an employee of the miller, insisted that the poet take supper and lodging at the house's expense.

During the meal Ebenezer pondered Mrs. Russecks's strange behavior. The only theory he could devise to account for both her knowledge of the state of things at Malden and her strong adverse reaction to his name was the not unlikely one that Russecks was affiliated with William Smith the cooper and Captain Mitchell's sinister traffic in vice. At length he mustered courage to approach the innkeeper.

"I say, friend, have you heard of Eben Cooke, that was wont to call himself Laureate of Maryland?"

"Eben Cooke?" The man's face brightened. "Why, that I have, sir; he's the wight that runs the Cooke's Point whorehouse with Bill Smith."

The poet's heart tingled; it appeared that his inference had some truth in it. "Aye, that's the man. But you've ne'er laid eyes on him, have you?"

"Indeed, Sir Benjamin, I've met the man but once, some days since——"

Ebenezer frowned, for he had been about to reveal himself. "You say you've met him?"

"Aye, that I did, sir, just once, in the very spot thou'rt standing now. An average-looking fellow he was, naught to set him off. Folks claimed he was looking for a wench that had run off from Malden—one o' the friskers, don't ye know —but I'll own he made no mention of't to me."

The innkeeper grinned. " 'Twas the Virgin he was after, we all knew well, and had he come a few days sooner we'd have steered him to her. But by then she was Lady Rumbly, don't ye know, and de'il the man of us would lead him to Billy's wife, for all she's a simple whore. 'Twas lucky Sir Harry wasn't about . . ." In defense of his characterization of Miss Bromly, which Ebenezer questioned, the innkeeper reaffirmed his conviction that she was a fugitive prostitute from Malden. The poet did not insist the contrary, both because he wished not to alienate the innkeeper and because he was suddenly struck by an alarming notion: could it be that the Church Creek Virgin was not really Miss Bromly at all, but poor Joan Toast? Certain features of the story definitely argued for the notion: the girl's competent defense of her chastity (had not Joan, on the night he abandoned her, proposed a life of mutual celibacy in London?), her general independence and toughness of spirit (which surely did not suggest the demure Miss Bromly), her understandable confusion of Billy Rumbly with Henry Burlingame, and, alas, even her final succumbing to abduction by an Indian. But perhaps the most revealing detail of all was that hysterical moment when "Miss Bromly" had insisted that her name was Anna Cooke: that Joan, driven mad with despair, should identify herself not only in the tavern but in her own mind with the person whose ring she wore, the person of whom she could very probably have learned to be supremely jealous—this struck him with a force like that of certainty, and his conscience groaned at the blow.

693

But his immediate objective, however trifling by comparison, made it necessary to postpone these reflections. He changed his mind about revealing his true identity and came to his point by a different route. " 'Tis not really Eben Cooke I am concerned with; I merely wished to test whether thou'rt a man of the world, so to speak. Now I am a stranger to this province, friend, but 'tis said a bachelor need no more sleep alone here than in London, thanks to a string of gay establishments like Malden. 'Tis only natural a man should wonder whether a genial house such as this . . ."

He allowed the innkeeper to complete the clause; the fellow's eyes were merry, but he shook his head.

"Nay, worse luck, Sir Benjamin; old Sir Harry ne'er durst make a regular stews o' the place for fear some clever Jack might roger Henrietta for a whore."

The poet reluctantly abandoned his theory—somewhat relieved, however, that the inn was not really a brothel, for he scarcely knew how he would have retreated otherwise from his inquiry.

"All the same, I'd not have ye think there's no sport to be had in Church Creek," the innkeeper continued. "How would it strike ye if I should say that the lady ye must apply to is the selfsame lady ye rode in with this noon?"

"Nay!"

"I swear't!" The innkeeper beamed triumphantly. "Her name is Mary Mungummory, the Traveling Whore o' Dorset —she's but the Mother Superior now, ye understand—and I'll wager the price of admission she can find some manner o'—— Hi, there! Speak of the devil!"

Ebenezer followed the man's eyes and saw that Mary had just entered the room and was looking worriedly about. He caught her eye, and as she approached his table the innkeeper excused himself, saluted her cordially, and declared with a wink that Sir Benjamin had business to discuss with her.

"I feigned to mistake this inn for a brothel," Ebenezer explained as soon as they were able to talk, and told her briefly of his hypothesis and its failure.

"I might have spared ye that fiction, had ye asked me," Mary said. "I vow, Mr. Cooke, I don't know what hath possessed poor Roxie!"

"Is she worse, then?"

"She is cousin-german to a Bedlamite!" The miller himself, she went on to say, was no better or worse than before, but Mrs. Russecks, so far from regaining her composure after Ebenezer's departure, had grown steadily more distracted and unreasonable: she fell by turn into fits of cursing, weeping, and apathy; Mary's attempts to divert her with stories of Henry Burlingame and Billy Rumbly had only provoked fresh outbursts; Henrietta herself had been screamed at and banished from the chamber.

"Methinks 'twas not you that set her off," Mary asserted, "else why would she treat Henrietta so harshly? What's more, she seems as wroth with herself as with any soul else; she tears her hair, and rakes her cheeks, and curses the day of her birth! Nay, Mr. Cooke, I am more persuaded than ever 'tis the shock o' the day's events hath fair unhinged her, naught more mysterious; but I fear this night she'll fling away the pins and ne'er hinge back."

Ebenezer was not convinced, but he could offer no more plausible hypothesis. He called for two glasses of beer, and when Mary had finished relating her news to the other patrons, he told her of his firm belief that the Church Creek Virgin was in fact Joan Toast. She scoffed at the notion at first, then listened in amazement, perplexity, and mounting concern.

"There's naught I can say to rebut ye," she admitted finally, "albeit I can't see why she pitched on the name *Meg Bromly*. Still, 'tis as good as another, I daresay."

"I am convinced 'tis she!" the poet declared, and tears started in his eyes. " 'Sheart, Mary, what miseries have I not brought on that girl? Would God I might fly to her this night and beg for retribution! Would Heav'n——"

An expression of horror on Mary's face arrested him; looking beyond him while he spoke as had the innkeeper, she too had seen someone come in, and her reaction was frightening to behold. Ebenezer's flesh crawled.

"Is't Harry Russecks?" he whispered.

"Dear Christ!" moaned Mary, and, expecting the worst, Ebenezer turned to see for himself. The new arrival was not Harry Russecks, but a slight statured gentleman whom the other patrons rose to greet. The poet's heart sprang up; he moved his mouth to call *"Henry!"* and realized just in time to check himself that this man was not the "Nicholas Lowe" Burlingame but the Burlingame of St. Giles, grown fifteen years older and tanned by the Maryland sun: that is to say, not Burlingame at all . . .

" 'Tis my Charley Mattassin come from the dead!" Mary cried aloud.

"Nay, Mary," Ebenezer whispered. " 'Tis Billy Rumbly!"

Everyone in the room was startled by the outburst. Rumbly himself broke off his salutations and looked over with a puzzled smile. Two of his friends murmured something, but he ignored them and came towards the poet's table, where, still smiling, he bowed slightly to Ebenezer and addressed the ashen-faced woman.

"I beg your pardon, madam, but I must know whether you did not speak the name *Charley Mattassin* just then." His voice, Ebenezer observed, was of the same timbre as Burlingame's, but the accent was more continental than English.

"Thou'rt the breathing image o' thy brother!" Mary replied, and began to weep unashamedly. The other patrons came over to see what was the trouble; Billy Rumbly politely requested that they permit him to learn for himself, and they retired.

"May I sit down with you, sir? I thank you. Now, my dear lady——"

"Pray let me explain, sir," Ebenezer ventured. " 'Tis a most happy coincidence that brought you hither tonight!"

"I quite agree," said Billy Rumbly. "As for explanation, there may be no call for one: my dear lady, can it be thou'rt Miss Mungummory?"

Mary's astonishment was followed immediately by apprehension. "Now, Mr. Rumbly, ye mustn't think hard o' me; I swear——"

"That you had naught to do with Mattassinemarough's death? Let *me* swear, Miss Mungummory, that none save Mattassin had aught to do with Mattassin's death. He destroyed himself—I appreciate that fact—and for all his fits of contrary passion, I know he died with your image in his heart." He smiled. "But say, how is't you knew I was his brother? Merely by reason of a certain likeness betwixt us?"

Mary was still too taken aback to muster a coherent answer, and so Ebenezer declared, "We've heard the tale of your adventures from the trapper Harvey Russecks, sir——"

"Dear Harvey! A consummate gentleman! Then thou'rt aware I was formerly called *Cohunkowprets,* the Bill-of-the-Goose; yet that doth not quite account for all."

"My business will explain the rest," Ebenezer said. "I am in Church Creek expressly to deliver you a message from the Tayac Chicamec."

For the first time, Billy Rumbly's composure was ruffled: his brow contracted, and his eyes flashed in a way that chilled the poet's blood, so often had he seen that angry flash in Burlingame's eyes.

"The Tayac Chicamec hath no messages that I care to hear," he said dangerously.

"Haply not, sir," the poet granted at once, "yet I must tell you that as a gentleman you cannot refuse to hear me: I swear to you that the lives of every man, woman, and child of this province are in your hands!"

Billy Rumbly fixed his attention on the glass of beer brought to him by the innkeeper; his anger seemed to have hardened into stubbornness.

"You speak of the coming war. I do not think of it."

Ebenezer had anticipated this difficulty; he sighed as though resigned to the Indian's obduracy. "Very well, sir, I shan't trespass farther on your good nature. I only hope my friendship with your brother Burlingame will make him less unreasonable than you."

The remark had its intended effect: Billy grabbed his hand and stared open-mouthed at him, as if scarcely daring to believe his ears.

"What cruel stratagem of my father's is this?"

"The stratagem is mine, sir, to persuade you to hear me out on a number of urgent matters; but what I said is nonetheless true. As 'twas my pleasure to inform the Tayac Chicamec, your younger brother, Henry Burlingame Third, is neither dead nor lost; he was my tutor in England for six years and at present is not many miles from this spot." Despite his fear of alienating the man, who rather intimidated him as well, his terrific responsibilities caused Ebenezer suddenly to lose patience. "Damn you, sir, put by your skepticism; 'tis mankind's side I'm on, not Chicamec's! Do you know this ring? Aye, 'tis the ring of Quassapelagh, that he gave me for saving his life whilst he was hiding in the cliffs. Ah, you've heard that tale before? Then you know that the wight I left to serve him also owed his life to me—a trussed-up Negro slave named Drepacca, that I believe hath been a friend of yours! Do you think I'll beg you to save my companions' lives by leading that monstrous rebellion? I come here with a plan, sir, not a plea; a plan to save both English and Ahatchwhoops!" He paused to regain his self-control and concluded in a calmer tone, "What's more, I wish to speak with you as one gentleman to another with regard to your wife, who I have reason to believe is a woman very precious to me; and if after all this you need still more evidence of my good intention, know that we may speak here at length without fear of interruption by your enemy the miller Russecks:

697

he is lying this moment at death's doorsill after a bout with me and my companion this afternoon."

Billy Rumbly was flabbergast. "Great Heavens, sir, you leave me breathless! My father, my wife, my long-lost brother—thou'rt setting my world a-spin!" He laughed. " 'Tis clear I misapprehended you, and I humbly beg your pardon, Mr.——"

"Cooke; Ebenezer Cooke, of Malden." The poet was relieved to observe that the name apparently meant nothing to Billy Rumbly.

"Mr. Cooke, sir." The Indian shook his hand warmly. "May I say at the outset, Mr. Cooke, that gossip to the contrary notwithstanding, my wife is as dear to me as you declare she is to you, and her condition (which I gather thou'rt aware of) is a matter of gravest concern to me. In fact, 'twas to seek advice from Mrs. Russecks on that subject I drove hither this evening—for which praise God!"

Mary, having by this time got the better of her emotions, explained that Mrs. Russecks was indisposed and excused herself to return to the patient's bedside.

"If ye still mean to call on Mrs. Rumbly," she said to Ebenezer, "we'll ride out first thing in the morning."

"Nay," Billy Rumbly protested, "you must be my guest tonight, sir, and tell me these wonders at your leisure; I shan't have it otherwise! And you, Miss Mungummory, if you really must go now, take my sympathies and regards to Mrs. Russecks and tell her I'll consult her another time; but you and I must speak together very soon about Mattassin—tomorrow, perhaps? I've much to ask and much to tell!"

Almost too carried away to speak, Mary managed some sort of acknowledgment and left the inn. Billy watched her intently until she was gone and then shook his head.

"I'll wager she was beautiful once! And even now, despite all—I don't presume to understand *her*, Mr. Cooke, but I quite understand my brother, I believe." He turned to the poet with a smile. "Now, sir, what say you? If your business with regard to my wife is not to duel for her affections, let's out at once for Tobacco Stick Bay; 'tis but four miles down the road, and I've a fair team to fetch us. Astonishing, this business about my brother!"

Ebenezer was altogether charmed. He had not suspected how deep was his anxiety at the prospect of encountering Billy Rumbly until now, when the man's amiability removed it. It was like meeting Henry Burlingame again after a long and discouraging separation—but a Burlingame whose formidability was not ambivalent; whose benevolence was unequivocal; in short, the gay, efficient Burlingame who had come to his rescue once in Magdalene College. There still remained the task of inducing him to save Bertrand and Captain Cairn, and the rather more ticklish problem of what to do about Joan Toast; but in the presence of Billy Rumbly—his princely animation, his mannered power—Ebenezer could not feel pessimistic, much less despairing. On the contrary, his flagging spirits soared; his face grew flushed with the ardor of gratitude, the warmth of reciprocal good feeling. While he donned his greatcoat, Billy Rumbly (who had never removed his own) declared to the house that Miss Mungummory's earlier commotion had been due to a simple case of mistaken identity: she had taken him for his late brother, Charley Mattassin, the misguided fellow who had been hanged for the murder of Mynheer Wilhelm Tick and family. Ebenezer was surprised at the man's candor, but Billy apparently knew his audience: although the revelation shocked them, their murmurs seemed commiserative rather than hostile.

"Now," Billy cried, "having blessed your wives with some gossip, let me bless you gentlemen with a dram!" When the drinks were distributed among the admiring patrons, he purchased in addition a "rundlet for the wagon," declaring that the day Sir Harry Russecks broke his head must not go uncelebrated. This sentiment was affirmed with loud hurrahs, and when the two men made their good nights and mounted Billy's wagon, Ebenezer felt himself envied by everyone in the tavern.

They paused briefly at the mill, where he introduced McEvoy to the object of their mission, announced his current plans, and learned that while Mrs. Russecks had finally been got to sleep, there was no change whatever in the miller's condition; then they set off westward along a dark and narrow path. The night was still and frosty; through the trees the poet spied the great triangle of Deneb, Vega, and Altair, though the constellations to which they belonged were obstructed from view.

"Our little drive takes half an hour," Billy said. "If I may request it, spare me the message from my father till later, as I can estimate its substance out of hand. But I must hear about this gentleman who claims to be my brother, and methinks 'twere better we spoke our minds on the subject of my wife ere we arrive. Yet stay: we durst not essay these weighty matters with dry throats; the first thing to do is take Lady Rundlet's maidenhead!"

"Marry," Ebenezer laughed, "thou'rt more a twin than a common brother to Henry Burlingame! How oft have I burned to hear some news he had for me, or tell him news of my own, and been obliged to sit through a chine of pork ere he'd give me satisfaction!"

They sampled the rundlet, and the good white Jamaica scalded the poet's innards most gratifyingly. Both the Indian and himself had availed themselves of lap robes, which, together with the rum and the absence of wind, kept them as comfortable as if the month were April instead of latest December. The team stepped leisurely in the frozen path, and the wagonwheels creaked and crunched with a pleasing sharpness. Ebenezer permitted his body to rock with the motion of the springs; the task of relating once again the story of Burlingame's quest and his own intricate history had previously appalled him, but in these circumstances it seemed a pleasant labor. He sighed as he commenced, but it was the sigh of a man certain that his story will give its bearers unusual pleasure. Making no mention of his doubts, reservations, disappointments, and astonishments, he told of Burlingame's rescue by Captain Salmon; his boyhood as sailorman, gypsy minstrel, and Cambridge scholar; his tenure at St. Giles in the Fields and the twins' affection for him; his adventures in the provinces as political agent and unwilling pirate; his rescue of the Russecks ladies; his vain endeavors to discover his parentage; and the poet's recent solution of that mystery.

"The question," he asserted near the end of his relation, "was who came 'twixt Sir Henry and Henry the Third, and how my friend came to be lightskinned as any Englishman, when neither Sir Henry's *Privie Journall* nor Captain John Smith's *Secret Historie* referred to any Lady Burlingame. E'en that last installment of the *Historie,* that your people call *The Book of English Devils,* did not resolve these questions, inasmuch as any offspring of Sir Henry and Pokatawertussan must needs be a blend of English and Ahatchwhoop —as is the Tayac Chicamec, in fact."

" 'Tis as much a mystery now as erst, for all I grasp it," Billy confessed. "Yet I have no doubts this fellow is in sooth my brother. Miraculous!"

"Aye, and no less so is the chance that gave me the key." He told of his visit with Burlingame to the Jesuit Thomas Smith, who had entertained them with the tale of Father

FitzMaurice. "When I spied Father Joseph's chests in the house of the Tayac Chicamec and learned the King had wed that martyr's offspring, I had the answer: 'tis by decree of the Law of Averages their union should have issue not alone like thyself, who have the same commingled blood as both thy parents, but also pure-blooded Indian and pure-blooded English, in equal number. In short, Mattassin and Henry Burlingame."

"What a gift you have presented me!" Billy exclaimed quietly. "A brother, to replace poor Mattassin! I am forever in your debt, sir! But what is his trade at present, that hath plied so many in the past, and where might I find him? For I mean to seek him out at once, whether in Cambridge Maryland or Cambridge England."

With his imminent plea for Billy's assistance in mind, Ebenezer replied that Burlingame was still very much engaged in provincial politics as an agent for Lord Baltimore, in whose service he had jeopardized his life time and again for the cause of justice. It was difficult to praise as anti-revolutionary a man who had lately changed allegiance to John Coode (and who for all Ebenezer knew might be the arch-rebel and insurrectionist himself), but the poet reasoned that Billy Rumbly would be more likely to assent to a plan of which he believed his long-lost brother would approve.

"As to where he is now, I am not certain, for his home is where'er the cause of civilization leads him. But my desire to find him is no less urgent than your own, for I know well he'd gamble his life to prevent a massacre." Here, though he had promised to save the story, he could not resist telling of the perilous circumstances under which he had learned about the coming attack, and of Chicamec's ransom terms for Bertrand and the aged sea-captain. "He wants a son with the power of Quassapelagh and Drepacca to lead the Ahatchwhoops in the insurrection. My prayer is that you or Henry, if not the twain of you, will deceive him in the name of peace and good will; take your place as King of the Ahatchwhoops and use your influence for the good of red man, black man, and white man alike. 'Twere not beyond question, methinks, if only you——"

"Ah, sir, your pledge, your pledge!" Billy held up his hand. "Let us proceed to the subject of my wife. Before you speak your business, may I assume thou'rt acquainted with the story of our—*courtship?*"

"Aye, from Harvey Russecks and from Mary Mungummory, who had it from Sir Harry's wife."

701

"Both excellent sources. Then you doubtless know I share your alarm at Miss Bromly's self-imposed degradation. I am not yet either a Christian or a legal denizen of the Province, sir, and thus cannot properly marry her as I wish to. But she would have none of't e'en were't possible; she wishes no more than the simple Ahatchwhoop rite I performed—the which neither I nor the laws of Maryland honor where one of the parties is English."

"Then in reality she is not your wife at all, save in the spirit of Common Law?"

Billy acknowledged that this was unhappily the case. "I freely own, what you know already, that I was prepared to ravish and abduct her after the old Ahatchwhoop manner. I hid in the woods near Sir Harry's mill and brought her to the window by means of certain noises, whereupon I revealed myself to her sight. The object of this is to terrify the victim, but so far from swooning away, Miss Bromly came out to me alone, and when I offered to attack her—ah well, 'tis enough to swear no attack was necessary: she came with me of her own choosing, and of her own choosing remains. Moreover, for all my pressing her to live like a proper gentlewoman, she hath transformed herself into a salvage—nay, worse: into a brute, that neither speaks nor grooms itself! You have heard tales that I torture her over the fire? I swear to you that I would not willingly harm a hair of her head, but she hath learned somewhere that Indian husbands are wont to truss a shrewish wife near a green-wood fire, to cure their ill temper, and she obliges me to rope and smoke her in like manner above the hearth."

Ebenezer clucked his tongue. "Alas, poor woman!"

Billy regarded him carefully and gave the reins a little snap. " 'Tis with reason I tell you these things, my friend. I would imagine there hath been some adverse sentiment regarding Miss Bromly and myself; for aught I know, despite your cordial air you may be her brother or her betrothed, come to take revenge for her abduction—she tells me naught of her former life or past connections." He did not mean to suggest, he went on to say, that he was devoid of responsibility in the affair: whatever Miss Bromly's past, it was he who had in ignorance assaulted her in Russecks's tavern and set out deliberately to ravish her afterwards; it was not impossible that her current state was a deranged one caused by the shock of his attacks. However, he dearly loved her and wished her well, and was willing to do anything to improve her condition or otherwise discharge his responsibility.

So disarmed was Ebenezer by the man's frank and friendly attitude that, though the thought of Joan's degradation stung him to tears, he could not muster anger against her abductor. "More virtuous men than I may call you to account," he said instead. "Only tell me this: doth the girl wear any sort of ring?"

"A ring? Aye, she hath one, that she kisses and curses by turns but will not speak of. 'Tis a silver seal of sorts: methinks 'twas designed to fend off evil spirits, for it hath the word *ban* or *bane* around the seal: *B-A-N-N-E*."

For a moment Ebenezer was puzzled: then he recognized the anagram. "Ah God, 'tis as I feared! I am more than the girl's betrothed, Mr. Rumbly; I am her husband and I came hither, among other reasons, to save her from your clutches! Howbeit, I am persuaded thou'rt even less to blame than you imagine: 'tis I, above all others, who am responsible for Joan Toast's sorry state—that is her true name, not Meg Bromly, and if you truly love and pity her, 'tis *you* should punish *me,* not vice versa." His former sense of well-being entirely flown, he apprised Billy of the history of his relationship with Joan Toast and his crowning injustice to her, which he attributed her flight from Malden and her current distracted state.

The Indian attended with great interest and sympathy. "You must forgive me if this question is improper, sir," he said, when the poet was finished. "I believe I understood you to say that albeit you married the woman thou'rt yet a virgin, did I not? Remarkable! And yet methinks you implied that Miss Toast, or Mrs. Cooke—how doth a gentleman say it?— that you are perhaps not the only man who hath enjoyed her companionship, and that some others, let us say, were not so tender of her honor as were you . . . Is that correct, or have I misconstrued your words?"

Ebenezer smiled. "No need to step lightly, sir. In London she was a whore."

"I see," Billy murmured, but his frown suggested that he was not altogether satisfied on the matter. "And of course thou'rt quite certain of these things?"

The poet could not suppress a grim amusement. "Belike thou'rt new to the ways of cultivated ladies, sir: a clever tart may whore herself to the very gate of Hell and then sell Lucifer first go at her maidenhead."

"Indeed. And yet the ring seems certain proof . . ." He allowed the sentence to trail off in vague perplexity. "Hi, here's an end to speculation: yonder stands my cabin."

The path had brought them out of the woods into a sizeable cleared field bounded on the north by a narrow bay. On the near end of the water-front stood a cabin, dimly lit, and several outbuildings. As they stabled the team and approached the house, Ebenezer grew increasingly nervous at the prospect of confronting Joan Toast; the most honorable course, he decided, was simply to present himself, humbly and without excuse, and leave the first reaction to her.

At the doorstep Billy Rumbly stopped and laid a hand on the poet's shoulder. "Let us quite understand each other, my friend: is it your intention to take my—that is, *your* wife, I suppose—is it your intention to take her from me for her own good?"

"That is my intention," Ebenezer admitted.

"By force, if need be?"

"I am neither armed nor inclined to violence, sir; my only weapon is persuasion, and 'tis not likely she'll even listen to me. Nor are you obliged to invite me in, under the circumstances; I'll not bring suit."

Billy chuckled. "Thou'rt a noble fellow! Very well, then, since we both love the woman and both feel answerable for her condition, let us both put her improvement above all personal considerations: we will put our separate cases and leave the choice to her. Belike she'll wash her hands of the twain of us!"

Ebenezer agreed, charmed anew by the civilization his host had acquired in so short time, and they entered the cabin. A single candle flickered near the door, and on the hearth the fire had burned to its last few coals; the room was obscure and chill.

"*Yehawkangrenepo!*" Billy called, and explained in an undertone, "She obliges me to call her by that name. *Yehawkangrenepo!*"

Now came a grunting and stirring from a straight-backed wooden bench before the fire; a woman sat up, her back to the door, and commenced rubbing her eyes and scratching in her wild dark hair. Her shift was ragged, filthy stuff, and she grunted and scratched about her person like a jackanapes picking fleas. Ebenezer felt faint at the wretched spectacle. The creature scratched her head again, rising from the bench as she did so, and the candle glinted briefly from her silver ring. The flash was barely perceptible, but it blinded the poet altogether to his resolve. He ran to throw himself at her feet.

"Joan Toast! Ah Christ, how I have wronged thee!"

At the sound of his voice the girl gasped; at sight of him lunging toward her she screamed and caught at the bench-

704

back for support. And then it was Ebenezer's turn to moan and stumble, for despite her changed appearance, the flickering candlelight, and the tears that made his vision swim, he saw when she turned that Billy Rumbly's mistress was neither Joan Toast nor Miss Meg Bromly, but his sister Anna.

16

A Sweeping Generalization Is Proposed Regarding the Conservation of Cultural Energy, and Demonstrated With the Aid of Rhetoric and Inadvertence

WHETHER FROM DESUETUDE or access of surprise, after her initial scream Anna's voice quite failed her. Brother and sister embraced in vast, unselfconscious relief at having found each other again, but even as Ebenezer comforted himself with her name and explained to bewildered Billy Rumbly, between sniffs and sobs, that she was his twin sister and not his wife, he felt her stiffen in his arms. At once his memory surrendered to the dreadful things he had learned from Burlingame, as well as the story, now newly appalling, of the Ahatchwhoop prince's courtship. The embrace became awkward; he made no effort to detain her when she pushed free of him and collapsed in tears on the bench.

"She is in sooth your sister?" Billy asked.

The poet nodded. "You must try to understand," he said, speaking with difficulty. "This is a painful moment for both of us . . . I can't explain just yet . . ."

"There will be time," Billy said. "For the present, my company is burdensome to all; I shall bid you *adieu* and return in time for breakfast."

"Nay!" Anna suddenly found her voice. The tears had marked courses through the dirt on her face. "This man is my husband," she declared to Ebenezer.

"Quite so," the poet murmured. " 'Tis I must go."

"I shan't allow it," Billy said firmly. "Whate'er the breach

705

betwixt you, 'tis a family matter and must be put right. In any case I've meant for some time to sleep in the barn: I have cause to believe a thief hath been pilfering from it lately." The pretext was unconvincing, but it went unchallenged. Billy laid his hand affectionately on Anna's head. "Prithee mend the family fences with forgiveness and good will; 'tis a great pity for brother and sister not to love each other. Nay, raise up your eyes! And you, sir: I am in your debt already for arousing this woman to speech, and more than thankful for the chance that hath enabled me to repay your gift of a brother with like coin. I beg you only to remember our agreement: in the morning you must tell me the news from Bloodsworth Island, and we shall see what is to be done on every head."

Anna hung her head and said nothing; Ebenezer too, though embarrassed by his own unwillingness to protest, was so eager for private conversation with his sister that he permitted Billy to make up the fire in the cabin and then leave for the cheerless barn. He scarcely dared look at Anna; the thought of her condition made him weep. For a while they sat on opposite ends of the bench and stared into the fire, occasionally sniffing or wiping their eyes.

"You have been to Malden?" he ventured at last. From the corner of his eye he saw her shake her head negatively.

"I met a Mr. Spurdance at the wharf in Cambridge . . ."

"Then you know my disgrace. And you must have encountered . . . my wife there too, since you have your ring again." His throat ached; the tears ran afresh, and he turned to Anna with great emotion. "I was obliged to marry her or perish of my seasoning, as our mother did; but 'twas not her doing, Anna; you mustn't think ill of her. 'Tis true she is a whore, but she followed me to Maryland out of love——"

Again he faltered, remembering Burlingame's assertion that Anna's motive was the same. " 'Tis on my account she hath the pox and is a slave to opium; she suffered unimaginable indignities to be with me, and nursed me back to health when I was ill, nor made any claim on me whatsoe'er—not e'en upon my chastity, I swear't! Her one wish, when all was lost, was that we fly together to London and live as brother and sister till her afflictions carried her off. And I, Anna—I betrayed that saintly woman most despicably! I stole away alone; abandoned her to die uncared for! 'Tis I you must despise, not poor Joan Toast!"

"Despise?" Anna seemed surprised. "How can I despise either of you, Eben? 'Twas through deception you lost Malden,

706

and honor as well as necessity required your marriage. I wish you had not abandoned her—'tis a hellish thing to be alone!"

She found it necessary to pause for some moments after this observation. Then, speaking carefully and avoiding his eyes, she asked how it happened that he was not in London. Had he known she was in Maryland? Did he understand that she had loved Henry Burlingame for a dozen years and had come to Maryland hoping to marry him? Did he appreciate that it was Bertrand's terrible news, and Mr. Spurdance's, and Joan Toast's, and her despair at ever finding either Henry or her brother, and the shock of being assaulted by a savage who miraculously resembled Burlingame, that had brought her to her present state? She dissolved in tears of shame. Ebenezer took her hand, but made no attempt to answer the questions.

"My story will take hours to repeat," he said gently, "and I've been telling divers parts to divers people these two days till I am weary of't. I'faith, Anna, there is so much to say! You wept once when we were first separated for an evening, and declared we'd ne'er catch up to each other again—I little dreamt the full import of that remark! Now 'tis no matter of hours or rooms that parts us; 'tis as if we were on twin mountaintops, with what an abyss between! We shall span it ere we leave this cabin, though it take a week of explanation —how fine a gentleman Billy is to give us some hours to make beginnings!—but methinks 'twere better to hear first what passed 'twixt you and Joan, and what the state of things at Malden is, now Father's there, for the smallest detail of my story may want an hour's gloss." By way of example he declared that the resemblance of Billy Rumbly and Henry Burlingame was no more miraculous than that of any other pair of brothers. Anna was almost dumb struck; she pleaded for more information, but Ebenezer was adamant.

"Please," he said, "have you not seen Henry at all? I must know these things ere I commence."

"Not at all," Anna sighed, "nor hath anyone in Cambridge or St. Mary's City: the name is foreign to them." And resigning herself to the postponement of her questions, she told of her great loneliness in St. Giles, her growing fear that Burlingame would never succeed in discovering his parentage (which discovery, she declared, he had made prerequisite to their marriage), and her final determination to leave their father to his querulousness, join Ebenezer at Malden, and either persuade Burlingame to abandon his research or else assist him in whatever way she could.

At this point Ebenezer interrupted; turning her face to his he said, "Dearest Anna, don't feel shame in your brother's presence! This bridge of ours must have piers of love and candor; else 'twill fall." What was on his mind was the love which she was alleged to feel for him, and about which he thought it imperative to reach an understanding from the first; however, he suddenly recalled Burlingame's assertion that Anna herself was at most only dimly aware of her strange obsession and possibly altogether oblivious to it. Her look of bewilderment seemed to confirm this assertion. "What I mean," he added lamely, "matters once reached a pass where Henry judged it necessary to take me altogether into his confidence . . . and in sooth, I have learned some things about him that you——" He could not go on; Anna blushed as deeply as he and veiled her eyes with her hand.

"And thou'rt aware that my husband resembles him in every particular," she said. "In short, I am no less virginal than thyself, and no more innocent."

"Let us speak no more of't!" Ebenezer begged.

"One more thing only." She removed her hand and regarded him seriously. Ebenezer felt certain that she was about to confess her unnatural passion—a prospect the more alarming because of his suspicion, vouched stoutly for by Burlingame, that to some extent he shared it—but instead she declared that he must not think her naïve with regard to Henry Burlingame. Hadn't she seen that he took his deepest pleasure in the two together? Hadn't he revolted her time and again at St. Giles by his amorous disquisitions on everything from asparagus-spears to bird dogs of both sexes? "Methinks 'tis easier to know another than to know thyself," she said. "There is little in Henry's character that is foreign to me." She smiled for the first time and blushed at a sudden recollection. "Dare I tell you something he neglected to? I asked him, ere the twain of you left London, wherefore you made so much of your virginity, when I longed so to have done with mine! And I said farther that were you he, the both of us would put an end to innocence."

Ebenezer shifted uncomfortably.

"His reply," Anna continued, watching Ebenezer's face, "was that you harbored in your breast a grand and secret passion for one woman that the world denied you, and had liefer remain a virgin than take second choice!"

"That is true to some extent," the poet granted. "Howbeit, 'twas not so much the *world* that denied me Joan Toast, as John McEvoy, and——"

"Stay, I did not finish. I shall confess, Eben, Henry's news inspired me with inordinate jealousy, albeit I knew we each would marry soon or late. 'Tis that we had been so close, you know . . . In any case, I demanded the name of this lady who had writ such a patent on your heart, and why you'd ne'er confided in your own dear sister that once knew your every whim and thought. Henry answered that you yourself scarce realized who she was, but that e'en if you did, the force of custom would seal your lips, inasmuch as the object of your passion was—your sister!"

Ebenezer sat upright. "Henry said that? I'Christ, there is no end to the man's nefariousness! Do you know, Anna, he told me the selfsame thing about you? I had learned of your affair with him, you see—this was before I knew of his impotence—and I was aflame with rage and envy——"

He cut his sentence short, but its implication hung clearly between them. The room was filled at once with tension and embarrassment, of a different order from what they had felt before; their positions on the bench were suddenly awkward; on pretext of scratching her leg, Anna slipped her hand from under his and averted her eyes.

"So," she said, and was obliged to clear her throat. "It would seem there was a mustard seed of truth in what he said to us."

For a time they could speak no more. The silence was painful, but Ebenezer could imagine no way to terminate it. Fortunately, Anna came to the rescue: in a mild, deliberate voice, as if no digression had occurred, she resumed the narrative of her journey from St. Giles, employing without comment the proposition that her motive had been to join Henry Burlingame. The poet's heart glowed.

"I had heard naught of his activities since 1687, when you and I abandoned him in London. Then last spring he approached me as he did you later on the Plymouth coach, disguised as Colonel Peter Sayer. When I was finally persuaded of his true identity, he told me the tale of his adventures in the provinces, his discovery of certain references to a namesake in Virginia, and the political intrigues to which he was party."

Ebenezer questioned her closely on this last subject, confessing his doubts about Burlingame's good will towards him and, what was vastly more important, his misgivings about the virtuousness of Lord Baltimore's cause and the viciousness of Coode's. It was then necessary to waive his earlier agenda and tell of Henry's impostures of both Charles Calvert and John Coode, and the transfer of his allegiance from the former to the latter; Bertrand Burton's conviction that Burlingame himself was John Coode; the evidence suggesting that Coode, Lord Baltimore, Burlingame, and Andrew Cooke himself—or some combination thereof—were involved in the deplorable traffic in prostitutes and opium of which Anna had learned from Benjamin Spurdance; and finally, Ebenezer's own sweeping suspicion that both Baltimore and Coode either did not exist save in Burlingame's impostures, or else existed as it were abstractly, uninvolved in and perhaps even ignorant of the schemes and causes attributed to them.

Anna listened with interest, but professed no great surprise at Burlingame's behavior. "As to whether Lord Baltimore and John Coode are real or figmentary," she declared, "I cannot say, albeit 'twere hard to believe that so general an assumption hath no truth in't. Neither can I say with confidence whether the two are in sooth opposed or in league, or opposed in some matters and allied in others, or which hath the right on his side. But I have cause to think that insofar as Henry hath any genuine interest in these matters, his sympathies are with neither of those men; nor doth he truly contradict himself by declaring first for one and then for the other. The man he really admires and serves, I do believe, is Governor Nicholson."

"Nicholson!" Ebenezer scoffed. "He is neither this nor that, from what I hear: he is no Papist, yet he fought for James at Hounslow Heath; he was Edmund Andros's lieutenant, and so differed with him that the two despise each other yet; Lord Baltimore chose him to be commissioned Royal Governor, thinking Nicholson shared his sympathies, but albeit Nicholson seems concerned with prosecuting Coode, he governs as if Lord Baltimore did not exist—which, to be sure, he may not."

Even as he articulated his objection, Ebenezer grew more and more persuaded of the likelihood of Anna's new hypothesis, until arguments began to sound like evidence in its favor. Burlingame had early confided that his purpose was to play off Coode and Andros against Nicholson to Baltimore's benefit—that is to say, "both ends against the middle." But was not Nicholson truly the man in the middle, and Baltimore the extremist? From all the reports of his impatience with dreamers and radicals, his hardheadedness, daring, irascibility, and efficiency, Nicholson's character seemed much more likely to appeal to Burlingame that Charles Calvert's. Moreover, while not an idealist, Nicholson was (now that

Ebenezer reflected on it) perhaps the only person of influence who had actually done anything to further the cause of culture and refinement, for example, in the Plantations: he had established the College of William and Mary during his tenure as lieutenant governor of Virginia, and had avowed his intention to found a similar institution in Anne Arundel Town, at public expense. Even the less creditable aspects of the man—his bastard origins, for instance, and that obscure erotic streak that alienated him from women and gave rise to rumors of everything from privateering to unnatural practices —Ebenezer could readily imagine to be attractive in Burlingame's eyes. In short, what began as a refutation ended as a complaint.

"Why could Henry not tell me this at the outset, as he told you?"

" 'Tis not mine to answer for him," Anna said soothingly, "but he did mistrust your enthusiasm, Eben—as well about virginity as about Lord Baltimore's commission. You know how he was wont to play devil's advocate at St. Giles; with Henry one never knows quite where one stands."

There was little in this explanation to console the poet, but he held his peace while Anna went on with the story of her passage to St. Mary's City and her discovery of Bertrand there posing as Laureate of Maryland, which Ebenezer had heard previously from Bertrand himself.

"I was obliged to put ashore at Church Creek," she said, "and hire a wagon-ride to Cambridge, whence I meant to make my way to Malden; but near the wharf at Cambridge I saw a wretched old beggar in conversation with some slattern of a woman, and albeit I had no idea who they were, I chanced to spy this ring on the woman's hand——"

"Ah, God!"

"She was showing it to the beggarman, and when he laughed at it she flew into a rage and cried, 'To Hell with ye, Ben Spurdance! He is my husband nonetheless, and for aught we know that villain may have been carrying him off!' " Upon recognizing the ring as her own, Anna said, she had understood from what Bertrand had told her that the frightful-looking woman must be her sister-in-law, and the reference to Ebenezer's being carried off by villains had greatly alarmed her. She had gone up to the pair and introduced herself, whereupon the woman, for all she had just been defending Ebenezer, now cursed him as a coward, a liar, and a pimp, flung the ring at Anna's feet, and left, declaring she must get back to Malden before the new whoremaster, An-

711

drew Cooke, came looking for her. This news, together with the testimony of Mr. Spurdance that Ebenezer had deserted his bride and returned with some other gentleman to England, had caused Anna to swoon away; Mr. Spurdance had revived her and told her of the state of things at Malden: that the cooper William Smith had transformed it into a den of sundry vices; that Master Andrew had arrived there with a party of strangers the day before, much concerned over his daughter's whereabouts and distraught by the news that Ebenezer had lost the estate, and upon seeing how matters actually stood, had become so enranged as to fall victim to something like apoplexy. He was temporarily confined to bed, where he spent his time cursing mankind in general, but it was not yet clear whether he was actually unable to regain possession of the estate or whether his wrath was occasioned merely by the distracted state of his affairs; similarly, it was not known whether or in what respect he was himself involved in Captain William Mitchell's activities.

Ebenezer shook his head. "Marry, what is to become of it?" He described the circumstances of the court-trial at Cambridge wherein he had innocently granted Cooke's Point away, and explained that the other man who had boarded the *Pilgrim* with him was Burlingame himself. "But my tale must wait till yours is done, inasmuch as it brings us to Billy Rumbly and my reason for being here. What did you then? Return to Church Creek?"

"Aye," Anna said. "I durst not show myself at Malden till I learned more about Father's position, nor durst I remain in Cambridge, or he'd surely hear of't. I begged Mr. Spurdance to say naught of having seen me, and he promised to pass on whate'er he learned, inasmuch as he too hath no small interest in Cooke's Point. Then I took lodging in Church Creek under Meg Bromly's name, hoping I'd learn ere my money was gone that it was safe to go to Father, or else find some clue to Henry's whereabouts." The end of her story reduced her again to tears. "You know the rest. . . ."

Ebenezer did his best to comfort her, though he too was far from tranquil. The discovery that Ebenezer and Burlingame were not forever lost made Anna frightfully ashamed of her present condition, which only utter despair could justify. On the other hand, she would not repudiate Billy Rumbly.

"You must remember," Ebenezer said, "he is not your husband in the eyes of God or Maryland law, nor e'en by the

712

custom of the Ahatchwhoops, inasmuch as the union hath not been consummated."

"I shall wed him properly now," Anna replied. "As for the matter of consummation, 'twere an overnice point in our case!"

Ebenezer declared his considerable affection for Billy, but averred that insomuch as Anna's condition at the time of choosing him had been far from responsible, she was under no moral obligation to maintain the connection. "Billy himself hath vouched for that: the 'bargain' you heard him allude to was our agreement that thou'rt free to leave or stay, whiche'er you choose. And Henry, after all——"

He pressed the point no farther, aware that his footing was precarious. And as he feared, although she chose not to remind him that her devotion to Burlingame was ambiguous, Anna declared very pointedly, "I have pledged myself to Billy, Eben; would you have me break my pledge? If e'er we part, 'twill be at his behest, not mine; I shall be as good a wife to him as I am able."

Much mortified, Ebenezer said no more; but the subject of his original mission in Church Creek suddenly seemed more crucial than ever to him. Since despite their weariness it was unlikely that either of them would be able to sleep, he proposed that he summon Billy in from the barn and devote the remainder of the night to exposing his plight and plans. It took no more than the assertion that innumerable lives were at stake to win Anna's approval of this proposal, and she insisted on fetching Billy herself.

She did not return at once; Ebenezer spent the uncomfortable interval sighing at the fire. Among his myriad reflections were a few that he readily identified as jealous, though he could not banish them: Why did he object, after all, to a marriage of Anna and Billy Rumbly, who appeared to have all the virtues and none of the vices of his brother?

When at last the two of them came in, Billy hurried to shake his hand.

"Your presence hath achieved what I could never," he declared with great emotion. "Whatever the outcome, my friend, I shall bless you for bringing her to herself."

He shook his head in awe at the spectacle of Anna washing her face and hands in the basin and deploring the state of her hair and clothes. Now that his mistress was a normal English girl, her presence, and Ebenezer's, seemed to intimidate him; he proposed to find them something to eat and was much abashed at Anna's insistence that preparing the food was not a husband's chore.

His discomfiture moved even Ebenezer to amusement and sympathy. "I'Christ, Anna, what can be done with this accursed salvage practice of eating a meal before every conversation?"

The absence of malice in his raillery had a magical effect: the others laughed, and Billy was put somewhat at ease; pipes were brought out; a bottle of wine was discovered in the sideboard. They dined in the best of humor on cold spareribs and muscatel. Anna recounted with much animation, for Billy's benefit, the salient points of the evening's conversation, and though her speech made Ebenezer wonder more than ever what had detained her so long outside, both men regarded her throughout with loving eyes.

"Anna Cooke of St. Giles in the Fields!" Billy marveled. "That wants some getting used to!"

The Indian's subdued, almost awkward voice and manner touched the poet deeply; he put down as unworthy the notion of somehow telling Billy about Anna's love for Burlingame. To divert his mind from it he posed to himself the question whether "cultural energy," so to speak, was conserved within a group after the fashion that physical energy, according to Professor Newton, was conserved within the universe. Was there, he wondered, some unreckoned law of compensation, whereby an access of cultivation on Billy's part reduced Anna to bestiality, and her improvement, which her paramour had so devoutly wished, necessarily brought him low? He decided that quite possibly there was, and lost interest in the question. As soon as the meal was done and fresh pipes were lit he sighed and said, "There was as pleasant an hour as I've spent since leaving London, but my pleasure is a guilty one: e'en as I stretch my legs here and McEvoy pays court to his new mistress, two hostages for our lives are shivering in a hut on Bloodsworth Island." He looked to Billy for approval. "With your permission, friend, I'll state my business now."

Billy shrugged his shoulders, so much in the manner of Burlingame that the wine-cup trembled in Anna's hands. "Methinks I can predict it," he said, and explained the situation unemotionally to Anna, ending with the history of his parentage and the fate of his two brothers. "My father is very old," he concluded, "and no match in strength and influence for Drepacca and Quassapelagh. Besides which, he hath been doubly unhappy in his sons, that not only are fated ne'er to carry on their line but seem driven as well to turn their backs upon their people and aspire to the very stars." Turning again to Ebenezer he said, "If I may hazard another guess, you and your party in some wise fell into my father's hands, and you saved your life by pledging to restore his long-lost son to him, or the son more lately lost, or both, to lead the Ahatchwhoops into battle. Is that the case?"

"That is the case," the poet admitted. "The Tayac Chicamec is much aggrieved by your defection, but what saved us was my news of Henry Burlingame. If 'tis not overbold of me to speak of such matters, your grandfather Sir Henry had clearly learnt some means of rising above his shortcomings on one occasion, inasmuch as he contrived to get your father on Pokatawertussan; now Chicamec believes that just as Sir Henry's defect was transmitted to his grandsons, so perhaps his magical remedy was transmitted as well——"

"The Rite of the Sacred Eggplant," Billy acknowledged with a smile. "Methinks 'tis but a vulgar superstition. In any case I know naught of't—worse luck!"

"Nay, but your brother Henry might, so Chicamec believes, inasmuch as he shares Sir Henry's blood and pigmentation."

"Whate'er this mystery of magical eggplants," Anna said carelessly, "if it hath the effect you mentioned, Henry Burlingame knows no more of't than doth Billy." At once she realized her slip, and crimsoned.

"Aye, that's plain enough," Ebenezer added quickly, "else he'd likely have a wife and family by this time, would he not?"

But it seemed clear that Billy had not missed the implication of Anna's remark. He said nothing—for one thing, Ebenezer deliberately gave him no opportunity—but his manner grew pensive, even brooding. No less than Anna, Ebenezer regretted the slip, for he sensed that it had damaged in advance the appeal he was about to make. Nevertheless he spoke on brightly, as if nothing had changed, only avoiding wherever possible any references to Burlingame.

"There is my plight," he declared, "e'en as you guessed it: if I fail to deliver Chicamec his son within thirty days—fewer than that, now—poor Bertrand and Captain Cairn will be dismembered and burnt at the stake—as well as I, for I have pledged myself to return if I fail, and I intend to."

"I am no longer an Ahatchwhoop," Billy muttered. "Had I wished to succeed my father I'd not have abandoned him. Nor do I see the virtue of trading the lives of your friends for those of all the white men in the Province."

"The war will come in any case," the poet insisted, "only Chicamec will have no hand in waging it. 'Tis not my object to deliver him a good general, but to prevent the war itself."

To this Billy replied, more sullenly yet, that for all he was a deserter, he had not sunk to the level of treason against his people.

" 'Tis not treason I have in mind," Ebenezer protested, not at all pleased with the way things were going. "My plan is not to betray the Ahatchwhoops, but to save them——"

Billy bristled. "Do you think your wretched militia is a match for Quassapelagh and Drepacca? By summer the Governor's scalp will hang from my father's ridgepole!"

"Please, sir, hear me out! If Drepacca makes his treaty with Monsieur Casteene and the Naked Indians, the English will be harried out of America, and 'twill be no chore to drive the French out after them; I grant that. But 'tis not the English case I plead: 'tis the case of humankind, of Civilization *versus* the Abyss of salvagery. Only think, sir: what you've acquired in less than a fortnight wanted two thousand years and more a-building; 'tis a most sweet liquor, is't not? Yet the mash whence man distilled it is two dozen centuries of toil and misery! What, will you drink your fill and throw away the flask, when your people hath such thirst? I grant the English have used you ill, but to drive them out is to drive yourself back into darkness."

Billy did not reply.

"All well, here is my plan," Ebenezer said resignedly. "Whilst I was in your father's town I marked a great rivalry betwixt Quassapelagh and Drepacca; they regard Chicamec as no more than a valuable figurehead, as't were, and vie with each other to dominate the triumvirate. But the fact is, neither hath the whole requirement of an emperor, do you think? Quassapelagh hath the loyalty of the Indians, but for all his virtues he falls short in cleverness and diplomacy; Drepacca is a brilliant fellow, but as yet hath little strength. . . ."

"Thou'rt a shrewd observer," Billy admitted. " 'Tis well for them the Tayac Chicamec is old, for he hath both wit and numbers in his favor."

"Precisely!" the poet exclaimed. "But he *is* old, and there's our opportunity! Thou'rt his son, and heir to both his genius and his influence; if he should abdicate in your favor, 'twould be no chore for you to play Quassapelagh and Drepacca against each other. Thou'rt the only one of the three who can rule alone. And i'faith, Billy, what blessing you could bring

716

to your people! The power to make war would still be yours, and in the plain and public face of't any governor in his senses will put an end to oppressing you; violence will give way to honest negotiation, and our two peoples may borrow each the best of the other's culture——"

"Why do you not apply to your good friend Burlingame instead?" Billy interrupted. "Belike your sister could hit on some subtle means of persuading him."

"Ah, dear Billy!" Anna cried. "I've had no chance yet to explain——"

"Apply to Burlingame I shall," Ebenezer broke in, "but not to go to Chicamec. In the first place he is English by nurture and appearance, a stranger to your people, and ne'er could win their trust; in the second, he is close to Governor Nicholson and hath great influence in the provinces; he can do your cause more good in Anne Arundel Town than on Bloodsworth Island." He searched his mind desperately for additional arguments. " 'Sheart, Billy, 'tis not as if you must live there forever! When your position is secure there'll be no need for your people to hide; you can rule just as well from here and live as you live now. As for Anna, she hath declared already——"

"Enough," Billy commanded, and rose from the bench. "The house belongs to Harvey Russecks, not to me; and the woman, as I gather, belongs to my brother."

"Go to!" pleaded Anna. "I shan't leave you!"

"Then follow me to the town of Chicamec," Billy said coldly. "The Ahatchwhoop women will tear you to pieces." He made a bow to Ebenezer. "I congratulate you, sir, on achieving both of your objectives: your sister now understands that she is no Indian, and I that I am no Englishman. I shall go back to Bloodsworth Island in a very few days."

Anna burst into tears. "Nay, if thou'rt English no more, then you must own me for thy lawful wife!"

"On that point, Miss Cooke, the code of the Ahatchwhoops is quite clear: the Tayac may take as many outland concubines as he pleases, but the blood of his wife should be untainted. Good night."

Ebenezer entreated him not to leave, but Billy (who now demanded that they call him Cohunkowprets) was adamant. " 'Tis near dawn now, and we've yet to sleep," he said. "I shall spend today putting my friend's property in order; tomorrow we'll return to Church Creek and thence to Bloodsworth Island."

Forbidding Anna to follow him, he left the cabin, whereupon Anna fell into a fit of weeping and cursing her inadvertence. Ebenezer's own feelings were mixed: on the one hand he was genuinely sorry that Billy's pride had been so injured, and concerned lest his stratagem misfire on that account; overbalancing these considerations, however, were his joy at finding and in a sense rescuing his sister, as well as succeeding, so it appeared, in his mission to save the lives of his companions. It was no easy matter to calm Anna's distress, but he was assisted by their mutual fatigue; after what seemed like hours of soothing talk he put an end to her tears, and when the first grey light appeared she was asleep on the bench.

17

Having Discovered One Unexpected Relative Already, the Poet Hears the Tale of the Invulnerable Castle and Acquires Another

THROUGHOUT THE AFTERNOON and evening both Ebenezer and his sister did their best to regain Billy's friendship, but though his bitterness seemed to have passed, he held steadfastly to his position and virtually ignored their presence as he worked about the cabin. His taciturnity was not the only change in Billy: overnight, as it were, he had discarded his *mufti* and become an Indian again. His English clothes he had exchanged for matchcoat and buckskin breeches (just as Anna, when she awoke, had exchanged her ragged shift for a proper English costume); his movements were those of a woodsman rather than a planter; even his skin seemed magically to have darkened, as Anna's had quite literally lightened under her diligent scouring. It was a difficult day, and Ebenezer welcomed the coming of nightfall, when Billy again retired to the barn and he and Anna talked for hours between their separate pallets in the dark, much as they had done in childhood. Next morning Billy closed the cabin and outbuildings, hitched up the team, and drove them silently to Church Creek. He would not enter the little settlement himself, but stopped a quarter of a mile from the inn.

"I'll wait here for one hour by the sun," he announced— the first words he'd spoken in two days. "Stay with your sister and send your companion to me if you want the hostages to live."

In vain Ebenezer protested that he had promised Chicamec to return in person; that Anna would be perfectly safe with Mrs. Russecks if the miller was not entirely recovered; that to send McEvoy in his place would make him look and feel a coward.

"One minute of your hour is spent" Billy observed, and turned away; to Anna's farewell he made no reply at all.

It was Ebenezer's intention to approach the village with caution, lest Harry Russecks be up and about his business, but upon reaching the inn he saw McEvoy and a considerable number of others gathered in plain sight in the nearby churchyard. Anna drew a scarf about her face to avoid being recognized as the Church Creek Virgin, and they went over to the gathering.

"Eben!" McEvoy cried upon recognizing him. "Dear Christ, but it's good to see ye back! I feared the salvage had done ye to death for stealing his bride!" He noticed Anna and went pale. "Is't you, Joan?" he whispered.

Ebenezer smiled. " 'Twas a more eventful journey than I'd supposed, John: his bride was not Joan Toast but my sister Anna, who is his bride no longer."

"What in Heav'n!"

"There's no time to explain now." Ebenezer glanced at the activity around the church door. "Since thou'rt not in hiding, I gather that Sir Harry is still bedridden."

"Nay, Eben, no longer," McEvoy said seriously. "Thou'rt just in time to attend his funeral!" The miller, he declared, had never recovered from his comatose state and had expired during the night after his fall. Mrs. Russecks was no longer hysterical, but seemed indifferent to the point of numbness; one was not certain that she quite understood what had happened. Henrietta was of course subdued by her mother's reaction, but the villagers were openly relieved to be rid of the tyrant.

"I share their sentiments," Anna declared with feeling. "He was a beast! But I feel sorry for Mrs. Russecks and Henrietta, who were so kind to me. Where are they now, Mr. McEvoy?"

McEvoy answered that they were inside the church, where the funeral was about to commence, and suggested that the three of them go in also.

"You should go," Ebenezer said to Anna, "but you and I have more urgent business, John: Billy Rumbly waits for us round yonder bend, to go to Bloodsworth Island. We daren't detain him."

Anna excused herself to comply with her brother's suggestion, and Ebenezer explained the situation to McEvoy as rapidly as possible. "We can only pray that Billy will do his best to prevent the war," he said at the end, "but in the meantime we must rescue Bertrand and the Captain."

"Aye, but when then, Eben? Whither do we go from there?"

"Anna swears that Henry Burlingame is a lieutenant of Governor Nicholson's," the poet replied. "Whether he is or not, methinks we should go to Anne Arundel Town with all haste and apprise the Governor of the coming insurrection. Beyond that I cannot see." He hesitated, uncertain how to broach the subject of Billy's ultimatum; but McEvoy took the matter out of his hands.

" 'Twere best only one of us went, Eben, and the other stay here. We heard rumors yesterday that a famous pirate fellow called Every, or Avery, is passing through on his way to the head o' the Bay and hath been foraging for provisions along his route. 'Tis not likely he'd come so far from open water, but the folk are up in arms, and the ladies will want some protection. Besides, ye'll want to be with your sister, will ye not?"

"Ah, John——"

"Nay, not a word, now! Ye know how it burthens me to owe my life to ye, Eben; give me this chance to remit a little on account."

Ebenezer sighed and confessed that he was not in a position to protest, inasmuch as Billy seemed to bear him a grudge. He promised to look after Henrietta and vowed that if the hostages had not arrived safely in four days he would bring the Maryland militia to Bloodsworth Island. McEvoy decided to leave without more ado; Ebenezer went with him to Billy's wagon, full of misgivings, saw him off, and returned to the churchyard.

For all the villagers' excitement, the next few days were happy and almost tranquil for Ebenezer and Anna. Indeed, the pirate-scare (based on Governor Nicholson's announcement that "Long Ben" Avery's ship *Phansie* and Captain

Day's brigantine *Josiah* had been sighted in Maryland waters) turned out to be a blessing in disguise. For one thing, the rumor of foraging privateers kept everyone indoors much of the time and thus, together with the diversion of Harry Russecks's death, spared Anna no end of embarrassment; by the same token it made it unnecessary for Ebenezer either to maintain the imposture of Sir Benjamin Oliver or to disclose his true identity. For another, although Henrietta, distressed as she was at the news of McEvoy's dangerous errand, was delighted to see "Miss Bromly" again and soon became fast friends with her, and although Anna and Mary Mungummory (who was also a houseguest) got on splendidly together, Mrs. Russecks seemed still much disturbed by the presence of the twins; Ebenezer sensed that she would probably not have taken them in as guests had not the other women insisted on male protection.

Her manner was strange and contradictory: in their company she was reserved, even slightly hostile, but whenever they ventured outside she seemed anxious for their safety and was clearly relieved when they returned uncaptured by pirates. There appeared to be little basis for Ebenezer's original fear that she abhorred him for his part in the miller's downfall; she accepted their condolence for her loss but admitted readily that all concerned, herself included, were better off for Sir Harry's demise, and insisted that neither Ebenezer nor McEvoy were in the least responsible for it. On the other hand, she would listen almost with irritation to the poet's account of his peregrinations since April last, and once when he was voicing his joy at being reunited with his sister, she left the room.

"I cannot fathom it," Anna said on that occasion. "She was so gracious before, and now—'tis as if the sight of us gives her pain!"

"Nay, child," Mary Mungummory chuckled, "I've long since given up Roxie as a mystery. None but the good Lord knows how Harry's death hath touched her—she hath yet to tell me clearly why she married the brute to begin with!"

"We must be patient," Henrietta said. "Try to forgive her, Anna."

"La, 'tis we must be forgiven," Ebenezer protested. "Your mother's a judicious soul, and whate'er the affront we've given her, 'tis plainly no trifle."

Henrietta smiled. "Since we agree 'tis a mystery, let's alter the maxim to suit the case: *Rien comprendre c'est pardonner —n'est-ce pas?*"

And there the matter rested, though the poet saw a troubling ambiguity in the proverb.

By way of posthumous retribution for his boorishness, the villagers resolved that Sir Harry's grave remain forever anonymous; with the consent of Mrs. Russecks, who declared her intention of removing to Anne Arundel Town in the near future, they dismantled the machinery of the tide-mill and, in lieu of inscribed granite, marked his resting place head and foot with the unadorned millstones. Henrietta, though she made no secret of her joy at being delivered from her father's despotism, visited the grave dutifully every day during this period, often accompanied by the twins. Mrs. Russecks would not go with them, pleading fear of the pirates; to get out of the house they were obliged to unbar the door, which she then barred behind them, and to re-enter they knocked three times and offered a password. Similar precautions were taken by most of the other villagers as well, on whom Sir Harry had been wont to press stories of his abuse at the hands of Captain Pound; on the way home from the churchyard one saw houses with every window boarded, and Henrietta declared that some people had nailed fast every door in their houses except one, which was kept heavily barred.

Now Ebenezer could scarcely believe that pirates would come so far upriver from the Chesapeake, nor had he ever heard of their assaulting a whole village in the English provinces; nevertheless, the responsibility for a houseful of women weighed heavily upon him—the more since he had no weapons except Sir Harry's old cutlass—and the general mood of alarm was contagious. On the third day of their visit, therefore, while taking tea with Anna, Henrietta, and Mary Mungummory, he suggested that they follow the example of the neighbors.

"After all, we're but one man with one sword; if the pirates really should come hither, they could have at us through two doors and a dozen windows."

For some reason this proposal amused Henrietta. " 'Twould make our house an invulnerable castle, would it not?"

"Very nearly, if you choose to think of't thus. Really, Henrietta, is't so humorous that I'm concerned for your safety?"

"Nay, Eben, 'tis not that at all. The fact is, our family hath had unhappy dealings with invulnerable castles in the past; otherwise my mother would be no orphan, and belike we'd not be named Russecks at all."

Everyone's curiosity was aroused by this remark; they demanded to hear the story.

"Ah, now, I've sworn not to speak of my family to Eben and Anna——" She smiled mischievously and whispered, "But if Mother's asleep I'll forswear myself—'tis a marvelous tale!"

She tiptoed upstairs to Mrs. Russecks's chamber and returned with the news that her mother was still napping soundly. "Now I've no idea why all this hath suddenly become such a dark secret, but when Eben left us to ride out to Billy Rumbly's, Mother made me swear to say naught of her family in his presence. Since I'd not dream of going counter to her wishes, you must swear to me you'll keep her secret. Do you swear?"

They did, much amused by her casuistry, and Henrietta, assuming the manner of a storyteller, began what she called *The Tale of the Invulnerable Castle*, as follows:

"Once on a time there lived in Paris a certain Count named Cecile Edouard, who had the bad judgment to be born into a family of Huguenots . . ."

Ebenezer suddenly frowned. "I say, Henrietta, have you e'er heard tell——"

"Ah, ah, ah!" the girl scolded. "Marry, Eben, thou'rt Laureate of this wretched province, and you know very well 'tis only a boor will interrupt a story!"

The poet laughed and withdrew his question, but his expression remained thoughtful.

"I was getting to the family scandal," Henrietta said with relish. "*Maman* wouldn't mind your knowing this; I've heard her tell it to others often enough, to mortify Papa when he bragged of her nobility. The fact is, albeit we know Monsieur Edouard was a bona fide count, his ancestry is lost to history, and there was a scandalous story among the workmen and servants at Edouardine——"

"Dear God, I was right!" Ebenezer cried. He half rose from his chair with excitement and then sat down again, his features dancing. "Tell me, Henrietta, was this man your—let me see—your grandfather? And was this Castle Edouardine here in Dorset County, not far from Cooke's Point?"

Henrietta feigned exasperation. "I declare, Anna, your brother must be taken in hand! What matter if you've heard the plot already?" she demanded of Ebenezer. "Dido knew the tale of Troy, but she had manners enough to hear't twice from Aeneas, nor e'er broke in with niggling questions."

"But you yourself don't realize——"

"Stop him, Anna, or I'll not say another word!"

By now everyone was laughing at Ebenezer's frustration and Henrietta's mock anger, even the poet himself.

"Very well," he said, "I'll hold my peace. But I must warn you: if your tale goes whither I guess, I'll steal your thunder with a postscript more marvelous by half."

" 'Tis your privilege, and may the cleverest liar win. But will you swear to interrupt me no more, on pain of hearing me read my verses if you do? Good, then let's return to the family scandal. I said there was a story that Cecile's mother had been a Jewess, nor any rich one, either, but a common chambermaid or washwoman in a noble Roman house. In the same house there was a Greek who had once tutored the Marchese's children, but had been reduced to the post of footman because of his depravity; 'tis said he got the young Jewess with child ere he was sent packing, and that subsequently she contrived to make a conquest of the Marchese himself and prevailed upon him to raise her bastard son as his own, there in the *palazzo*." Henrietta pointed out that this story shed no light whatever on Monsieur Edouard's metamorphosis from Roman to Parisian, Catholic to Huguenot, and natural son to nobleman. Nevertheless, she insisted, its odd particularity had the ring of truth. As for the mysterious changes of status, she added mischievously, was not their own Governor Nicholson the Duke of Bolton's bastard, and had he not enjoyed transmogrifications of faith and place no less astonishing?

"Whate'er his origin," she went on, "we know for a fact he was neither a hypocrite on the one hand nor a martyr on the other; when the Huguenots continued to be persecuted even after the Edict of Nantes, he refused to become a Papist, but fled from Paris to London and joined Oliver Cromwell's army. *Maman* says he fought bravely in divers campaigns, but cannot recollect which ones. In any case he left the Lord Protector's service in 1655, as abruptly as he had joined it, and came to Maryland." She sighed. "Now here's a weak spot in my *Edouardiad*, that Eben will surely pounce upon: the voyage of your proper hero like Ulysses or Aeneas is always fraught with trials, but Cecile—albeit he *did* sail east to west, as a hero ought—crossed without incident. He must have got a fortune somewhere in his past, for he cargoed three ships with naught but furniture, carpetings, ironwork, plate, flatware, gewgaws, and oddments for the house he meant to raise in the Plantations. What's more, he brought his wife Sophie along and the rest of his ménage as well: fifteen servants and *Maman*, his only child, who was seven or eight years old. The Province was only twenty-odd years old itself at the time, and had surely never beheld such a Croesus as my grandfather. In 1659 the Lord Proprietary patented him six hundred acres on the Choptank, and he moved across the Bay with his company and baggage to build a house."

Ebenezer shook his head in wonderment, but not at Henrietta's narrative. "Nay, Eben, you must wait as you promised," she said. "What you've heard is merely the preface, and now the tale proper commences."

There was among Monsieur's servants, she declared, an old fellow known only as Alfred, who had been his master's valet as long as anyone could remember. This Alfred was said to know Cecile more intimately than did Madame Edouard herself, and his master loathed him. Cecile was not such a fool as to be unaware of his own character, but his position enabled him to punish others for his shortcomings; yet he dared not cashier the valet and have done with it, not only because Alfred knew so much about him, but also because the servant, despite his menial status, seemed to have been endowed with uncommon acumen and foresight. Thus Monsieur never failed to heed his valet's counsel, for he was, like many another man, wise enough to recognize good sense when exposed to it, if not wise enough to conjure it for himself; but poor Alfred was ill rewarded for his services, inasmuch as each time his advice was taken, his master's resentment towards him increased.

"Now Cecile fell to the task of raising his house with wonderful haste and gusto. He brought with him to Edouardine a shallop's-load of carpenters, cabinet-makers, masons, and even glaziers, though his window glass and mirrors were still en route from London. In six months, whilst the family and workmen lived in cabins, an imposing wooden edifice was raised, with a large central section and two wings. Ordinarily such an army could have built the house more quickly, but it happened that Monsieur Edouard was possessed of a marvelous fear of salvages; time and again he halted the progress of his house and set his men to building a stockade fence about the grounds, or clearing away more trees on his point of land, or constructing earthworks against Indian attacks. Just how numerous and belligerent were the salvages thereabouts no one knew at the time, but certainly Alfred could have pointed out to Monsieur in a moment that such defenses were of the wrong sort. Howbeit, as I said before, he was the perfect servant; he ne'er durst proffer advice unless asked for't, and Cecile was too engrossed in building his palisades, terrepleins, and demilunes, ever to question their utility. In sooth, Indians were observed in the neighborhood from time to time, and albeit their motives may have been naught more sinister than curiosity, still their presence sufficed to send Cecile into a fresh fit of crenelations, embrasures, and machicoulis.

"When at length the house was finished, save for the window glass, he loaded Sophie, Alfred, and himself into a small boat and bade another servant row them some hundred yards offshore, the better to view Edouardine from its noblest elevation.

" 'Well, Sophie,' Monsieur demanded (I mean to invent these colloquies for the sake of interest, if the Laureate hath no objection)—'Well, now, Sophie,' he demanded, 'what do you say of Edouardine?' And Madame Edouard replied, ' 'Tis lovely, *mon cher.*'

" '*Lovely,* you say!' (Can't you see him turning red like Papa, and poor Sophie lowering her eyes?) '*Lovely,* you say! *C'est magnifique! Sans pareil!* And my *palissade!* Why, we are invulnerable!' And then he demanded to know whether Alfred too regarded Edouardine as merely *beau.*

" 'The house is superb, Monsieur,' I can hear Alfred saying —very calmly, you know. 'It is truly elegant.'

" 'Eh? You think so? That's more to the mark!' "

Ebenezer, Anna, and Mary Mungummory applauded Henrietta's lively mimicking of the Count and his timid valet.

" 'But if Monsieur will observe—'

" 'What's that? Observe what?'

" 'I think of the salvage Indians, Monsieur. . . .'

" 'Ah, you think of them? Did you hear that, Sophie? He thinks of *les sauvages,* doth this Alfred! And do you suppose I think of aught besides, idiot? Small chance they have of broaching my palisade!'

" 'None whate'er, Monsieur; but I fear they would not need to broach it.'

" 'And how is that, pray? Do you fancy they have artillery?'

"Whereupon Alfred must have cleared his throat and said politely, 'I have heard, Monsieur, that these salvages make use of flaming arrows in siege. Despite your clearing the trees, they could very well (if they'd a mind to) stand off yonder in the forest and throw such arrows over the palisade onto the house—which then must surely take fire, inasmuch as 'tis made of wood. Monsieur would be obliged to use many men to put out the fire, and thus leave the palisade weakly manned: the salvages would be upon us in short order. Always assuming, of course, that they are hostile.'

" 'Ridiculous!' I daresay Cecile came nigh to striking the valet for having mentioned such a possibility. But next day the carpenters, that were making ready to return to St. Mary's City, found themselves engaged for another three months, for the purpose of rebuilding the house they had just completed. Moreover, their new job involved no carpentry at all, but laying bricks. First Monsieur sent a party to explore the beaches for clay; when they found a good bed he set half his crew to digging, shaping, and firing, and the other half to mixing mortar and laying the finished bricks. What he did, in effect, was erect a new house of brick to encase the wooden one, leaving all the doors and windows in their original locations. It wanted four months instead of three to complete the job, during which period Indians were remarked more frequently than before, in ones and twos. The finished manor even *Maman* remembers as a formidable affair.

"When the last brick was in place, Monsieur Edouard assembled all his workmen and servants before the house. Some weeks earlier, one of their number—I'll have more to say of him anon: he was an English redemptioner so jealous of his master's favor that he changed his name from *James* to *Jacques*—this fellow had found a salvage bow and arrows in the woods nearby, and now Cecile instructed him to secure a resinous pine knot to the shaft of an arrow, down by the head, and set it ablaze, after what was held to be the manner of the Indians.

" 'Now fire,' he ordered Jacques. 'Shoot the arrow at my house, *s'il vous plaît*.' The redemptioner took aim and, being a reasonably good marksman, contrived to hit the great house some thirty feet distant. The arrow glanced off the bricks and fell to the ground.

" '*Voilà!*' Cecile shouted in Alfred's ear. 'Can they harm us now?'

" 'I see no likelihood that they will, Monsieur. So long as the salvages have a care to aim only at the walls, we are as secure as the Bastille.'

" 'What new folly is this you've hatched?'

" 'Should they shoot from the woods, Monsieur,' Alfred

727

ventured, 'as they assuredly would do, why then they must needs aim high, the more so since these fire-arrows are so heavy. Reason dictates that a high trajectory would be most likely to bring the arrows down upon the roof, and the roof is still made of wood.'

"For some moments Cecile could not find his voice, and the fellow with the bow, who was envious of Alfred's position in the household, offered to put his theory to the test; but Cecile snatched away the bow and dismissed the company, calling them idlers and ne'er-do-wells. On the following day the men found themselves dispatched in search of slate, for the purpose of recovering the roof. . . .

"Now it happens that there is not a piece of roofing slate in the whole of Dorset; the men combed the countryside and the riverbanks for days and discovered naught but a few hunting Indians here and there. These they joyfully reported to their employer, who grew so frightened that he scarcely durst venture beyond his *palissade*, and cursed Alfred with every breath. Finally he ordered the workmen to cover the peaked roof with large, flat bricks. Under the additional weight the rafters commenced to buckle; it became necessary to fashion heavy piers from whole logs to support them. The job required another month and immeasurable bother, inasmuch as portions of the floors and partitions had to be removed to accommodate the piers. Upon its completion the house looked secure indeed, if somewhat *grotesque:* it was during this period that the laborers dubbed it *The Castle* in jest, and Monsieur Edouard, for once more flattered than annoyed, renamed his property *Castlehaven*. Again the company was assembled before the main entrance, and obliging Jacques lobbed a new fire-arrow onto the roof. It struck the tiles, rolled down the slope, and came to rest upon a cornice, where it burned out.

" 'Well, sir?' Cecile demanded, and none replied. Alfred looked away.

" 'I command you to say truthfully, on pain of flogging: is my castle *invulnérable*? My Jacques shall fire where'er you wish!'

" 'I have no love for floggings, Monsieur.'

" 'Then you must command him.'

"Jacques, I imagine, was so pleased that he could scarcely manage to light a new fire-arrow and draw the bow. 'Into a window,' Alfred murmured, 'any window . . .' And he indicated with his arm the rows of open window frames on both floors of the house.

" 'Son of a harlot!' Cecile cried, and this time when he snatched the bow he took a cut at Alfred, who'd surely had his skull cracked had he not sprung back. The company dispersed, and Alfred was birched that night for the first time since, on his advice, the *ménage Edouard* had abandoned Paris. During the next week all the first-floor windows were bricked in, and those on the second floor were reduced to shuttered embrasures like cannon-ports. The absence of light and air made living downstairs intolerable, but so secure was Cecile in his fortress that he was actually smiling when he assembled everyone for the third time to witness his triumph over his servant.

" 'Have I left aught undone?'

" 'Naught, Monsieur, that I can imagine.'

" 'Ha, did you hear, *mes amis?* Monsieur Alfred hath assured me I am safe. I think he will detain you no longer. Make ready to depart.'

" 'Ah, Monsieur, I shouldn't dismiss them.'

"Cecile squeezed the valet's arm. 'Oh, you shouldn't, shouldn't you? And may your poor master hear the reason?'

" 'When the workmen are gone, Monsieur, you will have only your servants and yourself to defend the house: four men to a door. But the salvage, if he hath a fancy to attack us, will attack from every side——'

" 'Flog this man!' Cecile cried, and the fellow was dragged off by Jacques and the others. Then the overseer of the workmen enquired whether his men were free to go. 'Idiot!' Cecile thundered. 'Close up the doorways, all save one, and fix two stout crossbars to that!'

"In a day the final alterations were completed, and without risking another consultation with Alfred, Cecile sent the workmen back to St. Mary's City, where they doubtless still relate the tale of their curious labors. As soon as they were gone Monsieur entered his castle, inspected the three bricked-up doorways to make certain no cracks were left unsealed, swung the two great crossbars to and fro upon their pivots to assure himself of their adequacy, and ascended the dark stairs to his sitting-room—all the habitable rooms were perforce upstairs; only Cecile slept below, away from the window slits. He summoned Alfred to him.

" 'Is it not a pleasant thing to be altogether secure from the onslaughts of the salvage?'

"Alfred held his peace.

" 'Damn you, sir; speak up! Do we not rest here in a fortress in no way vulnerable?'

"Alfred went to one of the apertures and surveyed the scene below.

" 'Answer me! If there is a gap in my defenses (which of course there is not), I command you to tell me, or by our Lord I'll have you flayed alive!'

"Alfred was afraid to turn from the window, but he said, 'There is one, Monsieur.'

"Cecile sprang from his chair. 'Then tell me!'

" 'I should rather not, Monsieur, for the reason that it is irremediable.'

" 'You have gone mad!' Monsieur Edouard whispered. 'Nay, I see it! You say these things to torment me; to make me spend myself into poverty! I see the plot, sir!' He demanded again to be told, but Alfred durst not speak. At that moment there was a sound at the front door: someone entered, and in the room the two men heard the crossbars swing into place and soft footsteps ascend the stair. Monsieur Edouard came near to swooning.

" 'The salvages are in the house! How shall we escape?'

"Alfred's expression was apologetic. 'Where many exits are,' he said, 'are many entrances, Monsieur. Where but one entrance is, there is no exit.'

"Then the voice of Madame Edouard came meekly from the stair. 'Cecile? Would you please have Alfred attend those crossbars? I find them difficult to close.'

"Her husband made no reply, and Sophie, who was used to such rebuffs, presently returned downstairs. Alfred, meanwhile, had gone once more to the embrasure, and now Monsieur Edouard, his heart still pounding, crept up behind and caught him under the shoulders. The servant was old and frail; the master middle-aged and robust: albeit the opening was none too large, Cecile soon had his valet squeezed through it, and Alfred's head was entirely smashed upon the new brick terrace below.

" 'He fell,' Cecile announced to the household shortly after, and no one questioned him. That night Monsieur had his bedding shifted from the first floor up into the attic, under the rafters, where despite the poor ventilation he retired content beside the great hewn piers. Below, where the household slumbered, the single door was fastened with its double crossbars. Jacques, the new valet, assured his master that he was in every way invulnerable—and Cecile slept soundly."

Henrietta delivered the final sentence with her eyes closed and her voice sardonically hushed. There was a pause, and then Anna cried, "Is that the end, Henrietta?"

The girl pretended surprise. "Why of course it is! That is, the *tale* ends there—what could Homer add to't? As for the history, 'tis curious enough, but it hath the nature of an anticlimax. The Castle burned to the ground not long after, from the inside out, and my grandfather and grandmother burned with it. *Maman* was saved by Jacques, that some folk guessed had set the fire; he raised her in his own house till she married Papa, and pretended to be her uncle till the day he died. Don't you think a castle should last longer than that?"

The three listeners praised both the story itself and Henrietta's rendering of it; Ebenezer, in particular, was touched by her combination of spirit, beauty, and wit, and was surprised to discover among his feelings a certain envy for McEvoy.

" 'Twas a tale well told," he said, "and nicely pointed as one of Aesop's. Throw wide the doors and let the pirates in!" Henrietta reminded him of his promise to surpass it, and the poet's tone grew warm and serious. " 'Tis a chore that gives me pleasure, for it brings you closer to Anna and me than ever friendship could."

"Marry, then out with't!" Anna too regarded him wonderingly.

" 'Tis as rare and happy a turn as e'er the dice of Chance have thrown," Ebenezer said. "Your mother, Henrietta, is the same our father once saved from drowning in the Choptank! She—she was our wet nurse after Mother died a-bearing me and her own child died a-bearing, and till the fourth year of our life, when Father fetched us back to England, she was as much to us as any mother could be!" He finished his revelation with tears in his eyes.

"Dear Heav'n!" Mary whispered. "Is that true?" Anna and Henrietta clasped hands and regarded each other with astonishment.

Ebenezer nodded. "Aye, 'tis true, and haply it sheds some light upon Mrs. Russecks's shifting attitudes toward us. Father told me the story just before I left: Roxanne's uncle—that is to say, this rascal Jacques—must have been a man of Sir Harry's temper, inasmuch as he guarded her in the way Henrietta hath been guarded, and when Nature slipped through his defenses, as is her wont, he turned Roxanne out to starve." He related quickly what Andrew had told him of the rescue and Roxanne's unusual indenture-terms. "There were some lying rumors after Mother died that Roxanne had become his mistress," he concluded. "In part, 'twas to give these slanders the lie he left Cooke's Point for London. I recall his saying that Roxanne's 'uncle' had approached him with apologies and begged for her to come back to him; he was supposed to have arranged a good match for her."

Henrietta winced. "With Papa!" Mary shook her head and sighed.

"Aye," the poet affirmed. "This Jacques, evidently, was indebted to Harry Russecks and hoped thus to settle his obligations. To be sure, Roxanne had no need to consent; but she told me not long since that she had come to loathe all men, and wed Sir Harry in effect to mortify her sex and gratify this loathing. She was much attached to Anna and me, and I daresay she felt abandoned, in a sense. . . ."

"In every sense." Mrs. Russecks's voice came from the hallway stairs and was followed by the lady herself. Ebenezer rose quickly from his chair and apologized for speaking indiscreetly.

"Thou'rt guilty of nothing," Mrs. Russecks said, looking past him to her daughter. " 'Tis *you* that have been naughty, Henrietta, to tell tales out of school——" She got no farther, for Henrietta ran weeping to embrace her mother and beg forgiveness; yet it was clear that the girl's emotion was not contrition for any misdemeanor, but sympathy and love inspired by what she had learned. Mrs. Russecks kissed her forehead and turned her eyes for the first time, eager and yet pained, to the twins; she managed to control her feelings until Anna too was moved to embrace her, whereupon she cried "Sweet babes!" and surrendered to her tears.

There ensued a general chorus of weeping that for some minutes no other sound was heard in the millhouse. Everyone embraced everyone else in the spirit summed up by Ebenezer, the first to speak when the crest of the flood had passed and everyone was sniffling privately.

"Sunt lacrimae rerum," he declared, wiping his eyes.

But the day's surprises were not done. As soon as Mrs. Russecks had satisfied, for the moment, her hunger to embrace the twins and beg pardon for her previous aloofness— refraining, as did Ebenezer, from any illusion to her innocent attempt to seduce him, as well as to her own seduction by

Anna's supposed lover Burlingame, either of which in itself could account for her distress—she joined them at the tea table and said to Ebenezer, "You made good your vow to surpass Henrietta's story with a postscript, Eben (I'God, how can my babies have grown so! And what trials have they not suffered!); but I believe I may yet snatch back the prize with a postscript of my own. To begin with, that 'vicious lying gossip' about your father and myself—'twas gossip in sooth, and vicious, but it was no lie. For three years after poor Anne's death—that was their mother, Henrietta—Andrew and I mourned her together. But in the fourth year—i'faith, I loved him then, and hinted vainly at betrothal!—in the fourth year I was in sooth his mistress. Prithee forgive me for't!"

Both twins embraced her again and declared there was nothing to forgive. "On the contrary," Ebenezer said grimly, "'tis my father needs forgiving. I see now what you meant by saying you were abandoned in every sense."

"Nay," Mrs. Russecks said, "there is more . . ." She raised her eyes painfully to Mary, whose face suddenly changed from deep-frowned reflection to understanding.

"Ah, God, Roxie!"

Mrs. Russecks nodded. "You have guessed it, my dear." She sniffed, took both of Henrietta's hands in hers across the table, and looked unfalteringly at her daughter as she spoke. "Twice in my life I've loved a man. The first was Benjy Long, a pretty farmer-boy that lived near Uncle Jacques: he it was I gave my maidenhead to, when I was sixteen, and anon conceived his child; he it was ran off to sea when I would not cross my guardian's wishes, nor have I heard of him from that day to this; and he it is, methinks, that still hath letters-patent to my heart—though I daresay he's either long since fat and married or long since dead!" She laughed briefly and then grew sad again. "Shall I prove to you that time is no cure for folly? Often and often, when Andrew left me and when Harry would abuse me, I'd pray to little Benjy as to God, and to this hour my poor heart falters when a stranger comes to call——" She smiled at Ebenezer. "Especially if he calls himself Sir Benjamin!"

"Ah, Christ, forgive me!" Ebenezer pleaded. Mrs. Russecks indicated with a gesture that there was nothing to pardon and returned her attention to Henrietta. "That was my *first* love. Andrew was the other, and far the greater, but merely to think of him drives me near to madness . . ." She paused to recompose herself. "Let me put it thus, my dears: this second

733

love affair was in essence the first, save for two important differences. One, as you know already, is that my lover abandoned me . . ." She squeezed her daughter's hands. "The other is that this time the baby lived."

18

The Poet Wonders Whether the Course of Human History Is a Progress, a Drama, a Retrogression, a Cycle, an Undulation, a Vortex, a Right- or Left-Handed Spiral, a Mere Continuum, or What Have You. Certain Evidence Is Brought Forward, but of an Ambiguous and Inconclusive Nature

THE IMPORT OF MRS. Russecks's last remark occasioned a new round of joyful and sympathetic embraces. Mrs. Russecks apologized to Ebenezer and Anna for having transferred her resentment to them, and they apologized in turn for their father's ungentlemanly behavior of two dozen years earlier; Henrietta begged her mother's retroactive forgiveness for all the times she had inveighed against her for marrying Russecks, and Roxanne begged reciprocal forgiveness for having conceived her out of wedlock as well as for the double injury of subjecting her to Sir Harry's maltreatment and obliging her to believe she was his daughter. Even Mary was included, for the well-kept secret had caused occasional misunderstandings on both sides during her long friendship with the miller's wife. There being no wine on the premises, when all were shriven and embraced, a new pot of tea was boiled for celebratory use, and, alternately shy and demonstrative, the new relatives talked long into the evening. For all her avowed hatred of Andrew Cooke, Roxanne was exceedingly curious about his life in England and his present highly questionable position; that night, moreover, Anna and Henrietta, who slept together, must each have taken the other completely into her confidence, for Ebenezer was surprised to observe next morning that they spoke freely of Henry Burlingame. At breakfast the three young people were in almost hilarious spirits: Ebenezer traded Hudibrastics with Henrietta, whom he found to have a real gift for satire, and Anna declared herself totally unconcerned about the future—as far as she was concerned, Roxanne was *her* mother too, and she would be content if she never saw Malden or her father again. Roxanne and Mary looked on joyfully, wiping their eyes on an apron-hem from time to time.

By midmorning it had been decided that the Russeckses would travel with the Cookes to Anne Arundel Town as soon as McEvoy returned from Bloodsworth Island; there Roxanne and Henrietta would remain until the miller's estate was sold, whereupon they (and, Henrietta hinted demurely, perhaps McEvoy) would sail for England and a new life. Ebenezer would carry his urgent message to Governor Nicholson and, if the situation warranted, plead for gubernatorial restitution of his estate on grounds that it was being used for activities subversive to the welfare of the Province; if his appeal bore no fruit or his father proved unrelenting, he and Anna would leave Maryland also as members of Roxanne's family, and he would endeavor to find employment in London. Henry Burlingame and Joan Toast, though they weighed heavily on the twins' minds, were provisionally excluded from their plans, since the whereabouts of the former and the attitude of the latter were uncertain.

Their spirits were lifted even higher by the appearance, shortly after noontime, of McEvoy and Bertrand, who announced that Captain Cairn was waiting with his sloop in the creek to ferry them anywhere in the world. McEvoy kissed Henrietta ardently, and her mother as well, and Bertrand embraced his master with speechless gratitude.

"Would ye fancy it?" McEvoy laughed. "Those wretches thought we'd left 'em stranded! When they saw me ride in with old Bill-o'-the-Goose they reckoned I'd been captured again, and commenced to give ye whatfor!" His face darkened for a moment, and while Bertrand professed his delight at seeing Miss Anna safe and sound, he confided to Ebenezer, " 'Twas all Dick Parker and the others could manage to get us out alive. Our friend Billy Rumbly hath gone salvage altogether, and would have had us murthered on the spot!"

Ebenezer sighed. "I feared as much. I suppose he'll inflame the Ahatchwhoops farther."

"Aye." McEvoy displayed a new fishbone ring of the sort that had saved Ebenezer. "Chicamec gave me this for retrieving his son, and Dick Parker gave another to Bertrand, but I'd not give a farthing for its protection when the war comes —and 'twill come sooner now than before, with Master Cohunkowprets at the helm. I mean to sail out o' this miserable province the minute I have my freight, and Henrietta's going with me if I have to kidnap her." He blushed, for his last remark had chanced to fall into a pause in the general conversation and was heard by all.

"I hope you shan't need such measures." Ebenezer laughed. "Nor is't likely I'd permit you to treat my sister so unchivalrously!" He proceeded to dumfound his companion with the news of his relationship to Henrietta and the party's plans for the immediate future.

"I vow and declare, Eben, ye frighten me!" He looked at Henrietta with awe. "Nay, methinks I should steal her away all the sooner, ere ye discover me for your brother as well!"

As soon as all the salutation had been got over, Mrs. Russecks suggested that Bertrand be dispatched to summon the Captain for dinner as well as for protection from the pirates, against whose rumored presence the village had taken such a posture of defense. The valet was much alarmed by this last disclosure, but McEvoy scoffed at the idea.

"If there were any pirates about, they'd have taken us ere now; we were the only ship in sight from Limbo Straits to Church Creek! In any case, the Captain's not likely to be aboard; he wanted to recruit himself a crew that knows more about crewing than Bertrand and myself."

Everyone except Bertrand and Mrs. Russecks joined McEvoy in minimizing the threat of piracy, and upon Mary's offering, at dinner, to oversee the closing of the millhouse and the sale of the inn (which latter property she herself expressed some interest in), the party resolved to set sail for Anne Arundel Town that same afternoon if possible.

"The sooner I leave Church Creek behind, the better," Henrietta said, and McEvoy, perhaps less than altruistically, observed that Billy Rumbly's defection made it even more urgent to apprise Nicholson of the situation at once.

"Nonetheless," Roxanne declared, "I can't help trembling at the thought of pirates. All of us here, save Mary, have been captured once before and cruelly used, and escaped by the skin of our teeth: 'tis not likely we'll be so lucky a second time."

"Aye," the poet agreed. "But by the same token 'tis less than likely such a catastrophe could befall the same party twice in's life." He went on, partly in good-natured irony and partly to divert the woman from her fears, to speak of sundry theories of history—the retrogressive, held by Dante and Hesiod; the dramatic, held by the Hebrews and the Christian fathers; the progressive, held by Virgil; the cyclical, held by Plato and Ecclesiasticus; the undulatory, and even the vortical hypothesis entertained, according to Henry Burlingame, by a gloomy neo-Platonist of Christ's College, who believed that the cyclic periods of history were growing ever shorter and thus that at some non-unpredictable moment in the future the universe would go rigid and explode, just as the legendary bird called *Ouida* (so said Burlingame) was reputed to fly in ever-diminishing circles until at the end he disappeared into his own fundament. "The true and proper cyclist," he averred, "ought not to fear being taken again by pirates, inasmuch as his theory will loose him from their clutches as before; if you fear we'll be recaptured and done to death, 'tis plain you believe the course of things to be a sort of downward spiral—whether right- or left-handed I can't determine without farther enquiry."

By dint of these and like sophistical cajolements Mrs. Russecks was quieted; after dinner the women's trunks and chests were loaded onto Mary's wagon and drawn by Aphrodite through the desolate little village to a landing down on the creek, where Captain Cairn's sloop was moored.

"Hallo, where is the Captain?" Ebenezer asked.

"He said we were to wait aboard for him if he had trouble finding a crew," McEvoy said. "Methinks he'll have trouble finding *anyone* in yonder village!"

When they had transferred their gear from the wagon to the deck, Mary Mungummory declared with a wink at Ebenezer that, her errand in Church Creek having failed in its object, she too must needs address herself to the task of finding a crew. If she was successful, she said, her regular circuit of the county would bring her to Cooke's Point a few days hence, where she promised to plead the poet's case to Joan Toast, inquire as to the whereabouts of Henry Burlingame, and relay any news to Anne Arundel Town. She wished them all success in their embassy to the Governor, for her own sake as well as theirs, and after an exchange of the most affectionate farewells—especially with Roxanne, Henrietta, and Ebenezer—she returned up the path towards the settlement.

Ebenezer surveyed the familiar deck. "Thank Heav'n the weather's fine; my last voyage on this ship was a harrowing one!" He noticed that Bertrand, who had been unusually subdued throughout the day, now looked quite downcast, and asked him teasingly whether he had seen the Moor Boabdil in the myrtle bushes.

" 'Sheart, sir," the valet complained, "I had almost as lief be back with old Tom Pound as travel about in Maryland."

"Why, how is that?"

Bertrand replied that though he was eternally obliged to his master for, among other things, effecting his release from Bloodsworth Island, it was really a matter of frying-pan into fire, for old Colonel Robotham would surely do him to death upon discovering that Miss Lucy was wed not to the Poet Laureate at all, but to a servingman, whose astrolabe had already taken the alnicanter of her constellation.

"You've done the lass a great injustice," Ebenezer admitted, "but I'm scarcely the man to reprove you for't, and the Colonel is far from blameless in the matter himself. Methinks a marriage under such false pretense can be annulled e'en after consummation, and I've no great fear of Lucy's claim to Malden; but I pity the poor tart for being twice deceived with a babe in her belly. 'Tis your affair, of course; yet I could wish—— *God's body!*"

From the stern of the sloop, where McEvoy had taken the ladies to wait for the Captain's return, came a tumult of shrieks, squeals, and curses. Ebenezer hastened aft to investigate and found himself confronted by a man whose appearance from the tiny cabin set his knees a-tremble and prostrated Bertrand upon the deck: a stout little man dressed in black from beard to boots, with a pistol in one hand and an ebony stick in the other

"Well, marry come up!" the fellow marveled. "Will ye look who's here, Captain Scurry?"

His counterpart emerged onto the stern sheets, also brandishing a pistol and supporting himself on a stick. "I'cod, Captain Slye, we've a bloody crew to go with our pilot!" He drew closer and smiled evilly at Ebenezer. "I say, Captain Slye, 'tis the very wretch that fouled his drawers in the King o' the Seas!"

"The same," said Slye. "And that craven puppy yonder is

our friend the false laureate, that bilked us for a carriage-ride to Plymouth!"

The two rejoiced in the most unpleasant manner imaginable at having accidentally caught up with three old acquaintances—they had already recognized McEvoy as the redemptioner who had so plagued them on their last crossing. Captain Cairn, his countenance stricken, appeared on deck at their order, and the party was assembled in the waist of the vessel.

"God forgive me!" the Captain cried to Ebenezer. "I went to sign me a crew, and these rogues set upon me!"

"Now, now," Captain Scurry admonished, "there's no way to speak o' thy shipmates, sir! Our friend Captain Avery lies yonder in the lee o' James Island and wants a pilot up the Bay, and inasmuch as Captain Slye and myself was steering southwards, we promised to find him one."

"What do you mean to do with us?" Ebenezer asked.

"What do?" echoed Captain Slye. "Ah well, sir, as thou'rt the Laureate o' Maryland—ah, ye thought your friend John Coode would not betray ye, eh? What would ye say if I told ye he weren't John Coode at all, but merely one o' Coode's lieutenants? D'ye think I'd not know my own wife's father? Mark the man's trembling! Methinks he'll smirch his drawers anon! What *shall* we do with the merry lot, Captain Scurry?"

His partner chuckled. "Now, we might eat 'em alive for supper, Captain Slye, or we might put a ball in each jack's belly . . ."

"Set the women ashore," the poet said. "You've no quarrel with them."

Captain Scurry admitted that he had neither quarrel with nor appetite for any female on the planet, but that he would not impose his personal tastes upon Captain Avery and his crew, who having made a lengthy ocean crossing would not likely refuse the blandishments of three so toothsome ladies. He proposed to Captain Slye that the entire party, excluding Captain Cairn, be cargoed into the hold and their final disposition left to the pirates.

Having had no prior experience of privateers, Anna Cooke seemed merely dazed by what was taking place, but Roxanne and Henrietta clung to each other and redoubled their lamentations. To all entreaties the kidnapers replied with a sneer, and the prisoners were obliged to descend into the cramped and lightless hold of the sloop, which stank of oysters. Mc-

Evoy embraced Henrietta in an effort to comfort her, and Ebenezer did likewise Anna; Bertrand and Mrs. Russecks had to deal with their terrors unassisted, and it is surely to that latter's credit that she never once mentioned the downward-spiral theory of history, which was much on the anguished poet's conscience. Over their heads they heard Slye and Scurry agree to move the sloop from Church Creek out into Fishing Creek lest any villagers hear the prisoners' complaints, but to wait until nightfall before running down the Little Choptank to their rendezvous with Captain Avery.

A long while they languished in despair as black and exitless as their prison. Then when the sloop got under way Anna began to whimper, and her brother was moved to say, "What a wretched thing is happiness! How I contemn it! An interlude such as ours of the past few days—— 'Sheart, 'tis a waterhole in the desert track of life! The traveler mistrusts his fortune; shocked by the misery he hath passed, sickened by the misery yet to come, he rests but fitfully; the dates lie like pebbles in his stomach; the water turns foul upon his tongue. Thus him whose fancy gives purpose to the journey; but on this path, who is no pilgrim is perforce a vagrant, and woe to us less blest! For us 'tis causeless martyrdom, *ananabasis*, and when Chance vouchsafes some respite she earns our anger, not our gratitude. Show me the happy man who is neither foolish nor asleep!"

If his companions understood this apostrophe, they did not respond to it. Anna proposed that the three women destroy themselves at the earliest opportunity rather than suffer mass ravishment by the pirates. " 'Tis not that I choose death to dishonor," she explained. "My virginity means naught to me, but inasmuch as they'll surely murther us after, I'd as lief die now and have done with't. If Eben will not throttle me, I mean to drown myself the moment they fetch us on deck."

"La, girl," Mrs. Russecks scoffed from across the black enclosure, "put such notions out o' thy pretty head! Suppose Henrietta and I had taken our lives when Tom Pound captured us? We'd not be here today!"

There was general, if grim, laughter at the unintended irony of this remark, but Mrs. Russecks insisted that anything —even ten years as a sea-going concubine—was endurable so long as one could hope for ultimate improvement. "We've no assurance they mean to murther us," she said. "I'faith, we're not even raped yet!"

Sensing that Anna's resolve was beginning to falter, Eben-

740

ezer pursued this point. "Do you recall when we read Euripides with Henry, how we contemned *The Trojan Women* out of hand? Hecuba we called a self-pitying frump, and Andromache either a coward or a hypocrite. 'If she loves her Hector so, how is't she lets wretched Pyrrhus make her his whore? Why not take her own life and save the family honor?' What unrelenting moralists children are! But I tell you, Anna, I contemn the woman no more. We praise the martyr; he is our shame and our exemplar; but who among us fallen will embrace him? What's more, there is a high moral in Andromache; her tears indict the bloody circus of man's lust; her sigh drowns out the shouts of a thousand heroes, and her resignation turns Hellas into Vanity Fair."

Ebenezer himself was not so persuaded by this argument as he hoped Anna would be. Committing suicide merely to escape pain he could not but regard as cowardly, though he understood and sympathized with such cowardice; suicide as a point of honor, on the other hand, like martyrdom, made him uneasy. The martyr, it seemed to him, was in a sense unnatural, since blind Nature has neither codes nor causes; it was from this point of view that Andromache, like Ecclesiasticus, appeared the more sophisticated moralist, and heroes of every stamp seemed drunkards or madmen. Yet the very unNaturalness, the *hubris*, as it were, of heroism in general and martyrdom in particular were their most appealing qualities. Granted that the Earth, as Burlingame was fond of pointing out, is "a dust-mote whirling through the night," there was something brave, defiantly human, about the passengers on this mote who perished for some dream of Value. To die, to risk death, even to raise a finger for any Cause, was to pennon one's lance with the riband of Purpose, so the poet judged, and had about it the same high lunacy of a tilt with Manchegan windmills.

But if his words were not altogether heartfelt, his purpose was, and sensing that his arguments had had some effect on Anna, he returned to them several hours later when the sloop was under way again—presumably to James Island. "I beg you to think of one thing only: Reason aside, is there aught on earth you prize? Suppose us safe in Anne Arundel Town: what would you wish for then?"

"Some years of peace," Anna replied unhesitatingly. "I've no use any longer for estates or e'en for a husband, since—since Henry is denied me. What can they matter, after all that hath occurred? In time, perhaps, new goals may beckon,

741

but just now I should wish to live some years in utter peace."

Ebenezer stirred. "How my heart responds to that ambition! But stay, there is no point: if aught in life hath value to us, we must not give o'er its pursuit."

He felt Anna tremble. " 'Tis not worth the cost!"

"Nor is aught else."

She wet his hand with tears. "If I must suffer what I shall, then I amend my wish: I wish we two were the only folk on earth!"

"Eve and Adam?" The poet's face burned. "So be it; but we must be God as well, and build a universe to hold our Garden."

Anna squeezed his hand.

"What I mean," he said, "we must cling to life and search each moment for escape . . ."

Anna shook her head. "Anon they'll run you through and throw you to the fishes, and I . . . Nay, Eben! This present hour is all our future, and this black cave our only Garden. Anon they'll tear our innocence from us . . ."

He sensed her eyes upon him. "Dear God!"

Just then a shout came down from above, answered by another off in the distance: the rendezvous had been made.

"*Make haste!*" cried Anna.

The poet groaned. "You must forgive me——"

Anna shrieked and fled on hands and knees across the hold; a few minutes later, when the hatch-cover was lifted and a lantern held down the ladderway, Ebenezer saw her shuddering in the arms of Mrs. Russecks.

"Ah, now," said the lantern-bearer, "I do despise to be a spoilsport, but Captain Avery wishes to speak to the six of ye on deck. He hath offered to torture the ladies at once if ye do not come promptly and civilly, sirs."

After a moment's hesitation the prisoners complied, urged on by Henrietta and Mrs. Russecks. Night had fallen, and a strong, cold breeze had blown up out of the west; for all the turmoil in his head, Ebenezer was surprised to observe that the sloop had not anchored but only come up "in irons" some distance from the pirate ship, whose lights could be seen several hundred yards ahead. Slye and Scurry had picked up a small party, and the prisoners were instructed to stand fast amidships while the vessel was got under way again. The poet's heart lifted: could it be that they were not to be transferred to the other ship?

Captain Cairn, who happened to pass nearby, confirmed

his hope. "I'm to pilot their Captain up the Bay," he murmured, "lest his ship be spied and taken." He could say no more, for the pirates sent him aft to tend the mainsheet. Captain Slye and Captain Scurry bid the prisoners a sneering farewell and departed in a dinghy to their own ship, which presumably lay with Avery's *Phansie* in the lee of the island. Darkness prevented Ebenezer from seeing his new captor, who from the helm of the sloop ordered one of his two lieutenants to mind the jib sheet and the other—a gaunt, blond-bearded youth who looked more like a rustic than a pirate—to guard the prisoners. When Ebenezer moved to put his arm about Anna's shoulders she recoiled as if he were a pirate himself.

"Stand off, there, matey," the guard threatened. "Leave that little chore to us."

The women huddled together in the lee of the mast: the two younger ones still sniffed and whimpered, but Mrs. Russecks, seeing that their ordeal was not yet upon them, regained composure enough to embrace and comfort them both. Whatever the pirate captain had on his mind, it was clearly not so pressing as Captain Scurry (who had summoned the prisoners from the hold) had led them to believe; for more than an hour the three men stood mute and shivering before their guard's pistols while the sloop bowled northwards on a broad reach up the Chesapeake. The wind was fresh, the Bay quite rough; the moonlight was occulted by an easting scud. At last a voice from the helm said, "Very well, Mr. Shannon, fetch the gentlemen aft."

Fearful of what lay ahead, Ebenezer yearned to kiss Anna one last time; he hesitated, and in the end decided not to risk the guard's displeasure, but all the way aft he railed inwardly against his own timidity. The small light of the binnacle showed Captain Cairn standing tensely at the helm and revealed the countenance of the notorious Long Ben Avery: a sad-eyed, beagle-faced fellow, not at all fearsome to behold, who wore a modest brown beard and curled mustachios.

"Good evening, gentlemen," he said, scarcely raising his eyes from the compass. "I shan't detain ye long. Would ye say she lies abeam, Captain Cairn?"

"Off the starboard bow," the Captain grumbled. "If we don't run aground ye'll soon hear the surf to leeward."

"Excellent." The pirate captain frowned and sucked at his pipe. "Aye, there's the surf; thou'rt a rare good pilot, Captain Cairn! Now, gentlemen, I've but one question to put—— Ah, damn this tobacco!" He drew at the pipestem until the coals glowed yellow. "There we are. 'Tis a simple question, sirs, that ye may answer one at a time, commencing with the tall fellow: are ye, or have ye ever been, an able seaman?"

The pirate called Mr. Shannon prodded Ebenezer with his pistol, but the poet wanted no urging to reply; his heart glowed like the pipe coals with hope at their captor's gentlemanly air. "Nay, sir, I'm but a poor poet, with no craft save that of rhyming and no treasure save my dear sister yonder, for whose honor I'd trade my life! Dare I ask your pledge as one gentleman to another, sir, that no harm will be offered those ladies?"

"Ask the second gentleman, Mr. Shannon."

The guard poked Bertrand.

"Nay, master, 'fore God I am no seaman, nor aught else in the world but a simple servingman that curses the hour of his birth!"

"Very good." Captain Avery sighed, still watching the binnacle. "And you, sir?"

"This is but the third time I've been on shipboard, sir," McEvoy declared at once. "The first was as a redemptioner, kidnaped out o' London by Slye and Scurry; the second was as a passenger on this very ship this morning. I swear to ye, I know not my forepeak from my aft!"

"Cleverly put," Captain Avery approved. "Then it seems I cannot enlist ye for my crew. Mr. Shannon, will ye escort these pleasant gentlemen o'er the taffrail?"

Ebenezer stiffened as if struck, and Bertrand fell to his knees; even Captain Cairn seemed not to realize for a second what had been said. The guard gestured towards the taffrail with one of his pistols and nudged the trembling valet with his boot.

"There's a little island to leeward," observed Captain Avery. "With some luck and the sea behind ye, ye might manage it. Count five, Mr. Shannon, and shoot any gentleman who lingers."

"One," said Mr. Shannon. "Two."

McEvoy gave a great oath and kicked off his boots. "Farewell, Eben," he said. "Farewell, Henrietta!" He sprang over the rail and splashed into the sea astern.

"Three." Mr. Shannon smiled at the remaining two as they also removed their boots. An inquiring female voice called back from the mast, but the question was lost on the wind. Bertrand gave a final whimper and vaulted overboard.

"Four."

Ebenezer hastened to the taffrail. Hoping against hope, he called to the pirate captain's back, "Do I have your pledge, sir? About the ladies?"

"I pledge to swive your pleasant ladies from sprit to transom," said Long Ben Avery. "I pledge to give every jack o' my crew his slavering fill o' them, sir, and when they're done I pledge to carve your little sister into ship's-beef and salt her down for the larboard watch. Fire away, Mr. Shannon."

Given another ten seconds Ebenezer might have run forward to die at Anna's side, but under the inpulse of the sudden command he sprang wildly over the rail and smacked face-first into the icy water. The triple shock of the threat, the fall, and the cold came near to robbing him of his senses; he retched with anguish, coughed salt water from his throat, and after some moments of frantic indirection, caught sight of the sloop's light receding into the darkness. The waves slapped and tossed him; merely to float, as he had done once before in similar straits, would be to perish of the cold in short order. Taking his bearings from the sloop and the direction of the seas, he thrashed out for the island allegedly to the east.

"Halloo!" he called, and imagined that he heard an answer up the wind. A thought as chilling as the Bay occurred to him: what if there was no island after all? What if Long Ben Avery had fired their hopes as a cruel jest? In any case, if there *was* an island, it would have to be close, or he was a dead man; the following seas pushed him in the right direction but diminished by half the effectiveness of his stroke, and the low temperature robbed him of breath.

He was encouraged, a minute or two later, by a positive cry ahead: "This way! I'm standing on bottom!"

"McEvoy?" he called joyfully.

"Aye! Keep swimming! Don't give up! Where's Bertrand? *Bertrand!"*

From ahead and somewhat to the right of the poet came another response; not long afterwards the three men were panting and shivering together on a dark pebbled beach.

"Praise God, 'tis a miracle!" Bertrand cried. "Twice drowned by pirates and twice washed safe on an ocean isle! Methinks we could walk down the strand a bit and find Drakepecker once again!"

But McEvoy and Ebenezer were too sickened by the plight of the women to rejoice at their own good fortune. The poet

745

deemed it best to say nothing of Captain Avery's parting threat, since they were unable to prevent his carrying it out; even so, McEvoy vowed to devote the rest of his life to pursuing and assassinating the pirate.

By comparison with the air on their wet clothes, the Bay seemed tepid. "We must get out of the wind and make a fire," McEvoy said.

"We've no way to light one," Ebenezer pointed out listlessly. Now that he was safe, his mind was full of Anna's fate and their last interview; he began to wish that he had drowned.

"Then, let's build a shelter, ere we freeze," McEvoy said.

They hurried up onto the island proper, which appeared to be only a few hundred feet across; there they found loblolly pines, a few scrubby myrtles, and much underbrush, but not much likely-looking material for a shelter; nor was the growth an adequate windbreak. The leeward slope of the island was somewhat more comfortable, though even there it was unthinkable that they could long survive soaking wet in a forty-mile winter wind.

"M-marry, sirs, l-look yonder!" Bertrand cried, shaking with cold. " 'Tis a light!"

Indeed, out over the water to the east of them shone what appeared to be the lighted windows of a house. The distance was hard to estimate, but unless the structure was very small, McEvoy judged, it lay three or four miles away. In the face of Ebenezer's previous objection he declared that they must build a fire at once, set fire to the entire island if need be, to attract rescuers; else they'd be dead before sunrise.

"Let's scour the island," he proposed. "If we hit on naught better, why, we'll claw out a trench and bury ourselves together under evergreen boughs. Methinks we must prance and swing our arms about."

They decided to search together, in order to utilize the sooner anything they might come across. One man on the beach, one on the brush line, and one at the edge of the heavier growth, they proceeded northwards up the lee shore of the island. But their search seemed vain: every stick of wood was wet, and no one yet had proposed any means of ignition should it have proved dry. Moreover, the growth thinned out as they approached the northern end of the island, which appeared to be half a mile or so in length.

Not far from the point, Bertrand, who had been patrolling the brush lines, called for them to come at once and behold another miracle. "Lookee here, what I came nigh to breaking my toes on!"

At his feet they saw a longish black shape, which on closer approach they recognized as a stranded dinghy.

"I'faith!" cried McEvoy, scrabbling inside to examine it. "There's even an oar! She must have blown hither in a storm!"

"I doubt she's seaworthy," Ebenezer warned, observing that several inches of water stood in the bilge. "But we might use her for a shelter."

"Nay," McEvoy protested. "She might be tight, Eben, else the water would have leaked out, would it not? I say let's make a try at yonder light! But stay—we've only one oar."

"There's a trick called *sculling* . . ." Ebenezer offered doubtfully. "But i'Christ, John, listen to that chop—'tis like the ocean! We'd drown in five minutes!"

"But if we manage it, we're safe," McEvoy reminded him. "If we stay here, belike we'll freeze to death ere sunrise, and e'en if we do not, who's to say we'll be rescued in the morning?"

They pondered the alternatives briefly, and the third course of sending one of their number to bring assistance to the others.

" 'Twill take one man to scull and another to bail," Bertrand ventured. "We'd as lief die together, as apart, hadn't we, sirs?"

"Then I say let's drown together instead o' freezing," said McEvoy. *"What say ye, Eben?"*

The poet started, and saw by his companion's grim smile that McEvoy had formed the question deliberately. For an instant he forgot the frightful cold: he was at table in Locket's, where the eyes of Ben Oliver, Dick Merriweather, Tom Trent, and Joan Toast had joined McEvoy's to render him immobile; again, as then, he felt the weight of choice devolve upon him, peg him out like a tan yard hide in all directions. It was a queer moment: he felt as must a seasoned Alpinist brought back to a crag whence he fell of old and barely survived; many another and more formidable he has scaled since without a tremor, but this one turns his blood to water . . .

With some effort, Ebenezer threw off the memory. "I say we try for the house. Wind and waves are behind us, and for better or worse we'll have done with't in an hour."

However chilling this final observation, it spurred them to action. They overturned the dinghy to empty the bilge, dragged it down to the water, and launched it. McEvoy's reasoning proved correct: the water standing in the bilge had kept the chine- and keelson-seams tight. At Ebenezer's suggestion, who had learned something of rowing from Burlingame, Bertrand and McEvoy each equipped himself with half of a shingle discovered on the beach, both to assist in freeing out the water they were certain to ship and to help prevent the little boat from broaching to in the following seas.

Though he truly cared little now for his own safety, the burden of responsibility weighed heavy on the poet's heart. He knew so little about what he was doing, and they carried out his suggestions, on which their lives depended, as if he were Captain Cairn! But however meager his seamanship, it was apparently superior to Bertrand's and McEvoy's. And however great the burden, it was no longer an unfamiliar one: he grappled with it calmly, as with an old, well-known opponent, and wondered whether his sensibility had perhaps of late been toughened like the hands of an apprentice mason, by frequent laceration.

"Methinks 'twere best the twain of you sit forward, to keep the stern high. If sculling fails us, we'll paddle like salvages."

They clambered aboard, shivering violently from their new wetting; Ebenezer was able to pole out a hundred yards or so through shoal water before it became necessary to fit his oar between the transom tholes and commence sculling. Fortunately, the first mile or so was in the lee of the island; the relative stillness of the water gave him opportunity to get the knack of pitching the blade properly for thrust without losing his oar. But soon the island was too far behind to shelter them: the hissing seas rolled in astern—three, four, and five feet from trough to crest; as each overtook them the dinghy seemed to falter, intimidated, and then actually to be drawn backwards as if by undertow. Ebenezer would hold his breath—surely they would be pooped! But at the last instant the stern would be flung high and the dinghy thrust forward on the crest; the scanty freeboard disappeared; water sluiced over both gunwales; Bertrand and McEvoy bailed madly to keep afloat. Then the sea rushed on, and the dinghy would seem to slide backwards into the maw of the one behind. Each wave was a fresh terror; it seemed unthinkable that they should survive it, and even more that managing by some miracle to do so earned them not a second's respite. The helmsman's job was especially arduous and tricky: though the net motion of the dinghy was actually always forward, the approach of each new sea had the effect of sternway; instead of sculling, Ebenezer would be obliged to use the oar for a rudder to keep the boat from broaching to, and moreover would have to steer backwards, since the water was moving faster than the boat. Only at the crest could he scull for a stroke or two—but not a moment too long, or the dinghy would yaw in the next trough. The men were rapidly demoralized past speech; they toiled as if possessed, and when the moon broke the scud it lit three shocked faces staring wide-eyed at the monster overtaking them.

To turn back was out of the question, since even if some god should turn them around, they could make no windward headway. Yet after what seemed an hour of frantic labor and hairsbreadth escapes—perhaps actually no more than twenty minutes—the light ahead appeared no closer than before. What was worse, it seemed to have moved distinctly northward. It was Bertrand who first observed this distressing fact, and it moved him to speak for the first time in many minutes.

"Dear Father! What if it's a ship, and there's no land for miles?"

McEvoy offered an alternative hypothesis. "Belike the wind hath swung round a bit to the northwest. We may have to hike a few miles up the shore."

"There's e'en a happier possibility," Ebenezer said. "I scarce dare hope—— But stay! Do you hear a sound?"

They paused in their work to listen and were nearly taken under by the next wave.

"Aye, 'tis a surf!" Ebenezer cried joyously. "Neither we nor the light have changed course; 'tis that we're almost upon it!" What he wanted to explain was that though from the island they had steered as directly for the light as they were able, their actual course was somewhat to the south of it; from four or five miles distance the error (perhaps a few hundred feet) had been too small to notice, but as they drew very near, the angle between their course and the light tended to increase towards ninety degrees. Before he could elaborate, however, a wave greater than usual tossed the stern high and to larboard and lifted the oar from its tholes.

"She's broaching to!" he warned.

The others paddled to no purpose with their shingles. Ebenezer slammed the oar back between the pins and attempted to bring the stern into the seas by putting the "tiller" end hard over to larboard, as he had grown used to doing under sternway. But his action was out of phase, for the crest had passed and left the dinghy momentarily wayless in the trough: the motion of the oar was in fact a sculling stroke, and had the effect of bringing the stern even farther around. The next wave struck them fair on the starboard quarter, broached them to, and filled the boat ankle deep with water; the one after that, a white-capped five-footer, took them square abeam, and they were flailing once more in the icy Chesapeake. This time, however, their ordeal was brief: their feet struck seaweed and mud at once, and they found themselves less than a dozen yards from shore. They scrambled in, knocked down time and again by the hip-high breakers, and gained the beach at last, scarcely able to stand.

"We must make haste!" McEvoy gasped. "We may freeze yet!"

As fast as they could manage, stumbling and panting, they moved up the shore towards their beacon, now plainly recognizable as the lighted windows of a good-sized house. Not far from it, where the beach met the lawn of the house, stood a tall loblolly pine, at the foot of which they saw a conspicuous white object, like a large vertical stone. Ebenezer's hackles tingled. "Ah God!" he cried and summoned the last of his strength to sprint forward and embrace the grave. The feeble moon sufficed to show the inscription:

> *Anne Bowyer Cooke*
> *b. 1645 d. 1666*
> *Thus Far Hath the Lord*
> *Helped Us.*

The others came up behind. "What is it?"

Ebenezer would not turn his head. "My journey's done," he wept. "I have come full circle. Yonder's Malden; go and save yourselves."

Astonished, they read the gravestone, and when entreaty proved vain, they lifted Ebenezer by main strength from the grave. Once upon his feet, he offered them no resistance, but the last of his spirit seemed gone.

"Had I ne'er been brought to birth," he said, pointing to the stone, "that woman were alive today, and my sister with her, and my father a gentleman sot-weed planter, and the three of them happy in yonder house."

Bertrand was too near freezing to offer a reply, if he had any, but McEvoy—who likewise shook from head to foot with cold—led the poet off by the arm and said, "Go to, 'tis like the sin o' Father Adam, that we all have on our heads; we ne'er asked for't, but there it is, and do we choose to live, why, we must needs live with't."

Ebenezer had been used to seeing Malden a-bustle with deplorable activity after dark, but now only the parlor appeared to be occupied; the rest of the house, as well as the grounds and outbuildings—he peered with awful shame in the direction of the curing-house—was dark and quiet. As they went up the empty lawn toward the front door, which faced southwestwards to the grave and the Bay beyond, McEvoy, as much to warm himself, no doubt, as to comfort Ebenezer, went on to declare through chattering teeth that the single light was a good sign: without question it meant that Andrew Cooke had put his house in order and was waiting with his daughter-in-law for news of his prodigal son. He would be overjoyed to see them; they would be clothed and fed, and alarms would be dispatched at once to Anne Arundel Town to intercept Long Ben Avery.

"Stay." Ebenezer shook his head. "Such fables hurt too much beside the truth."

McEvoy released his arm angrily. "Still the virgin," he cried, "with no thought for any wight's loss save his own! Run down and die on yonder grave!"

Ebenezer shook his head: he wanted to explain to his injured companion that he suffered not from his loss alone, but from McEvoy's as well, and Anna's, and Andrew's, and even Bertrand's—from the general condition of things, in sum, for which he saw himself answerable—and that the pain of loss, however great, was as nothing beside the pain of responsibility for it. The fallen suffer from Adam's fall, he wanted to explain; but in that knowledge—which the Fall itself vouchsafed him—how more must Adam have suffered! But he was too gripped by cold and despair to essay such philosophy.

They reached the house.

"We'd best have a look through the window ere we knock," Bertrand said. "I'Christ, what will Master Andrew say to me, that was sent to be your adviser!"

They went to the lighted window of the parlor, from which they heard the sounds of masculine laughter and conversation.

McEvoy got there first. "Some men at cards," he reported, and then a look of sudden pain came into his face. "Dear God! Can that be poor Joan?"

Bertrand hastened up beside him. "Aye, that's the swine-maid, and yonder's Master Andrew in the periwig, but——"
Now he too showed great distress. "God's blood and body, Master Eben! 'Tis Colonel Robotham!"

But Ebenezer was at the window sill by this time, and beheld for himself these wonders and others by far more marvelous. Joan Toast, so beridden and devoured by her afflictions that she looked a leprous Bedlamite, was hobbling with a pitcher of ale towards a green baize table in the center of the parlor, about whose circumference five gentlemen sat at cards: the lawyer, physician, and minister of the gospel Richard Sowter, who sucked on his pipe and called upon various saints to witness the wretched hand he was being dealt; the cooper (and dealer) William Smith, who smiled grandly at the table and with his pipestem directed Joan to fill Andrew Cooke's glass; Bertrand's portly, sanguine father-in-law from Talbot County, Colonel George Robotham, who seemed preoccupied with something quite other than lanterloo; Andrew Cooke himself, grown thinner and older-looking since Ebenezer had seen him last, but more sharp-eyed than ever, grasping his cards in his good left hand and glancing like an old eagle at the others, as if they were not his adversaries but his prey; and finally, most appalling of all, at Andrew's withered right arm, joking as merrily over his cards as if he were back in Locket's—Henry Burlingame, still in the character he called Nicholas Lowe of Talbot!

"Very well, gentlemen," the cooper declared, having dealt four hands. "I share the fortunes of Mr. Sowter, I believe."

"Put it the other way about," Burlingame remarked, "and there'll be more truth than poetry in't when we get to court."

Sowter shook his head in mock despair. "St. Dominic's sparrow, neighbors! If our case were half as feeble as this miscarriage, we'd get no farther than the courthouse jakes with't, I swear!"

"As we all know ye shan't in any case," Burlingame taunted amiably, "inasmuch as the only *real* case to argue is the size of your bribe."

"Ah, lads, go to," said Andrew Cooke. "This talk of bribes and miscarriages alarms the Colonel!" He smiled sardonically at Colonel Robotham. "Do forgive my son his over-earnestness, George: 'tis a famous failing of the lad's, as I daresay your daughter hath remarked."

Outside the window, Bertrand gasped. "D'ye hear that,

Master Eben? He called that wight his son! An entire stranger!"

"There's something amiss," McEvoy agreed, "but they all seem peaceable enough." Without more ado he began to rap on the windowpanes. *"Hallo! Hallo! Let us in or we're dead men!"*

"Nay, i'Christ!" cried Bertrand, but he was too late; the startled players turned towards the window.

"Januarius's bubbling blood!"

"Look to't, Susan," the cooper ordered calmly, and Joan Toast set her pitcher on the sideboard.

"Ebenezer, my boy," said Andrew Cooke, "fetch thy pistol." Burlingame laid his cards face down on the baize and went to do as he was bid.

Joan Toast opened the door and thrust out a lantern. "Who is't?" she called listlessly.

"Run!" muttered Bertrand, and lit out across the lawn.

McEvoy drew back from the window and bit his underlip nervously. "What say ye, Eben?" he whispered. "Hadn't we best run for't?"

But the poet neither moved nor made reply, for the reason that at first sight of the strange assemblage in the parlor he had been dumfounded, brought back (or around, as the case may be) to that vulnerable condition of his youth which the cuisses of virginity, the cuirass of his laureatcship, were donned to shield; and when in addition he had witnessed his father addressing Burlingame—incredibly!—as "my son" and "Ebenezer," he had been frozen on the instant where he stood, not by the Bay wind but by the same black breeze that thrice before—in Magdalene College, in Locket's, and in his room in Pudding Lane—had sighed from the Pit to ice his bones.

"Who is't?" Joan repeated.

McEvoy stepped from behind Ebenezer so that the light from the parlor window illumined his face.

" 'Tis I, Joan Toast," he said uncertainly. " 'Tis Eben Cooke and John McEvoy. . . ."

Joan made a sound and clutched at the doorjamb; the lantern slipped to the ground and was extinguished. A man's voice came from the vestibule behind her. "What the Devil!"

"Haply we'd better flee, after all," McEvoy suggested. But Ebenezer, no longer even shivering, stood transfixed in his original position.

19

*The Poet Awakens from His Dream of Hell
to Be Judged in Life by Rhadamanthus*

FOR CENTURIES UPON CENTURIES, so it seemed to Ebenezer,
he had sojourned in the realm of Lucifer, where in penance
for Lust and Pride he underwent a double torture: the first
was to be transferred at short intervals from everlasting
flames to the ice of Cocytus, frozen by the wings of the King
of Hell himself; the second, less frequent but more painful,
was to see commingled and transfused before his eyes the
faces of Joan Toast and his sister Anna. Joan would bend
near him, her face unmarred and spirited as it had been in
London: her dress was fresh, her pox vanished; her eyes were
bright and tender—indeed, her face was not hers at all, but
Anna Cooke's! Then even as he watched his sister's face he
saw her eyes go red and dull, her teeth rot in the gums, her
flesh go raw with suppurating lesions—until at last, with Joan
Toast's face, she became Joan Toast, whereupon the cycle
would sometimes recommence. The metamorphosis invariably stole his breath; he would choke and cry out, thrash his
arms and legs about in the fire or the ice, and gibber blasphemies as obscure as Pluto's *"Papè Satan aleppe . . ."* It is not
difficult to imagine, therefore, with what joy he found Anna
quite unaltered when at length he opened his eyes and saw
her sitting near his bed, reading a book. The very magnitude
of his relief thwarted its expression; he fell at once into profoundest dreamless sleep.

Upon his second awakening he was more rational; he realized that he had been ill and delirious for some time—
whether a day or a month he could not guess—and that now
his fever was gone. It pleased him no end to see that his sister
was still in attendance at his bedside, since now he was quite
able to address her.

"Dearest Anna! How very kind of you to nurse me . . ."

He spoke no further, both because his sister, weeping joyfully, rushed from her chair to embrace him, and because he suddenly understood how incredible it was that she should be there, apparently safe and sound!

"I'faith, where am I?" he whispered. "How is't thou'rt here?"

"Too great a story!" Anna sobbed. "Thou'rt home in Malden, Eben, and God be praised thou'rt back among the living!" Without releasing him she called through the open doorway, "*Roxanne!* Come quick! Eben's awake!"

"Roxanne as well?" Ebenezer closed his eyes to gather strength.

"Thou'rt weak, poor thing! Marry, if you but knew how I wept when I learned what Captain Avery had done, and how I yearned to die with you, and how I feared you'd perish here at Malden and spoil the miracle—i'God, 'tis too much to tell!"

Mrs. Russecks and Henrietta came in from the hall, neither evidently the worse for their ordeal, and when their initial rejoicing subsided, the poet learned the circumstances of their escape.

" 'Twas an act of God, nor more nor less," Mrs. Russecks declared simply. "How else account for't? Long Ben Avery is Benjamin Long of Church Creek, my first and long-lost lover!" Immediately after dispatching the three male prisoners, she said, the privateer had summoned the women aft for the avowed purpose of taking his pleasure, but as it turned out, they suffered no more than a few prurient remarks, for upon learning first her Christian name and then, in response to closer inquiry, her maiden surname, his attitude had changed altogether: he had apologized for having thrown the men overboard, expressed his hope that they would reach Sharp's Island safely, and at the risk of his own life changed course for the mouth of the Severn, where he had bid them *adieu* and returned to his own ship, leaving Captain Cairn to ferry them singlehanded to Anne Arundel Town!

"We don't *know* 'twas Benjamin Long," Henrietta admitted. "He'd not answer Mother's questions. But I can't account for his behavior otherwise——"

"Of course it was my Benjy," Mrs. Russecks said. "The dear boy ran off to sea thirty years ago and turned pirate. 'Twas purely out o' shame he'd not own up to't." On this point she was calmly impervious to argument, and despite the staggering unlikelihood of the coincidence, Ebenezer had to admit that he could think of no hypothesis to account more reasonably for Long Ben Avery's sudden charity. He sat up to embrace them all by turns, and his sister again and again, and then lay back exhausted. His sojourn in Hell, he now learned, had actually lasted four days, during which he had hung in the balance between life and death; McEvoy and Bertrand had also been bedridden from the effects of exposure, though not comatose. The former was now quite recovered, but Bertrand, whom they had not located in the barn until the morning after, was still in grave condition.

"Thank Heav'n they're alive!" Ebenezer exclaimed. "What of Father, and Henry Burlingame, and the cooper? Do I hear them belowstairs?" Indeed, from the rooms below came the sound of several men's voices, apparently in argument.

"Aye," Anna said. "The fact is they're all under house arrest till the matter of our estate is settled! Governor Nicholson is much alarmed about the rebellion and the opium traffic, and hath put Cooke's Point under a sort of martial law till your recovery. In the meantime, everyone accuses everyone else, and no man knows whose title is valid." Directly upon their arrival in Anne Arundel Town, she explained, Captain Cairn and they had gone to the Governor's house, roused him from bed despite the hour, and reported as much as they could piece together of their kidnaping, the activity on Bloodsworth Island, and the vicious enterprise of which Malden had apparently become a regional headquarters. Thanks to the mention of the John Smith papers and Captain Cairn's reputation as a sober citizen of St. Mary's, Governor Nicholson had accepted their report at face value: two armed pinnaces had been dispatched in pursuit of Captain Avery's *Phansie*, and the President of the Council himself, Sir Thomas Lawrence, had set out with the ladies for Cooke's Point before dawn, empowered by the Governor to act as his proxy in any matters involving the welfare of the Province.

"And marry," Henrietta laughed, "what a jolly time we've had since!" Andrew Cooke, she declared, had suffered a series of such great and ambivalent surprises that for a time they had feared for his sanity: to begin with, his joy at finding Ebenezer alive had given way at once to wrath and no small embarrassment—the latter occasioned by his having sworn to all and sundry that "Nicholas Lowe," who in truth had befriended him a fortnight previously and told him that Ebenezer was dead, was the *real* Ebenezer Cooke, and that the so-called Laureate of Maryland who had given Cooke's Point away was a gross impostor. How had his dismay been compounded, then, when in the space of twenty-four hours he had learned that his "son" was apparently a highly placed agent of the Governor's; that Anna had been captured and freed by the notorious Long Ben Avery; and—perhaps most disconcerting of all—that she had brought with her his old mistress Roxanne Edouard and a young lady alleged to be his natural daughter!

"Beside these wonders," Henrietta said, "such trifles as the Bloodsworth insurrection are beneath his attention! Really, Brother Eben, 'tis a droll fellow we have for a father!"

"Henrietta!" Mrs. Russecks scolded. "Let us hasten to tell Sir Thomas that Mister Cooke is himself again, and will soon be strong enough to speak with him." She kissed the poet quite maternally. "Thank God for that!"

Anna was greatly amused. "Henrietta is a marvelous tease," she said to Ebenezer when they were alone again. "Roxanne hath warned her not to call us *brother* and *sister* or speak of Father as *her* father, but she doth it nonetheless to provoke him." By Roxanne's own admission, she said, Andrew had not known when he left her in 1670 that she was carrying his child; she had refrained from telling him lest he marry her under coercion, and so had been doubly embittered when he returned her to her "uncle" in Church Creek. "But ah, he loved her," Anna declared. "You should have seen him when we came in! So overjoyed to see her, he scarce had eyes for *me*, yet so ashamed of having left her —i'faith, he was crucified by shame! He ne'er once questioned that Henrietta was his daughter, but for days now hath gone from begging the whole world's pardon to raging at the lot of us as vultures and thieves, come to do him out of Malden! 'Tis a pitiful sight, Eben: we must forgive him."

Anna seemed to have been altered by her late experience: her face was drawn and weary as before, but her voice and manner reflected a new serenity, an acceptance of things difficult to accept—in short, a beatitude, for like Mrs. Russecks she reminded Ebenezer of one to whom a miracle, a vision or mystic grace, has lately been vouchsafed. The memory of their last exchange in the hold of Captain Cairn's sloop brought the blood to his face; he closed his eyes for shame and gripped her hand. Anna returned the pressure as if she read his thoughts clearly, and went on in her quiet voice to declare that despite Roxanne's coolness to Andrew's contrition, and her assertion that Benjamin Long, or Long Ben Avery, was the only man who ever truly won her heart, Henrietta and Anna agreed that she had by no means lost her affection for their father, but was too wise to grant her pardon overhastily.

Ebenezer smiled and shook his head. He was frightfully weak, but he could feel the balm of his good fortune working magically to restore his strength.

"What of you and Henry, Anna?" he inquired.

Anna lowered her eyes. "We have talked," she said, "— like this, with eyes averted. He was as confounded as Father when I walked in with Roxanne and Henrietta! He rejoiced at our safety and yearns to see you. I told him privily what I could of his father and brothers, and your fears for the safety of the Province; naturally he is ablaze with curiosity and cannot wait to set out for Bloodsworth Island—you know how Henry is—but he won't go till he talks to you. We've promised not to reveal his disguise, you know: even Sir Thomas calls him 'Mr. Lowe,' and Father thinks he's the finest fellow in the Province—he's supposed to be a friend of yours, that bemoans your loss and agreed to help Father get Malden back. The three of us, I suspect, will be much embarrassed by one another for some time . . . our situation is so hopeless . . ." She sniffed back a tear and made her voice more cheerful. "The others are quite delighted with each other, or at least resigned: Henrietta and John, Roxanne and Father; even Bertrand and the Robothams have a sort of truce: the Colonel still vows that Bertrand is you and presses his claim to Malden for fear of scandal, and Lucy, poor thing, hath not got long to her term and trembles at the thought of bearing a bastard. They know very well their claim's a fraud and they're as much to blame for't as Bertrand, but they're desperate, and Bertrand won't confess for fear the Colonel will murther him where he lies. 'Tis a splendid comedy."

Ebenezer heard the sounds of new excitement downstairs: his recovery had been announced.

"Tell me about my wife," he begged, and saw Anna try in vain to dissemble her shock at the deliberately chosen term.

"She hath not long to live . . ."

"Nay!" Ebenezer raised up onto his elbow. "Where is she, Anna?"

"The sight of you and John McEvoy was too much for her," Anna said. "She swooned in the vestibule and was fetched off to bed—'twas another grand moment for Father, you can fancy, the day he learned she was your wife (that he himself once paid six pounds to), and another when he learned she wasn't Susan Warren but the same woman you knew in London! He swears the match is null and void, and rants and rages; but withal he hath not abused her, if only because Henry——"

"No matter!" Ebenezer insisted; a number of people could be heard ascending the stairs. "Quickly, prithee, Anna! What is her condition?"

"The swoon was only the last straw on her back," Anna answered soberly. "Her—her *social disease* hath not improved, nor hath her need for devilish opium, nor hath her general health, that was long since spent out in the curing-house. Dr. Sowter hath examined her and declares she's a dying woman."

"I'God!" the poet moaned. "I must see her at once! I'll die before her!" Against Anna's protests he endeavored to get out of bed, but immediately upon sitting up grew dizzy and fell back on the pillow. "Poor wretch! Poor saintly, martyred wretch!"

His lamentations were cut short by a commotion of visitors led by Henrietta Russecks. First in were his father and Henry Burlingame.

"Dear Ebcn!" Henry cried, hurrying up to grasp both his hands. "What adventures are these you deserted me for?" He raised his head to Andrew, who stood uneasily on the other side of the bed. "Nay, tell me truly, Mr. Cooke: is't a bad son that saves a province?"

Ebenezer could only smile: his heart was full of sentiments too strong and various to permit reply. He and his father regarded each other silently and painfully. "I am heartily sorry, Father," he began after a moment, but his voice was choked at once.

Andrew laid his left hand on Ebenezer's brow—the first such solicitude in the poet's memory. "I told ye once in St. Giles, Eben: to beg forgiveness is the bad son's privilege, and to grant it the bad father's duty." To the room in general he announced, "The lad hath fever yet. State thy business and have done with't, Sir Thomas."

Three other men had come into the room: Richard Sowter, Colonel Robotham, and a courtly, white-wigged gentleman in his fifties who bowed slightly to Andrew and Ebenezer in turn.

"Thomas Lawrence, sir, of the Governor's Council," he

759

said, "and most honored to meet you! Pray forgive me for imposing on your rest and recuperation, so well deserved, but none knows better than yourself how grave and urgent is our business——"

Ebenezer waved off the apology. "My sister hath apprised me of your errand, for which thank God and Governor Nicholson! Our peril is greater than anyone suspects, sir, and the sooner dealt with, the better for all."

"Excellent. Then let me ask you whether you think yourself strong enough to speak this afternoon to Governor Nicholson and myself."

"Nicholson!" Sowter exclaimed. "St. Simon's saw, sirs!" Andrew too, and Colonel Robotham, seemed disquieted by the Council President's words.

Sir Thomas nodded. "Mister Lowe here hath informed me that the Governor went to Oxford yesterday and, being notified of Mister Cooke's rescue, plans to cross to Malden today. We expect him hourly. What say you, sir?"

"I am quite ready and most eager to report to him," Ebenezer said.

"Very good. The Province is in your debt, sir!"

"I say——" Colonel Robotham had become quite florid; his round eyes glanced uneasily from Ebenezer to Andrew to Sir Thomas. "I've no doubt this lad's a hero and hath business of great moment with the Governor; I've no wish to seem preoccupied in selfish concerns or appear ungrateful to His Majesty's secret operatives, whose work requires them to assume false names——"

"Out on't, George!" snapped Andrew. "Mister Lowe here may well be the Governor's agent, or King William's, or the Pope's, for aught I know, but this lad is my son Eben and there's an end on't! Heav'n forgive me for conniving with Mister Lowe to deceive the lot o' ye, and Heav'n be praised for bringing my son back from the dead, Malden or no Malden!"

"Enough," Sir Thomas ordered. "I remind you, Colonel, that the Province hath no small interest in this estate; 'twas to look into it I came hither in the beginning. If the Governor's willing, haply we can hold a hearing on that question this very day, now Mister Cooke is with us." He further reminded the entire party, and especially Richard Sowter, that they were forbidden to leave the premises until the matter had been disposed of.

"By the organ of St. Cecilia!" Sowter protested. "'Tis an nfracture o' *habeas corpus!* We'll hale ye to court, sir!"

"Your privilege," Sir Thomas replied. "In the meantime, lon't leave Cooke's Point: Mister Lowe hath communicated with Major Trippe, and as of this morning we have militia-men on the grounds."

This news occasioned general surprise; Colonel Robotham tugged at his mustache, and Sowter invoked Saints Hyginus and Polycarpus against such highhandedness on the part of public servants. Sir Thomas then requested everyone to leave the room except Anna, who had established herself as her brother's nurse, and "Mister Lowe," who declared it impera-tive that he not leave the key witness's bedside for a moment. Andrew seemed reluctant. "We shall have much to say," Ebe-nezer consoled him, "and years to say't. Just now I'm dead for want of food and sleep."

"I'll fetch broth for ye," his father grunted, and went out.

Ebenezer sighed. "He must soon be told who you are, Henry; I am sick unto death of false identities."

"I shall tell him," Burlingame promised, "now I know my-self. I'faith, 'tis miraculous, Eben! I can scarcely wait to lay hands on my father's book—what did he call it? *The Book of English Devils!* King of the Ahatchwhoops! Miraculous!" He held up a tutorial finger and smiled. "But not yet, Eben; nay, he oughtn't to know quite yet. My plan is to go to Bloods-worth Island as soon as possible—tomorrow, if we settle our business here today—and do what I can to pacify my father Chicamec and my brother—what was his name?"

Ebenezer smiled despite himself at his tutor's characteristic enthusiasm. "Cohunkowprets," he said. "It means 'Bill-o'-the-Goose.' "

"Cohunkowprets! Splendid name! Then I'll return here, pay court to your sister, and sue my good friend Andrew for her hand. If he consents, I'll tell him who I am and ask him again; if not, I'll go my way and ne'er disturb him with the truth. Is that agreeable to the twain of you?"

Ebenezer looked to his sister for reply. It was clear to him that her private conversations with Burlingame had dealt with matters more intimate than *The Book of English Devils;* he felt sure that Henry knew all that had transpired not only be-tween Anna and Billy Rumbly but also between Anna and himself. She caught her breath and shook her head, keeping her eyes down on the counterpane.

" 'Tis so futile, Henry . . . Whate'er could come of it?"

761

"Nay, how can you despair after such a miracle as Eben's stumbling on my parentage? Only let him gain his feet again and he'll solve that other riddle for me: the Magic of the Sacred Eggplant, or whatever!" He gave over his raillery and added seriously, "I proposed to Eben not long since that the three of us take a house in Pennsylvania; since Nature hath decreed that I be thwarted, and Convention hath rejected your appeal, where's the harm in being thwarted together? Let us live like sisters of mercy in our own little convent—aye, I'll convert you to Cosmophilism, my new religion for thwarted seekers after Truth, and we'll invent a gross of spiritual exercises——"

He went on in this vein until both Ebenezer and Anna were obliged to laugh, and the tension among them was temporarily dispelled. But Anna would not commit herself on the proposal. "Let us attend to first things first: come back alive from Bloodsworth Island, neither scalped nor converted to *their* religion, and we shall see what's to be done with ourselves."

"What came of your pilgrimage to John Coode?" Ebenezer asked Burlingame.

"Ah, my friend, you've much to forgive me for! How can I excuse myself for having deceived you so often, save that I put no faith in innocence? And to plead this is but to offend you farther . . ."

"No longer," Ebenezer assured him. "My innocence these days is severely technical! But what of Coode? Did you find him to be the savior you took him for?"

Burlingame sighed. "I ne'er found him at all." It had been his intention, he said, to establish himself as Coode's lieutenant (in the role of Nicholas Lowe), the better to learn what truth might lie in certain current rumors that Coode was organizing slaves and disaffected Indians for another rebellion, to be staged before Nicholson could institute proceedings against him on the evidence of the 1691 Assembly Journal. But in St. Mary's City, on the morning after the same stormy night that had carried Ebenezer to Bloodsworth Island, Burlingame had encountered Andrew Cooke himself, who he thought had crossed from Captain Mitchell's place to the Eastern Shore. By discreet inquiry, he learned that Andrew had fallen in with Colonel Robotham at Captain Mitchell's, and upon hearing the Colonel refer to Ebenezer as "my son-in-law in St. Mary's," had hastened to investigate as soon as he recovered from the shock.

"Well, friend," Burlingame went on, "I scarce knew what to think; I'd searched all night in vain for you and finally got word that Captain Cairn had sailed at dusk with the Laureate of Maryland and some long skinny fellow and was thought to be drowned in the storm. Your father had learned the state of things at Malden and was at his wit's end for loss of both his heirs and his estate." When it had seemed likely that Ebenezer was either dead or lost from sight, Burlingame had introduced himself to Andrew as Nicholas Lowe, "a steadfast friend of the Laureate," and declared further that it was he who had posed as Ebenezer, the better to cover his friend's escape. This news had redoubled Andrew's wrath; for some moments Burlingame had expected to be assaulted where he stood (in Vansweringen's Tavern). In order to pacify him, therefore, console him in some measure for his loss, and at the same time put himself in a better position to hear news of the twins and pursue his complex interests, Burlingame had made an ingenious proposal: he would continue to pose as Andrew's son; they would go to Cooke's Point together, declare both the grantor of Malden and the husband of Lucy Robotham to be impostors, and so refute the claims of colonel and cooper alike.

"Thus came we hither arm in arm, the best of friends, and save for one fruitless visit to Church Creek to chase down a rumor I caught wind of—you know the story? Is't not ironic? —save for that visit, I say, here we've sat to this day, waiting for word from you or Anna. As for the estate, Andrew and I threaten Smith and Sowter, and they threaten us in return, and of late the Colonel hath been threatening the lot of us; but no one durst go to court lest he lose his breeches, the case is such a tangle, or lest he find himself answerable for the whores and opium. What old Andrew's connection with *them* might be, if he hath any, e'en I can't judge."

"Thou'rt not John Coode thyself?" Anna asked half seriously.

Henry shrugged. "I have been, now and again; for that matter, I was once Francis Nicholson for half a day, and three Mattawoman tarts were ne'er the wiser. But this I'll swear: albeit 'tis hard for me to think such famous wights are pure and total fictions, to this hour I've not laid eyes on either Baltimore or Coode. It may be they are all that rumor swears: devils and demigods, whichever's which; or it may be they're simple clotpolls like ourselves, that have been legend'd

763

out of reasonable dimension; or it may be they're naught but the rumors and tales themselves."

"If that last is so," Ebenezer said, "Heav'n knows 'twere a potent life enough! When I reflect on the weight and power of such fictions beside my own poor shade of a self, that hath been so much disguised and counterfeited, methinks they have tenfold my substance!"

Burlingame smiled approval. "My lad hath gone to school with a better tutor than his old one! In any case, Francis Nicholson exists, that is neither a Coode nor a Calvert, and he counts Nick Lowe as the cleverest spy he knows. 'Twere indiscreet to press me farther."

There were still a number of questions on Ebenezer's mind, but at this point the cook—whom he recognized as the old Parisian trollop who had wept at his wedding—brought up his beef broth, and Burlingame took the opportunity to excuse himself.

"I must see to't the Governor's not murthered on your property, my dears." He kissed Anna lightly and unabashedly on the mouth, as husband kisses wife, and then, to the poet's surprise, kissed him also, but discreetly, upon the forehead, more as father might kiss son or, in more demonstrative latitudes, brother brother. "Thank almighty Zeus thou'rt back amongst the living!" he murmured. "Did I not once say there'd be great commotion at thy fall?"

Ebenezer protested with a smile that, ruined and spent though he was indubitably, as yet he was not officially among the fallen, nor did it appear likely that he would ever join their number. Burlingame responded with a characteristic shrug and departed.

"Heav'n knows our other problems are far more grave," Anna sighed, "but I cannot give o'er my concern for that man and for the three of us!"

"Will you marry him?" asked her brother.

Anna too shrugged her shoulders. "What is the use of't? As well go off with him, as I did with his brother, and live in sin." So peculiarly inapposite was the phrase, under the circumstances, that both twins had to smile. But then Anna shook her head. "What I most fear is that he'll not return from Bloodsworth Island."

This notion surprised Ebenezer. "You fear Billy Rumbly might do him in from jealousy? I'd not thought of that."

"Nay," said Anna. "Formidable as Billy may be, he is no match for Henry, and there's the danger."

764

Ebenezer saw her point and shivered: how slight and qualified were Henry's ties to the cause of Western Civilization (to say nothing of English colonialism!), than which his mind and interests were so enormously more complex that it seemed parochial by comparison! Had he not already been a pirate and perhaps an agent for Heaven knew what satanic conspiracy? Had he not extolled the virtues of every sort of perversity, and pointed out to Ebenezer man's perennial fascination with violence, destruction, and rapine? It was by no means unthinkable that, whatever his present intention, Burlingame would remain on Bloodsworth Island to ally his wits with those of Drepacca and Quassapelagh; and with three so canny, potent adversaries—not to mention John Coode and the shadowy Monsieur Casteene—God help the English colonies in America!

The broth did wonders for his strength; when he had finished it he sent Anna to express his contrition to Joan Toast and beg her to allow him an interview.

"She refuses," Anna reported a minute later. "She says she hath no quarrel with me, but wishes to die without having to endure the sight of another man. Not e'en Dr. Sowter may come near her anymore."

As always upon hearing news of her, Ebenezer was stung to the heart with shame. Nevertheless he took it as a good sign that Joan had at least not sunk into apathy: where belligerence lingered, he declared to Anna, life lingered also, and while his wife lived he did not abandon the hope, not of winning her forgiveness, to which he felt no title, but of demonstrating in her presence the extent of his wretchedness at having deserted her. In the meantime he summoned McEvoy, who after commiserating with him for Joan's condition, shaking his head at the miraculous coincidence of Long Ben Avery's identity (which he said quite substantiated Ebenezer's charge that Life is a shameless playwright), and rejoicing at the ladies' safety, assisted the poet down the hall to the chamber he shared with Bertrand Burton.

"The poor wretch bolted, don't ye know, for fear Colonel Robotham and your father would have his arse, and what with Joan swooned away in the vestibule, and yourself froze up like marble, and all the stir and commotion, they ne'er found him till morning, near dead of cold. E'en so they meant to put him with the servants, but Mister Lowe and I persuaded 'em to bed him with me. I fear the cold hath got to him, poor devil."

They found the valet awake, but far from healthy. His cheeks, though fanned with fever to an unnatural red, were pinched and drawn; his nose was more sharp than ever, and angled like a Semite's at the bridge; his eyes, round as always, and protruding, looked lusterless past his beak like a sick owl's eyes. Just as Burlingame had hurried forward to Ebenezer's bedside, so now the poet hastened to his valet's.

"Poor fellow! You ought ne'er to have left us!"

Bertrand smiled wryly. "I ought ne'er to have left Pudding Lane, sir," he said, his voice half croak and half whisper. "Your servingman had better face his Ralph Birdsalls than play at Laureates and Advisers, whate'er his gifts. Hadn't we a lark, though, the day we were Drakepecker's gods and thought we'd found the golden city?"

Ebenezer wanted to protest that his servant was talking like a doomed man, but he checked himself lest the figure be read for a prophecy.

"Indeed, that was a splendid day," he agreed. "And we shall have many another, Bertrand, you and I." He assured his man that neither Andrew nor himself felt anything but solicitude for his infirmity, from which they all prayed for his swift recovery. "As for the Colonel, he hath cause enough to be wrathful, and Lucy's case is pitiful enough, but Heaven knows they brought it upon themselves! In any case, they shan't lay a hand upon you. Get you well, man, and advise me, or let me freight you back to Betsy Birdsall!"

But the valet was not to be drawn from his mood: he sighed and, rendered incoherent by his fever, spoke unintelligibly of ratafia, Great Bears, and women's wiles. He would express lucidly his chagrin at not having guessed Betsy Birdsall's scheme to save him by unmanning her husband, and almost in the same breath begin to rave about Cibola, the Fortunate Islands, and the Sunken Land of Buss.

"Ye must own," he said slyly at one point, "I had some knack for playing poet. . . ."

"No knack, i'faith," Ebenezer wept. "A very genius!"

Bertrand lapsed once more into mild delirium, and at Anna's suggestion the two men left him to be attended by her and Mrs. Russecks. Ebenezer returned to his own room for a short nap, after which, and a heartier refection than his first, he declared himself ready to report if need be to God Himself.

"Then I shall send for Governor Nicholson to come up," replied Burlingame. "He arrived while you slept and hath given everyone the vapors by refusing to hear a word about the estate ere he speaks with you. But I resolved to make him wait till you had done eating."

Despite his apprehension at meeting the Governor, Ebenezer had to smile. "Did I tell you that your brother hath that same maddening habit?"

"Nay, that's marvelous! I cannot wait to end this tiresome business and fly to him!"

On this ambiguous note Henry went belowstairs; he returned very shortly afterwards in the wake of Francis Nicholson, Royal Governor of the Province of Maryland, a man of Burlingame's brief height and robust frame, though a dozen years older and somewhat gone to stomach. He had the plum-velvet breeches, the great French periwig, the fastidious manicure, and the baby-pink face of a dandy; but his great jaw and waspish eyes, the snap of his voice and the brusqueness of his manner, belied all foppery. He strode into the room without asking leave, leaned heavily upon his silver-headed stick, and peered at the patient through his glasses with a mixture of eagerness, curiosity, and skepticism, as if Ebenezer were one of those stranded whales to which his royal commission gave him title, and he was not certain whether the oil would be worth the flensing. Burlingame stood by, amused; Sir Thomas Lawrence, catching up breathlessly to the others, closed the door behind him.

"Good evening to you, Your Excellency," Ebenezer ventured. "I am Ebenezer Cooke."

" 'Sheart, ye had better be!" cried the Governor. His air was curt but not unkind, and he laughed along with the others. "So this is Charles Calvert's laureate, that we hear such a deal about!"

"Nay, Your Excellency, 'twas ne'er an honest title——"

"The Governor will have his jest," interposed Sir Thomas. "Mister Lowe hath apprised us already of the circumstances of your commission, Mister Cooke, and the sundry trials and impostures wherewith it burthened you."

" 'Tis not a bad idea at that," declared Nicholson, "albeit I'll wager old Baltimore did it merely to play at being king. Only give me time to found myself a college in Annapolis—that's what I call Anna Arundel Town—just grant me a year to build a school there, and whether these penny-pinching clotpolls like it or no, we'll have ourselves a book or two in Maryland! Aye, and belike a poet may find somewhat to sing about then, eh, Nick?"

"I daresay," Burlingame replied, and added, upon the Governor's further inquiring, that he had established communication with a certain Virginia printer and, in accordance with Nicholson's directive, was endeavoring to hire the fellow away from Governor Andros to set up shop in Maryland. For a time it looked as if Ebenezer had been forgotten, but without transition the Governor turned to him—indeed, turned *on* him, so formidable was the man's usual expression —and demanded to hear without ado the details of "this fantastical story of slaves and salvages." His apparent skepticism put the poet off at first—he commenced the story falteringly and with misgivings, almost doubting its truth himself—but he soon discovered that the Governor's incredulity was only a mannerism. "Absurd!" Nicholson would scoff on being told that Drepacca was in communication with the northern chiefs, but his pink brow would darken with concern; by the time he called the story of Burlingame's true name and parentage "a bold-arsed fraud and turdsome lie," Ebenezer was able to translate the obscenities accurately to read "the damn- 'dest miracle I e'er heard tell of!" In short, though he protested his utter disbelief at every pause in the poet's relation, Ebenezer felt confident, as did Burlingame, that he accepted every word of it: not only the grand perils of the Negro-Indian conspiracy and the traffic in whores and narcotics, but also such details as the illicit trade in redemptioners practised by Slye and Scurry, the depredations of Andros's "coast guard" Thomas Pound (upon learning of which he rubbed his hands in delighted anticipation of embarrassing his rival), and the duplicity of the *Poseidon*'s Captain Meech—whom, ironically, Nicholson had recently hired to cruise against illegal traders in the provincial sloop *Speedwell*.

"Sweet Mother o' Christ!" he swore at the end. "What a nest o' wolves and vipers I'm sent to govern!" He turned to his lieutenants. "What say ye, gentlemen: shall we make for Barbados and leave this scurfy province to the heathen? And you, you wretch!" He aimed his stick at Burlingame. "You go about posing as a proper Talbot gentleman, and all the while thou'rt a bloody salvage prince! Marry come up! Marry come up!"

Burlingame winked at Ebenezer. For some moments Governor Nicholson paced about the bedroom, stabbing at the floorboards with his stick. At length he stopped and glared at his Council President.

"Well, damn it, Tom, can we prosecute this Coode or not?

'Twill be one rascal the less to deal with, and then we can look to arming the militia." Aside to Ebenezer he confessed, "If the truth is known, we've more balls in our breeches than we have in the bloody armory."

Sir Thomas appealed to Burlingame for a reply and received a tongue-lashing from His Excellency for having to get his answers from "a red-skinned spy."

"We can prosecute whene'er we find him, sir," Burlingame declared, "but we'll need to choose our judges with care, and e'en so there's a chance he'll get off lightly." One portion of the 1691 Assembly Journal, the Province's most damning evidence against Coode and the "Protestant Associators," had yet to be retrieved, he explained; though its relevance to the tale of his own ancestry was presumably slight (it was that portion of Sir Henry Burlingame's *Privie Journall* which dealt, so William Smith had vaguely averred, with the Englishmen's escape from the Emperor Powhatan), its importance as evidence might be very great indeed. " 'Tis in the possession of that loutish cooper belowstairs," he concluded, "who will not part with't for love nor money. Howbeit, we may threaten it loose from him yet, and once I've seen it we shall look for the Reverend General Coode."

"We shall have it, right enough," Nicholson muttered, "ere this day is done. If I'm to be massacred by the heathen, I want to see that rascal Coode in Hell before me."

"There's a more worrisome business," said Burlingame. "You know as well as I that if the Negroes and salvages take a mind to, they can murther every white man in America by spring—more especially with three or four good generals." It was his intention, he said, to go in any case to Bloodsworth Island as soon as possible and present himself to the Tayac Chicamec and Cohunkowprets; there was every chance that they would doubt his identity, as he had no proof of it, but if by some miracle they should believe him, he would endeavor to depose his brother and set Quassapelagh and Drepacca against each other. Faction and intrigue, he was convinced, were the only weapons that could save the English until their position was stronger in America.

"Ye'll not live past your preamble," Nicholson scoffed. "The brutes are slow, but they're not stupid enough to bow to any Englishman that strolls in and declares he's their king."

"Ah, well, 'tis not a role that *any* Englishman could play. Not that I claim any special talent, sir—on the contrary, this role wants a most particular *shortcoming,* doth it not, Eben?"

He proceeded to describe quite candidly the congenital infirmity which he had inherited from Sir Henry Burlingame, his grandfather, and which he meant to employ by way of credentials on Bloodsworth Island. The Governor was astonished, sympathetic, and vulgarly amused by turns: he declared that the stratagem would surely fail nonetheless if the Indians had even one self-respecting skeptic in their number —"D'ye think old Ulysses would have scrupled to eunuch Sinon if he'd judged it to his purpose?" he demanded—but for the present, at least, he could offer no better proposal. He turned to Ebenezer, all the surliness gone for once from his face and manner, and asked, "Have ye aught else to tell me now, my boy? Ye have not? God bless ye, then, for your courage and reward ye for your trials: if thou'rt half as much a poet as thou'rt a man, ye deserve a better laureateship than Maryland's."

And having extended himself so vulnerably into sentiment, he retreated into character before the poet could find words to express his gratitude. "Now then, Tom, I want every wight and trollop on the premises assembled in the parlor, saving only that one poor devil that's mad with his fever. We'll hold us a fine court-baron here and now, as Charlie Calvert was wont to do when things grew tame, and rule on the patent to this estate ere moonrise."

"Very well, sir!" replied Sir Thomas. "But I must remind you what Judge Hammaker——"

"My arse to Hammaker, let him take a toast in't!" cried the Governor, and Ebenezer could not help recalling a certain libelous story once told him by Bertrand. "Stir thy stumps, there, Nicholas me lad—nay, what is't, now? *Henry?* I'Christ, a fit name for a codless Machiavel! Ring in the parishioners to be judged, Henry Burlingame: Tom here shall play old Minos, and I'll be Rhadamanthus!"

20

The Poet Commences His Day in Court

INASMUCH AS THE QUESTION of Malden's ownership had been
uppermost in everyone's mind for several days at least, it was
not long before Governor Nicholson was able to call his extraordinary court to order in the front parlor. All the interested parties were present, including at least one who seemed
to wish he was somewhere else: two troopers of the Dorchester County Militia, it was made known, had intercepted William Smith on the beach not far from the house, and the discomfort in his face belied his avowal that he had sought only
a breath of fresh air. The two judges established themselves at
the green baize table with their backs to the hearth and arranged the others in a large half circle about them; Henry
Burlingame was equipped with paper and quill and stationed
on Nicholson's left, opposite Sir Thomas, whence he surveyed
the assembled company with amusement.

Ebenezer, who had taken the trouble to dress himself for
the occasion, sat upon the arm of Anna's chair on the extreme right of the semicircle (as viewed from the judges' position); though he naturally desired that the title of Cooke's
Point should be returned to his father, all this past anxiety
had been washed out of him by the events and revelations of
his recent past: his excitement was that of mere anticipation.
In keeping with her new tranquility, Anna had brought a
piece of needlework with her, which seemed to absorb her
whole attention; one would have thought her altogether unin-
terested in the disposition of the estate. On her right sat Andrew Cooke, smoking his pipe so fiercely and steadily that the
wreathing smoke seemed to come not from his mouth but
through his pores. From time to time he cast great frowning
glances at his children, as if afraid they might vanish before
his eyes or change into someone else; for the rest, he stared

impatiently ahead at the table and sipped at a glass of the rum that Nicholson had ordered served around.

Never once did he turn his eyes to the leather couch beside him, where sat Roxanne Russecks, Henrietta, and John McEvoy. There was gossip, Anna had reported to Ebenezer, of a reconciliation between the old lovers. Neither of them would speak of the matter directly—Roxanne protested her eternal devotion to the memory of Benjamin Long, and Andrew protested his to the memory of Anne Bowyer Cooke—but the miller's widow, for all her serenity, was uncommonly full of life; her brown eyes flashed and she seemed always to be relishing some private joke. And Andrew, when his daughter had assured him that neither she nor Ebenezer would consider his remarriage an affront to their mother's memory, had been covered with confusion, and advised Anna to look to her own betrothal before arranging his. Ebenezer had not realized thitherto that his father was not so hopelessly ancient after all, but a mere mid-fifty or thereabouts—no older to Burlingame, for example, than Burlingame was to the twins—and still quite virile-looking despite his greying beard, his withered arm, and his late ill-health.

Beside Roxanne, in the middle of the group, sat the reunited lovers Henrietta and John McEvoy, about whom there were no rumors at all: they made no secret of their feelings for each other, and everyone assumed that their betrothal would soon be announced. On their right along the other arc sat Richard Sowter, William Smith, Lucy Robotham, and the Colonel, her father, in that order—rather, all sat except Colonel Robotham, who fussed floridly hither and thither behind the chair in which his daughter scowled with shame. The cooper glowered at his shoes and nodded impatiently from time to time at whatever Sowter whispered him: he would not look at all towards Ebenezer, or towards the militiaman in Scotch cloth, musket at the ready, whom Nicholson had promoted to sergeant-at-arms five minutes previously.

For want of a gavel, the Governor rapped the edge of the table with his stick.

"Very well, dammee, this court-baron is called to order. Our trusted friend Nick Lowe hath devised a clever code for taking down the spoken word, and on the strength of't we here appoint him clerk of this court."

Ebenezer saw a manifold opportunity in the situation. "If't please Your Excellency——" he ventured.

"It doth not," snapped Nicholson. "Ye'll have ample time to speak thy piece anon."

"'Tis with regard to the clerk," Ebenezer insisted. "In view of the extraordinary complexity of the business at hand, wherein the matter of identities hath such importance, methinks 'twere wise to establish a firm principle at the outset: that no actions be taken by the Court or testimony heard save under the true and bona fide identities of all concerned, lest doubt be cast on the legality of the Court's rulings. To this end I request Your Excellency to appoint and swear the clerk by's actual name."

Anna was understandably alarmed by this proposal, and the others—especially Andrew—were perplexed by it; but both Nicholson and Sir Thomas clearly appreciated the poet's strategy of establishing a precedent favorable to his case, and with a little nod Burlingame signaled his approval of Ebenezer's other intention.

"Unquestionably the wisest procedure," Nicholson agreed, and declared to the room: "Be't known that Nicholas Lowe is our good friend's *nom de guerre*, as't were, and we here appoint him clerk o' the court under his true name, Henry Burlingame the Third—do I have it right, Henry?"

Burlingame affirmed the identification with another nod, but his attention, like the twins', was on Andrew Cooke, who had gone white at mention of the name.

"Marry come up!" laughed McEvoy, unaware of the situation. "Is't really you, Henry? There's no end o' miracles these days! Did ye hear, Henrietta——"

Henrietta hushed him; Andrew had risen stiffly to his feet, glaring at Burlingame.

"As God is my witness!" he began, and was obliged to pause and swallow several times to contain his emotion. "I will see thee in Hell, Henry Burlingame——"

He advanced a step towards the table; Ebenezer moved forward and caught his arm.

"Sit down, Father: you've no just quarrel with Henry, nor ever did have. 'Tis I you must rail at, not Henry and Anna."

Andrew stared at his son's face incredulously, and at the hand that restrained him; but he made no move to go farther.

"Aye, go to, Andrew," said Mrs. Russecks. "Thou'rt the defendant in that affair, not the plaintiff. For that matter, a deceiver hath little ground to complain of deception."

"I quite agree!" said Colonel Robotham, and then cleared

his throat uncomfortably under a whimsical look from Burlingame.

Nicholson rapped for order. "Ye may settle your private differences anon," he declared. "Be seated, Mister Cooke."

Andrew did as he was bade; Roxanne leaned over to whisper something in his ear, and Anna patted her brother's hand admiringly. Ebenezer's pulse was still fast, but a wink from Henry Burlingame warmed his heart. A moment later, however, it was his turn to be shaken: the French kitchen woman came to the door with a whispered message, which was relayed to the Governor by the militiamen who blocked her entry; it seemed to consist of two parts, the first of which he acknowledged with a nod, the second with an oath.

"Ye'll be pleased to know, Madame Russecks," he announced, "thy friend Captain Avery hath given us the slip and is on his way to Philadelphia, where I'm sure he'll find snug harbor and no dearth o' companions."

Roxanne replied that neither her old affection for Long Ben Avery nor her recent obligation to him blinded her to the viciousness of his piracies; she would thank His Excellency to recall that it was she who had reported Avery's whereabouts, and not to embarrass her by insinuations of a relationship that did not exist.

"I quite agree," said Andrew. Ebenezer and Anna exchanged glances of surprise, and the Governor, who seemed impressed by Roxanne's spirit, nodded his apologies.

"I am farther advised that one of our invalids hath requested to join us, and inasmuch as Mr. Burlingame believes her to be a material witness on sundry points, I shall ask him to assist the sergeant-at-arms in fetching her down ere we commence."

Andrew, Roxanne, Henrietta, John McEvoy—all looked soberly at Ebenezer, whose features the news set into characteristic turmoil. For some moments he feared another onset of immobility, but at sight of Joan, borne in on the arms of her escorts like some wretch fetched fainting from a dungeon, he sprang from the chair arm.

"Ah God!"

All the men rose murmuring to their feet; Andrew touched his son's arm and cleared his throat once or twice by way of encouragement. It was indeed a disquieting sight: Joan's face and garments were free of dirt—Anna and Roxanne had seen to that—but her face was welted by disease, her teeth were in miserable condition, and her eyes—those brown eyes that had flashed so excellently in Locket's—were red and ruined. She was no older than Henrietta Russecks, but her malaise, together with her coarse woolen nightdress and tangled coiffure, made her look like a witch or ancient Bedlamite. McEvoy groaned at the spectacle, Lucy Robotham covered her eyes, Richard Sowter sniffed uncomfortably, and his client refused to look at all. Joan being too infirm to sit erect, she was wrapped in blankets on the couch by Henrietta, whose solicitude suggested that McEvoy had kept no secrets from her.

Not until she was settled on the couch did Joan acknowledge Ebenezer's anguished presence with a stare. "God help and forgive me!" the poet cried. He threw himself to his knees before the couch, pressed her hand to his mouth and wept upon it.

"Order! Order!" commanded Nicholson. "Ye may sit beside your wife if ye choose, Mister Cooke, but we'll ne'er have done with our business if we don't commence it. Whatever ill the wretch hath done ye, Mrs. Cooke, 'tis plain he's sorry for't. Do ye wish him to change place with Mrs. Russecks or leave ye be?"

"If wishes were buttercakes, beggars might bite," Joan replied, but though the proverb was tart, her voice was weak and hoarse. *"I ne'er fared worse than when I wished for my supper."*

"Whate'er ye please, then, Mister Cooke," the Governor said. "But smartly."

Mrs. Russecks drew Ebenezer to the place she had vacated, by Joan's head, and herself took the chair offered her by Andrew Cooke, who regarded his son gravely. Out of range of her eyes, Ebenezer retained Joan's spiritless hand in his own; he could not bear to look at the rest of the company, but to the left of him he heard Anna's needles clicking busily, and the sounds went into him like nails.

"Now," said Nicholson drily, "I trust we may get on with our business. The clerk will please give the oath to Andrew Cooke and commence the record."

"That man shan't swear me," Andrew declared. "I'd as lief take oath from the Devil."

"Any wight that won't stand forward and be sworn," Nicholson threatened, "forfeits his claim to his miserable estate here and now."

Andrew grudgingly took the oath.

"I object, Your Excellency," said Sowter. "The witness failed to raise his right hand."

"Objection be damned!" the Governor answered. "He can no more raise his hand than Henry here his cod, as any but a blackguard or addlepate might see. Now sit ye down, Mister Cooke: inasmuch as the lot of ye have some interest in the case and we've no regular courthouse to hear it in, I here declare this entire parlor to be our witness-box. Ye may answer from your seats."

"But St. Rosalie's kneebones, Your Excellency," Sowter protested. "Who is the accused and who the plaintiff?"

The Governor held a brief conference on this point with Sir Thomas Lawrence, who then announced that, owing to the unusual complexity of the claims and allegations, the proceedings would begin in the form of an inquest, to be turned into a proper trial as soon as issues were clarified.

" 'Tis no more than all of us were wont to do under the Lord Proprietary," he maintained. Sowter made no further objections, even when, as if to tempt him, Nicholson took the extraordinary step of administering the oath to everyone in the room simultaneously, obliging them to join hands in a chain from Burlingame, who held the Bible, and recite in chorus.

"Now, then, Mister Andrew Cooke——" He consulted a document on the table before him. "Do I understand that on the fifth day of March, in 1662, you acquired this tract of land from one Thomas Manning and Grace his wife for the sum of seven thousand pounds of tobacco, and that subsequently ye raised this house on't?"

Andrew affirmed the particulars of the transaction.

"And is it true that from 1670 till September last this property was managed for ye by one Benjamin Spurdance?"

"Aye."

"Where is this Spurdance?" Nicholson asked Burlingame. "Oughtn't he to be here?"

"We're endeavoring to find him," Henry said. "He seems to have disappeared."

Andrew then testified, in answer to the Governor's inquiries, that on the first of April, at his orders, Ebenezer had embarked from Plymouth to take full charge of the plantation, and that for reasons of convenience he had given his son full power of attorney in all matters pertinent thereto.

"And did he then, in the Circuit Court at Cambridge last September, grant Cooke's Point free and clear to William Smith?"

"Aye and he did, by good St. Wenceslaus," Sowter put in firmly. "Your Excellency hath the paper to prove it."

"He was deceived!" Andrew shouted. "He had no idea 'twas Malden, and what's more he had no authority to dispose of the property!"

"I fail to see why not," Sowter argued. "What matter could be more pertinent to the business of a planter than disposing of his plantation?"

Here Colonel Robotham joined the battle. "This entire question is beside the point, Your Excellency! The wight that granted Cooke's Point to Smith was an arrant impostor, as Mr. Cooke himself hath admitted, and my daughter's claim hath priority in any case—the *real* Ebenezer Cooke lost the property on a shipboard wager to the Reverend George Tubman in June, and Tubman conveyed the title to my daughter ere ever this other hoax was perpetrated!"

"A bald-arsed lie!" cried Sowter, and Andrew agreed.

Nicholson stood up and pounded his stick on the floor. "That will quite do, dammee! The inquest is finished!"

Even Burlingame was astonished by this announcement.

"'Tis scarce begun!" protested Andrew. "You've not heard aught of't yet!"

"Ye'll refrain from speaking out of order," said the Governor, "or be removed from this courtroom. We said at the outset that directly we found a clear defendant we'd end the inquest and commence the trial. The inquest is done."

Andrew beamed. "Then you agree I'm the true defendant, and 'tis for these thieves to prove their lying claims?"

"Not a bit of't," Nicholson answered. "*I* am the defendant —that is to say, the Province o' Maryland. We here confiscate the house and grounds together, dammee, and 'tis for the lot o' ye to show cause why we oughtn't to hold 'em in His Majesty's name."

"On what grounds?" Sowter demanded. "'Tis a travesty o' justice!"

Nicholson hesitated until Burlingame, who was clearly delighted by the move, whispered something to him.

"'Tis for the welfare o' the Province and His Majesty's plantations in America," he said then. "This house is alleged to be the center of a vicious traffic, which same traffic is alleged in turn to be managed by seditious and treasonable elements in the Province. 'Tis entirely within our rights as Governor to confiscate the property of traitors and suspected traitors pending trial o' the charges against 'em."

"St. Sever's tan yard! There are no charges against any-one!"

"Quite so," the Governor agreed. " 'Twere unjust to bring so grave a charge in a special court and without a hearing. In short, the lot o' ye are under house arrest for sedition pending your hearing, and there'll be no hearing till we settle the title to this estate!"

Sir Thomas himself was plainly dazzled.

"It hath no precedent!" the Colonel complained.

"On the contrary," Nicholson said triumphantly. " 'Tis the very trick Justice Holt employed for King William to snatch the charter o' Maryland from Baltimore."

The confiscation was promptly made official: Sir Thomas's status was changed from judge to counsel for the defense; Andrew, William Smith, and Lucy Robotham were named joint plaintiffs; and the case of *Cooke et al.* v. *Maryland* was declared open.

" 'Sheart, now!" laughed the Governor. "There's a piece o' courtsmanship to remember!" He then ruled that Colonel Robotham, as Lucy's counsel, should be heard first, since his claim antedated the others. The Colonel, much ill at ease, repeated the particulars of the gaming aboard the *Poseidon*, the final wager made prior to the Laureate's capture, by virtue of which the title to Cooke's Point passed to the Reverend George Tubman of Port Tobacco parish, the Reverend Tubman's marriage of Lucy (subsequently annulled as bigamous), her acquisition to the title of Cooke's Point, and finally her marriage to the Laureate himself.

Nicholson grunted. "Now see here, Colonel Robotham, thou'rt a responsible man, for all ye once served with Coode and Governor Copley; if I hadn't thought ye a friend o' Justice I'd ne'er have made ye Judge o' the Admiralty Court. Thou'rt an honest man and a just one: a credit to the wretched Province . . ."

"I thankee, sir," muttered the Colonel. "Heav'n knows I crave naught save justice———"

"Then lookee yonder at that skinny fellow on the couch and admit he is no more thy daughter's husband than I am, nor is he the wight that made the wager with George Tubman!"

"I never said he was," protested the Colonel. "Andrew Cooke himself hath declared to all of us———"

"We know his lying declarations," Nicholson interrupted,

"and we know as well as you do why he called Henry here his son."

This point Colonel Robotham granted freely. "He thought his son was dead and hoped to deceive me with an impostor. But if Your Excellency please, sir, my position is that a man who will disown his own son dead would as lief disown him alive, and as lief twice or thrice as once. My position, sir, is that when he learned how his son had gambled away his property, he conspired with Mister Lowe—or Burlingame, whiche'er it is—to defraud us; and that when my poor son-in-law appeared with his companions and Mister Burlingame was obliged to reveal himself, Mister Cooke callously bribed that wretch of a servant to pose in his place. I can produce witnesses a-plenty from the *Poseidon* to identify my daughter's husband as Ebenezer Cooke and that treacherous rascal as his valet; and they will swear, as I do now, that oft and oft on shipboard he would presume to his master's office."

The Governor shook his head. "I greatly fear, George, 'tis thy son-in-law upstairs that is the presumptuous servant. Much as I deplore the scandal of't, and pity ye the burthen of a short-heeled daughter, I am altogether convinced that this fellow here is the true Eben Cooke. In addition to the testimony of his father, his sister, and Mister Burlingame, I have here a sworn affidavit from Bertrand Burton, the man in yonder chamber, that Mister Burlingame had the foresight to acquire before the poor devil was o'erhauled by fever. I shall read it aloud and hand it round for your inspection."

He proceeded to read a confession, over Bertrand's signature, of the valet's several impostures of Ebenezer, his unauthorized wager with Tubman, and his fraudulent marriage to Lucy Robotham. Despite Ebenezer's overwrought condition, this gesture of atonement filled his heart.

" 'Tis but a farther deception!" the Colonel objected. "They have twisted a dying man's delirium to their ends!"

"Nay, George," Nicholson said gently. "He really is a servant named Bertrand Burton."

"Ah, marry!" Lucy moaned. Mrs. Russecks hurried to comfort her.

"But God's body!" The Colonel clenched his fists and snorted. "Behold my daughter, sir! Fraudulent or no, the match hath been consummated!"

"Beyond a reasonable doubt," the Governor agreed. "Methinks no Maryland court will dispute the match unless thy daughter sues for annulment, which is her clear prerogative. But her husband is Bertrand Burton, not Eben Cooke, and this Court here disallows her claim to any part o' this estate, either through marriage or through this forgery of Tubman's. D'ye have that, Burlingame?"

Henry nodded. Andrew and Richard Sowter smiled broadly at Colonel Robotham's defeat; and Ebenezer too, though he greatly pitied both father and daughter, felt relieved that at least one of the contenders was out of the field. The Governor advised the Colonel that he was free to leave or linger, as he pleased.

"I shall leave this instant," Colonel Robotham declared with great emotion, "least I commit murther on that lying lecher upstairs. God forgive him!"

Properly hospitable now that their quarrel was settled to his advantage, Andrew offered to see the Robothams to their carriage, but the Colonel refused the courtesy and escorted his tearful daughter from the room.

"So," said Nicholson with a sniff. "Now, may I assume we're all of a mind as to who is Eben Cooke and who is not? Excellent. Then as for the quarrel betwixt Mister Smith and Mister Andrew Cooke, methinks it hangs upon three main questions: a question o' law, a question o' fact, and another question o' law, in that order. Did Eben Cooke's power of attorney give him leave to dispose o' this estate? If so, did he dispose of it knowingly or in ignorance? And if in ignorance, is the conveyance nonetheless valid before the law? I ask ye now to address yourselves to the first question, gentlemen."

Andrew took the floor to plead that while in fact there was no stipulation in his son's commission specifically forbidding him to dispose of the estate, no reasonable man could question that such was the spirit of the thing—why would he apprentice the young man to Peter Paggen to learn the plantation trade, if he meant to dispose of his holdings in Maryland? But, he added, if anyone *were* carping enough to challenge his intent, he offered in evidence a transcript of his will and testament, prepared in 1693, wherein he bequeathed Cooke's Point to his children, share and share alike. Did that suggest to the Court that he meant for his son to dispose of the property? Andrew concluded with high indignation and a red face. When he was finished, Roxanne nodded her belief in the justice of his arguments and lent him her linen handkerchief to mop his brow.

"If't please Your Excellency," Sowter declared in his turn,

"my client freely grants Andrew Cooke's intention; we have no doubt whate'er that the young man was not instructed to dispose of Cooke's Point. But good St. Abdon, sir, the question hath to do with *authority*, not with instruction: I submit that if young Mister Cooke's commission lawfully empowered him to dispose of the property, the question of paternal sanction is immaterial."

The Governor rubbed his nose and sighed. "The Court agrees."

Sowter then obtained further concession from the Court that if in the management of the estate Ebenezer had found it expedient to lease, sell, or grant away some small portion of it, his action would be fully authorized by the phrase "all matters pertinent thereto"—since, after all, the very sot-weed for the sale of which the plantation existed was part and parcel of the estate. And having won this point, he declared that what applied to a part applied to the whole; to infer some arbitrary limitation from the language of the commission would be patently absurd.

"If Mister Eben had the right to sell one leaf o' sot-weed," Sowter concluded, "he had the right to sell the whole estate."

By way of rebuttal, Andrew maintained that to interpret so broadly the phrase "all matters pertinent thereto" was in effect to contradict it, for if the attorney disposed of the whole estate, he by that gesture disposed of his power of attorney as well.

"Which in sooth he did!" laughed Sowter. "We ne'er disputed that!"

Nicholson consulted Burlingame and Sir Thomas. "I greatly fear," he then declared, "the Court must find for Mister Sowter on this first question. 'Tis common practice for an overseer with power of attorney to deed away portions of an estate to indentured servants, for example, in fulfillment of their bonds—'twas just such a matter, as I recall, that Mister Spurdance was litigating with Mister Smith in the Cambridge Court. And albeit 'tis the custom of attorneys to consult the owners ere they make any large transaction, in the absence of any stipulation to the contrary the Court must rule that Eben Cooke was lawfully empowered to dispose o' the whole estate as he saw fit."

This was a hard blow for Andrew; Ebenezer was touched to observe more distress than anger in the look his father gave him.

"As to the second question," Nicholson proceeded grimly,

781

"let me merely enquire whether there is any difference of opinion. 'Tis thy contention, is't not, Mister Cooke, that the boy granted away his legacy unwittingly to Mister Smith?"

"Aye," said Andrew. "Eben himself will swear to't, as will ———" He hesitated, loath to pronounce Burlingame's name. "As will the clerk o' this Court and this unfortunate young lady here, whom my boy was coerced by Mister Smith into marrying. Both were eyewitnesses to the grant. Moreover, Your Excellency may consult the records of the Circuit Court, session of September last———"

"I have already," the Governor said. "Mister Sowter, is't thy intent to dispute this question of fact, or do ye allow that the grantor was unaware o' the nature of his grant?"

"We have no mind to dispute that fact," Sowter replied. "Howbeit———"

"Nay, now, spare me thy *howbeits* for the nonce, sir. To proceed, then: Ebenezer Cooke was fully within his rights as Andrew Cooke's attorney to grant away Cooke's Point to William Smith, but 'tis agreed by all parties that he did so unaware that it was his own estate he granted. I now ask Ebenezer Cooke to describe in full the circumstances o' the grant, and then we'll have an end to the tawdry business."

The poet released Joan's hand long enough to do as he was bid: he reviewed as clearly as he could recall them the details of his journey to Cambridge with Henry Burlingame; their dispute concerning the relationship of innocence to justice; his indignation at the conduct of Judge Hammaker's court; his intervention in the case of *Smith* v. *Spurdance* and the several stipulations of his verdict thereon.

" 'Twas an outrage against Justice I sought innocently to rectify," he concluded. "Howbeit, when my innocence was stripped from me I saw I had not rectified but perpetrated injustice: not only did I grant what was not mine to grant—I mean morally—but in so doing I ruined a good and faithful man, Ben Spurdance; and indirectly, by giving this house to William Smith to turn into a den of viciousness, I ruined many another man as well, for which God forgive me."

"I see," Nicholson smiled drily. "And may the Court infer that your estimation of innocence hath been revised somewhat in consequence?"

Though he knew there was nothing malicious in the question, Ebenezer could not return the smile. "The Court may," he answered quietly, and resumed his seat. Seldom had he felt more dispirited about himself than now, when, with many of his perils behind him, he had leisure to contemplate the destruction wrought by his innocence. He scarcely took notice of the fact that it was Joan who took *his* hand this time; he stole a guilty glance at his sister, whose rueful eyes said plainly that the gesture had not escaped her.

Nicholson next requested a preliminary statement from both Andrew Cooke and Richard Sowter on the question of the validity of the grant.

"My contentions are three, sir," Andrew declared. "I hold in the first place that Judge Hammaker had no authority to delegate his office to my son, who hath no reading in the law, and thus that the sentence imposed on Spurdance was unlawful; second, that e'en if the sentence was lawful, the grant was not, being made unknowingly; and third, that e'en should an innocent grant be ruled binding, the conditions of my son's were not fulfilled. That is to say, Smith was ordered to find a husband for the girl Susan Warren, supposedly his daughter; but I hold, sir, that her marriage to my son is null and void, on the double grounds that he was coerced into wedding her and that her name is not Susan Warren but Joan Toast. The stipulations being therefore unsatisfied, the grant must be revoked."

Impressed as he was by the persuasiveness of his father's case, Ebenezer was greatly perturbed by this last contention. "A word, Your Excellency!" he pleaded.

"Not now," said Nicholson. "The floor is Mister Sowter's."

Sowter then declared his intention to show first, by legal precedent, that it was within Judge Hammaker's rights, under special circumstances, to delegate the authority of the Bench in effect, since in fact he never relinquished it at all: what he had done, in other words, was grant Ebenezer the privilege of pronouncing a sentence which he then ratified and so made lawful, but which he could as easily have overriden; it was in truth no more than a consultation that Hammaker availed himself of, as a judge will often consult an expert and disinterested third party before ruling on a difficult civil suit (furthermore, he added in an aside to Andrew, it must be allowed that Ebenezer *was* a disinterested party; otherwise the grant was made knowingly and could scarcely be challenged). In the second place, he meant to demonstrate both by reason and by precedent what no man familiar with torts would seriously question: that a lawful contract lawfully signed is binding, it being the responsibility of the signatories to apprise themselves of its terms. Moreover, it would be a mockery of justice to hold that a breach of contract committed by Ben Spurdance was more reprehensible than the same breach committed by Messrs. Cooke and son; if in the Circuit Court's opinion William Smith was due the whole of Malden (less one and a half acres) in redress of his grievances, then surely it was no less his due for the fact that 'Squire Cooke and not poor Spurdance happened to own it—Spurdance too, the Court was to remember, had power of attorney, and was thus acting in Andrew's behalf when he deprived the cooper of his just reward. As for that feeble casuistry regarding the marriage——

"If't please Your Excellency," Burlingame interrupted at this point. "I am dry of ink." He showed Nicholson the paper on which he had been transcribing testimony. "See there, how I was obliged to leave Mister Sowter's period half-writ? I beg Your Excellency's leave to forage for another pot of ink and a better quill as well."

At first the Governor's expression was as impatient as were Sowter's and Andrew Cooke's, but something in Burlingame's face—which Ebenezer too remarked, but Sowter was prevented by his position from observing—led him to examine the page of testimony.

"Ah, well, 'tis a bother, Henry, but there's no help for't—besides, I daresay I'm not the only man here that hath been tendered a subpoena by Dame Nature." He rapped the table-edge and stood up. "This Court stands in recess for half an hour or thereabouts. Leave the room as ye please, but not the house."

21

The Poet Earns His Estate

As SOON AS COURT was recessed Richard Sowter and William Smith retired to another room, whereupon Burlingame, so far from going in search of ink, admitted cheerfully that his pot was half full, but dispatched the militiaman to find more for appearance's sake.

"Why is't ye tricked us?" Andrew demanded. "I strenuously object!"

Burlingame shrugged. "To save Anna's dowry," he said mischievously.

"I'd not want to lose my share of Cooke's Point."

"Nay, Henry," Anna scolded. "Go to!"

"I'll have somewhat to say to you anon, young lady," Andrew threatened. "Just now——"

"Just now we've a crisis on our hands, sir," Governor Nicholson broke in, "and not much time to make our plans."

"A crisis? Nonsense! You heard my arguments!"

"Aye, and Sowter's rebuttal, that leaves ye not a pot to piss in. Which vulgar trope reminds me——" He bowed to the ladies and excused himself.

"Nay, sir," urged Burlingame. " 'Tis important you hear this too."

"Ah, ah——" Nicholson waggled a finger. "I remind ye we have declared ourselves a court o' law, and 'tis popularly believed a judge should be impartial."

"As should a clerk," Andrew added sternly. "I'll win my case without thy assistance, Mister Burlingame."

"A fart for thy case!" cried Henry. "I care no more who owns this piece of dirt than doth Ebenezer, or thy daughter! 'Tis the Province I'm concerned with."

"Eh?" The Governor paused at the door. "How's that, Henry?"

Burlingame gathered all the men around the baize table for a conference.

" 'Tis about that portion of the Assembly Journal," he announced. "All of us here save you, Mister Cooke, are aware of its nature and importance—I shall ask you merely to accept His Excellency's word for't that without this document of Bill Smith's we may well lose a much graver case than this one, and belike the entire Province o' Maryland into the bargain! With the Journal complete we may yet not get our man, but at least we can prosecute."

"That is correct, sir," Nicholson assured Andrew. "But what of't, Henry?"

Burlingame smiled. "We've heard Mister Cooke's case and Mister Sowter's, sir, and you know as well as I that as they stand, Mister Cooke hath lost every point."

Andrew protested vigorously against this opinion, and Nicholson reminded Burlingame of the unethicality of asking a judge to commit himself before the pleadings were complete. But his smile suggested, to Ebenezer at least, that Andrew's case was perhaps by no means so strong as the poet had thought.

"Methinks I should tell you now, sir," Ebenezer said to his father, "I have no intentions of disavowing my marriage, whate'er the circumstances of't. Joan's state is my responsibility——" Here he waved away McEvoy's protests. "Nay, John, 'tis mine, and I'd not abandon her again for a thousand Maldens."

In vain did his father point out that she was a diseased and dying prostitute; in vain he turned from wrath to reasonableness to supplication, and returned to wrath. Ebenezer was adamant.

"Out on't, then!" his father cried at last. "Wed the whore a second time when our case is won, and be damned t'ye! All I beg is your leave to save Malden for ye!"

Now Ebenezer found himself caught between conflicting responsibilities and could see no way to reconcile them. It was a painful moment until Burlingame came to his rescue.

" 'Tis all beside the point in any case, gentlemen," Henry said. "If Sowter hath a brain in his thieving head he'll agree that the marriage is false (if you'll pardon me, Eben, 'tis as well your father knew the match hath ne'er been consummated). But the stipulation that required it was false for the same reason: Joan Toast isn't Susan Warren, and Susan Warren isn't Bill Smith's daughter, and there's an end on't! As for the other arguments, they simply hold no water; 'twill be light work for Sowter to rest his case on precedents. Do you agree, Tom? Thou'rt no judge now."

Sir Thomas Lawrence admitted that Andrew's case struck him as vulnerable and Sowter's relatively strong, but added that he thought Mister Cooke had overlooked the best line of attack. "If *I* were thy counsel," he told Andrew, "I'd appeal the *extremity* of the Circuit Court's ruling, not its legality. Admit that Spurdance was in the wrong, but plead for the damages to be lightened—say, to the terms of Smith's original indenture plus costs and a sop for's trouble."

Burlingame shook his head. "You don't see the problem, Tom. We don't want Sowter to win, but we dare not let him lose!"

"And why not, pray?" demanded Nicholson.

"For the best of reasons, sir," Burlingame replied calmly.

"You and I and Sir Thomas know very well that this court hath no more law in't than a bawdyhouse."

Ebenezer expressed his astonishment, and Andrew openly charged Burlingame with prevarication; but Sir Thomas blushed, and Governor Nicholson scowled uncomfortably.

"Ah, well now, Henry!" He glanced angrily about the room. "I'll own 'tis not the sort o' thing a governor doth every Tuesday—but 'tis done, dammee! If I choose to find for Smith I'll find for Smith, and if for Cooke then Cooke, arguments and precedents be damned! I doubt our friend Sowter will appeal to the Lords Commissioners!"

"I'm sure he won't," Henry agreed. "But when Judge Hammaker learns that you sat yourself down in this parlor one evening and reversed the ruling of his Circuit Court, you may rest on't *he'll* make a noise in London! And wouldn't Andros love the sound of't!"

"No more!" growled Nicholson. "The point is clear enough." His tone bade no good for Andrew's prospects.

"Well, God's blood!" that gentleman exclaimed. "I'd have ye recall, sirs, that *my* voice is as loud as Hammaker's with the Lords Commissioners! If this court hath no jurisdiction, ye'll be no better off for ruling against me!"

"Quite so," Burlingame agreed with a smile, "now that I've shown ye the way. Besides, we want the rest of the *Privie Journall* as well as the estate, if not more so. Sowter knows his client's position is shaky—Smith's attempt to run away shows that—but he also knows there's some connection 'twixt me and the Cookes. He's not sure of his ground, particularly with regard to our vice and sedition charges, and methinks his only motive in defending Smith's claim is to give his man more bargaining power when the time comes to bargain."

Nicholson fumed and worried his stick. "Ye might have mentioned this ere we set up court, you know!"

" 'Twere premature," Burlingame declared. "We have got rid of the Colonel already, and 'twas quite within your rights to seize Cooke's Point for the nonce—well done, in fact."

"Thou'rt too gracious!"

"But you daren't hold the property for long on such a pretext, and you daren't release it by court order to either party. 'Tis hence I warned you to recess."

Nicholson wiped his brow. "Devil take all barristers and law-books! What a province I could have me without 'em! What do we do now?"

Burlingame shrugged. "What do all good barristers do when they have no case, sir? We settle out o' court!"

"Stay!" Ebenezer warned. "Here they are."

Richard Sowter and William Smith came in from the next room. The cooper did indeed look unsure of his ground, but his counsel was as breezy as ever.

"Did ye scare up some ink, Mister Clerk? Splendid! By St. Ludwig, 'twere a pity such eloquence as Mister Cooke's went unrecorded!"

The party around the table dispersed. Observing with some surprise that Anna had moved to the couch and was deep in conversation with Joan, Ebenezer returned with his father to his earlier place. So dispirited was Andrew by the progress of events that he offered no resistance when his son took his arm and directed him gently to a seat.

"By'r leave, Your Excellency," Sowter asked, "may I proceed with my statement?"

Burlingame, Ebenezer noticed, had been conferring in whispers with the Governor and Sir Thomas Lawrence. Now he sat back and winked at Ebenezer as if there was nothing at all to be concerned about!

"Ye may not," Nicholson grumbled.

Sowter's face clouded. "Your Excellency?"

"The Court will rule on thy client's claim some other time," the Governor said. "Just now I'm fetching the twain of ye to Anne Arundel jail. The charges are conspiracy, sedition, and high treason, and after what Tim Mitchell here hath told me, I quite expect to see ye hanged ere the year is out!"

The surprise brought even the sullen cooper to his feet. "Tim Mitchell!"

"Aye, gentlemen." Burlingame smiled. "Captain Billy's pride and pleasure, till his real son came along." His hands were busy as he spoke, and his appearance changed magically. Off came the powdered periwig, to be replaced by a short black hairpiece; from his mouth he removed a curious device which, it turned out, had held three artificial teeth in position. Most uncannily of all, he seemed able to alter at will the set of his facial muscles: the curve of his cheeks and the flare of his nose changed shape before their eyes; his habitually furrowed brow grew smooth, but crow's-feet appeared where before there were none. Finally, his voice deepened and coarsened; he drew in upon himself so as to seem at least two inches shorter; his eyes took on a craftier cast—Nicholas Lowe, in a few miraculous seconds, had become Timothy Mitchell.

" 'Sbody!" exclaimed Sir Thomas Lawrence, and the Governor himself—though one supposed he must have witnessed such transformations of his agent before—was moved to shake his head.

" 'Tis a page of Ovid!" Ebenezer marveled. The others made similar expressions of their awe—except Smith and Sowter, who were dumb struck.

"Now, Mister Smith," Burlingame said grimly, "methinks ye know what straits thou'rt in if I testify against ye—if ye do not, I give ye leave to consult Mister Sowter, that will keep ye company in jail for's misdemeanors."

The cooper seemed ready to do violence, but Sowter waved his hand resignedly.

"Ye quite agree we've dagged ye? Splendid! Then attend me closely: 'tis my intention to expose for prosecution the entire traffic in opium and whores, the which hath paid for all of John Coode's mischief and haply Baltimore's as well. Whoe'er hath had a finger in't"—he smiled at Andrew—"shall be brought to account, regardless of his station——"

"St. Louis's wig, man!" Sowter complained. "Jail us and have done with't, but spare us this pious gloating!"

"Patience, Dick." Henry raised his finger. " 'Tis but my preamble to a bargain. On the strength of my deposition His Excellency hath instructed Sir Thomas to proceed against Coode, Bill Mitchell, and every traitor of a whoremaster in his company—with the possible exception of yourselves."

Smith's eyes narrowed, and Sowter's expression became calculating as Burlingame offered to waive the charges against them in return for the cooper's portion of the *Privie Journall,* on whose *verso* was believed to be Coode's record of confiscations and prosecutions during his brief tenure of office. The cooper agreed at once to the exchange, but Sowter restrained him.

"Only think of the consequences, Bill!" he warned. "D'ye think we'll live out the month when John Coode learns ye've let go the papers? Besides, methinks His Excellency must set great store by 'em to make us such an offer; and *What will fetch eleven pence,* don't ye know, *will as lightly fetch a shilling . . ."*

"Take 'em away, Sergeant," snapped Nicholson. "I'm sorry to disappoint ye, Henry, but I'll not dicker farther with traitors just to get your grandfather's diary."

"Stay!" Sowter cried at once. "We'll fetch ye the wretched papers! Only give us thy pledge in writing . . ."

Nicholson shook his head. "I'm not such a fool."

"Welladay! Then this much, at least, sir: we'll have no profit in our bargain if John Coode murthers us; grant us safe conduct to Virginia, and ye may have the papers."

Again Burlingame conferred in whispers with the Governor and Sir Thomas.

"His Excellency advises me to authorize safe exit for ye," Henry declared, "but not as a term of our first agreement. We'll fetch ye out o' Maryland in the morning if Smith relinquishes all claim to this estate."

"God bless ye, sir!" Andrew cried.

"'Sheart!" protested Sowter. "Ye'd bleed us dry!"

Nicholson grinned. "And 'twill not be Virginia we fetch ye to, either, but Pennsylvania. I've enemies enough in Virginia."

"What liars they are that call ye Papist!" William Smith exclaimed. "Thou'rt not even a proper Gentile!"

Sowter sighed. "We've no choice, Bill. Fetch the papers, and I'll draw up a conveyance."

The rest of the company cheered the news: Anna and Ebenezer embraced each other with relief; Andrew apologized stiffly to Burlingame and commended him for his strategy, as did Nicholson, Sir Thomas, and John McEvoy; Roxanne and Henrietta looked on approvingly. Only Joan Toast remained apathetic, and the sight of her blighted Ebenezer's joy.

The cooper left the room, under guard, and returned with a roll of yellowed papers, which Burlingame received eagerly. He and Sir Thomas made a cursory inspection of the *verso* and pronounced it sufficient evidence, when combined with the 1691 Assembly Journal, to institute proceedings against Coode and his associates. Then, while Sowter, Sir Thomas, and the Governor discussed the details of releasing Malden and ferrying the two men up the Bay to Pennsylvania, Burlingame took Ebenezer aside.

"D'ye recall the story I told ye on our way to Plymouth?" he asked excitedly. "How Sir Henry and Captain John were captured by Powhatan?"

Ebenezer smiled. "They struck some lewd bargain over the King's daughter, as I recall, but we ne'er learned the outcome of't. Is that the rest of the tale?"

"Aye, methinks our story is complete. Let's read it while Tom and the Governor attend those rascals."

And then and there, despite the general excitement in the

room, they read together the second and final portion of Sir Henry Burlingame's *Privie Journall*, which began (where the first had left off) with the author and Captain John Smith incarcerated in the Emperor Powhatan's village waiting for dawn, at which time the Captain was pledged to gamble their lives against his ability to do what the ablest young men of the town had found impossible: relieve Pocahontas of her maidenhood.

Two burlie Guards were plac'd over us [*had written Sir Henry*] and commission'd to provide our everie wish, and to slay us s^hd we offer to escape. My Captain then commenc'd to regale me with accounts, endlesse & lubricious, of divers maidens in exotick lands, that he had deflowr'd, till that I grewe so wearie, I did feign sleep. But watch'd him privilie, the night through.

Neare midnight, believing me fast asleep, my Captain did ryse up from his bed (like mine, a filthie pallet upon the grownd), and summon'd one of our Guards. Thereupon ensu'd a whisper'd colloquie, yet not so hush'd withal, but I heard the substance of it. Ever & anon he glanc'd to see, Whether I was asleep? And to all that were naught the wiser, so I was. But I kept one eye still a-squint, and both eares wide, and follow'd there conversation with passing ease. Smith declar'd, He was hungrie, the wch surpriz'd me not a little, seeing he had eate enough at the Emperours feest, to preserve the whole of Jamestowne through the Winter. He demanded to be brought food at once. The Salvage was loath to bestire him selfe, so it seem'd to me, the moreso when my Captain commenc'd to tell what dishes he crav'd; to witt: one egg-plant (that frute, that is call'd by some, Aubergine) with corne-floure wherein to cooke it, & water wherewith to drinke it downe . . .

"An eggplant!" Burlingame murmured.

He did maintaine, that onlie thus did white men prepare the frute of the egg-plant. W^ch I knewe for a lye.

The Salvage did pleade the houre of night and the season of yeere, but upon my Captains pressing the matter (besides bribing him with some bawble from his wicked pockett), he at last consented to steale an egg-plant and floure from the common store near the Emperours howse. Then departing, he was absent some while, during wch my Captain pac'd about the hutt, as might a man, whose wife was in travaile, not forgetting to certain him selfe, now & againe, that my sleep was sound & undisturb'd.

Whenas the Salvage did returne, with 2 dry'd egg-plants & a dishful of floure, not to mention an earthen jugg of water, my

791

Captain rewarded him with a second trinkett, and ask'd him to remove him selfe from the hutt, if it pleas'd him, and sett outside, for that white men (as he claim'd) never cook'd there food, but privilie. The Salvage did as he was bid, eager to contemplate his treasures, and left alone, my Captain straightway set to work upon the egg-plant, in the strangest manner I ever did behold. Forsooth, I was that amaz'd, that even some weeks thereafter, here in Jamestowne, what time I set to recording this narrative in my Journall-booke, it was no light matter to realize it was true. For had I not observ'd it my owne selfe, I had never believ'd it to be aught but the lewd construction of some dissolute fancie. Endlesse indeed, and beyond the ken of sober & continent men, are the practices and fowle receipts of those lustful persons, the votaries of the flesh, that still sett *Venus & Bacchus* over chast *Minerva*, and studie with scholars zeale all the tricks and dark refynements of carnallitie! I blush to committ the thing to paper, even to these the privie pages of my Journall. Wch it is my vow, no man shall lay eyes upon, while that I live.

"I say!" Burlingame exclaimed. "The rest of the page is gone, and part of the next! D'ye grasp what it is we have here, Eben?"

"You mean the matter of the Sacred Eggplant, that the Tayac Chicamec spoke of? 'Tis not impossible there's some connection . . ."

"I *know* there is! I'Christ, what this could mean!"

They read on, Burlingame with an expression of voracious, almost painful eagerness, and Ebenezer with the first stirrings of unease.

For this reason [*the narrative resumed after the break*] it was to my grand chagrinn, that coming to my senses some houres later, I discover'd I had assum'd in fact, that state wch theretofore I had feign'd; to witt: a sownd & recklesse sleep . . .

"God damn him!" Henry cried.

My repose was broken by the Salvage Guard & Keeper, and starting up, I found the Sunne alreadie risen. From without our hutt there came to my eares, the whooping & hollowing of many Salvages, and I guess'd, they were assembl'd for my Captains lustie tryall of there Princesse. My Captain, when I look'd at him, was fullie cloth'd, and no signs of the Aubergine or other things being apparent, I wonder'd whether the scene I had witness'd in the night just past, was a mere fantastick dreem, such as men are wont to suffer, when there death is neare to hand . . .

"Then he did witness it," Ebenezer offered, "whate'er it was."

"But the page is gone!"

It is true, *the* Journall *went on*, that when we left the hutt, under the eye of our Salvage Guards, and were led to the publick square, my Captain shew'd some hardshipp in walking, as if loath to keep his leggs together; but this deficiencie c^d as well be attributed to feare (wch it is well known, can loose a mans hold upon his reins), as to any strange behaviour of the evening past. And this former seem'd the more likelie, for that the scene before us was aught but a consoling one.

Round about the court-yard, in a circle, stood the people of the towne, hollowing & howling in a fearsome manner. Within the large circle thus form'd was a smaller, made up of tenne or a dozen of the Emperours Lieutenants. These were great brawnie Salvages, bedeck'd in feathers and paynted most grewsomelie, that donn'd in naught save these adornments, did leap and daunce about, issuing feerce screames, and brandishing there Tomahawkes. In the center of this smalle ring sat the Emperour Powhatan, rays'd above the crowd on a loftie chaire, and before him, upon a manner of altar stone, lay Pocahontas, stript & trust with throngs of hyde for the heethenish rites. Yet maugre the rudenesse of her position, the Princess seem'd not a whit alarm'd, but wore an huge smyle upon her face. Whereat I guess'd that this vile manner of presenting maidens for betrothal must be in common use among the Salvage nations, to such extent that, Habit being master of us all, they had got even to relish it, in there pagan sinfullnesse. W^ch notwithstanding, I was fill'd with trepidation, the more for that, marking the considerable manlinesse of those Salvages, that sprang about all nakedlie, and re-calling the modest endowment of my Captain (that for all his boasting, I had seen privilie to be but passing well equipt for Venereal exercise), I sawe no hope of his making good where they had fail'd. Forsooth, I had been in his place, I sh^d not have been able to summon the most tryfling manlinesse, for knowing those evil Tomahawkes stood readie to breake my head at the first sign of deficiencie.

Directly they spy'd us, all the Salvages redoubl'd there com-motion. The folk in the greate circle showted and clapt hands, the Lieutenant-Salvages leapt and hopt, even Pocahontas con-triv'd to joggle about on her pedestall. W^ch movements, consider-ing the manner wherein she was trust and tether'd, shew'd un-common suppleness of limb, and readiness for whatever might ensue.

We were fetch'd into the small circle and station'd before the

altar of *Venus* (to look whereon brought the blush to my
cheeks), whereupon the Salvages lay'd hands upon my Captain,
and with one jerk brought his breeches low. From where I
stood, wch chanc'd to be behind him, the sight was unprepossessing
enow, but the Salvages before all suddenlie put by there clamour.
The Emperour shaded his eyes from the morning Sunne, the
better to behold him, and Pocahontas, maugre her bonds (w^{ch}
netted her as fast as those, that *Vulcan* fashion'd for his faithless
spouse), this Pocahontas, I say, came neare to breaking her
necke with looking, and the unchast smyle, that erst had play'd
about her mowth, now vanish'd altogether.

My Captain then turning half around to see, Whether I was
at hand? I at last beheld the cause of all this wonder, and as
well the effect of his magick of the night past—the wch to relate,
must fetch me beyond all bownds of taste & decencie, but to
withhold, must betray the Truth and leave what follow'd veil'd in
mystery. To have done then, my Captains yard stood full erect,
and what erst had been more cause for pity than for astonishment, was now in verie sooth a frightful engine: such was the
virtue of his devilish brewe, that when now his codd stood readie
for the tilt, he rear'd his bulk not an inch below eleven, and
well-nigh three in diameter—a weapon of the Gods! Add to w^{ch},
it was all a fyrie hue, gave off a scent of clove & vanilla, and
appear'd as stout as that stone whereon its victim lay. A mightie
sownd went up from the populace; the Lieutenants, that had
doubtlesse been the Princesses former suitors, dropt to there
knees as in prayer; the Emperour started up in his high seate,
dismay'd by the fate about to befall his daughter; and as for
that same Pocahontas, she did swoone dead away.

Straight leapt my Captain to his work, whereof I can bring
myself to say naught save this: Mercifull, mercifull, the Providence, that kept the heethen maid aswoon, while that my Captain
did what none had done before! And so inordinatelie withal, that
anon the Emperour begg'd for an end to the tryall, lest his daughter
depart from this life. He declar'd my Captain victorious, rescinded
the decree of death hanging over us, dispers'd the companie, and
had Pocahontas remov'd to his howse, where for three days
thereafter she hung in the balance twixt life & death. A banquet
was then prepar'd for us, whereat Powhatan express'd his intent
to marrie his daughter to my Captain, inasmuch as no Salvage in
his trybe c^d match his virilitie. My Captain declyn'd, whereupon
the Emperour wax'd wroth, and w^d have return'd us to our hutt,
had not my Captain offer'd to instruct him in that mysterie,
whereby he had so increas'd him selfe. This more than satisfy'd
the Emperour, that s^{hd} have been long past such vanitie, and it
was on the best of terms, that we set out at last for Jamestowne.
With a troup of Salvages to assist us by the way.

Throughout the journie, as one might guess, my Captain bragg'd and strutted handsomelie. I was oblig'd to him for life, he declar'd, for that his deed had preserv'd the twain of us; and he offer'd to murther me, in some dark and dastard wise, if ever I noys'd about in Jamestowne the manner of our salvation. I c^d scarce protest, inasmuch he had in sooth preserv'd me, but it was bitter frute to eate, for that I must submitt to his browbeating and braggadocio without compleynt. In briefe, I was to feign I had been detain'd with Opecancanough, and my Captain alone led in unto the Emperour. Moreover, he made so bold as to shew me a written account of his salvation by Pocahontas, the wch he meant to include in his lying *Historie*: this version made no mention whatever of his scurrilous deflowring of the Princesse, but merelie imply'd, she was overcome by his manlie bearing & comelie face! It was this farce and travestie, then, wherein I was oblig'd to feign belief, and wch hath mov'd me, in hopes of pacifying my anguish'd conscience, to committ this true accounting to my Journall-booke. Whereon, I pray God, my Captain will never lay his lecherous eyes!

Here ended Sir Henry's *Privie Journall* except for one final entry, dated several weeks after his return to Jamestown and only a few months prior to his conscription for the fateful voyage up the Chesapcakc:

March, 1608: Pocahontas, the Emperours daughter, having at long last regayn'd full possession of her health, is ever at the gates of the towne, with a retinue of her people, enquiring after my Captain. He shuns her as much as possible, albeit in her absence, and in his *Historie*, he makes the finest speaches in her praise. The truth is, he feares his fowle adventure will out, and I suspect he is torn betwixt his reluctance to wed her (and thus make an honest woman of her), and his desire once againe to sate his lust on her. For albeit the verie sownd of his voice doth sicken my stomacke, so do I loathe him, yet he cannot contain his lewd exployt, but must still catch privilie my eare, and declare that hers was the most succulent flowr ever he pluckt, & cet., & cet.

As for the Princesse, she still lingers at the gate, all wystfullie, and sends him, by her attendants, woven basketts of great dry'd egg-plants . . .

"God's body!" Burlingame cried at the end. "Your Excellency, look here!"

Nicholson smiled from the green table, where he was completing the transaction with Sowter. "New matter against Coode, is't?"

"Coode be damned!" Burlingame replied. "Here, read it, sir! 'Tis all about the mysterious eggplant business I spoke of before! I'God, if only the recipe were there as well! 'Tis some encaustic, or aphrodisiac, don't ye think, Eben? That 'fyrie hue' sounds like *phlogosis* . . . But marry, what is the trick? I could save this miserable Province with it!"

"Go to, ye lose me!" Nicholson protested, as mystified as everyone else except Ebenezer; but when the contents of the *Journall* and their significance were explained to him, his face grew grave. " 'Twere a risky adventure even so," he declared, referring to Burlingame's proposed embassy to Bloodsworth Island, "but with this eggplant trick to confound 'em . . ."

"I could do it!" Burlingame insisted. "I'd be King of the Ahatchwhoops by the week's end if I had that recipe! *Smith!*" He turned upon the wondering cooper. "Where's the missing part of these papers? I swear you'll not leave the Province till we have it!"

To Ebenezer's surprise, before the cooper could protest his bewilderment, Joan Toast spoke up for the first time.

" 'Tis vain to threaten him," she said. "He hath no idea what you want, or where to find it. *I* stole those pages, and I mean to keep them."

Burlingame, Nicholson, and Sir Thomas all pleaded with her to surrender the missing passages, or at least to disclose the trick which Captain John Smith had employed to win the day in Virginia; they explained the gravity of the situation on Bloodsworth Island and Henry's strategy to forestall an insurrection—but to no avail.

"Look at me!" the girl cried bitterly. "Behold the fruits of lustfulness! Swived in my twelfth year, poxed in my twentieth, and dead in my twenty-first! Ravaged, ruined, raped, and betrayed! Woman's lot is wretched enough at best; d'ye think I'll pass on that murtherous receipt to make it worse?"

In vain then did Burlingame vow never to employ Smith's formula for carnal purposes, but only to demonstrate his identity to the Ahatchwhoops.

"The Devil was sick, the Devil a monk would be," Joan retorted. "The time will come when ye crave a child by Anna yonder, or some other . . . I shan't e'en make the vile stuff for ye myself!"

"Then it *is* some potion he takes!" cried Henry. "Or is't a sort of plaster?"

Nicholson pounded his stick on the floor. "We must know, girl! Name thy price for't!"

Joan laughed. "D'ye think to bribe the dead? Nay, sir, the

Great Tom Leech bites sore enough, God knows; I'll not give him more teeth than he hath already! But stay——" Her manner suddenly became shrewd, like Sowter's. "I may name my price, ye say?"

"Within reason, of course," the Governor affirmed. "What ye ask must be ours to give."

"Very well, then," Joan declared. "My price is Malden."

"Nay!" Andrew cried.

"Nay, prithee!" pleaded Ebenezer, who until then had found the discussion as embarrassing as had Anna.

"'Tis a hard price," Burlingame observed, regarding her curiously.

"Not for doing so great a disservice to my sex," Joan replied.

Now even McEvoy was moved to join the chorus of objections. "Whate'er will ye do with this estate, my dear?" he asked gently. "'Tis of no use to ye now. If there is someone ye wish to provide for, why, peradventure the Governor can make arrangements."

Joan turned her face to him, and her expression softened, if her resolution did not. "Ye know as well as I there's no one, John. Why d'ye ask? Can it be ye've forgot the whoremonger's first principle?" For the benefit of the others she repeated it: *"Ye may ask a whore her price, but not her reasons.* My price is the title to Cooke's Point, forever and aye: ye may take it or leave it."

Nicholson and Burlingame exchanged glances.

"Done," said the Governor. "Draw up the papers, Tom."

"Nay, b'm'faith!" cried Andrew. "'Tis unlawful! When Smith gave o'er his claim, the title reverted to me!"

"Not at all," said Burlingame. "It reverted to the Province."

"Damn ye, man! Whose side are ye on?"

"On the side of the Province, for the nonce," Henry answered. "Those pages are worth a brace of Maldens."

Andrew threatened to appeal to the Lords Commissioners, but the Governor was not to be intimidated.

"I've seldom stood on firmer ground than this," he declared. "When I move to save the Province ye may appeal to the King himself, for aught ye'll gain by't, and Godspeed. Where are the papers, Mrs. Cooke?"

Not until he heard the unfamiliar mode of address did Ebenezer have the least hint of Joan's motives. Now suddenly, though a hint was all he had, his backbone tingled; his heart glowed.

"Where are thine?" she demanded in reply, nor would she stir until Sir Thomas had conveyed the title to Cooke's Point into her possession. Then she calmly reached into her bodice and withdrew a tightly folded paper which, when she handed it to Burlingame for unfolding, proved to be three missing pages of the *Journall.*

" 'Sheart, Eben, look here!" Henry cried. "May he look, Joan?"

" 'Tis not mine to forbid," the girl said glumly, and seemed to relapse into her former apathy.

First [*read the missing fragment*] he pour'd a deale of water into the dish of floure, and worked the mess to a thick paste with his fingers. Then he set the remainder of the water, in its vessell, next the smalle fyre, wch the Salvage had been Christian enough to make us, against the cold. Whenas he sawe this water commence to steem and bubble, then drewe he from his pockett (wch forsooth must needs have been a spacious one!), divers ingredients, and added them to the paste. Of these I c^d name but few, forasmuch as I durst not discover to my Captain that my sleep was feign'd; but I did learn later from his boasting that it was a receipt much priz'd for a certain purpose (whereof I was as yet innocent) by the blackamoors of Africka, from whom he had learnt it. To witt: a quantitie of *Tightening Wood* (wch is to say, the bark of that tree, *Nux vomica,* wherefrom is got the brucine and strychnyne of apothecaries), 2 or 3 small dry'd pimyentoes (that the blackamoors call *Zozos*), a dozen peppercorns, and as many whole cloves, with 1 or 2 beanes of vanilla to give it fragrance. At the same time he boyl'd a second decoction of water mix'd with some dropps of oyl of mallow, to what end I c^d not guesse. These severall herbs and spyces, I s^hd add, he still carr'd on his person, not alone for their present employment, but as well to season his food, wch in his yeeres of fighting the Moors he had learnt to savour hott; and for this cause he did prevaile upon the masters of vessells, to fetch him such spyces from there ports of call in the Indies.

When that the paste was done, and the water fast aboyle in both vessells, my Captain busy'd him selfe with cutting the eggplant, and this in a singular wise. For it is the wont of men to lay hold of an Aubergine and slyce across the topp, to the end of making thinne rownd sections. But my Captain, drawing his knife from his waiste, did sever the frute into halves, splitting it lengthwise from top to bottom. Next he scor'd out a deep hollow ditch in either moietie, in such wise, but when the two halves were joyn'd, like halves of an iron-mould, the effect was of a deep cylindrick cavitie in the center, perhaps 3 inches in dyameter, and 7 or 8 in profunditie, for that it was an uncommon large egg-plant. All this I did observe with mounting curiositie, yet careful not to discover my pretence of sleep.

The strange brewes having cook'd a certain time, my Captain then remov'd them from the fyre. The first, that had in it all the spyces, he stirr'd and kneaded into the paste, till the whole took on the semblance of a plaister. He next disrob'd him selfe, and before my wondering eyes lay'd hands upon his member, drawing back that part, that the Children of Israel are wont to offer to *Jehovah*, and exposing the carnall *glans*. His codd thus bar'd (wch poets have liken'd to that Serpent, that did tempt Mother Eve in the Garden), he apply'd thereto the plaister, and lay'd it within the two halves of the egg-plant. There it linger'd some minutes, notwithstanding the ordeall must needs have been painfull, for all the spyce & hott things in the receipt. His face did wrythe & twist, as though it were straight into the fyre he had thrust his yard, and whenas he at last remov'd the Aubergine, and wash'd away the plaister with his oyl-of-mallow brewe, I cd observe with ease that his part was burnt in sooth! Moreover, he did seem loath to touch it for feare of the payne thereby occasion'd.

Now albeit this spectacle was far from edifying, to a man of good conscience & morall virtue, I yet must own, I took greate interest in it, both by reason of naturall curiositie, as well as to gage for my selfe the depths of my Captains depravitie. For it is still pleasing, to a Christian man, to suffer him selfe the studie of wickednesse, that he may content him selfe (without sinfull pride) upon the contrast thereof with his owne rectitude. To say naught of that truth, whereto *Augustine* and other Fathers beare witnesse: that true virtue lieth not in innocence, but in full knowledge of the Devils subtile arts . . .

Thus ended the fragment, having brought Sir Henry to his unintended sleep and rude awakening.

"I can do't!" Burlingame murmured. " 'Tis all I need!"

Ebenezer looked away, revolted not only by the narrative but by other, more immediate images. He observed that Anna too, though she had not read the *Journall*, was aware of its significance: her eyes were lowered; her cheeks aflame.

"Well, now," declared the Governor, rising from his place. "I think our business here is done, Tom. Fetch those rascals aboard my ship in the morning and see they're ferried to Pennsylvania."

The others stirred as well.

"La, Master Laureate!" Sowter jeered from across the

room. "The party's done, and thou'rt still as penceless as St. Giles!"

Andrew cursed, and Nicholson frowned uncomfortably.

"Thou'rt mistaken, Dick Sowter," Joan said from the couch.

Everyone turned to her at once.

"I've little time to live," she declared, "and a wife's estate passes to her husband when she dies."

Andrew gasped. "I'cod! D'ye hear that, Eben?"

All except Sowter and Smith rejoiced at this disclosure of her motive. Ebenezer rushed to embrace her, and Andrew wept for joy.

"Splendid girl! She is a very saint, Roxanne!"

But Joan turned away her face. "There remains but a single danger, that I can see," she said. "As hath been observed already today, a false marriage such as ours may be disallowed, and my bequests thus contested in the courts—inasmuch as it hath yet to be consummated."

The company fell silent; the twins drew back aghast.

"Dear Heav'n!" Roxanne whispered, and clutched at Andrew's arm. Burlingame's expression was fascinated.

The cooper laughed harshly. "Oh, my word! Ah! Ah! D'ye hear the wench, Sowter? She is the very Whore o' Babylon, and Cooke muyt swive her for's estate! Oh, ha! I'd not touch her with a sot-weed stick!"

"My boy——" Andrew spoke with difficulty to his son. "She hath—the social malady, don't ye know—and albeit I love Malden as I love my life, I'd ne'er think ill o' ye——"

"Stay," interrupted Burlingame. "Ye'll take her pox, Eben, but ye'll not die of't, methinks: belike 'tis a mere dev'lish clap and not the French disease. Marry, lad, inasmuch as Malden hangs in the balance——"

Ebenezer shook his head. " 'Tis of no importance, Henry. Whate'er she hath, she hath on my account, by reason of our ill-starred love. I little care now for my legacy, save that I must earn it. 'Tis *atonement* I crave: redemption for my sins against the girl, against my father, against Anna, e'en against you, Henry——"

"What sins?" protested Anna, coming to his side. "Of all men on the planet, Eben, thou'rt freest from sin! What else drew Joan half round the globe, do you think, through all those horrors, if not that quality in you that hath ruined me for other men and driven e'en Henry to near distraction——" She blushed, realizing she had spoken too much. "Thou'rt the very spirit of Innocence," she finished quietly.

"That is the crime I stand indicted for," her brother replied: "the crime of innocence, whereof the Knowledged must bear the burthen. There's the true Original Sin our souls are born in: not that Adam *learned,* but that he *had* to learn —in short, that he was innocent."

He sat on the edge of the couch and took Joan's hand. "Once before, this girl had shriven me of that sin, and I compounded it by deserting her. Whate'er the outcome, I rejoice at this second chance for absolution."

"Marry!" McEvoy said. "Ye mean to do't?"

"Aye."

Anna threw her arms about his neck and wept. "How I love you! The four of us will live here, and if Henry doth not stay on Bloodsworth Island——" Her voice failed; Burlingame drew her back gently from the couch.

Ebenezer kissed Joan's hand until at last she turned her haggard eyes to him.

"Thou'rt weary, Joan."

She closed her eyes. "Beyond imagining."

He stood up, still holding her hand. "I've not strength enough yet to carry you to our chamber . . ." He looked about awkwardly, his features dancing. All the women were in tears; the men either shook their heads, like McEvoy and the Governor, or winced, like Andrew, or merely frowned a grudging awe, like Smith and Sowter.

"I claim the honor!" Burlingame cried, and the spell was broken. Everyone stirred himself to cover the general embarrassment: Andrew and John McEvoy busied themselves comforting their women; Sir Thomas and the Governor assembled their papers and called for tobacco; Smith and Sowter, accompanied by the sergeant-at-arms, left the room.

Burlingame lifted Joan in his arms. "Good night all!" he called merrily. "Tell cook we'll want a wedding breakfast in the morning, Andrew!" As he headed for the hallway he added with a laugh, "See to what lengths the fallen go, to increase their number! Come along, Anna; this errand wants a chaperon."

Blushing, Anna took Ebenezer's arm, and the twins followed their chuckling tutor up the stairs.

"Ah, well now!" their father's voice cried from the parlor. "We've a deal to drink to, lords and ladies!" And addressing the unseen servant in the kitchen he called "Grace? *Grace!* 'Sblood, Grace, fetch us a rundlet!"

PART IV: THE AUTHOR APOLOGIZES TO HIS READERS; THE LAUREATE COMPOSES HIS EPITAPH

LEST IT BE OBJECTED by a certain stodgy variety of squint-minded antiquarians that he has in this lengthy history played more fast and loose with Clio, the chronicler's muse, than ever Captain John Smith dared, the Author here posits in advance, by way of surety, three blue-chip replies arranged in order of decreasing relevancy. In the first place be it remembered, as Burlingame himself observed, that we all invent our pasts, more or less, as we go along, at the dictates of Whim and Interest; the happenings of former times are a clay in the present moment that will-we, nill-we, the lot of us must sculpt. Thus Being does make Positivists of us all. Moreover, this Clio was already a scarred and crafty trollop when the Author found her; it wants a nice-honed casuist, with her sort, to separate seducer from seduced. But if, despite all, he is convicted at the Public Bar of having forced what slender virtue the strumpet may make claim to, then the Author joins with pleasure the most engaging company imaginable, his fellow fornicators, whose ranks include the noblest in poetry, prose, and politics; condemnation at such a bar, in short, on such a charge, does honor to artist and artifact alike, of the same order of magnitude as election to the *Index Librorum Prohibitorum* or suppression by the Watch and Ward.

Thus much for the rival claims of Fact and Fancy, which the artist, like Governor Nicholson, may override with fair impunity. However, when the litigants' claims are *formal*, rather than *substantial*, they pose a dilemma from which few tale-tellers escape without a goring. Such is the Author's present plight, as he who reads may judge.

The *story* of Ebenezer Cooke is told; Drama wants no more than his consent to Joan Toast's terms, their sundry implications being clear. All the rest is anticlimax: the stairs that take him up to the bridal-chamber take him down the steep incline of *dénouement*. To the *history*, on the other hand, there is so much more—all grounded on meager fact and solid fancy—that the Author must risk those rude *cornadas* to resume it, and trust that the Reader is interested enough in the fate of the twins, their tutor, Bertrand Burton, Slye and Scurry, and the rest, to indulge some pandering to Curiosity at Form's expense . . .

Andrew Cooke's conviction (which he voiced innumerable times in the course of that night's rundlet and next morning's wedding breakfast) that the sun had set on their troubles forever and would rise thenceforth not only on a happy and prosperous family, but on a happier and nobler Province as well, was—alas!—by no means entirely borne out by history. Indeed, with the possible exception of William Smith the cooper and Captain Mitchell the opium merchant—both of whom disappeared from Clio's stage not long afterwards, never to be heard from to this day—it cannot be said that the life of any of our characters was markedly blissful; some, to be sure, were rather more serene, but others took more or less turns for the worse, and a few were terminated far before their time.

Tom Tayloe, for example, the corpulent dealer in indentured servants, was released from his own servitude at Malden immediately upon promising to press no charges against McEvoy; one hoped his experience would lead him into a less unsavory trade, but within the week he was peddling redemptioners again all over Talbot County, and a few years later he was throttled to death on Tilghman's Island by one of his investments—a giant Scot with all of McEvoy's passion for liberty and none of his resourcefulness. No more fortunate was Benjamin Spurdance, "the man who had naught to lose": Andrew discovered him in the jail in Annapolis, serving a sentence for petty thievery, and restored him to his former position as overseer of the tobacco-fields on Cooke's Point, but vagrancy and despair had so debilitated him that, the very next winter, an ague robbed him forever of the only thing he had not previously lost.

It may be said of Colonel Robotham, who succumbed to a like infirmity in April of 1698, that Life owed him no more years; but who will not regret that his journey ended, not in disgrace—which, when complete, can be as refreshing as success—but in embarrassment? A collaborator in the revolution of '89 and a Councilman under both royal governors of Maryland, he and four similarly flexible statesmen fled cravenly to England in 1696, when Nicholson opened his prosecution of their former leader. To add to his humiliation, Lucy never found a husband. Her child, a girl, was born as it had been conceived, out of wedlock, and raised on the Colonel's estate by his widow. Lucy herself fell farther and farther from respectability: abandoning her child, she lived openly in Port Tobacco as the mistress of her seducer, the Reverend Mr. Tubman, until that gentleman and his colleague, the Reverend Peregrine Cony, were suspended by their bishop in 1698 on charges of drunkenness, gambling, and bigamy. Of her life thereafter nothing positive is known, but one is distressed to hear of a young prostitute in Russecks's Tavern (which Mary Mungummory purchased from Roxanne's estate and operated jointly with Harvey Russecks) who achieved some fame among the lower-Dorset trappers by reason of *"a Beare upon her bumm"*—could it have been a freckled Ursa Major?

At least the Colonel was spared the chore of arranging a second annulment for his daughter, inasmuch as she became a widow before she was a mother. Poor Bertrand, after that final lucid hour with Ebenezer, lapsed first into prolonged delirium, in the course of which he accepted the worship of "Good Saint Drakepecker," held forth as Poet Laureate of Brandon's Isle, and deflowered harems of Betsy Birdsalls and Lucy Robothams; then he sank into a coma, from which Burlingame and a physician strove in vain to rouse him, and three days later died in his bed at Malden. Ebenezer was greatly saddened by his death, not only because he felt some measure of responsibility for it, but also because the ordeals they had survived together had given him a genuine affection for his "adviser"; yet just as scarlet fever may cure a man of the vapors, so his distress as losing Bertrand was eclipsed by the far more grievous loss that followed on its heels: Joan Toast, as everyone expected, succumbed before the year was out—on the second night in November 1695, to be exact—but it was neither her opium nor her pox that carried her off. Without them, to be sure, she would have survived; they felled and disarmed her; but the *coup de grâce*—by one of those monstrous ironies that earlier had moved

Ebenezer to call Life a shameless playwright—was administered by childbirth! Hear the story:

After that evening which regained Cooke's Point for Ebenezer (and ended our plot) there was a general exodus from Malden. Governor Nicholson, Sir Thomas Lawrence, William Smith, and Richard Sowter sailed for Anne Arundel Town the next day, and the militiamen went their separate ways; Burlingame tarried until he could do no more for Bertrand and then struck out alone on his perilous embassy to Bloodsworth Island, promising to return in the spring and marry Anna—to which match her father had consented. John McEvoy and Henrietta, on whom Andrew also bestowed his blessing, were married soon after in the parlor at Malden (to the tearful joy of the Parisienne in the kitchen) and sailed for England as soon as Sir Harry's will was probated; moreover, contrary to the general expectation, Roxanne went with them, whether because her old love for Andrew had not got the better of her grievance, or because she deemed herself too old for further involvements or too scarred by her life with the brutish miller, or for some other, less evident reason. Andrew followed them, leaving Malden to the care of his son and Ben Spurdance, and it pleased the twins to conjecture that Roxanne meant to marry their father after all, but not before repaying him in his own coin. However, if Andrew entertained hopes of winning her by siege, they were never realized: on the income from her estate she toured Europe with her daughter and son-in-law. McEvoy went through the motions of studying music with Lotti in Venice, but apparently lost interest in composition; he and Henrietta lived a childless, leisurely life until September of 1715, when they and Roxanne, along with fifty other souls, set out from Piraeus in the ship *Duldoon,* bound for Cadiz, and were never heard from again.

By spring, then, everyone had left except the twins and Joan Toast, and life at Malden settled into a tranquil routine. Ebenezer did indeed contract his wife's malady, which, though virtually incurable, he contrived to hold in check by means of certain herbs and other pharmaceuticals provided him earlier by Burlingame, so that for the time at least he suffered only a mild discomfort; and after the first two weeks Joan's health grew too delicate to permit further physical relations with her husband. The three devoted most of their time to reading, music, and other gentle pursuits. The twins were as close as they had ever been at St. Giles, with the difference that their bond was inarticulate: those dark, unorthodox aspects of their affection which had so alarmed them in the recent past were ignored as if they had never existed; indeed, the simple spectator of their current life might well have inferred that the whole thing was but a creation of Burlingame's fancy, but a more sophisticated observer—or cynical, if you will—would raise an eyebrow at the relish with which Ebenezer confessed his earlier doubts of Henry's good will, and the zeal with which he now declared that Burlingame was "more than a friend; more e'en than a brother-in-law-to-be: he is my *brother*, Anna—aye, and hath been from the first!" And would this same cynic not smile at Anna's timid devotion to the invalid Joan, whom every morning she helped to wash and dress?

The equinox passed. In April, true to his word, Burlingame appeared at Malden, for all the world an Ahatchwhoop in dress and coiffure, and announced that, thanks to the spectacular effect of the Magic Aubergine (for which, owing to the season, he had substituted an Indian gourd), his expedition had achieved a large measure of success: he was positively enamored of his new-found family and much impressed by Quassapelagh and the able Drepacca—whose relations, he added, had deteriorated gratifyingly. He felt confident that he could get the better of them, but of his brother he was not so sure: Cohunkowprets, thirsty for blood, had the advantage of copper-colored skin, and the problem of deposing him was complicated by Burlingame's great love for him. His work there, Henry concluded, was not done; he had planted the seeds of faction, but after marrying Anna he would be obliged to return to the Island for the summer, to cultivate them properly.

His appearance disrupted the placid tenor of life at Malden. Anna had grown increasingly nervous with the coming spring, and now she seemed positively on the verge of hysteria: she could not sit still or permit a moment's lull in conversation; her moods were various as the faces of the Chesapeake, and changed more frequently and less predictably; a risqué remark—such as Ebenezer's, that he had seen dried Indian gourds in Spurdance's cabin on the property—was enough to send her weeping from the room, but on occasion she would tease her brother most unkindly about his infection and speculate, with deplorable bad taste, what effect the eggplant-plaster might have on it. Burlingame observed her behavior with great interest.

"You *do* want to wed me, Anna?" he asked at last.

"Of course!" she insisted. "But I'll own I'd rather wait till

the fall, when thou'rt done with the Salvages for ever and aye
. . ."

Henry smiled at Ebenezer. "As you wish, my love. Then methinks I'll leave tomorrow—*The sooner departed, the sooner returned*, as they say."

To what happened in the interval between this conversation, which took place at breakfast, and Burlingame's departure twenty-four hours later, Ebenezer could scarcely have been oblivious: the very resoluteness with which he banished the thought from his mind (only to have it recur more vividly each time) argues his awareness of the possibility; his sudden need to help Spurdance oversee the afternoon's planting argues his approval of the prospect; and his inability to sleep that night, even with cotton in his ears and the pillow over his head, argues his suspicion of the fact. Anna kept to her room next morning, and the poet was obliged to bid his friend good-bye for the two of them.

"The fall seems terribly distant," he observed at the last.

Henry smiled and shrugged his shoulders. "Not to the fallen," he replied. "*Adieu*, my friend: methinks that prophecy of Pope Clement's will come to pass."

These were his final words to the poet, not only for the day and season, but forever. Later that day Anna declared her fear that Burlingame would remain with the Ahatchwhoops all his life, and *much* later—in 1724—she confessed that she had sent him away herself in order to be, literally and exclusively, her brother's keeper. In any event, unless a certain fancy of Ebenezer's later years was actually the truth, they never saw or heard from their friend again. Whether owing to his efforts or not, the great insurrection did not materialize, though by 1696 it seemed so imminent that Nicholson raised the penalties for sedition almost monthly: even the loyal Piscataways, who had fed the very first settlers in 1634, were so inflamed—some said by Governor Andros of Virginia—that they abandoned their towns in southern Maryland, removed to the western mountains with their emperor (Ochotomaquath), and either starved, they being farmers rather than hunters, or were assimilated into northern groups. The great Five Nations, thanks to the efforts of Monsieur Casteene, General Frontenac, and perhaps Drepacca as well, were wooed away entirely from the English to the French, and the massacres of Schenectady and Albany would almost surely have been multiplied throughout the English provinces had the grand conspirators on Bloodsworth Island not been divided. The fact that Nicholson never mustered a force to attack the Island itself suggests both communication with and great faith in Henry Burlingame; by the end of the century the place was an uninhabited marsh, as it is today. One supposes that the Ahatchwhoops, under whatever leadership, migrated northward into Pennsylvania like the Nanticokes, and were in time subsumed into the Five Nations. On the ultimate fate of Quassapelagh, Drepacca, Cohunkowprets, and Burlingame, History is silent.

But though the twins' extraordinary friend departed, life at Malden never regained its former serenity. Anna remained in a highly nervous state; then in May it became apparent that during their brief cohabitation three months previously, Joan Toast had been impregnated by her husband. Here was a grave matter indeed, for if she carried the fetus to term, the labor of bearing it would surely kill her, and in any event the child would be born diseased; thus despite his sudden passionate desire for fatherhood, which he felt with an intensity that frightened him, Ebenezer was obliged to pray for a spontaneous early abortion. But not only were his prayers unanswered: as if in punishment for his having made them, Anna confessed in midsummer that she too was in a family way, and it took all the resources of the poet's rhetoric to dissuade her from ending her life!

"I—I'm a *fallen woman!*" she would lament, fascinated by the term. "Wholly disgraced!"

"Wholly," Ebenezer would agree: "as I have been since ever I came to Maryland! You must wed thy shame to mine or see me follow you to the grave!"

So it was that Anna remained at Malden, in relative seclusion, while among the servants and neighboring planters the most scandalous stories ran rife. Once Ebenezer returned ashen-faced from Cambridge and declared: "They're saying 'twas *I* got the twain of you with child!"

"What did you expect?" Anna replied. "They know naught of Henry, and 'tis unlikely I'd take Mister Spurdance for my lover."

"But why *me?*" Ebenezer cried. "Are people so evil-minded by nature? Or is't God's punishment to shame us as if we did in sooth what——"

Anna smiled grimly at his discomposure. "What ever and aye we've blushed to dream of? Haply it is, Eben; but if so, His sentence hath many a precedent. 'Tis the universal doubt of salvages and peasants, whether twins of different sexes have not sinned together in the womb; is't likely they'd think us guiltless now?"

But there is, it would appear, no shame so monstrous that one cannot learn to live with it in time: no visitors called at Malden, and Ebenezer's relations with his domestic staff and field hands grew cold and formal, but neither he nor Anna spoke again of suicide, even when it began to be clear that Burlingame was not going to return. In November Joan Toast died, and her infant daughter as well, from a breech-birth that would have carried off a much stronger woman; grief-stricken, Ebenezer buried the two of them down by the shore, beside his mother. The following January was Anna's term: her brief labor commenced late at night, and in the absence of professional assistance she was delivered of a healthy male child by Grace the cook (who had some experience of mid-wifery) and the poet himself. There being little likelihood that Andrew Cooke would ever return to Maryland or hear the scandal from a third party, Ebenezer thought it best not to cloud his father's old age with the truth: instead, he wrote that although Joan had expired in childbirth, their baby—a son christened *Andrew III*—had lived, and was being cared for by Anna. The old man, needless to say, was over-joyed.

This fiction, once established, had a marked effect on Ebenezer and his sister. Despite her shame, Anna seemed eminently suited in body and mind for motherhood: she had bloomed during pregnancy; her delivery had been easy; now her breasts were rich with milk, and lament as she might, she feasted upon her child as did he upon her, and grew plump and ruddy from the nursing. They did in fact name the child Andrew, and began to consider removing from Malden altogether as soon as feasible, "for the boy's sake . . ."

But this brings us near the end of the history, and it will be necessary to digress for a moment before reaching it if we are to learn the fate of that arch-mischiefmaker John Coode, of the saucy Governor who prosecuted him, and of Lord Baltimore's grand crusade to recover his charter to Maryland, which had been confiscated by King William.

Of Coode, then, whom Nicholson was wont to call "a diminutive Ferguson in point of Government; a Hobbist in point of Religion": already in November of 1694, while Ebenezer was ill and languishing at Malden, the Governor had demanded an account of Coode's disbursement of public revenue and had charged him with, among other misdemeanors, accepting an illegal award of four thousand pounds of tobacco from the Lower House for his services to the Rebellion, stealing the records of his criminal courts for 1691, embezzling public funds in the amount of five hundred thirty-two pounds two shillings and nine-pence as chief of the Protestant Associators (not to mention four hundred more as Receiver General for the Potomac and yet another seven hundred in bills of exchange as Collector for Wicomico River), impersonating a Papist priest and an Anglican rector, conspiring against Governor and King alike, and blaspheming against the Father, the Son, and the Holy Ghost. In July of 1696, on the strength of his new evidence, Nicholson instituted proceedings against him and took depositions from divers officials and citizens on the several charges, whereupon his quarry fled to the protection of Andros in Virginia. From there (so went the rumors, for few people claimed ever to have seen him with their own eyes) he communicated secretly with his agents, particularly Gerrard Slye and Sam Scurry—the former of whom he prompted to publish "Articles of Charge" against Nicholson to the Lords Justices in London, accusing the Governor of everything from Papism and unnatural practices to the murder of one Henry Denton, Clerk of the Council and "material witness to his misdeeds." Despite his problems with privateers in the Bay, Frenchmen on the border, Indians all about the Province, and various murrains and epidemics, Nicholson contrived during this period to found a college in Anne Arundel Town (whose name had become *Annapolis*), defend himself against Slye's charges, and finally, in the summer of 1698, order two sloops and a hundred men to capture Coode and Slye on the Potomac River. The lesser man was apprehended and brought to justice, whereupon he immediately pled coercion by his superior; but Coode himself eluded the trap.

One is pained to learn that at this point matters were removed from the doughty Governor's hands. In an action calculated to solve a number of problems at once, His Majesty commissioned Nicholson to replace his old rival, Sir Edmund Andros, in Virginia, who, having fallen out of royal favor by his attacks on Dr. Blair of William and Mary's College, was demoted to a minor governorship in the West Indies. In January of 1699 (1698 by the old calendar) the transfer was effected, and almost at once Coode was reported to have returned triumphantly to St. Mary's County. Some said he misjudged Nathaniel Blackiston, Nicholson's successor and a nephew of Coode's own brother-in-law, inasmuch as Blackiston actually arrested him in May of the same year; others maintained that such naïveté was unthinkable in so shrewd an intriguer. It was simple collusion, they claimed, and their cynicism seems justified when one learns that in July of the following year Coode was pardoned and released at his own request, and by 1708 was actually licensed to practice law in the St. Mary's County Court! But another view, less cynical and more subtle, was advanced by Ebenezer Cooke to his sister at the time: no trace had ever been found or mention made of Captain Scurry, he pointed out, since early in the trial of Captain Slye. Was it not entirely within the scope of possibility that the man arrested and pardoned under Coode's name was this same Scurry, either in collusion with Blackiston or otherwise? Ebenezer thought it was, and thus returned to the more basic question: did the "real" John Coode exist at all independently of his several impersonators, or was he merely a fiction created by his supposed collaborators for the purpose of shedding their responsibilities, just as businessmen incorporate limited-liability companies to answer for their adventures?

In any case, one knows that John Coode never attained the grand objectives attributed to him, and neither did that shadowy figure presumed to be at the other pole of morality, Lord Baltimore—at least not in his lifetime. For however ambiguous Charles Calvert's means and motives, if he existed at all (and if Burlingame did not entirely misrepresent him) one assumes at least that he was anxious to recover his family's proprietary rights to Maryland. This much granted, he must have died in 1715 a doubly disappointed man, for not only was Maryland under the rule of her sixth Royal Governor, but his son and heir, Benedict Leonard Calvert, had two years previously renounced Catholicism in favor of the Church of England, at the expense of his annual allowance of four hundred fifty pounds. It was this very defection, however, that set in progress a swift and dramatic change in the family fortunes: Charles Calvert died on the twentieth of February, and the outcast Benedict Leonard became the fourth Lord Baltimore; but less than two months later, on April 5, Benedict himself passed on, and the title was inherited by his sixteen-year-old son, also named Charles. Now this fifth Lord Baltimore was not only a Protestant like his father, but a handsome, dissolute courtier to boot, so well respected in the royal house for his abilities at pimping and intrigue that in time he became Gentleman of the Bedchamber to the Prince of Wales. With this array of qualifications in his favor, it took him exactly one month to do what his grandfather had not managed in twenty-five years: in May of 1715,

His Majesty George I restored to him the charter of Maryland, its almost monarchic original privileges intact.

These marvels alone, it seems to the Author, are sufficient evidence to convict Mistress Clio on the charge of shamelessness once lodged against her by our poet; what then is one to think on seeing this same young Baltimore, in 1728, offer to Ebenezer Cooke a bona fide commission as Poet and Laureate of Maryland? "On to Hecuba!" as our poet was wont to cry. Or, after the manner of his hybrid metaphors: let us plumb this muse's farce to its final deep and ring the curtain!

First, the Reader must know that after the burst of inspiration which drove him, during his convalescence at Malden in the winter of 1694, to compose not the promised *Marylandiad* but a Hudibrastic exposé of the ills that had befallen him, Ebenezer wrote no further verse for thirty-four years. Whether this fallowness was owing to the loss of his virginity, dissatisfaction with his talents, absence of inspiration, alteration of his personality, or some more subtle cause, it would be idle presumption to say, but Ebenezer was as astonished as will be the Reader to find that precisely during these decades his fame as a poet increased yearly! The manuscript of his attack on Maryland, one remembers, Ebenezer had taken with him on his shameful flight from Malden and entrusted, via Burlingame, to the captain of the bark *Pilgrim*. At the time, Ebenezer had been apprehensive over its safety and had exacted assurances from Burlingame that the captain would deliver it to a London printer; but in the rush of events thereafter, he forgot the poem entirely, and when, after the christening of Andrew III, Life eased its hold upon his throat, he only wondered disinterestedly whatever became of it.

His slight curiosity was gratified in 1709, when his father sent him a copy of *The Sot-Weed Factor* under the imprint of Benjamin Bragg, at the Sign of the Raven in Paternoster Row! The *Pilgrim*'s captain, Andrew explained in an accompanying letter, had delivered the manuscript to some other printer, who, seeing no profit in its publication, had passed it about as a curiosity. In time it had fallen into the hands of Messrs. Oliver, Trent, and Merriweather, Ebenezer's erstwhile companions, who, upon recognizing it as the work of their friend, created such a stir of interest that the printer decided to risk publishing it. At this point, however, Benjamin Bragg got wind of the matter and asserted a prior right to the poem, on the ground that its author was still in his debt for the very paper on which it was penned. There ensued an exchange of mild threats, at the end of which Bragg intimidated his rival into relinquishing the manuscript and brought out an edition of it at 6d. the copy. The first result, Andrew declared, was a vehement denial from the third Lord Baltimore that he had in any way commissioned Ebenezer Cooke—a perfect stranger to him—as Laureate of Maryland or anything else, and a repudiation of the entire contents of the poem. There were even rumors of a libel suit against the poet, to be brought by the Lord Proprietary at such time as the King saw fit to restore him his province; in time, however, the rumors had ceased, for some favorable notices of the poem began to appear that same year. Andrew included one in his letter: "A refreshing change from the usual false panegyrics upon the Plantations . . ." it read in part. ". . . admirable Hudibrastics . . . pointed wit . . . Lord Calvert's loss is Poesy's gain . . ."

"What a feather in thy cap!" Anna cheered upon reading it. "Nay, i'faith, 'tis a very plume, Eben!"

But her brother, surprised as he was to learn of his sudden notoriety, was unimpressed. In fact, he seemed more annoyed than pleased by the review.

"The shallow fop!" he exclaimed. "He nowhere grants the poem's *truth!* 'Twas not to wax my name I wrote it, but to wane Maryland's!"

Nevertheless, in the years that followed, *The Sot-Weed Factor* enjoyed a steady popularity among literate Londoners —though not at all of the sort its author wished for it. Critics spoke of it as a fine example of the satiric extravaganza currently in vogue; they praised its rhymes and wit; they applauded the characterizations and the farcical action—and not one of them took the poem seriously! Indeed, one writer, commenting on Lord Baltimore's wrath, observed:

> *It is a curious thing that Baltimore, so anxious to persuade us of the elegance of his former Palatinate, should so hardly use that Palatinate's first Poet, when the very poem he despises is our initial proof of Maryland's refinement. In sooth, it is no mean Plantation that hath given birth to such delicious wit as Mister Cooke's . . .*

Such accolades chagrined and wisened the poet, who accepted not a word of them. In 1711, when old Andrew died and Ebenezer was obliged to sail to London for the purpose of probating his father's will, he permitted himself to be wined and dined by Bragg and Ben Oliver, who had become his partner in the printing-house (Tom Trent, they informed him, had renounced poetry and the Established Church to become a Jesuit; Dick Merriweather, after wooing Death in a hundred unpublished odes and sonnets, had made such a conquest of that Dark Lady that at length, his horse rearing unexpectedly and throwing him to the cobbles, she had turned into an eternal embrace what he had meant as a mere flirtation), but to their entreaties for a sequel to the poem—*a Fur-and-Hide Factor* or *a Sot-Weed Factor's Revenge*—he turned a deaf ear.

Truth to tell, he had little to say any more in verse. From time to time a couplet would occur to him as he worked about his estate, but the tumultuous days and tranquil years behind him had either blunted his poetic gift or sharpened his critical faculties: *The Sot-Weed Factor* itself he came to see as an artless work, full of clumsy spleen, obscure allusions, and ponderous or merely foppish levities; and none of his later conceptions struck him as worthy of the pen. In 1717, deciding that whatever obligation he owed to his father was amply satisfied, he sold his moiety of Cooke's Point to one Edward Cooke—that same poor cuckold whose identity Ebenezer had once assumed to escape Captain Mitchell—and Anna hers to Major Henry Trippe of the Dorset militia; though "their" son Andrew III was by this time a man of twenty-one and had already sustained whatever wounds the scandal of his birth was likely to inflict, they moved first to Kent and later to Prince George's County. For income, Ebenezer—now in his early fifties—performed various clerical odd-jobs as deputy to Henry and Bennett Lowe, Receivers General of the Province, with whom he became associated (the Author regrets to say) by reason of his conviction that their brother Nicholas was actually Henry Burlingame. Anna, be it said, did not permit herself to share this delusion, though she indulged it in her brother; but Ebenezer grew more fixed in it every day. If, indeed, it *was* a delusion: Nicholas Lowe did not in the least resemble Burlingame's past impersonation of him or any other of the former tutor's disguises, but he was of the proper age and height, possessed a curious wit and broad education, and even displayed what can only be called "cosmophilist" tendencies now and again. Furthermore, to all of Ebenezer's hints and veiled inquiries he replied with a mischievous smile or even a shrug . . . But no! Like Anna, we shall resist the temptation to *folie à deux:* age has made our hero fond, like many another, and there's an end on it!

Two things occurred in 1728 to conclude our history. Old Charles Calvert was then a baker's dozen years under the sod and thus unable to savor, as did our poet in his sixty-second year, this final irony concerning *The Sot-Weed Factor:* that its net effect was precisely what Baltimore had hoped to gain from a *Marylandiad,* and precisely the reverse of its author's intention. Maryland, in part because of the well-known poem, acquired in the early eighteenth century a reputation for graciousness and refinement comparable to Virginia's, and a number of excellent families were induced to settle there. In recognition of this fact, the fifth Lord Baltimore (that famous young rake and dilettante referred to earlier) was moved to write a letter to the aging poet, from which the following excerpt will suffice:

> *My Grandfather & namesake, for all his unquestion'd Virtues, was no familiar of the Arts, and thwarted in his original purpose in calling you Laureat (wch be it said We are confident he did, notwithstanding his later denials thereof), he was unable to perceive the value of your gift to Maryland. We do hence mark it fit, that now, when a generation hath attested the merits of your work, you s^{hd} accept in fact, albeit belatedly, that office & title the qualifications whereto you have so long since fulfill'd. Namely, Poet & Laureat of the Province of Maryland . . .*

Ebenezer merely smiled at the invitation and shook his head at his sister's suggestion that he accept it.

"Nay, Anna, 'tis a poor climate for a poet, is Maryland's, nor is my talent hardy enough to live in't. Let Baltimore give his title to one whose pen deserves it; as for 'me, methinks I'll to the muse no more!"

But that same year saw the death of Nicholas Lowe, which so touched the poet (owing to his delusion) that he broke his vow and his long silence to publish, in the *Maryland Gazette,* an *Elegy on the Death of the Hon. Nicholas Lowe, Esq.,* containing sundry allusions to his ambivalent feelings towards that gentleman. Thereafter, either because he felt a ripening of his talents or merely because breaking one's vow, like losing one's innocence, is an irreparable affair which one had as well make the best of (the Reader will have to judge which), he was not sparing of his pen: in 1730 he brought out the long-awaited sequel, *Sot-Weed Redivivus,* or *The Planter's Looking-Glass,* which, alas, had not the success of its original; the following year he published another satirical narrative, this one dealing with Bacon's Rebellion in Virginia, and a revised (and emasculated) edition of *The Sot-Weed Factor*. In the spring of 1732, at the age of sixty-six, he succumbed to a sort of quinsy, and his beloved sister (who was to follow him not long after), in setting his affairs in order, discovered among his papers an epitaph, which, though undated, the Author presumes to be his final work, and appends for the benefit of interested scholars:

> *Here moulds a posing, foppish Actor,*
> *Author of* THE SOT-WEED FACTOR,
> *Falsely prais'd. Take Heed, who sees this*
> *Epitaph; look ye to* Jesus!
> *Labour not for Earthly Glory:*
> *Fame's a fickle Slut, and whory.*
> *From thy* Fancy's *chast Couch drive her:*
> *He's a Fool who'll strive to swive her!*
> E.C., G^{ent}, P^t & L^t of M^d

Regrettably, his heirs saw fit not to immortalize their sire with this inscription, but instead had his headstone graved with the usual piffle. However, either his warning got about or else his complaint was accurate that Maryland's air—in any case, Dorchester's—ill supports the delicate muse, for to the best of the Author's knowledge her marshes have spawned no poet since Ebenezer Cooke, Gentleman, Laureate of the Province.

ABOUT THE AUTHOR

JOHN BARTH, born May 27, 1930, in Cambridge, Maryland, was only twenty-six when his first novel was published. Titled *The Floating Opera*, it was the runner-up for the 1956 National Book Award. Mr. Barth's other works include *The End of the Road, Lost in the Funhouse, Chimera, Giles Goat-Boy,* and *The Sot-Weed Factor*. In 1965, a poll of two hundred prominent authors, critics, and editors placed John Barth among the best American novelists to emerge in the past twenty years.

John Barth holds an A.B. and an M.A. degree from Johns Hopkins University. From 1953 to 1965 he taught English at Pennsylvania State University. He is currently professor of English at the State University of New York at Buffalo. He is married and has three children.